## THE LOVE MACHINE
### Jacqueline Susann

"Jacqueline Susann is . . . an extraordinary publishing phenomenon. Seven years ago, she gave up acting to write a rather charming little book about her poodle. It was called **Every Night, Josephine!** and it sold quite nicely. Then, in 1966 [she wrote] her first novel, **Valley of the Dolls**. . . . The book sold 350,000 copies in hardcover and, far more astonishing, eight million copies in paperback. It is now among the top all-time best sellers and has just gone into its 53rd Bantam softcover printing . . . **THE LOVE MACHINE** is a far better book than **Valley**—better written, better plotted, better structured."

—Nora Ephron, **The New York Times Book Review**

"Sex is the most potent ingredient in Jacqueline Susann's books. And she is quite a love machine in her own right."

—Donald Zec, **London Daily Mirror**

D1637871

# The Love Machine

## Jacqueline Susann

BANTAM BOOKS

TORONTO · NEW YORK · LONDON

This is a work of fiction. All events and all
characters are products of the author's imagination.
Any resemblance to real events or real persons,
living or dead, is purely coincidental.

*This low-priced Bantam Book
has been completely reset in a type face
designed for easy reading, and was printed
from new plates. It contains the complete
text of the original hard-cover edition.*
NOT ONE WORD HAS BEEN OMITTED.

THE LOVE MACHINE
*A Bantam Book / published by arrangement with
Jacqueline Susann*

PRINTING HISTORY
*Simon & Schuster edition published May 1969*
2nd printing ............ *May 1969*    4th printing ............ *May 1969*
3rd printing ............ *May 1969*    5th printing ........ *August 1969*
*Excerpts appeared in* LADIES' HOME JOURNAL *May and June 1969*
*Bantam edition published July 1970
24 printings through March 1981*

*Bantam Books are published by Bantam Books, Inc. Its trade-
mark, consisting of the words "Bantam Books" and the por-
trayal of a bantam, is Registered in U.S. Patent and Trademark
Office and in other countries. Marca Registrada. Bantam
Books, Inc., 666 Fifth Avenue, New York, New York 10103.*

PRINTED IN THE UNITED STATES OF AMERICA

33 32 31 30 29 28 27 26 25 24

To Cārol Bjorkman

# PROLOGUE:

# THE
# LOVE
# MACHINE

☥

MAN CREATED THE MACHINE.

A Machine does not feel love, hate or fear; it does not suffer from ulcers, heart attacks or emotional disturbances.

Perhaps man's only chance of survival is to *become* a machine.

Some men have succeeded.

A machine who passes for a man often rules societies—a dictator is a power machine in his country. A dedicated artist can turn into a talent machine.

Sometimes this evolution occurs without the man realizing it.

Perhaps it happens the first time he says, "I am hurt," and his subconscious replies, "If I cut all feeling from my life—*I cannot be hurt!*"

Amanda would have laughed if you had told her this about Robin Stone—because Amanda was in love with him.

Robin Stone was a handsome man.

He could smile with his lips.

He could think without emotion.

He could make love to her with his body.

Robin Stone was The Love Machine.

# AMANDA

# ONE

A T NINE IN THE MORNING, she was standing on the steps in front of the Plaza Hotel, shivering in a linen dress. One of the clothespins that held the back of the dress together clattered to the ground. A dresser hurried to replace it, and the photographer used the time to reload his camera. The hairdresser quickly retouched a few stray hairs with a can of hair spray and the session resumed. The curious crowd that had gathered was delighted with this glimpse of one of the Beautiful People —a top fashion model, facing the blasting cold winds of March, in a lightweight summer dress. To add to the strangeness of the scene, there were cold-looking snowbanks on the hills of Central Park, reminders of a recent snowstorm. The crowd, comfortably bundled in winter coats, suddenly felt no envy for the shimmering creature they were watching who earned more money in a morning than they earned in a week.

Amanda was freezing, but she was impervious to the crowd. She was thinking of Robin Stone. Sometimes thinking of Robin Stone helped, especially when they had spent a wonderful night together.

This morning her thoughts were not comforting. She had not spent a wonderful night with Robin. She had not even heard from him. He had two lecture dates, one in Baltimore on Saturday, and one at some dinner in Philadelphia on Sunday. "I'll shoot my speech to them at seven and be back at New York by ten," he had promised.

"Then we'll go to the Lancer Bar and grab a hamburger."
She had sat around in full makeup until two in the
morning. Not even a phone call.

The photographer finished. The fashion coordinator
rushed to her with a coat and a container of coffee. She
went into the hotel and sank into a massive armchair in
the lobby and sipped the coffee. The icicles in her veins
began to thaw. She would survive. Thank God the rest of
the shots were indoors.

She finished the coffee and went up to the suite that
had been engaged for the session. The clothes were
hanging in a neat row. With the help of the dresser, she
slipped out of the linen dress and changed into a pair of
summer "at home" slacks. She adjusted the falsies in her
bra, then checked her makeup. The electricity crackled as
her comb went through the thickness of the soft honey-
colored hair. She had washed it herself yesterday and set
it the way Robin liked it, long and loose. This afternoon
she had a three-hour session scheduled with Alwayso
Cosmetics—they would probably reset it. Jerry Moss liked
her in an upsweep; he claimed it gave the product more
class.

At eleven o'clock she was closeted in the bathroom,
changing into her own clothes. She opened her large bag
and took out the container with toothbrush and tooth
paste. She brushed her teeth in up and down strokes. She
was doing the summer shades of lipstick for Alwayso
today. Thank God for her teeth, thank God for her hair.
And her face. Her legs were good, her hips were slim, she
was tall. God had been very good; He had only been
forgetful in one spot. She stared ruefully at the falsies in
her bra. She thought of all the women who had watched
her pose: working girls, housewives, heavy women,
thick-ankled women—they all had bosoms. Bosoms which
they took for granted. And she was flat as a boy.

Oddly enough this was an asset for the perfect model.
But it certainly was no asset in one's personal life. She
recalled the dismay she had felt when she was twelve
and most of the girls at school began to sprout small
"bumps" on top. She had run to Aunt Rose, Aunt Rose
who had laughed: "They'll come, honey, only let's hope
they don't get too big like your Aunt Rose's!"

But they *hadn't* come. When she was fourteen Aunt Rose had said, "Now, honey, the good Lord gave you a beautiful face and a good mind. Besides, it's more important for a man to love you for yourself, not your face or your body."

This simple logic was all very fine when she sat in the kitchen listening to Aunt Rose, when neither of them thought she would ever go to New York and meet the kind of people she knew now.

Like the singer—she never thought of Billy in any other way. She had been eighteen, just starting to model, when they met. She had played his records in high school. When she was twelve, she had stood in line for two hours when he was making a personal appearance at a local movie house. Seeing him in person at a party was like a dream. And it was even more unbelievable when he singled her out. As Billy put it to some of the columnists, "It was instant romance!" From that night on, she was part of his entourage. She had never seen this way of life —the nightclub openings, the round-the-clock chauffeur, the large groups he took everywhere, songwriters, agents, song pluggers, press agents. And although they had never laid eyes on her before, they just accepted her as part of the family. She was amazed at the whirlwind courtship and all the attending newspaper publicity. He held her hand and kissed her cheek as the camera snapped, and on the fifth night they finally wound up alone—in his hotel suite.

She had never been in a suite at the Waldorf Towers —at the time she was still living at the Barbizon Hotel for Women. She stood in the center of the room staring at all the flowers and the bottles of liquor. He kissed her, loosened his tie and beckoned her toward the bedroom. She meekly followed him. He took off his shirt and casually unzipped his pants. "Okay, angel, unwrap," he said.

She had felt panic as she slowly undressed down to her pants and bra. He walked over and kissed her lips, her neck, her shoulders, while his fingers fumbled with the bra. It fell to the floor. He stood back, his disappointment evident.

"Jesus, baby, put the bra back." He looked down at

himself and laughed. "Charlie here has already folded from shock."

She put the bra back on. She put on all her clothes and rushed out of the hotel. The following day he sent her flowers, besieged her with calls, pursued her. She relented and they had three wonderful weeks together. She went to bed with him, but she kept her bra on.

The singer returned to the Coast after three weeks. He never called her again. He salved his conscience by giving her a mink coat as a going-away present. She could still recall the amazement on his face when he found he had taken a virgin.

The newspaper publicity brought a call from the Nick Longworth agency. She signed with them and her career as a model was launched. He started her at twenty-five dollars an hour, and now, five years later, she was one of the top ten models in the country, booked solid at sixty dollars an hour. Nick Longworth made her study the fashion magazines, learn how to dress, practice her walk. She had moved from the Barbizon to a nice apartment on the East Side where she spent most of her evenings alone. She bought a television set and a Siamese cat. She concentrated on her work and studied the magazines. . . .

Robin Stone had exploded into her life at a charity ball. She had been chosen along with five other top models to appear in a fashion show for a charity ball at the Waldorf. Seats cost one hundred dollars. There was the usual dancing and entertainment in the Grand Ballroom; all the best people came. But there was one factor that set this ball apart from all the other similar glittering charity events: Mrs. Gregory Austin was head of the committee. Mrs. Gregory Austin's ball not only made all the newspapers, it also received television coverage on the local IBC station. And why not? Mr. Austin owned the IBC network.

The Grand Ballroom at the Waldorf was packed. Amanda and the other models were accorded the courtesy of "paying guests," since they were donating their time. Along with the five other girls, she sat at a table and nibbled at the dinner. IBC had placed six minor executives at the table as escorts for the girls. The men were attractive and bland. In the beginning, they made stabs at small talk, but gradually they fell into discussions of ratings and cancelations among themselves. Amanda barely listened. She covertly studied the table where Mrs. Gregory Austin sat with her friends. She recognized Judith Austin from her newspaper pictures and was secretly elated that Mrs. Austin's hair was tinted the exact color as her own. Amanda judged Judith Austin to be about forty, but she was very beautiful—small, elegant and perfectly understated. It was women like Mrs. Austin whom Amanda had tried to emulate in the early stages of learning how to dress—of course she still couldn't afford clothes like Mrs. Austin's, but she could get the copies.

After dinner she went to the dressing room to prepare for the fashion show. The IBC cameras were set up. The show would go on live for the local eleven o'clock news. She was sitting with the other models when there was a light knock on the door. Robin Stone came in.

The girls gave him their names. When she simply said, "Amanda," he wrote it down and waited. She smiled. "Just Amanda—that's all there is," she said. Their eyes met and he smiled. She stared at him as he went around the room, writing down the names of the other girls. He was very tall, and she liked the way he moved. She had caught him a few times on the local news before switching over to CBS and the late movie. Somewhere in the recesses of her mind she recalled he had once won a Pulitzer Prize as a newspaper reporter. Television certainly didn't do him justice. His hair was dark and thick, just beginning to tinge with gray. But it was his eyes. They suddenly caught her own, held them—almost as if he was appraising her. Then he flashed an easy grin and left the room.

She decided he was probably married to someone who looked like Mrs. Austin. By the time the show was over, Amanda had even pictured two small children who looked exactly like him.

She was completely dressed when he knocked on the door. "Hello, Miss One Name," he said with a grin. "Is there a Mr. One Name waiting for you at home or are you free to have a beer with me?"

She went to P.J.'s with Robin, toyed with a Coke and

watched him in amazement as he drank five vodkas and remained absolutely sober. And she followed him back to his apartment without a spoken word or suggestion on his part. The pressure of his hand carried the message, as if it was mutually understood.

It was almost as if she had been under hypnosis. She entered his apartment without any sense of apprehension, stood before him and undressed without giving a thought to her bosom. And when she hesitated with her bra, he walked over and removed it himself.

"Are you disappointed?" she asked.

He tossed the padded bra across the room. "Only cows need boobs!" Then he took her in his arms and gently leaned down and kissed her breasts. He was the only man who had ever done this. She held his head and trembled. . . .

That first night he had taken her gently and wordlessly, then when both their bodies were moist with exhaustion, he had held her close. "Want to be my girl?" he asked. Her answer came in the darkness as she clung to him with more fervor. He broke the embrace, and those clear blue eyes searched her face. His lips smiled, but the eyes were serious. "No strings, no promises, no questions—on *both* sides. Okay?"

She nodded mutely. Then he reached out and made love to her again, with a peculiar combination of violence and tenderness. At last they lay back, exhausted and fulfilled. She caught a glance at the clock on his night table. Three o'clock! She slid out of bed. He reached out and grabbed her wrist. "Where are you going!"

"Home. . . ."

He twisted her wrist and she cried out in pain. He said, "When you sleep with me, you *stay!* You don't leave!"

"But I have to. I'm wearing an evening dress!"

Without a word, he released her and got up and began to dress. "Then I'll spend the night at your place."

She smiled. "Afraid to sleep alone?"

His eyes went dark. "Don't ever say that! I sleep alone. But when I go to bed with a girl, I *sleep* with her!"

They went to her apartment, and he made love to her again. And as she fell asleep in his arms she was filled with a happiness so acute that she felt sympathy for every woman in the world because they would never know Robin Stone.

Now, after three months, even her Siamese cat, Slugger, had accepted Robin and snuggled against his feet at night.

Robin didn't make very much money, and he was away many weekends, doing lectures to augment his income. Amanda didn't mind not going to Colony or "21." She liked P.J.'s, the Lancer Bar, the Piccolo Italia, Robin's hangouts. She loved double features, and she was trying desperately to learn the difference between a Democrat and a Republican. Sometimes she would sit in the Lancer Bar for hours, while Robin discussed politics with Jerry Moss. Jerry lived in Greenwich and his agency handled the Alwayso cosmetics account. It was Robin's friendship with Jerry that had landed her the color layouts for Alwayso.

She stood before the mirror in the bathroom of the Plaza, slipped into her woolen dress and walked into the living room of the suite.

The makeshift dining table had been removed. The photographer was packing his equipment. His name was Ivan Greenberg, and he was a good friend. She waved to him and the people repacking the dresses and left the suite, a golden image, her long hair flying, the singer's burnished mink rippling as she ran down the hall.

She went to the phone in the lobby and checked with her exchange. No word from Robin. She dialed his number—it rang tonelessly, the kind of a ring that tells you no one is home. She hung up.

It was almost noon. Where on earth was he?

# TWO

H E WAS IN A SUITE at the Bellevue Stratford Hotel in Philadelphia.

He awoke slowly with the knowledge that the morning was all but gone. He heard pigeons murmuring on the ledge of the window. He opened his eyes and knew exactly where he was. Sometimes when he awoke in a motel he wasn't sure. Every motel room looked the same and he had to stop and recall the city, or even the name of the girl who slept beside him. But he was alone this morning, and this was not a motel. Good old Philadelphia and their Man of the Year dinner. They had sprung for a real suite.

He reached for his cigarettes on the night table. The pack was empty. There wasn't even a decent-sized butt in the ashtray. Then he saw the ashtray on the other side of the bed—long butts with orange lipstick on the tips.

He reached for the phone and ordered a double orange juice, coffee and two packs of cigarettes. He scrounged for the least damaged butt, scraped off the dead ash and lit it. There were longer butts in the other ashtray, with orange lipstick. He didn't take one. He got up and spilled the contents of that tray into the toilet. He watched them disappear, feeling he was also exorcising the girl. Damn it, he would have sworn she was single. He usually could spot them right away, the married women out for a secret thrill. This one had really fooled him, maybe because she was a cut above the average. Well, they were all one-night stands. Let their husbands worry. He grinned and looked at his watch—almost noon. He'd catch the two o'clock train back to New York.

Tonight he and Amanda would celebrate and drink a toast to Gregory Austin, the man who was taking him away from all this. It still seemed unreal, as hard to believe as the personal phone call from Austin himself at nine o'clock on Saturday morning. At first Robin had thought it was a gag—the chairman of the board of IBC calling a local newsman! Gregory laughed and told him to call him back on the IBC number to verify it. Robin did exactly that and Austin picked up the telephone on the first ring. Could Robin Stone come directly to his office? He was in Gregory Austin's office ten minutes later, his suitcase with him. He had to catch the noon train to Baltimore.

Austin was alone in his massive office. He came to the point immediately. How would Robin like to be the Head of Network News? He would also want Robin to bring in ideas for expanding the news department, and form his own team to cover the conventions in the summer. Robin liked the idea very much. But "Head of Network News"? The title was enigmatic. Morgan White was *President* of Network News. Randolph Lester was Vice-President. What, Robin asked, did "Head of Network News" *mean?* Well, it meant fifty thousand a year, more than double his present salary. And, as Austin put it, in answer to his question about the title, "Let's leave it this way for starters, shall we?"

It was one hell of a start. And when Austin learned Robin still had another year to go with his lecture contract, he simply made two phone calls, one to the lecture agency, the other to his lawyer, instructing him to buy out Robin's lecture contract. It had been as simple as that— simple and secretive. Robin was to stay away from IBC for a week. He was also to keep his mouth shut about the assignment. On the following Monday he was to come in and take over in the new job. Gregory Austin himself would handle the announcement his own way. . . .

He poured his coffee and lit a fresh cigarette. The weak wintry sun streamed through the hotel windows. A week from today he would be reporting at IBC for the new job. He took a long drag of his cigarette. Some of his good mood filtered away with the smoke. He ground out the cigarette. It conjured up the image of the girl with the orange lipstick. What was her name? Peggy? Betsy? Neither name hit a spark of recognition. But her name ended like that: Billie? Mollie? Lillie? The hell with it! It wasn't important. He sat back and pushed the coffee away. Once when he had come to New York for a weekend while he was still at Harvard, he had seen a show, *Lady in the Dark*. There was something about a girl hearing part of a tune—she could never get past the first few bars. The same thing occasionally happened to him. Only it wasn't a tune, it was a memory, a vision . . . He could never quite see it, but he sensed it. It was like being on the verge of an important recollection, and it left him with a sense of musky warmth, of happiness ending in panic. It didn't happen often, but it had happened last night, in one fast flash—no, *twice!* The first time had been when the girl had slipped into bed with him. The feel of her body, vibrant and soft—her breasts were magnificent. He didn't usually pay much attention to breasts—there was something childish to him about sucking a full breast. Why did men think of it as a sex act? It was a longing for Mama. There was something *weak* about a man who wanted to lay his head against a woman with big breasts. Robin dug blondes, clean and bright, slim and hard. There was a symmetry to their bodies that he found exciting.

But the girl last night had been a brunette, with beautiful full breasts. Oddly enough he had found himself excited. It was coming back to him now. He had shouted something when he hit the climax. But what was it? He never shouted ordinarily, not with Amanda, or any girl he stayed with. Yet he *knew* he had shouted something, just as he knew there had been other times when he had shouted and could not remember his words afterwards.

He lit a fresh cigarette and intentionally turned his thoughts to the new future that awaited him. This was a time for celebration. He had an entire week off.

He picked up the Philadelphia paper that had arrived with his breakfast. On page three he saw his picture with the man who had been honored, a balding corpulent judge. The caption read: ROBIN STONE, PULITZER PRIZE-WINNING NEWSMAN, TELEVISION PERSONALITY AND LECTURER, CAME TO PHILADELPHIA TO SPEAK AND HONOR JUDGE GARRISON B. OAKES, 1960 MAN OF THE YEAR.

He poured himself some fresh coffee and grinned. Sure he had come to honor the judge, a man he had never heard of. He had come because they paid Universal Lecture Agency five hundred bucks.

He sipped his coffee, cheerful in the knowledge that he would never have to lecture again. It had sounded so easy in the beginning. He had been doing the local IBC news for about a year when Clyde Watson, head of the Universal Lecture Agency, sent for him. The agency occupied an entire floor in a new building on Lexington Avenue. And Clyde Watson, sitting behind the massive walnut desk, looked like a trusted stockbroker. Everything was designed to put the victim at ease, even the paternal smile. "Mr. Stone, why should a Pulitzer Prize-winning columnist wind up doing a local news show?"

"Because I quit the Northern Press Association."

"Why did you quit? Because you had no New York outlet?"

"No. Not being in a New York paper didn't bother me. That's just good for free tickets to theaters and free tabs at restaurants. That's not my scene. I'm a writer. At least I think I am. But NPA allowed every editor in every small town to hack my column to bits. Sometimes they only ran three lines. Three lines of a column that had taken me six hours to write. Writing doesn't come easy to me. I sweat over it. And for some guy to toss six hours of my life into a wastebasket—" Robin shook his head as if he felt actual pain. "At least at IBC I'm able to be a news analyst and there's no editing. I've got complete freedom —just the usual station disclaimer at the end."

This time Watson's smile was accompanied by an approving nod. Then a sympathetic sigh. "But it doesn't pay well."

"Enough to live on. My needs are simple. A hotel room. Enough paper for my typewriter," this time Robin grinned like a small boy, "and I steal all the paper and carbon from IBC."

"Writing the great book?"

"Isn't everyone?"

"When do you get the time?"

"Weekends, sometimes at night."

Now there wasn't any smile on Watson's face. He was going in for the kill. "Isn't it difficult doing it piecemeal? How can you keep the flow going? Shouldn't a writer be able to take a year off and give his book total concentration?"

Robin lit a cigarette. His eyes met Clyde Watson's with merely a slight show of curiosity. Watson leaned closer. "Universal Lectures could book you on weekends. I'm sure we could ask for five hundred—maybe even work it up to seven fifty."

"Doing what?"

"You pick a subject. I've read your columns." Watson held up a file to prove his point. "You could talk about amusing incidents that occurred when you were a correspondent. Mix it with anything timely. Play it serious. Play it light. I can *promise* you a lot of work."

"Why would anyone come to see me?"

"Look in the mirror, Mr. Stone. Women's clubs book the guest artists. They've had it with the bald-headed professors or comedians without sex appeal. You'd bring some glamour into their lives. A war correspondent, a Pulitzer Prize-winner—you'd be in big demand at dinners and colleges."

"And when would this leave me time to write my book?"

"Shelve it for now. Forget it. At the rate you're going it will take years. But two years of lectures and you can save enough to take a year off. Go away somewhere. Then, who knows—maybe another Pulitzer Prize, for the book? You don't want to be a local newscaster all your life, do you?"

It had sounded great. Even with the thirty-five percent the agency would take out of his fee for booking the lectures. He signed eagerly. His first lecture was in Houston. Five hundred dollars. One seventy-five back to the agency. That left three twenty-five. Then he read the small print: he had to pay his fare and hotel room. On that first lecture he had cleared thirty-three dollars. When he tried to break his contract, Watson merely smiled blandly. Sure he could break it—if he paid it off. That had been a year ago: a year of traveling tourist in planes, sandwiching his six-foot-three-inch frame into a narrow little seat, all-night flights with fat women and crying babies as seat companions. And the terrible motels, except for a rare case like Philadelphia, when a good hotel suite was included in the deal.

Robin stared at the suite. It was a proper setting for his farewell performance. Thank God it was over: no more tourist planes, no more mingling with the guests . . . He could forget about the speech—the speech that had gotten so pat he could deliver it stoned. The laughs always came in the same place, the applause was always the same. In the end, even the towns looked the same. There was always the good-looking, toothy Junior League girl on the welcoming committee to greet him, eager to discuss Bellow and Mailer and the state of the arts. And after the first martini he knew she was going to wind up in the kip with him.

Well, he had humped his way across forty-six states. Now he was "Head of Network News."

With the first lecture money he had taken an apartment. Nothing fancy but it was better than his hotel room. But he never had a chance to spend any time in it. There was the new desk, the big stack of yellow paper, carbons, even a new electric typewriter to replace his tinny portable. But the job at IBC took up his days, booze and broads took care of the nights, the weekends were spent traveling. Well, that was over now. He'd do a hell of a job at IBC, save every damn cent. And he'd write that book.

Sometimes Robin wondered about his writing. Did he really have it? The Pulitzer Prize didn't prove anything. Journalism didn't mean you had a book in you. And it was a book he wanted to do. He'd show the effect of war on men in politics—the resurgence of Churchill, the emergence of generals as politicians, Eisenhower—de Gaulle. . . . After that, he wanted to write a political novel. But most of all he wanted to see his book become a reality, see the yellow paper transformed into text.

Material things meant little to him. When he saw Amanda purr as she showed him a new pair of shoes, he sometimes wondered about his own lack of interest in possessions. Perhaps it was because he had always had them, at any rate until his father had died, leaving the interest on a four-million estate to Kitty. Upon her death

the principal of the estate would be divided between his
sister Lisa and himself. Meanwhile on $12,000 a month,
the glorious Kitty was having a ball. Funny how he
always thought of his mother that way: "the glorious
Kitty." She was beautiful, small and blond—hell, she
might have red hair by now. Two years ago, when she
left for Rome, she was what he called a "plaid" blonde.
Kitty said it was frosted. He grinned at the memory. For a
fifty-nine-year-old broad she looked pretty good.

His life had been good as a kid—it had even been good
through college. The old man had lived long enough to
give Lisa the biggest wedding in Boston history and now
she was living in San Francisco, married to a crew-cut
idiot who was one of the richest real estate men on the
West Coast. She had two wonderful kids—God, he hadn't
seen them in five years. Lisa was . . . let's see he had been
seven when she was born—she must be thirty now, a
mother, all settled. And he was still on the loose. Well, he
liked it that way. Maybe it came from a crack his father
had made. He had been about twelve and his father had
taken him out on his first round of golf.

"Approach the game as if it was a subject at school,
like algebra—something you must master. You've got to
be good in the game, son. Many a business deal is consummated on a golf course."

"Does everything you learn have to help toward
making money?" Robin had asked.

"It sure does, if you want a wife and family," his father
answered. "When I was a kid I dreamed of being Clar-
ence Darrow. But then I fell in love with your mother
and settled for corporate law. I can't kick. I've become a
very rich man."

"But you loved criminal law, Dad."

"Once you have a family you can't do just what *you*
want. They become your primary responsibility."

Robin learned to play golf. He had a seven handicap
when he graduated from Harvard. He had wanted to
take a liberal arts course, then major in journalism. His
father had been against it, just as he had been furious
when he caught Robin reading Tolstoy and Nietzsche.

"That's not going to help you with law," he said.

"I don't want to be a lawyer."

Robin's father stared at him and left the room. The next day Kitty gently explained how he owed it to his father to make him proud. Jesus, it sometimes seemed the only word he heard was "owe." He *owed* it to his father to play football—it was a good image for a lawyer. So he broke every bone in his body to become the best quarter-back Harvard had that season. When he graduated in 1944, he might have gone into corporate law but he was twenty-one and there was a war on, so he enlisted in the Air Corps, promising to return and complete law school. But it hadn't happened that way. He saw a lot of action, got his captain's bars and landed on page two of the Boston papers when he was hit in the shoulder—at least *that* made the old man proud of him! It was a minor wound but it aggravated an old football injury and Robin had to remain in a hospital overseas. To ease the monotony he wrote about life in the hospital and the experiences of the other soldiers. He sent his copy to a friend who was with the Northern Press Association. They ran it, and his career as a journalist began.

When the war was over, he joined NPA as a full-time correspondent. Of course he got the usual arguments from both Kitty and his father. He *owed* it to his father to study law. Fortunately, Lisa had met Crew Cut and the entire household was spinning with the preparations for her wedding. Five days later, the old man dropped dead while playing squash. Well, that's the way he would have liked it, Robin thought. Dying with all his muscles intact and all his obligations to his family paid off.

Robin stood up and pushed the room-service table away. He was on his own, and he didn't owe anyone in the world a goddam thing. And he was determined to keep it that way.

He went into the bathroom and turned on the shower. The water sprayed hard and cold, knocking the last vestige of vodka from his brain. God, he had missed his Monday workout at the gym. And he had forgotten to call Jerry in New York and cancel the date. He grinned. Poor Jerry—he had probably gone to the gym alone. And Jerry hated the gym; he only went because Robin forced him to go. Oddly enough, Jerry didn't seem to mind being flabby at thirty-six.

Robin began to hum. He would call Jerry and Amanda as soon as he got into New York. They'd meet at the Lancer Bar and celebrate. But he wouldn't tell them what they were celebrating—Gregory Austin had said he wanted to handle the announcement himself.

He began lathering the shaving cream on his face. God, he thought, I'd give anything to know just what's happening at IBC this morning.

# THREE

TO EVERYONE AT IBC it began as an ordinary Monday morning. The "numbers" (as the weekly Nielsen ratings were called) were placed on every executive's desk. The first sign of disturbance came at ten o'clock. It was triggered by a simple message: "Gregory Austin would like to see Danton Miller in his office at ten thirty."

The message was transmitted from Mr. Austin's private secretary to Susie Morgan, Danton Miller's private secretary. Susie scribbled it on a pad and placed it on Mr. Miller's desk alongside of the Nielsen ratings. Then she headed for the Powder Room. She passed the secretaries in the "bullpen." They were immersed in their work; their typewriters had been clacking away since nine thirty. But the "Upper Echelon" (the VIPs' personal secretaries) arrived at ten, with dark glasses and no makeup. They checked in, letting their bosses know they had arrived, then dashed to the Powder Room. Twenty minutes later they emerged, looking like fashion models. One of the more progressive secretaries had even installed a large magnifying mirror.

The Powder Room was crowded when Susie arrived. As she spat into her mascara, she casually dropped her contribution to the gossip session. Gregory Austin had sent for Danton Miller! The first girl who left the Powder Room passed Susie's tidbit to a friend who worked in the legal department. In less than six minutes the news had traveled all through the building.

Ethel Evans was typing a release when the news hit the publicity department. She was so anxious to see Susie and get all the details that she didn't wait for the elevator. She ran down four flights and was breathless when she burst into the sixteenth-floor Powder Room. Susie was alone, adding a final dab of lip gloss, when Ethel found her.

"I hear your boss is getting his walking papers," she said.

Susie finished her lips. She picked up a comb and teased her bangs, conscious that Ethel was waiting for an answer. She hoped her voice contained the proper tone of boredom when she finally said, "Isn't that the usual Monday morning rumor?"

Ethel's eyes narrowed. "This time I hear it's on the level. Gregory has his weekly meeting with the heads of departments on Thursdays. To send for Dan on a Monday morning—well, everyone knows that has to mean the ax."

Susie suddenly felt concern. "Is that what they say upstairs?"

Ethel felt happier. She had gotten a reaction. She leaned against the wall and lit a cigarette. "It certainly figures. Have you gotten a load of the numbers?"

Susie back-combed her hair. Her hair didn't need it and she hated Ethel Evans. But if Danton Miller went, then *her* job went! She *had* to know if there was anything in the air. She knew Danton's job depended on the rise and fall of the numbers. It had never occurred to her that Gregory Austin's summons could be ominous. In the Powder Room she had imparted the news as further proof of Dan's importance. Now suddenly she felt panic. But she had to regain her poise—Ethel Evans was just a girl who worked in public relations. *She* was Danton Miller's private secretary! Her voice was calm when she answered. "Yes, Ethel, I've seen the numbers. But the ratings of network News are hardest hit. Morgan White is

President of News. *He* should be the man to worry. Not Danton Miller."

Ethel laughed. "Morgan White is related to the Austins. Nothing can hurt *him.* Your boyfriend is the one who's in trouble."

Susie colored slightly. It was true she dated Dan, but their relationship was confined to an occasional dinner at "21" or the opening of a Broadway show. Secretly she hoped something would come of it, but so far all he had done was give her a light kiss on the brow when he left her at her door. But she knew she was assumed to be "his girl." They had even been coupled together in a Broadway column. She loved the prestige it gave her among the other secretaries.

Ethel shrugged. "Well, I'm just tipping you off. You'd better gird yourself for a tough evening with the Great Danton. If he gets the sack, it'll be awfully drunk out."

Susie knew Dan had a reputation as a heavy drinker, but he never took more than two martinis with her, and she had never seen anything ruffle his calm. She looked at Ethel and smiled. "I don't think you have to worry about Dan. If he did lose this job, I'm sure he'd have plenty of offers."

"You weren't here when Colin Chase quote, retired, unquote. When they asked him about his plans, he said, 'when you're captain of a dirigible and the dirigible blows up, that's it. After all, how many other dirigibles are there to go to?'" Ethel waited for this line to make an impact, then added, "It can get very lonely and cold sitting out there at Lakehurst, waiting for another dirigible to come along."

Susie smiled. "I don't think Dan will go to Lakehurst."

"Honey, *every* place is Lakehurst when you have no dirigible. Colin Chase still sits in '21' or the Colony every day, having three-hour lunches, stalling until it's time to go to Louis and Armand's for cocktails."

Susie studied her hair in the mirror. Ethel gave up. "Okay, play it cool if you like, but I'll bet you a lunch that Dan will go. He's in real trouble."

Susie stood alone in the Powder Room. She was concerned for Dan. But she was even more concerned for herself. If a new man came in, he'd bring his own secretary. She couldn't go back to the "bullpen"! She'd have to job-hunt. . . .

Oh Lord, she had spent a whole week's salary buying a dress to wear with Dan at the Emmy Awards dinner next month. She was feeling panic now. She *had* seen the ratings. Everything was down. Network News was hardest hit, but Ethel was right—Morgan White was related to the Austins. Danton would be the fall guy. True, he had looked calm enough this morning when she placed the message on his desk, but you could never tell when Dan was worried. His Madison Avenue training and his ubiquitous catlike smile made him seem in total command.

In fact Dan *was* worried. He sensed disaster the moment he saw the ratings. And when Susie put the phone message before him he felt the blood drain from his stomach. He loved the job. It was stimulating and exciting. And as he reveled in his power, his fear of failure grew. You couldn't take chances when you put your job on the line. Presidents of other networks could take chances. They didn't work for a maniac like Gregory Austin, who fancied himself a combination of Bernard Baruch and David Merrick. What was he trying to prove? You couldn't be any bigger than Gregory, unless you were Robert Sarnoff or William Paley.

At ten twenty-seven he left his office and walked to the elevator. He looked down the hall at the impressive walnut door with the gold lettering: MORGAN WHITE. Everything seemed serene in there. Sure, Morgan was safe. Gregory Austin had chosen Danton Miller, Jr., as the sacrificial lamb.

He nodded briskly to the elevator boy as the car took him swiftly to the penthouse floor. He smiled evenly at Gregory Austin's secretary as she announced him. She returned his smile and motioned him to go inside. He envied her, serene and secure in her paneled and broad-loomed cubicle.

He entered the spacious reception room, where Gregory usually came out to greet VIPs—big sponsors or presidents of advertising agencies who were making multimillion-dollar buys of IBC air time. Beyond it was the conference room and Gregory's luxurious inner office.

If Gregory wanted to fire him, he'd probably be standing here, waiting to get it over with quickly. But Gregory wasn't here, so maybe it was a good sign. But what if Gregory wanted to make him wait and sweat? It could be a bad sign.

He sat on one of the leather couches and stared morosely at the handsome early American furniture. He glanced at the neat creases in the trousers of his Dunhill suit. God—right now, he was Danton Miller, Jr., President of Network Television. Five minutes from now he might be unemployed.

He took out his cigarette case. The slow burn of his ulcer warned him, but he took out a cigarette and tapped it against the case. He should have taken a tranquilizer before he left his office. He should have stayed on the wagon last night. Hell, he should have done a *lot* of things! He studied the cigarette case. He had selected it with great care. Three hundred dollars. Black baby alligator, trimmed with eighteen-karat gold. He could have gotten a solid gold one for the same price, but that wasn't the image of understated elegance he had styled for himself—the black suit, the black tie, the white shirt. He had twelve black suits, fifty black ties, all the same. Each tie had a small number in the lining so he could rotate them each day. A black suit simplified life: fine for the office, but equally presentable if an important dinner date came up. The cigarette case was a great prop. If he was asked to make a snap decision, he could reach for the cigarette case, select a cigarette, tap it against the case—it gave him time to think, to stall. It was also a substitute for cuticle picking, nail biting and other manifestations of nerves.

His hands felt damp. He didn't want to lose this job! This was power! There was no place to go after this, no place other than the Valhalla of ex-network presidents, the martini-laden four-hour daily lunch at "21."

He stared out the window. A watery sun was trying to shine. Spring would soon be here. This couch would be here in spring. Gregory's secretary would be here. But *he* would be gone. Suddenly he knew how a condemned man must feel as he walks to the electric chair and stares at the witnesses who must watch him die. He breathed deeply, as if savoring every last second of life; as if in a few seconds his life could be shot from under him. The large office, the trips to the Coast, the bungalow at the Beverly Hills Hotel, the broads. . . . He walked back to the couch. He didn't consciously believe in God, yet he sent up a small prayer—a promise. If he got through today without getting canned, things would be different. He'd make those numbers rise. He'd do it if he had to steal shows from other networks. He'd make it a twenty-four-hour-a-day job. He'd cut down on the booze, on the broads. This was a pledge—and he'd keep it. Hadn't he kept the rule he had set for himself against drinking at lunch? He had made that decision when he saw the disintegration of Lester Mark. Lester had headed a big advertising agency. Dan had watched him go from two to four to five martinis at lunch. Martinis bolster a man's confidence and loosen his tongue. He had watched Lester go from president of an advertising agency to vice-president of a lesser agency, from vice-president to unemployment, from there to full-time alcoholic.

Dan was convinced that the lunchtime martini was one of the worst occupational hazards of television. For this reason, he was strict in his abstinence during the day. What he did after hours he always considered his own business. But in this past year he had been doing it too much. Maybe that was why he had latched on to Susie Morgan, breaking another of his rules. (Keep your social life apart from your business.) Susie was too young for him, so he made no passes and stayed reasonably sober when he took her out. Besides, he couldn't really cope with a twenty-three-year-old: a girl that age has marriage spelled across her forehead. It was safer to get a hooker for sex or even jerk off. Girls like Susie were good for window dressing. He'd even give up the hookers if he held the job. He'd stay home several nights a week, just watch that goddam box, watch the competition, find out why IBC was lagging. Find out what the public really wanted. Oh, who the hell knew? Even the public didn't know.

The heavy door swung open and Gregory Austin walked in. Dan jumped up. Gregory was holding the ratings. He handed Dan the paper and motioned him to sit down. Dan studied the ratings as if seeing them for the first time. From the corner of his eye he watched Gregory pace up and down the room. Where did the man get the energy? Dan was ten years younger, yet he didn't walk with the same spring. Austin was not a tall man. Dan was five foot ten and he stood several inches higher than Gregory. Even Judith in her high heels sometimes appeared taller than Gregory. Yet there was a virility and a feeling of strength that emanated from him. His whole being crackled with excitement: the red hair, the freckles on the strong sun-tanned hands, his flat stomach, the quick movements, and the sudden disarming smile. The rumor was that he had led an active love life among the Hollywood starlets until he met Judith. After that, to Gregory, no other woman seemed to exist.

"What do you think of the numbers?" Gregory said suddenly.

Dan made a wry face.

"Notice anything particular?"

Dan took out the cigarette case. He tapped a cigarette.

Gregory reached over and took one, but ignored Dan's offer of a light. "Been off them for a week," he announced. "I just hold one in my mouth. It works. You should try it, Dan."

Dan lit his own cigarette and exhaled slowly. He made another vow to the God who watched over network presidents. If he walked out of this room with his job intact, he would never smoke again.

Gregory leaned over. The strong hand with the red-gold hairs pointed to the news ratings.

"We're in the cellar," Dan said, as if making a sudden discovery.

"Notice something else?"

Dan's ulcer stabbed him. His eyes kept riveting to the two variety shows that were in the bottom ten. Shows that he had recommended. But he forced himself to look at Gregory with a bland innocent stare.

Gregory Austin's finger impatiently tapped the page. "Look at our *local* news. Not only does it hold its own, but some nights it even outrates CBS, ABC and NBC. Know why? A man named Robin Stone!"

"I've caught him many times, he's excellent," Dan lied.

He had never seen the man or watched the eleven o'clock IBC news. Either he was loaded and fell asleep, or he turned to NBC and waited for the *Tonight* show.

"I've watched him every night for a month," Gregory stated. "Mrs. Austin thinks he's great. And it's the *women* who determine what channel their husbands pick for news. The man may win in the choice of any other show, but when it comes to the news, it's *her* choice. Because the news is the same on each network—it just depends on which newscaster you prefer to watch. That's why I've taken Robin Stone off local news. I intend to put him on our seven o'clock network show with Jim Bolt."

"Why keep Jim on at all?"

"He's got a contract to play out. Besides, I don't want Robin Stone stuck with just that spot. I have other plans for him. This man can be another Murrow, Cronkite, Huntley or Brinkley. We build him. And in turn he'll build the seven o'clock spot. By the end of this summer, his face will be known nationally. He'll be our anchor man at the conventions. We've got to build our news department. The only way to do it is with a personality. And Robin Stone is our man."

"Could be," Dan said slowly. He wondered what was coming next. This should be Morgan White's territory.

As if reading his thoughts, Gregory said, "Morgan White has to go." He said it quietly, without emotion.

Dan remained silent. This was a startling turn of events and he wondered why Gregory was confiding in him. Gregory kept everyone at a distance.

"Who would replace Morgan?"

Gregory stared at him. "What in hell have I been telling you? Do I have to lay it out? I don't want Robin Stone just as a performing newscaster. I want him to *head* the department."

"I think it's a marvelous idea." Dan was so relieved at his own stay of execution he could afford to be expansive.

"But I can't fire Morgan, he has to quit."

Dan nodded, still afraid to offer any comment.

"Morgan has no talent. But he has plenty of pride. It runs in the family. His mother and Mrs. Austin's mother were sisters. Great family—no business sense—but *great* pride. But that's what I'm counting on. When you leave here, I want you to send a memo to Morgan, announcing that you have hired Robin Stone as Head of Network News."

"Head of Network News?"

"There's no such job or title. I'm just creating it temporarily. Morgan will wonder what the hell it is, too. He'll come to you. You'll say that you created this job for Robin Stone in order to bolster the ratings. That Robin Stone will have a free hand in changing things in the news department—and will report directly to you. Get it?"

Dan nodded slowly. "Morgan will claim I'm butting into his department."

"Not butting in. As President of Network Television, you have the right to suggest changes in any department."

Dan smiled. "Suggest, but not *act.*"

"Let's not fool with semantics. Morgan will come running to me. I'll pretend it's a surprise, but I'll say that your job gives you the power to hire new personnel."

"Suppose Morgan doesn't quit?"

"He will," Gregory said. "I'm betting on it."

Then Gregory tossed aside his unlit cigarette and Dan stood up. The interview had ended. His life had been spared. He left the office with a new sense of security. His job was not in peril, and wouldn't be for some time. Gregory wanted him to be hatchet man on Morgan. He was dizzy at the thought of the new prestige this would give him in the business. Everyone knew Morgan's relationship with Gregory Austin. And now he, Danton Miller, Jr., would make the announcement that he had appointed Robin Stone as Head of Network News. They would actually believe that he was big enough to fire Morgan White and that Gregory Austin would sit back and accept it! The word would be out all over town: "Danton Miller, Jr., has autonomous power."

His hand shook as he wrote and rewrote the memo to Morgan White. After rephrasing it several times, he dictated it to Susie. He wondered how fast she'd get the news around the building. He sat back and reached for a cigarette, then, recalling his pledge, he tossed it unlit into the wastebasket.

He stood up and stared from his window. The sun was shining, the sky was almost a Wedgwood blue. Spring was coming and he'd be alive to greet it.

He turned around calmly as Morgan White burst into his office.

"What is all this about?" Morgan demanded.

"Sit down, Morgan. . . ." Dan reached for his cigarette case, hesitated, then snapped it open. Hell, if there was a God, He knew a man *had* to have a cigarette at a moment like this!

# FOUR

THE DAY AFTER the big announcement was made, business went on as usual at IBC. Robin Stone's picture appeared in *The New York Times* with a brief statement announcing his appointment as President of News replacing Morgan White, who had resigned. There was a sense of suspended apprehension in the news department as everyone waited for Robin Stone to appear. Robin had always been a loner, so there was one speculation that took all precedence—"What was Robin Stone really like?" The only person who had come near to socializing with him was Bill Kettner, a cameraman. On two occasions he had gone to a bar with Robin after the eleven o'clock news. On both occasions it was to watch a night ball game. Robin Stone liked baseball. He could also polish off three vodka martinis as if they were orange juice. This was the sum total of information that had been dredged together.

A few of the girls had seen him at P.J.'s, always with a pretty girl. Sometimes Jerry Moss was with them. Jerry Moss seemed to be his only male friend. They met every day at the Lancer Bar for a drink.

"Where in hell is the Lancer Bar?"

Jim Bolt said he thought it was on West Forty-eighth Street.

Sam Jackson was sure it was on First Avenue.

They looked it up in the phone book.

It was on East Fifty-fourth Street.

No one had ever been there.

On Wednesday afternoon, half the news department went to the Lancer Bar.

Robin Stone never showed.

On Thursday one of the researchers went there because he had liked the Lancer Bar.

Robin Stone was there.

With Jerry Moss and the most beautiful girl in the world.

There was nothing to do but wait for Robin Stone to make a move. It came late Friday afternoon. A message was placed on the desks of all news personnel:

> THERE WILL BE A MEETING IN THE CONFERENCE ROOM
> ON THE EIGHTEENTH FLOOR, MONDAY AT TEN THIRTY.
> ROBIN STONE

They began filing into the conference room at ten twenty. At ten twenty-five Ethel Evans entered. Jim Bolt glanced at her curiously. She had no business being here. But he was too concerned with his own problems to give her much thought. A new president meant a big shake-up. Yet he had to hand it to Ethel—barging in like this. He admired her guts and her easy confidence.

But Ethel wasn't as confident as she appeared. She noticed that most of the staff automatically took seats as if they had been assigned to them. It was a long room, the long table was the only furniture. Some extra chairs were against the wall. The door they had all come in by led to the outside hall. She stared at another door. A door that was ominously closed. Soon every seat was taken except the empty seat at the head of the table. Ethel hesitated, then she took a chair from against the wall, dragged it to the table and wedged it in between a researcher and a sportscaster.

At ten thirty Randolph Lester, Morgan's vice-president of News, entered the room. Ethel noticed that he looked fairly confident. Maybe Robin had given him some hint that his job was not in jeopardy. Randolph was wearing a black suit and black tie. The IBC image that Danton Miller had inspired. He smiled at them paternally. "Good morning, ladies and gentlemen," he said. "I know you've all shared IBC's excitement at the appointment of Mr. Stone to the presidency of News. Some of you have worked with him. Some of you will be meeting him for the first time. Both Mr. Gregory Austin and Mr. Danton Miller are proud to place all future news programming in Mr. Stone's hands. There will be some changes made—in fact, there will be *many* changes made. But I'm sure everyone will understand they reflect in no way on anyone's personal talent or accomplishment. The changes will be to extend our news coverage. To make for higher achievement."

"Why doesn't he just say higher ratings?" whispered someone near Ethel.

Someone else muttered, "See you in the unemployment-insurance line."

Randolph Lester continued, "IBC's policy has always been—" He stopped as the door opened and Robin Stone swung into the room.

There was a small spatter of applause, but something in Robin's eyes made it die before it began. Then he grinned and they all felt like ridiculous children who had done something foolish but were forgiven.

Robin Stone glanced down the table quickly, his eyes resting on no one. It was as if he was summing up the number of people, the room, the setting. Then he flashed an easy grin. Ethel noticed that everyone's resistance seemed to liquefy. The charisma of that grin was like a voltage of paralyzing electricity. To Ethel he was suddenly more desirable than any movie star. God, to break through that steel façade . . . to make this man tremble in her arms . . . to control him . . . even for a second! From her distance at the end of the table she could stare at him without catching his attention. She noticed suddenly that he smiled only with his mouth. His eyes were cold.

"I've studied the news operation," he said quietly. "Each and every one of you is good. But IBC is dragging in the ratings. We've got to add some juice to the operations. I'm a newsman—remember that. First, last and always. This is my first shot as an executive. But I will also function as a newsman. In the Air Force, when they finally stuck a couple of bars on my shoulder, I still flew a plane as a fighter pilot."

Ethel watched him intently as he spoke. He was handsome, cold-looking but handsome. He had to be almost six three, and not an inch of flesh to spare. She *had* to diet. He was grinning again. He could win the war with that smile alone.

"I intend to stay with the action here. This summer I want to build a top team to cover the conventions," Robin continued. "By then Andy Parino, from our Miami station, will be established on the network—he'll also be part of our convention team. I want to *add* to the combination—not eliminate." He turned to Randolph Lester. "But first of all, suppose we go round the table and you introduce everyone to me."

The two men walked around the table and Robin shook hands with each person. His friendly grin was intact, but his eyes were remote and his greeting impersonal. It was almost as if he had never seen any of them before.

When Lester's eyes rested on Ethel, he seemed surprised, hesitated a second, then quickly passed by her. The entire procedure went so quickly that Ethel was unaware of the deliberate slight. She watched them return to the head of the table. But Robin didn't sit down. His eyes scanned the table and rested on Ethel.

He pointed to her. "I don't believe we were introduced."

She stood up. "I'm Ethel Evans."

"What is your function?"

She felt her face grow warm. "I'm with the public relations office . . ."

"Then what are you doing here?" He was still smiling and his voice was gentle, but the eyes chilled her.

"Well . . . I thought . . . I mean, someone has to be assigned to News. To publicize any new ventures. I figured you'd need someone." She sat down quickly.

"When I want someone, I'll notify the publicity department," he said with the same half-smile. "Now suppose you return to wherever you came from." Every eye watched her as she walked out of the room.

Outside in the hall, Ethel leaned against the door. She felt physically sick. She wanted to run away from that conference room—she could hear him talking inside—but she stood there. She couldn't move . . . she was in a state of shock.

Then she heard Lester ask Robin whether he wanted Mondays set aside for the weekly meetings.

"There will be no weekly meetings," Robin answered. "I call them as I see them. But I want one thing changed —"

There was a second of silence. She knew everyone was leaning forward intently. Then Robin's voice: "Get rid of this table, I want a round one."

"A round one?" This was Lester.

"Yep. A great big round one. I don't like to sit or stand at the head of a table. I don't want seats assigned. If we work as a team, we sit as a team. Get me a big round table." There was a moment of silence, then everyone began to talk at once and she knew Robin had left the room. She heard them chattering with nervous relief. They'd begin to file out in a second! She dashed down the hall. She couldn't wait for the elevator—she didn't want to face them. She ran to the stairway and ducked into the Ladies' Room on another floor. Thank God, it was empty. She gripped the sink until her knuckles were white. Tears of humiliation ran down her face. "You son of a bitch, I hate you!" She started to sob. "I hate you!" She wiped her eyes and stared into the mirror. A fresh flow of tears spilled over. "Oh God," she begged, "why didn't you make me beautiful?"

# FIVE

A FTER HER DISASTROUS EVICTION from Robin's meeting, Ethel holed away in her office for the rest of the day. She didn't want to run into anyone in the halls—she was positive they were joking about her unceremonious departure.

She put the time to good use and typed out all the releases that had piled on her desk. At six thirty, the offices on the entire floor were empty. In her concentration on her work most of her humiliation had evaporated. Now she just felt drained—wrung out.

She took her mirror and tried to fix her makeup. She stared at herself disconsolately. Her face looked lousy. She put the cover on her typewriter and stood up. Her skirt was a mass of rolled wrinkles. It was too tight. Ethel sighed. Everything she ate went straight to her hips. She really had to go on a strict diet.

She took the elevator to the lobby. It was deserted but the coffee shop was still open. It was too late to go to Louis and Armand's on the pretense of looking for someone and maybe having a few laughs at the bar. Everyone she knew would be gone by now. The dinner crowd would be coming in. She went into the coffee shop and ordered black coffee. Usually she took cream and two sugars. The diet was officially on! She watched the waitress pour it into a cup. The girl's hands were red and cracked from washing dishes. She wondered about her. Didn't she have dreams? Didn't she hope to get somewhere? She had much more on the ball than Ethel, as far as looks went. She was slim and had a pretty face. Yet that girl was content to stand on her feet, slop up a wet counter, take crap from customers, smile at a dime tip— and Ethel Evans was making a hundred and fifty dollars a week!

She got out her compact and retouched her lipstick.

She was no beauty, but she got by. More than got by—but it would be nice to have a little something going in the looks department. Damn that separation in her teeth. And damn that lousy dentist who wanted three hundred dollars for a cap job. She had offered to sleep with him if he'd do it for free and he had thought she was joking. When she let him know she was serious, he pretended not to believe her. Then she realized he didn't *want* her! Dr. Irving Stein, a lousy little dentist, didn't want her! Ethel Evans who only fucked the big boys—who was known at IBC as the "celebrity-fucker"!

She walked out of the coffee shop and hesitated in the lobby. She didn't want to go home. This was the night her roommate bleached her hair and the whole place would be a mess. But it was a good arrangement, sharing an apartment with Lillian, who worked at the Benson-Ryan agency. Their hours were alike and they dug the same scene. They had met at Fire Island. That had been a great summer. Six girls had anted up to share a cottage. They called it the House of the Six Swingers. They had a blackboard and kept score. Every time one of them banged a guy, the others had to put a dollar in the kitty. And at the end of the summer the girl who had banged the most men won the pot. Lillian had beaten Ethel out by more than a dozen men. But then Lillian wasn't choosy. She was a good girl, a fun girl, but a slob. She'd even bang an assistant director. In Ethel's book, an A.D. couldn't qualify for anything but a few laughs at Louis and Armand's bar, if she was desperate.

She was suddenly conscious that the doorman was staring at her. She left the building and started to walk. Maybe she'd stop at P. J. Clarke's.

They were three deep at the bar and she connected with some agency men. She stood there for over an hour, exchanging dirty jokes, toying with one beer, her eyes watchful for some good prospect at the door. Someone who might buy her dinner. . . .

At seven thirty she saw Danton Miller walk in alone. She wondered where in hell was Susie. He looked straight through her without even nodding and joined some men at the other end of the bar.

Another hour passed and then as if a timer went off,

the agency men suddenly gulped down their drinks and raced to catch the last decent commuter train. And not one of the bastards picked up her check. She was hungry now. If she went inside and had a hamburger, Lillian would be through with the peroxide and jazz by the time she got home.

She sat alone at a small table and ate the hamburger. She was starving but she left half the roll. Damn, why had she had the beer? She weighed a hundred and forty now. Well, she had a small waistline and her boobs were sensational. Size thirty-eight—upright and firm. Her problem was her ass and thighs. If she didn't get it off now, she'd never lose it and next month she was going to be thirty. And still not married!

She could have been married, if she had wanted to settle for a civilian—the cameraman at CBS or the bartender in the Village. But Ethel wouldn't settle for anything less than a top celebrity. A one-night stand with a celebrity was preferable to a mediocre existence with a nobody. After all, when she held a movie star in her arms and he murmured, "Baby . . . baby," as his climax came, that moment made up for everything in the world. During that one moment she was beautiful—she was *someone*. She could forget who she was. . . .

She had always wanted to be beautiful, even as a child. Fat little Ethel Evanski from Hamtramck in Detroit. Eating mashed potatoes and fried onions, listening to everyone on the block talk Polish, playing potsy, double Dutch, double Irish, reading movie magazines, sending for genuine autographed pictures of Hedy Lamarr, Joan Crawford, Clark Gable. Sitting on the front steps and playing "The Game"—talking dreams and pretending they were real—with Helga Selanski, a stringy-haired little Polish kid the same age. The whole world was Polish on that block in Hamtramck. And the second-generation Poles seemed locked in, destined to marry their own kind. They went to movies and saw that there *was* another world, but it never occurred to them to try and enter it. But to Ethel, movies and the places she saw on the screen weren't merely two hours of silver escape.

Hollywood was a real place. New York and Broadway
actually existed. At night she would stay awake and listen
to the radio, and when the voice announced that the
music was emanating from the Cocoanut Grove in Hollywood, she would hug herself with excitement—at that
very second, the beautiful music she listened to was
being listened to by the famous stars who were there. For
that one moment, there almost seemed to be physical
contact, like she was *there*.

Ethel had always known she would leave Hamtramck.
Getting to New York was Phase One in her dreams. One
night when she and little Helga were listening to a band
coming from the Paradise Restaurant in New York, Ethel
began "The Game." Planning what she would wear
when she grew up and went to such a place—what movie
actor would escort her. Usually Helga played along with
The Game. But on this night, Helga suddenly protruded
her bony jaw and stated, "I'm not playing anymore. I'm
too big." Ethel had been surprised. Usually she could
make Helga do anything, but this time Helga was stub-
born. "My mother says we shouldn't talk and play like
this, it's time for us to be practical and not play make-believe games."

Ethel had answered, "It's *not* make-believe. I'm going
there someday, and I'll know movie stars and they'll take
me out—and kiss me." Helga had laughed. "Like fish!
Kiss you! Oh Ethel, I dee-double-dare you to say that to
anyone else on the block. You're not going anywhere.
You're going to stay right here like all the rest of us and
marry a nice Polish fella and have babies." Ethel's eyes
had narrowed. "I'm going to meet stars . . . go out with
them . . . maybe even marry one." Helga laughed. "See,
my mother's right. She says it's all right to talk about
Hollywood if we know we're just dreaming, but not to
believe that it's true. You're crazy. And you won't go out
with movie stars. You're Ethel Evanski and you're fat and
ugly and live in Hamtramck, and what movie star would
want to go out with you!"

Ethel had slapped Helga—hard. But she was frightened because she was afraid Helga might be telling the
truth. But she *wouldn't* stay on the block and marry a

nice Polish boy, raise kids and make mashed potatoes and onions! Why *had* her mother and father come from Poland if it was to live in a little Poland in Detroit?

The incident that triggered "The Game" into determined action was Peter Cinocek, a boy with protruding ears and large red hands who had "come to call" when she was sixteen. Peter was the son of a friend of Aunt Lotte's. He was a "real catch," half Polish, half Czech. Her mother and father had looked idiotic with delight at the prospect. She recalled how diligently her mother had cleaned the house. Everything had to be spotless the night Peter Cinocek came to call. She could still see them. Her mother nervously waiting, in a freshly ironed housedress. Her father skinny and bald, so old. God, he had only been thirty-eight. He had seemed worn and bloodless in her eyes, but her mother had appeared massive and strong.

She would never forget the night Peter Cinocek arrived. First she saw the big ears, then the pimples on his neck surrounding a great red boil that had not quite matured. But he could have been Clark Gable the way her mother had beamed as she placed a pitcher of lemonade on the porch and discreetly disappeared into the kitchen to wait.

Everyone on the block waited. Everyone in the small row of houses knew a "suitor" had come to call. She sat on the swing with Peter Cinocek. They sat in silence, listening to the creak of the swing, to the whispers of the neighbors on the porch that adjoined theirs. She could still see that house. A small cubicle, sandwiched in a long block of identical small frame houses. Every house had the same broken-down porch, the same small dinky dining room, the tiny living room, and the kitchen where everyone spent most of their time. And, oh God, the endless garbage pails and the cats that frequented the back alley. Even now she could still hear their mating sounds, and some disgruntled neighbor tossing out a pail of water to shut them up. Either their aim was bad or the cats were extremely passionate, because after a brief lull the mating yowls commenced again.

She thought back to that night when she sat on the creaking swing and listened to Peter Cinocek. He told her about his job at the A&P, then he took her hand in his. It felt moist and limp. And he told her how he hoped to have a home just like this and many many children. That's when she had bolted off the swing and run! Of course she came back, when she was sure the big-eared Peter had gone. Her folks had laughed. In Polish they kidded, "Little Ethel, she was scared of a boy. Ah, but she was born to have children—nice broad hips, she would have an easy time."

Ethel was silent, but she doubled her efforts at school and that summer she got a job in an office in downtown Detroit and became fairly efficient as a secretary. She never dated. But she was not unhappy. She was waiting. Saving all her money—and waiting.

When she was twenty she had saved five hundred dollars and she came to New York. Her final job in Detroit had been in the publicity department of a small advertising agency. In New York she landed in the secretarial pool at a large advertising agency. Ethel's big chance came the day a drunken movie idol who was appearing on one of the agency's shows wandered into the office. She had been thrilled to follow him back to his hotel. He had sobered instantly when he found he had taken a virgin. But he had been too drunk to remember that the virgin had practically raped him. He was frightened there might be repercussions. He offered her money. Ethel haughtily refused. It had been love, she insisted. His panic mounted. He was married and loved his wife. Was there anything he could do for her? Well, she explained she wasn't exactly thrilled being in the secretarial pool . . . He had acted immediately. With quick finesse and help from his agent he arranged for Ethel's transfer to the New York publicity office of his movie company.

This was smorgasbord for Ethel. She met a lot of drunken actors, even some sober actors. And she did it all for love. The word spread, and Ethel's career had begun. When an opening came in the publicity department at IBC, Ethel took it. After all, she had practically gone through the movie company's talent list. IBC offered more money and a whole new arena with its ever-changing shows. She was good at her work and superb at her hobby—her job was secure at IBC.

She was well aware that her reputation had traveled from coast to coast. She enjoyed the notoriety, even her title. One of the Six Swingers from Fire Island had gone to work in Los Angeles in the publicity department of Century Pictures. She and Ethel exchanged voluminous letters. Ethel described every detail of each current affair, gave the man a rating, and even included the size of his equipment. Ethel had a funny style and Yvonne, her correspondent, had Ethel's letters mimeoed and they passed freely around the office. When Ethel learned this, she took even greater pains to be more descriptive. It worked almost like a paid ad for her. Many big names called her when they came to New York. Famous men . . . beautiful men. . . .

Often she wished Helga could see her on some of her dates with the handsome stars. Helga must be faded and loaded with kids by now. Helga had married Peter Cinocek!

She looked up suddenly. Danton Miller was standing at her table. He was very drunk.

"Hello, baby," he said with his Cheshire smile.

She smiled casually. "Well, well, if it isn't City Lights."

"Meaning what?" he asked.

"Like the picture of the same name. You only recognize me when you're drunk."

Dan pulled up a chair. He laughed. "You're a funny girl." He waved for another drink. Then he looked at her with a grin. "They say you're the greatest. Do you think I should lay you?"

"*I* choose who I lay, Mr. President. But don't feel sad —I've got you on my list, if there's a slow night."

"Is tonight slow?"

"It started that way . . ."

He threw his arm around her. "You're an ugly broad. In fact, you're really a beast. But I hear you're the greatest. Want to come home with me?"

"You make it sound so romantic."

His eyes narrowed. "I hear you also have a big mouth. That you spread the word, give a Nielsen rating on every guy you lay."

She shrugged. "Why not? My ratings save some of my girl friends from shacking up with a blintz."

Dan's smile was ugly. "Who the hell are you to give a guy a rating?"

"Let's say I have an excellent basis for comparison."

"Want a drink?" he asked, as the waiter placed his Scotch before him.

She shook her head and watched him drain the glass. He stared at her. "You're getting prettier by the minute, Gargantua. And I'm getting curiouser and curiouser."

"You're also getting very drunk," she said,

"Yeah, time to go home. Maybe I'll take you home with me."

"You forget, Mr. President. *I* make the decision."

He was almost humble as he stared at her. "Well, wanna come?"

She thrilled at the glorious surge of power. He was begging now. "If I do, you have to send me home in a Carey car."

"I'll send you home in a Rolls-Royce if you're half as good as they say." He lumbered to his feet and signaled for his check. She was relieved to see he automatically picked up hers.

"Are you sure you're sober enough to enjoy it?" she asked.

"You *make* me enjoy it," he challenged. "I think it's about time someone gives a rating on *you*."

She stood staring at him on the street. "Forget it. I'm too great to waste on a drunk."

He grabbed her arm. "Scared? Maybe your reputation is phony. Probably is. How could you be any different from any other dame—unless at the finish your cunt plays 'The Star Spangled Banner'?"

"I think I'll show you, little man." She hailed a cab and helped him in.

He had a nice apartment in the East Seventies. Typically bachelor and typically executive. He led her directly into the bedroom and fumbled out of his clothes. She saw the surprise on his face as she undressed. Her perfect breasts always caused this reaction.

"Hey, baby, you're stacked." He held out his arms.

She came to him. "A little better than Susie Morgan, huh?"

"Wouldn't know," he mumbled. He threw her on the bed. His kiss was sloppy. He tried to mount her but he was limp. She slid out from under him and rolled him over.

"Take it easy, sonny," she said. "You may be president of the network, but you're just a boy to me. Now lie back. Ethel will show you what love is about."

She started making love to him. And as his excitement mounted, as he responded and whispered, "Baby, baby . . . you're the greatest," she forgot that tomorrow he would pass her in the hall without a nod. Right now she was making love to the president of IBC. And right now she *felt* beautiful. . . .

# SIX

D ANTON MILLER tossed the trade papers aside. He couldn't concentrate on a damn thing. He spun his chair around and faced the window. In one hour he was to have lunch with Gregory Austin. He had no inkling what it was about. No warning, just the goddam phone call and the impersonal voice of Gregory's secretary.

So far the ratings were about the same. News was still in the cellar, but the new guy, Andy Parino, had just started cutting in from Miami a week ago. He had to admit it gave the show an extra dimension. Well, that was their problem. He had his own. The variety show was canceled. He was positive the Western Gregory had handpicked to replace it would bomb. And he was determined to come in with a mid-season saver. That's why he had spent every night of the past week with two writers and a half-baked singer named Christie Lane.

Last week he had stumbled into the Copa to catch a well-known comic—Christie was merely the supporting act. At first Dan had paid no attention to this forty-year-old second-rater who looked like an old-time Coney

Island singing waiter. Dan had never heard of the bum. But as he watched him, an idea began to form. Suddenly Dan turned to Sig Hyman and Howie Harris, the two writers who had accompanied him, and said, "He's just right for what I want!" He knew they thought it was the whiskey talking. But the next morning he sent for them and told them he wanted to do a pilot with Christie Lane. They had stared at him with disbelief.

"Christie Lane! He's a stumblebum, he's over the hill," Sig Hyman stated.

Then Howie jumped in: "He can't even get a Saturday night at the Concord or Grossinger's off-season. Did you read the Copa show notices in *Variety?* Christie didn't even get a mention. The Copa girls' costumes did better than he did. He only plays New York as a filler-in when they've got a jumbo name. And those Irish ballads—" Howie rolled his eyes.

And Sig added the clincher: "Besides, he looks like my Uncle Charlie who lives in Astoria."

"That's just what I want!" Dan insisted. "Everyone has an Uncle Charlie they love."

Sig shook his head. "I hate my Uncle Charlie."

"Save the jokes for the script," Dan answered. Sig was right about Christie's looks. He looked like Mr. Average Man. He'd be perfect for a homey-type variety show. Sig and Howie gradually got the idea. They were top writers who had worked only for established stars. Three months ago Dan had given them each a year's contract to help him develop new shows.

"We make Christie the host," Dan had explained. "Form a stock company—girl singer, announcer, do sketches—and we make use of Christie's singing voice. If you close your eyes the bum sounds like Perry Como."

"I think he sounds more like Kate Smith," Sig said.

Dan smiled. "I tell you the timing is right. Television runs in cycles. With all the violence of *The Untouchables* and its imitators, the time is ripe for a show the entire family can watch. Christie Lane is a second-rater. But no one in TV knows him, so he'll be a new face. And we'll use a big guest star each week to attract ratings. I tell you it can work!"

Like many performers, Christie Lane had started in

burlesque. He could dance, sing, tell jokes, do sketches. He worked with Dan and the writers with hysterical eagerness. Dan guessed him to be about forty. He had sparse blond hair, a large homely face, and a medium frame that was beginning to show the hint of a potbelly. His ties were too loud, his lapels were too wide, the diamond ring on his pinky too big, the cuff links were the size of half-dollars, yet Dan sensed he could create a likable character out of this oddly assorted but talented man. He was an indefatigable worker. Whatever town he played, he quickly scurried about and managed to pick up extra club dates on the side. He lived out of two wardrobe trunks and when he was in New York, he stayed at the Astor Hotel.

By the end of the first week, Dan's conception of the show had begun to take form. Even the writers got "with it." They wouldn't change the awful ties, the wide lapels. Christie actually thought he dressed well. He liked the goddam ties. This was the key to his character, Dan told them. They'd pick some good songs for him to sing, but at the same time allow him to do something corny of his own choosing.

Dan had sent a brief synopsis of the show to Gregory last week. Perhaps the lunch was about the show. But Gregory wouldn't waste a lunch just to okay a pilot. He'd send down word to go ahead . . . or to kill it. He hoped Gregory gave him the green light. It would be grim to have put in all this time and work for nothing. He got a headache at just the thought of all those nights in the smoke-filled suite at the Astor. Christie and those cheap cigars. And always the ever-present show girl from the Copa or the Latin Quarter sitting patiently and wordlessly; reading the morning papers; waiting for Christie to be finished. And the stooges—the two alleged "writers" Christie carried with him. Eddie Flynn and Kenny Ditto. They were supposed to supply Christie with jokes. As far as Dan could see they were "gofors." "Hey, Eddie, go for some coffee." "Kenny, didya go for my cleaning?" Christie came from a world where a man proved his importance by the stooges he carried. Sometimes he paid Eddie and Kenny as little as fifty dollars a week. When things went well he paid them more. But they were "with him." He took them to nightclub openings, the racetrack, on tour, and now, as Christie had stated, "My boys must be put on the show as writers. They should each get two C's a week."

Dan had hidden his amusement and relief. Four hundred dollars a week tacked on to a budget was minuscule in a major television production. And it would make Christie indebted. Sig and Howie would get the major credit on the screen, and it was always easy to list additional dialogue in small letters in the crawl at the end of the show. Of course they were still far away from the pilot. But if Gregory gave him the Go signal, he could have a pilot on tape by August. He hoped to do the show live—tape it at the same time, so they could use it for delayed markets. They could save a lot of money doing it live and Dan would be a hero if he brought it off.

For a brief moment he felt good. Then he thought of the lunch and the ulcer pain began. What in hell was the lunch all about?

At twelve twenty-five he entered the elevator. The operator punched the button to Penthouse. Dan had once said P.H. also stood for Power House. The name had stuck among the executives. A man could be made or broken up there. Well, he was prepared for anything. He had taken two tranquilizers right after the phone call.

He walked directly to Gregory's private dining room. He noticed the table was set for three. He was just taking out a cigarette when Robin Stone entered. Gregory walked into the room and motioned them both to the table.

It was a sparse lunch. Gregory was on one of his health kicks. You never knew what to expect. Gregory had a chef who had worked at Maxim's in Paris. You could come there one day and enjoy a cheese soufflé and flaming French pancakes, sauce that stabbed an ulcer and delighted the taste. This usually happened when Gregory read that a contemporary had died in a plane crash, or was stricken with cancer or some similar inexorable disaster. Then Gregory would smoke, eat all the rich food and say, "Hell, a flowerpot could fall on my head tomorrow." This state of gastronomic luxury would continue until another contemporary had a heart attack. Then the Spartan regime commenced again. Gregory had been dedicated to this present health kick ever since his last bout of indigestion.

In the beginning the talk was general. They discussed the chances of any team against the Yankees, and the effect of the weather on their golf scores. This was a lousy April. Hot as hell one day, then wham, down in the forties.

Dan silently made his way through the grapefruit, the two lamb chops, the string beans, the sliced tomato. He passed up the fruit Jello. He wondered what Robin Stone was thinking. But most of all his sympathy went to the chef whose talent was being stifled with Gregory's present regime.

With the coffee, Gregory went into his life story. He told Robin about IBC. How he had created it. His early struggles building a new network. Robin listened attentively, asking an intelligent question now and then. And when Gregory complimented Robin on the Pulitzer Prize and even quoted from some of his past columns, Dan was properly impressed. The old man must think a lot of Robin Stone to do all this homework.

When Gregory put the unlit cigarette between his teeth, Dan sensed the real purpose of the lunch was about to begin.

"Robin has some pretty exciting ideas," Gregory said expansively. "It would come under network programming —that's why I invited you here today, Dan." Then he looked at Robin almost paternally.

Robin leaned across the table. His eyes met Dan's. His voice was direct. "I want to do a show called *In Depth*."

Dan reached for his cigarette case. The tone of Robin's voice had held no request. It was an announcement. He tapped the cigarette. So that was it. Gregory had already given Robin the go-ahead. This was just protocol, pretending to allow him to make the decision. He was supposed to nod and say fine! Well, fuck them—he wasn't going to make it that easy. He lit his cigarette and took a deep draw. As he exhaled, his smile was intact. "Good title," he said easily. "What would it be? A fifteen-minute news show?"

"A half-hour. Slated for Monday night at ten," Robin answered.

(The sons of bitches even had the time picked out!) Dan kept his voice even. "I think we have the new Western scheduled for that spot." He looked at Gregory.

Robin cut in like a knife. "Mr. Austin feels the *In Depth* show should go in there. It would prove IBC had integrity—expanding the news media to prime time, plus doing a new kind of news show. The Western can always go to another slot."

"Do you realize the money we'd lose? We have a chance to sell a cheap game show right after the Western. We'd have to give away the time following your kind of show." Dan was addressing Robin, but he was talking for Gregory's benefit.

"If the *In Depth* show comes off, you'll still get your prime time rate," Robin answered.

"Not on your life," Dan said coldly. "We also won't be able to get a sponsor interested in a half-hour news show." (He wondered why Gregory was just sitting there, letting him battle out this cockeyed idea with this egghead!)

Robin looked bored. "I know nothing about network sales. You can take that up with the sales department. My function at IBC is to bring some excitement and expansion into News programming, and I think this will be an exciting show. I intend to travel, to bring *In Depth* interviews to IBC about current world news. I might do some live shows out of New York or Los Angeles. I promise you this—I'll deliver a damn good news show that will be entertaining as well."

Dan couldn't believe what was happening. He looked at Gregory for support. Gregory smiled evasively.

"When would you put this show on?" Dan asked. It was too incredible to be true.

"October," Robin answered.

"Then you don't intend to go on camera before then?" Dan asked. "No seven o'clock news? No special coverage?"

"I intend to cover the conventions this summer."

"I assume you'll take Jim Bolt along. His face is well known, and he did a great job in fifty-six."

"He did a lousy job," Robin answered, with no change of emotion. "Jim is good with the seven o'clock news. But he shoots no juice or excitement at convention coverage. I'm forming my own team."

"Any ideas, or is this going to be another surprise?" Dan asked.

"I've got it fairly well planned in my own mind." Robin turned to Gregory Austin. "I'll take a team of four. The team will consist of Scott Henderson, Andy Parino, John Stevens from Washington and myself."

This time Gregory spoke up. "Why Andy Parino? He's not politically oriented. I like him coming in from Miami, but for a convention—?"

"Especially for the convention," Robin answered. "Andy went to college with Bob Kennedy."

"What's that got to do with it?" Dan asked.

"I think Jack Kennedy will be the Democratic candidate. Andy's friendship with the Kennedys might enable him to get us some back-door muscle."

Dan laughed. "I don't think Kennedy has a chance. He made his bid for Vice-President in fifty-six and lost. Stevenson will be the candidate."

Robin stared at him. "Stick to time costs and ratings, Dan. You know that scene. Politics and news are my bag. Stevenson is a good man, but he's going to be the bridesmaid at this convention."

Gregory cut in. "Dan—I'm for giving him a shot with this *In Depth* show. Ratings may be the name of the game, but we need some prestige. If Robin makes a name for himself with the convention coverage, the *In Depth* show might turn out to be a commercial hit as well."

"You think you can buck Cronkite, Huntley and Brinkley, men like that, at a convention?" Dan couldn't keep the sneer from his voice.

"I'll do my damnedest. With Andy Parino along, I might get to tape an interview with Jack Kennedy. If he is nominated, it will make an excellent *In Depth* opening show. Then you can bet that Mr. Nixon will be delighted to give me an interview, for equal time."

"Okay," Dan growled. "So you land yourself the candidates—that's two shows. What else do you plan to do? As I see it, so far it's just a platform for political candidates."

Robin's smile was easy. "I plan to go to London and do an interview with some of the top British stars—like Paul Scofield, Laurence Olivier. Then do one with an American star of equal stature and compare the different attitudes. In May, Princess Margaret will wed Tony Armstrong-Jones. I have a friend with UPI who's a close friend of Tony's. I'll shoot for an interview with him. I'm planning on leaving next week for San Quentin to try and tape an interview with Caryl Chessman. His latest execution date is scheduled for May second."

"He'll be granted another stay," Dan snapped.

"I don't think so," Robin answered. "And there's such a mounting feeling against capital punishment that it's important to do a show on the subject."

"I think it's a little too controversial," Dan argued. "I think all the subjects you've picked are too far out. The public won't go for this egghead crap!"

Robin grinned, but Dan noticed the coldness in his eyes. "I think you underestimate the public."

Dan smothered his anger. He went for the cigarette case again. By the time he lit one he was able to get the right note of condescension in his voice. "I think these ideas of yours are gallant and crusading. But while you're off knocking down windmills, I have to fight sponsors, juggle programs and worry about ratings. Before you take off on this safari, I think we should feel out some sponsors—after all, a network is team play. You can't grab the ball and run off like a steamroller and expect me to hold the line without knowing the signals. I like your spirit, your enthusiasm, but have you seen the schedule of NBC, CBS and ABC? We need variety shows to compete with them."

Robin's voice cut in like an icicle. "I'm not going to pump sunshine up your ass. I'm here to create excitement for the News end of IBC. Maybe your job is to sit around and see what hits on other networks—then try and come out with carbon copies of their hit shows. Okay, that's your route. Not *mine!*"

Gregory Austin's eyes were shining. He jumped up and clapped Robin on the shoulder. "I talked like that when I was your age. I had the same enthusiasm when I said I was going to start the fourth network. I broke rules, I hustled, I didn't listen to the doubters. Go ahead, Robin! I'll send word to Business Administration to okay all expenses. You bring back those shows. Dan and I will work things out from this end."

Robin grinned and started for the door. "I'll start things rolling right away. I'll be in touch with you, Mr. Austin, from all points." Then he left the room.

Dan was still sitting at the table. He stumbled awkwardly to his feet. Gregory Austin was staring after the closed door with unmasked admiration.

"He's quite a man," Gregory said.

"*If* things work out," Dan answered.

"They will! And even if they don't, at least he's in there pitching. Know something, Dan? I think I've just bought myself the greatest piece of manpower in the industry."

Dan left the office. He went back to his desk. The outline for the Chris Lane show was on his desk. Suddenly the whole idea seemed limp. The steely arrogance of Robin Stone deflated him. But he picked it up and put in a call for Sig and Howie. He set a meeting for four o'clock. God damn it—he had to make the Christie Lane show work. The *In Depth* show would fall flat on its ass, he was confident of that. But Gregory liked action. Okay, he'd give him a show too. Maybe it wouldn't have Tony Armstrong-Jones or a Kennedy, and maybe the *Times* would murder it, but he'd deliver a hot commercial show and a rating. And in the end, when the stockholders met, ratings were all that counted. Prestige didn't pay dividends. Only ratings paid dividends.

He kept Sig and Howie in his office until seven o'clock. When he let them go, he demanded that they bring him more than an outline—he wanted a rough draft of a script and format within ten days.

When the writers left, Dan suddenly decided to go out and get drunk. He sure as hell rated it. He walked over to "21" and stood against the bar. The regulars were there. He nodded and ordered a double Scotch. Something was bothering him, beyond and above the set-to with Robin. He searched his mind. It wasn't Gregory's admiration for the man, Gregory blew hot and cold with equal force. A few weeks of low ratings and he'd be very disenchanted with Robin Stone . . . no, something that had happened in that dining room had unsettled him. Yet he couldn't put his finger on it. He retraced all the conversation, but he couldn't find the cause. He ordered another double Scotch. Then he relived the luncheon again—every word, even Gregory's life story. He felt that if he only remembered, he would have the key and know where to fight and what to fight against. The battle with Robin was out in the open. Time would prove him the winner and he would emerge stronger than ever. It was as if he had stumbled across a key to a bigger danger and lost it.

He thought about Ethel. Maybe he'd really tie one on and let her come to his apartment and do the cold-cream job. With Ethel, you didn't have to bother about satisfying her—in fact he got the feeling that she liked it better when she didn't even have to undress. He almost began to feel good. But the nagging feeling persisted of something wrong in his universe—something to do with Robin Stone. Again, he went over the luncheon from the top, all the way to Robin's exit: "I'll start things going right away." Dan slammed the glass down with such force it broke against the bar. A polite waiter immediately wiped it up. The bartender poured another double and handed it to him. Dan took it. Christ, that was it! Robin's exit line: "I'll be in touch with you, Mr. Austin, from all points."

In touch with *you*, Mr. Austin!

Robin Stone was supposed to report to *him*, Danton Miller. And Danton Miller should report to Mr. Austin. The son of a bitch was sidestepping him, going over his head—right to Gregory himself. And Gregory had allowed it. Well that settled it—he'd *have* to make The Christie Lane show a smash. Now he had to come up with a winner.

He walked outside to the phone booth and called Ethel Evans.

"Want to meet me at my apartment?" he asked.

"I'm no call girl."

"Meaning what?"

"I haven't eaten."

"Okay, meet me at P.J.'s."

"Is that the only restaurant in town?"

"Honey"—he softened his voice—"it's eight thirty. I can't make it a late night. Next week, I'll take you anywhere you want to go."

"Is that a promise?"

"I swear on my Nielsens."

Ethel laughed. "Okay, I'll change to slacks."

"Why change?"

"Because whenever I see a girl walk into P.J.'s at nine, all caked up, it looks like she was disappointed. You know, had her hopes geared for Voisin or the Colony. But when she walks in wearing slacks, it looks like it's her decision."

"You've got everything figured out, haven't you?"

"Yes—even you, great man."

He laughed. He didn't want to argue with her. "Okay, Ethel, see you in half an hour."

He returned to the bar and finished his drink. He looked at his watch. It was bad enough to be seen with Ethel; he was not about to be seen waiting for her. He signaled for another double.

Someone tapped him on the shoulder. It was Susie Morgan. God, she looked so fresh and pretty.

"Dan, you know Tom Mathews?"

Dan found himself shaking hands with a sandy-haired giant. The name rang a bell. Yeah, he had just been appointed to the CBS legal department. Or was it NBC?

The giant almost broke his hand pumping it. Jesus, how young and hearty did he have to be!

"Dan, look!" Susie held out her hand. A microscopic diamond in a Tiffany setting was on the proper finger.

"Well, well, when did all this happen?"

"Tonight!" she said. "That is, I got the ring tonight. We've dated occasionally for a year and just started going steady the last three weeks. Isn't it wonderful, Dan!"

"Just great. Lemme buy you both a drink."

"No, we're having dinner upstairs with Tom's folks. But I heard you were in here and I wanted you to be the first to know."

"When do I lose you?" Dan asked.

"You don't. Unless you want to. We're getting married

in June, we'll have our honeymoon during our vacation. We both have two weeks coming. And, Dan, I'd love to continue to work for you until the lucky day when baby comes." She blushed and looked at the giant adoringly.

"You bet!" Dan nodded. "Let me know what you want for a wedding present."

He watched them as they left the room. It wasn't proper to be that happy. He had never been that happy in his life. . . .

But he had *power*. That was his kind of happiness. And he'd come up with a winner with the Christie Lane Show if it was the last thing he did. By then Robin Stone would have fallen on his ass with the *In Depth* show and there'd be a new president of News.

He looked at his watch. Holy God, ten o'clock. He signed his check and suddenly was aware that he was very drunk. He got into a cab and went home. So Ethel was waiting. So what? All he wanted to do was fall into bed. Let her wait. He didn't need to offer that cunt any explanations. She was a bum—and he was a big man!

# SEVEN

E THEL WAS WAITING. At ten thirty she called Dan. He answered after a few rings. "Who'sh this?"

"It's me, you drunken son of a bitch! I'm sitting at P.J.'s waiting for you!"

The receiver clicked in her ear. She stared at it for a moment, then slammed it down in fury. Christ! How had she ever allowed herself to get involved with him? Danton wasn't a movie star passing through on a one-night stand. And she didn't take any crap even from a movie star if he got out of line. She walked back to her table, paid her bill, and gave the place a final survey. She noticed everyone staring at a beautiful girl who had just entered the room, followed by two men. God, she was incredible-looking. They took the front table near the door. The girl looked familiar. Of course—she was on the cover of this month's *Vogue*. Ethel looked at the men. She had been so busy staring at the girl that she hadn't noticed them. One was Robin Stone, the other was Jerry Moss. She had met Jerry at a few agency parties.

She walked over to their table. "Hi, Jerry," she said with a smile.

He looked up and didn't rise. "Oh, hello there!" he said offhandedly.

She smiled at Robin. "I'm Ethel Evans. . . . We've met before. I'm with the publicity department of IBC."

Robin looked at her. He grinned slowly. "Sit down, Ethel, we can use another girl. This is Amanda."

Ethel smiled at her. The girl didn't return the smile. Her face was a mask but Ethel could feel the wave of resentment pour across the table. How can she be jealous of me? she thought. If I looked like that, I'd own the world.

Ethel took out a cigarette. Robin leaned across and lit it. She stared at him as the smoke curled toward his face. But he had switched his attention to his drink.

The silence at the table unnerved her. She felt Amanda's discontent, Jerry's uneasiness, and Robin's absorption with his drink.

"I just finished an assignment," Ethel said. Her voice sounded unnatural. She paused and almost whispered. "And then I stopped by to get a bite."

"No explanations," Robin said with the same easy grin. "You're here, relax." He caught the attention of the waiter. "What do you want, Ethel?"

She looked at his empty glass. She always made it a point to drink what the man drank. It started them off with at least one thing in common. "I'll have a beer," she said.

"Give the lady a beer," Robin said. "And bring me my glass of ice water."

The waiter brought the beer and a large glass of ice water. Robin took a long swallow. Amanda reached over and sipped it. She made a face and put it down vehemently. "Robin—" Her eyes were angry.

He grinned. "Don't you like ice water, baby?"

"That's straight vodka," she said.

Ethel felt a surge of excitement as she watched them curiously.

Robin took another long swallow. "So it is. I guess Mike made a mistake."

"You've got Mike trained," she said coldly. "Robin"—she leaned closer—"you said we'd be together tonight."

He threw his arm around her again. "We *are* together, baby!"

"I mean . . ." Her voice was low and pleading. "*Together*. Not with Jerry and another girl. I don't consider that being with you."

He rumpled her hair. "I got Ethel for Jerry. Now we're a foursome."

Amanda's face remained impassive. "Robin, I have an early booking for a color layout tomorrow. I should have stayed home and washed my hair and gone to bed early. But I came out to be with you. And now you're drinking."

"Aren't you having a good time?" he asked.

"I'd be better off home. You don't need me just to sit here and watch you drink."

Robin stared at her for a moment. Then the slow grin appeared. He turned to Ethel. "What time do you have to be up in the morning?"

"I don't need any beauty sleep," Ethel answered, "it wouldn't help."

Robin grinned. "Jerry—we've just switched girls."

Amanda grabbed her bag and stood up. "Robin, I want to go home."

"Sure, baby."

"Well?" Her eyes were too misty to be angry.

"Sit down," he said gently. "I like it here. I want to stay awhile." Amanda sat down reluctantly, her eyes challenging, awaiting his next move.

Jerry Moss stirred uneasily. "Ethel, maybe you and I should cut out. There's a swinging party a friend of mine is giving, just a few blocks from here—"

"I want you both to stay." Robin spoke quietly but it was a command. Then he drained his glass of vodka and ordered another. He turned and looked at Amanda with a tender smile. "She is beautiful, isn't she? And she should have sleep. I'm a thoughtless son of a bitch. Really want to pack it in, baby?"

She nodded, as if not trusting her voice.

He leaned over and kissed her on the head. Then he turned to Jerry. "Put Amanda in a cab, Jerry, then come back. After all, we can't let New York's top model lose her sleep while we do some serious drinking."

Amanda got up and walked out of the room. Jerry followed her helplessly. Every man at the bar stared as she walked to the door. When she got outside she crumpled. "Jerry, what did I do wrong? I love him, I love him so much. What did I do wrong?"

"Nothing, honey. He's just turned off for this evening. When he turns off no one can get through to him. He'll forget it by tomorrow." He whistled and tried to flag a cab.

"Make him realize I love him, Jerry. Don't let that ugly cow move in. She's trying to—isn't she?"

"Honey, Ethel Evans is a one-night stand for everyone. Robin knows the score. Now get a good night's sleep."

A cab pulled up. He opened the door.

"Jerry, I'm going back there. I can't let him—"

He pushed her into the cab. "Amanda, you've only known Robin a few months. I've known him for years. No one ever tells him what he can or can't do. You want to know what you did wrong? And I'm only guessing, but you made noises like a wife. You told him not to drink. Don't crowd him, Amanda. This man needs space. He was always that way. Even at college. Now go home, get your sleep, I'm sure it will be all over by tomorrow."

"Jerry, call me when you leave him. No matter how late it is—how can I sleep when we've parted like this! Please, I've got to know, even if he tells you he's had it with me—or if he winds up with that girl . . ."

"He won't tell me anything. You should know that."

Jerry was suddenly aware that the taxi driver was enjoying the scene while his meter was clicking. He gave him Amanda's address.

She rolled down the window. "Call me, Jerry"—she reached out and grabbed his arm—"*please.*"

He promised. Then he watched the cab disappear. He felt for Amanda. Robin hadn't been intentionally sadistic tonight. He had just turned off. Jerry had learned to recognize this trait in him. Maybe it was part of his charm. You could always count on Robin to do the unexpected. Like inviting Ethel Evans to join them.

"How about some hamburgers?" Jerry asked, as he returned to the table.

"You can afford to skip a meal," Robin said easily. "You missed gym twice last week."

"I live near here," Ethel said. "Why not come back to my place? I scramble crazy eggs." She looked at Jerry and added, "And I've got a very nice blond roommate. She might have a towel around her head but if we give her five minutes' warning, she can have the coffee going."

Robin stood up. "I'm not hungry. Jerry and I will walk you home. Then Jerry can walk me home." He picked up the bill and handed it to Jerry. "You sign it, junior. It's a write-off for you: entertaining a client."

Ethel lived at Fifty-seventh and First Avenue. She walked quickly trying to keep up with Robin's long strides. "You live near here?" she asked.

"I live on the river," he answered.

"Maybe we're neighbors—"

"It's a long river," he said.

They walked silently the rest of the way. For once Ethel found it hard going. He had a way of answering that seemed to curtail any added conversation. They stopped in front of her building. "Are you sure you don't want a nightcap?" she asked. "I have some hundred-proof vodka."

"No. I'm packing it in for now."

"Well, I guess I'll see you. I'm sure you're going to be very happy at IBC, and if there's anything I can do—"

His smile was slow. "I'm happy everywhere, baby. See you around." Then he walked off with Jerry stumbling after him.

Ethel stared at them as they rounded the corner. She wanted Robin so bad she physically ached. Why couldn't she look like Amanda? Why did she have to always kid and come on strong to get a man? What did it feel like to have a man actually call you and want you and look at you as if you were the most desirable woman in the world? She walked down to the river and knew the tears were running down her face. Oh God, it wasn't fair! It wasn't fair to put the heart and emotions of a beautiful woman into the body of a peasant. Why hadn't her emotions been as commonplace as her body? Then she could have settled for Peter Cinocek, maybe even been happy with him.

"Oh, God"—she said it aloud—"I just want to be someone, to have a man who *is* someone care about me. Is that too much to ask?" Suddenly she felt an unbearable loneliness. All the dreams, the one-night stands—but she had *nothing!* Sure, a nice apartment, beautiful compared to Hamtramck, but just a three-room modern place, shared with another lonely girl who also went after one-night stands. Sure it was great to hold a star in your arms, but the next night he was gone.

She walked back to her building. She was positive that Robin Stone was in Amanda's arms by now. She pushed this thought from her mind. No use making herself more miserable. There would be another night.

When Robin and Jerry left Ethel, they walked a few blocks in silence. They passed a bar and Robin said, "Let's cut in here and grab one for the road."

Jerry followed silently.

"Where do you put it?" he asked.

Instead of the usual silent grin, Robin stared at the glass seriously. "Christ, I went so long without drinking, I've got a lot of making up to do. I came from a health-oriented family. My father never touched it."

Jerry laughed. "And I used to think you were a swinger at college."

Robin stared at him as if seeing him for the first time. "Were you around Harvard at the same time?"

"Class before you," Jerry said meekly. He was glad no one else was around. Everyone knew he and Robin had gone to school together and thought their friendship dated back to that time. That was one of the disturbing things about Robin. He always seemed attentive, but you never knew whether anything you said registered. Suddenly Jerry was angry at his own submissiveness. He turned to Robin with a rare show of spirit. "Where in hell did you think we met?"

Robin rubbed his chin thoughtfully. "I never thought about it, Jerr. I meet so many people. Seems I just looked up one day at the Lancer Bar and there you were." Robin signaled for the check. They walked out in silence. Jerry walked Robin to the large apartment house on the river. It suddenly occurred to him he had never been to Robin's apartment. Either he walked him home, or they met at a bar.

When Robin casually said, "Come on up for a nightcap," Jerry felt embarrassed. It was as if those clear blue eyes had read his thoughts.

"It's pretty late," he mumbled.

Robin's smile was almost a sneer. "Wife waiting to give you hell?"

"No. It's just that I have a long drive ahead, and I have an early appointment in the morning."

"Suit yourself," Robin said.

"All right. One fast beer," Jerry conceded. He followed Robin into the elevator. He would put in a good word for Amanda, he told himself.

It was an attractive apartment. Surprisingly neat and well furnished.

"A girl I knew—before Amanda," Robin said, as he waved his hand around the room.

"Why did you treat Amanda so badly tonight? She loves you. Don't you feel anything for her?"

"No."

Jerry stared. "Tell me, Robin—do you ever feel *anything?* Have any emotions?"

"Maybe I feel a lot of things, but I'm not able to show it." Robin smiled. "I guess life would be a lot easier for me if I could. I'm like an Indian. If I get sick, I just turn and face the wall and stay there until I get better."

Jerry stood up. "Robin, you don't need anyone. But for what it's worth, I'm your friend. I don't know why, but I am."

"Bullshit—you're with me because you want to be. You just said it yourself. I don't need anyone."

"Didn't you ever feel any obligations toward anyone?" Jerry knew he was probing, but he was helpless to stop.

"Yep. In the war. A guy saved my life and he didn't even know me. He was in another plane. Suddenly he pointed to my right. A Messerschmitt was coming at me. I dived and got away. Two minutes later he got hit. I owe him a hell of an obligation. I owe him my life. I tried to find out who he was, but seven of our planes were knocked out that day. I would have done anything for that guy—even marry his widow if she'd have me. But I never knew who he was."

"Then you'd feel the same way about a surgeon?"

"Nope. That's his job to save me. I'd be paying him. But this guy in the plane, he didn't know me. He didn't have to save my life."

Jerry was silent. "What kind of an obligation do you expect from a friend?"

Robin's smile was tight. "I don't know. I never had one."

Jerry started for the door. "Robin, I'm not going to give you my scout knife, or wait until you cross the street against signals and save your life. But I am your friend and I'll toss you some free advice. Don't write Amanda off as just another broad. I don't know her well, but there's something about her—I can't say what it is, but I sense it. She's quite a girl."

Robin put down his glass and came across the room. "Good God, I forgot about the bird." He went into the kitchen and switched on the light. Jerry followed him. There was a large ornate birdcage on the floor. And at the bottom a miserable little baby sparrow sat, staring at them.

"I forgot to feed Sam," Robin said, as he dug out some bread.

"That's a sparrow, isn't it?" Jerry asked.

Robin came over with a piece of bread, a cup of water and an eyedropper. He reached into the cage and gently took out the bird. It nestled in his hand with confidence. "The little jerk tried to fly too soon. It fell out of its nest and landed on my terrace and broke a wing or something. Amanda saw it happen. Naturally she rushed out and bought a cage, and I'm its new mother. She can't take it home: she's got a Siamese cat. The damn thing can walk up walls."

He held the little bird gently and it opened its beak expectantly. Robin broke off some bread crumbs and fed the bird. Jerry's amazement increased when Robin took the eyedropper and dropped some water down its little beak. Robin smiled sheepishly. "This is the only way it can drink." He placed it back in the cage and closed the door. It sat there and stared at Robin gratefully, its bright little eyes fastened on the tall man.

"O.K., Sam, it's nighttime now," Robin said. He switched off the light and walked back to the bar. "I don't think it's in pain," he said. "It eats like a son of a bitch—if something's in pain it doesn't eat, does it?"

"I'm not familiar with birds," Jerry answered. "But I do know that a wild bird can't live in captivity."

"Listen, as soon as the little jerk mends, I send him on his way. He's a smart little bird with a mind of his own. Did you notice how he closed his bill after he had some crumbs, and demanded water?"

Jerry was tired. It seemed incongruous that a man like Robin would be so gentle with a sparrow and so callous to a woman. "Why not call Amanda and tell her the bird is okay?" he suggested.

"She's probably been sleeping for two hours," Robin answered. "Her career comes first. Look—don't worry about Amanda. She's been around the turf, she knows the score."

Robin was pouring himself another drink when Jerry left. It was late, but he decided to walk to the garage. It would clear his head. On impulse he stopped at a drugstore and called Amanda.

"Jerry—I'm so glad you called. Oh, Jerry, he wound up with that cow, didn't he?"

"For your edification, we left that cow at her door maybe twenty minutes after you left."

"But it's so late—what have you been doing? Why didn't you at least call and tell me? I would have been able to sleep."

"Well, we walked, then we stopped at a bar, then we walked to his place, then we drank and talked. And then we fed the goddam bird. When I left him he was extolling its virtues—how brilliant it is: it knows when it wants water."

She laughed in relief. "Oh, Jerry. Shall I call him?"

"No. Amanda, play it cool. Give it time."

"I know. I'm doing my best. You do all the right things automatically when your heart isn't involved. You play it cool without even trying. It's different when you care. I've never cared before. I'm in love with him, Jerry."

"Don't let him know."

Her laugh was forced. "It's crazy, isn't it? To love someone, and have to hide it. You're a man, Jerry. Did your wife play it cool? Is that how she got you?"

He laughed. "Mary wasn't a top model and I'm not Robin Stone. And if I don't get home, I may not have a wife. Good night, honey."

# EIGHT

THE FOLLOWING MORNING Robin awoke at seven. He felt good. No matter how much vodka he consumed, he had yet to experience his first hangover. He was properly grateful to whatever mysterious force in his metabolism created this phenomenon and decided to enjoy it while it lasted. He realized that one day he would wake up feeling like any other guy who drank too much. He went to the refrigerator and poured himself a large glass of orange juice. Then he got a crust of bread and lifted the cover off the birdcage. The sparrow was lying on its side, its eyes wide open, its body stiff with death. He picked it up and held it in the palm of his hand. Poor little fellow must have been busted up inside. "You never complained either, you little bastard," he said. "I like your style."

He threw on a pair of slacks and a sport shirt. Then he put the small body into a cellophane bag. He left the apartment and walked to the river. "A burial at sea, Sam. I can't offer you anything better than that." A battered gray barge was inching its way along. He tossed the little bag into the black water and watched it spin into the ripples created by the boat. "I'm sorry you didn't make it, fellow," he said. "But at least you have one true mourner, which is a lot more than most people can claim." He waited until the bag disappeared, then he walked back to the apartment.

He stood under a cold shower and when he turned off the water the phone was ringing. He quickly tied a towel around his waist and dripping water across the room, he grabbed the receiver.

"Did I wake you, Robin?" It was Amanda. "I have an early booking. I wanted to get you before I left."

He fished around for a cigarette.

"Robin—are you there?"

"Yep." He was searching the night table for matches. He found them on the floor.

"I'm sorry about last night."

"What about last night?"

"My walking out, but I just hated that girl and I guess I was tired and—"

"That was last night. Forget it."

"How about tonight?" she asked.

"Fine. Want to cook for me?"

"I'd love it," she said.

"Then it's a deal. Make it steak and that crazy salad."

"Robin, how's the bird?"

"It's dead."

"But it was alive last night!"

"It was?"

"Well—" She thought quickly. "I figure it had to be, or you would have told me."

"You're right. It kicked off sometime between two and five this morning. It was already stiff when I saw it."

"What did you do with it?"

"I tossed it in the river."

"You didn't!"

"What did you expect? Did you want it laid out at Campbell's?"

"No, but it sounds so callous. Oh, Robin, don't you ever feel anything?"

"Yep. Right now I feel wet."

"You know what you are? You're a cold son of a bitch." She said it as a statement of fact rather than in anger.

He laughed. She heard him drag on his cigarette.

There was a pause. "Robin—what do you want out of life?"

"Well, right now I want some eggs."

"You're impossible!" She laughed to break the mood.

"Then you'll be here at seven. Steak and salad. Is there anything else you want?"

"You."

She laughed and some of her confidence returned. "Oh, Robin, I forgot to tell you. Next week, I've been invited to the April in Paris Ball. They sent me two free tickets, and they cost a hundred dollars each. Will you take me?"

"Not on your life."

"But I *should* go . . ."

"Baby, I may not even be in town next week."

"Where are you going?"

"Maybe Miami, I want to start shaping up a team for the convention coverage with Andy Parino. He's with our O&O station down there."

"What's O&O?"

"Owned and operated. Each network is allowed to own and operate five stations. Want to come? Ever been to Miami?"

"Robin, I don't have vacations. I work all winter and summer."

"Which reminds me, I've got to work too. See you at dinner, baby. And for God's sake, keep that damn cat in the bathroom. He sat on my lap all through dinner last time."

She laughed. "He adores you. And, Robin—I love you." But he had already hung up.

Amanda grabbed a cab and headed for the Lancer Bar. That last job had run thirty-five minutes overtime. It meant a lot of money, but it also meant she didn't have time to go home and change. And she had wanted to wear the new pale blue raw silk. Robin was back from Miami and it was their last night together before he left for Los Angeles and the Democratic Convention.

Damn Nick Longworth! She had wanted to take ten days off and go to Los Angeles with Robin. It would have been so marvelous. Of course during the five days of convention she wouldn't see much of him. But after that he and Andy Parino were taking a few days off to play golf at Palm Springs. Robin's invitation had been casual, but he *had* invited her!

Nick had been adamant. She was getting to be one of

the hottest models in town. In the fall he was going to raise her fee again. He had too many important bookings for her in July. When she had explained this to Robin, she had longed for him to say, "To hell with the bookings —I'm your future." But he had only said, "Sure, baby, I keep forgetting how much money there is in the rag business." And he had meant it.

But Nick was right. She had worked hard to get into this bracket. She needed the money and if she missed out on a few important jobs, it was more than just losing the money—it was giving another girl a chance to hit! She was on her way to the top.

She looked at her watch. She was ten minutes late and the cab was inching along. She sat back and lit a cigarette. No use worrying. Andy Parino was probably with Robin anyway. He had been with them every night since he arrived from Miami. She liked Andy. He was very attractive, actually he was probably better-looking than Robin. But she accepted his looks with the same apathy she felt toward the handsome male models she occasionally posed with. Beautiful, but so what? Yet just thinking about Robin made her feel light-headed. She wanted to get out of the creeping cab and run. But it was hot and humid outside and her hair would be ruined.

Their last night together. No, she mustn't even think that way. He'd only be gone ten days. But ever since he'd become president of News he was always going off somewhere. He had been to Europe twice. She wondered if Andy would stick with them all evening. The last three nights they had met at the Lancer Bar, then gone to the Italian place and she didn't have Robin alone until midnight. And the last three nights he had done an awful lot of drinking. Yet no matter how much he drank, it never seemed to affect his lovemaking. But she liked it better when he was sober—then she knew it was the man whispering the endearments, not the vodka.

The dim light of the bar made her blink. "Over here, baby!" She heard Robin's voice and headed toward the booth in the back of the room. Both men stood up. Andy smiled in his open friendly way. But Robin's grin and the fleeting second when their eyes met and held obliterated

Andy, the bar, the noise—even her heartbeat seemed suspended in that one wonderful moment of intimacy no one else could share. Then she was sitting beside him, and he was back to talking politics with Andy. And the room and noise came into focus. She watched him as he talked. She wanted to touch him but she sat back, her face composed in the "Nick Longworth Look": slight smile—no movement of features—no lines.

The waiter placed a martini in front of her.

"I ordered it," Robin said, "I'm sure you can use it. It must be hell to stand under lights on a day like this."

She didn't like the taste of alcohol. In the old days (before Robin) she would order a Coke and blandly say, "I don't drink." But somehow her instincts had warned her that Robin would never stay with a girl who didn't drink. Most of the time she toyed with a drink. Sometimes she poured half of it into his glass. But today the martini felt cold and smooth. Maybe she was finally developing a taste for them.

Robin and Andy went back to the subject of the coming nomination. As the conversation continued, he unconsciously reached out and held her hand, which was his way of including her in a discussion that was over her head.

"Eleanor Roosevelt is coming as a last-ditch effort to help Stevenson, but he hasn't a chance," Robin commented. "It's a shame, he's a great man."

"Don't you like Kennedy?" Amanda asked. Actually she didn't care one way or another, but she felt she had to show some interest.

"I've met him. He has great magnetism. I intend to vote for him. I'm just saying it's too bad Stevenson is going to lose. It's very rare to have two good men on the scene at the same time. It happened with Willkie, but he was running against Roosevelt. Who knows what might have happened if Willkie had been born ten years later?"

Then they fell to discussing the Vice-presidential nominee. She heard the names, Symington, Humphrey, Meyner. . . . She sipped her drink and watched Robin's profile.

They went to the Italian place at nine. And when dinner was over and Andy suggested going to P.J.'s for a nightcap, to Amanda's delight Robin shook his head: "I'll have ten days of you, junior. This is my last night with my girl."

He was unusually tender that night. He ran his hand through her light hair and looked at her gently. "My lovely Amanda, you're so clean and sleek and beautiful." He held her close and stroked her neck. And he made love to her until they both broke away exhausted and fulfilled. Then he leaped up and pulled her out of bed. "Let's take a shower together."

They stood under the warm water. She didn't worry that her hair was soaked, that she had a job at ten in the morning. She hugged his wet body because now, this moment, was all that mattered. And when he reached out and turned on the cold water, she shrieked, but he laughed and held her close. After a moment her body grew used to it and it was wonderful. He kissed her with the water pouring on their faces. Then they got out of the shower and he grabbed a towel and wrapped it around them. She stood and stared into his eyes. "I love you, Robin."

He leaned across and kissed her. Then he kissed her neck, and her small flat breasts. He looked up. "I love your body, Amanda. It's clean and strong and wonderful."

He carried her back to the bedroom and made love to her again. Then they both fell asleep locked in an embrace.

Amanda awoke because Robin was lying on her arm. It was dark and her arm was numb. She eased it from under him. He moved slightly but did not wake. She saw the bright eyes of the Siamese cat glowing in the dark. Dear Lord, he had managed to push open the door. He inched forward and sprang on the bed. She held him quietly and nuzzled him. He purred in contentment. "I've got to put you back in the living room, Slugs," she whispered. "Robin doesn't like to wake up and find you around his neck."

She slipped out of bed carrying the cat. Robin stirred and his hand hit her empty pillow. "Don't leave me!" he shouted. "Please—don't leave me!"

She dropped the startled cat and rushed to his side.

"I'm here, Robin." She held him in her arms. He was shaking, staring into the darkness.

"Robin"—her fingers touched the cold dampness of his brow—"I'm here. I love you."

He shook his head like a man coming out of water. Then he looked at her and blinked as if he had just awakened. He grinned and pulled her to him. "What happened?"

She stared at him.

"I mean what in the hell are we doing sitting up like this in the middle of the night?"

"I was just putting the cat out and I was thirsty and then you yelled."

"I yelled?"

"You said, 'Don't leave me!' "

For a brief moment there was something close to fear in his eyes. Suddenly he smiled. "Well, don't go sneaking off again."

She clung to him. It was the first time she had ever seen him vulnerable. "I'll never leave you, Robin, never. I love you."

He held her away and laughed. He was in complete command again. "Leave me any time you want, baby. But not in the middle of the night."

She looked at him oddly. "But why?"

He stared into the darkness. "I don't know. I really don't know." Then he flashed his easy grin. "But you put an idea into my head. I'm thirsty too." He slapped her on the buttocks. "Come on, let's go into the kitchen and have a beer."

They drank the beer and he made love to her again.

The seasons melted into one another for Amanda. The early spring had brought Robin into her life. By summer their relationship had turned into a permanent blaze of excitement. He had been to Los Angeles and Chicago for the conventions. And each time he returned, she seemed to want him more than ever. Her love for Robin refused to find a level. It soared on and on to a peak of feverish infinity. And she was frightened of it because she knew Robin could not even begin to feel this kind of emotion. And the acclaim he received for his convention coverage did not add to her inner security. His new stature merely loomed as a threat—anything that took him away from her was a threat. If she ever lost him, she wouldn't want to go on. She fervently wished he was back doing local news.

In October they sat in his apartment and watched his first *In Depth* show together. Gregory Austin called to congratulate him. Andy Parino called from Miami to congratulate him. Andy had just met a young divorcee and was in love!

Robin laughed. "Sure, it figures. With all the girls in Miami, a nice Catholic boy like you has to fall for a divorcee."

"Maggie Stewart is different!" Andy had insisted. Of course, he admitted, his religion did create a few barriers, but it seemed that the main obstacle was the lady herself. She didn't want to get married. Andy had hired her to do a five-minute spot on their local news, and as he put it, at least they worked together.

Amanda listened quietly. Perhaps it was then that the first vague pattern of her plan began to form. It crystallized into action a few nights later when she giggled at the deadpan delivery of a girl doing a commercial on *The Late Show*.

"Don't knock it," Robin said. "It's not easy to be natural when the red eye of the camera is on you."

"What do you think I do?" she asked.

He pulled her to him and said, "You, my lovely one, pose for one shot fifty times until they finally catch you looking like the angel that you are. And if that doesn't work, there's always the airbrush and retouching."

Amanda thought about it. If she did a good commercial on television, perhaps Robin would really respect her. She talked to Nick Longworth about it. He laughed. "Dear girl, it's a brilliant idea. Except: one, you can't talk. That's a talent in itself. Two, you can't be one of many girls in a party scene. We only use neophyte models in that area. I have three booked for a beer commercial. The only thing you could do would be a big glamour product, and those kinds of commercials don't just drop in your lap. Usually they go after a Hollywood-type spokeswoman—one who can be glamorous and also sell the product."

On Christmas Eve they trimmed a tree in her apartment. Robin gave her a wristwatch. It was very tiny and very beautiful but without a hint of a diamond on it. She masked her disappointment. She had given him a cigarette case, a slim gold envelope with a facsimile of his handwriting. Jerry dropped by for a pre-Christmas drink before he hurried home to Greenwich. He brought champagne and a rubber squeak toy for Slugger.

That night as they were going to bed, Slugger leaped on the bed with his new toy. Amanda moved to collect the cat and put him in the living room. "Let him stay, it's Christmas Eve," Robin said. Then he added, "Oh, I forgot something." He went to his jacket which was sprawled on a chair and took out a flat box. "Merry Christmas, Slugger." He tossed the box on the bed. Amanda opened it. Tears came to her eyes as she looked at the soft black leather collar. It had silver bells and a little silver tag with his name engraved on it.

She threw her arms around Robin and hugged him. "You *do* like Slugger—"

He laughed. "Sure I do. I just don't like him sneaking up on me. This way those goddam bells will warn me of his approach." Then he took her in his arms and kissed her and they didn't even hear the silver bells as Slugger disdainfully leaped off the bed and left the room.

# NINE

I N JANUARY, the February replacements were announced in the television column of *The New York Times.* Dan smiled complacently when he saw that *The Christie Lane Show* was the lead story. He had sweated out the summer and literally wrung a good pilot out of Christie. And when Gregory viewed it and gave him the green light, Dan threw away the tranquilizers.

Tonight he would really celebrate. Unconsciously his thoughts went to Ethel. Maybe it had been a mistake assigning her to *The Christie Lane Show*. But hell, he had to pay her off some way. There was no one, but no one, who could compete with that dame in the feathers. She had flipped at the assignment. He knew it wasn't just the extra twenty-five bucks, the big attraction was the Hollywood guest star she would meet each week. Well, she was a good-natured nympho—and he sure as hell couldn't hump her more than twice a week. So if she wanted to slip in a Hollywood name on her free time, well, that was the least he could do for the bitch. And this way, maybe she'd lay off the "Take me to '21'." bit. Oddly enough, Ethel had no amorous inclinations toward Christie Lane. She said he gave her the creeps. "His skin is so pasty white, reminds me of a chicken's belly." From then on she referred to Christie behind his back as C.B.

Dan leaned back in his chair and his smile radiated contentment. All he had to do was wait until February. Then he'd bring in a big winner. He already had Alwayso as a sponsor. To go along with Christie as '"Mr. Average Man," Dan had lined up a plain-looking girl singer, a homespun announcer, and each week a big-name guest star would add some glamour. He had hired Artie Rylander, a top producer who had made his name in the fifties, doing live variety shows. Alwayso was going along, and doing their commercials "live." Once again, Dan reveled in his luck. A beautiful girl doing the commercials was the perfect contrast to the homey family format of *The Christie Lane Show*.

Right now Jerry's office was probably loaded with every beautiful model in town. Jerry intended to use a male "voice over," and have the model demonstrate the product. But as Jerry had said, they had to settle on one girl and stick with her. It was quite a problem.

Dan smiled. For months he had been closeted with Christie Lane, the "gofors," Sig and Howie, and Artie Rylander. And Jerry had an office stacked with beautiful models. He shook his head. He should have such problems.

But Jerry did have a problem. Amanda. Amanda with her cool Nordic features, her high cheekbones, the heavy blond hair, was perfect for the product; she had also done the Alwayso magazine layouts last year. Jerry wanted her for the show—but how would Robin take it if he hired her?

Would he say, "What the hell are you doing? Trying to suck up to me?" or, "That was damn nice of you, Jerry. I sure appreciate it."

Suddenly he hated himself. Dammit, the issue should be who was best for the job and not how Robin would feel! He sat and stared at the picture on his desk of Mary and the kids. Was he abnormal in his feelings about Robin? That was ridiculous! He had no sexual desire for Robin Stone! He just liked him, liked to be with him. But *why* did he like to be with him? Sometimes Robin treated him with the same offhand conviviality he tossed at Carmen, the bartender at the Lancer Bar. Then there were days when Robin hardly spoke to Jerry at all. Or then again, Robin could be gregarious, almost glad to see him: "Your drink is waiting, Jerr." Yet secretly, he had the suspicion that if he suddenly stopped calling Robin, stopped dropping in at the Lancer Bar at five, he would never be missed.

He pressed the buzzer and told his secretary to send Amanda in. A few seconds later she strolled through the door. God, she even walked like her damn cat. She was wearing a leopard coat, her blond hair streaming to her shoulders. Leopard! She also had a mink. All his wife had was an otter.

She sat down in the chair across from him, undaunted by the daylight that shot at her face. He had noticed that some of the older models always cautiously turned away from it. But Amanda's face was flawless and she knew it.

"You really want the job?" Jerry asked.

"Very much."

He stared at her. Jesus, she was even getting to talk like Robin. Short and to the point.

He saw her steal a glance at her watch. Sure, her time was valuable. Then he noticed the watch. Holy Christ—it was the Vacheron job, the tiniest watch he had ever seen. Mary had admired it in the window at Cartier's. But it cost over two thousand with the tax.

"That's a beautiful watch," he said.

She smiled. "Thank you. . . . Robin gave it to me for Christmas."

He was silent. He had sent Robin a case of a hundred-proof vodka. Robin hadn't even sent him a Christmas card.

Suddenly she leaned across the desk. Her eyes were urgent. "I want this job, Jerry. I want Robin to be proud of me." She gave him an imploring look. "Oh, Jerry, I love him. I can't live without him. You're his best friend. What do you think my chances are with Robin? It's been almost a year that we've been going together. And sometimes I think I'm no closer to him now than the first day we met. He's so unpredictable—what do you think, Jerry? Men confide in one another."

His entire mood changed. Suddenly he felt an odd sense of empathy with her. God, it must be hell for a girl to be in love with a man like Robin. He was glad he was a man. Glad he was just a friend to Robin.

"Jerry, I want to marry him," she said. "I want to have his children." Her face went tense. "You know what I've done with my evenings during the weeks he's away? I've taken a reading course at the New School. I've finished *Pickwick Papers*, and I've started on Chaucer. And when I tried to discuss them with Robin, he laughed and said he had no desire to be Professor Higgins. But I'll keep at it. Oh, Jerry—sometimes I wish I didn't love him this much. Even after he's spent the night with me, when he leaves the following morning, I snuggle against the towel he's used. Sometimes I fold it up and put it in my tote bag and carry it with me all day. And I reach for that towel and touch it. And it almost smells of him . . . and I get weak. I know it sounds silly, but I do this even when I know I'm going to meet him at the Lancer Bar that very day. And each time I walk in there I die because I think maybe he won't be there, yet he always is. And sometimes when I sit with him and he grins at me, I think, Oh God, can I just hold this moment, make it last forever. And that scares me because it means maybe I expect to lose him someday." She put her hands over her eyes as if to block out the thought.

Jerry felt his own eyes become moist in sympathy. "You won't lose him, Amanda, you're doing fine. You've held

him almost a year. That's a record in itself." Then he
handed her a contract. "I think you'll be just wonderful
for our product. And it's our pleasure to have you on the
show."

Tears threatened to spill down her face. She reached
for the pen and quickly scratched her name on the contract. When she held out her hand she was once more in
complete control.

He watched her as she left the office. Who would ever
dream that this supergirl, this perfect creature, was going
through a torturous love affair? It must be torture, loving
Robin Stone. Because any woman would know she never
really had him and sense that one day she must lose him.
He knew the Amandas would come and go, while he
would always be able to join Robin Stone at the Lancer
Bar.

Two weeks later Jerry paid his first visit to a psychiatrist. He had been making love to Mary with startling
infrequency. When she first brought it up, she had tried
to make light of it: "Hey, you with your work and your
golf on weekends—have you forgotten the woman you
love?"

He had looked properly startled. As if it had been an
oversight.

"Not once all summer," she said good-naturedly. "And
now it's the middle of September. Do I have to wait until
it's too cold for golf?"

He had made excuses, mumbling about how hectic the
start of a new season always was. September was pressure time.

In November he blamed it on commuting. The weather
was too hazardous to drive, and it was rough taking the
train each morning, rushing for the train home. No, it
wasn't because he was at the Lancer Bar with Robin
Stone. He *worked* late!

During the Christmas season he had more excuses. Everything was hectic. In January he had Alwayso to con-
tend with. The commercials had to be written, the
product selected for the first commercial—hair spray, or
the new iridescent nail polish? If these excuses appeased
Mary, they did not satisfy the nagging doubt that was

beginning to form in his own mind. Well, he *was* tired, the weather *was* lousy, and he had a cold that hung on. There were even times he blamed Mary's fat pink hair rollers. How was a guy supposed to be filled with desire when his wife slid into bed with fat pink rollers and a face loaded with night cream! To avoid arguments he kept silent. The atmosphere began to feel like a pressure cooker. And one night it exploded.

It happened on a Tuesday, a week after he had hired Amanda. He had spent the day checking the commercial copy. Everything went according to schedule. He had felt good. It had been one of those rare days, a day that had passed without any crisis. Even the weather was clear. He had taken the five-ten train and when he walked up the path to his house he suddenly felt a sense of well-being. It had snowed the day before. In New York it was already mashed into small banks of dull gray slush. But in Greenwich it looked like a Christmas card, clean and untouched. The lights that glowed in the windows beckoned warmth and hospitality. He entered and felt enveloped with contentment. The kids had yelled "Daddy! Daddy!" with pealing enthusiasm. He had played with them, enjoyed them, and felt relief when the maid took them off to bed. He had mixed martinis and had Mary's waiting when she came into the living room. He complimented her on her hair. She accepted the drink without smiling. "It's the same way I've been wearing it for a year." He refused to allow her lack of enthusiasm to penetrate his sense of tranquillity. "Well, it looks particularly good tonight," he said, as he raised his glass.

She stared at him suspiciously. "You're home on time. What happened? Did Robin Stone stand you up today?"

He was so angry he choked on his martini. Mary accused him of being flustered and he stormed out of the room. A tight knot of guilt began to form in his throat. Robin *had* stood him up. Well, not exactly, but when Amanda was in his office, she had begged off at four thirty, claiming she had a five o'clock modeling session. Secretly he had been pleased: Robin would be alone at the Lancer Bar. He called Robin the moment she left the office. "Lancer Bar at five?" he had asked.

Robin had laughed. "For Christ's sake, Jerry, it's my

first day back in town. Amanda is cooking for me. I'm skipping the bar today, see you tomorrow."

His face had burned with anger. But after a few minutes he cooled off. Big deal! So he'd see Robin tomorrow. And it was high time he surprised Mary for once and got home early.

Of course he had made up with Mary. She had come up to the bedroom waving a fresh martini as an overture of truce. That night Mary didn't cream her face or use the fat pink rollers, but when they went to bed together he couldn't get it up. This had never happened before! Sporadic as their sex life had been during the past year, the few times they had been together, it had always been fully consummated. She had turned away from him and he knew she was crying. He buried his own fears and apologized to Mary—blamed it on himself, on the martinis, on the pressures of the new Christie Lane Show. Then he even went for a checkup and asked for a B-12 shot. Dr. Anderson said he didn't need B-12. When he finally stammered his real problem, Dr. Anderson recommended Dr. Archie Gold.

He stormed out of the office. He didn't need a psychiatrist! God—if Robin ever dreamed he even considered such a thing he'd—well, he sure as hell wouldn't waste time on him. Robin would look at him in disgust, he'd be a weakling.

He didn't care what Dr. Anderson said. He didn't care how many healthy normal men went to psychiatrists when they stumbled on some kind of "block." He would never go to a shrink!

But it was Mary who broke down his resistance. She greeted him with a smile each night. She never wore the pink rollers anymore. He noticed she had new eye makeup. She took to snuggling against him in bed, and twice he had tried—but it hadn't worked. Now he was afraid to try. Each night he pretended to be exhausted. The moment he hit the bed he'd fake the even breathing of a man who has fallen asleep. Then he would lie awake and stare into the darkness as Mary crept into the bathroom and removed her diaphragm. He could hear her muffled sobs.

Dr. Archie Gold was surprisingly young. Subconsciously he had expected a guy with thick glasses, a beard, and a German accent. But Dr. Gold was clean-shaven and nice-looking in a subdued way. He accomplished very little in the first session. Jerry had come right to the point: "I can't make it with my wife in bed, yet I love her and there is no other girl. Now, where do we go from there?" Before he knew it the fifty minutes were over. He was stunned when Dr. Gold suggested three visits a week. Jerry had been positive that whatever was bugging him could be straightened out in an hour. It was ridiculous! But he thought of Mary—the muffled sobs in the bathroom. . . . O.K. Mondays, Wednesdays, Fridays.

On his third visit, he did the entire session on Robin Stone. Gradually Amanda crept into the sessions.

At the end of two weeks he felt better. After some intensive Freudian soul-searching and probing back to his childhood, he had come to some disturbing revelations. He had personality problems but he was not a fag! At least that subconscious gnawing doubt had been removed. They discussed his father, an enormous virile-looking man who had ignored him during his childhood. Then he suddenly began going with him to the football games, and his father had cheered for Robin Stone until he was hoarse. "Now, that boy's magnificent!" his father would shout. "That's what I call a man!" He recalled one specific incident when Robin had whipped through an impossible wall of players to score a touchdown. His father had leaped to his feet. "What a boy—that's it, son!"

Through Dr. Gold's gentle probings he recalled other fragments of ego-damaging evidence. When it was finally conceded that Jerry was not going to grow any taller than five feet nine, his father had snorted, "How could I have spawned such a shrimp? I'm six foot one. Christ, you take after your mother's family. The Baldwins are all puny."

O.K. At least he understood some things now. In trying to gain Robin's friendship, he was still seeking his father's approval. He was jubilant with this discovery. "I'm right in my diagnosis, aren't I?" he asked Dr. Gold. The cool gray eyes merely smiled. "You must answer your own questions" was the reply.

"What the hell do I pay you for if you don't give me the answers?" Jerry demanded.

"I'm not supposed to give answers," Dr. Gold said quietly. "I'm here to prod you into working things out and coming up with your own answers."

The week before the show opened he stepped up his visits to daily sessions. He gave up his lunch hour. Dr. Gold preferred to see him between five and six, but Jerry refused to give up the Lancer Bar. He insisted it was his only way of escaping tension—sitting with Robin, having a few drinks. But when he missed the train, he was torn with guilt for Mary and the dinner that was ruined.

On such occasions Jerry would be abrasive with Dr. Gold, demanding to know why he suffered such guilt. Why did he *have* to go to the Lancer Bar each day and sit with Robin, knowing he would suffer guilt toward Mary?

"I can't go on like this—wanting to please Mary, wanting to please myself. Why can't I be like Robin? Have no conscience, be free."

"From what you say about Robin Stone, I'd hardly say he was free."

"At least he's his own man. Even Amanda feels she has no real hold on him."

Then Jerry told Dr. Gold Amanda's searing confession about carrying Robin's towel; Dr. Gold lost his usually bland expression and shook his head. "She really needs help."

"Oh come on! She's just a highly sentimental girl in love!"

Dr. Gold frowned. "That's not love, that's an addiction. If a girl seemingly has all the attributes you give her, her relationship with Robin Stone should give her a sense of fulfillment. Not this kind of fantasizing. If he ever turned her against him . . ." Dr. Gold shook his head.

"You can't just sum up people this way. You don't know them!"

"When will Robin Stone be back?" Dr. Gold asked.

"Tomorrow. Why?"

"Suppose I meet you at your Lancer Bar. Then you can introduce me to Robin and Amanda."

Jerry stared at the ceiling. "But how would I explain you? I can't very well say, 'Hey, Robin, my shrink wants to case you.'"

Dr. Gold laughed. "It's conceivable we could be friends. We *are* about the same age."

"Could I say you're just a doctor, not a shrink?"

"Some of my best friends are people," Dr. Gold answered. "Couldn't you have one friend who is a psychiatrist?"

Jerry was nervous when he saw Dr. Gold walk into the Lancer Bar. Robin was on his third martini and today of all days Amanda was working and meeting Robin later at the Italian place for dinner.

"Oh, I forgot to tell you," Jerry said as Dr. Gold approached. "An old school buddy of mine is dropping by."

Jerry threw his arm around the doctor. "Archie"—the unfamiliar name almost stuck in his throat—"this is Robin Stone. Robin, Dr. Archie Gold."

Robin looked at the man with little interest. Robin was in one of his silent moods. He concentrated on his drink. Dr. Gold wasn't exactly loquacious either. His cool gray eyes calmly appraised Robin. Jerry began to babble nervously. Someone had to talk!

At one point Robin leaned across and said, "Are you a surgeon, Archie?"

"In a way," Dr. Gold answered.

"He cuts out ids." Jerry tried to make his voice light. "Would you believe it, Robin—Archie's a shrink. We ran into one another at a party and renewed old acquaintance and he told me—"

"Freudian?" Robin cut in, ignoring Jerry.

Dr. Gold nodded.

"Are you a psychiatrist or a psychoanalyst?"

"Both."

"You went through a hell of a long training—then you had to go through two years of personal analysis yourself, didn't you?"

Dr. Gold nodded.

"You're a good man," Robin said. "It must have taken a lot of guts to go through school with a moniker like Archibald. You must be very secure."

Dr. Gold laughed. "Insecure enough to shorten it to Archie."

"Were you always interested in this gaff?" Robin asked.

"Originally I wanted to be a neurosurgeon. But a neurologist often comes face to face with incurable illnesses. He can only prescribe medicine to ease the symptoms. But with analysis"—Dr. Gold's eyes suddenly became expressive—"he *can* cure the ill. The most gratifying thing in the world is to see a patient recover and begin to function, take his place in society and use his full potential. In analysis, there is always hope for a better tomorrow."

Robin grinned. "I know your bag, Doctor."

"My bag?"

Robin nodded. "You like people." He slapped a bill on the bar. "Hey, Carmen." The bartender came to him immediately. "This takes care of my tab. Give my friends another round and keep the rest for yourself." Then he held out his hand to Dr. Gold. "Sorry I have to shove off, but I have a date with my girl." He walked out of the bar.

Jerry stared after him. The bartender placed fresh drinks before them. "Compliments of Mr. Stone. Quite a guy, isn't he!"

Jerry turned to Dr. Gold. "Well?"

Dr. Gold smiled. "Like the bartender said, he's quite a guy."

Jerry couldn't conceal his pride. "What did I tell you? He got to you too, huh?"

"Of course. I wanted him to. I was more than receptive."

"You think he has any hangups—or bags?"

"I can't tell. On the surface, he's in complete control, and he seems to genuinely care for Amanda."

"How did you get that? He never even talked about her."

"When he left he said, 'I have a date with *my* girl'— possessive. He didn't say, 'I have a date with a girl,' which would be negating her importance, making her one of many."

"Do you think he likes me?" Jerry asked.

"No."

"*No?*" Jerry's voice held panic. "You mean he dislikes me?"

Dr. Gold shook his head. "He doesn't know you exist."

The control room was crowded. Jerry found a seat in the corner. In fifteen minutes *The Christie Lane Show* would go on the air—live! The entire day had been bedlam. Even Amanda had caught some of the tension. At the last rehearsal she had held the hair spray in the wrong hand and hidden the Alwayso label.

Christie Lane and his "gofors" seemed to be the only people unaffected with pre-show hysteria. They joked together, Christie mugged for the crew, the "gofors" went for sandwiches. They actually seemed to be enjoying the frenetic rehearsals.

The audience had already filed in. Amanda had said Robin was going to watch the show at home. Funny, Robin had never said a word, one way or another, about Amanda doing the commercial. Several times he had been tempted to ask her about Robin's reaction, but he couldn't without losing face.

Danton Miller entered, impeccable as ever in a black suit. Harvey Phillips, the agency director, rushed in. "Everything is shipshape, Mr. Moss. Amanda is upstairs having her makeup retouched. I told her to stick with the blue dress for the hair spray, and change to the green for the lipstick."

Jerry nodded. There was nothing to do but wait.

Dan told the director to click on the audio switch. The announcer had come onstage to do the usual corny warm-up. "Anyone here from New Jersey?" he asked. Several hands went up. "Well, the bus is waiting outside." The audience laughed good-naturedly. Jerry looked at his watch. Five minutes to air time.

Jerry suddenly began to wonder if the show would make it. It would be hard to tell even with the audience reaction. A studio audience loved every show. Why not— it was free. Tomorrow the reviews would come out, but reviews didn't matter in television. Nothing mattered but those damn numbers. They'd have to sweat it out for two weeks. Of course he would get an overnight rating, but it was the second week that counted.

Three minutes to air time. The door opened and Ethel Evans slipped in. Dan nodded coolly. Sig was the only one who stood up and offered her his seat, but Ethel waved it off. "I've got a photographer with me. Right

now he's taking some candids of Christie so I can service
them to the papers." She turned to Jerry. "After the show
I'll have him take some shots with Amanda and Christie."
She flounced out of the booth and headed backstage.

One minute to air time.

Suddenly there was complete silence in the control
room. Artie Rylander was standing, holding a stopwatch.
He threw his hand down, the orchestra went into a
theme, the announcer shouted, *"The Christie Lane
Show!"* The show was on.

Jerry decided to go backstage. There was nothing he
could do by remaining in the booth. His place was with
Amanda, in case she developed any last-minute jitters.

She was sitting in a small dressing room fidgeting with
her hair. Her cool smile gave him renewed confidence.
"Don't worry, Jerry, I'll hold the hair spray so you can
see the label. Sit down and relax, you look like a nervous
mother."

"I'm not worried about you, honey. It's the whole show.
Don't forget—*I'm* the one who made the recommenda-
tion to the sponsor. Did you watch any of the rehearsals?"

She wrinkled her nose. "For about ten minutes—until
Christie Lane started making idiotic mating calls." She
shuddered. Then seeing his face, she added, "But don't
go by me. As a man he's repulsive, but the audience will
probably love him."

The door opened and Ethel barged in. Amanda looked
at her. It was obvious she didn't place her. Ethel's glance
covered the room. She seemed surprised at finding just
Amanda and Jerry. Then she quickly smiled and held out
her hand. "Good luck, Amanda."

Amanda's expression was polite but curious. She knew
she had seen the girl somewhere.

"I'm Ethel Evans—we met at P.J.'s last year. I met you
with Jerry and Robin Stone."

"Oh yes." Amanda turned away and began spraying
her hair.

Ethel sat on the edge of the dressing table, her large
hips crowding Amanda. "It seems we're destined to be
thrown together."

Amanda backed away, and Jerry tapped Ethel's

shoulder. "Off, Ethel—you're blocking Amanda's light. Besides, this is not exactly the moment to renew old friendships."

Ethel's smile was friendly as she· got off the makeup table. "You'll be great, Amanda. They'll go hoarse whistling when you come on." She took off her coat and, without asking, hung it on the wall. "I've got to park this somewhere. Listen, I came by for two reasons: one, to wish you luck; two, I'd like you to take some pictures with Christie Lane after the show."

Amanda looked at Jerry who nodded slightly. Then she said, "All right, but it won't take long, will it?"

"Just three or four pops of the bulbs." Ethel started for the door. "I'll sit out front and watch the show. And look, Amanda, you've got to be a sensation. God, if I had your looks I'd own the world!"

Amanda felt herself thawing. There was an urgent honesty in Ethel's voice and she saw envy in her eyes. She said, "My aunt always taught me it takes more than looks to bring happiness."

"So did my mother," Ethel answered. "But that's a lot of shit. I've got an IQ of one thirty-six, and I'd trade it in for half a brain and a pretty face. And I'll bet anything that your fellow with *his* big brain would agree. By the way, is he coming to catch the show?"

"Robin, come *here?*" The idea of Robin sitting in a studio audience was so preposterous that Amanda laughed. "No, he's watching at home."

Amanda's cool detachment vanished the moment Ethel left the room. She reached out and grabbed Jerry's hand. "Oh, I hope he'll be proud of me. Has he said anything?"

"What has he said to you?" Jerry asked.

"He just laughed and said if I wanted to get into this rat race, it was my headache." Her eyes went to the large clock on the wall. "I'd better go down, the show's been on for ten minutes."

"You've got five minutes, maybe more."

"I know, but I want to phone Robin and remind him to watch. You know him—he might have made himself a few martinis, stretched out and fallen asleep."

The only phone in the theater was near the stage door. Jerry fidgeted as she stood and dialed in the drafty hall.

The music was blasting, the applause was strong, the show seemed to be going well. Amanda hung up as the dime fell into the coin-return box. "It's busy, Jerry. And I go on in a few minutes."

"Get going now, you've got to cross behind the curtain to your set."

"Wait—I'll try him once again."

"Beat it," he said almost gruffly. "You've got to be in place when the camera swings to you. Go check your props. I'll call him for you."

He waited until she disappeared behind the backdrop and appeared on the small set designed for Alwayso. Then he dialed Robin's number. The droning busy signal continued. He kept dialing until the actual moment of the commercial. "Damn Robin," he swore to himself. "He knows the girl is going on, why does he have to do this?"

He walked to the wings in time to give Amanda a smile of assurance. Her face lit up and he knew she interpreted it as a signal that he had reached Robin. She was poised and at ease when the camera came to her.

He watched her on the monitor. She photographed like an angel. No wonder she made so much money. She was breathless from nerves when it was over. "Was I all right?"

"Better than all right. Just great. Now you can relax for five minutes—then change, do the lipstick spot, and you're home."

"What did Robin say?"

"I didn't get him. The line was still busy."

Her eyes brightened ominously.

He grabbed her by the shoulder and steered her to the staircase. "Go up and change. And don't you dare cry and ruin your makeup."

"But, Jerry—"

"But what? He's home, at least you know that. And he was probably watching while he was on the goddam phone. It might have been an emergency, even an overseas call. War could be declared for all we know. Maybe an atom bomb dropped somewhere. Believe it or not, *The Christie Lane Show* is not the biggest happening in the universe. We only *act* as if we're discovering a cure for cancer in here."

Christie Lane ambled over. Bob Dixon was on stage doing his medley. "Didja hear that applause! And all for me! I'm the greatest!" He put his hand on Amanda's arm. "And you're the beautifulest. If you play your cards right, Uncle Christie just might take you out for a sandwich after the show."

"Take it easy," Jerry said, easing Christie's hand off Amanda's arm. "You haven't put Berle or Gleason out of business yet. And what's with the uncle bit?"

"Haven't you heard what Dan-the-man has been saying all these months? I'm the family image. I remind everyone of their uncle or husband." He turned his watery blue eyes on Amanda. "Doll, do I remind you of any relative? I hope not, because it would be incest with the thoughts I'm thinking." Before Amanda could answer, he said, "Well, the movie star has finished his off key number. Now watch the *real* pro go out and kill them." Then he dashed onstage. Amanda stood very still, as if she couldn't believe what had occurred. Then she turned and started for the phone.

Jerry stopped her. "Oh no, you don't. You've got exactly six minutes to change your dress and touch up your makeup. *After* the show, you can call him. And I'll bet you a late supper at '21' that he's watched you. As a matter of fact, I'll take you both there to celebrate."

"No, Jerry—I want to be alone with him tonight. I'll bring him some hamburgers." She looked toward the stage at Christie Lane and shrugged. "Maybe I'm crazy, but they do seem to like him." Then she ran up the stairs to her dressing room.

Amanda did the second commercial with equal ease. When the show ended, the small backstage area turned into a mob scene. Everyone was shoulder-punching one another. The sponsors, Danton Miller and the writers were clustered around Christie, shaking his hand. The cameraman was flashing pictures. Ethel came over and grabbed Amanda. "I want to get a picture of you with Christie."

Amanda broke away and raced to the telephone. Ethel followed her. "Can't it wait? This is important."

Amanda ignored her as she dialed. She was conscious of Ethel standing and glowering. Jerry came and stood

close at hand, protectively. This time there was no busy
signal. It rang once, twice, three times. After the tenth
ring, she hung up. Her dime returned. She dialed again.
The same monotonous ring, and Jerry and Ethel were
watching her. She could see the beginning of a smirk
come to Ethel's lips. She straightened up. She was Robin
Stone's girl! She wasn't going to let them see Robin
Stone's girl crumple. He wouldn't like that. When he held
her in his arms last night, their bodies close, he had
stroked her head and said, "You're just like me, baby—
resilient. No matter what anyone does to either of us, if
we hurt, we hurt inside and no one will know. We don't
cry on anyone's shoulders, or even to ourselves. That's
why we belong together." She forced herself to think of
this now, as the phone kept ringing to emptiness. She
hung up and casually took the dime from the coin box.
She faced Ethel and Jerry with a smile. "You know I'm
an idiot, I guess I was so nervous about the show that
I completely forgot—" She stopped, groping for some
alibi.

"Was it still busy?" Jerry asked sympathetically.

"Yes! And you know why? He told me he was going to
take the receiver off the hook so that no one would disturb him. And I forgot!" She turned to Ethel. "So let's
take the pictures, then I'll dash to his place as we
planned. And Jerry, would you be an angel and call
Cadi-Cars? Tell them to send a limo for me."

Then she walked toward Christie Lane and stood between him and Bob Dixon, flashed her brightest smile
and quickly squirmed out of Christie's arms as soon as
the picture was taken. Fortunately he was so mobbed
with the agency men he didn't see her slip away.

Jerry called for the car. He wondered about the phone
story and thought it odd that she would forget. But her
smile was too genuine. She was absolutely sparkling.

Ethel had also noticed Amanda's assurance. God, to be
going home to Robin Stone—!

But once Amanda was in the protective darkness of the
limousine, her smile dissolved. She gave the driver her
home address. Well—eight dollars shot down the drain
for the limo. And there were plenty of cabs around. But
this had been the only thing to do. She had gone off with

her head held high—she was Robin's girl, and this was the way he would want it.

Robin phoned bright and early the following morning. "Hello, star," he said lightly.

She had been awake half the night, vacillating between hating him, renouncing him, alibiing for him, and, through it all, wanting him. And she had promised herself to play it cool when and if he did call. But the early morning call caught her off guard.

"Where were you last night?" she demanded. (Oh Lord, this wasn't the way she had intended to act.)

"Watching you," he said, in his same bantering tone.

"You were not!" She was breaking every resolve, yet was powerless to stop. "Robin, I called you right before the commercial and the line was busy. I called you after the show and there was no answer."

"You're absolutely right. The damn phone started to ring just as the show went on the air. Not that I minded —it was Andy Parino, and I'd rather talk to him than listen to Christie Lane. But after I got off with Andy, someone else called. And I wanted to catch your great performance without any distractions, so the moment you came on, I turned off my phone."

"But you knew I'd call right after the show."

"As a matter of fact, I forgot I had turned the damned thing off."

"Well," she spluttered, "then why didn't you try me? I mean, even if you forgot you turned it off you could have called me. Didn't you figure I'd want to be with you after the show?"

"I know what it's like after a new show goes on. It's insanity backstage. I was positive that you'd be the center of attention with your sponsors. I thought you'd probably go off and celebrate with them."

"Robin!" she moaned in absolute helplessness. "I wanted to be with *you*. You're my guy, aren't you?"

"You bet I am." His voice was still light. "But that doesn't mean total commitment on either side. I don't own you, or your time."

"Don't you want to?" she asked. It was a wrong move, but she had to make a stab.

"No. Because I could never fulfill my end of the deal."

"Robin, I want to belong to you—totally. I want to give you all my time. You're all that matters to me. I love you. I know you don't want to get married," she rushed on, "but that doesn't mean I can't belong to you in every sense of the word!"

"I want you to be my girl, but I don't want to own you."

"But if I'm your girl, then you must know I want you to share everything with me. I want to be with you through everything—and when you can't be with me, I want to be home waiting until you come to me. I *want* to belong to you."

"I don't want you to get hurt." His voice was tight.

"I won't get hurt. And I won't nag—I swear."

"Then let's put it this way: *I* don't want to be hurt."

After a pause she said, "Who has hurt you, Robin?"

"What do you mean?"

"You can't be afraid of being hurt unless you've been hurt. That's why you've erected a steel door to put between us every now and then."

"I've never been hurt," he said. "Honestly, Amanda, I'd like to be able to tell you that some siren broke my heart when I was a boy in the war. But nothing like that ever happened. I've had girls—lots of them. I love girls, and I think I care for you more than I've cared for anyone."

"Then why do you hold back a part of yourself—and force me to do the same?"

"I don't know, I really don't know. Maybe I've got some crazy sense of self-preservation. Some instinct that tells me that if I didn't have that door, as you call it, I might get my head blown off." Then he laughed. "Oh hell, it's too early in the morning for soul-probing. Or maybe I haven't got a soul. Maybe if I opened that steel door, I'd find there was no one home."

"Robin, I'll never hurt you. I'll love you forever."

"Baby, nothing is forever."

"You mean you'll leave me?"

"I could go in a plane crash, a sniper's bullet could hit me—"

She laughed. "A bullet would bend if it hit you."

"Amanda." His voice was light, but she knew he was serious. "Love me, baby, but don't make me your life. You can't hold on to people. Even if they love you, they have to leave you."

"What are you trying to tell me?" She was dangerously close to tears.

"I'm just trying to explain how I feel. There are certain facts we all know: one, you can't hold on to people; two, one day you have to die. We all have to die—we know it, but we ignore it. Maybe we feel that if we don't think about it, it may not happen. But deep down we know it will. I feel much the same about that steel door. As long as it's there to clang shut, I can't get hurt."

"Have you ever tried to open it?"

"I'm trying right now, with you." His voice was quiet. "I've unhinged it because I care enough about you to want you to understand. But I'm slamming it shut right now."

"Robin, please don't! Love me all the way. I know what the door is—it slams on *feeling*. You've closed that part of your brain. You *feel* love . . . but you refuse to think about it."

"Perhaps. Just as I refuse to think about death. No matter when I go, even if I'm ninety, it will be a hell of a disappointment to have to check out. But maybe if I don't care about anything too much, I won't be too sorry to leave."

She was quiet. He had never opened up this much to her. She knew he was trying to say something else.

"Amanda, I do care about you. And I admire you, because I think you also have your own steel door. You're beautiful, you're ambitious, and you're independent. I couldn't love or respect a girl if I was her sole reason for existing. I think in a curious way, the rocks in your head fit the holes in mine. Now: are we squared away?"

She forced herself to laugh lightly. "Everything's fine. Unless you stand me up for dinner tonight. Then I'll bash those rocks in your head into little pebbles."

His laugh matched her own. "Well, I can't risk that. I hear you Southern belles swing a mean right."

"Southern? I never said I was from the South."

"You never tell me anything, my beautiful Amanda. Maybe that's part of your charm. But when you talk, every once in a while some Georgia or Alabama comes through."

"Wrong states." Then after a pause she said, "I never told you anything about myself, because you never asked. But I want you to know about me, I want you to know everything."

"Baby, nothing is as dull as a woman without a past. And once you know all the details there is no past. Just a long dreary confessional."

"But actually you don't know anything about me—aren't you curious?"

"Well, I knew you had been around the turf when we met—"

"Robin!"

"I mean it in the nicest way. I'm too old to start up with a virgin."

"There haven't been so many men, Robin."

"Careful. Don't disillusion me. I've always been hung up on broads like Marie Antoinette, Madame Pompadour —even Lucrezia Borgia. Now if you tell me there was just that nice boy you met at college, you'll ruin the whole thing."

"All right, then I won't tell you about the South American dictator who tried to kill himself over me, or the king who offered to give up his throne for me. Meanwhile, shall I do the steak and salad bit for tonight?"

He laughed. The mood was broken and she knew she had put him at ease.

"Okay, baby. Steak and salad, and I'll bring some wine. See you at seven."

She fell back into bed and cradled the phone. Oh God, she just couldn't go on playing games like this. But she knew she would, she had to, until she had gained his complete trust. Then his guard would relax, and. . . . She jumped out of bed and turned on her bath. She felt wonderful. Even though she had two rough sittings, this was a marvelous day. The greatest day in her life. Because she knew she had the key to Robin Stone. Play it cool, demand nothing. The less she demanded the more he would give. And soon he would find that he did belong to her—it would happen so gradually he wouldn't even be aware of it.

For the first time, she felt confident. She knew everything was going to be just fine.

# TEN

A MANDA'S NEW BURST OF HAPPY CONFIDENCE remained with her throughout the day. When a pose grew tiring, she relived her telephone conversation with Robin and forgot the lights, the kink in her neck and the pain in her back. Dimly she could hear the photographer say, "Yeah, baby, oh yeah, hold that look!"

Her final session ended at four. She checked with Nick Longworth's office.

"You'll like tomorrow's bookings," Nick sang out. "Eleven tomorrow at *Vogue*—and your old buddy Ivan Greenberg is doing the layout." She was delighted. The first job wasn't until eleven. That meant she could sleep until nine. She could make Robin breakfast. . . .

It was an unnaturally warm day for February. A haze hung in the sky and the air seemed thick enough to cut. It wasn't supposed to be healthy weather, but it was fifty-five degrees and she could walk without freezing and she was happy, and to her it was the most beautiful day in the world.

She went home, fed Slugger, set the table, made the salad and got the steaks ready.

She was never able to eat when she was with him, she just picked at everything. She had lost ten pounds during this year with Robin. Five foot seven and only weighed one hundred and eight. But it was great for photography and so far it hadn't affected her face.

She turned on the television set to IBC. Robin liked to watch Andy on the seven o'clock news. She usually sat snuggled in his arms while he watched, or sometimes she sat across the room and studied his profile. But tonight she'd watch it—she wanted to be interested in everything that concerned him.

Gregory Austin was also waiting for the seven o'clock news. Once again he had to hand it to Robin Stone. He had been right about using Andy Parino. Funny—he had actually brought Robin in to do news, and he was turning out to be one hell of an executive. Robin was a good man but he was a phantom—he rarely saw him. You'd think someone who traveled so much on IBC's money would at least check in and say hello when he returned. *In Depth* received excellent notices—the ratings were rising all the time—you'd think he'd want to take his bows.

Danton Miller always came fawning for *his* praise. The son of a bitch was on the phone the moment *The Christie Lane Show* went off the air. Well, it just proved you couldn't overrate the intelligence of the television audience. They were a bunch of slobs. *The Christie Lane Show* was a piece of tripe—Judith hadn't even been able to watch it! And the reviews in the morning papers were brutal. But the overnight Nielsen rating was sensational. Of course the two-week national Nielsen would tell the story.

He thought about this as he sat in the paneled den of his town house and switched on the built-in color set. To him, the best thing on television was the old technicolor movies on *The Late Show*. They didn't make girls like Rita, Alice Faye and Betty Grable anymore. Sometimes when he couldn't sleep, he'd raid the refrigerator and sit and watch the movie glamour girls he had been secretly in love with. He had Judith to thank for the color set. In fact, the entire den had been a surprise. She had it done last year while they were at Palm Beach. He had wondered about all those surreptitious calls—those quick trips she had to take to New York to see her dentist. And when they had returned from Palm Beach she had presented him with the den. Even had a big ribbon tacked on the door. He had been touched. Judith had great taste. The room was completely masculine. He knew that each piece of furniture had been carefully selected and had a history. The big world globe was supposed to have belonged to President Wilson. The desk was an antique. He didn't know the period, he didn't care about those things. He could tell you the exact date *Amos and Andy* went on radio, and proudly show you the set of earphones he had

built as a kid. But antiques, Oriental rugs, Ming vases—
that was Judith's world and she understood his taste and
didn't foist her own on him. She got him antiques, but by
God, they were strong ones, none of those faggy thin-
legged French jobs. "Your domain," Judith had said. "I'll
only come when I'm invited."

A frown crossed his forehead. He felt a vague feeling
of disharmony. He couldn't put his finger on it but he had
felt the same way when they had moved here from the
Park Avenue penthouse seven years ago. When Judith
had pointed out the two master bedrooms separated by a
small wall of closets: "Isn't this divine, Greg? Now you'll
have your own bedroom and I'll have mine. And we each
have our own bathroom."

He had liked the idea of "his" and "her" bathrooms, but
had suggested turning one of the bedrooms into a sitting
room. "I like sleeping in the same room with you, Judith."

She had laughed. "Don't worry, my love—I'll snuggle
with you each night as you read the *Wall Street Journal*.
But when I go to sleep, at least I'll sleep. I won't have to
poke you eight times during the night to tell you to stop
snoring."

She was right and it *was* practical. In the beginning he
hadn't really believed he snored—until the night he had
purposely set the tape recorder by his bed. The following
morning he was in a state of shock—he couldn't believe
those unearthly snorts had come from him. He had even
gone for medical advice. The doctor had laughed.
"Nothing wrong, Greg—everyone snores after they hit
forty. You're lucky you can afford two bedrooms. It's the
only civilized way to keep romance going in a middle-
aged marriage."

After she had given him his den, she had gradually
taken over the large library. Fancied it up, changed the
color scheme, the drapes and some of the furniture. He
hated the room now. It looked like one of those VIP
suites at the Waldorf Towers. His autographed pictures
of Eisenhower and Bernard Baruch had been transferred
to his den. Silver-framed pictures of her relatives had
replaced them on the fancy desk of the library. Oh what
the hell, why shouldn't she have her relatives on display?
She had the classy ones. Why shouldn't her twin sister

who was a bona fide princess have her mug in a silver frame? And the two little princesses she had begot. And it was right to have that oil painting of Judith's father over the fireplace. God, the old man looked like an ad for some vintage wine. Gregory had no pictures of his father. They didn't take pictures to put in silver frames in the North of Ireland. Besides, Judith needed a library. She and her social secretary worked there every morning. He smiled at the thought of the word "work" applied to Judith. But then, maybe it was work planning all the parties, heading the charities, staying on the best-dressed list. He had to hand it to Judith—her personal publicity had been so great that people actually believed she had a personal fortune of her own when she married the two-fisted self-made Irishman named Gregory Austin. He smiled. Sure, she was social, went to all the right schools and studied abroad, but the family didn't have a dime. The rush of publicity when her sister married that prince had elevated the two girls to sudden fame. And now he felt Judith actually believed she *had* been wealthy in her own right before her marriage. So what—it must have been tough for her, watching her friends make their debuts and scrounging to keep up with them. She had been dropped from the Social Register when she married him, but he had brought her a new kind of society—the society that broke through every social barrier. Celebrity society. Talent was the greatest equalizer in the world. A Danny Kaye could be presented at court. A top politician could dine with a king. And the chairman of the board of IBC was welcome everywhere. Judith was a great girl and he was damn glad he had been able to supply the one missing ingredient in her perfect life. Judith Austin *was* society today. She was more than society—she *created* society. She made fashions, she was on the front page of that newspaper all the dames liked—*Women's Wear*. Whatever she wore became a trend. He still couldn't believe she belonged to him. She still seemed unattainable. He had felt that way the first moment they met, and he still felt the same way.

It was two minutes to seven. He went to the bar and mixed a light Scotch-and-soda for himself, a vermouth on the rocks for Judith. He wondered how she could drink the stuff. It tasted like varnish. But Judith claimed that all the great beauties in Europe only drank wine or vermouth. Of course, Judith meant the great beauties over forty. Funny how a beautiful woman like Judith could have an age complex. She entered the den after knocking lightly. This tapping was a joke—asking permission to come into "his" den. But he went along with it. He realized in some way it nullified any guilt she felt for taking over the library.

She took her place on the twin leather chair across from him. And he thought as he did every night when he saw her sitting there, "God, she's a beautiful woman." She was forty-six and looked barely thirty-five. He felt a sudden swell of pride and sense of well-being. He loved the goddam den—it had become a part of their lives. Even if they were going to the theater or giving a dinner party, they had their drink together in his den while they watched the seven o'clock news. To Gregory Austin, nothing got going until *after* the seven o'clock news. And Judith had dutifully built their social life around this order.

The news began: "Good evening and welcome to *News at Seven*. We are saving the last five minutes of our program for an unscheduled appearance of the president of IBC News, the star of *In Depth*, Mr. Robin Stone."

"What the hell!" Gregory sat on the edge of his chair.

"Since when has Robin Stone appeared on the seven o'clock news?" Judith asked.

"Since one second ago when I heard the announcement."

"He's a very handsome man," Judith commented. "But when I watch him on *In Depth* I get the feeling that he takes extreme care to let nothing of himself ever leak out before the camera. How do you find him?"

"Exactly like he is on television. You hit it right on the head. He's an enigma. Great surface charm, but everything else locked in."

Judith's eyes glinted with a touch of interest. "Let's invite him to dinner one night. I'd like to meet him."

Gregory laughed. "You can't be serious."

"Why not? Several of my girl friends are dying to meet

him. He's never seen in public. And he's really catching on."

"Judith, you know my rule. I don't mix with hired help."

"When we go to the Coast we attend their parties."

"I do that because I figure you get a bang out of it. Besides, that's different. They're throwing the parties for us. We're not inviting them to our home. The New Year's Day bash we give takes care of them. And it's great that way. Makes them feel they're being presented at court."

She reached over and patted his hand. "For a man who was raised on Tenth Avenue, you're the biggest snob in the world."

"No, it's just business sense. Hell—I couldn't care less about dinner parties or social status. But anything that's hard to get is sought after."

She laughed. "Gregory, you're a wheeling-dealing bastard."

"I sure am. Even our New Year's Day party is no open house. Very few people from IBC make it."

She smiled. "The eggnog party is so square that it's *in*. And it was my idea. Do you know *Women's Wear Daily* said it was becoming an annual event? It even made Ernestine Carter's column in the London *Times*."

"I think we had too many show-business names this year."

"We need them, darling. A few of them add dash to the party. And it isn't easy, Greg, getting the right people together at that time of the year."

He waved his hand, and listened to a news item that interested him. She was silent until the commercial came on.

"Greg, when can we leave for Palm Beach? We're usually there by the end of January. But you insisted on staying in town for the premiere of that dreadful *Christie Lane Show*."

"I want to stay here for a few more weeks. I think we can build that show into a real winner. But you can go. I'll get there by the beginning of March at the latest."

"Then I'll leave Thursday—I'll have the house all set when you get there."

He nodded absently. The news had returned to the air.

Judith stared at the screen without really watching. "Well, I guess Robin Stone will have to keep until next New Year's Day . . ."

"Not even then." Gregory handed her his glass for a refill.

"Why not?"

"Because I'd have to invite all the presidents of the other departments. Christ, Danton Miller only made it for the first time this year." He leaned over and turned up the volume.

She handed him his drink. Then she hung over his shoulders. "Greg darling, my girl friends don't want to meet Danton Miller. But they *do* want to meet Robin Stone."

He patted her hand. "We'll see, that's a year away. Anything can happen by then."

Suddenly he sat forward. The camera came in for a tight closeup of Robin. Gregory could see why Judith's friends were interested. He was a hell of a good-looking guy.

"Good evening"— The clipped voice filled the room. "We've all been fascinated by the news story of a genuine adventure of modern-day piracy. I'm speaking of the Portuguese cruise ship *Santa Maria* that was seized at gunpoint in the Caribbean by twenty-four Portuguese and Spanish political exiles and six crew members. This raid was led by Henrique Galvão, a former Portuguese army captain. Three days ago, January thirty-first, Admiral Smith went aboard the *Santa Maria* thirty miles off Recife, Brazil, and held a mid-ocean conference with Galvão. Word has just reached me that Galvão has agreed to allow the passengers to leave the ship today. Galvão has been promised, along with his twenty-nine followers, asylum in Brazil by President Janio Quadros. There were also American tourists on board. But most of all, this reporter is interested in obtaining a filmed interview with Henrique Galvão. I am leaving tonight. I hope to bring back an *In Depth* interview with Galvão and perhaps some of the American passengers who were on the pirated ship. Good night, and thank you."

Gregory Austin clicked off the set in rage. "How dare he just take off like that without reporting to anyone!

Why wasn't I told? He just returned from London a few weeks ago. I want *live* shows, not tape—that's our main selling point against the competition."

"Robin can't do all his *In Depth* shows live, Greg. It's the world-famous people who give it stature. I, for one, would be fascinated to see an *In Depth* on this Galvão. I'd like to see the man who at sixty-five has the courage to pirate a luxury liner with six hundred passengers."

But Gregory was on the phone, demanding that the IBC operator track down Danton Miller. Five minutes later the call came through.

"Dan!" Gregory's face was red with anger. "I'm sure you have no idea what's going on. *You're* sitting at '21' relaxing—"

Danton's voice was cool. "Yes, I was relaxing on a nice sofa in the lobby, watching our IBC seven o'clock news."

"Well, did you know about Robin's trip to Brazil?"

"Why should I? He doesn't have to report to anyone but you."

Gregory's face went a shade darker. "Well, damn it, then why didn't he tell me?"

"Perhaps he tried. You weren't in the office today. I tried to reach you several times during the afternoon with some further reports on *The Christie Lane Show*. The out-of-town notices were great. I had them put on your desk."

Gregory's face went rigid with anger. "Yes, I *was* out this afternoon," he shouted. "And I have a right to be out one afternoon in a month!" (He had purchased two new horses and had driven to Westbury to see them.) "Goddammit," he went on, "you mean, if I'm not there one day the whole network falls apart?"

"I don't think the network is going to fall apart because one guy takes off for Brazil. Still I don't like the idea of Robin Stone using the seven o'clock news as a publicity bulletin for himself. Gregory, I don't like the president of *any* department having this kind of authority. But, unfortunately, Robin does not have to check with me. Since you were unavailable, the announcement might have been his way of telling you. It's faster than Western Union."

Gregory slammed down the receiver. Danton Miller's

obvious pleasure over the situation spiked his anger into a helpless rage. He stood staring into space, his fists clenched. Judith walked over and handed him a fresh drink. Then she smiled at him. "Aren't you being childish? The man has pulled a big coup, for *your* network. Everyone who heard the seven o'clock news will be looking forward to the interview. Now relax and have your drink. We're due at the Colony at eight fifteen for dinner."

"I'm dressed."

She patted his face gently. "I think you might have one tiny run-over with the electric razor. We're having dinner with Ambassador Ragil tonight. And he's got three Arabian horses you're keen on. So come on. Smile! Let me see the Austin charm."

His frown disappeared. "I guess I like to be Big Daddy all the way," he said grudgingly. "And you're right. Making that announcement was a superb piece of showmanship. It's just that it's *my* network—I created it, built it. I don't like anyone making decisions without my approval."

"You also don't like your trainer to buy horses unless you personally inspect them. Darling, you can't be everywhere."

He grinned. "You're always right, Judith."

She smiled. "And I think by next New Year's Day Robin Stone will be big enough to rate an invitation. . . ."

When Amanda heard the news, she stood staring at the set. It couldn't be true. Any second the buzzer would ring and Robin would be standing at the door. He was probably on his way now, and she'd drive to the airport with him.

She waited ten minutes. By eight fifteen she had smoked six cigarettes. She called his apartment. It rang monotonously. She dialed IBC. They had no idea of what flight Mr. Stone was using, but suggested she try Pan Am.

At eight thirty the phone rang. She banged her ankle against the table, rushing to it.

"This is Ivan the Terrible."

Her face fell. She loved Ivan Greenberg, but tears ran down her face from disappointment.

"You there, Mandy?"

"Yes." Her voice was low.

"Oh—did I interrupt anything?"

"No, I was just watching television."

He laughed. "That's right, now that you're a big TV star you've got to keep up with the competition."

"Ivan, I adore you, but I want to keep my line open. I'm expecting an important call."

"Okay, pussycat, I know—I heard the seven o'clock news—the Great Stone Man is off, so I thought you might grab a hamburger with me."

"I've got to get off the phone, Ivan."

"All right, get a good night's sleep—we have an eleven o'clock sitting tomorrow."

She sat and stared at the phone. At nine fifteen she checked with Pan Am. Yes, there was a Mr. Robin Stone booked on the nine o'clock flight. The flight had gone on schedule—it had been airborne for fifteen minutes. She flopped into a chair while the tears ran down her face in black rivulets. Her mascara was all but gone and her false lashes were coming loose. She pulled them off and put them on the coffee table.

She got up slowly and walked into the living room. She had to talk to someone. Ivan had always been her confidant.

She dialed nervously and gasped in relief when he picked it up on the second ring.

"Ivan, I want that hamburger."

"Great, I was just leaving. Meet me at the Tiger Inn: it's a new joint on First Avenue, at Fifty-third. Right near you."

"No, you get the hamburgers and bring them here."

"Oh, I dig. Torture time."

"Please, Ivan, I've got steaks if you like, and a salad—"

"No, baby, if you stay home it'll be like real hysterics —and that means swollen eyelids tomorrow. Not when you're sitting for me, pussycat. I had to work an hour on the lights when the Stone Man took off for London a few weeks back. You want a hamburger, meet me at the Tiger Inn. At least there you'll have to keep your composure."

"I look awful. It would take me an hour to redo my eyes."

"Since when have you run out of dark glasses?"

"Okay." She felt too weary to resist. "I'll be there in fifteen minutes."

The Tiger Inn was enjoying a flash of popularity. It was almost filled. Amanda recognized some models and some advertising men. She toyed with a hamburger and stared at Ivan, mutely demanding an answer.

He scratched his beard. "There's no answer. He loves you this morning—and disappears this evening. With all the great cats in this town, you have to pick a character like Robin Stone. I mean, it's not even your *scene*. After all, who is he, what is he? Just a newscaster."

"He's not just a newscaster. He's president of IBC News!"

He shrugged. "Big deal! I bet if I mentioned both your names at every table here, they'd all know you and say 'Robin *who?*' When you walk into a restaurant, everyone knows you. But Robin Stone?"

Her smile was weak. "Robin doesn't care about things like that. We don't even go to the right restaurants! He has an Italian place he adores and the Lancer Bar. Sometimes I cook."

"God, what a thrilling life you have."

"I love it, Ivan! Look, I've been in this town *five* years. I've seen every place and nothing matters but being with the man you care about. I love him."

"Why?"

She scratched Robin's initials on the wet paper napkin. "I wish I knew."

"Is he better than anyone else in the feathers? Like, does he have a new scene?"

She turned her head away and the tears slid down under the rims of her dark glasses.

"Cool it, Mandy," he said. "Those cats across the room are staring."

"I don't care. I don't know them."

"But they know you! Christ, baby, you're on two covers this month. You're really hot. Enjoy it—make it pay!"

"Who cares?"

"*You'd* better care. It's a cinch that Robin Stone isn't about to pay your rent or buy you any fur coats. Maybe making money doesn't mean anything to you? Or maybe you have rich relatives or something like that going for you."

"No, I have to work. My mother's dead. I was raised by an aunt. I have to support her now."

"Then you'd better get with it! Make this year pay off. Because next year there could be a new girl. If you make it to the very top—play it smart and establish a top salary —you'll be a top model for maybe ten years."

The tears slipped down her cheeks again. "But it's not going to get me Robin."

He stared at her. "What's your scene, baby? Self-destruction? You enjoy sitting around and crying for him? Is that going to turn him on?"

"You don't think I've already lost him?"

"I only wish you had. Because he's bad news. A guy who walks through life without getting turned on destroys everything he touches."

"No, I ruined it. I know I did, this morning on the phone. I smothered him."

"Mandy, you're sick. Look, nothing is ruined. Maybe he's not so bad. Maybe *you're* just some kind of nut."

"Why? Because I'm hurt? I have a *right* to be. Look what he did to me!"

"Okay, what did he do? He left on a job without calling to say goodbye. Big deal! How many times have I done the same thing? And you've understood, because we're friends."

"That's different than love," she argued.

"You mean love fucks up everything."

She managed a weak laugh.

"Look, maybe Robin is a nice cat. I'm only reading him from you. But you should work your pretty little ass off to be a big smash. Make him proud of you—that's the way to hold a guy!"

"Oh, Ivan, you make it sound so simple. In a few minutes you'll have me waiting for his cable to arrive."

"Could happen. But you'll be a loser if you just sit around crying. Let word get to him that you're having a ball."

"Then he'd have a real excuse for dropping me."

"The way it sounds, this cat doesn't need an excuse for

anything. He does what he wants to do. Try playing it cool. Go out with other guys while he's away."

"With whom?" she demanded.

"I'm not running an escort service, pussycat. You must know plenty of guys."

She shook her head. "I've been seeing no one but Robin for a year."

"You mean no one else has ever made a pass?"

She smiled slightly. "No one that I've paid any attention to, including that horrible Christie Lane. But that wasn't a real pass. He just asked me out."

"You could do worse."

She looked at him to see if he meant it. When she realized he was serious, she made a wry face.

"What's so bad about Christie Lane?"

"You saw the show. He hasn't an ounce of sex appeal. He's a slob."

"Well, I wouldn't exactly rush and ask him to pose for *Esquire*. He's a nice average guy who happens to be a big star."

"He's not a star. I mean he's star of *The Christie Lane Show*. But did you see the notice in the *Times?* He has to be canceled after thirteen weeks."

"In thirteen weeks you could get a hell of a lot of publicity going out with him."

"But I can't stand him."

"I'm not telling you to go to bed with him. Just let some of his publicity wash off on you."

"But it wouldn't be right to go out with him just for publicity."

He took her chin in his hand. "You're a nice girl. A nice, *stupid* girl with an unlined face. A nice, stupid girl who thinks that face will stay intact forever. Honey, I'm thirty-eight and I can still get all the eighteen-year-old chicks I want. And when I'm forty-eight or fifty-eight with gray in my beard, I'll still get them. But when *you're* thirty-eight, you'll only get high-fashion jobs—full length, that is. If you've taken care of yourself! But no more face ads, or hands—the ugly brown age freckles will have started. And even a slob like Christie Lane won't look at you. But right now, and maybe for the next ten years, you can have anything and anyone."

"Except the only man I want."

He sighed. "Look, I know you're a sweet, regular girl or I wouldn't be sitting here wasting all this time when I've got a lot of work piled up and three chicks I could score with at the drop of a dime. Face it—Robin doesn't function like other people. He's like a great big beautiful machine. Fight back, baby, it's your only chance."

She nodded absently and scribbled the initials R.S. on the table with the swizzle stick.

## ELEVEN

JERRY MOSS ALSO WAS OUTRAGED at Robin's departure. He had checked with Robin at lunch and Robin had said, "Lancer's at five."

Jerry had waited until seven and only found out what had happened from Mary, who had accidentally heard Robin on the seven o'clock news.

He had a long session with Dr. Gold the following day. No, Dr. Gold did not think Robin was intentionally sadistic—he felt most of Robin's actions were based on an unconscious effort to avoid close ties with anyone. He demanded nothing of his friends and in turn wanted no demands made on him.

Amanda's talk with Ivan had helped her. When she arrived to do the second *Christie Lane Show* she had worked herself from deep depression into a state of self-righteous anger. The rehearsals had the same frantic excitement but the tension was gone. There was a sense of fun and goodwill, a certain confidence that permeates the atmosphere when there is the smell of a hit.

This time, when Christie Lane asked her to go out after the show, she accepted. They went to Danny's Hideaway with his "gofors" and Agnes, a show girl from the Latin Quarter who obviously belonged to one of them. Amanda sat beside Christie, but aside from asking her, "What do you want to eat, doll?" no other conversation passed between them. Jack E. Leonard, Milton Berle and several other comedians came by to congratulate Christie. He was thrilled with the attention and tried to trade jokes with them. Then, as he watched Milton Berle walk down the room to the front table, he said to Eddie Flynn, "I think we're sitting in left field."

The show girl said in a tinny voice, "No, Chris, honest. As long as you make this room, you're in good shape. It's known as the Cub Room. The squares with the brown-and-white shoes sit in the other rooms. This is the *in* room."

"How would you know?" Christie snarled.

"I know," she said calmly, loading butter on a bread-stick. "I once came here with a square—oh, long before I met you, lover," she said as she gave Eddie's arm a reassuring pat. "And we were led right into another room. I dug right away where all the action went on when I saw all the celebrities being shown in here. But the square, he was from Minnesota, he had no idea. He collected matches to take home and was happy as a clam."

"Yeah, but Berle has the front table. And look, the McGuire sisters are at the other."

"Marty Allen is sitting along the side." This was Kenny Ditto.

"Yeah—but up *front* on the side. Someday I'm gonna sit at the front table. And someday I'll go to the '21' Club."

Amanda was surprised. "Haven't you ever been there?"

"Once," Christie said. "I had a date and all she wanted was dinner at the '21' Club. I called and made a reservation. Then, wham—upstairs left field, in a corner. And like Agnes said, the girl I was with didn't know the difference. She collected matches, too. But I *knew*." He seemed thoughtful. "I got to get my name in the columns. That Ethel Evans isn't any good—Eddie, tomorrow we start with our own press agent. Smell around, find out who'll work for a C-note a week. All he has to do is get me three column mentions a week. Nothing else."

It continued on throughout dinner. Christie Lane and his "gofors" plotting his career. The show girl ate every-

thing in sight. Amanda learned that Kenny Ditto's name
was really Kenneth Kenneth—Christie had tacked the
Ditto on, and Kenny was thinking of legalizing it. Kenny
Ditto was a better name for a writer, it stood out on the
crawl on the show.

Amanda sat with them feeling strangely isolated, yet
relieved at being left to herself. When they drove up to
her apartment building, Christie remained in the cab and
let Eddie take her to the door. He shouted out, "How
about tomorrow night, doll? There's an opening at the
Copa."

"Call me," and she dashed into the building.

He called the following morning and she accepted the
date. It was better than sitting home moping about
Robin. That night Christie exuded confidence. The Copa
was his "home ground." They had a ringside table. She
was crammed in among Christie, the "gofors," and the
new press agent—a skinny boy who worked for one of
the major publicity firms. He explained that no decent
press agent would take on an account for that money, but
if Christie paid in cash he would "moonlight" and deliver
the three column mentions a week.

After the Copa, Christie wanted to go to the Brasserie,
but Amanda begged off, pleading an early call. The following morning, Ivan called to congratulate her on an
item in Ronnie Wolfe's column which stated she and
Christie were the new big romance in town. "Now you're
making sense," he said. She was frightened at first, but
when three more days passed with no word from Robin,
she decided to see Christie again. It was another nightclub opening, another table filled with the "gofors," the
press agent and a second-rate dance team who had
latched on, hoping for a guest shot on Christie's show.

The night of the third Christie Lane telecast was
charged with excitement. The two-week Nielsens had
come out—Christie Lane was in the top twenty! The
sponsors appeared, Danton Miller was shaking everyone's
hand, everyone was congratulating everyone. Alwayso
gave Dan an immediate renewal for the following season.
Thirty-nine weeks firm. That night Danton Miller threw a
little victory party at "21" after the show. Christie unloaded his "gofors" and took Amanda. Jerry Moss came

with his wife. They had a table downstairs in the middle section and although none of the captains knew Christie Lane, everyone knew Danton Miller and some of them even knew Jerry Moss. At one point in the evening, Danton Miller tried to make the proper small talk with Amanda. He complimented her and said she was excellent on the commercials.

"I'm used to a camera," she said modestly. "My real feat was learning to hold the lipstick without letting my hand shake."

"Have you ever acted? Pictures? The stage?"

"No, just modeled."

He looked thoughtful. "But it seems to me I've heard of you—"

"Perhaps in magazines," she said.

Suddenly he snapped his fingers. "Robin Stone! Didn't I see your name coupled with his?"

"I've gone out with him," she said carefully.

"Where the hell is he? And when is he coming back?" Dan asked.

"He went to Brazil." She was conscious that Jerry had stopped talking and had turned his attention to them.

Dan waved his hand. "That tape from Brazil came in over a week ago. Then he sent us one from France. He actually saw de Gaulle." He shook his head in amazement. "But now I hear he's in London."

She sipped her Coke and kept her expression bland. "I imagine he's getting wonderful tapes over there."

Danton smiled. "The ratings are pretty good, and for a news show it's solid. But your new boyfriend is our jumbo!" Dan looked at Christie and smiled.

Her new boyfriend! She suddenly felt she was going to be sick—physically sick. She was grateful that it was an early evening. Dan had a limousine and they dropped her off first. But Ivan was right. Two days later one of the afternoon papers carried a feature story on Christie Lane. The caption was THE MAN WHO LIVES NEXT DOOR. Amanda's picture was featured in a three-column cut: "The man who lives next door doesn't date the girl next door—he dates the top cover girl!" Christie was quoted as saying, "We've just been dating a few weeks, but man, I'm really hung on her." She threw the papers down in disgust. And she slammed down the phone on Ivan when he said, "Now you're getting smart, baby."

She reread the story. It was horrible—horrible! She stared at the open, vacant face of Christie Lane and felt nausea. So far they had been surrounded with stooges and comics and backslappers. But what would happen if there ever came a time when they were alone?

A few minutes later the phone rang and a jubilant Christie bellowed, "Doll—did you see the jazz in the papers? Well, this is only the beginning. Christie is going up, up, and up. And tonight we celebrate. Alone. I got Danton to get us a good table at '21' for cocktails and then we're going to dinner at El Morocco. Danton is fixing it—so we sit in the right place and not in Squaresville."

"I'm sorry, Christie," she answered. "I have a late booking, and a very early appointment tomorrow morning."

"Break it. You're going out with the new King—"

"I can't cancel my bookings. I earn too much money."

"Doll, whatever you lose, I'll pay you! What's the total?"

She thought quickly. She had no early bookings and her last appointment was at five. "Well, three hours tonight, and two tomorrow morning."

"Okay—what's the tab?"

She could hear him chewing on one of those foul cigars. She started calculating. "Between three hundred and seventy-five and four hundred dollars."

He whistled. "You make that kind of loot?"

"I get seventy-five dollars an hour."

"You're fulla shit!"

She clicked the receiver in his ear.

Two minutes later he rang back. "Doll, forgive me. It's just an expression. I mean, you knocked me on my ass. Eddie's girl, Aggie, well, she models for those confession magazines—and she gets ten bucks an hour. Fifteen if she wears a bathing suit, and twenty if she shows her tits."

"I don't do that kind of modeling."

"Maybe I better wise Aggie up. If there's this kind of

cash in modeling, what the hell is she doing posing for that crummy kind of dough?"

"Christie, I have to leave, I'm late as it is—"

"You're right. Listen, doll, for that kind of money, you need your sleep. We'll make the big leagues another night. But I have to keep the '21' bit—a lady from *Life* magazine is coming to have a drink with me. It's a shame you can't make it, you could cash in on the publicity if *Life* decides to do me."

"I'm sorry, Christie."

She hung up and resolved never to go out with him again. Never!

Then Ivan called. "I guess by now you've read *all* the papers," he said. "Well, at least the Christie Lane story saves your face, pussycat."

"What do you mean?"

"I thought America's top model would automatically go to the society columns first—you mean you haven't seen them?"

"No." She began rustling through the papers.

"Page twenty-seven. I'll hang on while you cut your wrists."

Robin's familiar grin hit her immediately. He had his arm around someone called Baroness Ericka von Gratz.

"Are you still there, pussycat?"

"Do you enjoy being sadistic, Ivan?"

"No, Amanda." His voice was low and serious. "I just want you to face facts. I'll be home if you need me."

She hung up slowly and stared at the paper. Baroness Ericka von Gratz was attractive. Robin was relaxed, from the look of it. She read the story:

Baroness Ericka von Gratz has not been around London since the death of her husband, Baron Kurt von Gratz. Those of us who have missed the fashionable pair are delighted to know she has come out of her mourning since the arrival of Robin Stone, American television journalist. The baron was killed in the Monte Carlo races, and for some time it was feared the lovely baroness would not recover from her mental depression. But for the past ten days she has gone to the theater and several intimate dinner parties with Mr. Stone. And now the pair have gone off to Switzer-

land to stay with the Ramey Blacktons in their Swiss
chalet. Skiing or romancing—it's hard to tell—but
everyone is delighted that our lovely Ericka is smiling
again.

She thumbed through the other paper. There was another picture of Robin and the baroness. She threw herself on the bed and sobbed. She pounded the pillow as if
she were slashing at Robin's smiling face. Then, with a
sudden change of mood, she sat up. Good Lord, she had
a three o'clock sitting for Halston and his new summer
hats! She rushed and got ice cubes, wrapped them in a
towel and put them on her eyes. Then she ran the hot
water for compresses: if she alternated with the hot and
cold on her eyes for half an hour, she would look all
right. She had to keep the appointment—she wasn't going
to lose a job because of Robin. He certainly wasn't pin-
ing away for her!

Then, with another swift change of mood, she dialed
Christie Lane. He answered immediately. "Doll, I was
just half out of the door on my way to the Friars. You just
caught me."

"I've canceled my late bookings," she said.

"Look, I was only kidding when I said I'd make it
up—I can't afford that kind of scratch." He sounded
frightened.

"I'm not asking you to pay me. I just suddenly decided
I was working too hard."

His voice changed immediately. "Oh, great! So everything's still on. Meet me at '21' at six-thirty. That's when
the broad from *Life* will be there."

The evening went off easier than she had expected.
The waiters had obviously been primed by Danton
Miller. The table at "21" was in the center section downstairs. She forced herself to drink a Scotch—it might
make the evening more palatable. The girl from *Life* was
extremely nice. She explained that she had been sent over
to "talk" to Christie about an interview. Then she was to
write her impressions and the senior editors would decide
whether they wanted to follow it up and assign someone
to do a story.

Christie managed a weak laugh. "This is a new slant—

being interviewed for an interview! How classy can a magazine be!" The unexpected humiliation deflated his ego. Amanda suddenly realized that most of his bravado was merely a pretense to cover his terrible insecurity. Her heart went out to him. She reached over and took his hand.

The girl from *Life* was also sensitive to his mood. She forced an easy laugh. "They do this with everyone, Mr. Lane. Why, just last week I did research on an important senator and the editors turned the story down."

Some of Christie's self-assurance returned. He insisted that she accompany them to El Morocco. Amanda realized that he was desperate for the story. He told the reporter about his humble beginnings, the early poverty, the honky-tonk nightclubs he had played. To Amanda's surprise, the girl was actually interested. As she began to take notes, Christie's enthusiasm soared. He threw his arm around Amanda and winked at the reporter: "Imagine a bum like me winding up with a fancy society-type cover girl!"

At the end of the evening, Amanda asked to be dropped off first. She closed the door wearily as she entered her apartment. She was bone-tired. It was an effort to take off her clothes. She wanted to flop on the bed and go right to sleep. She took off her makeup and automatically began the hundred strokes on her heavy blond hair. She stared at the brush. Good Lord, it was filled with hair. She'd have to stop using the Alwayso spray. No matter how much Jerry praised it, the stuff was murdering her hair. She dropped the can into the wastebasket. She finally fell into bed and was gratified that she was so tired—at least she wouldn't lie awake and think of Robin and the baroness.

She spent the next four evenings with Christie, followed by a reporter from *Life* and his photographer. But she couldn't forget Robin Stone. At the end of the week, the *Life* story was finished. It looked fairly certain that they would use it. But as the reporter had said, you couldn't be positive until it was "locked in." The final shots were taken while she was doing her commercial on the show.

Christie stood backstage with her and watched them

leave. "It's in the bag!" he said, throwing his arm around her. "Tonight we're really going to celebrate. And we've got something even more important to celebrate—the new ratings just came out. Now I'm in the top ten! Do you hear that, doll? Two weeks ago I was number nineteen. This week I'm number eight! Only seven shows to beat! We gotta celebrate. And there's something else: we never really been alone. Tonight, you and me, we're gonna go to Danny's Hideaway together—alone."

When they were ushered to the front table, Christie was like a child in his happiness. To Amanda it seemed as if the ratings had been posted on the front page of *The New York Times.* The entire restaurant seemed to know. Everyone, including Cliff, the public relations man, stopped by to congratulate him. Christie basked in his new glory. He called out to other performers, left her alone several times while he "table-hopped." Then he ordered steaks for both of them. She sat stiffly and picked at her food, while he ate with enthusiasm, his elbow on the table, his head lowered to the food. When he had finished, he used two fingers to dig for a fragment of food lodged between his back teeth.

He stared at her half-eaten steak. "Something wrong with the meat?"

"No, I've had enough. I'll get a doggy bag."

"You got a dog?"

"A cat."

"I hate cats." Then he smiled. "Does it jump on your bed at night?"

"Yes, it snuggles with me."

"Then tonight we go to my place." He looked at her dress. It was a beaded sheath she had worn on the show. "We'll stop at your place and you can feed the cat and change your dress."

"Why do I change my dress?"

He grinned awkwardly. "Well, look, doll, tomorrow morning how's it gonna look, you traipsing through the Astor lobby in that getup?"

"I have no intention of traipsing through the Astor lobby. Tomorrow morning I will be in my own bed."

"Oh, you mean you want to do it—and go home?"

"I want to go home. Now."

"What about the fucking?"

She colored visibly. "Chris, I don't want to get up and walk out on you. But if you ever use that language again, that is exactly what I will do."

"Come on, doll, you know it don't mean anything when I say things like that. But I'll be careful. Shit, I was raised backstage, I learned those words when most kids were reciting nursery rhymes. Tell you what—every time I say one of them words, I'll give you a buck. No, better make it a quarter. With a buck a throw and my vocabulary—you could retire."

She managed a smile. He was trying to be nice. It wasn't his fault that she felt such physical revulsion for him, but she longed to get away from him. "Chris, I want to go home, alone. I have a headache, it's been a long day."

"Oh sure, you stood around holding up that heavy lipstick. I only sing and dance and do sketches."

"But you're talented. You've been doing it all your life. I panic every time I see those three cameras coming at me. And facing that audience—it takes a lot out of me. You're born to it."

"Maybe. All right, we'll let the fuck—the lovemaking —go till tomorrow night. No, I got a benefit tomorrow, maybe the following night. Is that a date?"

"I don't know—"

"Whadya mean?"

"I just don't leap into things like this."

"We been going together a long time—"

"Three weeks and four days." (It had been four weeks and four days since Robin left.)

"Hey, you must care to number the days like that. Well then, when? Or are you still carrying a torch for Robin Stone?"

She knew she had reacted visibly. The question had caught her off guard.

He seemed pleased. "Oh, I been doing my own investigating."

"It's no secret that I've gone out with Robin Stone. He's a very good friend. An old friend. I've known him over a year."

"Then you're not carrying the torch?"

"Who ever told you that?"

"Ethel Evans."

She was silent. She had no idea that Ethel was so perceptive. Only this evening, while Ethel was backstage, she had acted as if she hadn't a thought in the world for anyone but Christie Lane.

Christie mistook her silence for bewilderment. "You remember Ethel Evans—the big-assed publicity dame with the loud mouth. She's laid every guy from coast to coast and brags about it. God, did you see her tonight? Falling all over the guest star. She's living up to her title: the Celebrity Fucker."

"Maybe it's men like you who make her bad news," she answered.

"Meaning what?"

"Hanging such a title on her and spreading gossip. After all, have you ever had an affair with her?"

"No, but everyone I know has had her—every big shot, I mean."

"Then you're giving lip service to something you've only heard."

"Why the big defense for that big-assed dame? You should hear her knock you."

"Take me home," she said tightly.

"Oh, Jesus. Doll, I'm sorry." He took her hand and looked at her intently. He placed her hand on his chest. "I go for you, Mandy—this is the first time I've ever said it and meant it. I really go for you. And it could be for keeps."

She saw the large blue eyes pleading. The open, homely face was vulnerable and she knew he was telling the truth. Tonight on the air he had intentionally sung "Mandy"—the song Al Jolson made famous. When he got to the line "Mandy, there's a minister handy," he had turned and looked right at her in the wings. The camera crew had gone crazy trying to change shots. She didn't want to hurt him, she *knew* what hurt was—she had been living with it for so long. She patted his hand. "Look, Chris, you're going to be a big star, you've got everything good ahead for you. You'll have millions of girls, nice girls, beautiful girls—"

"I don't want *them*. I want *you*."

"Chris, we've only been out together a few times. You couldn't love me, you don't *know* me."

"Doll, I've knocked around plenty. I've seen the dregs —low-down nightclubs, low-down girls. All my life I wanted something better. That's why I stayed single-o this long. I'd grab off a hooker when I needed it, but I never made no emotional attachment. See what I mean? Then, wham! Along comes this show—and you! All in one package. For the first time I'm in the big leagues, with a hit show and a lady at my side. Oh, I've seen ladies before—classy broads at benefits I've played—so I can tell the real McCoy. Only all the ones I've seen have been buck-toothed and flat-chested. But you're the whole package—and I want you."

She blanched, thinking of her small breasts. But what difference did it make? He'd never know. She looked at him with candor. "I like you, Chris. But I'm not in love with you."

"That's enough for me," he said. "I'm willing to wait. But just promise me one thing: give me a chance. Go out with me, date me, and eventually you'll want to go to bed with me. And if it works out—it'll be for keeps. Maybe it'll even be marriage." He stopped her objections. "Wait. Just wait—that's all I ask."

She knew what he was feeling. And if letting him hope made him happy, what harm would it do? At least tonight he would go to bed with a dream. Eventually he would be a big star—and the bigger he got, the less she would matter.

She kissed him good night outside her apartment. When she let herself in, she found a telegram had been slipped under the door. She picked it up and opened it lethargically—probably an invitation to a new discothèque:

ARRIVING AT IDLEWILD AT 2 A.M. YOUR TIME, TWA FLIGHT 3. NOW IF YOU ARE REALLY MY GIRL, YOU'LL HIRE A CAR AND BE IN IT.     ROBIN.

She looked at her watch. Eleven forty-five. Oh, thank God, she could make it! She rushed to the phone and ordered a car. She'd never be able to figure Robin. He

wouldn't waste a dime to call and say goodbye, yet he'd
send a wire to announce his arrival. She would have time
to change her makeup, her dress—she had to look her
best when she met him. She was singing as she rubbed
the cream on her face. And for the first time in four
weeks and four days she wasn't the least bit tired.

She stood at Gate 7. The plane had just arrived. Passengers began to disembark. She saw Robin immediately.
He was different from other men. Other men walked.
Robin sort of sailed through people. He dropped his
attaché case and threw his arms around her. "How's the
new television star?" he asked.

"Thrilled to see the world's greatest newsman." She
matched his tone and vowed not to mention the baroness.

He put his arm around her and walked to the car.

"I don't understand," she said. "I thought you were in
London. But your wire came from Los Angeles."

"I took the polar route and stopped off in Los Angeles
for a few days." He reached into his pocket and handed
her a small package. "A gift for you—I forgot to declare
it. I'm a smuggler."

In the car, she snuggled against him and opened the
package. It was a beautiful antique Wedgwood cigarette
box. She knew it was expensive, but she would have
preferred something half the price and more personal.

"I hope you still smoke." He laughed, reached for a
crumpled pack of English cigarettes and offered her one.

She inhaled and almost choked on the strong tobacco.
He took it away from her and kissed her lips lightly.
"Miss me?"

"Well—you took off leaving me with two steaks. I
didn't know whether to miss you or kill you."

He stared at her absently, as if trying to recall.

"I mean, you could have called me and said, 'Hey,
baby, take the steaks out of the oven, I can't make it.'"

"Didn't I?" He seemed genuinely surprised.

"Forget it. The cat had a marvelous meal."

"But you knew I had gone." He seemed vaguely trou-
bled.

"Well, I heard you announce it on the air. But, Robin,
you were gone for so long."

He put his arm around her and drew her closer. "Well, now I'm back. Tired?"

She clung to him. "Never for you."

His kiss was long and deep. His eyes were gentle and he touched her face with his hands almost like a blind man trying to see. "My lovely Amanda. You are beautiful."

"Robin, while you were away I went out with Christie Lane." He appeared to be trying to place the name. She added, "The star of the show."

"Oh. Yes, I hear he's catching on big. I've kept up with the ratings."

"My name was coupled with his in the columns."

"Did it raise your modeling fee?" His grin was friendly. She shrugged. "It's quite high."

"Good."

She looked at him. "People—well, some people—think I'm his girl. I wanted you to know it's just talk. I didn't want it to bother you."

"Why should it bother me?"

"I thought it might. . . ."

He lit another cigarette.

"I guess I was foolish to worry," she said.

He laughed. "You're a celebrity. Celebrities get their names in columns."

"And you don't mind that I went out with Chris?"

"Why should I? I wasn't exactly a hermit in London."

She pulled away from him and turned toward the window. She stared at the darkness of the night and the cars flashing by in the opposite lane. He reached out and took her hand. She pulled it away.

"Robin, are you trying to hurt me?"

"No." He was looking at her honestly. "Nor are you trying to hurt me."

"But I'm your girl—aren't I?"

"You bet you are." (That damned grin of his.) "But, Amanda, I never said I wanted you on a leash."

"You mean you don't mind that I went out with him, or you wouldn't mind if I continued to see him?"

"Of course I wouldn't mind."

"What if I slept with him?"

"That's up to you."

"Would you care?"

"If you told me—yes, I would care."

"You mean you'd want me to hide it."

"All right, Amanda: are you sleeping with him?"

"No. But he wants me to. He even talks about marriage."

"Suit yourself. . . ."

"Robin, tell the driver to stop at my place first."

"Why?"

"I want to go home—alone."

He pulled her back into his arms. "Baby—you came all the way out to Idlewild to meet me. Why the switch?"

"Robin, don't you see that—" Suddenly he kissed her and she stopped trying to explain.

They spent the night together, locked in one another's arms. There was no more talk about Christie Lane. It was as if Robin had never been away—it was like it had been in the beginning. Like it was every time they were alone, in bed. Urgent, exciting and tender.

Later as they lay together smoking and relaxed in a peaceful closeness, she said, "Who is the baroness?" It had just slipped out. She regretted it instantly.

His expression didn't change. "A broad."

"Now, Robin, I read about her, she's a baroness."

"Oh, the title is real, but she's a broad. One of those kids spawned during the war. At twelve she was doing it with GIs for candy bars. Then she married the baron—he was a fag, also a voyeur. Ericka knew all the tricks. She's not a bad girl, she's got a bona fide title, money for the first time and she likes to swing. I met her at an orgy."

She sat up in the darkness. "An orgy!"

"They're very large in London. I hear they're catching on in Los Angeles, too."

"And you like that sort of thing?"

He grinned. "What's not to like about it? It's better than television over there. They only have two channels, you know."

"Robin, be serious."

"I am. Did you ever meet Ike Ryan?"

The name was familiar. Suddenly she recalled. He was

an American film producer who was based in Italy and France, and was making quite a name for himself.

"You'll like him. We met in London. I was feeling rotten. The weather was getting me down and he invited me to one of his parties. There were three Italian movie actresses, the baroness, Ike and me. It was ladies' night in a Turkish bath."

"And you participated?"

"Sure, why not? First I watched the girls with each other, then Ike and I lay back and the harem took care of us. Ericka was the best—trust the Germans to perfect any art—so I carted her off for myself. But Ike's a real good guy. He's going to L.A. to set up his own company. He'll give that town a shot in the arm."

"With orgies?"

"No, with pictures. He's a gambler, and he has great style. He's also good-looking. Women like him."

"I think he's disgusting."

"Why?"

"Because, I mean, to do things like that!"

He laughed. "Am I disgusting?"

"No. I think you're like a bad little boy who feels he's being very daring. But this Ike Ryan, he originated it—"

"Baby, it started way back with the Greeks."

"And you'd want me to meet a man like that? Be seen out in public with him? If I were seen with him and you, everyone would think I was that kind of a girl. Would you want that?"

He turned and looked at her very seriously. "No, Amanda, I promise you: I'll never take you out with Ike Ryan."

Then he had gotten up and taken a sleeping pill along with a beer. "I'm still on European time. I'm overtired. Want one?"

"No, I have to be up at ten."

He got back into bed and took her in his arms. "My beautiful Amanda, it's good to be with you. Don't wake me when you leave in the morning. I have a busy afternoon ahead—mail piled up, appointments—I need some sleep."

In the morning she dressed and left his apartment quickly. She was tired that day and not very good in her

work. And her hair was coming out again. She called
Nick and asked him for a dermatologist. He laughed.
"You're molting, darling. It's just nerves."

"It probably is," she said. "Robin's back."

"Call your doctor and get a B-12 shot or something—
and for God's sake, don't spend every night making love."

"I don't have a doctor." She laughed. "I've never
needed one. Do you know someone good?"

"Amanda my love, you are so young and healthy it's
disgusting. I have six doctors. One for throat and ears,
one for my prostate, one for my slipped disc. Want my
advice, stay away from them all. Get a good night's sleep,
and once that *Life* story comes out all your worries will
be over."

He was probably right. She was finished with her work
by three. She went home to take a nap. Slugger jumped
into bed and curled up in her arms. She kissed his tawny
head. "It's not night, darling. We're just resting." He
purred gravelly in contentment. "You're the only male
who's reliable, darling, but Robin's back and when he
comes tonight, don't hate me for exiling you into the
living room."

She knew she had slept. She sat up with a jolt. It was
dark—she tried to orient herself. What day was it? Suddenly she remembered. She turned on the light. Nine
o'clock. Slugger jumped off of the bed and growled, demanding dinner.

Nine o'clock! And Robin hadn't called! She checked
with her service. No calls. She dialed Robin. After ten
empty rings she clicked the receiver. She didn't sleep the
rest of the night. Slugger, sensing something was wrong,
nestled close to her.

The following day she waited until six, then she called
him. After all, he might be ill. He answered, and he was
fine. It was just all the desk work that had piled up. He
said he would call tomorrow.

The following morning she caught his name as she
scanned one of the columns:

Ike Ryan and Robin Stone were at El Morocco with
two beautiful Italian actresses. Their names were too

long for this reporter to remember, but he'll never forget their faces and their—wow!

She threw the paper on the floor. He had been feeling her out, knowing Ike Ryan was coming to town. Oh Lord, why had she said she wouldn't be seen with him?

That night she went out with Christie. They went to Danny's. She was very quiet and Christie was disgruntled: they had been seated at a small table along the wall. One of the front tables was occupied by a group of Hollywood celebrities. The other was empty, with a RESERVED sign prominently displayed.

"Probably some other Hollywood joker," he said, eyeing the table enviously. "Why is everyone so impressed with movie people? I bet more people know me than most of the stars in Hollywood."

She tried to cheer him; no use both of them being miserable. "Christie, this is a marvelous table. I like being in the center of the room, you can see everyone."

"I belong at the best table everywhere!"

"Wherever you sit is automatically the best table," she said.

He stared at her. "You believe that?"

"It's more important if *you* do."

He grinned and ordered their dinner. After a short time his good humor returned. "The *Life* story is locked in," he said. He looked at her longingly. "Mandy, right now there's something I want more than *Life*. How do I have to prove myself? I love you. I feel like a jerky high-school boy, sitting just holding your hand. I been doing a lot of thinking. How *can* you get to love me if you don't sleep with me? I know there's no one else. Eddie was trying to tell me that the word around was that you were dead-stuck on Robin Stone. But I read the column today. . . ."

"Chris, since you brought it up, I think I ought to tell you—" She stopped, her attention suddenly riveted to the four people who were being shown to the front table. Danny himself was ushering them in. Two beautiful girls, two men. And one of the men was Robin!

She felt that strange light-headedness that often comes with shock. Robin was lighting the girl's cigarette and giving her that very private grin. The other man was probably Ike Ryan.

"Tell me what, doll?"

Chris was staring at her. She knew she had to say something, but she was powerless to remove her eyes from Robin. She saw him lean over and kiss the girl on the tip of her nose. Then he laughed.

"Oh, look who has my table," Chris said. "I watched him one night—wanted to take a gander at my competition. I tell you, I couldn't watch more than ten minutes. He was yelling about Cuba and all that kind of shit, and some jerk was agreeing with him. Big deal. Did you get a load of his ratings against mine?"

"He's in the top twenty-five, that's excellent for a news show." She wondered why she was defending him.

"I'm gonna be number one, you watch. And everyone treats me like I'm number one—except you."

"I—I like you very much."

"Then put up or shut up."

"I want to go home." She really felt ill. Robin was listening to the girl with his head bent close.

"Oh, doll, let's not fight. I love you, but we've got to make it together."

"Take me home. . . ."

He looked at her oddly. "If I take you home, that's it. I know when I'm licked."

She watched him sign the check. They would have to pass Robin's table. Chris stopped at almost every table on the way out, greeting people loudly. She knew Robin had to notice her. When they passed his table, he stood up. He wasn't the least embarrassed. In fact, he seemed actually glad to see her. He congratulated Chris on his show, and introduced everyone at the table. The two girls were both Francesca something—Italian starlets—and the man was Ike Ryan. She was surprised when Ike stood up. He was six feet tall, with black hair and blue eyes. He was tanned, strong-looking, good-looking; nothing like she had envisioned.

"So this is *the* Amanda?" He turned to the two girls and spoke Italian. The girls nodded and smiled at her. Then Ike said, "I just told them what a big shot you are, Amanda."

"Tell 'em about me," Christie said.

Ike laughed. "I don't have to. They know who you are. They've been glued to the television set since they got here."

It seemed an eternity, but they finally left. Amanda shot one last glance at Robin, hoping to find some message in his eyes, but he was talking and the girl was smiling. Obviously she understood *some* English.

Christie was glum as he hailed a cab. Suddenly she took his arm. "I'll go back to your place, Christie."

He was pathetically exuberant. "Oh, doll—but hey, what about the fancy dress? Want to stop off at your place and change?"

"No, I'll leave you after—after we do it."

"No, I'll even go along with the cat. We'll go to your place. I got no place to go tomorrow. Then I can stay there and you can get up whenever you want."

Her flesh began to crawl. "No, there's a cameraman coming up tomorrow, early. It's only ten-thirty now, so if I go to your place, and leave in a few hours, it will work out."

"But I want to be with you all night—hold you in my arms."

She fought back her feeling of nausea. She had deliberately chosen the Astor as the lesser of the evils. At least she could get up and leave when it was over.

"It has to be this way," she said quietly.

"Doll, I'll take it any way I can get it. Oh boy, are you gonna be happy! I'm the greatest—wait till you see."

She was positive that everyone in the Astor lobby knew her plans as she walked to the elevator. She felt that even the taxi driver had looked at her in contempt when she got out of the cab. But how many times she had sailed through Robin's lobby, even greeted his doorman with a cheery good morning—it had all seemed so natural and wonderful. . . . No. She mustn't think of Robin, not now.

She walked into the bathroom of Christie's suite and took off all of her clothes. She stared at her flat breasts, then walked into the bedroom defiantly. He was lying on the bed in his shorts, looking at the racing form. His jaw dropped in disappointment. "No tits!" Her eyes were cold—challenging him. He laughed and held out his arms. "Well! I guess it proves that all the classy ladies are skinny. At least you haven't got buck teeth. But come on over—you won't be disappointed at the size of my joint. Look what good old Chris has for you. . . ."

She submitted to his embrace in the darkness. She lay back while he panted and gyrated through her. She knew he was trying to please her. Oh God, if he went on for hours, nothing would happen. He could never rouse her —ever. She prayed for him to get it over. He suddenly leaped off her and fell to his side, groaning. After a few minutes he said, "Don't worry, doll, I pulled out in time. I won't knock you up."

She lay there quietly. He took her in his arms. His body was clammy with perspiration. "I didn't make you come, did I?" he said.

"Chris, I—" She stopped.

"Don't worry, let me catch my breath and I'll go down on you."

"No, Chris. It was wonderful! I was just nervous, that's all. Next time I'll wear something, don't worry."

"Listen, I've decided. We're gonna get married. At the end of the season. I've got six weeks booked in Vegas this summer for big money. We'll get married there. You'll have a ball, it'll be our honeymoon. So don't wear anything: if you get pregnant, great—we'll get married even sooner."

"No, I don't want to have a baby until after we're married. I wouldn't want people to think that was the reason."

"Listen, doll, I'm forty-seven. I'm leveling with you. Everyone thinks I'm forty. Even Eddie and Kenny don't know. But since you're gonna be my wife, I want you to know the real scene. I been careful with money all my life. I always made my forty or fifty thousand for the last fifteen years. And no matter what I made, I put half of it away. By the time I'm sixty, I'll have a million in annuities. Twenty years ago I met this guy in Chicago, he's a big tax expert. I got his kid out of some trouble, nothing serious, a slight car accident. But I had connections and I squared the rap and the kid's father, this Lou Goldberg, was so grateful that he became my father, mother, lawyer, tax man, everything. He said to me right then that I was a second-class talent, but if I listened to him, I'd wind up a first-class citizen. And he started taking half my money—I was maybe only earning a couple C-notes a week then—but Lou invested it. By now I got quite a portfolio—stuff like IBM that does nothing but double. Now that I've made it big, Lou still takes half. And if this keeps up—my new success, I mean—well, in a few years I'll have not one but two million. And the way he's investing it, I'll have over six thousand a month tax-free, without even touching the principal. We can leave that to our kid. Now that I've got you, everything will be perfect. And I want us to start having a kid right away, so when I'm sixty, at least I'll still be able to go to ball games with him and see him go to college like I never did. Don't ever tell anyone, but I never got past sixth grade—I was hawking candy in burlesque when I was twelve. But our kid will have everything!"

She lay very still. What had she done! This poor idiot. . . .

She suddenly got out of bed and went into the bathroom and dressed. Chris was dressing when she came out.

"Don't bother," she begged. "I can get a cab." She was anxious to get away. She couldn't bear his lovesick eyes.

"Nah, it's still early. I'll take you home and then drop by the Stage Deli. Eddie and Kenny will probably be there. I'll have a cup of coffee with them and kibitz. I'm so happy I can't sleep—I want to tell it to the world."

She let him hold her hand on the ride home. He kissed her good night at the elevator. Then she went into her apartment—ran to the bathroom and threw up.

Robin called the following day. He never mentioned the Italian girls. He was leaving that afternoon for Los Angeles with Ike Ryan. He wanted to do an *In Depth* on Ike. He felt it would be more exciting if it were filmed on location. In Ike's office, on the set. From there he was flying back to London on the polar route, and he had no idea when he'd return. She never mentioned the baroness or the Italian starlet, and he never mentioned Christie Lane.

# TWELVE

O N MAY FIRST, Amanda awoke fifteen minutes
    before her "wake-up" call. Tomorrow *Life* magazine
would be on every newsstand, but the Plaza Hotel always
got *Time* and *Life* a day earlier. She dressed quickly. For
the past six weeks she had vacillated between eagerness
and apprehension. Everyone was waiting for the *Life*
story. Christie felt it would make him an international
celebrity. Nick Longworth was all set to raise her fee to a
hundred an hour.

She took a cab to the Plaza and dashed into the lobby.
The bright red cover caught her eye as she approached
the newsstand. She dropped the money on the counter
and walked quickly to a large easy chair in the lobby
near the Palm Court.

It was a ten-page spread with a big headline: THE
CHRISTIE LANE PHENOMENON. She was featured with
Christie in four pictures and there was one of her alone,
posing for Ivan in a chiffon dress in Central Park. And it
was no wind machine swirling that dress—she would
never forget how cold it had been that day. As she read,
she was pleased that the reporter had been unusually
perceptive. There was a graphic description of the way
she had stood facing the March wind without flinching.
It took a peculiar kind of strength to be a model, he
noted. It was all very complimentary to her. And although it painted Christie as a man of the people, it slyly
revealed his bad grammar, his flamboyancy, his total absorption with his new fame. (So far—so good, she
thought.) She read on:

> To go along with his new prominence, Christie Lane
> has taken himself a girl fit to be the consort of the
> new top minstrel man of television. A beautiful
> cover girl—Amanda. She is not just the girl he loves.

She is a symbol. Proof that the world of second-rate
nightclubs is a thing of the past. Because Amanda is
definitely first-rate. And after seeing them together,
they are not the incongruous pair one might think.
Christie Lane worships the elegance of this beautiful girl. And perhaps the lovely Amanda finds reality
with Christie Lane. When a girl stands outdoors in
thirty-degree temperatures, wearing a chiffon dress
and a Palm Beach smile, she probably welcomes
the honesty of a man like Christie Lane. Perhaps
she is anxious to toss away the June-in-January world
of a fashion model to find a real world with this
very real man.

She shut the magazine. That last line! How would
Robin take it? She walked out into the bright sunlight.
Although she dated Christie and occasionally went to bed
with him, she felt she barely knew him. They were never
alone, except for the torturous few hours together at the
Astor. Christie spent at least two nights a week with his
writers; there were benefits, interviews—all time-con-
suming, all part of being a star. Yet he was planning to
marry her in Vegas! She had let him talk—the summer
had seemed so far away. But now it was May!

She had to break with Christie Lane! She had only
continued seeing him because of her loneliness and
longing for Robin. She could never really care about
anyone else. But at least she was making Christie
happy. . . .

The story in *Life* caused a great deal of excitement.
She actually felt famous, especially on the nights after the
show, when she came out of the stage door and all the
autograph kids called her by name. But she didn't hear a
word from Robin, until the Sunday before Decoration
Day. She had just hung up on Christie. He was playing
Decoration Day at Grossinger's for a fabulous fee. He
had wanted her to go along with him—but she refused.

"Ah, come on," he pleaded. "We'll have a ball. Even
Aggie is taking off from the Latin Quarter—"

"I can't afford to lose the money. Besides, I'm not Aggie
—I'm not a camp follower."

"What's with the camp-follower crap? We're getting married this summer."

"*If* and *when* we're married, I'll go to places where you play. Right now I'm staying in New York and keeping my modeling appointments. I'm not going anywhere as part of the Christie Lane caravan."

"Ah, shit, you and your highfalutin ideas. I hadda go fall in love with a lady!" He hung up, disgruntled but not angry.

After she had hung up, she thought about it. Why hadn't she just said, "I'm never going to marry you"? Because she was frightened! She was frightened of what would happen if Robin ever disappeared for good. She would go to pieces. She had tried breaking with Christie once, told him she was never going to see him again. The break lasted only five days. . . . At least with Christie she was able to keep her sanity. There was always a night-club opening or a benefit, and being with Christie was better than being alone.

The phone rang. She picked it up lethargically, thinking it was Christie calling back to make one last plea. The crisp voice caught her off balance: "Hello, Celebrity."

"Robin! Oh, Robin! Where are you?"

"I just came in. I've been away, covering the Eichmann trial. I just read all about you on the plane—caught up with all the back issues of *Life*—and, by God, there you were!"

"What did you think of it?" She forced herself to sound casual.

"Just great," he said with enthusiasm. "It makes you sound almost as exciting as you really are."

Her throat was tight—but she kept her voice light. "You almost sound like you missed me."

"I did."

She barely listened. She was planning their evening. It was five o'clock—too late to wash her hair, but she could put on a fall. She hoped they would stay in. Thank God it was Sunday—Jerry was in the country and couldn't tag along. She had steaks in the freezer, but she was out of vodka.

"Are you still as beautiful as ever?" he was asking.

"Come see for yourself."

"Fine. Meet me at the Lancer Bar tomorrow at seven."

She was so disappointed she couldn't speak.

He took her silence for indecision. His voice was light. "Or has Christie Lane cut me out of the picture?"

"No—but he's asked me to marry him."

"He might be a good bet at that. His show will go on forever."

"Would you care, Robin, if I married Christie Lane?"

"Sure I'd care. I'd hate like hell to lose you. But I can't compete against marriage."

"Why not?"

"Look, baby, there's only one reason for marriage, and that's to have kids. I don't want any kids."

"Why?"

"They're one hell of a responsibility."

"In what way?"

"Look, Amanda—I have to be loose, be able to pick up and go. You can do that with a girl, even a wife. But you can't do it to a kid. What kind of a father would I make?"

She was trembling. Marriage had always been a subject he had refused to discuss. But now they were actually discussing it.

"Oh, Robin, I think you'd make a marvelous father."

"A father should be with his kid."

"Did your father leave you?"

"No, he had nine-to-five hours. And Kitty was a good mother: we had nurses and cooks, but she was always there. And that's the way it *should* be."

"Then I don't understand—what makes you feel you would run out?"

"My work, baby," he said tightly. "And although it's never happened to me, I know that if I was a kid and my father wasn't there it would kill me—I know it. Don't ask me why, I just feel it."

"Robin, we don't have to have children now...."

"Then why get married?" he asked.

"To be together."

"We're together, except when I need to be alone. Like tonight—I've got a desk piled with mail. I feel like tossing it all in the basket. I may do just that." There was a pause. "I just did. The bills will arrive again, and I don't think they'll turn off the electricity if I'm one month late."

"All right, the mail is gone. Now we can be together tonight," she said.

"Amanda, that's why I'm against marriage. I *want* to be alone tonight." His voice suddenly became gentle. "Do you understand now, Amanda? I'm not geared for marriage. I like things the way they are."

"And the little setups Ike Ryan arranges!"

"Ike Ryan—now where did you drag that name from? I haven't seen or thought of him in ages."

"And what about the baroness? Or is that a name you haven't thought of in months?" She knew she was destroying herself, but she couldn't help it.

"Amanda darling, another awful thing about marriage is explanations. I don't owe you any, nor do you owe me any. Now, how about tomorrow? Are you free?"

"I'll *make* myself free." Her voice was sullen.

"Good girl."

"Are you here for some time? Or are you flying off somewhere?"

"Baby, I'm so tired of traveling, I never want to leave again. I'm going to stay put until fall."

"That's good." Her gloom evaporated. "We go off the air in two weeks."

"Oh, that reminds me, Jerry Moss invited me up to Greenwich for the July Fourth weekend. They have a great house and a pool. Would you like to come?"

"I'd love it, Robin."

"Great! See you tomorrow night."

She sat very quietly for a long time. She lay awake half the night. The following morning, she called Jerry Moss at nine o'clock.

"Jerry, I've got to see you. It's urgent."

"I'll probably see you at the Lancer Bar. I'm meeting Robin there at five."

"I'm not getting there until seven. But I've got to see you *alone*. It's very important!"

"Lunch?"

"No, I have a twelve o'clock session. Can I come to your office? Say, ten o'clock?"

"It's a date. I'll even have coffee waiting for you."

She sat across the desk from Jerry and sipped the coffee. She told him about Chris, implying that there had been no intimacy between them. In a way it wasn't a lie —there was no intimacy. She merely lay back, gritted her teeth and submitted to him.

Then she said, "That's why I had to come to you, Jerry. You're the only one who can help me."

He looked startled. "Me?"

"If I go to Vegas with Chris, I'll have to marry him. If I *don't* go to Vegas, I'll lose him."

Jerry nodded. "It's a simple decision. A sure bet against a long shot."

"I want a chance at that long shot," she said. "Robin will be in town all summer. He's invited me to your place for July Fourth."

Jerry was silent. Then he said, "Go to Vegas, honey— marry Chris. Don't waste any more time on Robin."

"Why? Has he told you something I don't know?"

"No, but look—did you ever hear of Ike Ryan?"

"I know all about Ike Ryan. But he doesn't see him—or do those things anymore."

Jerry smiled. "I have a friend who's a psychiatrist. When Robin told me about the action he got with Ike, I happened to bring it up with him and he said that Robin probably hates women."

"That's ridiculous!" she snapped. "This friend of yours doesn't even *know* Robin. How can he come up with a statement like that!"

"He's *met* Robin—"

"Are you trying to hint that Robin's queer?" Now she was actually angry.

"No. I'm saying that as people—as friends—he likes men. He digs women, but only for sex—he doesn't really like them. He's actually hostile to them."

"And you think that's true?"

"Yes. But I think Robin likes *you*—as much as he can like a woman. He'll force your hand eventually; *you'll* be the one to break this up."

"Jerry. . . ." Her eyes were soft. "Help me. . . ."

"How can I help you?"

"Keep me from going to Vegas with Christie. You can tell Christie I've signed a contract for the commercials on

the summer replacement show and I have to stay here
and do them live."

He looked at her. "Go to Vegas, Amanda. Christie Lane
is offering you a future, a real life, kids—the works."

"Jerry," she was pleading. "I want one last chance with
Robin."

"I thought you had more class, Amanda. Where's your
gambling spirit? If I cared that much for someone, I'd
toss the dice and go for broke. Give up Christie Lane.
Shoot for Robin! So you lose a chance for a good marriage and security. If you were thirty-five, I'd say you
couldn't risk it. But you're young, and you must have
plenty of money saved."

"I don't save any. I can't."

Jerry shrugged. "Then stop buying all those 'name'
clothes. God, Mary buys things in Greenwich for forty-
five dollars."

"Mary doesn't make a hundred dollars an hour. And
don't forget, I use my clothes on the show. Being well
dressed is part of my business. And I'm *scared* of not
having money, Jerry, scared of being without it."

"In my book, a girl with two men in love with her
shouldn't worry about being alone. And a girl who makes
a hundred dollars an hour shouldn't worry about not
having money."

She clenched her hands. "Jerry, have you ever been
poor? I mean *dirt*-poor. I was. I was white trash. It kills
me when Chris talks about Miami, and how he played
small clubs, and how he vowed to play the big time in
the big hotels. I was born in Miami—in a charity ward.
My mother was a Finnish chambermaid in one of those
fancy hotels. I suppose she must have been pretty. I only
remember her as being skinny and tired. But one of those
rich men who stayed at that hotel must have thought she
was pretty. I don't even know who my father was. I just
know he was some rich man who could afford to spend
the winter in Miami and knock up some little chambermaid. After I was born we lived in what they called
Niggertown, because the only woman who was decent to
my mother was a colored girl who worked in the hotel. It
was a shanty, a tar flat—you pass them when you drive to
the airport. This woman—her name was Rose—she got

my mother to the charity hospital when I was born. And then we lived with her. I called her Aunt Rose, she's the finest woman I've ever known. Later on, when my mother worked at night, Aunt Rose would come home and make supper and see that I studied and hear my prayers. My mother died when I was six. Aunt Rose paid for the funeral and kept me with her just like I was her child. She made me finish high school—she worked for me, she clothed me—then she sent me to New York on a bus with fifty dollars she had saved." Amanda stopped and the tears overflowed.

"I'm sure you've repaid the fifty," he said.

"I sent her fifty dollars a *week* in the beginning. But it would take me a lifetime to repay her for her love. A year and a half ago, Aunt Rose had a stroke. I rushed down to Florida—it was right before I met Robin—and I got her into a hospital. It wasn't easy, they weren't exactly thrilled about having a sick old colored woman. But I met a sympathetic doctor, and he helped me get her in a private room. Naturally she had no hospital insurance, nothing. She was there for six weeks—that cost four thousand dollars with nurses and therapy. You try explaining that to the Bureau of Internal Revenue. 'Is she a relation, a dependent?' they ask. 'No: just someone I love.' But they figure she has Social Security, like one hundred and fifteen a month or something, and she can go in a charity ward. But according to law she's not my kin—I wasn't adopted. And those heartless guys down there, they see someone like me come in and they think, 'A model, one hundred an hour—she makes more in a day than I make in a week.'"

"Where is she now?" Jerry asked.

"That's just it. I couldn't leave her alone, even when she was discharged from the hospital. I tried to get someone to care for her, but it didn't work. So I brought her up here to a nursing home on Long Island. That cost a hundred a week. Okay, it was fine, and I visited her every week. Then about eight months ago she had a massive stroke. I had to move her to another nursing home where she gets round-the-clock care. And now I'm paying two hundred and fifty dollars a week."

"Do you still visit her every week?"

She shook her head. "It hurts too much, and she doesn't even know I'm there. I go about once a month and on New Year's Day. I always used to call her on New Year's Eve when I first came to New York—and once I couldn't get through because the circuits were tied up, and I was frantic. And she said, 'Child, you call me on New Year's Day from now on. I don't want to ruin your night having you worry about getting to a phone.'"

Amanda sat up straight. "I grew up knowing the power of money, Jerry. Money enabled my unknown father to get out of town and go through life without even knowing me. *Lack* of money made my mother afraid to fight. And the only thing that is giving Aunt Rose some comfort now is *money*. So you see, Jerry, I can't gamble. I have to go for the sure thing. But I've earned the right to have a chance at the one man in the world I love! I can't settle for Christie without trying for Robin first."

He went over to the small bar he kept in the office and poured two shots of Scotch. He handed her one. "Amanda, I think Alwayso should do their commercials live this summer. I order you to stay here in town." He clicked his glass against hers. "I'll do my part, honey," he said. "Here's to the Fourth of July and a long, wonderful summer. We'll have a ball."

She managed a faint smile. "I hope so—because in the fall I'll have to make a decision."

The summer was over. She had been with Robin every night. Sometimes they went to the Hamptons for weekends. On Labor Day weekend they remained in New York. They went to Greenwich Village, walked down the narrow streets, sat for hours in a coffee bar on Cornelia Street.

Now it was October—the new season had begun. *The Christie Lane Show* was back on the air. *In Depth* had started its second season. Christie was demanding that she set a date for the marriage and Robin was off again on his sporadic trips. It was as if the summer had never happened. In spite of her vow, she knew she would go on —putting off Christie, waiting and hoping for Robin. She lost the few pounds she had gained during the summer

—yet whenever Robin returned she felt fine. She couldn't make a decision—she waited.

Oddly enough, it was the sponsor who forced her to decide: On the fifteenth of January Alwayso was moving the show to California for the rest of the season.

"We go out as man and wife!" Christie insisted. "We stop off in Chicago and get married!"

"I won't get married on the way to anywhere. If I go to California, we'll get married out there," she replied.

The decision to move the show had been made the week before Christmas. And Robin was in London.

On Christmas Eve she met Jerry at the Lancer Bar for a drink. Jerry wasn't happy about California either. It meant spending a great deal of time out there. . . .

They both stared morosely at the bar with its cheerful little Christmas tree, and the false snow and the holly that was strung across the mirror. Their eyes met. She raised her glass. "Merry Christmas, Jerry."

"You look drawn, Amanda."

"I feel drawn and quartered," she said.

He reached out and took her hand. "Look, honey, you can't play a waiting game any longer. Put it to Robin on New Year's Day."

"Why then? How do I know I'll see him?"

"Hasn't Chris been invited to Mrs. Austin's New Year's Day party?"

She managed a smile. "Has he ever! That's all he talks about. He acts as if it's a command performance at Buckingham Palace."

"In a way, it is. Judith Austin rarely extends invitations to people at IBC. This year seems to be an exception. Danton Miller was kind of surprised that Robin was also invited. And I happen to know Robin is flying back New Year's Eve. He kidded me about celebrating it twice due to the time change. Robin will be at Mrs. Austin's. He won't dare turn it down."

"And what do I do?" she asked. "Walk up to him and say, 'It's now or never, Robin'?"

"Something like that."

"I can't—I'm not going to that party."

"Why, hasn't Chris asked you?"

"Of course he has. But I always spend New Year's Day with Aunt Rose. Of course I haven't told that to Chris. He knows nothing about it. I just plan to have a headache that day."

"But you said she doesn't recognize you, Amanda."

"I know, but I sit with her, and feed her—and New Year's Day, well, that's our day together."

"Will she know whether it's January first or January second?" Jerry asked.

"I'll know, Jerry."

"Look: go to the party, Amanda. And put it on the line to Robin. Get a clear-cut yes or no out of him. If it's no, then write him off. Two years is long enough to wait for anyone, even Robin. And you can visit your aunt the following day."

She seemed thoughtful. Then she nodded. "Okay, this is it!" She crossed her fingers. "Here's to nineteen sixty-two—either I make it, or I'm through! God, I'm a poet. Let's have a vodka martini, Jerry, the kind Robin drinks —and let's wish that bastard a Merry Christmas wherever he is!"

# THIRTEEN

THE INVITATION to the Austin New Year's Day party read "Eggnog, Four to Seven." Chris wanted to pick Amanda up at three thirty. She insisted on making it four thirty.

"But, doll, we're supposed to be there at four."

"Which means no one comes until five. And anyone who is really anyone arrives at six."

He grudgingly agreed. "Who knows from all this classy protocol? I guess I really need a wife like you."

By three o'clock she had tried on six different outfits. The black dress was flattering—she could wear it with a string of pearls and Robin's gold watch. Funny about the watch—everyone seemed to admire it, maybe because it was so tiny. Nick Longworth said it was very expensive.

Chris had given her a gold charm bracelet for Christmas. She hated it, but she knew she had to wear it. She stared at the disc that said *Mandy and Chris*—it was so heavy and it clanked on everything. It definitely wouldn't go with the black dress.

She took out the Chanel suit. It was one of Ohrbach's line-for-line copies. Even the real Chanel cloth. But Judith Austin would be able to tell the difference. She probably had the original. Well, she wasn't out to impress Mrs. Austin. And Jerry had been right. She had watched IBC's *News at Noon.* They had a shot of Robin arriving at Idlewild at six that morning.

She had it all planned. It would be easy to slip away from Christie at a cocktail party. She'd go directly to Robin and say, "I want to talk to you tonight. It's urgent." She'd arrange to meet him later, after she unloaded Chris. And tonight it would be settled—one way or another. Chris thought she was all set for the Coast, but Jerry had given her a contract that she did not have to sign until the end of the week. Oh God, it had to work! In the last few weeks she had reversed many of her ideas about Christie. He was not just a simple good-natured slob. In some ways, especially concerning money, he could be absolutely cold-blooded. The other night, his fishy eyes had gone to a steely gray when he said, "You're playing it real cute, doll. Lou Goldberg tipped me off about you. Lou says you've been stalling our marriage date waiting for a shot like this."

"I don't understand," she said.

"You want to marry me in California—they got community property out there. If we divorce you'd get half of everything."

Since the thought had never occurred to her, the amazement on her face was real. "If I marry you, it's for keeps," she said.

"You bet it's for keeps." He had grinned. "And what's mine is yours—as soon as we have our kid."

Lou Goldberg had come to New York over Christmas. He was a nice man in his early sixties. She had tried to be pleasant, but she wasn't a very good actress and Lou's sharp eyes had taken in everything—the way she "allowed" Chris to hold her hand, her lack of spontaneous affection.

Today she *should* be with Aunt Rose—New Year's Day was a big visiting day at the nursing home. Maybe they wouldn't feed Aunt Rose her dinner, thinking she would be there to do it. Well, she'd call from the party just to make sure.

About twenty people had arrived when they entered the Austin town house. Its dark quiet luxury was impressive. The butler took their coats and directed them to the large living room. Amanda recognized a senator, several socialites, several movie stars, and a top comedy star from CBS (she had read that IBC was after him). She also saw Danton Miller, and in the corner, chatting earnestly with Mrs. Austin, was Ike Ryan. Amanda recognized him immediately. In the past few months Ike Ryan had exploded on the Hollywood scene. His flamboyant style made good copy. His first major picture was in the final stages of editing. The publicity began when he signed one of Hollywood's top glamour girls to star in it. She had immediately left her husband and embarked on a wild romance with Ike Ryan. The moment the picture was finished, he had dumped her, and taken up with a new little starlet whom he promised to feature in his next film. The rejected star tried sleeping pills but was saved when she phoned her estranged husband. A few weeks later the young starlet also tried sleeping pills and was saved by Ike whom she called at the zero hour. Ike had made the front pages—swearing he had come to Hollywood to be a producer, not a lover. He had tried all that once before, he stated. He had married the girl he went to school with in Newark. They had been divorced five years ago. Now he was immersed only in his work. Sure he fell in love—every day. But not for keeps.

He was good-looking in a rugged way. His mother had been Jewish, his father a second-rate Irish prizefighter. Ike talked about this in his interviews, claiming he had the best from both sides. Amanda guessed him to be forty. He was tanned, with some gray beginning to show at the temples in his black hair. His nose was short and puggish, giving a boyish quality to his square-jawed face. Judith Austin seemed captivated with him.

This surprised Amanda. Judith Austin was everything that Amanda wanted to be. She was slim and elegant, her ash-blond hair twisted into a French knot, and she wore a velvet "at home" gown. Amanda had seen it in *Vogue* and knew it cost twelve hundred dollars. She noticed that Mrs. Austin wore very little jewelry—small pearl earrings, nothing else. Then her eye was caught by the enormous pear-shaped diamond that hung loosely on her finger. It had to be at least thirty carats.

She and Christie stood alone, oddly isolated in the crowded room. Danton Miller saw them and came over and graciously made some small talk. Chris clung eagerly to Danton and the two men launched into a discussion of ratings.

Amanda looked around the room. It was a wonderful house. Aunt Rose would be thrilled if she could see her here now! She suddenly thought of the nursing home. She excused herself and asked the butler for a telephone. He led her to the library and closed the door. She looked around her, awed by the dignity of the beautiful room. She went to the desk and ran her fingers over it gently. It looked French. She saw all the buttons on the phone and the blank cardboard where the number should be. Unlisted—naturally. She stared at the picture of Judith in the silver frame, then leaned closer. It was signed "Consuelo," in that funny backhand style all society women had. Of course, this was her twin sister—the princess! She dialed the nursing home. It was busy. She sat down and opened the silver box on the table and lit a cigarette. She studied the other silver frame that showed the two little princesses taken when they were about ten and twelve. Maybe they were debutantes by now, beautiful debutantes in Europe without a care in the world. She tried the nursing home again. It was still busy.

The door opened. It was Ike Ryan. He grinned. "I saw you slip out. As soon as I could break away I came looking for you. I'm Ike Ryan. We met at Danny's Hideaway last year."

She hoped her blank stare told him she had no recollection of the incident. Then in a detached voice she said,

"I came in here to make a phone call, but the number I'm trying to get is busy."

He waved his hand. "That's what I'm after too. Mind if I use it?" Before she could answer, he reached over and took the phone and began to dial. He stopped midway and turned to her. "Hey, are you free after this party?"

She shook her head.

He went back to his dialing. "Then I'll put through this call. I guess you're serious about that joker you came with. You were with him at Danny's when we met."

"I do the commercials on *The Christie Lane Show*." She wondered if Robin had ever mentioned her to Ike Ryan.

His number answered. "Joy, hi, sweetheart, want to make it for dinner at nine? I'll send my car for you. We got three parties we can go to, or we might wind up at the Sixth Avenue Delicatessen. Depends how I feel. What? Sure I do—would I stop in the middle of a business deal to call if I didn't? Okay, toots." He clicked the phone and turned to Amanda. "See what you've missed?"

She smiled wryly.

He stared at her. "I like you. Most broads fall all over me."

"I'm not a broad. I have a contract to go to California for some TV commercials, and the 'joker' who brought me here happens to be very much in love with me."

He smiled. "Where you staying on the Coast?"

"At the Beverly Hills, if I go—"

"*If* you go? I thought you had a contract."

"I do. I haven't signed it yet."

"What's the *efsher?*"

"*Efsher?*"

He smiled. "It's a Yid word. My old lady used to use it. It loses in the translation but I'll try and give you an example of *efsher*. Let's see. Oh yes! My sister was a beast before I sprung for the nose job which finally landed her a husband. But before that she never got dates. And so one weekend she was going to Grossinger's with several girls she knew, all pigs like herself—you know the type. No, you wouldn't. Virgin Jewish girls past twenty-five. Hysterical! Real losers. The kind that's stopped hoping. My sister was one of them. So this weekend I remember my sister was packing slacks, a tennis racket, a bathing suit, and my mom said, 'What, no pretty dresses?' My sister said, 'Look, Mom, I've been to these places. There are never any unattached men. So this time I'm going to relax. I'll play tennis. I'm going for a rest, not to look.' Then my mom walked over with my sister's best dress, plunked it in the suitcase and said, 'Take it, *efsher.*'"

Amanda laughed. She found herself warming up to Ike Ryan.

"Get it?" he asked. "*Efsher* means 'maybe'—a possibility, a dim hope. What's your *efsher*, toots?" Then, as if sensing her change of attitude, he said, "Listen, want to change your mind about tonight? I can always cancel that date I just made."

"I don't break dates," she said.

"Neither do I when I *care* about them." He stared at her intently. Then he smiled. "Come to the Coast, toots. I think we got a future together."

The room suddenly seemed so empty after he left. She realized it was after six. Robin might have arrived. She quickly dialed the nursing home. Still busy! She checked her makeup and returned to the party. She'd try later.

The large room had filled and spilled over to the drawing room and the dining room. She wandered into each room, scanning every face, but Robin wasn't there. She found Chris, rooted to the same spot, still talking to Danton Miller. Danton seemed relieved to see her and immediately broke away.

"Where the hell you been?" Chris asked, as soon as they were alone.

"Combing my hair," she said coldly.

"You been gone twenty minutes. Dan Miller was stuck standing with me."

"Well, if you're such a big star, where are all your fans?"

Chris stared at all the famous people in the room. "It's funny," he sighed. "I know everyone I see, but I see no one I know. Doll, let's go. I don't belong here."

"Oh, Chris, at least try and look like you're enjoying yourself."

"Why? Where's there a rule that says we gotta enjoy

it? So we were invited—Eddie Flynn *also* invited us to a party. He's giving it in his suite at the Edison. Some of the kids from the Copa are coming—it's for Aggie because she quit the line at the Latin Quarter to go to the Coast with Eddie. Now, that's a party that'll have some laughs."

She looked toward the door. Her heart quickened. But no, it was just another tall man. . . .

At eight fifteen Amanda finally gave in and allowed Chris to drag her to Eddie's party at the Edison. The Copa girls and the Latin Quarter girls had gone to do their dinner shows. Amanda sat on the couch and started to drink Scotch. Chris was relaxed—this was his kind of party. He brought over some pastrami sandwiches.

"Here, doll, this is better than that fancy food at the Austins'."

She refused and poured another Scotch. "Better eat," Chris warned her, cramming the sandwich into his mouth. "I've had three of these, so I don't feel like dinner."

"I'm not hungry," Amanda said.

Agnes joined her on the couch. "Is that how you models keep your figures?" she asked. "You're making a big mistake. The corned beef is to die over."

"I'm just not hungry," Amanda said. The Scotch suddenly made her feel drowsy and she yawned.

Agnes looked at her sympathetically. "Too much New Year's Eve, last night?"

"No, not really. Chris played a club date. It was very quiet really—that is, if you can call the Grand Ballroom at the Waldorf quiet."

"Last year me and Eddie were with Chris at the Fontainebleau. Oh, none of us lived there. Chris was playing a club date. That was before the show started on the air. You know something? Me and Eddie, we had more fun before we made it big on television. I mean—there were laughs. That's the way it should be on holidays."

"I don't like New Year's Eve or any holiday," Amanda said.

By eleven o'clock she was quite drunk. Chris wanted to go someplace for coffee but he finally agreed to take her home.

He held the cab while he walked her to the door. This was a courtesy she had finally drummed into him but he still thought it was ridiculous. "Maybe you get your kicks hearing that meter running," he said.

"Ike Ryan has a car and chauffeur," she said.

"Just a rented job," he snapped.

"But he doesn't use cabs—"

"That'll be the day, when I pay eight bucks an hour while a chauffeur sits around and listens to the radio." He kissed her quickly, conscious that the taxi meter was clicking. "Remember, doll—when I'm sixty, we'll have it made. A guy like Ike Ryan might go down the drain."

She stumbled as she let herself into the apartment. She felt a queasy feeling in her stomach and the beginning of a monumental headache. She checked with her answering service. One message, from the nursing home. Sure you can bet they had called—those nurses were waiting for the twenty-dollar bills she passed around on New Year's Day.

But no call from Robin! Well, this was it. No more— what was that word?—*efsher*. Yes, no more *efsher*. She'd go to California! She'd *marry* Chris! Suddenly she went rigid as a new thought came into focus. Then she went limp with shock. California! Who would visit Aunt Rose? She always went once a month—always on a different day, at a different hour, to check on her. If she went away, they'd leave her neglected. Why hadn't she thought of this until now? Because until this minute she had never actually believed she would go. She hadn't even bothered to sublet her apartment. She had still hoped for Robin.

She thought for a moment, then on impulse she dialed Jerry at home. His wife answered. Amanda apologized for the late call but explained it was urgent.

"Jerry—I can't go to California."

He sounded elated. "It worked, huh? I told you to put it on the line with him!"

"He never showed," she said slowly.

"Then why don't you go to California?"

"It has nothing to do with Robin," she said wearily. "Jerry—it just hit me. I've been so busy thinking of myself, of Robin, of Chris. I forgot about Aunt Rose. I can't just take off. Who will visit her?"

"I'm sure there must be good nursing homes on the Coast."

"But, Jerry—how could I move her?"

"Get Chris to charter a private plane. Get a nurse to go along with you."

"He doesn't know about Aunt Rose and I don't know how he'd take it."

"Listen, Amanda—Chris has come up the hard way. If anything he'll respect you twice as much. And it will make him happy to be able to help you."

"Oh, Jerry, if Chris does that, I'll try to love him. And I'll be good to him. I really will. I'll make him happy. I'm going to call him right now."

Christie's phone didn't answer. That meant he was at the Copa bar, the Stage, Lindy's or Toots Shor. She tried them all and finally located him at Toots Shor.

"Chris, can you come here? I want to talk to you."

"Doll, I'm sitting with Toots, and Ronnie Wolfe just joined us. I want to get a plug in his column."

"I have to talk to you."

"Jesus, everyone is here. It's jumping. Come on, doll, grab a cab."

"Chris, I can't talk with all those people. This is important. It's about us, our future."

"Jesus—all night we were together. At the Austins' you just stood there like a lump. Why didn't you talk to me then? We had plenty of privacy. People stayed away from us in droves."

"Are you coming, Chris?"

"Doll, I'll be there in, say, half an hour."

"No." The Scotch was hitting her. She felt groggy. "Now, while I'm still awake. This is important. Come right away."

"Okay, I'll be there."

"Hurry."

"Is it all right with you if I stop and take a leak first?"

She clicked the phone. Then she undressed. He probably would want to go to bed with her. Well, if he would arrange to bring Aunt Rose to Los Angeles, to a good nursing home, he could sleep with her every night. She'd even try and respond.

She put on a robe, combed her hair, fixed her makeup and put in her diaphragm.

Chris finally arrived. He took off his coat and took her in his arms and began to kiss her.

"Chris, later. I want to talk to you."

"We'll talk, but after—" He pulled the string of her robe and it fell open. He stopped suddenly. "Okay, you win. I don't want to make love to a statue. For all the action I'm getting, I could look at *Playboy* and jerk off."

She closed her robe and crossed the room. "Sit down, Chris, I've got quite a bit to say."

He sat very still while she spoke. She told him everything, omitting nothing. His eyes widened as he listened, then he shook his head in sympathy.

"You poor kid, you had it as rough as me."

Tears came to her eyes. "Then you'll help me, Chris?"

"Doll, how can I help?"

"Move Aunt Rose to the Coast!"

"You must be kidding!" he said. "You know what that will cost? We can't take a sick dinge on the plane!"

"Don't you dare call Aunt Rose that."

"All right! Even if she was snow-white, you still can't take a person with a stroke on a plane."

"You can *charter* a plane."

"Sure, for thousands of bucks!"

"Well . . . you certainly have enough money."

He stared at her. Then he stood up and paced the room. He whirled around, his finger shooting out at her. "Are you crazy! I got a cousin, a first cousin, a flesh-and-blood cousin, and he wanted to borrow two thousand to buy into a business and I turned him down. Know why? Because I'm like you. No one ever did anything for little Chris. My folks were poor too. My old man was in burlesque. He cheated on my old lady. She cheated on him, they both split, remarried—neither of them wanted me. I made it on my own from the time I was twelve. I got a half brother. I don't give him a dime! Because if it was all reversed, I know damn well he wouldn't give me the right time."

"Then you won't do it?" she asked.

"Kee-rist! Next thing I know, you'll want Aunt Rose to move in after we're married, stretcher and all."

"If she got better, why not?"

"Because I won't let my family poach on me—and I'm not about to lay out my money for an old——lady I never met. This could cost maybe ten thousand!"

"It might," she said coldly.

"Do you know how hard I work to make ten thou?"

"I heard you got that every week as a raise."

His eyes narrowed. "You been doing a Dun and Bradstreet on me?"

"Everyone knows the sponsor gave you a ten-thousand-dollar raise. You made sure that it got into every column."

"Well, the government gets seventy percent. See, that's what I mean. For me to lay out ten thou, I have to make a fortune."

"All right, Chris, please go."

He crossed the room and grabbed her. "Amanda, doll, I love you. I'm not cheap. Look, let's say we have a kid and it wasn't feeling right, I'd toss out ten thou in a second to the right specialist. Everything I got will be for you and the kid. But no relatives. Especially someone who's not even a blood relative," he added.

"She's like my mother!"

"Holy shit!" he exploded. "Only to me could this happen! I think I've found me the classiest broad in the world. And suddenly as a little dividend you spring a black relative on me—not even a healthy one we could pass off as the maid! Doll, when you say you want to talk, you sure don't fuck around!"

"Get out, Chris."

"I'll go, but you sleep on it. And don't get sullen and think I don't love you. I love you plenty—and I'm a liberal too! I figured maybe you came from some fancy family. Here I was, always apologizing about my background—and you coolly tell me you're illegitimate, you were raised by a black chambermaid, and does it matter to me. Not a bit! I still love you and I want to marry you. But I ain't forcing my crummy family down your throat, and you can't force yours on me. When we're married, the money we spend will be on *our* kid. But one thing, Mandy—" He stopped. "Jesus—even that name sounds lousy now. The next thing I know you'll want to name our kid Rastus. From now on no one calls you Mandy. It's *Amanda*. Did your aunt tag that on you?"

"No," she said quietly. "My real name is Rose. Nick Longworth changed it when I started to model. Rose Jones wasn't glamorous. He thought Amanda sounded English—Noel Coward and all that."

"Well, it did until I learned about dear old Aunt Rose. Look, doll, I shared dressing rooms with colored acts. They're my friends. Eventually things will change. I hope they do. But I'm not big enough to go on a one-man crusade. Let someone else do it, and I'll join. But all my life I've been an almost-was. I played every crummy joint in the world. Loads of guys have done the same and never risen above it. But I've made it. And I'm offering it to you! But just you! Not your aunt, my cousin, my half-brother—it's us all the way."

He grabbed his coat and started for the door. "We forget tonight, understand? It never happened. I don't know no Aunt Rose. You're Amanda, the top model—we've got it made together." He slammed the door.

She sat very still for a few minutes. Then she got up and poured herself a drink. Oddly enough she understood how Chris felt. Well, it proved one thing—she couldn't afford the luxury of love. Because no one really cared. Everyone was out for number one! She'd never see Christie Lane again or Robin Stone! She'd quit the show, tell Nick to concentrate on getting her bookings, even if she had to cut her price. She felt no guilt about Christie now. She'd work, take care of Aunt Rose, and marry the first decent man who came along so that she could have a child and give it a decent start in life. She took a sleeping pill, set the alarm and turned off her phone.

The alarm went off at nine. Her head ached. She reached for the phone to check with her service, then changed her mind. If there were any calls, they would only be trouble.

She took a cab to Queens. The small lobby of the nursing home was half empty. A few old women sat and watched television in wheelchairs. One woman was doing a child's jigsaw puzzle. Another just sat and stared into space. An attendant was taking down a moth-eaten Christmas tree.

She went to the elevator and pushed the button to the third floor. She never announced herself. It was best not to give them any warning.

She opened the door of the room. The bed was stripped.

Miss Stevenson, the supervisor, came rushing in. She looked upset.

"We called you last night," Miss Stevenson said.

"I tried to call in," Amanda said. "The line was busy. Why have you moved Aunt Rose?" She suddenly panicked. "Is she worse?"

"She's dead," Miss Stevenson said.

Amanda screamed. Then she flew at the woman and grabbed her. "What happened? How?" Amanda shouted.

"At six o'clock when we brought her dinner, she suddenly sat up. Her eyes were bright. She said, 'Where's little Rosie?' We told her you were coming. She lay back and smiled. She said, 'I'll eat with little Rosie. I don't like to eat alone. When she gets home from school we'll eat—'"

Amanda began to sob. "She thought she was in the past. But she might have recognized me."

Miss Stevenson shrugged. "When it seemed you weren't coming, we tried to get her to eat. But she kept saying, 'I'm waiting for my child.' Then at eight we came back, and she was sitting up just as we had left her. She was dead. We called you—"

"Where is she?" Amanda asked.

"In the morgue."

"The morgue!"

"We couldn't keep her here."

Amanda dashed to the elevator. Miss Stevenson followed. "I'll give you the address. You can make your funeral arrangements from there."

She made arrangements for the cremation and services. Then she went home, turned off the phone and slept.

When Jerry called the following day, she told him what had happened.

Jerry tried to hide the relief in his voice, but he said it

was for the best. "Now you can go to California with a clear conscience," he said.

"Yes, Jerry, I can go to California."

She finished an entire bottle of Scotch that night. Then she stared at herself in the mirror. "Well, that's it. Now you belong to no one! No one gives a good goddam about you. It's a rotten world!"

Then she fell into bed and sobbed. "Oh, Robin, Robin, where were you? What kind of a man are you? I stayed at that party waiting for you, while Aunt Rose was waiting for me. I could have been with her—she *would* have recognized me, died in my arms, knowing someone cared."

She buried her face in the pillow. "I hate you, Robin Stone! I was waiting for you while Aunt Rose died, and where were you? Oh God—where were you!"

He had been watching the Rose Bowl game. He had reached the apartment at seven in the morning, fallen into bed and slept until noon. When he awoke he went to the refrigerator, took two hard-boiled eggs and a can of beer into the living room, turned on the television set and stretched out on the couch. He took the remote control and clicked through the stations. He stopped at IBC. They were covering the pre-football-game pageantry. There was the usual fanfare, the floats, the interview with Miss Orange Blossom or whatever she was. They were always the same type: long-limbed sunny-looking girls who might have been weaned on double orange juice. In fact this one looked like her mother's milk had been orange juice. The nice white teeth, the clean hair, the nervous smile. Well, she'd have one day of glory, a week of local popularity and three pages in a scrapbook to show her children.

He stared at the girl with little interest. She was saying she wanted lots and lots of children. God, wouldn't it be wonderful if just once one of them said, "Oh, I just want to fuck!" He pitied the poor girl who was interviewing her. He could only see the back of her neck but she had a good voice. He caught a quick glance of her profile as she signed off: "This is Maggie Stewart with Dodie Castle,

Miss Orange Blossom of 1962—and now back to Andy Parino."

Andy came on to interview an old-time football player. Robin switched to CBS to catch the game, then he switched to NBC. He was restless. He turned to Channel 11, watched an old movie and dozed off. When he awoke he clicked off the set and dialed Amanda, stopped midway and hung up. She was probably out, and besides, he wanted to cool it with her anyway. He was tired . . . the weather in London had been very bad, but that English girl had been a real swinger, and when he got her with the baroness she had gone right along with the scene. Ike Ryan had introduced him to the orgy game. Hell, they weren't orgies—they were just group sex. Ike Ryan had a theory about making a girl become part of an orgy. You make her do it with you, then with a friend while you watch, then with another girl—and by then you've cut her down to size. Once she's gone along with that scene, she can't play games—none of that "send me flowers" jazz. You've reduced her to what every woman is, once you've stripped off the fancy manners: a broad.

Maybe he should try it with Amanda. That would sure as hell cut off the marriage talk. But something in him went against the idea. Because somehow he knew she *would* go along with it—she would do anything to hold him. But she wouldn't forget it like the baroness or the English girl. And he didn't want to hurt Amanda. God, in the beginning he had felt so safe with her. But lately she seemed always on the brink of bursting at the seams. Well, it was time to cut out. He had given her plenty of reason—he always liked the girl to be the one to walk; at least it left her pride intact. Maybe this thing with Christie Lane would really work out.

He picked up the phone and asked for the IBC tie line. He got Andy in the control room and wished him a Happy New Year.

"How's Miss Orange Blossom?" he asked.

"Chicken-chested and knock-kneed," Andy answered.

"She sure as hell looked good on camera."

"Maggie made her look good."

"Maggie?"

"Maggie Stewart—you probably only caught the back of her head. She's just great!"

Robin smiled. "Sounds like there's something really going with the two of you."

"There is. I'd like you to meet her. Why not come down for a few days? You could use a vacation. The golf is great here."

"I never need a vacation. I enjoy every day as it comes. I've just come back from Europe with some great tapes. Now I want to do some live shows. Listen, chum, don't go marrying this girl until I case her!"

"I'd marry her tomorrow if she agreed."

"Andy, I'll bet you anything she's just another broad." Andy's voice was hard. "Don't kid about Maggie!"

"Happy New Year, sucker," Robin said, and hung up.

He lit a cigarette. He thought of all the nights he and Andy had roamed up and down the Seventy-ninth Street Causeway together, stopping off at each bar, winding up with girls, swapping the girls in the middle of the evening. . . .

He threw on his coat and went out into the night. It was cold and clear. He walked down Third Avenue, all the way to Forty-second Street. He cut across town and hit Broadway. He stared at the glaring row of movie houses and pizza joints.

He passed a movie house, bought a ticket and walked in. A man from the next aisle came and sat beside him. After a few minutes Robin felt an overcoat tossed casually on his leg. Then a timid hand groped along his thigh. He got up and changed his seat. Five minutes later a stout Negro girl with a blond wig nestled close to him. "Want a good time, honey? Right here? I put my coat over you and do the greatest hand job you ever had. Five bucks."

He changed seats again. He sat next to two teen-aged girls. Suddenly one of them whispered, "Give me ten dollars." He stared at her as if she was insane. She couldn't be more than fifteen. Her friend was the same age. He ignored her. "Give me ten dollars or I'll scream out in the theater that you tried to feel me up. I'm a minor—you'll get into trouble."

He got up and dashed out of the theater. He walked a

few blocks and stopped at an all-night cafeteria for some coffee. He reached into his pocket—Christ! His wallet was gone. Who had it been? The fag with the overcoat? The hooker? The delinquent teenagers? He turned up his collar and walked home.

# FOURTEEN

T HE CROWD AT THE POLO BAR at the Beverly Hills Hotel was thinning out. But it was still too noisy to try and make a long-distance call. Jerry decided to make it from his room. God, he hated this town, but the show had climbed to the number-two spot. It had been a good move switching the show to the Coast for the second half of the season. But there'd be three more months in the land of eternal sunshine, palm trees and loneliness.

He went to his room and placed a call to Mary. Thank God for the summer replacement show—he'd have to go back and help make the decision. That meant an entire week in New York. He wouldn't even mind the commuter train.

The operator rang him back—the line in Greenwich was busy. He canceled the call. He was meeting Christie and Amanda at Chasen's at eight thirty. It was one of the rare nights that Amanda had agreed to go out. She was always tired lately. Her room was down the hall, and like clockwork the DO NOT DISTURB sign went on her door every night at eight thirty. Of course she did have long hours—she had picked up most of the top modeling assignments in California. Christie Lane was vehement about California. He insisted the whole town closed down at ten thirty. Night after night he sat in a large rented house playing gin with Eddie Flynn and Kenny Ditto. Christie wasn't comfortable at any of the Hollywood places. He claimed he never got a decent table. He had sulked for weeks when Amanda refused to go through with the Valentine's Day wedding. She insisted she didn't want to get married and rush back to work—she wanted a real honeymoon. Christie had finally agreed. Now they planned to get married the day after the show went off for the summer.

Jerry wondered about Amanda. She was with Christie the night of the show, and perhaps a couple of nights during the week. She refused to make the Hollywood scene, wouldn't go to the Cocoanut Grove or any of the openings that Christie adored. So Chris roamed Hollywood with Kenny, Eddie and the show girl. Each night they wound up at the drugstore at the Beverly Wilshire Hotel, hoping to run into some comics or other displaced New Yorkers who missed the midnight coffee klatches of the East. According to Chris, this was his first shot at California, and his last! He'd finish out the season, but he had served notice on the sponsors that he would do all the shows from New York the following season. Jerry was all for it—he was as lonely as Chris.

But Amanda didn't seem to miss New York at all. She had never looked better, and she was getting some interest from picture producers. Her entire attitude seemed to have changed—as if the California climate had effected some change of chemistry in her personality. Her easy smile was always there, but Jerry felt there was something missing in their relationship. It was almost as if they had never known one another. He had given up asking her to dinner. She always made the same plea: "I'd love it, Jerry, but I'm tired and I'm doing a big layout tomorrow." Well, maybe he had been exorcised along with Robin. She never mentioned his name or asked about him.

Jerry looked at his watch—eight forty-five. Christie and Amanda must be furious. He put in a call to Chasen's. Christie came on right away. "Where in hell are you?"

"I'm waiting for a call from New York. I'll be a little late."

"Then we'll cancel. I'll wander over to Schwab's." Christie sounded glum.

"Why, it's not as if you're waiting alone. You've got Amanda."

"She conked out."

"What happened?"

"She called me an hour ago. She has a sore throat—must be from the smog. So she took a sleeping pill and went to bed. I'm sitting here all alone. Jesus, this is a real hick town—no one goes out except on weekends. And if you're not in pictures you don't mean a damn thing out here. Hey, Alfie and his pack just came in—"

"Alfie?"

"Jerry, you're not with it. Alfred Knight."

"Oh, the English actor."

"Christ! You'd think he was *Sir* Alfred the way everyone's jumping around here. You should see what's going on. I had a reservation. Know where they put me? In left field. But Alfie boy, who just happens to waltz in, gets the big front table, the number-one spot. I think he's a switch-hitter. I not only hate the town—I also hate the people."

"Cheer up," Jerry laughed. "June will be here before you know it."

"I can't wait."

Jerry hung up and sat on the bed and lit another cigarette. Maybe Amanda would have something from Room Service with him. He called her.

She was polite, but she refused his invitation.

"I couldn't eat, Jerry, my throat is sore and I have a swollen gland in my neck. I'm coming down with something, and the show is in two days. I want to look all right—it would be terrible if I missed it."

He hung up and felt vaguely let down.

He suddenly felt hemmed in, and lonely. He opened the French doors onto the lanai garden outside his room. Amanda raved about her garden. She said it was wonderful to lie out there at night and look at the stars. He stepped into the patio of the garden. The night sounds of the crickets seemed intensified by the silent darkness. Amanda's garden was three doors down. Suddenly his loneliness engulfed him. He had to talk to someone. Maybe she wasn't asleep. He didn't want to ring and disturb her, but a pill didn't always work—he knew from experience. He went out to his garden hoping to see if her lights were on. No luck! Each patio was enclosed by a high wooden wall. He tried his gate—it was stiff, but he got it open. He walked down the path toward her patio.

Suddenly he heard another gate being opened. He ducked behind one of the giant palm trees. It was Amanda. She came out and looked around cautiously. She was wearing slacks and a loose sweater. She was heading toward the bungalows. On impulse, he followed her. She stopped in front of one of the bungalows and looked around. Jerry knew he was hidden by the darkness and the massive foliage. She tapped on the door. Ike Ryan opened it.

"Jesus, babe, where in hell have you been?"

"I wanted to wait a reasonable time in case Christie called back. I just turned off my phone."

"When are you going to unload the bum?"

"As soon as the show goes off. I might as well finish the season with no hard feelings."

The door closed. In the shadow of the window he saw them embrace.

He called Room Service and tried to watch television. But his thoughts were on the bungalow across the way. It was two o'clock when he heard the scraping sound of her patio gate. No wonder she was always too tired to go out—a swollen gland!

Actually she did have a swollen gland. Ike had noticed it too. When she returned to her room she stared at herself in the mirror. Her makeup was messed up. Ike was not the most gentle lover in the world, but she was sure he cared about her. He kept at her to break up with Christie. When she explained that the show was her main source of income, he said, "Listen, toots, you'll never have to worry about a buck as long as you're with me." But that wasn't exactly a marriage proposal. Well, she'd stall till June, then ask him right out. And if he didn't want to marry her, she'd marry Chris. It wouldn't matter too much, one way or another. Suddenly she was tired; all the blood seemed to drain from her. She had been taking amphetamines. They pepped her up—of course they killed her appetite, but she forced herself to eat. But tonight she had hardly been able to pick at her food. There were little cold sores on her gums and on the roof of her mouth. Maybe a penicillin shot would help, or a good night's sleep. She fell into bed.

The following morning she felt worse. When she brushed her teeth, her gums bled. She was alarmed—this was some kind of infection. She called Jerry. Yes, he knew a doctor, but from her symptoms it sounded like a general run-down condition. "Maybe it's trench mouth," he said.

"Oh God, Jerry, where would I have gotten that?"

"I can't imagine," he said coldly. "After all, you stay home every night."

She noticed the tinge of sarcasm in his voice. "Well, I guess I better see a doctor."

"Wait until after the show tomorrow. Meanwhile, gargle with peroxide-and-water. I had it once, it's not such a big deal." Then he hung up.

She took two amphetamines before she left for her modeling job. They gave her some energy but her heart was racing. The photographer drove her to Malibu. She stood in the bathing suit while the shots were set up. The sun was beating down on her, but she got on the water skis and managed to hang on. They completed the shot on the first take. The photographer wanted one more to play it safe. She felt wobbly as she got back on the skis. The boat began to move, the photographer followed in his boat, she bent her knees and held the rope, then pulled herself straight as the boat gathered speed. Suddenly everything seemed to sway—the sun was falling into the sea, and she felt the cool softness of the ocean close over her.

When she opened her eyes, she was on the beach—wrapped in a blanket. Everyone was staring at her with concern.

"I guess I just blacked out," she said.

She spent the rest of the day and night in bed. When she woke the following day her face was fine and her mouth seemed better, but her legs were black-and-blue. She must have bruised them when she fell—probably banged them against the skis in the water. Thank goodness she could wear a long dress on the show!

The following day she felt worse. The sores had returned to her mouth, but it was the bruises that frightened her. They had fused into one alarming pattern of purple covering her entire legs from the ankles to the thighs. When Christie called, she told him about it.

"Well, you're the one who wants to go out on those crazy jobs. According to the law of averages you shoulda died of pneumonia two years ago. Standing in summer clothes in zero weather! You're run-down. And anyone would be bruised if they fell with water skis."

"Chris, find me a doctor . . ."

"Look, doll, I'm meeting with the writers in ten minutes. Then I got a UP interview. There must be a croaker connected with that fancy hotel."

The doctor in the hotel was out on call. She was desperate now. She canceled her afternoon booking. She was supposed to pose in tennis shorts but makeup couldn't cover her legs. She was dozing off when Ike Ryan called. At first she was evasive, then she told him the truth.

"Don't move, toots. I'll be right over with the best doctor in L.A."

In less than twenty minutes Ike appeared accompanied by a middle-aged man carrying the usual satchel. "This is Dr. Aronson. I'll leave you two alone. But I'll be right out in the hall, so just holler if he gets fresh." His wink at the doctor proved they were friends of long standing.

Dr. Aronson examined her with impersonal casualness. He checked her heart and her pulse and nodded approvingly. She began to relax. His easy attitude told her nothing was radically wrong. He looked into her mouth with a light. "How long have you had these blisters?"

"Just for a few days. But it's my legs that worry me."

He felt her neck, and nodded. There was no change of expression on his face when he examined her purple-blotched legs.

She explained about the water-skiing accident. "Do you think that's what it is?"

"It's hard for me to tell. These things are probably all unrelated, but I'd like to put you into the hospital for a few days. When was the last time you had a blood test?"

"Never." She was suddenly frightened. "Doctor—is something really wrong?"

He smiled. "I doubt it. Probably just a case of old-fashioned anemia—all you fashionable girls lack blood. But I want to rule out a few things."

"Like what?"

"Well, mononucleosis for one thing—there's a lot of it around. You have some of the symptoms—fatigue, the bruises, headaches."

"Couldn't I have the tests in your office? I'm afraid of hospitals."

"If you like. I'll give Ike the address and we'll arrange for them tomorrow."

She watched him as he left the room. She felt better. She went into the bathroom and combed her hair. She really looked awful, and Ike would be back any second. She put on some lipstick, added some mascara, then settled into bed.

Ike came into her room with a big smile. "Pack your bag, put in your prettiest nightgowns, and be all set when I get back. I'm going down to the bookstore and buy you all the top novels."

"Where am I going?"

"To the hospital—and no back talk. Listen, toots, the doc thinks you may have mononucleosis. If you have, you'll infect the whole damn hotel—you won't even be able to get room service. Besides, he feels you should have complete bed rest, maybe even some transfusions to build you up."

"But a hospital—Ike, I've never been sick!"

"You aren't sick now, but this is Hollywood, toots. Everything is done larger than life. And if you're Ike Ryan's girl you don't schlepp to a doctor's office for tests. You lie in state like a duchess. I've ordered the biggest corner room. Listen, for a few days live it up. I'm footing the bills—it's a cinch a broad like you has no hospital insurance."

"No, I've always been healthy."

"Okay. You be ready when I get back. And just leave word you've gone to Frisco for a job. And that you'll be back in time to do the show."

Jerry was waiting at the Lancer Bar. At this moment he should have been in Los Angeles attending the Christie Lane rehearsal, but he had decided to stretch his week in

New York to ten days. It was two o'clock in Los Angeles now; the bedlam was just beginning. He sipped his martini and waved as Robin approached the bar.

After his second martini, he knew he was going to miss the last decent train home. Robin was telling him about a new idea he had for a news show when the bartender signaled Jerry to the phone. He was surprised. "For me? I never leave word that I'm here."

Robin smiled. "Your wife is probably tracking you down."

It was Christie Lane. "Listen, Jerry, I called your office and you were gone for the day. I called your home and your wife said to try you here. Jesus, am I glad I got you. Amanda ain't doing the show tonight. We put in a rush call and got a model. She'll get by, but I think you should do something about it."

"Where is she?"

"It's all a mystery to me. The other day she disappeared. Just left word she was going to Frisco on a job. Then today she calls and calmly announces she can't do the show. This was at nine in the morning yet! And where is she? In the hospital."

"Hospital!"

"Relax, nothing is wrong. I threw a raincoat over my p.j.'s and tore over. And there she was, in a big sunny room, the place filled with flowers, all made up, looking gorgeous. She claims she's anemic and isn't leaving until she gets all built up."

"Well, she must need it if she's there, Christie. A hospital doesn't let someone check in for no reason."

"In Hollywood? Are you kidding! Half the broads in this town check in for what they call nervous exhaustion. It's really to catch up on their beauty sleep. Look, I saw Mandy—she never looked better."

"I'll be out the end of the week, Christie. And look, don't worry about Amanda. I'm sure it's not serious."

"I'm not worried—I'm goddam mad. Even if she's just doing a commercial, she's part of a show. And you don't just skip a show for a rest cure. I know it sounds corny, but I played joints when I had flu. I sang when my throat was killing me. I don't go along with anyone who goofs on a show. This is a business I love. It's given me everything I've got. And she's got to respect that. What kind of a marriage will we have if she thinks she can just casually cancel a show like she used to with some of her modeling bookings? You know what I mean?"

"I'll talk to her when I get back."

He hung up and went back to the bar. Robin listened carefully as Jerry told the story.

"She's not the type to just check into a hospital," Robin said.

"Ike Ryan is behind this," Jerry muttered.

"What has Ike to do with it?"

Before he realized it, he was telling about Amanda's secret visits to Ike's cottage. "If you ask me," Jerry went on, "I think the sore throat was just a buildup—I'll bet you anything Ike knocked her up and she's there for an abortion. What do you think?"

Robin frowned. "I think you're a goddam pussyfooted sneak!" Then he slammed down a bill on the bar and walked out.

Amanda was still in the hospital when Jerry arrived on the Coast. She was propped up in bed, looking beautiful, in full makeup. But he was startled when he saw the large bottle of blood and the needle attached to her arm. She noticed his surprise and smiled. "Don't let it bother you. I'm just taking my bag of tomato juice."

"Why the blood transfusion?" he asked as he sat on the edge of a chair.

"So I can get back to your show faster."

Suddenly the door opened and Ike Ryan burst in. "Hi, toots, I got you all the trades and a new book." He looked at Jerry curiously when Amanda introduced them. Then he held out his hand. "I've heard a lot about you. Amanda says you've been a hell of a good friend."

"We go back together," Jerry said weakly. The man's energy overwhelmed him. In an effort to reinforce his authority he said, "This is all very nice, and I know Amanda is enjoying the attention, but she *does* have an obligation to me—and above all, to the show." He turned to Amanda. "When do you plan to leave?"

"The doctor thinks at the end of the week . . ."

"She'll go when she's completely rested," Ike snapped.

Jerry stood up. "Then perhaps we ought to find a permanent replacement for the rest of the season." (God, he hated himself for acting this way!)

"No," Amanda begged. "Oh, Jerry, no, please—I'll be back next week. Maybe even this week." She looked pleadingly at Ike.

He shrugged. "Whatever you want, toots. Listen, I've got some calls to make. I'll use the booth down the hall. Goodbye, friend." He looked at Jerry coldly.

The moment they were alone, Jerry's manner changed. His voice was sincere and earnest. "Look, Amanda, maybe you *should* quit the show. This guy seems crazy about you."

"He hasn't asked me to marry him . . ."

He groaned. "We're back to that game again?"

Her face went taut. "Look, Jerry, right now Ike wants me because he knows Chris wants me. But if I'm without a job, without Chris, Ike might suddenly get disenchanted with me."

"Where did you get all that faith and trust?"

"I was born with it," she said coldly. Then her eyes went soft. "Jerry, I'll be back. I feel wonderful already. I guess I needed this rest. I've been going at such a pace for six years. Do you realize I've never had a vacation?"

He patted her on the head. "Relax, honey, the job is yours for life. I'll call you tomorrow."

He left the room and walked down the hall. Ike Ryan was waiting for him. "In here, buddy," he said, motioning to the small waiting room.

"I have to get to my office," Jerry said.

"Not until we have a little talk. You're some fine friend. She hasn't got enough trouble—you have to threaten her, yet."

"Anemia isn't that serious," Jerry said.

"She only *thinks* she has anemia." Ike stared at him. "I'm gonna trust you. No one knows this. Just Doc Aronson and me. And nobody is *gonna* know it—especially Amanda. She's got leukemia!"

Jerry sank on the couch. His hands were shaking as he reached for a cigarette. Then he looked up, his eyes straining for hope. "I've heard of people who live a long time with leukemia."

"Not the kind she has."

"How long has she got?"

"It might be minutes. It might be six months."

Jerry turned away but his composure broke. He hated himself, but he sobbed openly. Ike sat beside him and clasped his shoulder. "Look, they're trying a new drug. I've had it flown here. It costs a thousand a shot. She started on it two days ago and her blood count has gone up. It's too early to hope, but if things go right . . ."

"You mean she has a chance?"

"She has a chance to *walk* out instead of going out in a box. She has a chance for a remission, maybe six months —and who knows, by then they might find the cure, or another miracle drug."

"What can I do?" Jerry asked.

"Just keep your mouth shut. Make Christie Lane stop heckling her with this show-must-go-on jazz! And you tell her the job is waiting."

"I already have."

Ike shook his head. "The damnedest thing is, if the drug works the doc says it will be dramatic. She'll be fine in like a week. For how long, no one knows. Why in hell does she want to work? She's got so little time."

"Because she thinks you might ask her to marry you— but only if she's working and is independent."

"Oh, for Christ's sake." Ike Ryan got up and walked to the window.

Jerry started for the door. "But as you say, she won't last more than six months. You don't have to worry about that. And it's better if she *does* work. She'll believe the anemia story then."

Ike turned and held out his hand. They shook solemnly. "If anyone knows about this, I'll break your head in," he said.

Jerry promised but he knew he was going to break his word. He was going to tell Robin. Amanda had so little time—and Robin was the only man who mattered to her. He could tell she liked Ike, *liked* him, but she never looked at him the way she had looked at Robin. But he would sit on it for a few days and see how she reacted to the new drug.

Ike Ryan watched him leave, then he walked slowly

down the hall to Amanda's room. He stood very straight and forced a smile on his face, then he opened the door and sailed in. A nurse was removing the needle from Amanda's arm.

"Tonight I'll bring champagne and some new books, but now I got to get to work." He started for the door, then turned. "By the way, toots, there's something I meant to ask you and it always slipped my mind. Will you marry me? You don't have to give me your answer for at least ten minutes. I'll call you when I get to the studio."

Amanda responded to the new drug. Within a week her blood count was normal—she was in a state of remission. Ike was jubilant, but Dr. Aronson warned him—a remission was not a cure.

"But for the time, she can live a normal life, right?" Ike asked.

"Let her do anything she wants. God knows how long she'll feel this well," the doctor replied. "But I want her to come to the office every week for a blood test. We've got to watch her red-corpuscle count."

"Every week? She's going to get suspicious."

"No, she's in excellent spirits and she has no idea anything is seriously wrong."

Ike came to bring her home from the hospital. "I just rented a palace on Canyon Drive. Wait till you see the joint—I moved in yesterday. It's got everything—even a cook and butler. When do you want to get married, toots?"

"When I finish the show."

"You kidding? That's six weeks away."

"It would be rough working with Christie if he knew."

"Who says you have to work with him? Quit the damn show."

"That wouldn't be fair to Jerry—he gave me the show when I wanted it. The girls they tried while I was gone weren't right. They're all so thrilled that I'm making it back for tomorrow's show."

"I still think you should wait a week or so."

"Ike, I've had almost three weeks' rest. I feel marvelous." The happiness suddenly faded from her eyes.

"But Dr. Aronson said I have to have blood tests every week. Why?"

Ike shrugged. "Probably to make sure you don't lose all this health."

"Well, I'm going to eat liver every day. And I've been reading about blood—all the things that are good for you."

"Now don't start practicing medicine," he said.

She tucked her arm in his and the chauffeur took her bag. "Ike, I'm so relieved. I'll admit it now: I was scared when I came in. I've never been sick before, and when I was lying there that first day, I thought, 'Wouldn't it be awful to have to check out now . . . to die without ever having a child.' I'm so grateful that I'm well. And I know what it is to be unhappy, to be hurt. That's why I want to finish out the show."

Ike dropped her at her hotel. The moment he reached his office he called Jerry. "You've got to make her quit the show—she thinks she owes it to you to finish the season. She's got so little time, I don't want her to throw away an hour—let alone six weeks. Yet if I force it, she may get suspicious. Think of something!"

Jerry stared at the smog-laden sky, at the pale sun trying to burn its way through. It wasn't like the summer sun in Greenwich—or the sparkling orange sun they had in the fall. Amanda would never see that sun again or know the clear cold of the winter. Tears came to his eyes.

He reached for the phone. Robin's secretary announced that Mr. Stone was in conference. "Tell her to get Mr. Stone *out* of conference," Jerry shouted to the long-distance operator. "This is an emergency!" After a few minutes Robin came on.

"Yes, Jerry."

"Are you sitting down, Robin?"

"Come to the point. I have ten people waiting in the conference room."

"Amanda has leukemia."

There was a terrible silence. Then Robin said, "Does she know?"

"Only three people know—the doctor, Ike Ryan and me. You make the fourth. She's been given some drug and it's worked wonders. She's even doing the show to-

morrow. But they give her six months top. I thought
you'd like to know."

"Thanks, Jerry." He hung up.

Amanda enjoyed her first day back at the hotel. The
suite was filled with flowers. Dozens of roses from Ike,
gladiolas from the hotel, a plant from the cast, and some
cheap spring flowers from Christie. His note said, "Am
taking publicity pictures—call you at six. Love, Christie."
At four o'clock a waiter arrived with a baked potato
loaded with Iranian caviar and sour cream. The note
read, "To hold you till I get there for dinner. Love, Ike."

She reveled in the luxury and ate the potato, but she
knew she would have to start watching her weight. She
had gained five pounds in the hospital. The phone rang at
six and she picked it up lethargically. It had to be
Christie.

"Hello, star—how are you?" The voice crackled across
the line.

For a moment she couldn't speak. It was Robin, just
like that, with no explanation for not ever calling. . . .

"I've just come home from the hospital." She finally
found her voice.

"What was the matter?"

"Anemia. I'm fine now. Didn't Jerry tell you?"

"I've been away, I haven't talked to Jerry. Listen, baby,
I have some business in L.A. and I'm flying out Sunday. I
should get there around five your time. Think you can
spare an evening for an old friend?"

"I'd be delighted, Robin."

"Good. Dinner on Sunday—that's a date."

She hung up and lay back against the pillow. No need
to get excited. He probably only had a few days and
figured there was good old Amanda, just waiting. So he
had called. Why not? She was a sure thing—it was easier
than calling around and finding someone.

After all, Hollywood wasn't his territory. He didn't
know too many people and he didn't want to waste an
evening. Well, she'd see him—you *bet* she'd see him—
and she'd show him how it felt when someone else called

the shots. But how? Stand him up? Keep him waiting at Chasen's all alone?

She thought about it for an hour. Suddenly she knew what she was going to do—it would be wonderful! She couldn't wait until Sunday.

# FIFTEEN

R OBIN CHECKED INTO THE BEVERLY HILLS HOTEL at five o'clock. The desk clerk handed him an envelope. Inside was a hastily scrawled note from Amanda:

> Dear Robin, It's my birthday and Ike Ryan is having a few people drop by. I have to get there early because I'm guest of honor. I can't wait to see you.

When he got settled in his suite he reread Amanda's note. There was a phone number and an address on North Canyon Drive. His first inclination was to call and leave word that he'd wait for her at the hotel. He hated cocktail parties. Then he abruptly changed his mind. From now on it was going to be whatever Amanda wanted. He reached in his pocket to check the small gold circlet—if they could break away from this party early enough, they'd fly to Tijuana and get married. He called the doorman and ordered a cab.

North Canyon Drive was a maze of parked cars. He paid the driver and walked up the driveway. Hollywood homes were deceiving in appearance: the front was always modest. But when you entered, there was an explosion of unbelievable splendor in the back. Ike's home was no exception. The marble entrance hall was crowded, the enormous living room had the usual enormous bar and people were clustered around it three deep. Glass doors opened onto a patio with an Olympic-size swimming pool—there was even a tennis court. He felt slightly disoriented, unprepared for the mob scene he had stumbled upon. Then he grinned: he should have known better. This was Ike's idea of a little gathering. He saw familiar faces, faces he had seen on the wide screen. There was enough earning power in this room to support a small country—actors, producers, heads of studios and directors, even the top screenwriters, and the usual assortment of beautiful girls.

Suddenly Amanda crossed the room to greet him. He had forgotten how lovely she was. Death couldn't be lodged in that slim wonderful body!

"Robin!" She threw her arms around him. He was surprised at her open display of affection. "Robin, you're here! It's wonderful to see you. Oh, but you don't know many people." She broke the embrace, took his hand and shouted, "Hey, everybody—*quiet!*"

The room grew still.

"I want you to meet Robin Stone. He came all the way from New York. You all know who Robin Stone is." Her voice was derisive. "You must know—he's the star of *In Depth!*" Her gaze was innocent. "None of you seem impressed, but he's a very big man in New York."

A few people pretended to recognize him with feeble nods, then turned back to their own conversations. Robin's lack of expression hid his surprise at her odd behavior. But Amanda merely shrugged.

"That's Hollywood for you," she said lightly. "They still refuse to recognize that television is here to stay. And as for news programs—darling, news is something they only hear on radio when they drive to the studio, and only if it butts into a music program. So forgive them, angel, if they don't recognize and fawn over you. Paul Newman, Gregory Peck, Elizabeth Taylor—that's the name of the game in this town."

She led him to the bar for a drink. Ike Ryan greeted him warmly, then crossed the room to greet a director who had just entered. Amanda handed Robin a glass. "Filled with your favorite brand of ice water—only this is one-hundred proof, imported."

Suddenly there was silence. Then a swelling murmur

grew as everyone stared at the handsome young man who had entered.

"Oh, look!" Amanda cried. "Ike even got the Big Dipper to come." Her eyes shone as Ike led the handsome, bronzed man to the bar.

"You know this good-looking bum?" Ike asked with a grin.

Amanda's smile went coy. "Oh, Ike, everyone knows Dip Nelson. I'm honored that you came, Mr. Nelson. Ike ran your new picture for me when I was in the hospital."

Dip looked slightly embarrassed. Robin was embarrassed too. He wondered what in hell had gotten into Amanda. Then she said, "Oh, Dip, this is Robin Stone, an old, old friend. He's like family, aren't you, Robin?"

Dip shook hands with Robin, then several women crowded around him and he was literally carried across the room.

"Poor Dip, he hasn't a chance with those women," Amanda said.

Ike smiled. "The Big Dipper can take care of himself. No talent—just brawn, dimples, and looks. But he's hot box office now, and that's all that counts."

Amanda nudged Ike. "Darling, speaking of box office ... look who just came in!"

Robin watched as Ike and Amanda went to greet a slim good-looking man—Alfred Knight, the English actor who had made such an impact on Hollywood. He searched the crowd for Chris Lane and spotted him across the room in a corner. Poor Chris—he not only looked like an outsider, but he'd soon need a program to be able to tell the players. He still thought he was engaged to Amanda. Robin finished off the vodka, got a refill and remained at the bar. It promised to be a very entertaining night.

The caterers began setting up tables around the pool. And suddenly it hit Robin that Amanda's birthday was in February. Or was it January? It had to be one of those months—he remembered celebrating it during a snowstorm.

He was just starting on his fourth vodka when there was a loud roll of drums. Amanda was standing in the center of the room.

"Everyone! I—we—have an announcement!"

Amanda held up her hand. There was a large diamond on her finger. "Ike gave this to me today—but it's not a birthday present. In fact it's not my birthday at all, it's just our way of announcing our engagement!"

Everyone began to talk at once. Christie Lane looked like an animal that had been impaled. He stood there, mute and glassy-eyed. One of the guests ran to the piano and began to play *Lohengrin*. Gradually the crowd returned to their original groups and resumed their conversation and drinking. From across the room, for one instant Amanda's eyes met Robin's. Their glance held; her eyes were dark with triumph. He raised his glass in a silent toast. Then she turned and let Alfie Knight waft her to another part of the room. Robin saw Ike crossing to the den. He put down his drink and went after him.

Ike smiled as Robin approached. "Well, you gotta admit I'm a barrel full of surprises."

"I want a few words with you, chum."

"What? No congratulations?"

"Where can we go? This won't take long."

Ike signaled a waiter for drinks, then led Robin to the pool area which was deserted.

"Okay, shoot. What's on your mind?" Ike said.

"Amanda."

"That's right, you had a swing around with her once." Ike swallowed his shot of bourbon neat. Then he stared at Robin's untouched drink. "Aren't you going to toast the groom?"

"I know about Amanda," Robin said quietly.

Ike's eyes narrowed. "What do you know?"

"Jerry Moss is a friend of mine."

"I'll kill that little punk. I told him to keep his mouth shut."

"Stop playing the tough guy. Jerry did what he thought was best. I came out here to ask Amanda to marry me."

"She doesn't need your charity," Ike snapped.

"Is that what you're giving her?"

"You said it—I didn't."

"Ike, we've shared the same scene, and I'm not knocking it. I like it too. But Amanda won't go that route. She can't, and especially not now."

Ike's smile was cold. "If I didn't like you so much I'd

knock the shit out of you. Just what kind of a bastard do you think I am?"

"No special kind, just a bastard. I don't want Amanda to get hurt."

Ike looked at him curiously. "Are you in love with her?"

"I care about her—I care about making the rest of her life happy."

Ike nodded. "Then we're both coming in on the same beam."

"You mean that?"

Ike leaned across the table. "Look, this is no time for fun and games. This is the truth game. Are you in love with her? Just tell me that, tell me you love her and I'll send for Amanda right now and give you your shot. Let the best man win. But if you're here to make some grandstand gesture, forget it. She doesn't need any favors from you—when the time comes, I think I have a better setup to give her what she needs."

"All right, chum, since we're playing the truth game" —Robin's face was grim—"are *you* in love with her? Seems to me you haven't answered that question."

Ike stood up and stared at the dark pool. "Of course I'm not in love with her," he said quietly. "But then, neither are you."

"That's the way I figured it from the start," Robin said. "Then why the marriage bit?"

"Why not?" Ike asked.

"As I see it, she'll tie you down. Stop some of your action."

Ike smiled. "She can help my image."

"I don't get you."

"Maybe you didn't read the newspapers. Last month my wife—my ex-wife, we've been divorced for five years —did the Dutch act: pills. Thank God she did it in Wisconsin. She was there visiting my son over the Easter holidays. He goes to school there. She took pills—a whole fucking bottle—and left a note saying she couldn't live without me. Thank God for Joey, that's my kid. He grabbed the note and sent for me. I schmeared around some money and we made it look accidental." Ike sighed. "Five years I haven't seen that broad. I never loved her

—we went to school together, and she gave me her all in our senior year. We got married, only she never grew with me—always chewing my ass off, wanting me to sell ties for her uncle. I stuck it out till Joey was twelve—then I walked. I've been sending her all the money a dame could use. Christ, I even agreed that her alimony would continue if she remarried. So she spends all this time living in the past, then decides to get back at me by taking her life.

"You should have seen that note—made me the biggest shit ever. Joey and I burned it, but there have been snide rumors around this town that she committed suicide. Then there were two crazy broads who also tried it—I don't get it, what's with these dames and sleeping pills? I'm not that big a lover. Then a scandal magazine tagged me: 'For Ike Ryan—dames are dyin'.' It's just this crazy business: there are no men out here. They'll latch on to a doorknob if it wears pants. Half the big stars in there, the women, are here with their fag hairdressers. Anyway, my reputation isn't exactly sympathetic. I can use a little good press. When Amanda goes, people will look at me in a different light. They'll realize I made the last months of a doomed girl happy ones—great ones. I'm gonna give her the biggest razzle-dazzle whirl any girl ever had. And when they close the lid on her pretty puss, at least she'll have gone out in style."

Robin sat in a stunned silence. Then he said hoarsely, "You're using her. You son of a bitch—you're using her."

"Let's say I need her, but not half as much as she needs me." Ike came close, his face hard. "Listen, I've seen *you* operate. You have ice water for blood, so don't sit in judgment on me. She digs me, and I'm going to make her goddam happy. I'll charter planes, fly her all over the world. I'm gonna load her with diamonds. What can you do for her? Fuck her? So can I. Although God knows how long she'll have the strength for that. But can you let her go out in the style I'm offering? I know about her past—and I think she rates Roman candles right now. Can you top it, newsman?"

Robin stood up. His eyes were as hard as Ike's. The two men faced one another. "No, I can't. But you better live up to it. Make damn sure it's not just talk. Otherwise,

I'll find you, Ike—no matter where you are—and I'll break every bone in your body."

For a moment their eyes locked in tense silence. Ike smiled and held out his hand. "It's a deal." He turned and went back to the house. Robin hadn't taken his hand. He sank into a deck chair and sipped his drink. He felt wrung out and empty. Ike didn't care for Amanda; Ike cared for his own image. Yet what difference did "caring" make? Results were all that counted. He looked at his watch. It was still early; he could get the midnight plane out.

"Too late for a tan." He looked up. It was Dip Nelson.

Robin grinned. "I guess I could use some sun."

Dip lit a cigarette. "Boy, is that a grind in there! You from New York?"

Robin nodded.

"I thought so. Are you in this racket?"

"No, thank God."

He stared at Robin speculatively. "Let me guess—a relative of the bride?"

"Distant." Then he added, "Incidentally, count me as one of your fans. I've seen some of your pictures. You handle a horse very well."

Dip looked at him oddly. "You putting me on?"

"Not at all."

"Then what kind of a line is that? What about my acting?"

"That's pretty lousy." Robin smiled.

For a split second Dip wavered between anger and action. Then he laughed and held out his hand. "Well, at least you're an honest man."

"I don't think acting really counts," Robin said. "It's star quality that makes it in pictures, and from the reception you got in that room, you obviously have it."

Dip shrugged. "Like you said, I did the horse routine for years. One crappy Western after another, then suddenly they came into vogue, and I'm a star. But it's my new picture that's causing all the excitement. It opens in New York next week. I play a Madison Avenue anti-hero type. The works: skinny tie, gray suit, like you. Hey, is that your racket?"

"In a way."

"Oh-oh, here comes Bebe. Let's duck out of here."

"Who's Bebe?"

"Her husband's a top producer. Come on, want to blow this party?"

"You must be reading my mind," said Robin.

"Follow me!" Dip headed for the cabanas. They slipped into the dark dressing room. "Now stay very quiet. She's too loaded to come this far."

They stood quietly in the silent darkness while the producer's wife wobbled around the pool calling for Dip. Finally she gave up and went inside.

Dip loosened his collar. "Boy, there's nothing worse than a menopause broad in heat. Listen: between you and I, don't let the movie-star bit put you off base. I'm a one-woman man. Oh, I may have to fuck a little to get certain parts, but I don't go after a broad like Bebe like some of these male whores out here."

He shivered. "There's nothing worse: a forty-year-old with the figure of a twenty-year-old until you get them in the sack—then it's like Jello. Everywhere you touch, you sink in—soft thighs, flabby belly, flopping tits."

"Sounds like you've had experience."

"It was either 'ride a horse' forever or ride Claire Hall for one picture. So I rode Claire and became a star. Come on, the coast is clear. We can duck out through the hedge."

He led Robin to the longest Cadillac he had ever seen.

"Like it?" Dip asked proudly.

"It sure as hell is impressive," Robin answered.

"Custom-made: the only gold convertible in town. I mean real gold—this is twenty-two-karat paint, and the leather is gold kid. It's part of the image I'm building. The golden man—gold hair, gold car. The leather alone cost me two G's."

The car eased down the lane. Dip headed down Sunset Boulevard. "You got any special plans?"

Robin smiled. "Just the midnight plane back to New York."

"A guy like you must feel out of place in this town."

"A guy like me certainly does."

"It's just a matter of being a winner, then you're secure

even in Bombay. My old lady taught me that. She died in the motion-picture relief home."

"I'm sorry."

Dip waved his hand. "Look, she never had it so good. I hadn't made it yet, so we had no choice. But it's a great setup. They have their own cottages, they sit around and talk shop. She was an extra; my old man was a stunt man for Fred Thompson and Tom Mix. One of the best. That was before I was born. He taught me to ride. He got killed on a stunt and my mother was stuck supporting me. And she wasn't young. I was a change-of-life kid. They say they're always brighter. Would you believe it— I never went to high school?"

"It hasn't seemed to hurt you," Robin said.

"Sometimes I miss it, like when I'm not sure about my English. Scripts are fine, they're all written . . . but those interviews—I know I murder the English because sometimes the interviewers think I'm putting them on and they tell me to stop with the cowboy twang."

"You can cut off at the next turn and drop me at the Beverly Hills Hotel, if it's not out of your way," Robin said.

"What's your rush? It's only seven o'clock. Or have you something lined up?"

"No, but I'm sure you have."

Dip grinned. "You bet I have! We're going to catch my girl—she sings in a place on the Strip. Wait till you see her, she's only nineteen and all woman."

"Won't I be butting in?"

"Nah. Besides, I want you to remember your one night in Hollywood. I know how you felt at that party. I once was on the outside looking in. And no one helped me. It was so bad I just stood and talked to the piano player. I stood there so long that someone asked me to sing. They thought I was part of the combo. When I saw you tonight I thought, There's a guy who's lost, and I, Dip Nelson, I'm Mr. Big—I am the action. And I figured I wasn't going to be like all the crumbs who were part of the action when I was nobody. I was damned if I'd dress up that bitch Amanda's party. I had to put in an appearance for Ike Ryan. So I showed, and blowed. But at least I'll show you a little fun."

"Well, you've more than done your bit," Robin said. "There's no reason to entertain me the rest of the evening. That's going beyond the call of duty."

"Nah, what the hell. I'd be sitting alone while Pauli sang anyway. She's in this lousy joint, but she belts out a song better than Garland or anyone you ever heard. She'll make it, you'll see. Only I got to give her some class first. She's real basic. She was a virgin when I met her, there's no one in her life but me. But we can't get married until I have three hot pictures under my belt. See, I'm today's sensation, but only with one picture. The next two will tell the story. And when they click, I can marry Pauli. No studio will be able to tell me what to do. And meanwhile I can smooth out some of her rough edges. I'm not apologizing for her—she's all talent and heart. Wait till you see her, you'll dig."

He slid the car up to a small restaurant. "She only makes seventy-five clams a week, but at least they let her sing what she wants to, and she doesn't have to mix with the customers."

The owner greeted Dip effusively and led him to a banquet table along the wall. The place was half filled. Men sat in sport shirts, most of the girls wore slacks. There were about twenty people at the bar, mostly beer customers.

"She goes on in about ten minutes, then she'll join us." He saw Robin glance at his watch. "You sure you haven't got a date tonight?"

"No, it's just that I have to check out of my hotel."

"I'll drive you to the airport."

"Oh, that's not necessary."

Dip flashed a big grin. "When I go, pal, I go all the way. Say, what's your racket in New York—advertising agency you said, huh?"

"No. I'm with International Broadcasting."

"The only thing I watch on TV is the movies. I figure I can learn from them. What do you do at IBC?"

"News."

"You a researcher or something? You write?"

"At times."

"I bet you went to college, huh?"

Robin smiled. "Does it show?"

"Yeah, you carry yourself pretty good. But college—that's a time waster, unless you want to be a lawyer or a doctor. I want to be a superstar! God, I can taste it, I want it so bad. I want to be able to tell everyone to go fuck themselves!"

"What about Pauli?"

"She's with me all the way, old buddy. And when we get married, if she just wants to be a wife and no career, hell, I won't push her. She's loaded with talent. But all she wants is to marry me and have a lot of babies. What about you—I guess you have a wife and a couple of kids?"

"No."

"Just a girl you're hung on to?"

"No, not even that."

Dip looked at him suddenly. "How come? Hey, you're straight, aren't you?"

Robin laughed outright. "I think women are wonderful."

"Then what's your hangup? I mean, at your age you should be married and have kids. Now me, I'm only twenty-six."

Robin's grin disconcerted him.

"Okay—so I'm thirty-one. But I can get by for twenty-six, can't I?"

"In the Hollywood light."

"Say, that's good. How old are you?"

"Forty in August."

"And no marriage ever?"

"Nope."

"And no serious girl?"

"I had one, but she got engaged."

Dip shook his head sympathetically. "Hit you hard, I bet. It's rough to find a real girl—especially out here. Every dame is out for number one."

"And you're not?" Robin asked.

Dip looked hurt. "You're goddam right, I am. But have I crapped you on *one* thing? I pull the act when it's for my career. But when I'm with people I like, I level."

"And you like me?"

"Yeah, I guess I do. Say, I don't even know your name."

"Robin Stone."

Dip looked at him suspiciously. "You're sure you're not light on your feet? Look, if you are, Pauli will spot it in a second. She can spot a fag a mile away." Suddenly he punched Robin's arm. "She's coming on now. Wait till you see this explosion of talent!"

Robin leaned forward as the slim young girl came into the spotlight. She had red curly hair and he guessed by the freckles on her shoulders that it was natural. Her nose was short and almost comically upturned. Her mouth was large, her eyes saucerwide and innocently blue. But when she sang, he was disappointed. Her voice was true, but she was ordinary. A garbled imitation of Garland and Lena. He had heard a hundred girls like Pauli, only they were better-looking. The only time she held his attention was with her takeoff on Carol Channing. Then she came to life—she had a definite comic flair. Her set ended to scattered applause and wild whistling from Dip. He thumped Robin on the back. "Now I ask you—is she beautiful? Has she got class? Turns the whole joint into the Waldorf the minute she steps onstage!"

Both men stood up as the girl came to the table. "This is my fiancée, Pauli. Pauli, say hello to Robin."

She smiled slightly and sat down. Then she looked at Robin curiously.

"He's from New York," Dip said quickly.

"Oh, listen, Dip, your press agent wants you to call him as soon as you come in," Pauli said, without listening.

Dip got up. "You two talk. Robin's at IBC."

Pauli watched him as he left the table. Then she turned to Robin. "What are you doing with Dip?"

"We met at a party."

Her eyes narrowed. "What's a guy in mechanics got in common with Dip?"

"Mechanics?"

"Didn't he say you worked with IBM?"

"IBC: International Broadcasting."

"Oh. Say, have you any pull to get me a guest shot on the Chris Lane show?" He decided he didn't like her, but he owed it to Dip. "Yes, I might be able to swing it."

Her eyes lit up. "Honest—could you really?" Then she looked suspicious. "What do you do at IBC?"

"The news."

"Like Huntley and Brinkley?"

"In a way."

"Then how come I never heard of you? I watch the seven o'clock news a lot. I know who Walter Cronkite is, but not you."

He smiled. "You've ruined my whole evening."

"How can you get me on *The Christie Lane Show?*"

"I can ask him."

Her stare was calculative. Then on the wild chance that he might be leveling, the saucer eyes went soft. "If you'd ask him, I mean, if you'd swing it, I'd—well, I'd do anything to get on that show."

"Anything?" Robin smiled and held her eyes.

Her stare was level. "Yes, if that's what you want."

"And what do you want?"

"To blow this crumb joint."

"Dip will arrange that eventually."

She shrugged. "Look, you just met him. I mean, you and him aren't buddy-buddy, because I never heard him mention you before."

"You're batting a thousand."

"Well, look, just between the two of us"—her voice lowered—"Laurence Olivier he's not. So he's handsome, but he has no talent. So far he's been lucky."

"I gathered from Dip that you had no ambitions—just wanted to get married and make babies."

She waved her hand in disgust. "Would any girl in her right mind stand up here and sing to these crumbs three times a night if she didn't know she was going to make it big? I *know* I've got it."

"Where does Dip fit in?"

"I dig him. I really do. I gave him my virginity. Honest to God. I was pure when we met. But I know Dip. He lives and breathes his career. He wouldn't last two minutes with a girl who had her own interest at heart. He wants to be the big shot all the way. So I pretend I'm nothing. Most of the time I sit and listen to how great things are going for him. And I'm burning inside me because I know *I'm* the one who's great. And there he is, going to the top because of his looks. That's all he has. Not a brain in his head."

"He wants to help you. He told me so," Robin said.

"Yeah, he talks. But words are cheap. Look—about the Chris Lane show, can you arrange it?"

"If I do, will you be grateful?"

"Mister—I take it you got a wife?"

"Maybe."

"Well, you get me on the Chris Lane show and anytime, anyplace, you just snap your fingers and I'll be there. I pay off—I got a big sense of honor." He reached for a cigarette. She picked up the matches and lit it for him. She leaned across and said, "Well, is it a deal?"

He smiled. "You know, you little bitch," he said softly, "it would almost be worth it—for Dip's sake."

"I don't get it."

Robin's grin was easy. He kept his voice even. "You're right about one thing: Dip hasn't a brain in his head, or else he would have seen through you. He thinks you're an angel. But you're a broad. No, not even a broad—you're a rough, no-talent cunt."

He stood up and smiled. His quiet calm seemed to infuriate her. "If you think I'm scared you'll tell Dip all these things, forget it. You open your stinking mouth and I'll tell him you made a pass at me."

"Tell Dip I got a phone call." He put down a ten-dollar bill.

"What's that for?" she asked.

"I think the going rate for a call girl is a hundred. Take this as a down payment. I think you're on your way." He walked out of the club.

# SIXTEEN

CHRISTIE LANE FINISHED THE SHOW the first week in June. He left for New York the following day.

On July fourth Amanda and Ike were married in Las Vegas. The front pages of all the tabloids featured pictures of the wedding—Amanda and Ike surrounded by several stars who were playing Vegas. They were flying to Europe for a honeymoon.

Chris held a wake in his suite at the Astor Hotel. Eddie, Kenny, and Agnes sat with him. He paced up and down. He cried. He talked: "God, if only I could get drunk. But I don't like booze."

"Let's go out on the town," Eddie suggested.

"I played it so straight with her," Chris kept repeating; "I even helped her find a place here to board her goddam cat."

"I wonder what'll happen to the cat," Agnes asked.

"I hope it croaks—it was the only thing she really cared about."

"I bet she sends for the cat when she comes back from Europe," Agnes said.

"Who gives a shit!" Christie roared.

"Well, you brought it up," she answered.

"I played it so straight with her," Chris repeated. "Why did she do it? Look at me . . . I'm better-looking than Ike Ryan."

"Whaaat?" This was Agnes.

Chris whirled on her. "You think he's good-looking?"

"He's sexy-looking," she said sullenly.

Eddie shot her a murderous look. "Hey, Aggie, you looking to be replaced? This is no time for funnies."

"I still think he's sexy-looking," she said stubbornly.

"Look, Chris," Kenny cut in, "how's about us getting a table at the Copa? I know some of the kids in the line. They got three new dancers. One is gorgeous, only nineteen. I bet she'd like you. She's a nice girl."

Chris kicked the coffee table so hard the leg came off and it collapsed. "Nice girl! I *had* a nice girl—a gorgeous girl! Christ, she'd give me a dirty look if I said a bad word in front of her. And she turns out to be the worst double-crossing cooze around. No dame in burlesque would act like that. I'm through being a nice guy and I want no part of *nice* girls. I want a bum! I'll treat her like a bum and no one will get hurt. Just find me the biggest bum in town—the best joint-copper!"

"Call for Ethel Evans—" Eddie chanted, mimicking a pageboy.

Chris snapped his fingers. "That's it!"

Eddie laughed. "Oh, come on—I was kidding. Listen, Chris, if you want a bum at least get a pretty one. There's a dame in town from Frisco—"

"I don't want a pretty bum, or a dame from Frisco. I want Ethel!"

"But she's a beast," Kenny said.

"I don't want a beauty queen. I want a fucker! Get me Ethel!" His eyes narrowed. "If I'm seen with a cunt like her, *that* will show them. They'll figure Amanda couldn't mean much to me if I could wind up enjoying a broad like Ethel. Get her!"

Eddie called Jerry Moss in Greenwich. Jerry sighed and promised to do his best. He located Ethel in Fire Island.

"What is this, a gag?" she demanded.

"No, Christie Lane *personally* asked to see you."

"That's a quaint way of putting it!"

"Ethel, you've boffed every guest star on Christie's show."

"I missed a few. Don't forget they did the last half of the season from the Coast."

"They're not going to the Coast next season."

"Great. I'll get a new diaphragm."

"Ethel, our star is unhappy. He wants *you.*"

"But I don't want him."

"I'm asking you to go into town."

Her voice was icy. "Is that an order?"

"Let's say it's a *request.*"

"The answer is no."

"Then perhaps I'll have to call Danton Miller and ask him to take you off the show." Jerry hated himself, but he had to make one last-ditch effort.

Her laugh was nasty. "I can always handle Danton."

"Not against a sponsor. And whether you like it or not, Ethel, that's what I am."

"Really? I thought you were Robin Stone's personal maid."

He kept his voice even. "I am not dealing in personalities with you."

"Oh, excuse me. I guess this is all impersonal—you calling me and telling me to come in town to fuck Chris Lane."

"Put whatever connotation on it you wish. You earned your reputation. And it's not my job to be on the phone with you on July Fourth either. I'm doing it because I'm part of the Christie Lane show. Obviously you have no idea of teamwork."

"Oh, cut the agency shit," she snapped. "I want you to get this straight. I'm not a call girl. When I hump a guy, it's because I dig him. For a year and a half Chris Lane never looked at me twice—thank God! And now all of a sudden I'm Elizabeth Taylor. What's the big deal?"

"Amanda married Ike Ryan today."

There was a pause. Then she laughed. "Hey, your friend Robin Stone must be upset too! Now why don't I go console *him?* I'd even swim back for that."

"Are you coming in?"

She sighed. "Okay. Where do I find lover boy?"

"At the Astor."

She laughed. "Wouldn't you know? All my life I've waited to meet someone who actually lived at the Astor!"

Christie was alone when she arrived. "Hey. What's the big idea?" he asked. "You're in slacks."

"You didn't expect me to walk in nude, did you?"

He didn't smile. "No, but the gang is at the Copa. I was waiting to take you over and join them."

She stared at him. "The Copa?"

"Come on!" he ordered. "We'll grab a cab and go to your place. I want you to change into a dress so we can go to the Copa."

He sat in her living room thumbing through a magazine while she dressed.

In the cab, he sat huddled on the other side of the seat, morose and uncommunicative, but once they entered the Copa, his entire personality changed. He flashed a broad smile, held her arm and introduced her to everyone they met with a proprietary air. He held her hand through the show; he even lit her cigarette. She sat through it all grimly. She had seen the show, she was tired and she wanted to get the evening over with.

It was close to three when they returned to the Astor. She had never had such a grueling time. The Copa, then the Copa bar, the Brasserie and a stop at the Stage Delicatessen. Now they were alone. She undressed silently. He was already naked, lying expectantly on the bed. She looked at him and felt a crawling revulsion. There was something so repulsive about a man without a hard on. How had Amanda done it? To go from a man like Robin Stone to this slob!

She walked to the side of the bed, completely naked. He couldn't mask his amazement as he stared at her enormous, well-shaped breasts.

"Hey, doll, for an ugly dame you sure got a build." He grabbed her rear. "Now if you'd just lose some of that ass, you'd almost have a great figure."

She pulled away from him. His hands were clammy. She didn't want him to touch her.

"You have any shaving cream?" she asked.

"Sure, why?"

She went to the bathroom and returned with the container. She spread the shaving cream all over her hands. "Now lie back, you big television star."

In less than five minutes he lay spent and groaning. She slipped into the bathroom and dressed quickly. When she returned to the bedroom he was lying motionless, his eyes closed.

"So long, Chris." She couldn't get out fast enough.

He reached out and grabbed her hand. "Doll, I never had it like that. But it's not fair, I mean, nothing happened for you. Christ, I never even got to touch you."

"That's all right," she said softly. "I know you felt blue tonight. I just wanted to make you forget, make you happy."

He pulled her down to the bed. Then he stared at her. "You know, that's the nicest thing anyone ever said to me. Look, I appreciate it. I know you came all the way in from Fire Island tonight. Is there anything I can do?"

She longed to say, "Just forget about me and leave me alone." But she merely smiled.

He pulled her down. "Give us a kiss."

His lips were soft and blubbery. She managed to pull away without showing her repugnance. Then she leaned down and kissed his sweaty brow and dashed from the apartment without even asking for cab fare.

He called her the next morning and invited her to dinner. She had nothing better to do, so she accepted. He took her out every night for two weeks. The columns began coupling their names together. He invited her to accompany them to Atlantic City when he went to play the Five Hundred Club. She was beginning to enjoy the sudden personal publicity she was getting as Christie Lane's girl. She had never been anyone's "girl." So she went along. Her picture appeared with Chris in one of the morning papers, showing them in a rolling chair on the boardwalk, hinting of an "engagement."

Jerry Moss grew slightly apprehensive. He called Christie in Atlantic City.

"Christie, you're not serious about this girl?"

"Of course not. Listen, Jerry, Dan's got the first two shows for the new season fairly set. Who are you getting to replace—" He stopped.

"We'll use a different girl each week," Jerry said. "But I want to talk to you about Ethel."

"Yeah?"

"You know her reputation."

"So?"

"Do you think it's smart bringing her to Atlantic City? The columns are writing about you and Ethel. She's not good for your image. The public wants to see you coupled with a nice girl, a beautiful girl."

"Listen, buster, I went with a *nice* girl, a beautiful girl. Maybe the public was happy, but I got my brains kicked in. The public wasn't around to hold my cock the night Amanda got married. But Ethel Evans was!"

"Everyone in the business knows about Ethel," Jerry argued. "So far the public knows nothing. But after this engagement rumor in the newspapers, the public will want to know more. And how will it look to the public to know their family man goes with a whore!"

"Don't say that!" Chris said roughly. "She never took a dime from a guy!"

"Chris, are you taking her seriously? I mean, you're leaving for Vegas in a few weeks. You're not taking her there, are you?"

"Too much plane fare involved. It ain't exactly Atlantic City where we hire a car and all pile in."

"Then you're not serious about her."

"Of course not. But I know one thing. She's there when I want her. She's nice to me. She doesn't cheat. And she hasn't been with another guy since I started dating her. And anything I want to do is okay with her. I'm relaxed with Ethel." He paused as if recalling something. Then he laughed. "Take Ethel to Vegas! That's like bringing a tuna-fish sandwich to Danny's Hideaway."

It had been a dull summer for Ethel. She worked on a variety show that featured new talent. She didn't dig guitar-playing groups. Even the guest stars were youth-oriented. She was relieved when Labor Day arrived. When Christie Lane returned to New York she was almost glad to see him.

She was with him constantly during the month of September. The show didn't start till October and he had most of his evenings free. She was bored to death with Kenny and Eddie and Agnes. She hated the Copa bar, the Chinese restaurants (always the cheapest ones), but most of all she hated the racetrack. He never offered to place a bet for her, so out of boredom she placed two-dollar show bets of her own and occasionally won sixty cents. She loathed any physical contact with him, but to her relief she soon realized he wasn't a highly sexed man. Twice a week more than satisfied him, then he would lie back and read the racing form.

She was really marking time until the show would begin and new guest stars would arrive. Then she would give Christie and his stooges the brush.

A week before the opening show, two television magazines came out with stories on Christie, featuring Ethel Evans.

Jerry sat in his office and stared at the pictures of the smiling couple—God, they really looked like a pair of bookends! But now he really had to take some action. This thing was getting out of hand. He made an appointment to meet Danton Miller for lunch.

At first Dan was amused. "Come on, Jerry, you're borrowing trouble. The hicks in the sticks never heard of Ethel."

Jerry snapped his knuckles. "Dan, this is serious. Tom

Carruthers is a Baptist as well as a sponsor. He didn't even approve of some of the rock singers we had on the summer replacement show. So far he thinks Ethel is a nice homespun girl. He's even had her to dinner with *Mrs.* Carruthers. If one of those scandal magazines ever decides to do some real research on Ethel, we're dead! She's got a girl friend on the Coast who saved all her letters with ratings of the stars in the kip. She's had them mimeoed and passes them around. If those letters ever got into print! Incidentally, Dan, I hear your 'rating' is listed, too."

Dan's smile disappeared.

"Look, Dan, I'm not a prude. That kind of publicity might help a swinging singer, but not our little old minstrel man. He appeals to a family-type audience. Carruthers even wants to try for an earlier time spot next season so that more kids can watch. He wants to stay with Christie Lane for life. You've got a gold mine with this show—and we can't let Ethel stand in the way. It's too big a risk."

Dan poured himself a second cup of coffee. Jerry Moss was making sense. One shot of notoriety and the Christie Lane-type sponsorship would pull out. They had gone along with the Amanda "romance" because it represented the Walter Mitty dream of every average Joe. A plain guy winding up with the most beautiful girl in the world. If Christie could do it, anything was possible. He gave people hope. They had fantasized with him even more when Amanda jilted him for the flamboyant Ike Ryan. And now they were latching on to Ethel Evans because she looked like the average girl. Jerry was right! It really was a mess!

The luncheon ended with his ulcer burning and his promise to step in and end the Ethel Evans-Christie Lane relationship immediately.

Dan thought about the situation for several days. He knew he'd have to take her off the show. Jesus, what had she said in her letter about him? He called the publicity department. He was informed that she could be reached at the beauty parlor. Beauty parlor! It would take a plastic surgeon to help her. He took the phone number and placed the call.

"Hi!" She sounded very cheerful.

"Is today some kind of holiday I don't know about? Why the unsolicited afternoon off?"

She laughed. "I go steady now and have to look nice. And tonight's the big night."

"Tonight?" He suddenly remembered. The TV Golden Personality Award. IBC had taken a table. Next to the Emmy, this was the biggest TV event.

"Are you going?" he asked. He knew it was a stupid question—of course she was going.

"Are you?" she countered.

"I have to. Chris is up for an award, so is Robin Stone, and Gregory Austin is on the dais."

"I guess I'll see you then—we'll probably be sitting at the same table. Oh, by the way, Dan, what was it you called me about?"

"Maybe I wanted to ask you to go with me," he said. This was not the moment to give her the ultimatum. It had to be done in person.

Her laugh was not nice. "Let's stop playing games. My hair is wet and I want to get back under the dryer. What's the reason for the call?"

"I'll talk about it tomorrow."

"We do the show tomorrow. I'll be busy, and Carruthers is giving a little party after the show."

"Only you won't be going," he said. He knew his timing was bad, but this was too much.

"Come again?"

"Tonight will be your last public or private appearance with Chris."

She was silent for a moment. Then she said, "Are you jealous?"

"This is an official order."

"By whom?"

"Me! *The Christie Lane Show* belongs to IBC. It's my duty to protect a property. Let's just say your image is not right for a family-type show. So after tonight I want you to give Chris the air."

"And suppose I don't?"

"Then you're fired from IBC."

She was silent.

"Do you hear me, Ethel?"

Her voice was hard. "Okay, sonny boy. Sure you can get me fired. But maybe I don't care. IBC isn't the only game in town. There's always CBS, NBC and ABC."

"Not if I spread the word about why you were fired."

"You mean it's illegal to boff Christie Lane—or presidents of networks?"

"No. But sending pornographic writing through the mail is. I happen to have some copies of letters you wrote to a girl friend in Los Angeles giving graphic and clinical reports on your sex life."

She tried to brazen it out. "Okay—so I won't work. It'll give me more time for Christie."

He laughed. "From what I understand, generosity is not one of Christie Lane's virtues. But maybe you know another side of him. After all, I forget how close you are. Maybe he'll set you up in an apartment, give you an allowance."

"You son of a bitch!" Her voice stabbed through the phone.

"Look. Dump Christie. Your job stays and I'll see that you get assigned to another show."

"I'll make a deal," she said. "Get me the Robin Stone show and Christie Lane won't be able to get me on the phone."

Dan was thoughtful. "We offered to assign someone to him way back, but he refused. Let me see what I can do. I promise I'll try and swing it. If not, there are other shows."

"I said the Robin Stone show."

"I'm afraid you're not in a position to call the shots. I'll *try* and get you Robin Stone. But remember, tonight is the last time you see Christie Lane. You make an appearance at his show tomorrow, and you're through!"

That night she dressed with care. Her hair had grown longer and she had added an auburn tint. The green dress was good—low-cut and showed her breasts to full advantage. Her hips were still too large, but the full skirt hid them. She appraised herself in the mirror and she was pleased. She was no Amanda, but if she remembered not to smile and show that damn separation between her teeth, she didn't look bad. Not bad at all. . . .

The Grand Ballroom of the Waldorf was jammed.

Chris led her in and shouted greetings to every table he passed. The dais was impressive: stacked with heads of all the networks, some Broadway stars, the mayor, and a motion-picture executive. Ethel spotted Gregory Austin and his beautiful wife in the center of the dais. A columnist was talking to her. Her head was bent almost as if she was giving audience, rather than listening. Ethel followed Chris to the IBC table, directly in front of the dais. Dan Miller was already seated. He was with a thirtyish-looking brunette. Trust Dan to dig up the right type for tonight. Almost like he called an agent and said, "Send me a society type—black dress, pearls, not too big on the boobs." There were two empty seats beside her. Could they be for Robin Stone? They had to be—all the others were taken. That meant he'd be sitting right next to her. She hadn't counted on such a windfall.

He arrived late with an exquisite girl, Inger Gustar, a new German actress. Ethel took out a cigarette. Christie made no move, but to her amazement, Robin held out his lighter.

"I admire your taste," she said quietly. "I saw her picture last week. She can't act, but it doesn't matter." When he didn't answer, Ethel pressed on. "Is this serious or just something new?" She tried to make her voice bantering.

He smiled and said, "Eat your grapefruit."

"I don't like grapefruit."

"It's good for you." He didn't look up.

"I *don't* always like the things that are good for me."

The music began. Robin suddenly stood up. "Okay, Ethel, let's try it."

She flushed with delight. Could that mean she had finally gotten through to him? Maybe the green dress and the red tint to her hair had helped more than she thought. He danced for a few minutes in silence. She pressed closer to him. He pulled away and looked at her. His face was void of any expression and his lips barely seemed to move. But the words came out cold and clear.

"Listen, you silly broad, don't you know that maybe for the first time in your life you have a chance at the brass ring? I gave you credit for some brains—now use them, and try and come up a winner."

"Maybe I'm not interested in brass rings."

"Meaning what?"

"Meaning Christie Lane doesn't appeal to me."

He threw back his head and laughed. "You really are choosy. I like your guts anyway."

"And I like everything about you." Her voice was insinuating and soft.

She felt his body stiffen. Without looking at her he said, "Sorry, no dice."

"Why?"

He pulled away and looked at her. "Because I'm choosy too."

She stared at him. "Why do you hate me?"

"I don't hate you. Let's say that until now the only thing I felt about you was that you had a fair amount of brainpower and nerve. But now I'm beginning to wonder. You've got Christie Lane, don't sell him short. He may not be Sinatra, but his show is hot. He'll last a long long time."

"Robin, tell me something. Why did you ask me to dance?"

"Because it's going to be a long night and I'm not up to ten or twelve veiled propositions from you. I thought I'd set the record straight right off. The answer is no."

She looked at the German girl dancing near them. "No for tonight." She smiled.

"No for any night."

"Why?" She looked into his eyes.

"Want me to be frank?"

"Yes." She smiled without showing her teeth.

"I couldn't get it up for you, baby—it's as simple as that."

Her face went tense. "I didn't know you had problems. So that's your hangup."

He smiled. "It would be with you."

"Maybe that's why Amanda blew you off for Ike Ryan. The great Robin Stone—all charm, all talk, no action. She even cheated on you with Chris."

He stopped dancing and took her arm. "I think we'd better go back to the table."

Her smile was evil. She refused to move. "Oh, did I hit you where it hurts, Mr. Stone?"

"I feel no pain, baby. I just don't think you're entitled

to gossip about Amanda." Once again he tried to lead her off the floor, but she forced him into a dancing position.

"Robin, give me a chance. Try it with me just once! No strings! You can have me whenever you snap your fingers. And I'm good insurance. I'll satisfy you—you'll never lose your head over a girl like Amanda again."

He looked at her with a strange smile. "And I'll bet you're healthy as a horse."

"I've never been sick in my life."

He nodded. "It figures."

She looked at him evenly. "Well?"

"Ethel"—he almost sighed—"send in your first team with Chris Lane!"

"I can't." She shook her head. "It's not up to me—I've been given orders to cut out."

He was genuinely interested. "By whom?"

"Danton Miller. Sure, it's great for him to bang me whenever he wants, but this afternoon he informed me I am to give up Chris—seems we are getting too much publicity. I'm not good for the family image and if I don't follow his orders he's going to fire me."

"What are you going to do?"

Well, at least she had his interest. Maybe this was the tactic—don't come on strong, play it for sympathy. Why not? She had tried everything else. She tried to work some tears to her eyes but nothing happened. She said, "What can I do?" and looked at him helplessly.

"You're losing me with the Shirley Temple bit. If you're a broad, act like one, don't suddenly turn girlish and beg for sympathy." He grinned at her. "You've been playing a man's game, with a man's rules. I'd put you up against Danton Miller any day."

She stared at him curiously. "You mean I should fight Dan Miller?" She shook her head. "I haven't a chance—unless you give me a job working on your show. You said I have a brain—let's forget sex for now. Give me a chance, Robin. I can do a lot for your show. I can get you important publicity."

"Forget it." He cut her short. "I'm not a performer—"

"But let me be assigned to your show. I'll type, do anything you want."

"Nope."

"Why not?" She was pleading.

"Because I give nothing out of charity, pity or sympathy."

"What about friendship?"

"We are not friends."

"I'll be your friend. I'll do anything for you—just name it."

"Well, right now there's nothing I want more out of life than to end this dance."

She broke away from him and stared with hate. "Robin Stone—I hope you rot in hell!"

His grin was easy. He took her arm and led her off the floor. "That's it, baby, get some spirit. I like you better this way." They had reached the table. He thanked her for the dance with a pleasant smile.

It was a long dull evening. Chris was chosen as the outstanding personality in a new show. Robin's *In Depth* show won the news category. When the speeches were over the curtains on the opposite side of the room parted, the band played a fanfare and everyone groaned inwardly as they turned their chairs to watch the entertainment.

Robin grabbed the German girl and they ducked out the moment the lights dimmed. But Chris remained at the table along with the other IBC personnel and watched the show.

Ethel stared at the two empty chairs. Who the hell was *he* to have the independence to walk out? Even Danton Miller sat and watched the tedious show. Chris wouldn't have dared to leave and Chris was twice as important as Robin Stone. Come to think of it, Chris was even more important than Dan Miller. Dan could get fired any time —and right now he was in favor *because* of Chris! How dare he threaten her! As long as she had Chris she was bigger than Danton Miller. And bigger than Robin Stone. Suddenly she realized that Chris was the only thing she had going for her. She was thirty-one. She couldn't just keep going on humping any celebrity that came along. In a few years they wouldn't want her.

She sat in the darkness oblivious to the polite laughter of the audience, as the new idea took hold and grew. Why should she give Chris the air? Sleeping with him was one thing—but to be Mrs. Christie Lane! The enormity of the idea was overwhelming. Of course it would be a long hard pull. She'd have to plant the idea gradually. Then she could tell them all to fuck off. Dan—Robin—the whole world. *Mrs.* Christie Lane! Mrs. TV Star! Mrs. *Power!*

It was three in the morning when they reached the Astor. Chris had offered to drop her at her own apartment. "I have to be at rehearsal at eleven tomorrow, doll."

"Let me come and just sleep with you. We don't have to have sex, I want to be with you, Chris."

His homely face broke into a smile. "Sure, doll. I just thought you'd be more comfortable in your own place, changing and all, because you got to be at rehearsal tomorrow too."

"That's just it—I don't."

He turned to her in the darkened cab. "Come again?"

"I'll tell you when we're upstairs."

She undressed silently and slipped into bed with him. He was looking at the racing form. His stomach was billowing over his shorts, a cigar was clamped between his teeth. He motioned to the twin bed. "Sleep in there, doll. No humping tonight."

"I just want to cling to you, Chris." She put her arms around his flabby body.

He looked at her. "Say, you're acting funny. What's up?"

She burst into tears. She was surprised how easily they came. She was thinking of the humiliation Robin Stone had caused her, and the tears grew into full-fledged sobs.

"Doll—for Chrissakes what's the matter? Did I do something? Tell me."

"Oh no, Chris, it's just that this is our last night together." She sobbed in earnest now. She was sobbing for all the rejections, all the men she had loved for just one night, all the love she had never had.

"What in hell are you talking about?" He put his arms around her and clumsily tried to pat her head. God, she even hated the smell of him, cheap shaving cologne and sweat, but she managed to think of Robin on the dance

floor. She thought of the German girl who was probably
in his arms, and her sobs increased in volume.

"Doll, tell me, I can't stand to see you like this. You're
the strongest girl in the world. I was telling that to Kenny
the other day. I said, 'That Ethel—she'd kill for me.'
What's this shit about this being our last night together?'"

She looked at him with the tears running down her
face. "Chris, how do you feel about me?"

He rubbed her hair and gazed into space thoughtfully.
"I dunno, doll, I never give it much thought. I like you.
We have a ball together. You're a good sport—"

She started to sob again. This pig—he was rejecting
her too!

"Now, doll, I mean look—I wouldn't let myself fall in
love. Once is enough. But there's no other girl. You're
with me as long as you want to be. Like Kenny and
Eddie. So what's all this talk about our last night?"

She turned away and stared straight ahead of her.
"Chris, you know about my past."

The color came to his face.

"That's just it," she sobbed. "But that's not the real me.
What you know *now* is the real me. You're afraid of
getting hurt because of Amanda—well, it happened to
me. A boy in college, we were engaged. I was a virgin,
and he walked out on me. I was so hurt, I decided to
screw every man in the world, just to get even with him.
I hated him, I hated life, I hated myself. Until you came
along—then it was as if I was purged. I met a fine human
being, I really cared. I began to like myself, and the real
Ethel Evans emerged. All the past was a put-on. What
I've been to you is really what I am."

"I understand, doll, and I'm even beginning to forget
about your past. So what's the big deal? Am I asking
questions?"

"No, but, Chris—before you came along, I—I went
with Danton Miller."

He sat up straight. "Oh shit, him too! Didn't you miss
anyone?"

"Chris, Dan really dug me. He got jealous of everyone
I went with. He put me on your show so he could keep
an eye on me. He was livid when Jerry arranged for us to
date. But he figured it would be a one-night stand. He

had no idea I'd really fall in love with you. Now he's jealous."

"Fuck him!"

"That's just what he wants."

"You're kidding!"

"No, he called me today, and told me he didn't want me to see you anymore. That he wants me to hold myself free just for him. I told him to go fuck himself and he said I'm to give you the air tonight. I'm not to go near your show—if I do, he'll have me fired from IBC. If I give you the air, I can stay. He'll even get me other shows with more money. But I can't do it, Chris—I can't live without you."

"I'll talk to Dan tomorrow."

"He'll deny it, and you'll have an enemy. He says he made you and he can break you."

Christie's jaw tightened. Ethel realized she had made a wrong move. Chris was still insecure. Dammit, he was afraid of Dan Miller.

"He can't touch you, Chris—you're the greatest. But he can get rid of me. It seems I wrote a lot of silly letters to a girl I thought was my friend—about some of my romances. Dan has copies of the letters."

"You know, some dames have a big mouth, but you got a big typewriter. Why in fuck did you ever write letters? You can hurt the guys too."

"I know, and maybe God is punishing me. But how did I know Yvonne would have copies made? Why doesn't God pay *her* back? I wrote them on the spur of the moment, as a joke. But that's all past. My problem is now."

"Okay, so you quit the show," Chris said.

"Then what?"

"You could get another job—CBS, NBC, any of the networks."

"No, Dan would blackball me. I'm finished."

"I'll get you a job, and right now."

"Chris, it's three thirty."

"Who gives a shit!" He picked up the phone and asked for a number. After a few rings, Ethel heard a sleep-filled voice answer. "Herbie? Chris Lane. I know it's late, but look, sweetheart, I'm a man who acts on impulse. It seems to me the other day at the track you said you'd give anything just for the prestige of having your office handle my public relations. Well, I just might give you the chance. Starting tomorrow."

Herbie's staccato voice rattled through the phone. He was elated. He'd do a hell of a job. He'd be at rehearsal at eleven.

"Hold it, Herbie. There's a few stipulations that go with the deal. I'll pay three bills a week—I don't care what the going rate is. You got a crummy office on Broadway with some borscht comics and a few dance teams. But if you got Christie Lane, you're in the big leagues. And I may be able to throw some work to your cockamamie clients. Only there's a deal goes with it: you got to hire Ethel Evans. Sure she's with IBC, but I want her to quit and just work for me. Only *you* pay her. How much—a C a week?" He looked at Ethel. She shook her head frantically. "That's chickenshit, Herbie, one twenty-five?" She shook her head again. "Wait a minute, Herbie." He turned to Ethel. "What do you want—opera?"

"I get a base pay of one fifty at IBC, twenty-five extra for doing your show—that's one seventy-five."

"Herbie, one seventy-five and it's a deal. So it only leaves you one and a quarter, but look at the prestige, baby. Well, I see your point, okay, one fifty." He ignored the elbow Ethel jabbed into him. "Sure, Herbie, she'll be at your office at ten tomorrow."

"You mean with all your big pull, I'm taking a cut?" she asked.

"The man is right, you can't make more than he makes out of the deal. Now relax. At IBC you have to work on a lot of shows. With Herbie it's just me, and you can live on one fifty."

Ethel was furious. She knew Herbie . . . he'd make her punch a time clock and the hours would be murder. Her job at IBC had prestige. Herbie ran a shlock outfit. Everything was all botched up, but she was stuck now.

"Chris, I've signed my death notice, you know that."

"Why? I just got you a new job."

"At IBC I had fringe benefits—hospitalization, nice clean air-conditioned offices."

"So you got me. Isn't that what you wanted?"

She snuggled close to him. "You know that. I gave up IBC for you—I could have stayed, done other shows. But I gave it up to work for Herbie Shine. But what are you doing for me?"

"Are you crazy? Didn't I just get you a job?"

"I want to be your girl."

"Christ, everyone knows it."

"I mean officially—can't we at least say we're engaged?"

He put down the racing form. "Forget it! I'm not marrying you, Ethel. If and when I get married, I want a decent girl. I want kids. Your cooze is like the Lincoln Tunnel, everyone's been through it."

"And I suppose Amanda was a decent girl . . ."

"She was a bum, but I thought she was decent. At least I know about you."

"And you don't think a girl can change?"

"Maybe. We'll see." He picked up the racing form.

"Chris, just give me a chance—please!"

"Am I throwing you outa bed? You're with me—wherever we go—aren't you?"

She threw her arms around him. "Oh, Chris, I don't just love you, I worship you. You're my God, my Lord, my king. You're my life!"

She crawled down to the bottom of the bed and began running her tongue along his toes. It nauseated her, but she tried to pretend he was one of the movie stars she had adored.

He started to laugh. "Hey, that feels good. I never had nothing like that."

"Lie down. I want to make love to every part of you. To show you how I worship and adore you. I always will —no matter what you do. I'll always love you. I love you so much. . . ." She began moaning and making love to him. Later when he lay back panting and wet with perspiration he said, "But, doll, that's not right. I came like crazy. Jesus—right down to my toes. But nothing happened with you."

"Are you mad?" she said. "I came twice, just making love to you."

"You're kidding!"

"Chris, don't you understand? I love you. You excite me, I come just when I touch you."

He put his arm around her and rubbed her hair. "Well, how about that! You're sure a crazy dame, but I like it." He belched loudly and he picked up the racing form.

"Hey, it's after four and I got to do my homework. You better get in the other bed and go to sleep. You got to get up early and give Dan your notice and go to Herbie's office. Go to sleep, doll."

She went into the other bed and turned her back on him. She gritted her teeth and said, "I love you, Chris."

He got out of the bed and headed for the bathroom. On the way he patted her buttocks. "I love you too, doll. Only don't forget, I'm—I'm forty-two, and I got a big career that got started late in life. And that's all that counts to me." Then leaving the door open, he sat on the toilet and had an explosive bowel movement. She threw the covers over her head. The pig! And she had to crawl to him! But she'd get even. She'd marry him! If it was the last thing she did—then she'd tell everyone to fuck off. Especially him!

Ethel ripped the copy from the typewriter and flung it on Herbie Shine's desk. She stood there, her eyes narrowed, as the small compact balding little man read it carefully.

"It's okay," he said slowly. "But you don't give the address of the restaurant."

"Herbie, it's a general release for the columns. Either the name 'Lario's' catches, or forget it. No column prints the address."

"But this joint is off the beaten track. We got to make people aware of it."

"If they'd spring for an opening party and have some celebrities and all the columnists, they'd make every paper. But they're like all your accounts—too cheap to do things right."

"On that you're right, especially my jumbo account, Mr. Christie Lane. He's the cheapest of them all. Lario's is a small place. They can't afford to go for all that free booze and food for a party. But better make some of those IBC people go there, also Christie Lane."

"Look. Chris is paying you on his own. He hated that last restaurant you handled, the one on Twelfth Street you made me drag him to—cost him three bucks in cab fare each way. I didn't hear the end of it for days."

"He also stiffed the waiters," Herbie said.

"Chris figures when he's on the cuff it's all the way."

"Anyone knows you still take care of a captain and a waiter."

"Not Chris."

"Well, why don't you tell him!"

"I'm not running an Emily Post course." She put her coat on.

"It's only four o'clock. What kind of banker's hours do you think you're keeping around here? You didn't come in till ten fifteen this morning."

"When I was at IBC I often came in at ten thirty, and I left when I wanted to. Sometimes I was in at nine and left at six. Look, Herbie, I'm good at my job. I get my work done and make my own hours. Next thing I know, you'll want me to punch a time clock."

"I'm not IBC. I have three people working for me. We handle twelve accounts. You make more than the other two and you work half the hours I do."

"Then fire me."

He stared at her with an ugly smile. "I'd love to. And you know it! But we both need Chris Lane—and you're not walking out of here at four o'clock."

"Watch me."

"Okay—then I'll dock you."

"Then I won't walk out. But when I arrive at Ike Ryan's big opening tonight, with my hair not done, Chris is going to ask some questions. And I'll tell him about the classy job he got me."

"Go get your hair done, you bitch."

She smiled and walked out of the room. He watched her broad hips wiggle, and like everyone else he wondered what Chris Lane saw in her.

Ethel knew a lot of people were wondering what Chris Lane saw in her. She sat in the Copa bar, trying to smile as Eddie and Kenny cracked jokes. She hated Chris more than ever tonight. Every important person was at the opening-night party Ike Ryan had thrown. Okay, so there was bad blood between Chris and Amanda, then at least they could have gone to Sardi's where the other first-nighters would be. But Chris didn't feel comfortable in Sardi's. He got a back table. He was a selfish tight bastard! She glanced at her dress. It was two years old. When she had hinted for a new dress for the opening, his eyes had narrowed: "What kind of crap is that? I buy all your meals, your rent isn't high. With one fifty a week you should dress like a fashion plate. Besides, Lou Goldberg just made me take another annuity."

Lou Goldberg was the key. He was coming in next week. She had to charm him and convince him that she was good for Chris. She opened her compact and added some lipstick. She simply *had* to get her teeth capped. She had hinted in every way about a mink coat for Christmas, but of course it fell on deaf ears with Chris. Well, she'd just wait till Lou Goldberg came to town—then she'd really send in the first team.

She sat tense as the dentist put the Novocain needle into her gum, even though she knew it really wouldn't hurt. She relaxed and soon the stonelike feeling crept into her lip, her mouth and even up to her nose. It was happening! She was going to have the teeth capped. And she had Lou Goldberg to thank for it. She lay back and shut her eyes as the dentist approached with the drill. She heard the buzz against her teeth. She felt nothing. She tried not to think that two healthy teeth were in the process of being ground into stumps. But it had to be done to close that goddam separation.

She thought about Lou Goldberg. Their evening together had been successful beyond her wildest expectations. She had planned it perfectly. She stayed late at the office intentionally and dashed into Dinty Moore's in the oppossum coat and blue wool dress. "I'm so sorry I didn't get home to change," she apologized, "but Mr. Shine is a slave driver. And I wanted to look my best for you, Mr. Goldberg. Chris talks about you so much—I almost feel as if I know you."

He was a nice-looking man. Tall, gray-haired, older than Chris. But he was slim and walked like a younger

man. It hadn't been easy. In the beginning Lou Goldberg
was suspicious and guarded. She played it guileless and
warm. Her entire conversation centered on Chris—his
career, his talent, how she admired the way he took his
success, how lucky he was to have the advice of Lou
Goldberg, how he didn't splurge to put up a false front
like some performers. "Everyone loves Chris now," she
said. "They'd love him even if he wasn't big, because he's
*nice*. And I guess he could always get work. But it's later
that a man needs security. If he's ill, no one cares then
but his family. And he's lucky to have *you* for family, Mr.
Goldberg."

She had watched Lou Goldberg melt before her eyes.
His guard dissolved and he looked at her with warm
interest. Soon he was asking questions—personal questions. That meant he was interested. She played it direct
and simple. Her parents were Polish, good God-fearing
people who went to church every Sunday. Yes, they were
still alive. They lived in Hamtramck. She almost choked
as she explained she sent them fifty dollars every week.
And Lou had swallowed it. God, if she sent them fifty a
month, her father would retire!

Lou Goldberg beamed approvingly. "I like that, most
girls don't think of their families. They just use their
money to put things on their backs."

"That's because they want to impress people," she said.
"I was afraid to come here in this dress, but then I realized you wouldn't care. Not from the things Chris has
told me about you. You size people up as soon as you
meet them. He said you could always spot a phony a mile
away."

"I usually can," he said happily. "And you're a real
girl."

"Thank you," she said modestly. "My whole life has
changed, just knowing Chris. I wasn't always this way. I
did some rather stupid things. But I was young, and
wanted to feel beautiful." She laughed. "I know I can
never be, but it doesn't matter now. If Chris loves me,
that's all I want."

Lou reached out and patted her hand. "You're quite
nice-looking, my dear."

Ethel pointed to her front teeth. "Not with this . . ."

"But that could be fixed," Lou said. "Dentists do marvelous jobs today."

She nodded. "But it costs at least three hundred dollars."

Lou looked at Chris meaningfully. Chris evaded the glance. Ethel pretended the subject was over and returned to her hamburger.

"Chris, I want you to have Ethel's teeth done," Lou said.

"Oh, she looks fine to me this way."

"It's for *her* sake. If she doesn't feel she looks well—"

And so it had been arranged. Lou had written the check himself.

"I'll take this out of your money, Chris," he said, as he handed Ethel the check. Then he laughed. "You know, I taught this boy to be thrifty, but sometimes he overdoes it. Chris, you really should get some new suits."

"I got three new ones—I use them on TV. And I'm working on a deal. A tailor downtown told me he'll furnish me all the suits free if I give him a credit. Dan Miller said no plugs, but when I renegotiate my contract next year I'm gonna insist."

"You can take it off income tax," Lou insisted.

"Sure, but if I can get them free, why not?"

Chris wanted everything free. Ethel lay back, her face numb, the dentist's drill humming away. She had swung it! When she had won Lou Goldberg's confidence, Chris's whole attitude had changed. He actually believed she *was* reborn. As he had put it, "I feel like God. I recreated you from a bum into a lady!" And she smiled and held his hand. . . . God, she had wanted to slap his smug idiotic face—but she was getting the teeth, and they'd be ready in time for the dinner at the Waldorf. Of course she was a long way from getting *him.* Some of the columns hinted they were engaged, but marriage was still the last thing on his mind. She had toyed with the idea of getting pregnant, but he was one step ahead of her. He wouldn't let her use a diaphragm. The few times he actually made the effort to do anything, he used a condom. Mostly he just lay back and let her make love to him! He actually believed she came from just touching him. . . . Well, at least she had the teeth and Lou Goldberg's approval.

That was a good start. And she would buy a new dress for the dinner.

The dinner at the Waldorf was exactly like all the other dinners at the Waldorf. Dan Miller arrived, escorting an exact replica of his other conservative "date." Only this one had frosted hair. There were two empty seats at their table . . . Robin Stone never appeared. Ethel was sorry she had sprung for the dress. The only eventful moment had been her introduction to Mrs. Gregory Austin. This had occurred as they waited for their coats at the checkroom. Ethel had been properly humble, Mrs. Austin properly gracious as she complimented Chris on his show.

Chris reveled in it as he undressed that night. "Didja hear Gregory Austin himself come over and tell me I'm the greatest? And he didn't have to. He went out of his way to tell me. You know he coulda just nodded. He's known for that, you know—staying apart from his stars. Jesus, I'll never forget his New Year's Day party. I think he nodded to me once and wondered who the hell I was." Chris flopped on the bed stark-naked. "Come on, baby, make my lob come to life. After all, it's an honor for you to be able to please the King."

She ignored him and undressed slowly. Chris gazed into space complacently. "Know something? That name isn't good enough. The King. There are a lot of kings—there's a King of England, of Greece, of Sweden, of—well, there's plenty of Kings. But there's only one Chris Lane. I got to get a tag."

"You could always try God for size."

"Nah, that's sacrilegious." He thought about it. "Hey, how about 'fantastic'! Yeah—that's it: Mr. Fantastic. Start getting that tag put after my name in the columns, baby. I *am* fantastic. Didja notice even Mrs. Austin told me how much she enjoyed me? That's because I'm the greatest—"

"She'd think you were the cheapest, if she knew how I worked for Herbie Shine and the hours I put in."

"She'd be more shocked if you were a kept woman," he growled. "There's nothing unrespectable about working."

"Ha! Everyone knows you're banging me. They think you're too cheap to keep anyone."

"No one says I'm cheap."

"I'm the living proof. I've been your girl for almost five months. They laugh at my clothes but they're not laughing at *me*—they're laughing at you!" Then as she saw the color come to his face, she felt perhaps she had gone too far. She softened her voice. "Look, I don't care whether you give me anything or not. It's just that Herbie Shine. He's been needling me, hinting that you're cheap, that if you weren't, you wouldn't have me working in an office like his. And it's such a crummy office, Chris. I don't think he should handle you. Eventually you should have Cully and Hayes."

"At a G a week?"

"You can afford it."

"That's pissing money away. They get you invited to all the fancy parties but not a line in a column. At least Herbie gets me a few column plugs."

"But Herbie can't get you lined up with any magazine stories."

"The IBC publicity office takes care of that. I only want column mentions from Herbie."

"You're paying Herbie three hundred a week for column mentions."

"Actually one fifty. The other one fifty goes for your salary."

"That's what *you* think—I work on ten other accounts for him. And you're paying for that!"

"The son of a bitch," he said softly.

"Chris. Hire me and unload Herbie!"

His smile was nasty. "You mean I should pay you three hundred a week? It doesn't add up. This way I got both you and Herbie working for me."

"Herbie doesn't lift a finger for you. He just makes you go to his crappy restaurants and gets your name in a column that way. And the restaurant is paying him. Look, Chris, pay me two hundred—that's a hundred less than you pay Herbie. And I'd do the same job. I know all the columnists—I can place all the items for you. And I'd be free to be with you whenever you wanted and keep your hours. Like last week I had to leave you at two at the

Copa because Herbie had an early assignment for me on one of *his* accounts. This way I could stay up all hours, and Herbie won't be taking your money and laughing behind your back."

His eyes narrowed. "That lousy little punk." He was silent. Suddenly he smiled. "Okay, doll, you got yourself a deal. I paid Herbie until the end of the week. Get your paycheck on Friday, then tell Herbie to go fuck himself. Tell him Chris said so."

She leaped on him and covered his face with kisses. "Oh, Chris, I love you, you are my master, my life!"

"Okay, now dive. Make Mr. Fantastic happy."

After Chris was satisfied he settled with his racing form, and she browsed through the morning papers. She leafed through the *Daily News* and stopped at page three. There was a big picture of Amanda being carried on a stretcher to the hospital. Ike was holding her hand. Even on the stretcher Amanda looked beautiful. She read the story carefully. Amanda had collapsed at a party. The diagnosis was internal hemorrhaging from an ulcer. Her condition was listed as "satisfactory." Ethel carefully hid the paper. Chris hadn't mentioned Amanda in a long time; she was sure he was over her. She wondered how Robin had felt when she married Ike. Then she thought of the two empty chairs at the table tonight. She had to admire his nerve. How did he have the guts not to show—?

# SEVENTEEN

ROBIN HAD INTENDED TO SHOW. He had told Tina, the new pride of Century Pictures, to be ready at eight. He had even ordered a car. He was glad he had gone to that movie opening last week. Usually he ducked those things, but he had started back on his book and had worked every night for several weeks. He was in the mood for some relaxation. And God had created Tina St.

Claire for just that purpose. She was a beautiful brainless
idiot who had come to New York to promote a picture.
She only had a small part but the stars had been unavailable, so Tina St. Claire, Georgia hopeful turned starlet,
had agreed to go on the junket. And *go* she had—San
Francisco, Houston, Dallas, St. Louis, Philadelphia, and
finally New York. This film company had staffed her with
a press agent, a studio-loaned wardrobe, and a suite at
the St. Regis which she barely had time to see. In three
days she had done seven television appearances, ten radio
shows, four newspaper interviews and had appeared at a
department store to autograph the sound-track album.
(That had hurt her ego more than her feet: she had stood
for two hours and no one had come.) Then the whole
thing had culminated in the premiere and an opening-
night party at which the press agent handed her a return
ticket (tourist) to Los Angeles along with instructions to
check out of the hotel the following day.

She had been heartbroken. After two bourbon-and-
Cokes at the party, she had met Robin and told him her
tale of misery. "Heah I've worked my li'l ole butt off, and
I have to go right back. Foah what! To jes sit and wait
till another small part comes up! My first trip to New
Yoak and I declare I haven't seen a thing!"

"Stay on," Robin offered. "I'll show you around."

"How? I can't afford that hotel. I just have ten dollahs
hard cash and my plane ticket back. I only make one
twenty-five a week! Would you believe it? My sister is a
waitress in Chicago and she makes moah!"

Two bourbon-and-Cokes later she checked out of the
St. Regis and into his apartment. For a week Robin lived
amidst mascara, eye shadow and pancake litter. He
couldn't believe a girl who wound up looking fresh and
natural could use so much gook on her face. She had
more paintbrushes than an artist. He had been forced to
move his manuscript to the office. According to Tina, his
desk had the best light for putting on her eyelashes.
Actually he found he liked working in the office. From
five until seven he could turn off the phones and accom-
plish a great deal.

He took the page from the typewriter and looked at his
watch. Quarter to seven. Time to pack it in. Tina was

leaving in four days and he could go back to working nights in his apartment. She was a hell of a girl, but he was not sorry that her stay was drawing to a close. She was his equal in every way. Insatiable in bed, asked no questions, made no demands.

He put the manuscript away and lit a cigarette. He didn't want to go to the Waldorf. But it was Mrs. Austin's charity and he had to show. Well, he'd grab Tina and duck out after the speeches. He had promised to take her to El Morocco. It wasn't his scene, but he owed it to the little nympho! He used the electric shaver in his office because Tina had also established a beachhead in the bathroom. She kept her night creams and douche bag there. He plugged in his razor and turned on the television for the seven o'clock news.

He had just finished shaving when Andy Parino came on. He was talking heatedly about another saucer sighting. Robin listened without too much interest until the saucer pictures flashed on. They were blurred, but by God, it looked like the real thing. He walked over to the set—he could swear he saw portholes on the damn thing.

"The Pentagon claims it was a weather balloon." Andy's voice was derisive. "If that is the truth, then why have they sent a man from Project Bluebook down here to investigate? Do we dare presume that in the vast universe ours is the *only* planet to breed life? Why, even our sun is not as good as some of the other suns. It's a Cepheid, an inferior star in the galaxy. Why shouldn't a planet in another solar system harbor human life perhaps twenty million years more advanced than ours? It is time we had a real investigation—and threw the findings open to the public."

Robin was fascinated. He had to talk to Andy.

It was getting late, but what the hell, they'd get to the Waldorf at eight thirty. He got Andy on the tie line and complimented him on the saucer picture, then asked for more details.

"It's exactly as I told it on the air," Andy said.

"You told it good, baby. Who wrote it?"

There was a moment of silence. Then Andy said, "Maggie Stewart." When Robin failed to respond, he added, "You know, I've told you about her."

"She sounds like a smart girl."

"I still can't get her to marry me—"

"Well, like I said, she sounds smart. How's the weather down there?"

"Seventy degrees, clear as a bell."

"It's thirty here and looks like rain."

"Know something, Robin? If I was president of News, I'd make it my business to find news in nice warm places in winter and cool places in summer."

"I wish I could."

"Well, I got to run. Maggie's probably sitting at the bar at the Gold Coast. It's right on the bay. You can see all the yachts pull up. Man, it's great. You sit at the window and stare at the moon and water."

"You've got it made." Robin's voice was filled with envy. "I've got to climb into black tie and make it to the Waldorf."

"You're crazy, you only live once. Why not come down here for a few days and unwind?"

"I wish I could."

"Well, I've got to run. This guy who sighted the saucer is joining us for dinner. He's no crackpot. Teaches high-school math, so he was even able to approximate its speed. I figure it might make a good show—maybe on a Sunday afternoon."

"Wait a minute!" Robin said. "It might make a hell of an *In Depth*. Let's say we got your math teacher and a few other creditable sighters from different parts of the country, with pictures. And we got some of those guys from the Pentagon on, and really shot the questions to them—"

"Want me to send you all the stuff?" Andy asked.

"No, I'll come down. I want to talk to this teacher."

"When will you be down?"

"Tonight."

There was a pause. Then Andy said, "Tonight?"

Robin laughed. "I'm taking your advice. I need a few days of sun."

"Okay, I'll get you a suite at the Diplomat. It's near my apartment, and it has a great golf course. I'll have a limo meet you."

"See you at twelve thirty then."

"No, Robin—you'll see a big black empty limousine. I told you, I have a date with Maggie."

Robin laughed. "You son of a bitch! You shacking up together?"

"When you see Maggie, you'll know better than to ask anything like that. We don't even live in the same building."

"Okay, Andy. See you tomorrow morning."

It was eight fifteen when Robin let himself into his apartment. Tina was standing in an evening dress, her long red hair done up in Grecian style. "Honey"—she danced around him—"yoah'll nevah guess what. The studio tole me I have an extra week before I have to report—isn't that divine? But, lovah, it's late, I have youah tux all laid out. The car is waitin'—"

He went into the bedroom and pulled out a suitcase. Tina followed him.

"I've got to go to Miami," he said.

"When?"

"Tonight. Want to come?"

Her face wrinkled into a pout. "Honey, ah live in Los Angeles. Los Angeles is just Miami with smog."

She stared in amazement as he went to the phone and made his plane reservations.

"Robin, you just cain't flip off lak this. What about this big dinnah for your boss?"

"I'll send a wire tomorrow with a proper apology." He picked up his bag, grabbed his overcoat and started for the door. He tossed some bills on the table. "There's about a hundred there!"

"When will you be back?"

"In about four or five days."

She smiled. "Oh—then I'll still be heah."

He looked at her. "Don't be."

She stared at him in bewilderment. "I thought you *liked* me."

"Baby, let's put it this way: we met on a pleasure cruise on the Caribbean. This is the first port of call, and you're getting off."

"What would you do if I decided to stay on the boat?"

"Toss you overboard."

"You wouldn't!"

He grinned. "Sure I would. It's *my* boat." He kissed her forehead. "Four days—then out!" She was still staring when he left the apartment.

The limousine was waiting at the airport in Florida. The suite at the hotel was in order; there was even ice and a bottle of vodka. The note said: "Call you in the morning. Have a good night's sleep. Andy."

He sent down for the Miami papers. He undressed, poured himself a light drink and settled comfortably in bed. The picture of the smiling girl on page two looked familiar—Amanda! It was one of her fashion shots, her head thrown back, a wind machine tossing the hair. The caption said HOMETOWN BEAUTY ILL. He read the story quickly and placed a call to Ike Ryan in Los Angeles.

"Is it serious?" Robin asked, when Ike came on the line.

"With her every fucking second is serious. She's been living on borrowed time since last May."

"But I mean—" Robin stopped.

"No, it's not curtains. Look, I've learned to live with death, I've been dying a little every day. You know what it's like, Robin, to see a girl looking gorgeous—the goddam illness makes her even more beautiful. Makes her skin like china. I watch her, I can see when she's tired and pretends not to be. I can also see something like the beginning of fear in her eyes. She knows it's not natural to be this tired. I kid her and pretend I'm tired too. I blame it on California, the change of air, the smog, everything. Oh, what the hell. Thank God she's rallied. They've given her two pints of blood. Tomorrow they're starting a new drug. The doctor thinks it will work, and with luck she'll have another few months of remission."

"Ike, she's made it since April—that's eight months more than they predicted in the beginning."

"I know, and I tell myself she'll have another remission. But the damn leukemia cells build up a resistance to the drug. Comes a day when you've gone through all the drugs—and that's it."

"Ike, she has no idea, has she?"

"Yes, and no. She's suspicious. She'd be an idiot if she wasn't, what with a blood test every week. And a bone-marrow test every month. Christ, I saw her get it once and I almost fainted—they stuck a needle right into her bone. And she never bats an eye. Later I asked her if it hurt and would you believe it, this girl just smiles and nods yes. When she asks me why the test has to be *every* week, I just toss it off and say I want a strong broad and a rush job done on it. But she asks funny little questions. And I catch her reading all the medical columns in the newspapers. Deep down, she knows something's dead wrong, but she doesn't want to believe it. And she's always smiling, always worrying about me. I tell you, Robin, I've learned a lot from this girl. She's got more gallantry than anyone I've ever met. I never really knew what that word meant until Amanda came along. She's scared to death and never shows it. Know what she said tonight? She looked at me and said, 'Oh, my poor Ike, what a drag I am. You wanted to go to Palm Springs.'"

Ike's voice broke. "I love her, Robin. I didn't go into this thing loving her. I did it for lousy stinking selfish reasons. I thought she'd have six months and then quietly lie down and die. I planned to give her a ball while she lasted—then a big send-off, and I'd take bows. I looked at it like I was booking a show, for a limited run. Does that make you want to puke? Boy, all those little broads that I've pushed around can sure have the last laugh now. For the first time in my stinking life, I'm really in love. Robin, I'd give every cent I got if they could cure her." Ike was sobbing openly.

"Is there anything I can do?" Robin felt helpless, hearing a man cry, a man like Ike. Yet there was nothing he could say.

"Christ," Ike said. "I haven't cried since my old lady died. I'm sorry I let it out on you. It's just that this is the first time I've been able to talk about it. No one knows but just you and me, Jerry and the doctor. And I have to keep playing it light for Amanda. It's been all locked up inside me. I'm sorry."

"Ike, I'm at the Diplomat Hotel in Miami Beach. Call me every night if you like. We'll talk."

"Nope. Tonight helped—but that's it. I can take everything except when she asks me to give her a baby. She wants a kid so much. You should see her with that cat. She talks to it, babies it."

"That cat has a lot of class," Robin said.

There was a pause. Ike's voice was low. "Robin, tell me something. You and me—we've met broads—loads of them, real bitches. Wanna bet they'll live to a hundred? But this kid who never had a break, never did a wrong thing to anyone? . . . why? What's the answer?"

"It's like rolling dice, I guess," Robin said slowly. "The hungry guy with his life's savings on the line comes up with snake eyes. If Paul Getty ever picked up the dice, he'd probably make ten straight passes."

"No, there's got to be more to it than that. I'm not a religious guy, but I tell you these last eight months have made me stop and think. I don't mean I'm gonna rush into a church or a synagogue, but there has to be a reason for things. She's only twenty-five, Robin, just twenty-five. I got twenty years on her. What in hell have I ever done to get double her span? I can't believe that maybe a year from now she'll be gone, leaving nothing but some eight-by-ten glossies to prove that she was around. Why should she go when there's so much beauty in her, so much life to be lived, so much love that she has to give?"

"Maybe just what she's done for you in these past months is reason enough for her existence. A lot of people pass through this world and leave no mark."

"I know one thing," Ike said. "I'm going to make this the greatest Christmas she's ever had. Robin—I want you to come. You've got to! I want to make it a slam-bang Christmas."

Robin was silent. He hated illness—and seeing Amanda and knowing . . .

Ike felt his hesitation. "Maybe I'm being selfish," he said. "You probably have your own family to be with. It's just that I want to give her every possible kick, make every second count."

"I'll be there," Robin said.

II

# MAGGIE

# EIGHTEEN

A T TWO A.M. Maggie Stewart was still awake. She
had smoked an entire pack of cigarettes. For three
hours she had paced back and forth—from the living
room to the small terrace overlooking the bay. She liked
facing the bay—the ocean was enormous and empty, but
the bay sparkled with life. It was dotted with large
yachts—their flickering lights sent shimmering reflections
in the dark water. She envied the contentment of the
people sleeping on them: it must be like a large cradle
with waves lapping against the side—the easy lilt of the
boat. She clenched the railing of the terrace until her
knuckles went white.

Robin Stone was here! In the same city. They would
come face to face tomorrow. What would she say? What
would he say? Oddly enough her mind raced back to
Hudson. For the first time in almost a year and a half she
allowed herself to think about him. Long ago, or rather,
right after her marriage to Hudson, she had learned it
was best to ignore unhappiness. Thinking about it nour-
ished it and kept it alive. Tonight, for the first time, she
allowed the image of Hudson Stewart to come into focus.
She saw his face, his smile that had gradually turned
bitter—and then that ugly final frightening smile. That
was the last she had seen of him—that terrible smile
before she blacked out. It seemed so long ago, when she
had lived in that big house as Mrs. Hudson Stewart III.
Why was it that men were forgiven for anything—but a
woman had to go by the rules?

She had married Hudson when she was twenty-one.
Officially it had lasted three years. It was hard to recall

just what she had felt in the beginning. She had wanted to be an actress. It was a dream that began when she was a child, the first time she had seen Rita Hayworth on the screen. It had crystallized when she saw her first legitimate show at the Forrest Theater. The living actors on the stage made everything in pictures pallid and unreal. This was what she would become. She made this decision when she was twelve and announced it at dinner. Her parents smiled and dismissed it as another adolescent phase. But she joined an amateur theater group while she attended high school and instead of going to dances, she spent her weekends studying Chekhov. The real explosion came when she announced she had no intention of going to college—she intended to go to New York and try for the theater. Her mother went into convulsive sobs. "Oh, Maggie," she sobbed, "you've been accepted at Vassar. You know how I've stinted and saved to send you to college!"

"I don't want to go to college. I want to act!"

"It costs money to live in New York—it could take a year or more before you got a job. What would you live on?"

"The money you've put away for Vassar. Just give me half of it."

"Oh, no! I won't give you money to go to New York and sleep around with actors and dirty old men who produce shows. Maggie—no nice girl goes to New York."

"Grace Kelly went to New York—she was a nice girl."

Her mother was adamant: "She was one in a million. And she was rich. Oh, Maggie, I never had a chance to go to college. Your father had to work his way through. It was our dream to send our daughter to the best school. Please—go to Vassar, then when you graduate, if you still want to go to New York—well, you'll still only be twenty-one."

And so she had gone to Vassar. She met Hudson when she was in her senior year. She thought him fairly attractive but her mother had gone wild with excitement. "Oh, Maggie, this is everything I've ever dreamed of! One of the best families in Philadelphia, and so much money. If only the Stewarts will accept us. After all, we're respected, and your father is a doctor."

"I've only had two dates with him, Mother, and I *still* want to go to New York."

"New York!" Her mother's voice became shrill. "Listen, young lady, get those ideas out of your head. I saved to send you to Vassar. I knew as soon as you told me you were rooming with Lucy Fenton that things were going to work out—you *had* to meet the right boys through Lucy!"

"I'm going to New York."

"On what?"

"Well—I'll get a job to support myself, and then try for the theater."

"And just what kind of a job do you think you could get, my fine lady? You can't type. You aren't trained for a thing. I should never have let you join that acting group in high school, but I thought you would get it out of your system. And don't think I didn't notice the moonstruck way you looked at that foreign-looking boy."

"Adam was born right here in Philadelphia!"

"Then he needed a bath and a haircut!"

She was amazed that her mother remembered Adam. She had never mentioned him. He had been a member of the Theater Arts group she had belonged to in high school. He had gone to New York and just this season he had come to Philadelphia with a real Broadway show. Of course it was a road company and he was only assistant stage manager. But he had made it. He was a real professional. The play had remained for a three-month run and she had seen him every weekend. Even Lucy thought he was divine. And then, the night before the play closed, Adam had asked her to come back to the hotel with him. She had hesitated—then tucked her arm into his: "I'll spend the night with you because I realize I want to spend my life with you. But we can't get married until I finish college. My mother will have a fit as it is. She never believed I'd go to New York and really try for a career. At least I've got to please her by graduating."

He had taken her face in his hands. "Maggie, I'm really dead stuck on you. But—look, honey, in New York I live in the Village with two other guys. Half the time I'm living on unemployment insurance. I can't even afford my own apartment, let alone a wife."

"You mean you intended to sleep with me and run?"

He laughed. "I run to Detroit, then Cleveland, then St. Louis, then back to New York, and hope my agent has lined up a job in summer stock. I want to get a crack at directing. It'll mean one of the lesser companies—and no money. Yes, Maggie, I'm running. An actor has to keep running all the time. But I'm not running out on you. That's the difference. You can always trace me through Equity."

"But what about *us?* What would we have together?"

"As much as any two people struggling in the theater can have. I'm hung on you, maybe I even love you. But you can't plan in this business. It's not a nine-to-five job, no steady salary coming in. No time for babies, a nice apartment. But if you want to come to New York after college—fine. I'll show you the ropes—get you to my agent. Maybe we can even shack up together."

"What about marriage?"

He had brushed her hair lightly with his hand. "Don't leave Philadelphia, Maggie. Not if you think that way. Either you're an actress or you're a wife."

"Can't I be both?"

"Not with a struggling director. It couldn't work. Actors and actresses are *dedicated.* They go hungry— they work—they dream—"

"Don't they fall in love?" she asked.

"All the time. And if they love, they go to bed together, but if a job comes along that separates them, well, that's the way it is. But an actress never feels alone because that burning thing inside called talent keeps her going."

"I want to go to bed with you, Adam," she said.

He paused. "Maggie . . . you have gone to bed with a guy before?"

Her eyes challenged him. "I'm not one of those burning actresses yet. I still have a nice clean bedroom all to myself."

"Then let's keep it that way. If and when you get to New York, look me up."

Hudson's entrance into her life, coupled with her graduation from Vassar, made their six months together so frenetic that she barely had time to analyze her emotions. She tried not to be influenced by her mother's pathetic eagerness but she was caught up and carried along by the excitement Hudson brought into her life. The country club; her first visit to the racetrack; the two-week vacation in Ocean City as house guest of Mr. and Mrs. Hudson Stewart II.

In September their engagement was announced and Hudson gave her a seven-carat emerald-cut diamond. Her picture appeared in the *Inquirer* and the *Bulletin.*

She found herself "going along" as if it was a production at the Theater Arts and Hudson was an actor playing opposite her and at the end of the third act the curtain would fall, she'd hear the applause and it would be over.

But as the date of the wedding grew closer, she suddenly realized that when the curtain came down, she would be Mrs. Hudson Stewart III. Oddly enough her mood became one of tranquil acceptance, until she had lunch with Lucy, a week before the wedding.

They were sitting at the Warwick, discussing the plans for the wedding, when Lucy casually said, "Have you ever heard from that actor—Adam? I saw him on a TV commercial the other day. He had no lines, he was shaving, but I'd never forget those eyes of his. He's rugged-looking. Jewish men are supposed to be exciting."

"Jewish?" It had never occurred to her.

"Adam Bergman," Lucy reminded her. "I remember one night he was talking—you were probably too starry-eyed to hear him—and he said an agent had suggested he change his name, because Bergman was too Jewish. And Adam said, 'I'll stick with it; Ingrid did all right.' " When Maggie didn't answer, Lucy added, "I guess that's life. We all fall in love with the wrong man. And it's all right, just so long as you *marry* the right one and settle down and have babies. Especially you—you'll get a million every time you have one. Hudson's father's already given Hudson's sister two million. That's why she's been pregnant two years in a row. Bud and I have to wait until my father dies."

"But you love Bud, don't you?"

"He's nice enough."

"Nice?" Maggie didn't hide her surprise.

Lucy smiled. "I don't have your looks, Maggie. I just have family name and lots of money."

"Oh, Lucy, you are—" Maggie stopped.

Lucy cut in with a smile. "Don't you dare say 'personable' or that I have brains. I do have brains, and there's nothing I can do about my looks because they're not bad enough. That's why I picked you as a roommate, Maggie. I thought, If I room with the most beautiful girl in school some of it has to rub off on me. And that was when I first began to get some attention. I met Harry that summer. He was a desk clerk at a hotel in Newport. Can you imagine *my* mother letting me marry Harry Reilly who lives in the Bronx and goes to NYU? Not that Harry was asking me to. But in the fall I met Bud, and my mother is happy as a clam. I guess I am too—we'll have a good life. But at least I had two glorious months with Harry."

"You mean you—" Maggie stopped.

"Of course we went all the way. Didn't you with Adam?"

Maggie shook her head.

"Oh Lord. Maggie, you're an idiot. Why not? A girl should go to bed with a man she's ape about at least once in her life."

"But how will you explain it to Bud? I mean not being—"

"That's archaic. You mean about the bleeding and all? I'm getting measured for a diaphragm; I'll just tell Bud the doctor deflowered me."

"But won't he be able to tell?"

"I can fake it. I'll just remember my first night with Harry. I'll lie back and play dumb, whimper a bit, tense myself, and it will work. Want to know something? I never even bled with Harry. But I was hard to get into— I guess that's the virgin bit. Poor Harry broke two rubbers before he made it. And I'll see to it that Bud has a hard time—the first night, anyway."

Maggie hadn't had to fake anything with Hudson. Even the pain was real. Hudson had been rough. He tried to enter her immediately. It had hurt—and she had hated the whole thing. And it was the same the second

night, and the third. They were on the *Liberté* en route
to Paris for their honeymoon. The cabin was luxurious,
but she was taking Bonamine and felt drowsy. Perhaps
things would be better once they left the boat. At the
George V in Paris, it was even worse. Hudson drank a lot
and fell on her each night, without even an attempt at
tenderness or affection. He satisfied himself and immediately fell into a dead sleep.

When they returned to Philadelphia and settled in the
beautiful home near Paoli, she had thought things would
be different. Hudson returned to work, she hired a staff,
gave dinner parties, went to the club for golf lessons, and
joined committees of various charities. Her pictures made
the society sections of all the newspapers. She was the
new young leader of Philadelphia society. Hudson was
like a stallion, methodically taking her in bed each night.
He never bothered to kiss her or touch her breasts anymore. In the beginning, she had felt she was at fault for
not reaching her climax, but as the months passed she
lost hope. She only longed for some display of affection in
their nightly ritual. When she tried to feel Lucy out, she
was answered with a shrug. "Sometimes it works with
me, sometimes it doesn't. But I moan and pretend it's
wonderful anyway. How is it with you and Hudson?"

"Oh great," Maggie had said quickly. "But as you say,
it doesn't happen with me all the time either."

"Look—it hasn't happened with us for three months.
*My* climax, I mean. Yet I'm two months pregnant. So
obviously it doesn't have anything to do with making
babies. But you'd better make Hudson go easy on his
drinking. That can make a man temporarily impotent."

Maggie felt that a baby would change things between
them. On the surface everything was fine. He was polite
in public, he held her close when they danced, but they
had nothing between them when they were alone.

She learned about Sherry at the end of their first year
of marriage. Hudson had been going to New York alone
on business frequently the last two months. On this night
she was in the bedroom, dressing for dinner. Hudson was
waiting downstairs. The phone rang. She was late, and
continued to fuss with her hair knowing that the maid
would pick it up. It continued to ring. Then through one

of the odd timings of fate, she picked it up just as
Hudson picked up the extension downstairs. She was
about to hang up when she heard a female voice whisper;
"Huddie? I had to call you."

She felt oddly calm as she listened. Hudson's voice was
also conspirational. "Dammit Sherry, I told you never to
call me at home."

"Huddie—this is urgent."

"Can't it wait until tomorrow? Call me at the office."

"I can't, because I'll be at work then, and I can't call
long distance—even if I reverse charges some of the girls
would hear. Can anyone hear me? Is your wife around?"

"She will be soon. What do you want?"

"Huddie, the test came back, I'm definitely preg."

"Christ, again!"

"Well, I can't help it if the diaphragm slips. And you
won't wear anything."

"Same doctor still in Jersey?"

"Yes, but he's upped his price to a thousand."

"Well—do it."

"Huddie, he wants cash. I made an appointment for
next Monday."

"Okay. I'll get to New York on Sunday and give you
the cash—no, I better make it during the week. Maggie
might get suspicious if I go on Sunday. Make it
Thursday. I'll be at your place at eight. God, I wish my
wife was as fertile as you. Your baby is costing me a
thousand to unload—hers would get me a million."

He clicked the receiver. Maggie stood and waited until
the girl's phone clicked. Then she hung up slowly. She
felt numb. Something like this had never occurred to her.
She read about it happening to other people—but it
couldn't happen to her. Yet if she confronted him, what
good would it do? She was twenty-two, equipped to do
nothing. A divorcée in Philadelphia, even with alimony,
was a lonely woman. She was stuck. There was no place
to go.

She remained silent about Sherry but she joined a little-theater group. Hudson didn't object. He was delighted
with the avalanche of free evenings. The program director from the local IBC station came backstage after
the second production and offered her a television job as

a Weather Girl. Her first impulse was to turn it down, until she realized it would give her something to do every day.

She took her job seriously. She watched television, especially the network shows. She went to a diction teacher every day and her improvement was swift. After six months she was promoted to the news department and a daily half-hour show of her own. It was called *Maggie About Town.* She did interviews with celebrities —local and national—covering everything from fashion to politics. Within a short time she became a personality in her own right. Heads turned as she entered a restaurant or theater with Hudson. His attitude toward her success was one of scornful amusement.

He had replaced Sherry with a girl named Irma who worked in his office. He no longer bothered with elaborate excuses on his evenings out. Yet he methodically made love to her three times a week. She submitted with impassive silence. More than ever, she wanted a child.

So the marriage had stretched out—for almost three lifeless years. But she did not get pregnant even though all the tests proved she was thoroughly capable. She sometimes wondered if they could just go on drifting like this. Something had to end this aimless relationship.

It came about by accident. For months the Man of the Year dinner had been extensively planned. It was scheduled for the first Sunday in March. As a local celebrity, Maggie was on the committee and required to sit on the dais. The mayor would also be there, and Judge Oakes who was about to retire was to be honored. Robin Stone had been booked as guest speaker.

Maggie had read Robin Stone's columns. In her small experience in Philadelphia with interviews, she had learned that people rarely resembled the image projected in their work. But Robin Stone's picture fit the image of his column: strong, clipped, virile, hard-hitting. She wondered what the man himself would be like.

At six o'clock she was dressed and waiting. Hudson had not come home. He always spent Sunday at the country club. She called and found that he had not been there all day. She should have known—that was just another excuse to be with his girl of the moment.

Well, she was *not* going to miss the cocktail party. It might be her only chance to actually meet Robin Stone. After the dinner, the guests of honor usually dashed for a train. She looked at her watch. If she left immediately, she could make it. That meant Hudson would have to come in on his own.

When she got to the hotel, she went directly to the Gold Room. Robin Stone was surrounded. He was holding a martini and smiling politely.

Maggie accepted a lukewarm Scotch with soda from one of the trays. Judge Oakes came to her. "Come with me, I'll introduce you to our guest speaker. We've all lost our wives to him."

When Judge Oakes presented her, Robin smiled. "A newsgirl? Come now—you look too beautiful to be an egghead." Then with no warning, he inched her away from the group and took her arm. "There's no ice in your drink."

"It is pretty dreadful," she answered.

He swallowed the rest of the martini. "So was this." He put his glass in the Judge's hand. "Take care of this for me. Come on, newsgirl, we'll get you some ice." He led her across the room. "Don't look back," he muttered. "Are they following us?"

"I doubt it, just glaring in stunned surprise." She laughed.

He walked behind the bar and said to the surprised bartender, "Mind if I make my own?" Before the man could answer, Robin was pouring a large amount of vodka into the pitcher. He looked at Maggie. "Want me to reinforce your Scotch—or will you try a Stone special?"

"The Stone special." She knew she was being stupid. She hated martinis. She also knew she was staring at him like an idiot. *Enjoy this second, she thought. Tomorrow you'll be sitting with Hudson—back in your own dreary world, and Robin Stone will be in another hotel, in another city, mixing another martini.*

He handed her the glass. "Here's to you, newsgirl." He took her arm and they crossed the room and settled on a small couch.

She knew every woman in the room was staring at her.

But once again she felt that odd new reckless freedom. Let them stare! But *she* couldn't just sit and stare at him. She had to say something.

"I read that you'd given up your column and gone on a lecture tour. But I miss the column." She felt it sounded forced and unnatural.

He shrugged. "They were probably chopped to mincemeat when they got here."

"No, sometimes they were quite long. But I suppose you like doing this better." He swallowed his drink and then reached over and took her untouched martini. "No, newsgirl—I don't like this better. I just do it for money."

He offered her a cigarette and lit it. "And what do you do on that little box?"

"News—women's angle mostly."

"And I'll bet they watch you and listen to you."

"Is that so incredible?" she asked.

"No, it's television. Wonderful thing, that little box," he said. "It's created a race of beautiful people."

"But don't you think *seeing* people makes it more personal—creates a better understanding?"

He shrugged. "Oh, it creates a love for certain people. The whole world loves Lucy, Ed Sullivan and Bob Hope. At the moment. But they're fickle—remember how they loved Uncle Miltie? Tell me, newsgirl, whom do *you* love on television?"

"I'd love you—" She stopped, horrified.

He grinned. "You're the first sensible girl I've ever met. You get right to the bottom line."

"I mean I'd love your thinking, your views."

He finished the drink. "Don't qualify it, newsgirl, or you'll ruin everything between us. The world is full of hedging broads. I like your style. Come on, let's get a refill."

She followed him as he carried the empty glasses back to the bar and marveled at the ease with which he had polished off both their drinks. He made two more and handed her one. She took a sip and tried not to make a face. It was almost straight vodka. People joined them and most of the women gradually drifted back; once again he was surrounded. He was polite, answered their questions, but he held her arm and never left her side.

Her eyes kept drifting to the door. Suddenly she prayed
that Hudson wouldn't appear.

There was a small tinkling chime. The chairman of the
committee clapped his hands.

"Where do you sit, newsgirl?" Robin asked.

"I guess at the other end." She heard her name. "That's
me." She broke away and got into line.

Robin tapped the chairman who stood beside him.
"How would you like to change seats with my newsgirl?
Both you and Judge Oakes are very attractive but I didn't
travel ninety miles to sit between the two of you when I
have a chance to have a lovely lady at my side."

As they entered the ballroom, Robin steered her to the
seat next to his on the dais. Maggie felt the entire audience was staring. Robin ordered fresh martinis. His capacity seemed unlimited. Three martinis and Hudson
would be clobbered. Robin appeared absolutely sober.
But no one could consume so many martinis without
feeling something.

She saw Hudson enter and take his seat at the far end
of the dais. As he sat down, she knew the man next to
him was explaining the unexpected change in the seating
arrangements. And she couldn't help but be pleased at
the surprise on his face.

She heard the chairman introduce Robin. Just as Robin
was about to stand, he leaned over and whispered to her,
"Listen, newsgirl, I'm going to pack this in as quickly as I
can. I have a suite here if I want it. They've been more
than generous, your Philadelphia organization. If you'll
cut out and meet me there, I'll stay over. Otherwise, I'm
going to run for the eleven-thirty train when all this is
over."

He rose and waited for the applause to die down. Then
he leaned over and said in her ear, "Come on, newsgirl,
give me the bottom line."

"I'll be there."

"Good girl, Suite 17B. Wait a decent interval after I
leave—and then come up."

He made his speech, and the award was finally presented to Judge Oakes. Guests from the ballroom congratulated the judge. Newspapermen asked him to pose
with Robin and the women surrounded him. He signed a

few menus for them, looked at his watch and said he was expecting an overseas call. He shook hands with Judge Oakes, waved at everyone and left.

It was eleven o'clock. Hudson walked down from his spot on the dais and sat in Robin's empty seat. "Was the cocktail party a big thrill?"

"I enjoyed it," she said.

"Let's go."

She was suddenly frantic. How could she have promised Robin Stone? What had gotten into her? She couldn't even blame it on the martini . . . she had just sipped it. She had no intention of going to his room!

"This is the last dinner I'll ever come to," Hudson said. "And you complain about Saturday night at the country club. At least I have a few laughs there. And we mingle with our own kind."

"It's part of my job," she said.

"Job?" he sneered. "Which reminds me—we're going to have to do something about that. Too many people are talking about it. Dad says some of his friends think it looks bad, you sitting across a mike interviewing all those types. That writer you talked with last week looked like a real Commie."

She didn't answer. Hudson talked this way every now and then and it passed. It was better to let him rant on. He drained the glass and deliberately refilled it.

"You really don't care about me, do you, Hudson?"

He poured himself another drink and sighed heavily. "Oh, it's not you. It's us. . . . Our families. . . . Sometimes I feel I've had it. . . . But don't worry, I won't leave you. Where can I go? Neither of us can have any real freedom until you get knocked up a few times. Christ, that's the least you could do."

She stood up. "Hudson, you make me feel sick."

"Come off it. I saw that mother of yours at the wedding, beaming. And your father, all handshakes and cigars. What were they so happy about? Hello, young lovers? Not on your life! It was the Stewart money. But you're not keeping your half of the bargain. You're supposed to have babies." He stared at her. "Maybe we should go home and try tonight."

"Maybe if you didn't drink so much," she said.

"Maybe I have to drink to get excited about you. I'm a man, I can't fake it." She walked out. He followed sullenly. At the checkroom they ran into Bud and Lucy. Lucy was pregnant again. She was also slightly drunk.

"We're going to the Embassy. Want to come?"

Hudson stared enviously at Lucy's stomach. "Sure, why not!" He grabbed Maggie by the arm and they all crowded into the elevator.

Bud's chauffeur was waiting. "Leave your cars," Lucy suggested. "We'll come back for them."

The Embassy was crowded. They sat in the smoke-filled room, squeezed around a tiny table. Some members from the country club were at the next table. They decided to put the two tables together. There were some jokes among the men, a bottle of Scotch was put on the table and Maggie sat hemmed in thinking of the man in Suite 17B.

She *had* to call him. She would tell him the truth, that she had accepted in a moment of crazy impulse, that she was married. It wasn't fair to make Robin Stone sit and wait. He worked too hard.

She stood up suddenly. "I have to powder my nose." There had to be a phone in the Ladies' Room.

"I'll go with you," Lucy said as she lumbered to her feet. "I'm dying to hear what Robin Stone said. I saw him lean over and speak to you several times. Coming, Edna?" she called to one of the girls.

The group headed for the Powder Room. There was an open phone. An attendant was sitting near it. It was hopeless. She patched up her makeup and was noncommittal about Robin Stone. They had talked about television, she explained. She tried to hang back, but Lucy and Edna waited. When they returned to their table there was no sign of Hudson. Then she saw him across the room—sitting at a table with a group of people, his arm around a girl. She recognized the girl, a new member of the club, a recent bride. Hudson's arm was gently massaging her bare back. Her husband sat across from her and did not see it. Suddenly Maggie stood up.

"Sit down," Lucy hissed. "Maggie, you know it means nothing. Hud always has to prove his charm with every new member."

"I'm going . . ."

Bud grabbed her arm. "Maggie, you've got nothing to be concerned about. That's June Tolland. She's mad for her husband."

She broke away and ran. She didn't stop running until she reached the street. Then she walked to the corner, hailed a cab and told the driver to go to the Bellevue Stratford Hotel.

She rang the bell of Suite 17B. It was a loud ring, an empty ring. She glanced at her watch. Twelve fifteen. Maybe he had left, or gone to sleep. She rang again, then she turned and started down the hall. Suddenly the door swung open. He was holding a glass. "Come on in, newsgirl, I'm on the phone."

She entered the living room of the suite. He motioned to the bottle of vodka and went to the phone. It was obvious he was talking business, something to do with clauses in a contract. She went through the motions of mixing herself a drink. He had taken off his jacket. His shirt clung to him and she saw the small initials, R.S., near his chest. His tie was loose and he talked earnestly and to the point. She noticed the bottle of vodka was half empty and once again she wondered at his capacity. He finally hung up. "Sorry to keep you waiting, but then, you didn't exactly break any track records getting here."

"Where do you go tomorrow?" She suddenly felt shy and nervous.

"New York. No more lectures ever again."

"Why do they call them lectures?" she asked. "I mean, tonight—you were wonderful, you talked about everything. Your adventures overseas, people—"

"I suppose it dates back to when some fink actually went out with slide pictures and—oh, who the hell cares." He put down his drink and held out his arms. "Come on, newsgirl, aren't you going to kiss me?"

She felt like a schoolgirl. "My name is Maggie Stewart," she said. Then she was in his arms.

He made love to her three times that night. He held her close and whispered endearments. He caressed her. He treated her like a virgin. And for the first time she realized what it was like when a man made love for the sole purpose of trying to make a woman happy. She reached a climax the very first time. And then it happened again. And the third time she fell back in gratified exhaustion. He held her close and kissed her gently. Then as he began to caress her again she pulled away.

He buried his face in her breasts. "It's been different tonight. I'm very drunk—tomorrow I may not remember any of this. . . . But I want you to know, this is different."

She lay very still. Somehow she knew he was telling the truth. She was afraid to move, afraid to break the spell. The cool crisp Robin Stone suddenly seemed so vulnerable. In the dim light she stared at his face against her breasts—she wanted to remember every second, she would always remember, especially the word he yelled each time at the climax.

He pulled away suddenly, kissed her, reached out and lit two cigarettes and handed one to her. "It's two thirty." He nodded toward the phone. "If you have to be up at any special time, leave a call. I've got nothing to do but catch a train to New York. What time do you have to be at work?"

"Eleven."

"How's nine thirty? I'll get up with you and we can have breakfast together."

"No, I—I have to leave now."

"*No!*" It was a command—but his eyes were almost pleading. "Don't leave me!" he said.

"I have to, Robin." She jumped out of bed and ran to the bathroom. She dressed quickly and when she returned to the bedroom he was lying back against the pillows. He seemed completely composed. He lit a cigarette, then looked at her oddly.

"Who are you running off to? Husband or lover?"

"Husband," she said, trying to meet his eyes. They were so amazingly blue and cold.

He inhaled deeply and blew the smoke to the ceiling. Then he said, "Did you risk anything coming here tonight?"

"Nothing, except my marriage."

"Newsgirl, come here." He held out his hand. She came to him and he looked at her as if trying to see into her brain. "I want you to know something. I didn't know you were married."

"Don't feel guilty," she said gently.

His laugh was odd. "Guilty, hell! I think it's funny. . . . So long, newsgirl."

"My name is Maggie Stewart."

"Baby, there's another name for girls like you." He leaned over and ground out the cigarette.

She stood at his bed for a moment. "Robin, tonight was different for me too, it meant something, it meant an awful lot. I want you to believe that."

Suddenly he threw his arms around her waist and buried his head in her dress. His voice was low and urgent. "Then don't leave me! You keep saying you love me, but you leave me!"

She had never said she loved him! She gently pried herself loose and looked at him in amazement. Their eyes met but he seemed to be looking somewhere far off as if he was in a self-induced trance. She decided the vodka had finally hit him. He couldn't know or mean what he was saying.

"Robin, I've got to leave you—but I'll never forget you."

He blinked and then stared as if seeing her for the first time. "I'm sleepy. Good night, newsgirl." Then he switched off the light, turned on his side and promptly fell asleep. She stood there unable to believe it. He was not faking. He *was* asleep.

She drove home with mixed feelings. The whole thing had been insane. He was two men and they never seemed to fuse except when he made love to her. Well, he had said it himself: tomorrow he would not even remember it, she would be just another girl on one of his whistle stops. But did he act this way with all girls? It didn't matter. The only thing that counted was tonight.

She let herself into the house quietly. It was four o'clock.

She crept into the bedroom. It was dark; in the shadows she saw Hudson's empty bed. Luck was with her. He hadn't gotten home yet. She undressed quickly. She had just turned off the lights when she heard the crunch of gravel in the garage path. She pretended sleep when he crept into the room. His cautiousness amused her. The way he lurched around the room, trying not to arouse her. Soon she heard him snoring in deep drunken sleep.

For the next two weeks she plunged into her work and pushed Robin Stone from her thoughts. She had almost succeeded until the day she opened her diary to check an appointment and saw "Curse due." She was four days late! And Hudson hadn't come near her in three weeks. Robin Stone! She had taken no precautions with him. Hudson had brainwashed her into actually thinking she couldn't get pregnant.

She buried her face in her hands. She didn't want to get rid of it! Robin's baby would be a baby conceived in love. . . . And Hudson wanted a baby. Oh, no! It was an outrageous thought! . . . But why not? What could be gained in telling Hudson the truth? It would hurt Hudson—and the baby. She stood up with sudden determination. She was going to have it!

When a week passed and her period did not come, she faced the real task of getting Hudson to make love to her. He had never stayed away this long. The model must be wearing him out, or perhaps he had found a new interest. When Hudson was in the flush of a new romance, he never came near her.

That night she snuggled against him in bed but he pushed her away.

She bit her lip in the darkness. "I want a baby, Hudson." She put her arms around him and tried to kiss him. He turned his head. "Okay, but cut the love crap, honey. We're playing for babies now—so let's fuck."

She went to the doctor when she had missed her second period. He called her the following day and congratulated her. She was six weeks pregnant. She decided to wait a few weeks before breaking the news to Hudson.

A few nights later they were having one of their rare evenings at home alone. He was quiet throughout dinner. But the surliness that had become part of his personality was not in evidence. He was calm, thoughtful. He was almost gentle when he suggested they go upstairs to the den and have an after-dinner drink. He sat on the couch and watched her as she poured the brandy. He took his glass, sipped it thoughtfully, then said, "Can you get away from your little television chores in about three months?"

"I could get a leave—but why?"

"I've told Dad you're pregnant."

She looked at him in amazement. Then she realized Dr. Blazer had probably told him. She had told the doctor she wanted to keep it a secret because of her work but he probably never thought she wanted to keep it from Hudson. This accounted for his new mood. Her smile was filled with relief. Her instinct had been right. A baby would change things.

"Hudson, there's no need to go away. I could work almost up to the date if the camera just gets head shots of me."

He looked at her curiously. "And how do we explain to Dad and to everyone your nice flat tummy?"

"But I'll—"

"We can't fake it. Everyone has to think it's the real thing. Even Bud and Lucy. One slipup, and Dad will find out. I've got it all worked out. We tell him we want a trip around the world as a pregnancy present. Because after the child is born, we won't feel free to leave it. Then we'll say it was premature and have it born in Paris."

"I don't understand, Hudson. I want my baby born here."

His old sneer returned. "Don't get carried away with the game. I merely *told* him you were pregnant. That doesn't make it so."

He got up and poured himself another glass of brandy. "I've made all the arrangements. We can get a baby in Paris. The doctor I talked to has a contact there. They even match the looks of both parents. There are three babies up for adoption that will be born in seven months. We just pay all the mother's hospitalization, first class. The mother turns the baby over immediately—she never even sees it or knows what sex it is, or who gets it. I've asked for a boy. Then we get a new birth certificate and it's made out as our baby. And the lucky little bastard not only nets us a million, but comes up with dual citizenship if he wants it. Then we return to America in triumph."

She laughed with relief. She got up from the couch and

walked over to him. "Hudson, now it's my turn for a surprise. All these elaborate plans—you don't need them."

"What do you mean?"

"I really am pregnant."

"Say that again," he snapped.

"I'm *pregnant*." She didn't like the way he was staring at her.

His hand lashed across her face. "Bitch! Whose is it?"

"It's mine, ours—" She felt her lip begin to swell, and the taste of blood in her mouth. He came closer and grabbed her shoulders and shook her. "Tell me, you whore—whose bastard are you trying to pass off on me?" His hand whipped across her face again. "Tell me, or I'll beat it out of you!"

She broke from him and ran out of the room. He dashed after her and caught her in the hall. "Tell me! Whose bastard are you carrying?"

"What difference does it make to you?" she sobbed. "You were willing to take someone else's in Paris; at least this is mine."

The anger suddenly drained from his face. A slow smile came to his lips. He pushed her back into the den. "You're right. You're absolutely right. You bet I'll let you have it. In fact you're going to have one every year, for the next ten years. Then if you're a good girl, I'll give you a divorce with a nice fat alimony."

"No." She sat on the couch and looked at him with a calm she didn't feel. "It's not going to work. I won't raise my baby in an atmosphere of hate between us. I want a divorce now."

"I won't give you a dime."

"You don't have to," she said wearily. "I'll live with my family. I'll make enough on television to provide for the baby."

"Not when I get through with you."

"What do you mean?"

"That baby means a million bucks to me. Either you have it, and give it to me, or you'll never work again. I'll smear you through every newspaper. You'll be through on TV and your family won't be able to face anyone in this town."

She put her head in her hands. "Oh, Hudson, why?

Why did it have to be like this? I made a mistake—one night, one man. It never happened before. It will never happen again. I wanted it to work with us. But you've made me so miserable, I didn't even feel like a woman with you. Perhaps what I did was wrong. I'm not going to bring up the things I know about you." Her voice broke. "I thought we still had a chance. I guess I was crazy, but I thought it would make you happy having a baby. I thought it might bring us together. And that once the strain was off you, we'd have more babies—babies of our own—"

"You idiot! Can't I get it through to you? I'm sterile!" he yelled. "I took tests last week—I'm sterile, I can never make babies!"

"But what about those abortions you paid for?"

"How do you know?"

"I know."

He pulled her off the couch. "So you had detectives on me!" He slapped her face. "Well, I was taken! All those broads I paid off who said I knocked them up—they took me! Like you just tried to do. But now I know: I'm sterile."

She pulled away from him. Her tears streaked her face and she knew her lip was cut. But she felt sorry for him. She started to leave the room. He grabbed her roughly. "Where are you going?"

"To pack," she said quietly. "I can't stay in this house with you."

"Why?" he said nastily. "You stayed all along when you knew what I was up to—we're even now. Two of a kind. It might even work better this way. We'll each go our own way—as long as my father never hears about it."

"I don't want to live like that."

"Then how do you account for the little bastard in your belly?"

"I knew about you . . . and all your girls. Then I met someone. I don't know how it happened. I guess I needed someone who cared—even if it was just one night. To know he cared for me . . . was aware that I existed . . . even if it was just for a few hours."

He slapped her again. "This is what you need?" His hand shot across her face again. Her head rocked back in pain. Then with one quick dart she broke from him and ran out of the room. He ran after her. "I'll beat the hell out of you—is that what you were looking for? I used to beat Sherry with a strap, she liked it." He began to unstrap his belt.

She screamed and hoped the servants would hear. She ran down the hall. His belt was in his hand—the alligator belt she had given him for Christmas. He lashed out at her. It caught her in the neck. She saw the hate and perversion on his face and knew real terror. She backed away from him and screamed. Where were the servants? He was insane! The belt hit her face, just missing her eye. He could blind her! She backed away in panic and felt herself falling backwards down the stairs. She hoped in that split second she might break her neck and die instantly and never have to see his face again. And then she was lying there at the bottom of the stairs. Hudson was staring at her legs. She felt the first clutch of pain. She clung to her stomach. She felt the blood running down her legs. Then she felt the slap of his hand across her face. "You dirty bitch—you've just leaked away a million dollars."

It was suddenly cold on the terrace. She walked into the living room and poured herself a Scotch. It all seemed to have happened in another world, yet it was barely two years ago. She dimly recalled the jangling of the ambulance, the week in the hospital, the way no one had questioned the lacerations on her face and neck, the polite way the doctor pretended to believe it was a result of the accidental fall—and the fight everyone put up about her decision for an immediate divorce. Everyone but Hudson. Her mother thought she was having a nervous breakdown. Losing a baby often did that. Even Lucy had pleaded with her to reconsider.

She had decided on Florida for the divorce. It would take three months, and she wanted the sun and time to rest, time to heal the hurt she felt—help her plan a new start. She took a leave of absence from the station.

Although Hudson's attorneys had agreed to pay all the divorce costs, including her stay in Florida, she took a small apartment, and lived frugally. After two months, she felt no hurt—just emptiness: Hudson no longer existed; but she was young and her strength returned, and soon the idleness began to pall.

She applied at the local TV station. Andy Parino had put her on immediately. She liked Andy. She wanted to care. To care meant you were alive. They drifted into an easy comfortable love affair. Andy made her feel good—made her enjoy being a woman. But Hudson had killed or destroyed some part of her. The part that made her really care.

After a few months, she felt secure. Andy cared for her and she liked her job. It was time to throw off this self-induced lethargy. Time to *feel*—to dream and hope—and she had tried, but nothing happened. It was as if Hudson had paralyzed all her emotions. When Andy asked her to marry him, she refused.

And now tonight, for the first time, she had felt the stirring of life. She was going to see Robin Stone again. She couldn't wait to see the expression in his eyes when they met. . . .

# NINETEEN

MAGGIE SAT at the Gold Coast bar and wondered if she looked as nervous as she felt. Andy had spent the day on the golf course with Robin. Robin had told him to assign his seven o'clock news to a staff announcer for the next few days. She looked at her watch—they should be here any second. She lit a cigarette and suddenly realized she had a fresh one going in the ashtray. She hastily stubbed it out. She felt like a schoolgirl—a schoolgirl waiting to come face to face with her first love. But she was nervous. Any second Andy would walk in with Robin Stone, and they would meet. She stubbed out the second cigarette.

She caught sight of herself in the mirror across the bar. The even tan of her skin blended into the beige silk dress. Her skin had been so white in Philadelphia. When Robin

had let his hands run over her breasts, he had said,
"White, white, mother-white skin." But the tan was more
flattering. She knew she was beautiful. She had always
known it. But she regarded it as merely a statistic: one
was either tall or short, homely or beautiful. Until now,
her beauty had not given her any pleasure. If anything, it
had caused disaster. But tonight she was suddenly glad
she was beautiful. She had dressed carefully—the dress
matching the tone of her skin seemed to emphasize the
green of her eyes. Cat's eyes. Andy called her his black
panther. Tonight she felt like a panther—taut, crouched,
ready to spring!

It had been her idea to meet here. She didn't want a
jumbled meeting in the dark of a car. She wanted them
both to walk in. She wanted to see Robin's look of surprise. . . . This time she would have command of the
situation.

She was just finishing her drink when she saw Andy
come through the door—alone. She kept her face impassive as he joined her at the bar and ordered a Scotch. She
was damned if she'd ask. But where *was* he!

"Sorry I'm late, Maggie," Andy said.

"That's all right." Finally she couldn't stand it.
"Where's your friend?"

"The big TV star?" Andy took a long swallow of his
drink.

"Isn't he coming?" She wanted to kill Andy for making
her draw it out of him.

"Maybe. You should see the commotion he caused at
the Diplomat—you'd think he was Cary Grant. Seems
like everyone watches that show of his, at least everyone
we ran into on the golf course."

Maggie lit another cigarette. She had never allowed
herself to watch Robin's show. That had been a part of
the cure. Like not thinking about Hudson or the past. Of
course he was famous now. That had never occurred to
her before.

"On every hole he had to stop and sign an autograph,"
Andy was saying. (She could still recall how he had tried
to hide his annoyance at the Bellevue when he was
forced to sign those menus.)

"It was a big bore," Andy went on, "until the little blonde caught up with him on the seventeenth hole."

She snapped to attention. "Who?"

Andy shrugged. "A guest at the hotel. She couldn't have been more than nineteen or twenty. She left her own foursome to get Robin's autograph and never rejoined them. She walked the rest of the way with us, right down to the eighteenth hole." Andy laughed. "Betty Lou, yeah, that's her name." He raised his glass. "Here's to Betty Lou—she earned me twenty bucks." He took a long swallow of his drink and went on.

"She came on so strong for Robin that she made him forget the game. When he sees a good-looking broad it's like a radar beam, and dear little Betty Lou laid it right on the line. Robin dug her. He also dug a big divot, landed in a trap and wound up taking a seven on the hole. Until then he had been only four over par. That's how I won my twenty bucks. Let's go inside, I'm starving."

They were about to order when Andy was called to the phone. He returned with a grin. "The great lover is on his way."

It was almost nine o'clock when Maggie saw Robin stride into the restaurant. He looked clean and fresh. Then she saw the little blond girl. Maggie knew instantly that she had been to bed with Robin. Her hair had lost its shape and her makeup looked patched.

Andy stood up. "Hi, Betty Lou." He hugged her like a lifelong buddy. Then he turned. "This is Maggie Stewart. Maggie, Robin Stone."

He looked at her with an easy smile. "Andy tells me you also play golf. You'll have to come with us one afternoon."

"I have a twenty-five handicap," she said. "I'm afraid I'm not in your league."

"Oh, that's the same as me," Betty Lou pealed. "We can have a real foursome."

Robin ordered two vodka martinis. Betty Lou acted as if she not only owned Robin Stone but had known him all her life. Robin was casually attentive. He lit her cigarette, ignored her in conversation, yet intuitively let her know that he was glad she was with him. Maggie saw him reach for the girl's hand and occasionally flash her a grin, but his entire conversation was directed to Andy.

Suddenly Maggie wondered if Betty Lou had been an intentional ruse on Robin's part, to make the "confrontation" easier. Andy must have told him about their relationship.

In an effort to go along with Robin, Betty Lou joined him in a second martini. The first one had left its mark. The second was lethal. By the end of dinner, she was leaning on her elbow, her hair falling into the spaghetti. She looked at everyone with glazed eyes. Robin suddenly noticed her condition. "Too much sun and golf, sometimes that's a bad combination with alcohol."

Maggie liked his defense of the girl he had just met. They all helped her out of the restaurant and piled her into Robin's car. After they dropped Betty Lou off, Robin insisted they go to the Diplomat for a nightcap.

They sat at a small table. Robin toasted Andy. "To you, chum—thanks for the first vacation I've had in years. And to your lovely lady." He looked at Maggie. Their eyes met. Her stare was challenging but his blue eyes returned an innocent gaze. Then he said, "I've been hearing nothing but raves about you. You're every bit as lovely as Andy said. And your report on the UFOs fascinates me. I read it today. Where'd you get the information, and how do you know so much about the subject?"

"I've always been fascinated with it," she answered.

"Let's all meet at your office tomorrow at eleven, Andy. You and Miss—" He stopped and looked at Maggie. He seemed to draw a blank.

"Maggie," Andy said quietly. "Maggie Stewart."

Robin smiled. "I'm awful with names. Well, let's all meet and kick this thing around. See if there's a network show in it."

They finished their drink and said good night in the lobby. Maggie watched Robin stride to the elevator.

She was silent as they drove away. In the darkness of the car Andy said, "Look, don't be hurt because Robin forgot your name. That's the way he is. Unless he's banging a girl, he doesn't know she's alive."

"Take me home, Andy."

He drove silently down the drive. "Headache again?" His voice was cold.

"I'm tired."

He was sullen as he stopped in front of her apartment. She didn't even try to appease him. She jumped out of the car and ran into the building. She didn't wait for the elevator, just ran up the two flights of stairs to her apartment. Once inside, she slammed the door and leaned against it. Tears ran down her face. Then her sobs came in dry choking gasps. Not only didn't he remember her name—he didn't remember that they had ever met before!

Maggie made an effort to study the script. She hadn't looked at it since Robin's arrival. Of course the first performance at the Players' Club was still three weeks off— but she wanted to be good. After all, this was Eugene O'Neill, and Hy Mandel was coming from California to see her. Probably nothing would come of it. The director of an independent film company had seen her on television and asked her if she was interested in a screen test. She said she was interested in becoming an actress—but no screen test. She couldn't take time from her television show to fly to California. Perhaps it had been her lack of interest that had caused him to pursue it. He had called Hy Mandel, a top Hollywood agent, and put in a rave about her. And now he was actually coming to see her perform in a semiprofessional group.

Well, after tonight she'd have plenty of time to concentrate on O'Neill.

This was Robin Stone's final night in town. He hadn't seen Betty Lou again. The second night he had come up with a swimming teacher named Anna. Then there was a divorcée named Beatrice. Then he had chartered a boat for three days and gone off alone to fish. He had returned this afternoon and Andy told her they'd have dinner together. She wondered who'd be his date—Betty Lou? Anna? Or the divorcée?

Andy called just as she was finishing her makeup. He was in high spirits. "I've just had a long talk with Robin. Guess what! He doesn't want to do the saucer thing as an *In Depth*. He wants to make it a special on its own—and he wants us to work on it. That'll mean a trip to New York and all expenses paid!"

"I hope it doesn't happen while I'm doing the O'Neill play."

"Maggie, twenty-six is a little old for a girl to tackle Hollywood. You belong right here—with me."

"Andy, I—" She had to tell him it was all over between them. That there never had really been anything.

But he cut in. "Listen, Maggie, don't say anything to Robin about Amanda."

"Amanda?"

"The girl whose picture I showed you in the newspaper the day before yesterday."

"Oh, the one who died of leukemia?"

"Yes. She was a friend of Robin's. He was on the boat when it happened and probably doesn't know about it. There's nothing he can do: the funeral was today, so why ruin his vacation?"

"But she was married to Ike Ryan," Maggie said.

"Yes, but she and Robin were a big deal for a long time. He went with her for almost two years."

Maggie thought about it as she finished her makeup. Two years—that meant Amanda had been his girl the night they had been together at the Bellevue. Her eyes narrowed as she stared at herself in the mirror. "All right, you fool. You're acting like a twenty-six-year-old virgin! Did you secretly nurture the idea that you had really been something special to Robin Stone?"

She parked her car at the Diplomat. She was aware that several men turned to stare as she walked through the lobby. Had they been staring like this all along? Had she been living in such a vacuum that she had never noticed? Suddenly she felt a current of excitement as she walked into the bar. Robin stood up and smiled. "Andy will be right back. He's being a cruise director. I'm booked out on the noon flight tomorrow but he's trying to switch me to a later plane so we can get in one last round of golf." He signaled the waiter. "What's it going to be? The usual Scotch?"

She nodded. "And who is your date tonight? The usual divorcée?" The strange inner excitement gave her voice just the right tone of flippancy.

He grinned. "You're my date tonight. You and Andy. I just want to drink and relax with two good friends. Maybe even get smashed."

Andy's smile was victorious when he returned to the table. "You're all set. Six o'clock tomorrow. Personally, I think you're crazy going back. Ellie, my connection with National, says it's fifteen degrees in New York. And Santa Claus is coming to town. All that slush and those Santas standing in front of department stores with tinny little bells, and no taxis—" He shook his head and shuddered.

Robin stared at his empty glass and signaled for another drink. "I'd like to stay, but I have a very special date Christmas night in Los Angeles."

Robin had four martinis. Maggie toyed with her second Scotch and once again marveled at his capacity. But he had appeared perfectly sober that night in Philadelphia when he admitted he was very drunk. Drunk enough not even to remember her! They went to the Fontainebleau and caught Sammy Davis. She had a steak. Robin ignored food, and methodically drank vodka. Andy tried to keep up with him.

They wound up at a bar on the Seventy-ninth Street Causeway. The place was heavy with smoke. Robin had a bottle of vodka placed at the table. Maggie stuck to Scotch. It was too noisy to attempt conversation. Robin drank silently and Andy sloshed at his drink.

At one in the morning Andy passed out. Maggie and Robin struggled to help him into the car.

Robin said, "We'll dump him at his place, then I'll drop you."

"But my car's at the Diplomat," she said.

"No sweat, take a cab there tomorrow. Put it on expenses—tell Andy he okayed it before he passed out." She directed him to Andy's building. Robin tried to lift Andy out of the car. "He's a dead weight," he groaned. "Come on, Maggie, I need some help." Between them they half carried, half dragged Andy to his apartment. Robin dropped him on the bed and loosened his tie. Maggie stared at him with concern. She had never seen anyone pass out from drinking. Robin's smile was reassuring. "Not even one of your flying saucers could wake him now. He'll feel horrible in the morning—but he'll live."

They returned to the car. "I'm just a few blocks away, that long low building down there," she said.

"How about going somewhere for a nightcap first?"

She directed him to a small bar nearby. The owner recognized Robin, placed the bottle of vodka on the bar and immediately launched into a discussion on professional football. Maggie sat with a watery Scotch and listened. It was incredible—Robin seemed absolutely sober.

They closed the bar and he drove her to her apartment. For a moment they sat in the darkened car.

"Do you have any vodka up there?" he asked.

"No, just Scotch."

"Too bad. Good night, Maggie, it's been great."

"Good night, Robin." She turned toward the door, then impulsively turned back and kissed him. Then she dashed out of the car and rushed to her apartment.

She felt exhilarated. If a man wanted to kiss a girl, he just upped and did it. This time, she had taken the initiative. She felt as if she had struck out for female emancipation. She had broken one of the ironclad rules. From now on she was going to break a lot of rules. She sang as she undressed. She started to put on her nightgown, then tossed it aside. From now on she would sleep in the nude. She always wanted to, but it hadn't seemed proper. She went to the bureau drawer and took out all the filmy nightgowns and put them in a shopping bag. Tomorrow the maid would have a bonanza. She slid into bed and turned off the lights. The cold sheets felt wonderful—she felt a sense of freedom she had never known. She wasn't sleepy but she shut her eyes. . . .

Someone was banging on her door. She switched on the light and looked at the clock. Only four thirty. She must have just fallen asleep. The banging became more insistent. She threw on her robe and opened the door, leaving the safety chain intact. Robin Stone was standing there, brandishing a bottle of vodka.

"I've brought my own nightcap!" he said.

She let him in.

"It was in my room, gift of the management. But I didn't feel like drinking alone."

"Do you want some ice?"

"No, I'll drink it neat."

She handed him a glass and sat on the couch and watched him drink. Suddenly he turned to her. "I'm smashed."

She smiled slightly. A pulse began to beat in her throat.

"Want me, baby?" he asked.

She got up from the couch and walked across the room. "I want you," she said slowly. "But not tonight."

"It's got to be tonight—I'm leaving tomorrow."

"Put it off a day."

"What will make tomorrow any different than today?"

"I want you to remember me!"

"Be good, baby, then I'll never forget you."

She turned and faced him. "Sorry, but I've already auditioned."

His eyes were mildly curious. Suddenly he was at her side, and with a swift movement opened her robe. She grabbed at it, but he wrenched it off. He stood back, staring at her speculatively. She fought her embarrassment and met his gaze defiantly.

"Big beautiful tits," he said. "I hate big tits." With another quick unexpected move, he lifted her in his arms, carried her into the bedroom and flung her on the bed. "I hate brunettes, too." He took off his coat and loosened his tie. She was frightened suddenly. There was an odd expression in his eyes—as if he was looking at her without seeing her. She jumped up, but he pushed her down. "You're not leaving me. I'm a big boy now." He sounded strange, as if he was talking to himself. His eyes had the stare of a sightless man.

She watched him undress. She could make a dash for it, call for help—but she felt frozen with curiosity. Perhaps this was the way a victim of a murderer felt. Paralyzed—unable to resist. He stripped off his clothes and came to her. He sat on the bed and stared at her with strange expressionless eyes, and when he leaned over and kissed her gently, her fear evaporated and she responded eagerly. He stretched out beside her, their bodies close. She felt him sigh—his body relaxed. His mouth searched for her breasts. She clung to him—every resolve disappeared. She was fused with excitement and emotion, and when he took her, she reached a climax with him. And as he clung to her he shouted the same three words he had shouted in Philadelphia: *"Mutter!* Mother! *Mother!"*

Then he fell off her. In the darkness she saw the same glazed look in his eyes. He caressed her cheek and smiled slightly. "I'm smashed, baby—but this was different, this is not like the others."

"You said that to me once before in Philadelphia."

"Did I?" He showed no reaction.

She snuggled against him. "Robin, has it been different with many girls?"

"No . . . yes . . . I don't know." He sounded drowsy. "Just don't leave me." He held her close. "Promise me that—never leave me."

She clung to him in the darkness. All right, she told herself. This is your chance. Throw him out of bed. Say "Goodbye, newsman." But she couldn't.

"I'll never leave you, Robin, I swear."

He was half asleep. "You're just saying that."

"No, I've never said that to anyone in my life. I promise. I love you."

"No, you'll leave me . . . to go . . ."

"To go where?" She had to know.

But he was asleep.

She saw the sky lighten and she lay there wide-awake. She stared at his handsome head. His cheek was warm against her breast. It didn't seem possible. He was *here* —sleeping in her arms. He belonged to her! She was glad she had told him about Philadelphia. He had asked her not to leave him then. And she had—perhaps he had been really hurt. That would explain tonight: in his drunken state he thought she was still married—of course! She felt she would explode with happiness.

She lay there half dozing, waking every few minutes to stare at the man in her arms to reassure herself that it had really happened. She saw the streaks of dawn—and marveled at the suddenness with which the sun claimed the sky, the sea gulls calling to one another, announcing a new day. It *was* a new day, a wonderful day! The sun filtered into the room; soon it would reach the man in her arms. She had forgotten to draw the drapes last night.

She eased herself out of bed and tiptoed across the room. Soon the cool darkness covered the room. It was nine o'clock. She slipped into the bathroom. She wanted him to sleep off all the vodka. She wanted him to feel good when he awoke. She caught a glimpse of herself in the mirror. Good Lord—she must have been in a daze last night, she had never bothered to remove her makeup. She was glad she had wakened first. Her lipstick and mascara were smeared. She creamed her face, took a shower and put on light makeup. She pulled her hair back into a ponytail and put on a blouse and slacks and went into the kitchen. Did he like eggs? Bacon? Maybe the smell of it would make him ill after all that vodka. She put the coffee on and opened a jar of tomato juice. That was supposed to be good for a hangover. She left the frying pan out—if he wanted eggs she'd make them. God, she'd do anything for him.

It was almost noon when she heard him stir. She poured some tomato juice into a glass and brought it to him in the bedroom. He groped for it in the darkness. She watched him as he drained the glass. Then she drew the drapes. The sunlight flooded the room. He blinked several times and looked around the room.

"Good God. Maggie!" He looked at the bed, then back at her. "How did I get here?"

"You arrived on your own at four thirty in the morning."

Like a somnambulist he handed back the empty glass. "Did we—yes, I guess we did." He stared at the bed. Then he shook his head. "Sometimes when I get very drunk, I draw blanks. I'm sorry, Maggie." Suddenly his eyes went dark with anger. "Why did you let me in?"

She fought the panic that was choking her.

"Oh God!" He ran his hand through his hair. "I can't remember. I can't remember."

She felt the tears roll down her face, but her anger kept her from breaking down. "That's the oldest line in the world, Robin. But you can use it, if it makes you feel better! The shower is in there."

She stalked into the living room and poured herself some coffee. Some of her anger dissolved. The bewilderment in his eyes *had* been real. Suddenly she knew he was telling the truth. He didn't remember.

He walked into the living room, knotting his tie. His coat was on his arm. He dropped it on the couch and took the cup of coffee she handed him.

"If you want eggs, or toast—" she said.

He shook his head. "I'm sorry as hell about all this, Maggie. Sorry for what I did to Andy. And most of all sorry because of you. Look—I'm leaving. You don't have to tell Andy. I'll make it up to him—I'll find a way."

"What about me?"

He looked at her. "You knew what you were doing. Andy didn't. He's your guy."

"I'm not in love with Andy."

He grinned. "And I suppose you're madly in love with me."

"Yes, I am."

He laughed, almost as if it was a private joke. "I must be a whiz when I'm smashed."

"You mean this has happened often."

"Not often. But it *has* happened before, maybe two or three times. And each time, it scares the hell out of me. But this is the first time I've ever been confronted with the evidence. Usually I wake up and know something has happened, something I can't quite remember. It's usually after I've really been on a bender. But last night I thought I was safe, that I could tie on a load—there was just you and Andy. What the hell happened to him?"

"He passed out."

"Yes, I remember that. I think that's the last thing I do remember."

"You don't remember any of the things you said to me?"

His blue eyes were candid. "Was I awful?"

Tears came to her eyes. "No, you were nicer than anyone I've ever known."

He put down the coffee and stood up. "Maggie, I'm sorry. Really sorry."

She looked at him. "Robin, do I mean anything to you?"

"I like you. So I'm going to give it to you straight. You're a bright beautiful girl, but you're not my type."

"I'm not your—" She couldn't get it out.

"Maggie, I don't know what motivated me to come here. I don't know what I said, or what I did. . . . And, oh Jesus, I'm sorry I've hurt you." Then he came to her. He touched her hair softly but she pulled away. "Look, Maggie, you and Andy pretend this never happened."

"Please go! I told you—it's over with Andy. It was over before last night."

"It will be rough on him. He cares about you."

"I'm not right for him. I don't want him. Please, get out."

"I'm going to transfer him to New York," he said suddenly. "There's not enough news coming out of here anyway. What about you—do you want to work in New York?"

"Oh for heaven's sake, stop playing God!"

He looked into her eyes. "Maggie, I wish I could buy back last night. This hasn't happened to me in a long time. The last time was in Philadelphia."

She stared at him. "You remember that?"

He shook his head. "She was gone when I woke up. I just remember she wore orange lipstick."

"I wear orange lipstick."

His eyes widened with disbelief.

She nodded mutely. "It's insane. I was doing the news there."

"Jesus—are you following me?"

She felt outraged with anger and humiliation. Before she realized it her hand lashed out across his face.

His smile was sad. "I guess I deserved that. . . . You must really hate me, Maggie—all these days we've been together and I never remembered."

"I don't hate you," she said coldly. "I hate myself. I hate all women who act like sentimental idiots or lose control. I'm sorry I hit you. You're not worth it."

"Don't try to be hard, it's not your natural behavior."

"How do you know what my natural behavior is? How can you know anything about me! You've made love to me twice and don't remember. Who are you to tell anyone what I am? Who are *you? What* are you?"

"I don't know, I really don't know." Then he turned and left the apartment.

# TWENTY

WHEN ROBIN LEFT Maggie's apartment he checked out of the hotel and went directly to the airport.
New York was clear and mild. The temperature was in the low forties. Idlewild Airport was crammed with good-humored holiday travelers. Robin hailed a cab and reached his apartment just before the heavy traffic jam began. He promised himself to go on the wagon until Christmas Eve in Los Angeles.

There was no important mail. The apartment was neat. He felt oddly depressed. He opened a can of tomato juice and placed a call to Ike Ryan. Amanda was probably out of the hospital by now.

"Where the hell have you been? *Now* you call!" Ike's voice was flat and oddly indifferent.

"How are things?" Robin asked cheerfully.

"'Just call me if you need me, Ike!'" Ike mimicked. "Oh, brother . . . did I call! I called you for two days!"

"I was on a boat. Why didn't you leave a message?"

Ike sighed. "What good would it have done? You blew the funeral."

Robin hoped he hadn't heard correctly. "What funeral?"

"It was in all the papers. Don't tell me you didn't know."

"Ike—for Christ's sake. I just came back to New York. What happened?"

Ike's voice was leaden. "Amanda was buried day before yesterday."

"But just a week ago you said she was coming along fine."

"That's what we thought. The day she died . . . even that morning she looked great. I arrived at the hospital around eleven. She was sitting in bed—all made up—in a beautiful dressing gown, addressing Christmas cards. The drug was working. I expected to take her home in a few days. Suddenly she dropped the pen and her eyes went blank. I ran to the door and yelled for nurses, doctors. Within seconds the room was filled with people. The doctor gave her an injection, and then she fell back asleep. I sat there for three hours before she opened her eyes. She saw me and smiled faintly. I held her in my arms and told her everything was gonna be fine. Then she looked at me, clear-eyed again, and said, 'Ike, I know, I know!'" Ike paused.

"Know what, Ike?" Robin asked.

"Oh Christ, who knows? I think she was telling me she knew that she was dying. I rang for the nurse. She came with the needle but Amanda pushed her away. She clung to me, like she knew there wasn't much time. She looked at me and said, 'Robin, take care of Slugger—please, Robin.' Then she lost consciousness. The nurse said to me, 'She didn't know what she was saying, she was talking in the past.'

"She woke again about an hour later with that sweet smile on her face. She reached for my hand. God, Robin, those eyes were so scared and big. She said, 'Ike, I love you. I love *you*.' Then she closed her eyes and never regained consciousness. She died an hour later."

"Ike, her last words were for you. That should give you some comfort."

"If she had said, 'Ike, I love you,' period, then it would have been fine. But she didn't. She said, 'I love you, I love *you*.' As if she had to try and convince me it was me she loved and not you. That was part of the sweetness and gallantry of Amanda. She knew it was the end, and she wanted to leave me with something positive to cling to."

"Ike—don't brood on it. She didn't know what she was saying."

"Yeah. Say, is it all right with you if I keep the cat?"

"The cat?"

"Well, by right it's yours. Because, conscious or not, she said for you to take care of Slugger. And I'd respect her wishes right down to the end. But I want the cat—it's like having a part of her."

"Oh, for God's sake," Robin said. "Of course the cat belongs to you."

"I've been sleeping with it every night," Ike said. "The cat senses something is wrong. We're both lost souls."

"Ike, give the cat a saucer of milk and sleep with a blonde."

"With my luck, I'm doing a war picture. Not a broad in it. Just twenty guys who all look like John Wayne. But what the hell—I guess I'll be okay. Merry Christmas, Robin."

"Sure. Same to you, Ike."

He hung up and sank back in the chair. Amanda was dead . . . it didn't seem possible. She couldn't have cared about him. Ike was just off balance with his misery. Poor guy, what a lousy Christmas he would have. The thought of Christmas wasn't exactly a cheerful idea to him either. Suddenly he had an urgent desire to spend Christmas with someone he cared about. Who was there? His mother? His sister? Well, Kitty was in Rome, and Lisa— God, he hadn't seen her in ages. He didn't even know what her kids looked like. He put in a call to San Francisco.

Lisa sounded genuinely surprised. "Robin! I can't believe it. *You* calling me. I know—you're getting married."

"Lisa dear, it's a week before Christmas—and odd as it may seem, I do occasionally think of my family. Especially around this time of the year. How are the kids? And good old Crew Cut?"

"Still crew-cut and still the most wonderful man in the world. Robin, I should be angry at you—all the times you've been to Los Angeles and never called. We're only an hour away by plane. Kate and Dickie would love to see you. You've just caught us. We leave in an hour for Palm Springs. We've become tennis nuts. Going to spend the holidays there with Dick's family. When are we going to see you?"

"Next time I'm in L.A., I promise." He paused. "How's the glorious Kitty?"

She didn't answer immediately. Then she said, "Robin, why do you always call her that?"

"I don't know. Maybe after the old man died."

"You mean my father."

"Come on, Lisa: how's Kitty?"

"Why *do* you call her Kitty?"

He laughed. "Okay, what is Mummy up to these days? Is that better?"

"She was a good mother to you, Robin."

"She sure was, and I'm glad that she's having a ball. How is she?"

"Not well. She has what they call walking coronaries—mild little heart attacks. She was hospitalized for a month. She's all right but the doctor warned her not to overdo things. She carries nitroglycerin tablets. And she moved into a big house in Rome. Of course there's someone else on the scene now—this one is twenty-two. I think he's a fag. She says he cooks for her, waits on her hand and foot and adores her. She gives him an allowance. Can you stand it?"

"I think it's great," Robin said. "What do you want her to do, have an arthritic old man creaking around? I'm like Kitty, I also like them young and attractive."

"Don't you ever want children and a home of your own?"

"Hell, no—and I'll tell you something. I don't think the glorious Kitty did either. I think she had us because it was the thing to do."

"Don't say that!" she said hotly.

"Oh come off it, Lisa. We always had a nurse, at least you did. I can still remember how frightened Kitty was when she had to hold you. And I can't remember her ever holding me when I was a baby. I think we were just part of the scheme—a boy and a girl to go with the house."

"She loved kids," Lisa snapped. "She wanted children so much, she had almost given up when I arrived."

"Shows you how much I mattered," he said lightly.

"No. It was different. After all, we are seven years apart. She wanted a house full of kids. She almost died having me, and she had three miscarriages after me."

"How come I never knew any of this?"

"I never knew about it either. But a year after Dad died, she came to visit us for a short time. I was three months pregnant with Kate. And she said, 'Don't just have one, Lisa—or even two. Have a house full of children. I have so much money to leave to you and Robin. You both can afford many children. And life means nothing without them.' That's when she told me a lot of things. I wanted her to live with us but she was dead set against it. She said I had my own husband and life—and it was up to her to make her own. She was determined to live in Europe."

"I guess girls are closer to their mothers," he said quietly.

"I don't know, but I do know children are important. Mother knew that. I wish you felt the same way."

"Well—happy Palm Springs and Merry Christmas."

"Same to you. I guess you'll wind up surrounded by blondes. But have a nice holiday, Robin." She clicked the receiver.

He rubbed his head thoughtfully. The holiday season stretched ahead. The idea of the saucer special was beginning to take form in his mind, but he knew nothing could be accomplished until after the first of the year. Meanwhile there was Christmas to get through. He could go to Los Angeles and try to help Ike out of the doldrums, but the idea of sitting and rehashing Ike's frustration over Amanda was depressing.

He called a model he had dated. She had gone to West Virginia for the holidays. He tried an airline hostess. Her plane was two hours late, but her roommate was available. He arranged to meet her at the Lancer Bar. She was a nice-looking clean-cut kid. They had a few drinks together. He stuck to beer. He bought her a steak. She was ready to go home with him, but he dropped her back at her own apartment. He took a long walk, then he watched *The Late Show* and fell asleep. He awoke at four in the morning. He was damp with sweat and although he couldn't remember, he was aware that he had had a nightmare. He lit a cigarette. Four in the morning; that meant it was ten o'clock in Rome. The more he thought about it, the more sense it made. He placed a call. The voice that answered was masculine and spoke in stilted English.

"Mrs. Stone, please," Robin said.

"Please, she is still asleep. May I take the message?"

"Who is this?"

"May I in turn ask the same question?"

"I'm her son. Robin Stone. Now who the hell are you?"

"Oh." The voice took on a tone of warmth. "I have heard much about you. I am Sergio, an excellent friend of Mrs. Stone's."

"Well, look, excellent friend, I'm going to grab the first flight I can get for Rome. I want to spend Christmas with my mother. How is she feeling?"

"She is quite well, but she will feel even better when she hears this news."

Robin kept his voice cold. If this was a sample of the charm these gigolo types dished out, no wonder so many women were taken in. This one was getting to him right through the phone. "Look, excellent friend, you can save me a cable if you reserve a room for me at the Excelsior."

"I do not understand—"

"The Excelsior. It's a big hotel on the Via Veneto."

"I know the hotel well, but why should you stay there? Your mother has a very large *palazzo*, ten bedrooms. She would be most hurt if you did not stay with her."

"Ten bedrooms!"

"It is a nice villa. Very restful for her."

I'll bet, Robin thought; plenty of freedom for little Sergio to have his boyfriends as house guests. But he remained silent.

Sergio said, "If you will wire the time of your flight, I will meet you."

"That's not necessary."

"But it will be a pleasure."

"Okay, chum, you really earn your keep, don't you?"

"I am looking forward to our meeting."

The plane landed at eleven at night, Rome time. Robin was suddenly grateful for the time difference. He could greet Kitty and go directly to sleep. In a way he wished he could stay at a hotel. The role of house guest wasn't to his liking, even if it was his own mother's home. After all, a *palazzo* in Rome with Sergio was a far cry from the rambling brownstone he and Lisa had shared with Kitty in Boston. And he was sure Sergio in no way resembled his father.

He saw the handsome young man in the skinny pants the moment he got off the plane. As Robin came through the gates, he rushed to him and tried to take his hand luggage.

Robin waved him off. "I'm not decrepit, junior."

"My name is Sergio. May I call you Robin?"

"Why not?" They walked toward the baggage area. The boy was exceptionally handsome, better-looking than any movie star. Definitely light on his feet but he didn't swish. And he had more than just the looks and accent going for him. His manner was right—eager and enthusiastic, yet not subservient. The son of a bitch acted like he actually was glad to meet him. And he was a whiz with the baggage—whatever it was that he was rattling in Italian sure as hell worked. Immigration stamped his passport; and while everyone else fought and tried to find their luggage, Sergio merely peeled off some lire, and within seconds a bent old porter came up with Robin's bags and piled them into a long red Jaguar. Robin was silent as they sped along the modern highway that led into town.

"Nice car," he finally said.

"It belongs to your mother."

"I'm sure she speeds around in it every day," he said acidly.

"No—I drive. She had a large chauffeur-driven Rolls, but in Rome such a large car in our traffic is not good. And the chauffeur—" Sergio rolled his eyes toward heaven. "He had arrangements with gas stations. He was making much money off your mother. Now I do the driving."

"And you've found a cut-rate gas station, I'm sure."

"Cut-rate?"

"Forget it, Sergio—how is my mother?"

"I think she is more well than she has been for a long time. And your arriving has made her so very happy. We are planning a big Christmas party in your honor. Your mother likes parties, and I think it is good for her, makes her dress nice. And when a woman dresses up and looks beautiful, she feels well."

Robin sat back and watched Sergio navigate through the tiny squealing cars and jammed traffic in the center of the city. Gradually they eased their way into a less congested area and headed for the Appian Way. Sergio drove into an enormous tree-lined drive. Robin whistled. "Looks like Nero's summer palace. What's the rent on this place?"

"No rent," Sergio said. "Kitty bought it. Very nice—yes?"

Kitty was waiting in the large marble entrance hall. Robin embraced her gently. She seemed smaller than he remembered, but her face was smooth and unlined. At first glance, standing there in the red velvet hostess pajamas, she looked to be about thirty. She led him into an enormous drawing room. The floors were pink marble and frescoes lined the high walls. Sergio disappeared, and Kitty led him to the couch. "Oh, Robin—it's so good to see you." He stared at her tenderly. Suddenly he was so damn glad she was his mother. He saw the age spots on the hands that contrasted so incongruously with the young unlined face. And yet, sitting here with him, she suddenly seemed like a little old woman. Her body seemed to collapse—even the smooth face looked old.

Then Sergio entered and he witnessed an amazing transformation. Kitty sat up. Her body seemed vibrant—she grew two inches, her smile was young—she *was* young as she accepted the glass of champagne Sergio offered.

"I made for you vodka martini on the ice," Sergio said. "Kitty said this is what you drink. Is it made correct?"

Robin took a long swallow. It was incredible. The son of a bitch made a better martini than the bartender at Lancer's. Sergio disappeared again and Kitty took both of Robin's hands. "I'm a bit tired, but tomorrow we'll catch up on everything. Oh, Sergio, you are sweet." The boy had returned with a tray of cold lobster.

Robin dipped a piece into some sauce. He suddenly realized that he was hungry. Sergio had no end of talents. He stared at the young man, standing straight and erect near the fireplace, and wondered what made a boy who had everything going for him turn queer. If it was money he wanted, there had to be young Italian heiresses who would go for a guy with his looks. Why tie up with an older woman? Easy: an older woman was grateful for any small favors. Grateful enough to let him have an occasional boy on the side.

"You called just in time," Kitty was saying. "We already had our plane tickets for Switzerland. I had promised Sergio ten days of skiing."

Robin's face showed his concern. "Why didn't you tell me I was interrupting something?"

She waved her hand. "Oh, it didn't matter one way or the other to me. Heaven knows I don't ski. Poor Sergio was the one who had looked forward to the trip. But it was his decision not to go. When I woke up, he announced that you were coming and that he had already canceled our reservation at the lodge."

Robin looked at Sergio. The young man shrugged. "I think perhaps the air is too thin for Kitty anyhow. With her heart, maybe she should not go to the Alps."

"Nonsense! The doctor said it was all right!" Kitty said. "But this is much nicer. We're all together. And—has Sergio told you?—we're going to have a big party Christmas day. I'm making a list. Of course many people will be away on holiday, but all the strays who are stuck in Rome will be here. And, Robin, you are going to stay until after New Year's. After all, we gave up the Alps for you, so don't dare run off."

"But if I stay for a few days you could still go to Switzerland."

"No. We'd never get reservations now. As it was, we had to make them months in advance. So now you have to stay."

Kitty put down her glass. "Time for me to go to sleep." Robin stood up but she waved her hand. "Now you finish your drink. It's late for me, darling, but you're still on American time, so you can't be sleepy." She kissed him lightly. Sergio came and took her arm and she looked at him gently. "He's a nice boy, Robin. He's made me very happy. He could be my son." She turned to him suddenly. "How old are you, Robin?"

"I hit the big one last August."

"Forty." She smiled. "Suddenly that seems so young. But it isn't young when a man hasn't married." Her eyes were questioning.

"I guess I can't find anyone as attractive as you."

She shook her head. "Don't wait too long. Children are very important."

"Sure," he said hollowly. "That's why you need Sergio. We're a big comfort to you, Lisa and me."

"Robin, a mother really loves her children only if she loves them enough to let go. I didn't have children as annuities against loneliness in my old age. They were part of my youth—the wonderful thing I had with your father. Now they must have their youth and their children." She sighed. "Those years—they are the really happy ones of one's life. I see that now as I look back. Don't let it slip by you, Robin." Then she left the room with Sergio at her side. He watched them disappear at the top of the stairs.

He poured himself a shot of straight vodka. He was tired but he wasn't eager to go to bed. He had nothing to read . . . and this strange new sense of loneliness persisted. His glance went to the top of the winding stairs. Were Kitty and Sergio making love? He shivered. It was a mild night—but he was cold. He walked over to the fire. Maybe it was the goddam marble. He shivered again.

"I lit the fire in your room."

He turned—Sergio was standing at the foot of the stairs.

"I didn't hear you," Robin said. "You sure pussyfoot around."

"I intentionally wear rubber soles. Kitty often takes small unexpected naps. And I do not wish my footsteps to disturb her."

Robin walked back to the couch. Sergio sat beside him. Robin moved away and looked at the young man. "Look, Sergio, let's get this straight right from the start. Get your pleasure with my mother or with boys. Just don't get any ideas about me."

"Forty is late to be unmarried."

Robin laughed without mirth. "Good thinking. But you're off base. I dig girls, buddy—I dig them so much that I never intend to settle for just one." The dark-brown liquid gaze of the man unsettled him. "Look, why aren't you in bed with the glorious Kitty? That's what you're getting paid to do."

"I am with her because I like her."

"Yeah, I like her too. But I left her when I was your age, and she was a lot younger and prettier."

Sergio smiled. "But she is *not* my mother. There is love between us—but not the kind you think. Your mother does not want sex, she wants affection, someone to be with her. I care for her. I will always be very good to her."

"You do that, Sergy." Robin's voice was tight. He found himself reevaluating the boy. He no longer resented him. In a crazy kind of way he thought Kitty was lucky. He felt a surge of gratitude toward Sergio.

"Tell me about your work in the States," Sergio said.

"There's nothing to tell . . . I'm in news broadcasting."

"Don't you like it?"

Robin shrugged. "It will do—it's a job."

Robin poured himself some more vodka. The young man jumped up and brought him the ice bucket.

"Everyone has to have a job," Robin said slowly.

"We are a Catholic country and there is no divorce. Poor people have bambinos. So they must have a job and work hard—even at jobs they do not like. But the man of affluence, he does not have just a job. He works at a business of his choosing. He enjoys life. All businesses and shops close every day from noon until three. A man of means enjoys life over here. At lunch he goes to his mistress. He has a long lunch—wine—he makes love. Then at night he goes to his wife, and he relaxes again. But you Americans—you take jobs you do not care about. Tell me, do you ever take wine with lunch?"

Robin laughed. "The idea would never occur to me."

"But why? Your mother will leave you so much money —why should you work so hard at just a job?"

"I don't work that hard. Maybe we do rush a lot, but we also don't expect to be supported by women. Lovers or mothers."

Robin watched, but the implication missed its mark. Sergio's expression never changed.

"Will you work on this news job all your life?" The question was asked with sincere interest.

"Nope. One day I'll take off and write a book."

Sergio's eyes lit up. "I read all the time. Kitty is helping me much with education. I had so little. I am reading

Wells's *Outline of History* now. Do you write like Mr. Wells?"

"I'm writing like me—which is the only way, good or bad. Trouble is, I sandwich it in during odd hours."

"I think you should give up this job and come and live with us. You could write here and we would all be very happy together. Please, Robin, it would make Kitty happy, and I would like it much."

Robin smiled. "I'm too big for a roommate, friend."

"Oh, you would have your own room. We would block off a suite for you. And on vacation you could go skiing with me. Please, Robin!"

"Sergio, the last time anyone looked at me like that we went to bed for three days. Only difference was, it was a girl. Now cut it."

"It shows?"

"You're damn right it shows."

"Does it bother you?"

"If you want me to stay—cut it."

Sergio sighed. "I understand. It's just that you are—everything that I would dream to find in a man. I cannot help it, any more than a girl could help it if she saw you. Yet if a girl stared at you this way, you would not hate her. I stare at you from the heart. I cannot help the way my emotions go. But do not worry." He held out his hand. "Shake, Robin. We'll be friends."

Robin was surprised at Sergio's firm grasp. "That's a deal." He put down his glass and started up the stairs. "Oh, by the way, where do you sleep, chum?"

"Down the hall. In an adjoining room to your mother."

Robin's grin was slow. Sergio's eyes were serious. "She has a heart condition. I think I should be within calling distance."

"Good night, Sergio—you've outdistanced me."

Sergio smiled and walked toward the fireplace. "I'll put out the fire. The servants arrive at seven. I left a thermos of hot coffee on your night table on the chance you might awake earlier."

Robin laughed as he started up the steps. "I'm glad there's only one of you, Sergio. If there were many more you might put girls out of business."

Kitty spent the next few days immersed in elaborate preparations for Christmas. Food had to be purchased, wines, Christmas ornaments, a tree. Each day she gave Robin and Sergio a list and sent them off like two children. Robin relaxed and entered into the spirit of it all. Sergio drove and knew all the right shops. Often they were forced to stop and have a long lunch while they waited for the shops to reopen. Robin found himself enjoying the leisurely pace. He even drank wine. He had fallen into an easy relationship with Sergio. The boy was gentle and kind. He began to feel a paternal affection toward him.

Sergio asked eager questions about the States. He was interested in New York, Chicago, but it was Hollywood that seemed to hypnotize him. He had devoured fan magazines. The beach houses and lavish estates amazed him. "In Rome, maybe three or four people live so magnificently. In Hollywood, *everyone* has their own swimming pool. That would be a wonderful life. Here I have no chance for the cinema, so many young men look like me —but in Hollywood I would be different."

"Can you act?" Robin asked.

"Do you have to act for pictures?" The eyes were innocent. "I hear it is made in little pieces, and the director tells you what to do."

"Well, there's a little more than that to it. Why not study drama? Kitty wouldn't mind."

Sergio shrugged. "It is just a dream. I am happy being with Kitty. And these last few days, Robin, they have been the happiest of my life."

The day before Christmas, Sergio dragged him to a jewelry shop on the Via Sistina. The owner of the shop, a fat balding man, quivered with excitement when he saw Sergio.

"Sergio, you have come back," the man said.

"I want to see the mirror," Sergio said coldly.

"Oh yes, you bad boy. I told you it was yours if you wanted it." He reached in a case and brought out a beautiful little Florentine gold mirror. Sergio stared at it with admiration.

"What in hell is it?" Robin asked. He was growing uncomfortable. The owner of the shop was staring at

Sergio hungrily, yet Sergio seemed impervious to the man's attention.

"Kitty admired it," Sergio said. "She saw it a month ago. It's a mirror for her purse. I tried to save, but I only have half the money."

"Sergio"—the man's voice was oozing oil—"I told you, pay what you can. The rest will be a gift from me."

Sergio ignored him. He pulled out some crumpled lire. "Robin, I need—well, twenty American dollars more would do it. Can it be a present from both of us to Kitty?"

Robin nodded. He handed the owner the money, and with a shrug of disappointment the fat man disappeared to wrap the gift. Robin walked around the store staring at the various cases of jewelry on display. Sergio followed. "He has very beautiful things—he is a collector."

"Seems like jewelry isn't the only thing he collects."

Sergio's eyes drooped mournfully. "He is famous for his presents to young boys."

Robin laughed. "Sergio, the way he looked at you—you've got it made. Hold out for marriage."

"I never met him until I came to find the price of the mirror. He offered it to me for nothing if I . . ."

"Why not, Sergy? He's not much older than Kitty."

"I would have to sleep with him."

"Well?"

"I only sleep with someone who attracts me."

Robin walked away. The boy was giving homosexuality a crazy kind of dignity. Sergio followed him. "That is true, Robin. I have had only a few friends. There has been no one since my last friend became ill."

"And how soon will you leave Kitty for another friend?"

"I will not leave her. It is not easy for me. The men that I could love, they love women. I will not take up with any man just because he is homosexual. I would rather be with Kitty."

"Stay with her, Sergio. I promise you, if and when Kitty goes, I'll see that you get an allowance for life."

Sergio shrugged. "Money is not everything to me." He paused. "But would you buy me a Christmas present so I can remember you?"

They were standing near a tray of diamond-studded men's wristwatches. A glint of suspicion came to Robin's eyes. "Okay, chum, what is it that catches those big brown eyes?"

"Over here." Sergio led Robin to a case that held some gold slave bracelets. "I have always wanted one of these."

Robin suppressed a smile. The bracelets were about eighteen dollars. He waved his hand. "Take your pick." The boy was childlike in his enthusiasm. He finally selected the least expensive one. Plain gold links with a nameplate.

"Can I have my name put on the front? There is extra cost for that."

Robin smiled. "Go the whole route. Put on whatever you like." Sergio actually clapped his hands. He lapsed into excited Italian with the owner of the shop. Robin browsed through the store. Suddenly his attention was caught by a black-enameled panther with green jeweled eyes staring up from the case.

He beckoned the salesman. "How much is that?"

"Four thousand."

"Lire?" Robin asked.

"Dollars."

"For that!"

The young salesman immediately placed it on a piece of white velvet. "It is the most beautiful pin in Rome. It comes from India. A maharaja had it made. It is three hundred years old. The emeralds in the eyes are priceless. You would not have to pay duty as it is an antique."

He stared at the panther. The jeweled eyes were the exact color of . . . He turned away. Then with a quick change of heart, he told the man to wrap it up. Hell— why not? He sure owed Maggie something after that night. As he wrote the traveler's check it occurred to him he had never spent this kind of money for anything. Yet oddly enough he felt exhilarated. He put the box in his pocket. Then he went to collect Sergio, who refused to go until he got a written guarantee that the engraving on the bracelet would be ready at closing time that day.

Robin couldn't remember a nicer Christmas Eve. The fireplace was crackling, the tree reached to the ceiling—

they even popped corn to string on the tree. At midnight they opened the gifts. Kitty had given both Robin and Sergio diamond cuff links. Robin was embarrassed and touched at the small gold St. Christopher medal Sergio gave to him. "It has been blessed," Sergio explained, "you travel so much." Kitty was delighted with her gift. She toasted them both with champagne and throughout the evening Sergio kept staring at the shiny new bracelet on his wrist.

The following day the villa overflowed with guests. Robin drank a lot and wound up in an apartment facing the Borghese gardens with a beautiful Yugoslavian girl whose husband was in Spain on business. They spent the following afternoon making love. He returned to Kitty's *palazzo* exhausted, but very content.

The week passed quickly.

Sergio drove him to the airport. "Call me if she doesn't feel right. And, Sergio, make her get checkups. She won't tell you when she's not feeling well—she doesn't want to act like an old woman—but call the doctor if there's the slightest suspicion."

"Trust me, Robin." They were walking to the gate. Robin's luggage had been checked, the flight had been announced. "And, Robin—perhaps you should see a doctor, too."

"Hell, I'm strong as a horse."

"I mean another kind."

Robin stopped suddenly. "What are you getting at?"

"Something is bothering you. Two nights in a row you shouted in your sleep. Last night I ran to your room—"

"What did I say?"

"You were thrashing about in the bed, asleep, but with a hurt sad expression on your face. You were hugging the pillow and shouting, 'Don't leave me! Please!' "

"Too much vodka," Robin said. Then he shook hands and boarded the plane. But he thought about it on the trip home. He thought about it when he showed the pin at customs and had to pay an enormous tax—if he ever saw that son of a bitch on the Via Sistina again who had said *no duty!* And he kept thinking about it on the taxi ride home. The whole thing didn't add up. At the height of his affair with Amanda he had never bought her such an expensive present. And here he was with a four-thousand-dollar trinket for a girl he couldn't even get it up for unless he was drunk. Maybe it was guilt, but four thousand bucks plus duty was a hell of a high price to pay for one night. A night he couldn't even remember.

# TWENTY-ONE

H E WENT INTO IMMEDIATE ACTION the moment he returned to New York. He notified the legal department to draw up a contract for Andy Parino. He mailed it to him with a short note stating his offer to join the network in New York. He also mailed the panther pin to Maggie with a note saying, "A belated Merry Christmas—Robin." Three days later Andy phoned and eagerly accepted the offer.

"Sure you won't miss anything down there?" Robin asked.

"Hell, no. It's all washed up with Maggie and me anyhow."

"I'm sorry."

"No, it just wasn't in the cards. She's—well, she's too complicated for me. Right now she's rehearsing like crazy —some Hollywood agent is coming to catch her in a play. I want a girl who puts me ahead of Eugene O'Neill."

"Fine. I'll assign you to Network News—you'll still work with Jim Bolt. And you can start sitting in on my *In Depth* taping sessions to get the feel of it. In a month or so, I'll let you try one. By next season I hope to turn it over to you and go on to something new."

"I've been running all your tapes and studying them. I don't know whether it's going to be that easy to step in your shoes."

"Do your own thing—and they'll buy it."

"Thanks for the vote of confidence. I'll sure try my damnedest!"

By the end of the week, Robin had caught up with all

his back work, and scheduled a taping for *In Depth*. He looked at his appointment pad—the afternoon was free. He unlocked his desk drawer and took out his manuscript. It seemed years since he had looked at it. Well—tonight he'd take it home and work on it, and lay off the vodka. He hadn't been to the Lancer Bar since he returned.

His secretary came in with a package. He had to sign for it. He scribbled his signature and stared at the brown-paper wrapping. It was heavily stamped and insured. He opened it and found the Italian leather box with the black panther pin. There was a typewritten note: "I only accept gifts from friends."

He tore up the note and put the box in a small wall safe where he kept his contracts and private papers.

He put the book back in his desk drawer and left the office. When he arrived at the Lancer Bar, Carmen the bartender was effusive in his greeting. "Mr. Stone, it's been so long! The usual?"

"Make it a double to celebrate my return," Robin said.

He finished the drink quickly and ordered another. This was going to be one of those nights. He was beginning to hate the nights. He knew he had dreams . . . several times he had awakened in a sweat. But he couldn't remember them. He hadn't remembered his dreams in Rome, yet Sergio said he had shouted two nights in a row. He finished the second drink and ordered another. Maggie sending back the pin bugged him. But why should it? She didn't mean anything to him. Nothing seemed to add up lately. Maybe Sergio had something. He crossed the room and picked up the phone book. Why not? It was worth a visit to a shrink to stop the dreams. He leafed through the pages. There sure were a hell of a lot of Golds but there couldn't be more than one Archibald Gold. He found it listed on Park Avenue. He hesitated a moment, then quickly dialed the number. Dr. Archie Gold picked up on the second ring.

"This is Robin Stone."

"Yes."

"I'd like to see you."

"Professionally or personally?"

There was a pause. "I guess professionally."

"Could you ring me back at six? I have a patient."

Robin hung up and walked back to the bar. He finished his second drink; then exactly at six he rang Archie.

"Okay, Doc, when can I see you?"

He heard the ruffling pages and knew the doctor was going through his appointment book. "I have a few openings," he said. "Some of my patients have gone south for the winter. Would you like to come next Monday? I could put aside ten o'clock. We could start with three visits a week."

Robin's laugh was hollow. "I don't want a course. Just one shot will do. I want to talk to you about a specific problem. Why don't you come over to the Lancer Bar for a drink? I'll pay for the drink and your time—like it was an office visit."

"I'm afraid that's not the way I work."

"I talk better when I'm drinking," Robin said.

"I listen better in my office," the doctor replied.

"Then forget it."

"I'm sorry. But you know my number if you change your mind."

"What time is your last appointment tonight?"

"My last patient is due now."

"That means you're free at seven."

"I plan to go home at seven."

"Archie—I'll come to your office if you'll see me tonight."

Dr. Gold was not misled by Robin's casual tone. From a man like Robin, the phone call itself was a cry for help.

"All right, Robin, seven o'clock. You have my address?"

"Yep. And listen, Archie old boy, one word of this to your friend Jerry and I'll break your head in."

"I never discuss my patients. But if you have any doubts perhaps you should go to another doctor. There are several good men I could recommend."

"No, Archie baby, you're my man. See you at seven."

Robin sat across the desk from Dr. Gold. The whole idea struck him as ridiculous. He never opened up to anyone—how could he tell this placid-looking stranger what was bugging him?

Dr. Gold recognized the silence and smiled. "Sometimes it's easier to talk about intimate things with someone you don't know. That's why bartenders are the recipients of so many confidences. In a way the psychiatrist and the bartender have a great deal in common. We remain in our spot; you only have to see us when *you* want to. You don't run into us in your day-to-day living."

Robin laughed. "You've made your point. Okay—it's as simple as this. There's a girl." He paused. "I can't get her out of my mind—but I don't dig her. That's what's so crazy."

"When you say you don't dig her—do you mean you dislike her?"

"No, I do like her. I like her a lot. But I can't make it with her in bed."

"Have you ever tried?"

Robin shrugged. "Seems when I was pissy-eyed drunk I went after her on two separate occasions, and judging from her reactions, I was pretty good."

"Then what makes you say you can't make it with her?"

Robin lit a cigarette and exhaled thoughtfully. "Well, the first time it happened I woke up the following morning and she was gone. I couldn't even recall her face —or her name. I just knew that she was a brunette with big tits. And something disturbed me when I thought about it that morning. I couldn't remember a thing, yet I sensed I had done something or said something I shouldn't have. Then to compound the felony, I run into the lady two years later and have absolutely no recollection that we had ever met. She was making it with a buddy of mine. I thought she was beautiful, good company, and she was with him. Which was fine with me, because, like I said, she wasn't my type. We double-dated a few nights—then I went off for some fishing, alone. On my last night there, I went out with them. It started out as a great evening, only I got roaring drunk. My buddy passed out and I wound up with the lady. I have no recollection of being with her—except that I woke up the following morning in her bed. And I must have made it with her pretty good because there she was making breakfast and chirping little mating calls."

"What was your feeling about her?" Dr. Gold asked.

Robin shuddered. "Fright. It was almost like waking

up and finding you were with a boy, or a child—someone you *shouldn't* have gone to bed with. And because I did like her, I leveled with her." He ground out the cigarette. "I was rough. I told her how I felt. She was so damn beautiful, yet when I thought of sex with her I felt this sudden revulsion, and I knew I couldn't make it."

"Revulsion for her?"

"No. Revulsion about sex—as if doing it with her would be dirty, incestuous. Yet I like her. Maybe I like her more than any girl I've met. But I can't feel a physical drive for her."

"And you want to go to bed with her, or—let me put it this way: you would like to have this hangup, as you put it, removed so that you can fulfill a relationship with her."

"Wrong again. I don't care if I never see her again. But I don't like dark areas in my brain. This girl is beautiful —why should I feel this way? And it's happened before, just in a few isolated cases, but always with a brunette. Only they were never quite the caliber of this girl and fortunately I never saw them again. This thing with Maggie—it was an accident. I just happened to get roaring drunk."

"Just happened? Were you drinking an unusual drink? Something you were unaccustomed to?"

"No, vodka. That's what I always stick with."

"Were you aware that you were ordering too many drinks?"

"I guess I was."

"Let's go back to the first time with this girl. Two years ago. Were you very drunk when you met her?"

"No, but I was drinking."

"And then you purposely proceeded to get drunk?"

"Purposely?"

Dr. Gold smiled. "It would seem that way. I wouldn't say you were the kind of a man who is caught off guard."

Robin looked thoughtful. "You mean that subconsciously I wanted this girl and intentionally got drunk so I could make it with her?" When Dr. Gold didn't answer, Robin shook his head. "Doesn't add up—because I don't dig this type of girl. Why would I want to make it with her? Drunk or sober, she's not my type."

"What is your type?"

"Slim, golden, clean hard-bodied girls. I like the smell of gold hair. Maggie is sultry—like a jungle cat."

"Have you ever been in love?"

He shrugged. "Hung on girls, sure. But I've always been able to walk away from it. Know something, Archie. Everyone is *not* heterosexual or homosexual. There are people who are just plain sexual. They dig the bed scene, but don't necessarily fall *in* love. Take Amanda: she was great. I thought we had a marvelous relationship. Yet from what Jerry told me, I hurt her very badly. But I was never aware of it. I only cut out toward the end when she tried to swallow me. And even then I was only cooling it —but I had no idea that all along I'd been hurting her."

"You really never knew?"

"That's right. If I took off to tape a show in Europe and didn't write, I figured she knew the score—that I was coming back, and it would be to her. And when I did come back, I couldn't wait to get into the feathers with her. It was great."

"Yet you are conscious that you have hurt this other girl, Maggie."

Robin nodded. "Yes."

"Why would you be unaware that you were hurting Amanda, whom you really desired, yet be so painfully aware of this girl you don't care about?"

"That's why I'm here, Archie. *You* tell me."

"What did your mother look like?"

"Oh Christ, let's not go into the Freudian jazz. I had a healthy happy childhood. Kitty is blond, nice, clean—" He stopped.

"And your father?"

"He was a hell of an outgoing guy. Strong, all muscles. I have a nice kid sister. Everything was shipshape in my childhood. We're only wasting time there."

"All right . . . father, mother, sister. All healthy relationships. Let's locate the dark stranger. Was it a nurse? A schoolteacher?"

"My first teacher was a hunchback. That was kindergarten. My nurse—well, I must have had one, but I can't recall. There were servants—a chauffeur took me to school. There was a nurse when Lisa was born—a gray-haired job."

"Was there any rivalry between you and your sister?"

"Hell, no. I was her big brother. I was protective of her. She looked like a tiny Kitty: blond, white and clean."

"Do you resemble Kitty?"

Robin frowned. "I have her blue eyes, but my hair is dark like my father's, although now it's turning gray pretty fast."

"Let's go back to before Lisa was born. What is the first memory you have?"

"Kindergarten."

"Before that."

"None."

"You must be able to recall something. Everyone remembers one small incident in early childhood. A pet, a playmate, happiness, disaster."

Robin shook his head. Dr. Gold pursued: "A conversation, a prayer?"

Robin snapped his fingers. "Yes—one thing. Maybe it was a conversation, but it was just a line and I can't remember who said it: 'Men don't cry. If you cry you're not a man, you're a baby.' For some reason it stuck with me. I believed it. I believed that if I didn't cry I could have anything I wanted. Whoever said it must have made an impression on me because I never cried after that."

"You've never cried?"

"Not that I can recall." Robin smiled. "Oh, I'll go to a corny movie and get a lump in my throat. But in my own personal life"—he shook his head—"never."

Dr. Gold looked at his watch. "It's five to eight. Would you care to make an appointment for next Monday? My fee is thirty-five dollars an hour."

Robin's expression was one of disbelief. "You must be some kind of a nut. I've been here almost an hour, to discuss a girl that I have some hangup about. We've solved nothing—and you want me to come back."

"Robin, it's not natural to be unable to recall anything in your childhood."

"Five years old is not exactly middle-aged."

"No, but you should be able to recollect some incident that occurred before, unless—"

"Unless what?"

"Unless you are intentionally blocking it out."

Robin leaned across the desk. "Archie, I swear to God, I have not blocked out anything. Maybe I have a lousy memory—or did it ever occur to you that perhaps nothing ever happened that was worth recalling?"

Archie shook his head. "Very often when something traumatic happens, the brain automatically builds amnesia as scar tissue."

Robin walked toward the door. He turned to the doctor. "Look, I lived in a nice big house, with two nice parents and a pretty little sister. No skeletons in my closet. Maybe that's the bit. Maybe things went too smooth, maybe kindergarten was the first jolt I got—the hunchback teacher—maybe that's why my memory starts there."

"Who told you a man doesn't cry?"

"I don't know."

"Was it before kindergarten?"

"It had to be, because I didn't cry in kindergarten when the other kids did. They were all scared of the teacher—the poor bitch."

"Then who said it?"

"Archie, I don't know. But whoever it was, I bless them. I don't like to see men cry. I don't even like to see women or babies cry."

"Robin, I'd like to try you on hypnosis."

"Are you crazy? Look, Doc, I was in the war and got shot up a bit. I can think of a hell of a lot of things I went through that could have loosened some screws, but I came through in one piece. I came here to get one specific question answered. You come up zero. Okay. Be a sport and admit it. Don't try to make good by digging back into my childhood to see if a nurse belted me when I was two or three for messing up my toys. Maybe she did and maybe she had black hair and green eyes and big tits—okay?"

"You know where to find me if you decide to try it my way," Dr. Gold said.

Robin grinned. "Thanks, but I think it's easier and less expensive to duck if I run into a green-eyed brunette." He closed the door and walked into the night. Dr. Gold stared at the notes he had made, and put them in a folder. He would not destroy them: Robin Stone would return.

Robin glanced at the February Nielsens. The news department was finally giving the other networks real competition. This week it was second in its time period. *In Depth* was still in the top twenty-five. He had given Andy a shot at it last week and it had gone well. He studied the presentation of the saucer project—the research staff had come up with some exciting new angles. It would make a hell of a show.

He met with Danton Miller the following day and explained his intention of easing out of *In Depth* and letting Andy take over permanently the following season. Oddly enough, Dan raised no objections.

"Giving up acting?" he said with a smile. "Your adoring public won't like that."

"I intend to do a news special once a month," Robin explained. "Take some subject that no one will touch. Dig into it, lay it bare. This could be the first." He handed Dan the saucer presentation. Dan read it carefully.

"Sounds like a Sunday afternoon project—it might grab the kids," Dan said. "But it's not a nighttime show."

"I think it is. Why not try one shot in May or June in prime time, when the big shows are having reruns? That should be an honest test."

"If you like, I'll slate it for a Sunday afternoon, April or May. But not at night."

"I don't want Sunday afternoon," Robin said. "You know damn well it would get no rating. The baseball games would kill it. I'm looking for sponsor interest for the fall."

Dan smiled. "If you want to line up a staff and put this science-fiction crap on tape, that's up to you. But it has no place in my network planning."

Robin reached over and picked up the phone. Dan's secretary came on. "Would you call Mr. Gregory Austin. Tell him Robin Stone and Danton Miller would like to see him at his earliest convenience."

Dan's face drained of color. He recovered quickly and

forced a smile. "That was a bad move," he said easily. "You just went over my head."

"But not behind your back." For a moment their eyes locked in silence. When the phone rang it seemed unnaturally loud. Dan reached for it. The secretary announced that Mr. Austin could see them immediately.

Robin stood up. "Coming, chum?"

Dan's eyes narrowed. "Seems like I have no choice." Then he smiled. "I'm curious to see Gregory's reaction to your Buck Rogers drama. He'll realize I've vetoed it—and Gregory doesn't like having his time wasted to act as referee. That's why I'm president of Network Television. My decision on matters like this is final. But I think I'll let you dig your own grave."

Dan sat back as Robin outlined the saucer project to Gregory. When he had finished, Gregory turned to Dan. "I gather you're against it."

Dan smiled and held his fingers together pyramid style. "Robin would like to do a show like this next season. One a month—in prime time."

Gregory looked at Robin questioningly. "A saucer show every month?"

Robin laughed. "No, I want to do an hour of television comparable to a *Life* magazine spread on a subject that's in the news. Saucers, politics—anything that's timely or newsworthy. Instead of doing a personality—like our half hour on *In Depth*—we do a subject, for an hour. An important movie could be filming—we'd go on location, talk with the stars, the director, the author. We could go into the private life of a television personality—take Christie Lane. The public keeps asking what he's really like—"

The mention of Christie Lane brought a sudden look of concern to Gregory's eyes. He turned to Dan. "That reminds me, we only have Christie signed for another season. Has anyone done anything about getting him signed to a new long-term contract?"

"We've started the negotiations," Dan said. "He wants to start reruns the end of April so he can pick up all that Vegas money. He's also booked some fairs. He gets ten thousand a night for them. He's still doing the shows live, but we've been taping them for the rerun bank. And next season he wants to go to tape—he's secure enough now. There's no problem there. But Cliff Dorne says we're miles apart in money—in what he's asking and what we want to give. We've agreed to give him a big raise, but he wants to form his own company—split ownership of the show with us. And he wants ownership of his tapes after the first rerun to sell to the independents. Plus many other fringe benefits. It's not going to be easy—both NBC and CBS are hot on his tail."

The secretary crept in and announced that Mrs. Austin was calling. Gregory rose. "I'll take it in the other room." Both men watched him disappear into the inner office. Dan was the first to break the silence. He leaned across and tapped Robin on the knee. His voice was low. "Listen to me: I hope you've learned a lesson. You've had a chance to look behind the scenes of network planning. There's more to it than being an Ivy League reporter. You've bored Gregory with your piddling science-fiction show. You've taken up my time and his. You are president of News. I am president of Network Television. I work alone —I'm not looking for a partner."

Robin laughed. "This sounds like a Madison Avenue version of a Chicago gang war: You have the South Side and I take the North Side."

"I have *both* sides. You have News, period. And you don't mix into programming. I'm not a newsboy playing part-time actor, part-time executive. This is my life—not a hobby. And no one cuts into it."

"I have no desire to shoot for any of your marbles. But I am president of News and I have a show that I think should go on. You have to give me the time. If you say no, then I have to—"

"You have to pass! Get it? Pass! The next time I say I don't want a show—you pass. There are to be no more calls to Gregory Austin!"

Robin's grin was easy. "Well then, Mr. President, just don't pass too quickly."

Gregory Austin returned. "Sorry, gentlemen. I never let personal calls interfere with business, but then Mrs. Austin is my most important business." His face softened as his thoughts reverted to his wife. Then he cleared his throat, and his expression took on the matters at hand. "I was telling Mrs. Austin your idea about the saucer special. She was intrigued. I never realized that there is a romanticism to space that appeals to women. Go ahead with the saucer project, Dan. Slate it in May in place of one of Christie's reruns. If it gets a rating, then we'll talk about a monthly series." He looked at Dan. "I'll work with Cliff Dorne on the Christie Lane renewal. Anything else on the agenda?"

Dan stood up. "I guess that's about it."

Gregory waited until both men reached the door—then almost as an afterthought he said, "Oh, Robin, would you wait one moment. There's something I want to talk to you about."

Dan left and Robin eased himself into a chair. Gregory stared after the closed door and smiled. "Dan's a good man. An ambitious man. Hell, we all are. That's why he's good. I like the idea of you thinking of other projects. Only from here on, if they're outside the news department, come to me first—and I'll pass them on to Dan as my idea. It will keep peace in our little family."

Robin smiled. "I'm still new at network protocol." He made no move to leave, because he sensed this wasn't the real reason Gregory had detained him.

"Robin"—Gregory's manner was suddenly oddly shy—"I know this seems like trivia, and it has nothing to do with the line of duty—but what happened to you on January first?"

Robin's brow creased. January first. . . . So far as he could recollect, Sergio had driven him to the airport.

Gregory lit a cigarette. "Gained ten pounds," he said sheepishly, "so I'm back smoking—just until I knock off the weight." Then he said, "Our eggnog party."

Robin's expression was blank.

Gregory studied the ash on his cigarette. "You've been invited two years in a row. Not only haven't you shown, but you've never even sent a note of regret."

"Good God! How rude of me! I was in Rome this year, and the year before I think I was—" He frowned, trying to recall. "I was in Europe then, yes, I remember, I returned on New Year's Day. And there was all that mail. I'm ashamed to tell you what I did with it—on both

occasions. I stared at it, and then dumped it all into the
wastebasket. After all, no one expects you to answer
Christmas cards, and I figured the bills would come again
the following month. I guess Mrs. Austin's invitation was
among them. I'll write to her immediately."

Gregory smiled. "I assumed it was a misunderstanding.
But you know how women are. Mrs. Austin was wondering if it was a personal slight."

"That's the last thing I would want her to think. The
hell with a note—may I call her?"

"Of course." Gregory scribbled down the number.

Robin returned to his office and placed the call to Mrs.
Austin.

"Now, Robin Stone," she said, "you didn't have to call.
I know this is Gregory's doing."

"It is—and I'm grateful that he told me. I've been out
of the country on both occasions of your New Year's Day
parties."

She laughed when he told her of the way he had dis-
posed of his mail. "I think that's a marvelous idea," she
said. "I wish I had the nerve to do it. I'd miss so many
dull events."

"Mrs. Austin, I promise you—next year I shall go
through every Christmas card, searching for your invitation."

"Oh come now, Robin." She paused. "Forgive my infor-
mality, but we do watch your show. I feel as if I know
you."

"Mrs. Austin, I promise, no matter where I am, on
January first, nineteen sixty-four, we have a definite
date."

Her laugh filtered through the phone. "I certainly hope
we're not going to have to wait that long to meet."

"I hope not. But I want you to know, I like eggnog. I
really do."

"I'm sure Gregory has told you he hates it. Oh, Robin"
—he heard the rustle of paper—"I'm having a small
dinner party March first. We've just returned from Palm
Beach—the weather has been so unreliable there that
we've decided to stay in New York. Would you like to
come?"

How had he gotten into this? But he had those two

goddam New Year's Days to make up. "I'd be delighted, Mrs. Austin."

"Oh, my sister will be in town. The dinner is really in her honor. The prince couldn't get away. Shall I make you her dinner partner, or is there someone you would care to bring?"

"I'd like to bring a young lady," he said quickly.

Without pausing, she said, "That will be fine. Eight thirty, March first, black tie."

He hung up and stared at the phone. Well, so the princess was here solo. He was not about to step into the role of the "personable extra man"! If he passed inspection as her dinner partner there would be other invitations. This way he had nipped it at the start. But now he had to dig up a girl. Well, he had ten days . . . he'd think of someone.

He forgot about Mrs. Austin in the week that followed. He spent two days in Washington for the saucer project. He had selected a director and a producer and had set March fifteenth as the tentative taping date. Everything was in order. Everything except the one call he had to make. Maggie Stewart. He didn't *have* to call her, but her story on the sighting in Florida had sparked the entire idea. Andy was set to do a segment and he *had* promised Maggie that she'd participate in the show. He put in the call. When she came on the line he wasted no time on amenities. He explained the setup and asked if she was interested.

She was equally impersonal. "Of course I'd be interested in doing the show. When do you want me there?"

"As soon as possible!"

"Today is the twenty-fifth. How is March first? That will give the station time to get someone to fill in for me."

"March first is fine." He turned to his appointment pad and saw the notation: "Dinner party at the Austins'." "Maggie, I know you don't owe me anything, but you could do me one hell of a favor."

"Yes?"

"Come in February twenty-eighth and bring an evening dress."

"For the show?"

"No, for a dinner party on March first. I want you to go with me."

"Sorry, I'm coming in to work."

"You're absolutely right. But, well, I'd wish you come. It's a black-tie dinner at the Austins'."

She hesitated. "You really want me to go with you?"

"Yes, I do."

She laughed and her voice lost some of its reserve. "Well, it just so happens that I have a smashing dress that I'm dying to wear."

"Thanks, Maggie. Wire the time of your arrival. I'll send a car to meet you at the airport. And I'll book a reservation for you at the Plaza."

He called the Plaza to reserve a room, and suddenly decided to change it to a suite. Business Affairs would probably chew his ass off, but she rated it. Everyone lived well on IBC's expense account—why not Maggie?

Her wire arrived on the morning of the twenty-eighth: ARRIVING AT IDLEWILD AT 5. NORTHEAST AIRLINES FLIGHT 24. MAGGIE STEWART.

He ordered a car; then on a last-minute impulse he called Jerry Moss. "Can you be loose at four? I have to meet a girl at Idlewild. I have a car—"

"And?"

"And I don't want to meet her alone."

"Since when did you need a chaperone?"

"Jerr—I have my reasons."

"Okay, I'll meet you in front of the IBC building at four."

It was close to eleven o'clock and Robin was drinking slowly and steadily. Jerry finished his coffee. The whole evening had been crazy. This Maggie Stewart was the most incredibly beautiful girl he had ever seen. Yet she had greeted Robin as if she barely knew him. And when Jerry suggested they all have a drink at the Lancer Bar, both Robin and Maggie had refused simultaneously. They had dropped her at the Plaza and then Robin had dragged him to Louise's for dinner. The restaurant had almost emptied, yet Robin sat toying with his drink. Long John Nebel stopped by on his way to do his all-night show.

"I listen to him when I can't sleep," Robin said. "He's tied to another network or I'd use him on the saucer show. He knows all about that jazz."

Robin ordered another drink and lapsed into silence. Jerry sensed Robin's mood and didn't try to pry. But what was all this about listening to Long John Nebel? That meant he wasn't sleeping well—it also meant he wasn't bedding down with a chick. You listened to Long John when you were lonely, or afraid of sleep. Robin an insomniac? This was a new twist.

Suddenly Jerry said, "Look, Robin, I don't know what's bugging you, but this Maggie Stewart is really special. If you blow this, there's something wrong with you."

"There's not a goddamned thing wrong with me," Robin snarled. "And get this straight. There's nothing between Maggie Stewart and me. I just brought her here because she's good at her job."

Jerry got up. "If you want to stay and drink all night, do it alone. I sat with you because I thought you needed me."

"I don't need anyone," Robin answered. "Run home to your wife."

Jerry started from the table, then he turned back. "Look, Robin, I'm not going to blow off at you, because I realize there's something eating you. You haven't been the same since Florida. And whether you admit it or not, it's tied up with that girl." Then he walked out.

Robin sat and drank until the restaurant closed. Then he walked home and turned on the radio. It was easier to fall asleep with the radio, you didn't wake up with the light of television glaring at you. He poured himself another stiff vodka. This was the first night he had tied one on since his visit to Archie. He got into bed and listened to Long John. He drifted off to sleep just as Long John was talking about some water you had to drink. Water. . . . That was a nice thought. . . . Think of a boat, he told himself, a boat and water. . . . A nice bunk. . . . Sleep. . . . Sleep. . . . He was on a boat, in a bunk. The bunk turned into a large bed. Maggie was holding him, stroking him, telling him everything was going to be all right. He felt good. He believed her. Then she slipped out of bed and Jerry was waiting in the other room. She was balling with

Jerry! He came running in—she led him back to bed and snuggled against him and told him it was just a bad dream. She kept stroking his head. . . . He relaxed. . . . She was warm. . . . Then he heard her leave the large bed again, heard her giggling in the other room. He walked in . . . Jerry was gone. She was sitting on the couch with Danton Miller. Dan was sucking at her breast . . . Danton looked up and laughed. "He's jealous," Dan said. Maggie didn't smile. Her face was serious. "Go back to bed and stay there." It was a command. And for some crazy reason he knew he had to obey her.

He woke up. Christ, it was four in the morning. Another one of those dreams—John Nebel was still talking. Robin switched to an album station and finally drifted off to sleep.

He picked up Maggie the following evening. She was right, the dress was a knockout and he felt guilty because the dinner party at the Austins' was stiff and formal and dull. Everyone was pleasant, but small talk always got him down. He sat at Judith Austin's left and struggled to keep his attention from straying. Somehow he managed to be attentive, ask the proper questions when she spoke of her charities or the weather at Palm Beach. His eyes roamed down the long table to Maggie. She was stashed between a neurosurgeon and a stock-market specialist. He envied her easy graciousness and wondered what the hell she was finding to talk about with them.

Later, when he stood in the lobby of her hotel and thanked her for "helping him out," he noticed that every man who passed turned to stare at her. Why not? She looked better than any movie star. Suddenly he said, "How about a drink? I think you deserve one."

"I take it you're on the wagon—I noticed how you toyed with the sauterne at the Austins'. Are you even afraid to have wine when you're with me?" The green eyes stared at him with a tinge of mockery.

He took her arm and led her to the Oak Room.

He signaled the waiter. "The lady will have Scotch. Bring me a double vodka."

"You don't have to prove anything," she said. "I'm aware of your weaknesses."

"Drinking is not one of them," he said tightly.

"Oh, I was beginning to think you had lost that talent, too."

He waited until the waiter put down the drinks. Then he reached out and took her hand. "I want us to be friends, Maggie."

She let her hand remain in his and their eyes met. "We can never be friends, Robin."

"You still hate me?"

"I wish I did. Oh God, I only wish I did. . . ."

He withdrew his hand abruptly and drank the vodka straight, in one long swallow. Then he signaled for the check.

"I have a lot of work piled up at home," he said as he signed the check.

"You don't have to lie," she said. "You haven't so far. Why start now?"

"No, it's true. I'm moonlighting—working on a book. I've set a goal to write five pages every night, no matter when I get home."

She looked at him with interest. "Is that your secret ambition?"

"I try and tell myself it is."

"Isn't it?"

He suddenly looked very tired. "Maggie, I don't know what the hell I want or don't want."

Her expression softened. "Are you unhappy, Robin?"

"Who said I was unhappy?"

"Anyone who doesn't know what he wants is afraid to find out. It's as simple as that. Unless he's frightened of his own secret thoughts."

"Thanks, Doctor, I'll call you when I need your couch again." He stood up and helped her with her coat.

Maggie went to her room and tossed her evening bag on the bed in anger. Just when everything had been going so great! Her eyes dimmed. Why kid herself? Everything was going nowhere. It was all in her mind. And she was going to put him right out of her thoughts. His invitation to the Austins' had stirred false hope. He had just needed a presentable date. It was as simple as that. Well, she had the whole weekend to herself and she was not going to sit in her room and hope he'd call! She'd get

up early—see a matinée—see a double feature at night.
She would not be here if he called. And when she walked
into the office on Monday, she'd act as if she barely knew
him. She took a sleeping pill, left a DO NOT DISTURB sign on
the door, and a wake-up call for ten.

It seemed as if she had only slept a few minutes when
she heard the wake-up call. She tried to reach for the
receiver, but the sleeping pill made her arm as leaden as
her head. It rang again. With a supreme effort she managed to pick up the receiver. The impersonal voice of the
operator said, "I know you have a DO NOT DISTURB sign but
a telegram has arrived marked 'Urgent, deliver at once.'"

She sat up and switched on the light. It was only seven
fifteen. "Send it up," she mumbled. She got out of bed
and put on a robe. She still slept in the nude—even the
cold weather could not change that.

She signed for the telegram. As she walked back into
the bedroom a sudden feeling of apprehension took hold
of her. She had been too sleepy to think, but who would
send her a telegram? Was her mother or father ill? She
ripped it open. She read it quickly—she couldn't believe
it!

> STELLA LEIGH PREGNANT. MUST BE REPLACED IM-
> MEDIATELY. HAVE SOLD CENTURY PICTURES ON USING
> YOU. TRIED TO REACH YOU BY PHONE FOR THE LAST SIX
> HOURS. NO ANSWER. CALL COLLECT AS SOON AS YOU RE-
> CEIVE THIS. HY MANDEL.

She put in the call to Hy Mandel and did not reverse
the charges. Let Mr. Robin Stone and IBC pay for that
too! She heard Hy's voice as the operator informed him
long distance was calling. Poor Hy—it was only five in
the morning out there. Well, he said to call immediately.

"Maggie!" He had snapped awake immediately. "How
fast can you get out here?"

"Hold on," she said easily. "What is the part? And how
much does it pay?"

"What is the part? Does Stella Leigh play bit parts?
It's the lead—opposite Alfie Knight. They've been
shooting around Stella for a week. She thought she had a
virus, throwing up all the time. The shmuck didn't even

know she was pregnant. Now look, Century is way behind schedule as it is. I've gotten them to give you a straight twenty thousand for the part, plus an option for another picture at terms to be discussed. They'll also pay for a suite at the Beverly Hills Hotel."

"Oh, Hy, how did you ever swing it?"

"To tell the truth, I had almost given up. You and your attitude about no screen test. I raved about you in the O'Neill play, but no one would listen. And yesterday when we got the news about Stella, I tried again. Frankly I didn't think we had a chance, but the director got excited and said you were exactly what he wanted—a new face."

"Who is he? And how does he even know what I look like?"

"Haven't I got your pictures spread all over Hollywood?"

"Oh, Hy—I hope I don't let you down."

"You won't. Listen. In the O'Neill play you didn't exactly give Geraldine Page anything to worry about. A big dramatic stage star you're not. But you've got something: personality, a flash, and *that's* star quality. It doesn't always take talent to be a star, but it takes some intangible thing. I think you got it. I remember when Ava Gardner came out here—she was just a kid, but she had that same something you've got. The way she moved. You remind me of her. That's what I told the director."

"Oh Lord," she laughed. "That poor man—he's going to be disappointed."

"Nah, wait till he sees you. And he's about the hottest director in town right now. He just finished a smash picture and Century nabbed him for Alfie: Adam Bergman."

"Adam!"

"You know him?"

"I worked with him once, way back, in a little-theater group. Oh, Hy, I'm so thrilled."

"Listen, can you get here tonight? It would give you all day Sunday to read the script and get set. Monday they want you right away for wardrobe and makeup tests. I'll make the reservation at the hotel out here."

"Yes! Yes! I can leave today."

"Okay. As soon as you get the flight, wire me the number and the time of your arrival. I'll meet you."

She hung up and tried to assemble her thoughts. She felt exhilarated. She would see Adam again! She was delighted about that. But she was even more delighted to be walking out on Mr. Robin Stone.

Robin returned to his office after viewing the saucer tape. The more he thought about the show, the more he was convinced that it should go on in September and be the first of a series of a new type of show. He could make it a happening. That was it! He got up and paced his office. A *Happening*—that would be the title! If he could only sell Gregory on it—but he needed some other "Happening" ideas to throw at him at the same time. He thought about Christie Lane: What was the chemistry that had suddenly turned him into a national idol? Why hadn't he been an idol five years ago when he was doing the same songs in saloons? It would make a great hour. *The Happening of Christie Lane*. He'd do interviews with nightclub owners who had played him when he was a second-rater, interview his "gofors," Christie's family— he had to have some kind of a family—even interview that awful Ethel Evans he was going with. And there had to be all kinds of interesting characters connected with his past.

He put his plan into action by making an unofficial visit to the penthouse floor the following morning.

"Robin—without realizing it, you've come up with just the bait we need!" Gregory's voice crackled with enthusiasm. "We're in the middle of a six-lawyer hassle trying to get Christie to sign a new contract. He's playing it cute, but if we tell him we'll do an hour special on him with you moderating it, Robin, it's—" He stopped, at a loss for complimentary adjectives. "Don't say a word to anyone about this. Especially Dan. Let me talk to Christie myself. Of course you won't mind if I pretend this comes right from the top of my head. I'll throw it in at lunch tomorrow. I'm even going to have the slob and his lawyers meet with me and my lawyers in the private dining room. I'll tell him no network has ever done this for a star—and they haven't either! We'll make this the first Happening and let the saucer special follow."

Three days later the trades carried the news that Christie Lane had signed a new five-year deal with IBC. The following day Gregory sent for Robin and Danton Miller and outlined the idea of the special.

Dan listened carefully. Robin watched his reactions. He was positive Dan remembered that he had suggested a Christie Lane show for the series. But Gregory was acting as if the idea had suddenly struck him a few days ago. Dan wasn't fooled. Robin knew that. But Dan would have to play the game and go along; the Cheshire smile appeared, he nodded approvingly. Then a slight frown appeared, signaling that his thoughts had run into an obstacle.

"I think the conception is brilliant, Gregory, especially as it has locked Christie in for IBC. But I'm just wondering if Robin is the man to moderate the show. No offense, Robin. It's just that your image doesn't actually go with divulging the life of a man like Christie Lane. We need a top star to present Christie—a Danny Thomas, or Red Skelton. Someone who'd have empathy with him."

Gregory was caught off guard. It made sense. Dan's smile was openly victorious. Robin leaned forward. His expression was bland and his voice even. "I disagree."

Dan's smile remained fixed. His voice was patronizing. "I'm sorry. But as President of Network Television, I know a little more of what appeals to the public than a newsman who spends half the year in Europe."

Robin didn't smile. "I agree that you know about programming. But I think you know absolutely nothing about human nature. You put on a star with Christie Lane and you rob him of the spotlight. It becomes the Danny Thomas or Red Skelton show featuring Christie Lane. It is to be *his* show, about *him,* with no one overshadowing him in any way."

Gregory stood up. "He's absolutely right, Dan! Put on another star as emcee and you have another variety show. This is the first show of a series I want Robin to do."

Dan nodded tightly, then turned to Robin. "Lay low on the romance angle," he warned.

"The public wants romance," Robin answered.

"His romance won't bear close scrutiny," Dan said.

"It'll only make him more colorful," Robin insisted.

"No romance!" Dan snapped. "Besides, the public isn't interested in Christie's love life."

Gregory interrupted. "You're wrong again, Dan. Christie has to have a girl. Personally I'm always suspicious of a man who is over forty and has never been married. With Christie it's understandable—he's always been a gypsy. But we need the girl angle now. Who is she and what's wrong with her?"

"Ethel Evans," Dan said. "She used to work in publicity for us. She's one step removed from a hooker."

"Can't we find some other girl?" Gregory asked. "Why not give him a lot of girls? Hire beautiful models, link him with several."

"Ethel would never stand for it," Dan said. "And if you're going to use girls, you have to use her too. The public has read too much about her."

"What's she doing now, besides laying him?" Gregory asked.

Dan laughed. "Believe it or not, she's his personal press agent!"

"Fine," Robin interrupted. "Let's make her just that in the special. Every star has a Girl Friday!"

Dan nodded slowly. "It's an angle—it sure as hell would white-wash everything. We can't dismiss her from his life; she's been in too many fan magazines with him as it is."

Robin smiled. "Fine. Now it's your problem to make Christie Lane buy it."

Dan's laugh was ugly. "Oh, he'll buy it—but will Ethel?"

# TWENTY-TWO

THE PRESENCE OF DANTON MILLER at the Hotel Astor somehow seemed to emphasize the shoddiness of the room. Ethel stared at a stain on the carpet and wondered why Christie always wound up with one of the rattiest suites in the place. Probably because he always asked for the one that cost the least. And there was Dan, incongruously elegant, sitting in a faded club chair. And Christie, oblivious of the expression on Dan's face when he had seen the suite, sat puffing away at a cigar. Ethel was coiled tight as a spring. Her suspicions had been aroused when Dan casually phoned and said he'd drop by to talk over the mechanics of the special. Dan wasn't the type to just "drop by." And what was all this crap about "mechanics"? It was going to be Christie's life—his friends, the people he knew on the way up. His Happening! That's all she had been hearing for the past two weeks. Christie acted like he was being immortalized. But she could understand his excitement. As star of *The Christie Lane Show*, he appeared in a format. He sang songs, played in sketches, introduced guest stars. But the Happening was *him*. Everyone on it would be talking about *him*, no buildups for Hollywood guests— just *him!* The "gofors" were even springing for new suits. And Agnes kept dropping gentle hints. Oh, she didn't expect to *really* be on it, she claimed, "but when all my friends kid me about being a camp follower, I just tell them I'd rather be a tiny part of Christie's life than the star in anyone else's." Christie hadn't given her the nod yet, but Ethel sensed he'd give in. And gradually, Ethel had even been caught in the general excitement. She started a rigid diet and bought two dresses to wear on the show. But the full impact of her own importance on the show never really occurred to her until Danton Miller "casually dropped by."

Ethel sat and listened silently as Dan spoke about the special. To Ethel's amazement, his enthusiasm matched Christie's. Everything he said whetted Christie's appetite, inflated his ego. As he talked, the event of Christie's Happening took on the proportions of an Academy Award feature. It had to win the Emmy. When he got to the "mechanics" her eyes narrowed. And as she listened, her worst suspicions were realized. All the fancy footwork was just a cover-up. Dan's prime objective was to de-emphasize her—throw a smoke screen around the real role she played in his life. She couldn't believe it! She listened as Dan casually explained about the models they would hire to act as Christie's dates. The debutante who had already agreed to attend the opening of Aqueduct with him. The great shots they'd get with Christie visiting her father's stables.

"It gives you another dimension," Dan was saying. "Christie Lane is not just everyone's Uncle Harry—beautiful girls are attracted to him, debutantes adore him. We've even dug up a poetess and we'll show the two of you browsing around Doubleday's. Christie Lane is erudite! Of course Ethel will play an important role on the show. We'll have shots of her handling your mail, on the phone making your appointments—"

Ethel fastened her eyes to a sun spot that was working its way across the faded rug. This was the final humiliation. Lumping her with the "gofors." But when you got down to it, what else was she? They serviced him by running errands, she serviced him in bed. They even earned the same kind of money. For the first time in her life she felt defeated. She even lost the will to fight. Maybe it was Dan's supercilious manner, maybe it was the suite, but suddenly she felt as shabby as the soot-stained drapes that hung limply on the grayish windows. She suddenly saw herself through Danton Miller's eyes, and she wanted to run! Oh God, what had happened to fat little Ethel Evanski who sat on a stoop in Hamtramck and had the dream? How had she turned into Ethel Evans who sat in a smoke-filled suite at the Astor listening to Danton Miller evasively and politely plotting to alibi her presence in Christie's life? How had it all happened? She had only wanted to be someone—was that so wrong? She wanted to burst into tears, lunge at Danton Miller, scratch that snobbish smile off his face. . . . How could he sit there and look so impeccable and spotless? Who the hell was he to intimate she wasn't good enough to be Christie's girl? Dan had slept with her. Why hadn't it soiled him and his goddam black suit? But she remained silent. Because everything Dan said made sense. With the models, the debutante and the poetess, it *would* make a better show. And to Christie the show was all that mattered. That was one argument she could never win. Oddly enough, she didn't care what anyone in the business thought. They would all know it was a cover-up. But for the first time she thought of her mother and father, and even Helga. In their eyes, she was "engaged" to Christie Lane. How would it look when they saw Christie with all the glamour girls, and fat little Ethel Evanski sitting on the sideline with the "hired help"? She fastened her eyes to the sun spot on the rug. She didn't dare look up. Her throat was tight and she was dangerously close to tears. Christie's lusterless eyes were objective and thoughtful. Dan was still going strong, coming on for a big flash finish. Then he leaned forward. "Well, Christie, what do you think?"

Christie bit off a piece of his cigar and spat it on the floor. "I think it stinks."

Ethel looked up. Dan was too surprised to answer.

"What is this shit with me and the debutante or a poet? Everyone knows Ethel is my girl."

Ethel's lips parted in amazement. The slob was actually sticking up for her!

Dan shrugged. "Of course you go with Ethel. I know it, and you know it. But we've all done a lot of thinking about this Happening and the conclusion is unanimous. They think it will make a more exciting show if you are seen with many girls instead of one."

"Are we doing a glamour show, or the Happening of Christie Lane?" he asked.

"It's better for the ratings if we can combine them both."

"My show is in the top five, right? And it's not because of models or debutantes—it's *me!*"

Dan nodded. "But, Christie, let's not forget you do

have big-name guest stars on your show, pretty girls for the commercials, and an occasional girl singer to do a duet with you."

"What about Ethel?" Christie's voice was gravel-hard.

"Ethel is very attractive," Dan said quickly. "As a matter of fact, Ethel, I've never seen you look better." His smile was indulgent. She answered it with a baleful glance.

Christie ignored the byplay. "So?" he demanded.

"We're afraid of scandal magazines. So far we've been lucky—but just let one of them start with Ethel's love life, and they'll all leap on the wagon."

"I'd sue them," Christie said. "She's been with no one but me for almost a year. I can prove it."

"I'm afraid you'd only be proving their point. Yes, Ethel's been *with* you—living with you! That's why they figured the 'girl Friday' was such a good gimmick. It would explain *why* she is with you so much."

"Wait a minute!" Christie waved the cigar. "Who the fuck is *they?*"

Dan took out the cigarette case. "Let's put it this way, Christie. Robin Stone is *also* part of this show. If the scandal magazines hit at him on his first show because of Ethel, he could lose his blue-chip sponsor on the entire series. You've got to remember there is a large world outside of New York, Chicago and Los Angeles—a world where people go to church every Sunday, get married and celebrate golden anniversaries. Those people love you. You come into their living rooms. You can't blatantly state: 'This is the girl I live with—take it or else.'"

Dan took advantage of Christie's silence, and forged on with renewed emphasis. "No matter how you look at it, Christie, it adds up to this: you can't take the chance of acknowledging Ethel as your girl on the special."

"Okay. She won't be my girl," Christie said quietly. "She'll be my wife."

Dan's face lost its usual bland expression. His lips parted—but no words came. Ethel leaned forward—there had to be a catch!

Christie nodded, as if to affirm the decision to himself. "Yeah, you heard me. I'm gonna marry Ethel."

Dan had recovered from his initial shock and managed

a weak attempt at his feline smile. Christie sat back as if the matter was settled, but Ethel sensed the battle had just begun. Dan was marshaling his forces, readying for another attack.

It came immediately. "Funny." Dan's tone was almost melancholy. "I had you down in my book as one of the great romantics."

"A what?" Christie asked.

"A man who would only love one woman all his life. I was positive that's the way it was with you and Amanda. The night she died I was even afraid you might cancel the show. But you're a pro. I knew how you felt, but you realized that life goes on. When a man loses the only thing that matters, he finds a substitute—a temporary replacement."

For the first time Ethel understood the temporary insanity of blind fury that caused murder. She wanted to leap at Dan's throat. But this was no time for her to come on tough—not as long as Christie was carrying the ball. She clutched the arm of the sofa until her knuckles went white. And dredging her resources for a final gust of control, she managed a voice as cautious as his own: "You seem to forget, dear Danton, that Amanda had left Chris for Ike Ryan. She died as Mrs. Ike Ryan, not as Christie's girl."

Dan's tone was conciliatory. "Ah, but the greatest lovers of all are the lovers who lose and go on loving. To me Christie Lane is that kind of a man."

Christie jumped up. "What is this bullshit? Is that your idea of a great lover? To me it sounds like a number-one shmuck! A shmuck who sits around weeping for a broad that walked out on him! Oh no, Danny boy, I'm Christie Lane. I'm a big one, Buster! I came up the hard way— I've gotten real kicks in the gut. One little blond broad is no earth-shattering event in *my* life." He walked over to Ethel and took her hand. "Take a good look, Mr. Miller —this is a real broad. A great broad. Sure, Ethel and I started out as just two people on the town together. But after a few dates I forgot I ever knew Amanda."

Dan's smile was sad. "I reread the *Life* story just the other day, and it really got me. Especially when you said Amanda was the only girl you ever thought about marrying. The girl you wanted to have a child with." He sighed. "But it's really too bad, the Amanda thing was going to make a great part of your special."

"What has Amanda got to do with my special?" Christie asked.

Dan's voice was low and intense: "We were going to show blowups of the pictures you took together for *Life*. Get a clip of Amanda doing the commercial—and use the tape of that great moment when you sang 'Mandy' to her. Remember—when we cut to the wings and took a close-up of her face listening to you?" Dan shook his head sadly. "Can you see it? There wouldn't be a dry eye in the audience. Every newspaper in the country would write about it—the special with the love story of the century. Amanda—the only girl in Christie's life. And when she married someone else, he bore her no ill will. But when she died, a little bit of him died with her. The public will lap it up. That explains the models, the debutante—because after Amanda, there can't be any *one* girl in Christie Lane's life. Then, as you sing, the announcer's voice will say, 'Women love to listen to Christie sing—but Christie will always sing his love songs to a girl who can never hear them.' Then we show you on the town, proving that you're trying to forget. Christie, the public adores a lover; they'll dismiss the fact that she married Ike Ryan. They were only married for a short time. Tell me, how many girls do you recall being with Sinatra? There've been plenty—but the fans think he still sings only to Ava Gardner. The lyrics take on a stronger meaning—the world loves a lover, especially if he's lost someone. We can say that Ethel Evans is your most constant companion, that she cared for Amanda too—they were friends and worked on the show together, she understands the loss you've gone through. Christie, can't you see it?"

Christie's expression was bland. "You should be a movie writer, Dan." Then his voice went hard. "What kind of shit-kicking show do you expect me to do? Is *this* the Christie Lane Happening? The story of a man who came up the hard way, who was still just a second-rater when he hit his fortieth birthday? Everyone wrote him off—and two years later he made it big! *There's* your story—the heart of it—right there! That's the Christie Lane *Happening*. Get it? My Happening—about *me!* If the day ever comes when I need to rattle a dead girl's bones to have a show, then I'll sell shit! But right now I'm selling my talent, my life. And neither you nor Mr. Robin Stone is going to dictate to me what I am. I am me! Get it? *Me!* And I'm marrying the only broad I care about— Ethel Evans."

Dan walked to the door. "I'm sorry. Perhaps I just took the *Life* story too seriously—all that talk about how much you wanted a baby with Amanda, so it would look like her, be like her. . . ."

"Bullshit!" Christie yelled. "You bet your ass I want a kid. I want a son. I want to give him everything I didn't have. And Ethel and I will have one hell of a kid together!"

Dan bowed slightly. "May I wish you both happiness. I think it's wonderful. Christie, after listening to you, I've changed my mind. You and Ethel—well, one might almost say it's a marriage made in heaven." Then he left the room.

Christie stared after the closed door for a moment. Then he turned and started toward the bedroom. Without glancing at Ethel, he said, "Call Lou Goldberg. Tell him to come to town. Call Kenny and Eddie. Tell them to find out about blood tests and all that jazz. Call the mayor. See if we can get him to marry us." He disappeared into the bedroom.

Ethel sat on the couch. She couldn't believe it. He really meant it! She was going to be *Mrs.* Christie Lane. She looked up as Christie came from the bedroom, carrying his topcoat.

"Well, what are you sitting there for?" he asked. "Don't you want to get married?" Then as she nodded mutely, he snapped his fingers. "Well, move it—start making the arrangements."

She leaped from the couch and with one convulsive dash landed in his arms. "Oh, Christie." Her tears were genuine. "You really mean it?"

He seemed embarrassed as he gently broke her embrace. "Sure, sure. Now make the calls, doll." He started for the door.

"But where are you going?"

He paused. Then with a weak smile he said, "I'm gonna buy us wedding rings."

When Christie left the Astor he walked uptown. He reached Forty-seventh Street, and headed toward the block known as jewelers' row. Several guys he knew had booths—the Edelmans always gave him good bargains when he sprung for gold cuff links for the writers and crew at Christmas. He saw them through the window as he passed their store. He waved and wondered why he hadn't stopped. But he continued to walk east. He found himself heading toward Fifth Avenue. His pace quickened as he slowly became aware of his subconscious destination. He broke into a run. By the time he reached Fiftieth Street he was short of breath. He hesitated for a moment, then slowly walked up the stone steps of St. Patrick's Cathedral.

Christie had been born a Catholic. He accepted this fact the way a person accepts the color of his skin. He didn't practice the religion, he couldn't even remember his catechism though he had known it by heart when he took his first communion. But with his parents' divorce his formal religious training had come to an abrupt end. His mother had remarried—the guy was a Baptist and his half brother was raised as a Baptist. Or was it Methodist? He hadn't gotten along with his stepfather and had left home at fourteen. Now, as he stood in the soft darkness of St. Patrick's Cathedral, all the forgotten rituals slowly came back from his memory. Unconsciously he dipped his fingers in the holy water and made the sign of the cross. He walked past tiers and tiers of burning candles and gazed at the Stations of the Cross. He saw a woman enter one of the small confessionals. Suddenly he had an overwhelming urge to make a confession. He approached a confessional nervously. Then he stopped. It had been so long. The last time he had gone was when he was fourteen, after the first time he got laid. He had hoped that the act of confession might prevent him from getting the clap. He had been so eager to get into the girl, he hadn't realized what a beast she was until it was over. But what could you expect in a doorway for fifty cents? A woman came out of a confessional and crossed to a pew. He watched her kneel and take out her rosary. Her eyes closed, her lips moved as she fingered each bead. All he had to do was go in, kneel: "Forgive me, Father, for I have sinned." He walked into the confessional, knelt and mumbled, "Forgive me, Father, for I have sinned."

"Yes, my son?"

Dimly he saw the shadowy outline of the priest behind the screen.

"I have committed many mortal sins," Christie began. "I have lived with a woman who is not my wife. I have taken the Lord's name in vain."

"Do you intend to make amends?"

"Yes, Father. I am going to marry this woman and have a child and I will—" He stopped. He wanted to say, "I will love and cherish her," but the words stuck in his throat. He jumped up and rushed out of the confessional. He walked to the front of the church. He knew there must be a side exit somewhere. His gaze wandered along the wall where the rows and rows of lighted candles wavered in the dim light. Several people were kneeling before the Virgin Mary. He wandered down the side of the church toward the back. Under each statue was a blaze of lighted candles. It looked like a sea of light—each flame representing a personal prayer. Suddenly he passed an altar that was dark. It took him a moment to realize that only one solitary flame flickered—*one* candle among two trays of unlit candles. It glowed, defiant and proud in its pathetic loneliness. It didn't seem fair—the only saint in the whole place who wasn't doing any business. He looked at the plaque. St. Andrew.

He looked around to make sure no one was watching, then he slipped to his knees. The stone steps were hard. He put his head in his hands, then he looked up. "Okay, Andy, old pal, I'm gonna give you my business. From the look of things you got nothing much to do but listen to me. This one lone candle you've got going for you is almost burned out, so you probably already attended to it." He stood up. Was he nutty or something? Talking like it was real, talking to plaster. . . . Besides, there were no saints. They were just radical nuts who got killed for a cause. And what did it all matter in the end? They were dust and gone, and people were still sinning and fighting

and dying. Like Amanda. Amanda. . . . He stopped and
the tears came to his eyes. He put his face in his hands
and sobbed quietly. "Oh, Mandy," he whispered, "I didn't
mean a thing I said in that room. Oh, dear God, if there
is a heaven and You are listening, tell her I didn't mean
it. Mandy, can you hear me, doll? I love you. I never
loved no one else. I never will. And it doesn't matter that
you didn't love me. I loved you and that's all that counts.
Maybe that's why I'm marrying Ethel. I loved you and
you went off with someone and it hurt. I guess I kind of
remembered it today and suddenly I thought—why
should I hurt Ethel? I don't love her, but she loves me. So
why not make her happy? So you see, doll, indirectly,
you're the reason Ethel is gonna be happy. And when I
have my kid, then I'll be happy. Why is it like this,
Mandy? Why does Ethel love me and I loved you, and
oh shit—excuse me doll—but why can't people love together? But I'm gonna give my kid everything. . . . And
look, Mandy, maybe when I walk outa here I'll think I'm
crazy, but right now, this very second, I believe you can
hear me. And I believe this St. Andrew is with you, and
maybe there is something after we kick off. I can't start
being a knee bender and going to Mass, but I'll tell you
this—I'll raise my kid as a Catholic, and I'll never say a
wrong word in front of him. And, doll, I'll never stop
loving you. I think you know it, don't you, Mandy?
You're not down in the earth in a box. You're up there
somewhere—and you're happy. I can feel it. Jesus—I *can*
feel it!" He paused and for a moment her lovely face
seemed so close and she was smiling. He smiled too.

"Okay, doll, take care of yourself up there. And who
knows? If there *is* a second time around, maybe we'll
make it together." He shut his eyes. "St. Andrew, help me
be a good father. And give me a good healthy son." He
stood up, then suddenly he knelt again. "And by the way,
thank the Head Man up there for all the luck He's
thrown my way. And pray for my intentions."

He stood up and dropped a quarter in the box, took a
taper and lit a candle. Now two candles flickered together. But oddly enough the one extra light seemed to
make the tiers of gray unlit candles more prominent. He
gazed at the statue of St. Andrew. "I know how you feel

—like I did when I played to empty nightclubs with maybe two tables taken. I used to look at those white cloths on all the empty tables and go snow-blind." He reached into his pocket and took out a dollar, jammed it into the box and lit four more candles. It still looked meager compared to the other saints. Christie shrugged. "What the hell, I'm not gonna be chintzy." He took out a twenty-dollar bill and stuffed it in the box. Then he studiously lit every candle. He stood back and proudly surveyed the effect. "Andy, old boy—when them priests come around to check the house tonight, are they gonna be surprised—you're gonna have the biggest Nielsen of them all!" Then he walked back to the wholesale district and bought two gold wedding bands.

The wedding received enormous press and television coverage. Even the events leading up to the nuptials made news. Lou Goldberg took over the second floor of Danny's and threw a tremendous "bachelor" party for Christie. Every male star who was in New York attended. The columnists printed some of the jokes told at the dinner. Television comics pulled good-natured gags about it. But there was not one joke pulled about Ethel. They all sensed that the slightest stab could blow the lid off the pressure cooker, which held Ethel's past.

But Ethel had several bad moments. The first hurdle was the arrival of her mother and father a week before the wedding. Christie sprung for a double room at the Astor. Ethel didn't argue on the "room" bit. Her parents had never been to a hotel, they probably wouldn't know what to do with a suite anyway. As it was, she had to warn her mother *not* to make the beds. She had been stunned when she met them at Penn Station. (Of course they wouldn't fly! The idea of New York was traumatic enough!) But she couldn't believe that these two tiny people were her folks. Had they shrunk?

They were awed with the Astor, speechless at meeting Christie, and viewed the city itself in terrified fascination. They insisted she take them to the top of the Empire State Building. (She had never been there herself.) And then there was the boat ride around New York. They *had* to see the Statue of Liberty. Next on the list—sure they had a list; half of Hamtramck had worked on it—was

Radio City. The picture was okay, but to sit through that stage show! They adored it. She was relieved when the "gofors" took over with Grant's Tomb, the hansom ride in Central Park and the trip across the George Washington Bridge. At first she was volubly grateful to them until it suddenly hit her as the future Mrs. Christie Lane: they were *her* "gofors" too. Meanwhile, she used this respite to cover the stores in search of a suitable wedding dress. It had to be on the conservative side. It was wild—Christie's sudden decision that they get married by a priest. But it was a good sign—he really meant it to stick. As far as she was concerned, she would have been married by a witch doctor as long as it was legal. She had talked to Father Kelly—no, she didn't have to convert, just promise to raise the children as Catholics. *Children!* He'd get one child. *One!* But not until she was ready. She was thirty-two and had spent too many years hunting bargain clothes and watching the right side of the menu. For the first time she was going to have a wonderful wardrobe, take massages, go to the best beauty parlors. She wasn't about to spend six months in maternity clothes. Not right now. Not when she was finally getting everything she ever wanted.

They were married the first week in May in a double ring ceremony at St. Patrick's Cathedral, with her folks, Lou Goldberg, the "gofors" and Aggie in attendance. Christie wanted it that way, and until the final "I do" was said, she wasn't going to argue a single point. When the ceremony was over, everyone kissed everyone. Suddenly she noticed that Christie had slipped away. She saw him crossing to the other side of the church. She followed him curiously, stood at a distance and saw him kneel at an altar. The nut was lighting *every* candle! And he put twenty dollars in the box! She returned to the wedding group without his seeing her. She hadn't realized how much he cared for her. For Christie to part with twenty bucks—it had to be love. But then, a lot of men who were penurious changed after marriage. This was a good omen.

Christie took everyone to dinner, and then they all went to the station to see her folks off. That night when

she went to Christie's suite at the Astor, she was registered at the front desk for the first time.

She made no comment about spending her honeymoon
at the Astor. Christie was immersed in the special and
then they were going to Vegas for six weeks. That was
the time to make all the future plans. She'd tell him to
deposit five thousand in her checking account every
month—maybe ten. After all, he had a great new deal at
IBC for next season. And she would call a renting agent
before she left and have them line up a duplex on Park
Avenue.

She spent the first week of her married life sitting in
the darkened theater watching Christie tape the Happening. Her part with Christie would be location shots:
restaurants, theaters. Right now they were re-creating the
atmosphere of his TV show so he could sing a few songs.
Ethel had quickly contacted a renting agent, an elegant
woman named Mrs. Rudin, who arrived at rehearsal one
day with floor plans for several excellent apartments.
Christie ambled over during a break. Ethel introduced
him to Mrs. Rudin. He listened quietly while Ethel explained. Then he clamped his teeth on his cigar. "Listen,
lady, roll all them blueprints up and forget it. Ethel and
I are plenty comfortable at the Astor."

Ethel's face burned with silent rage. She waited until
the woman left. Then she cornered him backstage. "How
dare you do that?" she demanded.

"Do what?"

"Embarrass me in front of a renting agent."

"Then don't bring them around and you won't be embarrassed."

"But we have to get an apartment."

"What for?"

"Christie, do you expect me to always live at the Astor
with your two wardrobe trunks in the living room, one
dinky closet for both of us, one bathroom—"

"Listen, I seen the joint you and Lillian shared. That
wasn't exactly the Ritz."

"I wasn't Mrs. Christie Lane then."

"Well *Mr.* Christie Lane is happy at the Astor."

She decided this was not the place to fight it out. She
had the whole summer to wear him down. "I'm going to

Saks to buy a bathing suit for Vegas. Oh, by the way, I want a checking account."

"So open one."

"I need something to put in it."

"You've been earning two hundred a week before we were married. I was talking it over with Lou. He'll still send you the same check each week. You can keep doing my publicity—you got nothing else to do anyhow."

"But what about my spending money?"

"Two hundred bucks isn't exactly chicken feed. Besides, now that you don't have to kick in your half of the rent to Lillian you'll have more money. Two hundred a week is plenty of spending money. Some families of eight live on that."

She sank into a seat in the empty theater. Suddenly she felt as if she had been tricked—like hitting an oil well and waking up the next morning to find it had run dry. And when the special was finished and they left for Vegas, the feeling persisted. Bellboys and motel managers called her Mrs. Lane. Other than that her life hadn't changed. Actually her life had been better *before* the marriage. There had always been a few nights a week that belonged to her—nights where she could sleep in the privacy of her apartment with Lillian. Now she spent every second with Christie, the "gofors" and Agnes. And in the fall, back in New York, it would still be the Copa bar, Jilly's and dinners with the "gofors." But she was damned if she'd go back to the Astor.

She brought it up to Christie one night after the show. "What's wrong with the Astor?" he demanded.

"I don't want to live there."

"Where do you want to live?"

"In a nice apartment, with a dining room, a terrace and *two* bathrooms!"

"All those rooms for just the two of us? I took a house in Hollywood once, but Eddie, Kenny and Aggie lived with me. And even then we had too much space. Look, once we have a kid, then we'll talk about apartments. Sure, with my kid I'll want a dining room. I want him to learn right, but as long as there's just you and me, it'll be a hotel suite."

The following night she didn't wear her diaphragm.

# TWENTY-THREE

R OBIN SAW THE PICTURE OF MAGGIE in the morning paper while he was having his coffee. He read the caption: MAGGIE STEWART, CENTURY'S NEWEST YOUNG STAR, IN NEW YORK TODAY TO DO LOCATION SHOTS FOR "THE TARGET."

Her makeup was a little more pronounced, her hair was longer, but she looked great. Suddenly he had an insatiable urge to see her. He placed a call to the Plaza. She was registered, but her room didn't answer. He left word that he had called.

He was in the middle of a meeting when his secretary quietly entered the room and placed a note before him: "Miss Stewart on the phone." He waved her off and went on with the meeting. It was five o'clock before he had the chance to return her call.

"Hi!" She sounded impersonal and cheerful.

"How's the big movie star?"

"Beat. I'm playing a high-fashion model whose life is in jeopardy. In the opening scene an attempt is made on my life while I'm shooting fashions in Central Park. Naturally, in true Hollywood form, we're shooting it last. That's why I'm here."

"It sounds exciting."

"I hope it is. As soon as this scene is finished they'll start to edit and score the picture."

"Have you another lined up?"

"I've had several offers but my agent wants me to wait until this one comes out. It's a gamble. If I'm good I'll get much more money and offers of better parts. But if I flop, I'll lose the things that I could grab now."

"It sounds like a rough decision," Robin said.

"I'm a gambler," she said. "I'm going to wait."

"Good girl. By the way, how long will you be in town?"

"Just three days."

"Want to have a hamburger with me at P.J.'s?" It had slipped out before he realized it.

"Why not? Room service takes forever. Just give me time to get out of eight layers of pancake and into a shower."

"Seven o'clock all right?"

"Fine. I'll meet you there." She hung up.

Robin stared at the phone thoughtfully. She hadn't even given him the chance to offer to pick her up. Was she intentionally playing it cool? Then that meant she still had ideas. . . . He quickly put in a call to Jerry Moss.

At seven thirty they were still waiting for her at P.J.'s. "Maybe she's standing me up," Robin said with a smile.

Jerry looked at him curiously. "What's with you and this girl?"

"Absolutely nothing. We're just friends—almost old acquaintances, you might say."

"Then why are you afraid to be alone with her?"

"Afraid?"

"Last time she was in, you made damn sure I was with you when you met her plane."

Robin sipped his beer. "Look, chum, she was once Andy Parino's girl. They had just broken up when she came here that time. I didn't want him to think I was horning in on him. That's probably why I asked you along. I don't recall."

"Oh, that explains everything. And tonight I'm here to protect you from Adam Bergman?"

Robin's glance was direct and curious. "Adam Bergman?"

"This season's bright young director," Jerry explained. "He did that show that won all the awards on Broadway last year. I forget the name—about a lesbian and a fag. Mary and I walked out after the first act, but he's the new sensation." Robin didn't answer. "Funny," Jerry went on, "maybe I'm old-fashioned but I like plays that have a plot—you know, beginning, middle and end. But today —" He stopped, as he heard the buzz that went through the room. Everyone's attention was focused on Maggie, who was walking toward them. Robin stood up. She pretended to remember Jerry, but he was positive she did not. She did not apologize for being late. She ordered a bowl of chili and rummaged through her bag for a cigarette.

"I'd offer you one of mine, but I've given them up," Robin said.

"Then you'll have to get me a pack, I forgot mine."

For some reason it pleased Jerry to see Robin jump up and go to the cigarette machine. He returned with the cigarettes, opened the pack and held a match for her.

"When did you give them up?" she asked.

"Two days ago."

"Why?"

"Just wanted to prove I could kick them."

She nodded as if she completely understood. When she finished the chili she said, "I'd like a beer, then I'm afraid I'll have to leave. Early call tomorrow."

Robin ordered the beer. A mob was queuing up at the door. Suddenly Robin jumped up. "Excuse me—I see a friend of mine."

They watched him go to the door and greet a couple who were standing in line. In a few minutes he returned, bringing them with him.

"Maggie Stewart, Jerry Moss; this is Dip Nelson and Pauli—" He turned to the girl. "I'm sorry, Pauli. I don't remember your last name."

"It's Nelson now."

"Congratulations." Robin signaled for some chairs. "I think we can all squeeze in here."

"I just want to eat and run," Pauli said as she sank into a chair. "Man, am I tired. We've been rehearsing all day —we've got only three weeks before our break-in date."

"We're doing a nightclub act," Dip explained. "We're breaking it in at a country club in Baltimore. No money, just to iron out the kinks. Then our first big date is July Fourth weekend at the Concord. We get five big ones for the one night."

"That's big money, isn't it?" Robin asked.

"Yeah, but the act is costing us over twenty-five thousand."

"Twenty-five thousand!" Robin's amazement was real.

"Why do you think we rehearse eight hours a day at

Nola Studios?" Pauli demanded. "Hey, waiter, two chilis, two cheeseburgers and two Cokes."

"See, we have special material," Dip explained. "Choreography, all the jazz. Pauli's a good dancer and it breaks up the singing bit. We've got two weeks booked in Vegas at fifteen thousand a week. That'll get us more than even. Then Reno, and in September the Persian Room at the Plaza. That's what really counts—the New York reviews."

"Why the big interest in a nightclub act?" Robin asked.

"Did you see my last two pictures?" Dip asked.

"I certainly did."

"Well, then you must know they were bombs."

Robin grinned. "No, I can pretty much tell what will go on TV, but I go to movies to unwind."

"Well, you musta seen the grosses in *Variety*," Pauli cut in.

"I don't read the picture news."

"Look, I know the picture business," Dip said. "I may not know much about anything else, but when my agent comes to me with an offer for an independent at only one hundred thou, I said, 'Dip—now's the time to go!'"

"Well, with that kind of money you have no worries." Robin wanted to turn the conversation into more general areas to include Maggie and Jerry.

"Are you kidding!" Dip said. "I bought her old man and old lady a house."

"A dumperino," Pauli said. "A small place in Los Angeles. Don't act like maybe you set them up in Truesdale. . . ."

"But I bought it outright, didn't I? Forty-nine thousand isn't chopped liver. So no matter what ever happens to us, they'll be fine. And I bought us a house—you should see it. The furniture and decorator set me back a hundred G's. Right in Bel Air. I hated to leave it. But you got to leave before you cool off. We'll be a smash with our act and Hollywood will be on its knees, and the Big Dipper will be right back on top."

"With Pauli right beside you," she said.

"Right with me. Like I said when we got married. We're a team—for keeps."

"See, I won't take a screen test," Pauli confided to the table at large.

"I agree." It was the first word Maggie had said.

Pauli looked at her curiously. "Oh, you in the business?"

"She's playing the lead in Alfred Knight's new movie," Robin explained.

"Oh." Pauli looked at Maggie as if seeing her for the first time. "Yeah, that's right, you're the girl who's having the big affair with Adam Bergman."

Maggie's expression never changed. It was Dip who looked horrified.

For a few moments there was an uncomfortable silence, but Pauli was completely occupied with her hamburger. When she popped the final morsel into her mouth, she said, "Get the check, Dip, I got to get some sleep. We got another eight-hour rehearsal session tomorrow."

Robin smiled. "It's my pleasure to buy the hamburgers. Just think, I'll be able to say I knew *the* Pauli Nelson before she became a star."

She turned and faced him squarely. "Know something? I don't have to take this shit from you. Who in hell are you anyway? Dip made me watch the *In Depth* show. Big deal! I noticed they kicked you off it—another guy's doing it now."

"Pauli!" Dip grabbed her arm. "Robin, I'm sorry. And listen—I *am* sorry you lost *In Depth*. Got anything in the works?"

Robin smiled. "A new show in the fall, called a Happening."

Dip looked genuinely relieved. "I'm glad, buddy boy. You're like the Big Dipper. They can't keep us down, right? Same network?" When Robin nodded, Dip said, "Well, listen, how well do you know Andy Parino?"

"Quite well."

"That's where you can help me, old pal of mine!" Dip flashed his bright smile. "Before we open at the Plaza, if you could swing it so we get interviewed on the *In Depth* show—Pauli and me?"

"If you want it, you've got it."

"No kidding?"

"My word."

Dip stood up. "I'll call you when we get back to town."

When they left the restaurant, Robin took Maggie's arm. "Come on, Jerry and I will walk you home."

"I don't want to walk."

"Jerry, hail a cab for the lady," Robin said.

"Jerry, *don't* hail a cab for the lady," she said, imitating his tone; "the lady has her own car." They suddenly noticed the large limousine that was waiting.

"Thanks for the hamburger and fascinating table talk. I'll try and return the hospitality if you're ever in California."

Jerry watched the car disappear down Third Avenue.

"She really digs you," he said quietly.

"Sure, she's mad about me." Robin's voice was hard.

"No—I mean it. She's an actress, don't forget. And probably a good one, because tonight she was playing one hell of a role."

"What do you mean?"

"She sure wasn't the same girl I met at the airport last February. And no girl changes that much in three months."

"Maybe this Adam what's-his-name has made the difference."

"Maybe."

"Let's cut over to the Lancer Bar and have a drink," Robin said.

"No, I'm cutting down to the station; I can still catch the last train home. If I were you, I'd call Maggie Stewart and ask to buy her a nightcap at the Plaza alone."

"No, thanks."

Jerry stopped. "Tell me, Robin, is she like the cigarettes?"

"I don't get you."

"What in hell are you trying to prove by giving up Maggie Stewart?"

Maggie left town and Robin threw himself into his work. He did four pages on his book every night. Tina St. Claire arrived for a week to promote another picture. He let her move in, enjoyed having her in bed each night, but when she left he felt the same relief at reclaiming his apartment. He worked hard on the Happening series and lost all sense of time or days. And suddenly he stared at his desk calendar and realized that July Fourth was coming up. It fell on a Thursday—that meant a long empty weekend. There wasn't even anyone he particularly wanted to shack up with. Jerry Moss was elated when Robin lethargically agreed to come out to Greenwich. Robin realized it meant an endless round of parties, but they had a swimming pool and he might be able to get in a few rounds of golf.

Maggie's wire arrived July second:

> ARRIVING JULY THIRD TO DO SOME TELEVISION PROMOTION FOR THE PICTURE. DO YOU REALLY THINK ELIZABETH TAYLOR STARTED THIS WAY? WILL BE IN TOWN FOR A FEW DAYS. MAYBE YOU CAN CUE ME ON MY AD LIBS. MAGGIE.

He called Jerry and canceled the weekend. On Wednesday he left his office at five. When he got home he called the Plaza. He learned she had checked in two hours earlier but had left to tape *The Johnny Carson Show*. Well, it was a muggy night, and the weekend stretched ahead. No sweat.

He called her on Thursday. She was out. He left a message and went out and shagged some golf balls.

On Friday he left two messages.

On Saturday he didn't bother to call.

His phone rang Sunday morning at nine. The hell with her! Let *her* spend the day alone. He waited until the exchange picked it up on the third ring. He took a shower, then dialed back his exchange for the message.

A Mr. Jerry Moss had called from Greenwich.

He felt oddly let down. Now, what would Jerry want at nine o'clock on a Sunday morning? He returned the call.

"Are you enjoying yourself in hot sunny New York?" Jerry asked.

"I'm getting a lot of work done."

"You missed a lot of great parties. Rick Russell threw a big one last night. You know who he is—a big wheeler-dealer who puts corporations together. Even has his own airline."

"I can see it all," Robin said. "Outdoors, tents, Japanese lanterns, drunks, mosquitoes."

Jerry laughed. "All of that, plus a friend of yours who was guest of honor: Maggie Stewart."

"What was she doing there?"

"Drinking, dancing, slapping mosquitoes like all of us. Rick Russell is celebrating his fifth divorce. He's not bad-looking, especially when you think of all those millions. Seems they met on the plane coming in from Los Angeles and he's stuck to her ever since. He's sending her to Chicago today in his private plane."

"I like to see a lady travel in style. By the way, Jerry, what did you call me about?"

There was a pause. "Why, I—I thought you'd want to know about Maggie."

"Why?"

"I, well—" Jerry sounded uncomfortable.

"If you thought I cared about her, this would be a rotten play on your part. Trying to give me some lumps, Jerry?"

"Oh no, I know you don't care about the girl," Jerry said quickly.

"Then why waste my time with this call?" And Robin clicked the phone.

He went to a double feature in the afternoon. When he came out it was dark. The streets were empty. Tomorrow the noise of traffic would shriek through the air. But right now the city belonged to him. He stopped at a Nedick's on Third Avenue and had a hot dog. Then he walked aimlessly crosstown. He reached Fifth Avenue and found himself in front of the Plaza.

"Want some fun, mister?" The remark came from a short plump overbleached woman in her forties. She was holding the arm of a skinny red-haired girl who couldn't have been more than nineteen. The young girl was obviously a novice. The older woman shoved her toward Robin. "Fifty bucks, and she has a room."

The girl was wearing a sleazy dress. Her skin was acne-scarred under the heavy makeup. Robin started past them. The blond madam grabbed his arm. "Forty—how's that? Come on, you look like a fellow who needs a little relaxation."

"I'm too relaxed," Robin said and walked away. He hadn't gotten halfway up the block before he was approached by another girl. Not bad-looking either.

"Fifty bucks for a trip to heaven, mister?"

He laughed and continued to walk. Obviously fifty bucks was the going rate. And Central Park South was now their beat. He passed the Hampshire House. Another girl sidled up but he quickened his pace. He suddenly remembered a bookstore on Seventh Avenue that was open at night. He'd buy something light, grab a sandwich and go home and read.

"Want a good time, mister?" He was standing face to face with an Amazon.

She was a mean-looking broad—she had to be over six feet tall. Her dyed jet-black hair was teased into a massive beehive. It was a warm night but she carried a mink stole. Her black eyes were beady, her nose was long and narrow. A big woman . . . big tits. . . . Suddenly a thousand lights seemed to explode in his head. His smile went slack.

She smiled too. "Fifty bucks and I got a room."

"I got a better offer down the street."

She shrugged. "Elsie's breaking in a new one. She's only turned three tricks since she got here. And from what I hear, she still belongs back with the coal miners in Scranton. I can really give you a good time."

"Maybe I should make you pay me," he said. "I'm supposed to be a pretty good stud."

"With me it's women for pleasure, men for business," she said.

"A dike, huh? Well you're an honest cunt, at that."

"And you're a good-looking bastard. Okay, I'll make it forty bucks."

"No favors. I'll pay the full rate. Where's your room?"

"Come with me, lover." She tucked her arm through his and they walked toward Seventh Avenue. She had a room in a dark building on Fifty-eighth Street. It was obvious she didn't live there. From the darkness of the building, it was also obvious that most of the rooms were rented for a similar purpose. The lobby was deserted and a self-service elevator wheezed its way to the third floor. There was a dampness in the hall and the paint was peeling off the small door she opened. "It's not a palace— I call it my work room."

He stepped into the narrow bedroom. A black shade covered a curtainless window. There was a bed, a sink and a small bathroom with a stall shower and a toilet. The overhead light seemed unnaturally bright. She smiled and methodically began to undress. Everything she wore was designed for her trade. The black lace brassiere with holes that bared the large brown nipples. She wore no pants, just a tight black lacy garter belt that left an ugly red mark against her large white stomach.

"Like it with the black stockings on or off?" she asked.

"Everything off." He hardly recognized the voice as his own as he began undressing quickly.

She took a dirty towel and wiped the bright lipstick off her mouth. Her massive body was amazingly well proportioned. "Hand over the fifty, lover, that's ground rules."

He went through his pants and handed her two twenties and a ten. She tucked it into her purse. "Okay, lover, do anything you like. Just try not to muss the hair or the eyelashes. The evening's young and I'm hoping to turn a few more tricks tonight."

He grabbed her and threw her on the bed. His movements were strong and direct. She whimpered slightly. "Hey, lover—take it easy. What are you trying to prove?"

Just as he reached his climax, he withdrew.

"You didn't have to do that. I'm wearing something," she said.

"I wouldn't chance letting a little bastard get born like this," he muttered.

She looked at her watch. "You did that in three minutes flat. You're entitled to another shot." She leaned over and began to run her tongue along his body. He pushed her away, turned her on her stomach and stabbed into her again.

He kept ramming into her, driven by a fury he did not understand. When he finally rolled off her, she jumped off the bed and went to the sink. She grumbled as she washed her stomach. "Jesus, for a classy-looking guy, you play rough."

He lay on the bed staring vacantly into space. She stood before the sink, a mass of white nudity, and applied her lipstick. "Okay, mister—start moving it. Time to go home to your wife. I bet you don't dare try any of this stuff with her, huh? Just nice ordinary fucking."

"I have no wife," he said tonelessly.

"Well, go home to your mother then—I'll bet you live with her. Guys like you always do."

He leaped up and grabbed her by the hair.

"Hey, take it easy lover—be careful of the hair. I told you, I still got work to do. Now go home to Mommy."

His fist cracked at her jaw. For a fleeting moment, before the pain telegraphed itself, her eyes stared at him in almost childish bewilderment. Then as the pain stabbed through her consciousness her mouth parted with a moan and she dashed toward the bathroom. He caught her by the arm.

"Please," she whimpered. "You know I can't make any noise, it'd bring the cops. Please—let me go."

He grabbed her huge breasts in his hands and put his mouth to them.

"You're biting me," she moaned, struggling to get away. "You've had your fifty bucks' worth!" With a final burst of strength she pushed her knee in his groin and broke away. He came after her. For the first time there was fear in her eyes. "Look, mister," she shouted, "I'll give you back your money! Go home to your mother! Suck *her* breasts!"

"*What did you say?*"

Sensing she had found his weakness, she lost her fright. She pulled her naked body to its full height. "I know about you mama's boys—you're closet queens, but you want Mama! Do I look like Mama, sonny boy? Well, go home to her. This mama has to work now."

Once again his fist crashed at her jaw. Only this time he did not stop. He kept slamming at her. Blood was streaming from her nose and mouth. A broken bridge-work fell to the floor. He felt her jaw crack, and he kept hitting her until he felt pain in his knuckles. He stopped to look at them curiously and she slumped to the floor. He stared at his hand as if it didn't belong to him. It was covered with her blood. He looked at the limp form on the floor. He walked to the bed, lay down, and passed out.

When he opened his eyes, he saw the light on the ceiling and the shadowy bodies of three dead moths who had been lured under the glass. Then he saw the bloody sheets. He sat up and stared curiously at his raw knuckles. Suddenly he saw the massive inert girl on the floor. Oh God—this time it hadn't been just a nightmare. It had actually happened. He got off the bed and approached the enormous limp body. Her lips were grotesquely swollen, a trickle of blood was running out of her mouth, blood from her nose was crusted on her upper lip. He leaned over her. She was still breathing. Good God—what had he done! He dressed quickly. Then he reached in his pocket—he only had thirty dollars. That wasn't enough. This girl had to go to the hospital. And he couldn't just leave her. He looked around the room. No phone. He peered out into the hall—nothing there. He had to get her a doctor. There had to be a phone booth down the street.

The lobby was still deserted. He walked out of the building and the darkness of Fifty-eighth Street folded around him. He headed toward the drugstore at the corner. He had to phone for help.

"Hey, buddy boy, what are you doing around here?" It was Dip Nelson in an open convertible.

Robin walked over to the car. "I'm in trouble," he said tonelessly.

"Aren't we all?" Dip laughed. "We played at the Concord last night and we bombed."

"Dip . . . do you have any cash on you?"

"Have I ever—ten C's and a check. Why?"

"Dip—give me the thousand in cash, I'll give you a check."

"Get in the car and tell me about it." They drove through the park and Dip listened silently. When Robin finished, Dip said, "Let's take first things first. One, do you think she'll recognize you? I mean, suppose she's seen you on TV, then what?"

Robin shrugged. "Then the shit hits the fan."

Dip shook his head in wonderment. "Buddy, I don't know how they let you cross the street alone. If you want to make it to the top, you got to see to it that the shit *never* hits the fan! Look—it would be your word against hers. Would anyone take the word of a prostitute against a solid citizen?" He looked at the clock in the car. "It's ten thirty. What time would you say all this happened?"

Robin shrugged. "I went to a movie; I'm not wearing a watch, but it was dark when I came out."

"Then it had to be about eight thirty, maybe nine. We'll get our alibi set for eight just to play it safe."

"Alibi?"

"Me, sweetheart. The Big Dipper is your alibi. *If* you need one. We say I went to your apartment at seven thirty. We sat around and talked shop, then we took a drive. When I check the car in at the garage, I'll make sure someone there notices us."

"But what about the girl?" Robin asked. "She's out cold."

"Whores never die. She'll be out on the street tomorrow as good as new."

Robin shook his head. "I hurt her pretty bad. I just can't let her lie there."

"What ever made you pick her up? Christ, I saw you with the most beautiful broad in the world at P.J.'s."

"I don't know, I can remember seeing her—then something like a rocket went off in my head and the rest is as if I dreamed it."

"Look—want some advice? Leave her be. What's one whore more or less?"

Robin suddenly gripped the door. Dip looked at him oddly. "Anything wrong, pal?"

"Dip—did you ever have a crazy feeling as if you had gone through something before, heard the same words, even though it's just happened?"

"Sure, there's some kind of name for it. Has to do with the mind—getting something a beat late. It happens to everyone. There's even a song about it called 'Where or When.'"

"Maybe," Robin said slowly.

"So cut her from your mind. Make like it never happened," Dip said.

"No—I can't. She's a human being . . . she might even have a kid."

"I thought you said she was a self-admitted lesbo?"

"Yes, of course. You're right."

Dip drove the car down Fifty-sixth Street and pulled into the brightly lit garage. The attendant leaped to greet him. "How did she drive, Mr. Nelson?"

"Like an angel," Dip said. "As a matter of fact my friend and I have been driving around in her since seven thirty. You recognize him, don't you? Robin Stone—remember the *In Depth* show?"

The attendant nodded as a concession to Dip. Then he said, "Mr. Nelson, did you remember to bring that autographed picture you promised—for my daughter Betty?"

"Would I forget?" Dip opened the glove compartment and handed him a manila envelope. "All signed with love and kisses."

They left the garage and Robin started back toward Fifty-eighth Street. Dip hurried after him and tried to talk him out of it. "Look—she could be up there turning another trick by now."

"I only pray to God she is," Robin muttered. They stopped before the dark building. Dip looked around cautiously. "Well, maybe I'm as nutty as you, because I'm gonna go up there with you. Come on, let's go."

Once again the self-service elevator creaked its way to the third floor. The door was slightly ajar just as Robin had left it. They both stared at the unconscious woman on the floor. Dip let out a low whistle. "She's a big one."

"Give me the thousand," Robin said. "I'll put it in her purse. Then we'll call the doctor from the outside."

"Sure, and the doctor puts her in the hospital and she comes to and rats on you."

"But she didn't recognize me."

"Buddy—when a whore has a thousand bucks on her, they're gonna ask a lot of questions. So she describes you, and that's how trouble could start."

"What else can we do?" Robin asked.

"You stay here, buddy boy, the Big Dipper has an idea. Lock that door. When I come back I'll give it two short knocks. Don't open for anything else." Before Robin could answer, he was gone.

Robin sat on the bed and stared at the massive white body on the floor. He cradled his head in his arms. The poor bitch. What had gotten into him? This was the first time he had ever tried it with a brunette sober. And the last! Good God, suppose it had been Maggie.

She stirred and moaned. He got off the bed and put a pillow under her head. Then he took his handkerchief, held it under the cold-water tap and tried to wipe the crusted blood off her lip. He stroked the hair from her face. "I'm sorry," he whispered. She half opened her eyes, moaned, and once again lapsed into unconsciousness. "I'm sorry, you dumb whore, I'm sorry. Oh Jesus, I'm sorry."

He opened the door when he heard the two quick taps. Dip brandished a bottle of gleaming red capsules. "Did I ever come up with an idea."

"Seconals?" Robin asked.

Dip nodded. "Now, we just have to get them down Brünnhilde."

"It will kill her."

"I only got eight. She can't die from eight. A human being, maybe—but it would take dynamite to put that whale away."

"But why the pills?"

"We get her on the bed, the empty pill bottle beside her—it's got no label so it can't be traced. Then we go out and put in a call to the police. I'll fake the voice, say I had a date to get laid, and found her this way. I'll say she always threatened the Dutch act. That's the way most whores end up anyhow, unless a guy like you does it for them. Then the ambulance will come and cart her to Bellevue, pump her stomach, and by the time she comes to they'll never believe anything she tells them nor will they care. And while she's there they'll patch up whatever damage you've done. Now all we gotta do is get Primo Carnera on the bed."

She was a dead weight. They were both out of breath

when they finally propped her up. Dip forced the pills into her mouth and slugged the water down her throat. She gurgled and the pills and water came sliding down her face. Dip pushed them back, shoved more water into her mouth. Robin held her head up so she wouldn't choke. His shirt was damp and he watched in agony until Dip finally got the pills down her.

"Okay, let's scram," Dip said. "Wait—" He took out a handkerchief and started wiping the place for fingerprints. He flashed Robin a wink. "All those B detective pictures I did are finally paying off. I know all the shticks. Did you touch anything, buddy boy?" Dip took a small leather case from his pocket. In it were a slim gold comb, a nail file and a nail clipper. Robin stared in horrified fascination as Dip cut her long red claws. Then he methodically cleaned the rest of her nails with a file.

"That's in case any of your hair was in it." He stared around the room. "I think that covers it." Then, using a handkerchief, Dip went into her bag and took out her wallet. "Her name is Anna-Marie Woods. She lives on Bleecker Street."

"Give me that address." Robin took the driver's license and jotted down the name and address. Then he handed it back to Dipper who replaced it in her bag. "She's got close to a hundred bucks on her—here, take it."

"Are you crazy!" Robin pushed it away.

"You didn't write down her address so you can take her dancing, did you? You want to send her some money, right? Well, you can also add this to it. Otherwise it's a cinch some orderly or patient will steal it from her at Bellevue."

Robin took the money and nodded dumbly. He understood why Dip had made it in pictures. He was constantly trying to outthink the next person. Maybe you had to when you came up the hard way.

They left the room cautiously. Their luck held and they reached the street without meeting anyone. Dip made the call, but Robin refused to leave until he was certain help arrived. Dip was against it, but they stood in a doorway across the street. Within ten minutes they heard the sirens. Three police cars pulled up before the house. Two minutes later an ambulance arrived. From nowhere a large crowd gathered—it seemed to Robin as if they emerged from the ground. "I've got to go over and see if she's alive," he whispered.

Dip started with him, but Robin pushed him back. "Now who's not thinking? With that blond hair and Hollywood tan, you'd have the crowd forgetting the ambulance and mobbing you for autographs. No one will recognize me."

"Don't be too sure," Dip hissed.

"From the look of them, I can be sure. And I'm also sure they saw *all* your B detective pictures." Robin crossed the street and mingled with the curious onlookers. A few minutes later the ambulance attendants came down with the stretcher. He breathed easier. Her head wasn't covered—that meant she was still alive.

He returned to Dip after the ambulance clanged its way through the red light and the crowd dispersed. Dip took his arm. "Okay, buddy boy, I think you've had a big night. You better go to bed now, alone."

Robin stared at him. "Dip, what can I do for you? Name it."

"Forget it." Dip jabbed him on the arm. "Pauli and I have it made. In September you can get us on *In Depth* before we open at the Persian Room. Now—let's hail separate cabs a few blocks from here. We follow the B pictures to the very end."

Robin got home and took a sleeping pill. An hour later he took another and washed it down with vodka. Within moments he fell into a hard sleep. When he awoke the following morning, he called Dr. Archie Gold. "This is Robin Stone. I think I'm ready for the full course."

# TWENTY-FOUR

R OBIN looked relaxed and in complete command of
   himself as he sat across from Dr. Gold.

"Have you ever picked up a prostitute before?"

"Never."

"Have you ever thought about it?"

"Never."

"And you say you passed up one that was fairly attractive. What made you go for this one?"

Robin squashed his cigarette. "That's why I'm here. She was a brunette."

Archie's gray eyes held a faint show of interest. "Could you have been testing yourself for Maggie?"

"What do you mean?"

"You'd have nothing to lose but your fifty dollars if you didn't get an erection with the prostitute."

Robin shook his head. "No, I don't think it was that at all. Something funny exploded in my head when she approached me. From the moment I went with her, I felt as if I was dreaming."

Dr. Gold studied his notes. "You know, the last time you were here, I told you I wanted to put you under hypnosis. I still do."

"That's ridiculous—we can certainly talk things out. . . ."

"I don't want to waste my time and your money. I'd like to put you under and use a tape recorder. Then you can hear your answers, and perhaps we can go from there." He noticed the frown appear on Robin's face. "When we talked last January, we hit a block. You can't go back to your early childhood. It's not that you refuse to remember—you *can't* remember. And until now, you have separated sex from love. You have no ability to put them together. What you feel for Maggie is the desire to love. Yet love *with* sex seems incestuous to you. We've got to find out the reason. There's not a clue in anything that you've told me in the last visit. And I assume you held nothing back." He paused. "Robin, how old are you?"

"I'll be forty-one next month."

"Have you ever thought of marriage?"

"No. Why should I?"

"Every man naturally assumes that one day he will marry. When did you first become aware that you wanted to be a loner?" Dr. Gold asked.

"I don't know. It was something I always felt."

"There we go again," Archie said triumphantly. "Something you *felt*—when? How? Don't you see, we have to go back." He stood up. "Robin, we're only going in circles. I think you've had enough for today. Come in tomorrow. Do you think you can give me three hours?"

"Three hours?"

"I want to put you under and use a tape recorder. After we both listen to the tape, I have a feeling we'll cut right through to the core of the problem."

"We'll have to make it in the evening," Robin said. "Would six be all right?"

"I'll see you here at six."

The following day Robin scanned the newspapers to see if there was anything about Anna-Marie. He finally found a brief mention on the fifth page of the *News*:

A woman was found brutally beaten in a furnished room on West 58th Street. Police arrived after receiving an anonymous phone call. She did not live in the room and offered no explanation for being there. She was taken to Bellevue where it was discovered she had a long record for prostitution. No charges are brought against her, and she has been unable to name her unknown assailant. Her condition is not serious and she will be discharged from Bellevue tomorrow.

Robin went to the bank, withdrew two thousand dollars in small bills and sent it to her home address in a plain manila envelope. He still had reservations about the hypnotism deal, but he arrived at Dr. Gold's office at six. When his eyes rested on the tape recorder he felt a small chill of apprehension. "You actually think this is going to work?"

"I hope so," Archie answered. "Take off your coat and loosen your tie."

Robin took out his cigarettes. "Might as well get comfortable. Do I use the couch? I'll even try that if it will help."

"No, sit there, in the straight chair. And forget the cigarettes. Robin, you're not going to fight it, are you?"

"Listen, neither of us has time to play games."

"Fine! Now I want you to clear your mind. Fasten your attention to that seascape on the wall. All you see is the water . . . your feet are relaxing . . . all sense of feeling is leaving them . . . your legs are also floating . . . the feeling is creeping up through your body . . . you are weightless . . . your hands will drop at your side . . . your head and neck are relaxed . . . your eyes will close. Close your eyes, Robin. Now . . . you see nothing but darkness . . . it is velvet darkness . . . you are falling asleep. . . ."

Robin was aware that Dr. Gold had dimmed the lights. He was positive it was not going to work, but he followed Dr. Gold's instructions. He stared at the damned seascape. He told himself all feeling was leaving him. He pushed every thought from his mind but the quiet voice of Dr. Gold. . . . He could hear Archie's voice. It wasn't going to work. He could still hear Archie's voice. The darkness behind his eyes was heavy . . . but it wasn't going to work. . . .

He opened his eyes. He was on the couch. He sat up and stared aimlessly around the room and reached for his cigarettes. "How did I get over here? A few seconds ago I was on that chair."

"That was two and a half hours ago."

Robin jumped up. "What time is it?"

"Quarter of nine. You arrived here at six."

Robin picked up the telephone and dialed for the correct time. The singsong voice said, "At the tone, it will be eight forty-seven." He hung up and looked at Dr. Gold in total disbelief. The doctor smiled at him.

Robin looked at the tape recorder questioningly. Dr. Gold nodded.

"Well, for God's sake—play it for me!"

"You've had enough for one night. I want to listen to it myself alone tonight. Then tomorrow I'll play it for you."

"Did I make sense?" Robin asked.

"You made some startling revelations."

"For Christ's sake, play it for me. How can I sleep tonight wondering about this?"

Dr. Gold placed two green pills in an envelope. "Take these when you get home. Can you be in my office at six tomorrow?"

The pills worked. He had a good night's sleep, but he was tense and impatient the following day. He chained-smoked and found it impossible to concentrate on the work at hand. By the time he reached Dr. Gold's office, he was taut with nerves.

"Robin," said Dr. Gold, "before we start, I want you to bear this in mind. People tell the truth under deep hypnosis. Every word you hear on that tape will be your voice. At times it may even sound strange because I took you back to your childhood and you even spoke as a child. But I want you to listen with an open mind and not fight anything you hear."

Dr. Gold walked to the machine. "Ready?"

Robin nodded and sat down. The hum of the tape began. The first voice was Dr. Gold's:

DR. GOLD: Robin, you are under . . . you will hear my voice and react to everything I tell you to do. Now get up from that chair and walk to the couch. Good. Now lie down, Robin. We are going back . . . way back . . . you are a little boy. You are five years old . . . you are in bed. . . .

ROBIN: Yes, I am in bed.

Robin sat on the edge of the chair and stabbed his cigarette out. Jesus, the voice was younger and lighter—but it was *his* voice!

DR. GOLD: You are in bed. What kind of a bed is it?

ROBIN: A nice bed. Kitty is kissing me good night.

DR. GOLD: Robin, you are four years old. You are in bed. . . . (*Silence on the tape*)

DR. GOLD: Robin, you are four years old . . . four years old. . . .

ROBIN: Why do you call me Robin? My name is Conrad.

DR. GOLD: All right, Conrad. You are in bed . . . what do you see?

ROBIN: Mama is in bed with me, but . . .

DR. GOLD: But what?

ROBIN: She only pretends to stay, until I am asleep. Then she leaves me. She leaves me every night.

DR. GOLD: How do you know she leaves you?

ROBIN: Because I always wake up and hear her in the other room . . . when she's with them.

DR. GOLD: Who is "them"?

ROBIN: I don't know.

DR. GOLD: Where is your father?

ROBIN: We haven't got a father.

DR. GOLD: We?

ROBIN: My mother and me . . . we have no one. Just us . . . and them.

DR. GOLD: Who is "them"?

ROBIN: Lots of times it's Charlie. Sometimes it's others.

DR. GOLD: They come to visit your mother?

ROBIN: Yes . . . but they wait until I'm asleep.

DR. GOLD: What do you do when you hear them out there?

ROBIN: Nothing anymore. Not after Charlie slapped me.

DR. GOLD: When did Charlie slap you?

ROBIN: A while back . . . when I came in and found him on top of Mama on the couch.

DR. GOLD: Does she still go into the living room after you're asleep?

ROBIN: Yes, but not with Charlie. She never let him come back again. On account of him hitting me. And I'm the only man she loves . . . we only have each other . . . no one in the world cares about us . . . we just have each other. . . .

DR. GOLD: How old are you?

ROBIN: I'll be four tomorrow, August twentieth. And my mother is going to take me to Boston to see the pigeons on the Commons. . . .

DR. GOLD: Where do you live?

ROBIN: In Providence, Rhode Island.

DR. GOLD: Aren't you going to have a birthday party with your little friends?

ROBIN: We have no friends. There's just us.

DR. GOLD: Rob—Conrad, it is a week after your birthday. What are you doing?

ROBIN: I'm still mad at my mother.

DR. GOLD: Why?

ROBIN: A man came on my birthday. He knocked on the door just as we were leaving for Boston. Mama said we were going out . . . for him to come back later that night. He gave her some money and said someone had sent him. Mama gave me a nickel and told me to go to the corner for ice cream and to sit on the stoop and not come in till she sent for me. I was sitting there eating my ice-cream cone and a big boy came by and took it from me. I ran inside . . . Mama was in our bed . . . the man was with her. I'm mad at her. No one sleeps during the day. It was my birthday. She yelled at me . . . told me to go out. . . . (*Silence on the tape*)

DR. GOLD: Conrad, it is Thanksgiving. You are four . . . what are you doing?

ROBIN: Mama made a goose. People with large families have turkeys. But we're a little family, just us . . . so we have a goose. But we have cranberry sauce with real berries in it . . . and she's making the goose just like she had it when she was a little girl in Hamburg.

DR. GOLD: Conrad, were you ever in Hamburg?

ROBIN: No. My mother was born there. Lots of sailors were there, and that's when she met *him*. And he brought her to America and married her.

DR. GOLD: And then you were born? He was your father?

ROBIN: No. He got killed. He wasn't my father. He was just the man my mother married. He wasn't any good. She told me. He worked and drove a truck selling whiskey and that wasn't allowed. And one night everyone in his truck got shot. And Mama was all alone. See, there wasn't even me . . . or anyone. She was alone. But the man who owned all the trucks told my mother not to worry. And he sent lots of men to visit her and cheer her up and give her money and a year later God sent me to her.

DR. GOLD: Did your mother know which man was your father?

ROBIN: I told you . . . we had no father. Just Mother and me. And we moved a lot because policemen don't like a little boy living alone with his mother without a father, and if they catch us they'll put me in a home away from Mother and send her back to Hamburg. But she's saving her money and then one day we will *both* go back to Hamburg and live with my *Grossmutter* . . . and I will have children to play with and not be alone. See, right now, that is why I am not allowed to get friendly with children in the neighborhood, because they would ask questions about my father . . . and then they would tell the police I had no father. . . .

DR. GOLD: Conrad, it is a week after Thanksgiving, at night. What are you doing?

ROBIN: I am in bed, but Mother is in the other room with George. He's been here every night. He says he will get us passports and he gives Mother money every night.

DR. GOLD: Who is George?

ROBIN: One of them. . . .

DR. GOLD: Conrad, it is two weeks after Thanksgiving, at night. Is your mother with George?

ROBIN: No . . . *He* was there.

DR. GOLD: Who is he?

ROBIN: Another man.

DR. GOLD: Who was the other man?

ROBIN: I don't know. I woke up and felt the bed empty and knew Mother was in the next room. I was hungry and wanted the coconut cookies she kept in the icebox. I had to go through the living room to get to the kitchen. So I tiptoed in because I remember when Charlie slapped me . . . and Mother gets mad if I don't stay in bed. . . .

DR. GOLD: Who was with your mother?

ROBIN: I never saw him before. He was on his knees on the couch . . . bending over Mother.

DR. GOLD: What was he doing?

ROBIN: His hands were on her neck. I stood very quiet and watched. Then he got up and left. He didn't even say goodbye to Mama. I walked over to the couch and she was asleep . . . only she wasn't really asleep, her eyes were open and she pretended to be asleep. And when I shook her she rolled off the couch and she was lying on the floor with her tongue hanging funny and falling to the side and her hair all dark and messed up. I loved to sleep against her breasts . . . they were so soft and warm under her nightgown. I didn't know what they looked like before, and they look so ugly now without the nightgown. I hate them! And her hair is black and looks too black against her face, and her eyes look funny, they look right at me as if they don't see me. I'm scared. "*Mutter*. Mother . . . *Mother!*" (*Silence on the tape*)

DR. GOLD: It is the next day. Where are you?

ROBIN: In a big room . . . everyone is asking me questions. I keep asking for Mama. They want to know what the man looked like. I want Mama. I want my mother. Then a big lady in white comes and takes me into a room where there are a lot of children. And she tells me this is where I will live. And that all the other little boys in the room are like me . . . they have no mothers. I ask did my mother go to Hamburg and she says no. And one boy says, "Your mother is dead." And I ask, "Did Mother go to the angels?" And the big lady in the white dress laughs and says, "Not your mother, sonny. Bad people don't go with the angels, and she deserves what she got, bringing a kid like you into this world with the life she led!"

And I . . . I hit her . . . I hit her. . . . (the voice

screams. Then after a pause the voice continues.)
Everything is going dark . . . but people are coming
around me. But I'm not crying . . . Mama said I was
a man and men don't cry. I won't cry . . . I won't say
anything . . . I won't eat . . . I won't listen to them.
Then they'll have to bring me back to my mother.
This is what she meant. . . . They found we had no
father . . . they've taken me to this big home . . .
away from her. But I won't think about it . . . I won't
listen to them. . . . (*There is silence on the tape*)

DR. GOLD: Conrad, it is Christmas. Where are you?

ROBIN: (*in a faint voice*) It is dark . . . I'm asleep . . .
dark . . . dark. . . . There is a tube like a little straw
in my arm . . . but it doesn't hurt . . . nothing hurts . . .
I sleep . . . sleep. . . . Ever since that bad dark lady
left me to go to Hamburg . . . she never loved me . . .
I will sleep and not think of her . . . she was bad. . . .

DR. GOLD: It is two weeks later, Conrad. Where are you?

ROBIN: I am sitting up in a big bed with sides around
it. Two ladies in white are with me and one is very
glad that I am sitting up. She asks me my name. I
have no name. I don't know where I am. A man in a
white coat comes and looks in my eyes with a light.
He is nice . . . they bring me ice cream. . . .

DR. GOLD: It is your fifth birthday, Conrad. Where are
you?

ROBIN: Why do you call me Conrad? My name is Robin
Stone, and I'm having a birthday party. And Mommy
and Daddy and all my friends are watching me
blow out the candles.

DR. GOLD: Do you like Mommy?

ROBIN: Of course. I was sick, did you know that? When
Mommy and Daddy came and took me from the
hospital I didn't even know them. But I do now.

DR. GOLD: What does Mommy look like?

ROBIN: She's pretty and nice and has yellow hair and
her name is Kitty.

Dr. Gold clicked off the set. "The rest goes exactly as
you stated—Lisa being born, all the rest of it."
Robin sat back. His shirt was drenched, his face was

drained of color. He looked at Dr. Gold. "What does it mean?"

Dr. Gold's gaze was direct. "It's pretty obvious, isn't it?"

Robin stood up. "It's a pack of lies!"

The doctor's expression was sympathetic. "I knew how you'd feel. At nine o'clock this morning, I phoned the Providence *Journal*. They went through the back issues for Thanksgiving 1928. They finally found this item: 'Police broke into an apartment, after receiving an anonymous phone call. A woman was found strangled and her four-year-old child was sleeping on her breast. The woman had been dead seven hours. She had been charged with prostitution several times, but never convicted. Police believe it was the killer who called, but there are no clues, as the child is the only one who saw the murderer and cannot describe the killer.'"

"And that's it?" Robin asked.

"One more item. Three days later." Archie continued: "'Police tried to show pictures of various sex offenders to the child, but he seems to be in a comatose state. He is at the Good Shelter Home in Providence, Rhode Island.'"

Robin walked to the window. "So I'm not me. I'm a little bastard named Conrad." He turned and stared at Archie. "Why did you do this to me? Why? Wasn't I better off not knowing?"

"Better off picking up strange prostitutes and almost killing them? Better off not being able to have a decent relationship with a woman?"

"I could have stayed away from whores. I was happy as I was."

"Were you? I also doubt if you could have stayed away from whores. Maggie's rejection of you caused something to stir which set off a chain reaction. And when you saw the prostitute, you unconsciously felt the old anger at your mother for leaving you—for being a 'bad woman.' There was, as you put it, an explosion in your brain. You acted out a dream fantasy, of hate and love."

"Why would I hate? That kid on the tape loved his mother!"

"Of course he loved her. Too much. There was no one

else in his life but her. Yet young as he was, his subconscious knew he had to hate to survive. But even hate can be painful, so he chose to forget—with self-induced amnesia. When you saw the prostitute, something from your subconscious came through—hate. When you met Maggie, the subconscious also stirred—love. The love you felt for your mother. You also saw Maggie as a beautiful girl *you* desired. But the subconscious rebelled. That's why you had to get drunk to be able to have sex with her. Sober, your subconscious ties her up with Mama."

"And now because you tell me this I'll walk out of here and be able to lay Maggie?"

"It's not that simple. Eventually yes. After you've learned to understand your drives, your desires, and what motivates them. When that happens, you won't need a clean antiseptic-looking girl to rouse you and a girl like Maggie to love from a distance. You will be able to give love and accept love in a total fulfillment."

"Archie, I'm going to be forty-one. It's a little late for a personality change. I think I'd rather have gone on grabbing a nice blond dish when I felt the urge." He sank into a chair. "Jesus, I'm not me—Kitty's not my mother. I don't know who my father was. I don't even know who my mother was." His laugh was forced. "And I pitied Amanda! Me! The lowest kind of bastard there is. I'm Conrad who?"

"You *are* Robin Stone. A name does not make a man. But you've been living with some of Conrad's scarred emotions. Get them out, air them. Keep the good ones, discard the wrong ones."

"What would be the wrong ones?"

"The hate for his real mother."

"Oh, she was a charmer," Robin said. "At least Amanda's mother did it with one guy. Mine was a bum."

"She was a poor little German girl alone in a strange country. Obviously the man she married worked for a bootlegger. When he was killed the boss probably set her up as a prostitute. And don't forget, when you were born she could have gotten rid of you. Dumped you into an orphanage in the very beginning. But she loved you—tried to give you a home, tried to save money to take you back to the only world she knew. She loved you, Robin."

He clenched his fists. "Why in hell didn't Kitty tell me? Why did she raise me to believe I was her own child?"

"It's obvious you went into shock. When you came out of it, you had complete loss of memory. To tell you that you were adopted might have reactivated the bad memories, which—young as you were—you wanted to blot out. She probably was advised *not* to tell you." He saw a hard gleam come into Robin's eyes.

"Look here, Robin, I don't want you to feel one second of self-pity. You're a very lucky man. You had a mother who loved you. And Kitty who loved you enough to adopt you and keep the secret from you. A man who has been given that much love has no right to skim through life giving nothing of himself."

Robin stood up. "As I see it, I've no right to skim through life *making* nothing of myself."

"What do you mean?"

"Lisa knows the truth—something she said makes me realize that. And of course Kitty knows. She probably is worried about me—that I might revert to type or collapse. She feels I need protection. That I'm weak. They think I need a wife and children as an anchor. God, I've gone through the last thirty-five years on a pass. Kitty and Lisa secretly pity me. Well, I don't need pity. And I don't need a wife. I don't need a child—I don't need anyone. Including you! Get it! I don't need *anyone!* And from here on in, no one gives me one goddam thing—I'm going to get it for myself." He grabbed his jacket and tore out of the office.

# TWENTY-FIVE

MAGGIE stretched out in the large bed. She smiled as she heard Adam's loud baritone reverberating from the bathroom. She wanted to get a good night's sleep. Tomorrow was Sunday and Adam had promised to work with her on the new script. Just thinking about it

brought on the fear. The fear she had been living with
ever since Karl Heinz Brandt had selected her to star in
his new picture. It was all very well for Adam to tell her
not to be frightened about working with Karl Heinz but
she was terrified. Karl Heinz was known for his
sadistic attitude toward actors. He would humiliate
the biggest stars to get a performance from them.
She pushed the thought from her mind and picked up a
copy of weekly *Variety*. Somehow there never seemed
time to read anything other than the daily trades.
You read them while they were doing your hair or
makeup. How long had it been since she had
read a newspaper? The gossip columnists attacked
her for living openly with Adam Bergman at his
beach house. They unearthed the fact that she had once
been Mrs. Hudson Stewart. They condemned a "nice" girl
for flagrantly ignoring matrimony. Oddly enough, the
publicity enhanced her value. She was becoming a "personality." And when Karl Heinz selected her to star in his
new picture, the new avalanche of publicity turned her
into a "hot" property.

One national magazine called her the "Lady of the
Dunes," and ran a photograph of her, walking barefoot
with Adam in the moonlight along the beach in Malibu.
Her constant refusal of invitations to all the "right" parties had also caused her to become a bit of a legend.
Actually, she didn't go because she was scared to death.
She enjoyed living with Adam, she enjoyed working with
him, she enjoyed him in bed. And neither of them ever
thought about marriage. The subject was never even discussed.

She thought about this as she leafed through *Variety*.
When she came to the television section, she lit a cigarette and scanned every item carefully. She checked the
ratings. Christie Lane was number one! Robin's Happening show was in the top twenty.

She had heard from him last February—he was planning a Happening on the world of fashion. The communi-
cation was merely a typed letter offering her expenses,
first-class accommodations at the Plaza and a fee of five
thousand dollars if she wanted to guest-star as the com-

mentator. She had typed a letter on a piece of Century's stationery, explaining that Miss Stewart's television fee was twenty-five thousand, but unfortunately her picture commitments would prevent any negotiations for a television appearance. Then she had signed it "Jane Biando, secretary to Miss Stewart."

Adam came out of the shower with a towel around his waist. She watched him as he combed his hair. She told herself she was very lucky. She adored Adam. Then why did she always subconsciously think of Robin? Did she still want him? Yes, dammit, she did! Maybe Alfie Knight had explained it best. He was in love with Gavin Moore, the designer, yet he had gone wildly on the make for her during the picture. And when it was over he continued to call her. One day he said, "Luv, you may *just* have to have an affair with me and get me back to being a happy well-adjusted homosexual."

"Now, Alfie, you're not in love with me," she had answered.

"Of course not. I adore Gavin. He's the love of my life —this season. But, luv, when I'm in a picture I have to mesmerize myself into being in love with my leading lady so I'll come across butch. Unfortunately, it sometimes works too well, and when the picture is over, I have to rush to Palm Springs to get the lady off my back. But you've been so distant that you've become an obsession with me."

She had told this to Adam and he had laughed. "You owe it to him, he made you look great in the picture. And an obsession is the worst type of sickness. With an obsession, you've got to come to grips with it—not let it smolder and take hold of you."

"You mean you'd let me sleep with Alfie?" She was teasing.

"Sure, if you let me watch." He meant it.

To her amazement, she had called Alfie and told him Adam's offer. Alfie accepted eagerly. He came to the beach house and made love to her while Adam lay beside them on the bed. The crazy part of it was that she felt no shame. And when it was over, she watched while Alfie made love to Adam. And it all seemed perfectly normal

and relaxed. Afterwards, they all went into the kitchen
and made scrambled eggs. And they remained the best of
friends.

Perhaps Adam had a point. Alfie was back with Gavin
but her obsession about Robin Stone was still festering.
She was positive that one day they would get together.
He would be tanked up on vodka—that was the only way
it could happen. And when he yelled *"Mutter,*
Mother, *Mother,"* she'd leap out of bed and throw a
pitcher of cold water on him. Let him try and say
he'd had a blackout after that!

Adam cut into her thoughts by dropping the towel and
coming to her. When it was over they raced into the
ocean, and when they went back to the house she curled
into Adam's arms and fell asleep and dreamed of Robin.

They flew to San Francisco to catch the sneak preview
of the picture. She sat clutching Adam's arm while he
nibbled the buttered popcorn. Karl Heinz sat in front of
them with a young ingenue. A few other members of the
cast sat across the aisle.

She watched the film intently and wished she could be
objective enough to analyze her performance. She knew
that she had never looked as exciting—the cinematog-
ráphy was fantastic. She was all eyes, cheekbones and
windswept hair. The clothes were fantastic. Adam had
complained that she was too thin, but it certainly paid off
on the screen. She shifted nervously in her seat. The big
scene was coming. When it began she peered cautiously
at the audience. She couldn't believe it—people were
actually affected by her performance.

And then the music swelled and the picture was over.
Adam grabbed her hand, whispering as they ran up the
aisle of the theater, "Baby, you've turned into one hell of
an actress. That last scene really had it." They got out of
the theater just as the audience was beginning to spill
into the aisles. They stood across the street and waited
for Karl Heinz and the others. Maggie was still apprehensive until Karl Heinz approached. His face was beaming.
He held out his arms and kissed her.

A week after the sneak preview, Hy Mandel, her agent, met her in the Polo Lounge at the Beverly Hills Hotel. He waited until they had ordered a drink, then he tossed the new contract to her with a flourish. "We did it, honey! When the heads of Century lamped the screening of the new epic, they realized it was stupid to try and force you to stay with the old deal at seventy-five thousand a picture. Like I said, 'Gentlemen—she'll do these pictures for you as an unhappy actress. And what will happen? She'll be unhappy and she'll be lousy. And you'll destroy a potential star. What will the stockholders say to that? Especially since it's now a road-show picture— three and a half hours with an intermission yet. *Starring* Maggie Stewart.' I hammered it home. How will it look, I asked them, if they didn't know how to take a star another director created, and continue to build her. And it worked! Look at the new terms—two hundred and fifty thousand apiece for the next two pictures, and three hundred thousand for the third, plus twenty percent of the net profits!"

She nodded and sipped her Bloody Mary. Hy rushed on. "Now look, principal photography on the new picture won't start until February. They want you back January fifteenth for wardrobe."

"January fifteenth! How wonderful! It's only December tenth!"

"That's right. We've arranged a nice little vacation for you."

She looked at him suspiciously. He laughed. "So maybe it isn't exactly a vacation, but we had to give a little to get. Now, there's going to be a tremendous opening of *The Torn Lady* in New York, and—"

"*The Torn Lady?*" She wrinkled her nose. "Is that the title they've settled on?"

"Don't knock it, honey. When it was called *Henderson,* that automatically geared it toward the male star. This way, it's your picture."

She smiled. "All right. Now what's the hitch? What do I have to do?"

"Well, it's not really anything rough—a trip to New York to attend the opening isn't exactly factory work."

"It also means interviews, television shows, and not a minute to myself."

"Wrong again. The picture opens December twenty-sixth. You don't have to be in New York until the twenty-second."

"And I work from the twenty-second straight through the big gala opening night."

"Yes, but meanwhile you're free from now until the twenty-second. And if you want to go to New York earlier and see some shows, they'll spring for that. Or if you want to stay on a week after . . . it means a vacation either way. As long as you're back here the fifteenth. Why not go now? It's all on Century."

She shook her head. "I think I'll stay at the beach and just rest. The good weather is still holding out."

"Maggie"—he paused—"I don't want you to stay at the beach—with Adam."

She looked at him curiously. "Everyone knows I live with Adam."

"Why don't you two kids get married?"

"I don't want to."

"Then why live with him?"

"I'm lonely. I'll stay with him until I—" She stopped.

"Till you find the right man? Maggie, did it ever occur to you that you won't find anyone else as long as you stay with Adam?"

"I've found him."

Hy stared at her with unmasked surprise.

"I found him four years ago," she went on, "but—"

"He's married?"

She shook her head. "Hy, let's forget it. I'm happy with my work, happy with Adam."

"I'm sixty years old," he said slowly. "I've been married to Rhoda for thirty-two years. Rhoda is fifty-nine. At the time I married her I had a small office on West Forty-sixth Street and Rhoda was teaching school. When we got married she was a twenty-seven-year-old virgin and I wasn't surprised. We expected girls to be virgins in those days. Today a twenty-seven-year-old virgin would be a freak. Today a guy who is true to his wife is a freak. Well, I'm one of those freaks. So maybe Rhoda is twenty pounds overweight. And maybe I've slowed down—it's been two or three years since Rhoda and I slept together. But we have a good life. We got grown children and grandchildren and we still have a double bed and we enjoy lying in it together and sometimes even holding hands when we watch television. But we hold hands with a different kind of love now. Ever since I got to be a top agent out here—and now especially since you've become so hot—I suddenly find I'm being given the eye by twenty-one-year-old beautiful shiksas. These same little shiksas wouldn't have given me the right time when I was in my prime. There was one just the other day—I never saw such a body. She bent down and all but dropped the boobies on my desk. But you know something? I look in the mirror each morning when I shave. I see a guy with too little hair and too much belly. Maybe if I took on the little blonde I'd get it up pretty good. Maybe we'd roll together in bed. But who am I kidding? She's not rolling with me because of my profile. It's my connections she wants. So I say, Hy, is it worth it? And I say no. But I've seen other guys my age get tied up with girls younger than their married daughters. But I will say they don't flaunt it. They go to La Rue Saturday night with their wives. They go to Hillcrest every Sunday with their wives. See what I mean? If they want it on the side, okay—but they keep up some semblance of a front for the children and the wife. Maggie, you have no children —but you have a public, and there are a lot of people who still think like me and they won't pay three dollars to go see a beautiful girl crying over dying and leaving her child and husband when they know she's flagrantly living at a beachhouse without a wedding ring."

"I've spent enough of my life living up to conventions and rules," she said sullenly.

His sigh was heavy. "Maggie, what is it with you kids today? Am I that out of touch? Look, all I ask is for you to marry Adam, or get your own place. Then sleep with him, run up and down the beach with him—but please get your own place."

She laughed. "All right, Hy, when I come back from

New York, I'll check into this hotel. Meanwhile, you can look for an apartment for me."

"It just so happens, I've already accidentally stumbled on just such a place. A furnished apartment at the Melton Towers—four hundred a month, switchboard service, right in Beverly Hills. Come. I'll drive you there."

She saw the apartment. It was perfect for her needs—a large living room, full kitchen, master bedroom, small den with a wetbar. The manager who showed the apartment had the lease all drawn up. Maggie laughed when she realized Hy had chosen the apartment before their talk. The next day Adam helped her move. He stayed at the beach, as he was blocking out the script for a new picture.

After two days alone in the new apartment, she grew fidgety. Adam was leaving the following week for location shots in Arizona. She'd be alone in Los Angeles. She called Hy and told him that if the studio still wanted to pay her way, she'd go to New York and do the publicity.

Adam took her to the airport. She posed for the airlines publicity man. Then Adam took her to the TWA Ambassadors lounge for a drink. "I'll be away for three months with the picture," he said. "When I come back, I'll move in with you. It's a nice apartment. Besides, it gets too damn cold at the beach in March."

She stared at the planes being serviced on the airfield. "I told you what Hy said."

He smiled. "Well, tell him I'm a nice Jewish boy, too. We might as well get married, Maggie. I think it could work. You won't mind if I shack up once in a while with another dame."

"I don't think I want marriage to be that way," she said slowly.

"Oh, you want it all neat and orderly like the kind you had in Philadelphia?"

"No, but I don't want to be *part* of a marriage—like the apartment, the furniture. I want you to be jealous of me, Adam."

"You didn't exactly blindfold yourself when Alfie was in bed with us."

"But don't you understand—that wasn't the real me."

He looked at her with his intense direct stare. "Cut the shit, Maggie. No one goes back. The girl that slept with Alfie is you. Now suddenly you start getting dewy-eyed about what you want in a marriage. What we've had at the beach is what there is to marriage in our kind of life."

He took her silence as acceptance and reached for her hand. "We'll get married when I come back from Arizona. I'll release it to the press after I leave you today."

She pulled her hand away. "Don't you dare!" Her eyes flashed in anger. "I'm not about to throw my life down the drain living with you and pretending that acting is art. It's a business! But there's more to life than living this business every second, and making excuses for sexual deviations because we're artists. I want a husband, not a bright young director who smokes pot and makes it with a boy occasionally for kicks."

His expression was grim. "When you sound off, you don't try to sugar-coat it." He snapped his fingers. "Just like that—we're through."

"Maybe we really never got started, Adam."

"Well, good luck. But the beach house is always waiting."

A press agent named Sid Goff from Century Pictures was waiting when Maggie's plane landed at Kennedy Airport in New York. The photographers moved in and the bulbs went off. Sid took her hand luggage and escorted her to the long black limousine the studio had ordered. The press followed and bombarded her with questions while the luggage was stored in the trunk. There was one final flash of cameras, the car pulled away from the airport and she leaned back and relaxed.

"Don't let all that action fool you," Sid Goff said glumly. "We may not make a paper."

"What are you talking about?" she asked.

"Diana Williams is due in on the next flight. She'll probably grab all the newspaper space tomorrow."

"I thought she was doing a TV series," Maggie said.

"It's been canceled—so now she suddenly wants to do a Broadway show. Ike Ryan has signed her. It goes into rehearsal in February."

Maggie smiled. "Well, don't be concerned. All Century cares about is press coverage on the day of the premiere."

"That's what *you* think," Sid said mournfully. "If we don't make the papers with pictures of your arrival, I'll be able to hear the screams from California without a telephone. We have some TV shows lined up—also newspaper interviews." He fumbled in his pocket for an envelope and handed her the typed schedule. "Then as I understand it, you can stay on until January fourteenth if you like, and Century will pick up the tab. We've got you booked at the Plaza until the twenty-sixth. If you want to stay on, be sure to let the hotel know right away."

She scanned the schedule he handed her. "This is incredible," she said. "I don't even get Christmas off—you've got two parties I'm supposed to attend."

"John Maxwell is one of Century's biggest stockholders. He has a big duplex at River House. It'll be loaded with rich civilians, but he likes celebrities and he definitely put in a request for you. The one at The Forum you've got to make—all the press will be there. It's Ike Ryan's party for Diana Williams."

"I don't go to parties," she said.

Sid Goff stared at her unable to believe he had heard correctly.

They drove in silence for a few minutes. Then he said, "Miss Stewart, I was given to understand that your agent had told Century that you would be available to promote the picture and grab all the publicity you could. This is Karl Heinz Brandt's picture for Living Arts Productions. Century is springing for the trip to build you into a star for themselves."

"I realize that," she said quietly. "And I agree to all interviews and television appearances. But there is no stipulation that says I have to make appearances at parties for stockholders. If Mr. Maxwell wants me to come, my fee is twenty-five thousand for an appearance."

Sid Goff leaned forward and studied his shoes. "Okay, Miss Stewart, maybe you have a point about John Maxwell. They really can't force you to go there. But there will be a lot of news coverage at Diana Williams' party. Please—at least make an appearance there."

She looked at his worried frown and relented. He had a job to do, and if making an appearance at Diana Williams' party would help, why not? But she was damned if she'd appear at John Maxwell's.

Since she had four days free before the interviews began, she invited her parents to New York. She saw to it that they had theater tickets and took them to dinner. Sid Goff arranged for tables, limousines, and keeping the fans at bay. Her parents returned to Philadelphia the day before Christmas in a state of subdued shock about their daughter's newly acquired fame.

She felt unbearably lonely Christmas Day. She had a tiny tree her family had brought for her and a wilted poinsettia plant . . . compliments of the studio. The endless Christmas carols on radio only depressed her more. She almost welcomed the idea of the Christmas party for Diana Williams at The Forum—at least it would get her out of the hotel suite.

Sid Goff called for her at five. "We only have to stay an hour," he told her. "Then you can cut out and join your friends and do whatever you wish."

"What are you doing later, Sid?" she asked.

"The same as you—cutting back to be with people I really like. My wife and her family. They're holding dinner for me until I get there."

The Forum was mobbed. Several cameras went off in her face as she entered. Ike Ryan's press agent cornered her to pose with Ike and Diana Williams. Maggie was amazed at Diana's appearance. She couldn't be forty, yet she was so burned-out looking. Thin, too thin. And her charged exuberance seemed to teeter on the verge of hysteria. She was too happy, too friendly—and the glass of orange juice in her hand was spiked with gin. Maggie posed with her. They exchanged the usual compliments. Maggie felt so young and healthy beside the girl. She also felt compassion. Everyone was dancing attendance on Diana but when the haunted eyes looked back at people, they didn't really focus.

Maggie was just passing the bar and heading for the door when she came face to face with the tall bronzed man who was entering. He stared in disbelief, then the familiar smile came to his eyes. She couldn't believe it. Robin Stone at a Christmas party for Diana Williams!

He grabbed her hands as his own astonishment turned into delight. "Hello, star!"

"Hello, Robin." She managed a cool smile.

"Maggie, you look marvelous."

Sid Goff moved off discreetly, but Maggie knew he was dreaming of the turkey dinner and his family. "I've got to leave," she said. "I have some other appointments."

His grin was filled with understanding. "I'm here on business too. I'm trying to talk Diana Williams into doing a Happening show. It's a murderous project, even if she agrees, but Ike Ryan is a friend of mine. I'd film the first day of rehearsal on the bare stage with the work light, then catch Philadelphia and the dress rehearsal and the New York·opening night, and cut to interviews with Diana and Ike and the cast—" He stopped. "I'm sorry, Maggie—this is a hell of a way to tell you I'm glad to see you."

Maggie laughed, then she turned and looked at Diana. "Do you think she still has it?"

Robin's expression was odd. "I thought you'd be the last person to judge talent by Hollywood standards. Diana Williams is one of a kind. Diana bad is better than most Hollywood stars good. She started on Broadway almost twenty years ago when she was seventeen. Diana wasn't created with camera angles, Klieg lights and press agents."

"I think I really must leave now," she said coldly.

He caught her arm. "I must say this is a great start. How did we get into all this?" He smiled. "Let's get to more important matters. When can I see you?"

"I don't know." Suddenly she smiled challengingly. "The premiere of my new movie is tomorrow night. Maybe you'd like to see what Klieg lights and press agents can do. Would you like to escort me?"

"I don't like wearing black tie to movies. I enjoy seeing my movies when I eat popcorn. How about the next night?"

She looked at him evenly. "I'm talking about tomorrow night. I never plan too far ahead."

Their eyes held for a moment. Then he flashed the familiar grin.

"Okay, baby, for you I'll give up the popcorn. What time shall I pick you up and where?"

"Eight o'clock at the Plaza. The movie starts at eight thirty, but there is television coverage first. Unfortunately I have to be there."

"No sweat. I'll be there at eight."

The press agent reappeared and escorted her to the door. Robin watched her leave, then he made his way across the room to Diana Williams.

At five to eight she began to get nervous. It was ridiculous to worry, she told herself. Above all, Robin was a gentleman. He wouldn't stand her up—and besides he wasn't supposed to arrive until eight. At three minutes to eight she wondered if she should put in a call to Sid Goff and have him stand by.

The phone rang sharply at eight. Robin was in the lobby. She took one last glance at herself in the mirror. He would probably loathe the way she looked: the white beaded dress (borrowed from the studio), the white mink coat (on loan to the studio from a Hollywood furrier), and the long black hair, lengthened by a "fall" (courtesy of the studio hairdresser who had arrived at her suite to recreate a hair style she wore in the film). It was crazy, she decided as she rode down the elevator. She had tons of hair—why did it have to hang down the middle of her back? And the large diamond-and-emerald earrings (also on loan and heavily insured) made her feel topheavy.

Robin smiled when she stepped out of the elevator. Oddly enough the slight nod that accompanied his smile seemed filled with approval. They didn't speak until they got through the autograph fans in front of the Plaza who braved the cold and snapped her picture and demanded autographs. When they were finally settled in the limousine, she leaned back, then sat forward quickly. "Good God, I'll lose my hair."

He laughed with her. "I thought it had grown since yesterday."

"Is it too much?" she asked hesitantly.

"It's marvelous," he said. "Look—regard the entire thing as a costume ball. That's what it is really. You're playing a movie star—give 'em their money's worth. If you're going to do it, go all the way."

The crush at the theater was frightening. Their limousine had to stand in line for fifteen minutes as bejeweled occupants of other cars alighted. When the mink-clad women who stepped out were unrecognized by the fans, there was a groan of disappointment. Maggie peered at them cautiously from the safety of the car. Wooden barricades and police forced back the crowd. Across the street a truck held a huge Klieg light. A red carpet was actually on the sidewalk. Newspaper cameramen were waiting anxiously, looking curiously disoriented in their tuxedos. As her car finally reached the entrance, the press swarmed forward. The crowd cheered and surged forward breaking through the police line. A few hands reached out to touch the white mink, voices yelled "Maggie, Maggie—" Sid Goff and another press agent surrounded her protectively. She looked for Robin. He had disappeared. She was frantic. She felt herself being swept toward the tall man who was handling the microphone. She was standing beside him. Bulbs were flashing. The television lights were being held by hand. The TV camera moved in. Oh God, where was Robin?

And then somehow, Sid Goff was helping her off the stand and she was ushered into the lobby and Robin was waiting with that wonderful grin that said he understood just how it was. He held her arm and they braved the well-dressed audience who were all congregated in the lobby staring at one another. She made her way to her seat, which seemed to be a cue for the audience to follow and begin the frantic search for their seats as the lights went low and the music and credits began to roll.

When the final scene came on, Sid Goff sneaked down the aisle and beckoned to them. In a half crawl they ducked out of their seats and rushed up the aisle. They reached their car just as the doors of the theater opened and disgorged the glittering audience.

Robin took her hand. "I think you handled it beauti-

fully. And you were excellent in the picture. Now tell me
—is there more to this awful night, or are you free?"

"There's a champagne supper at the Americana Hotel."

"Naturally."

Then they both laughed. Suddenly the idea of sitting in
the brightly lit ballroom at a table with Karl Heinz and
the leading man and his wife and posing for more pictures seemed unbearable.

"I'm not going," she said suddenly.

"Good girl. How about the Oak Room of your hotel?"

"No, I have a better idea. These earrings have to go
into the vault anyhow, and if I don't take off some of this
hair, I'm going to have a blinding headache. Suppose I
change into slacks and we go to P.J.'s?"

"You are the most brilliant girl in the world. But you
can't be the only one who gets out of these trappings.
Tell you what—I'll drop you and leave the car. When
you are ready, you can come and pick me up."

Twenty minutes later she was back in the car, bundled
in slacks and a white lamb sport coat. She wore dark
glasses and smoked nervously as they drove to his apartment building on the East River. He was waiting outside,
and he walked briskly to the car. He was wearing a white
sweater and gray pants and no overcoat. As he slid in
beside her, he said, "Even P.J.'s isn't private enough. How
about the Lancer Bar?"

She nodded and the driver headed toward Fifty-fourth
Street. The place was empty except for a young couple
who sat in the back booth drinking beer and holding
hands. Robin ordered a Scotch for her, a martini for
himself, and two large steaks.

Then he led her to a secluded table. He raised his
glass: "This picture will do you a lot of good, Maggie."

"But did you think I was good?"

"Let's put it this way—you'll convince the critics that
you can act."

"That means *you* don't think I can?"

"Does it matter?"

She smiled. "I'm curious."

Her pursed his lips thoughtfully. "Baby, you can't act

your way out of a barrel. But it doesn't matter—you
photograph like a goddess. You'll have a big future."

"Don't you believe there is any such thing as star
quality? That's all I hear out there."

"Yes, but she's got to be a genius or a nut."

"Maybe I still qualify."

He laughed. "I don't mean IQ genius—I mean emotional genius. Maybe there's a thin line between genius
and madness, and thank God you don't fit into either
category. Diana Williams is a genius and a nut. And a
poor lost soul. Come to think of it, I don't think I've ever
met a happy adjusted genius." He reached across the
table and took her hands. "Thank God you're just a beautiful lady who through some crazy fluke has fallen into an
incredible bit of luck. But you're not a nut—you're everything a man thinks of when he dreams of the ideal girl."

She held her breath and waited for the disclaimer, the
veiled insult that would knock her down. But their eyes
met and he did not smile.

It was one o'clock when they left the Lancer Bar. "Do
you have many appointments for tomorrow?" he asked.

She shook her head. "I'm on my own from here on in."

His pleasure was real. "How long can you stay in
town?"

"Until the fourteenth of January, if I wish."

The car had pulled up to the Plaza. He looked at her
earnestly. "I wish it. Can we have dinner together tomorrow?"

"I'd love it, Robin."

He kissed her gently and led her to the elevator. "I'll
call you before noon. Sleep well." And then the elevator
door closed and he was gone.

She heard the phone ring at eleven. She let it ring a
few times. It had to be Robin and she wanted to be fully
awake. When she answered it, the even tones of the desk
clerk asked her at what time she expected to check out.

"I'm not checking out," she said angrily. "I'm staying on
for at least two weeks." Then she hung up and punched
the pillow into place. She would go back to sleep—she
didn't want to wake up until Robin called. But the phone
jangled again. This time it was the assistant manager.

The smooth voice was apologetic. "Miss Stewart, your reservation ends today. We were told that you would notify us if you intended staying on. Unfortunately the hotel is one hundred percent booked. Had you told us—"

She was wide-awake now. Good Lord, she had forgotten. Well, she'd find another hotel. The assistant manager was eager to be helpful. He would personally try to relocate her. Fifteen minutes later he called back. "Miss Stewart, the situation is very tight. The Regency, Pierre, St. Regis, Navarro, Hampshire House—all of them are booked solid, not even a double room is available, let alone a suite. I haven't tried the commercial hotels, I didn't know how you would feel."

"Thank you very much. I'll see if Century can do something." She put in a call to Sid Goff. When she told him the situation, he seemed totally defeated. "Maggie, I warned you to let them know. Let me get on the phone and see what I can do."

She was packing when Robin called. She explained her predicament. "I'll probably wind up in Brooklyn, the way things look. Sid Goff hasn't called back yet, and if he can't come up with something, no one can."

"Tell Sid Goff to forget it," he said. "I'll take care of it."

Twenty minutes later he called from the lobby and told her to send down her bags.

The limousine was waiting. When they were settled in the car he gave the driver his home address. She looked at him curiously.

"It isn't the Regency," he said. "But a maid does come in every day and it's comfortable enough—even for a star like you. I'll stay at the club."

"Robin, I can't do this to you."

"You haven't. *I've* done it."

She liked the apartment. Unconsciously her eyes drifted toward the king-sized bed and she wondered how many occupants it had known. He handed her a key. "Feel free to come and go as you choose. I'll come by to take you to dinner." He pointed to the bar. "All I ask in lieu of rental is your services as a bartender. If you want to be my girl you've got to learn to make a vodka martini.

Three ounces vodka, a drop of vermouth, and no lemon peel. I like olives."

She started obediently toward the bar. "Maggie!" He laughed. "It's just past noon. I'm talking about this evening."

She had the martinis ready at seven. She had also bought two steaks and some frozen asparagus. After dinner they watched television and he held her hand as they snuggled on the couch. When the eleven o'clock news came on, he went to the kitchen and brought back two cans of beer. Then he said, "This is *your* place. Tell me when you want me to leave."

"Whenever you want to go," she said.

He pulled her to him. "I don't want to go—"

He took her in his arms and kissed her. All right now, she told herself: tell him *you* don't feel in the mood and *he* doesn't rouse *you!* But she clung to him and returned his kiss and when they went to the king-sized bed they came together eagerly. But this time his tenderness was not caused by the vodka, and when the moment came and his body went tense he didn't shout *Mother*—and she didn't throw the pitcher of cold water on him.

The next five days with Robin were unbelievable. They went out to dinner each night. Sometimes they bundled up and took a long walk and once they went to a double feature at a local movie, but each night they made love and fell asleep in each other's arms.

She thought about it now as she watched him sleep. She slid out of bed, put the coffee on and stared out at the grayness of the East River. She had never been this happy and she had fourteen more days. But why only fourteen days—why not forever? Robin was in love with her, there was no doubt about it. They had never discussed that terrible morning in Miami; somehow she sensed it was a closed subject. But what they were having now was no one-night stand. He was comfortable with her, he enjoyed being with her—maybe it was up to her to make the first move. Of course it was! How could he ask her to give up her career? She'd have to make him understand that for the first time in her life she was happy.

"It is a terrible-looking river on a gray morning." He had come into the kitchen and was standing behind her. He leaned down and kissed her neck. "Come to think of it, it's a lousy-looking river even on a beautiful day. The sun seems to point out its failings. Those awful little islands, and the tugboats."

She turned around and hugged him. "It's a *beautiful* river. Robin, I want to marry you."

He held her off and smiled. "I must say this is an auspicious way to start a new year."

"It would work, Robin, really it would."

"Perhaps. But not right now—"

"If you're thinking about my career, I've thought it all out." He smiled and reached for the coffee. "I'll make eggs," she said quickly, "and there's orange juice."

"Stop making noises like a wife," he said easily. Then he took his coffee cup and disappeared into the bedroom. She didn't follow him. She sat at the small table and stared at the river and sipped her coffee. Well, he hadn't said no—but he certainly was far from enthused at the idea.

Ten minutes later he came into the kitchen. She looked up in surprise. He was wearing a turtleneck sweater and had his overcoat on his arm. "I'll be back in an hour, I have some work to do." He leaned over and kissed her head.

"On New Year's Day!"

"There's a tape at the office I have to edit. I work better when I'm alone, especially when the whole building is empty—it gives me a sense of privacy. And, Maggie, I hate to impose on you, but do you think you could face an eggnog party at five?"

"An eggnog party?"

"Mrs. Austin's New Year's Day party—I've blown it three times in a row. At least I remembered to send a wire last year. But I've got to make an appearance this time."

"Oh, Robin, I sent back most of the fancy wardrobe. It was all borrowed finery and I've been living in a beach house—all I own is slacks and a few black dresses. What is in that closet is *it!*"

"I like a girl who travels light. The black dress will be fine."

"But it's a wool dress—"

"Maggie"—he came to her and stroked her face—"you'd pass anywhere in anything. Now, go do the dishes and help earn your keep."

Then he left the apartment.

It was cold but he walked. Archie Gold hadn't wanted to come out, but Robin had been insistent. He was sure Maggie hadn't heard him on the phone, the kitchen was at the other end of the apartment and he had kept his voice low.

He reached the office just as Archie arrived. "Robin, I don't come out like this for my regular patients. You walked out on me a year and a half ago, and now you suddenly call and tell me an emergency has come up."

Robin eased into a chair. "I need your advice. Maggie Stewart is in town. We made it together. It was great—she's living with me."

Archie lit his pipe. "Then there is no problem."

"The hell there isn't! She wants to get married."

"Most girls do."

"It wouldn't work. Look, there's more to marriage than shacking up with a girl. That is, for a girl like Maggie. In the past five days she's told me everything about her life —her first marriage, her past relationship with Parino, the guy in California, and the beach house. She's leveled all the way."

"And what have you done?"

"I've listened, chum. And I'm not about to talk. Let's see, how would I start? Oh by the way—my name isn't really Robin Stone."

"It is legally your name."

"Sure—but somewhere inside of me there's a little bastard named Conrad. *That's* me, too. And Maggie wants kids . . . the whole works." Suddenly Robin slammed his fist on the desk. "Dammit, Archie! I was going great until I met you—I enjoyed sex, I operated just fine!"

"You operated as a machine. Now Conrad is fighting to

merge with Robin. The man that kept Conrad locked away wasn't alive—he felt nothing. You admitted that yourself. And now for the first time you're at odds with yourself. But it's a healthy sign: You're feeling emotions, conflict, worry. And that's normal."

"I liked it better the other way. I told you when I walked out of here last time that I'd make the name Robin Stone count for something. And I will. But I don't need Conrad! I want to forget about him."

"Robin, why don't you go to Hamburg?"

"What the hell would I do there?"

"You know your mother's name. Look up her family— maybe your origins would surprise you."

"Conrad's mother was a whore!" He spat it out.

"She *became* a whore. To support Conrad. You may discover that you're proud to be Conrad!"

Robin stood up. "God damn you, can't you understand —I don't *want* to know Conrad. I don't want to worry about hurting Maggie Stewart! I don't want to miss her when she goes to the Coast. I don't want to miss or need *anyone!* I never have before . . . and I never will."

Dr. Gold stood up. "Robin, don't run out on yourself! Can't you see what's happening? You've started the process of giving—of combining love with sex. The experience has upset you. That's normal. But don't run from it. Of course there will be problems—but the day you can turn to someone and say *I need you* will be the day you become a complete person. And Maggie is that someone. Robin—don't shut her out."

But Robin had already slammed the door.

It was cold, but Robin walked back to his apartment. His mind was blank and he felt a strange calm. Maggie was in the living room, wearing the black dress. He looked at her curiously. "What time is it?" he asked.

"Four thirty."

He smiled, but his eyes were cold. "Well, take off the dress. We've got a good hour before we have to show at that party." Then he took her into the bedroom and made love to her. When it was over he looked at her with a detached smile. He seemed oddly pleased with himself.

"You don't know it, my girl," he said evenly, "but Robin Stone just made love to you, and it worked."

"It's always worked," she said softly.

"This time it was different." Then he slapped her bare bottom. "Move it, baby, we're due at an eggnog party."

**III**

# JUDITH

# TWENTY-SIX

J UDITH AUSTIN STEPPED OUT OF THE TUB.
She caught sight of her body in the mirrored walls . . .
she studied every angle. She was reed-thin, but dieted
constantly. At fifty, one didn't dare chance the risk of
spreading. Connie was lucky—she skied, on the Alps and
on the water, and she was firm as a rock. It had been nice
having Connie around, but thank God she had gone back
to Italy to spend Christmas with the prince and the
children. It had been an endless round of parties. Everyone was so damned impressed with a title. She shook
her leg before the mirror. Yes, the flesh on her thigh was
getting soft. Connie's thighs were like a rock. Maybe she
should take up some sport. But the sun and wind had
caused fine wrinkles in Connie's skin. Judith leaned closer
to the mirror: just a few tiny lines around the eyes. In a
good light she could pass for thirty-eight, maybe even
thirty-six. She headed the best-dressed list and was still
known as one of the most beautiful women in New York.
And Connie's last visit had unleashed a new burst of
national publicity—"the most beautiful twin sisters in the
world."

Judith wondered if Connie was still in love with Vittorio. She sat down on the stool and toweled herself
slowly as the realization hit her. Three years had passed
without a breath of romance in her life. Three years ago
she had broken off the thing with Chuck.

They had met during the summer at Quogue. Chuck
was a golf pro, twenty-eight, blond. It had started when
she took some lessons on her short irons. He put his arms

around her waist to keep her from pivoting. "It's all in the hands with a wedge, Mrs. Austin." Their eyes met, and that's how it began. During the summer, Gregory came out for long weekends and she had planned on getting Chuck transferred to the club at Palm Beach. Everything was divine until he made that remark: "Judith, wouldn't I be great doing the golf commentary on TV, like Jimmy Demaret or Cary Middlecoff?" It had disturbed her, but she had forced herself to dismiss it.

He had taken the job in Palm Beach. She arrived on January second, and for three weeks it had been wonderful. Gregory was still in New York, and each night Chuck crept into her mansion through the side entrance. Then he mentioned the television idea again. She had been intentionally vague. He shrugged. "Well then, maybe I'll try for tournament golf and go out on tour."

On tour? That offered all kinds of interesting possibilities. She might pop off and join him occasionally. He described the tournaments he wanted to enter—of course he'd have to practice every day for about a month or he'd never make the cut: "I'd need about ten or fifteen thousand," he said.

She stared at him. "Ten or fifteen thousand what?"

"Dollars. It costs money to hit the tournament trail. If I won any big purse I'd pay you back."

That had been the end of Chuck. She had refused to take his calls after that night.

It was the first time a man had ever gone after her with any ulterior motive. That had been three years ago— three years with nothing exciting in her life. Nothing but Gregory. She really loved Gregory, but she wasn't *in* love with him. And being in love was the only thing that made life worth living. She would never have married Gregory if it hadn't been for Connie.

The beautiful Logan twins: Judith and Consuelo. Daughters of Elizabeth and Cornelius Logan. A beautiful couple, beautiful twin daughters, a magnificent heritage. They had everything—except money. She would never forget their "poverty." Somehow the Logans always managed to live in the "right" apartment; she and Connie went to the "right" schools, and although it was whispered that Cornelius Logan had lost everything in the crash, everyone knew that Grandmother Logan still had enormous wealth. Grandmother Logan had paid for the big coming-out ball. She had also paid for the girls' first trip to Europe on their twenty-first birthday. Connie had met Vittorio. Judith had come back empty-handed.

Judith was twenty-six when she met Gregory Austin. She had seen his picture in the newspapers and knew he dated movie actresses, society women and debutantes. He was thirty-six, unmarried, and owned a radio network. He bragged about his lack of formal education: "I never finished high school, but I can read the stock-market pages better than Bernard Baruch." His first job had been a runner on Wall Street. When the market crashed, he made his first million selling short. With the profits he bought a small radio station in upstate New York, continued to buy stock when it hit the all-time low, sold when it climbed, and with each big financial gain purchased a new radio station. When he was thirty he formed the IBC network. His cocky manner and flamboyant behavior made him a colorful personality. His quotes made good newspaper copy. He enjoyed women, but marriage was the last thing on his mind, until he met Judith Logan. Perhaps it was her lack of interest that challenged him. Gregory always sought the unattainable.

Judith went out with him a few times because of his persistence and was amazed to find herself suddenly in the "news." She was even more amazed when her closest friends wanted to throw small dinner parties for "that fascinating red-headed spitfire." And when Consuelo wrote and said she had met him in London and found him sexy and exciting, Judith suddenly looked at Gregory Austin in a new light. She also realized that he *was* offering her a kingdom—there was no coat of arms, but in some circles the IBC crest was even more impressive. He opened the door to a world of opulent spending. Vittorio had money, but Connie's jewelry was "family" jewelry that had to be passed on to her children and their children. Gregory presented Judith with a twenty-five-carat diamond engagement ring, a diamond necklace as a wedding present, and fifty thousand dollars to open her

checking account. The wedding itself made both the society pages and theatrical columns.

Gregory was stunned to find he had married a virgin.
He bought her the Palm Beach estate to celebrate their
first year of marriage. He presented her with a diamond
bracelet at the end of the second year. By the end of the
third year, there was nothing else he could give her. And
by then, the only thing she really wanted was romance.
Sex with Gregory had been a complete disappointment.
She had no basis for comparison, yet somehow she sensed
she would discover romance when the proper moment
presented itself. It happened when she was thirty-two.
She decided to go to Paris to visit Connie. The war was
over, everyone was in a festive mood, and Judith was
anxious to show off her jewels and furs to Connie. Gregory couldn't get away but he sent her off with his best
wishes and an enormous letter of credit. She met the
opera star on the boat trip over. She skipped Paris and
they stayed in London together. She never saw Connie
and it never occurred to Gregory to ask why her letters
bore English postage stamps.

After that it had been easy. There had been the Italian
movie star, then for two years there had been the English
playwright, then the French diplomat. . . . Dear Connie
had proved valuable in the long run—one could always
dash to Europe to visit one's sister: twins were supposed
to be close. Of course Connie had been extracting her
pound of flesh lately—all these visits to the States. . . .
But in the last three years she had not gone to "visit
Connie" at all. She sat and thought about it now—three
years of *nothing*.

She finished her makeup and stood up and surveyed
her naked body. In the beginning she had been unhappy
because she hadn't been able to get pregnant. She had
tried desperately until she was thirty, even considered
adopting a baby, but Gregory was forty and didn't really
care. "The network is our baby," he would say. And a
child was a responsibility. . . . Now, as she stared at her
flat stomach, she was suddenly glad there were no stretch
marks. But her breasts *were* sagging and her thighs were
getting loose. She held her arms over head. There, that

looked fine—and in bed when she lay down they went into place. But her stomach was soft, even though it was flat. . . .

She went to her closet and reached for the purple velvet dress, then with a sudden change of mind decided on the red lamé hostess gown. And she'd wear the gold-and-ruby necklace. For the first time in ages, she felt a sense of anticipation in choosing a dress. An inner excitement had been building subconsciously for three days, ever since Robin Stone's note of acceptance arrived.

Until this moment Judith had refused to acknowledge it even to herself: she was dressing for Robin Stone. Suddenly she realized that she had wanted him since she first set eyes on him. Yes, she wanted Robin Stone! This would be her last and most exciting romance. But she knew she would have to make the first move, let him know in a terribly subtle way that she was interested. A man like Robin would take it from there. It was an ideal situation. It offered unlimited possibilities. He traveled so much. She could easily meet him abroad.

At four thirty she went downstairs to check the bar and hors d'oeuvres. At four forty-five Gregory appeared in his smoking jacket. He looked tired—well, Palm Beach would straighten him out. At five o'clock the first guests arrived. Naturally it was the senator and his wife. Why did the dull ones always arrive first? You were trapped talking to them until other guests arrived. But when the butler ushered the middle-aged couple into the living room, Judith's smile was brilliant.

"Hello, Senator. No, my dear, you are *not* early. You are just divinely punctual and I'm so glad. It will give us time for some chitchat."

Danton Miller arrived ten minutes later. He was alone. For once, Judith was glad to see him. It gave her an excuse to escape from the senator. Soon the door chimes grew constant. Within twenty minutes the crowd filled the living room and began to spill into the library and dining room. The party was on.

Robin Stone arrived at six. She floated across the room and held out her hands.

"You kept your promise." Her smile was radiant and

she accepted the introduction to Maggie as if she had never seen her before. Then she eased away to greet new guests. That damn girl! She was so tall and beautiful! Judith held herself erect. She had felt small and dumpy beside Maggie Stewart. She moved effortlessly through the room greeting people, talking with them. . . . And through it all she kept one eye on Robin Stone and Maggie Stewart. Oh Lord, there was Christie Lane with his dreadful wife. Gregory had insisted she invite them. The girl—Ethel, yes, that was her name—was talking to Maggie Stewart. Chris was standing like a wooden Indian. Oh marvelous—Robin had moved off to talk to the senator.

This was her chance. She eased her way to his side. Then with casual deliberation, she took his arm and said, "This is your first time here. Would you like the tour?"

"Tour?"

"Yes." She led him from the room to the outer hall. "Most guests like to see houses. And they rarely get beyond the living room, library and dining room." She stopped at a heavy oak door. "This is off limits to guests but I'd like you to see it. It's Gregory's den, his pride and joy."

"The house is deceptive," Robin said. "It's quite large, isn't it?"

Her laugh was easy and light. "Don't you know? It's really two brownstones—we broke the entire wall that separated the houses and wound up with fifteen large rooms instead of thirty small ones."

Robin looked around the den with obvious approval. "Good room for a man."

Her face was wistful. "Unfortunately he spends too much time here."

He nodded. "I imagine he thinks his problems out."

"Do you hole away like that too?"

He smiled. "My problems are on a smaller scale. I have just one department to worry about. Gregory has the entire network."

She threw her hands up in mock despair. "Is business the only kind of problems men have? I envy you."

His grin was noncommittal.

"A woman's problems can't be obliterated by a drink and an hour of deep thought in a den," she said.

"Maybe she hasn't tried," Robin answered.

"How do you erase loneliness, Robin?"

He looked at her curiously. For one second their eyes met. Her stare was challenging, with a hint of intimacy. Her voice was low when she spoke. "Robin, I love Gregory. In the beginning of our marriage we had something very wonderful. But now he's married to IBC. He's much older than I . . . the excitement of the network is enough for him. He brings his problems home—sometimes I feel I don't exist for him. I see him in crowds, at parties, at dinners. I know he loves me, but I'm just part of his empire. I feel so lonely and isolated. I'm not the type of woman who plays cards or enjoys meeting other women for lunch."

"Everyone has their own kind of loneliness," Robin said.

"But why should they? Life is so short. We're young for such a short time. I always believe if you don't hurt anyone, that's all that counts." She shrugged helplessly. "Gregory played the market when he was young, and he once said, 'It's the biggest and best crap game in the world,' but he doesn't play the market anymore—now the 'numbers,' as he puts it, are his big excitement. But a woman *can't* exist that way. She needs affection." She looked down at her hands and twisted the large ring. "I've found it perhaps once or twice." She looked at him. "It never took anything away from Gregory. It never touched my love for him. It was a different kind of love. I just gave someone something that Gregory didn't have the time or sensitivity to accept." Then in a small voice she said, "I don't know why I'm telling you all this. I hardly know you." Her smile was suddenly shy. "But friendship is not just a matter of time, it's a matter of understanding."

He took her by the shoulders and grinned. "Judith, you are a lovely woman, but I'd advise you to be careful whom you open up to like this."

Her eyes looked up to him appealingly. "I don't open

up like this. I never have before—I don't know what's the matter with me, Robin."

He turned her around and steered her toward the door. "Too much eggnog," he said with a smile. "Now, let's get back to your guests. That's one way of not being lonely."

Her stare was direct. "Is that the only solution?"

He took her arm and led her back to the living room. "I'm with a young lady who might get very lonely in this crowd. Happy New Year, Judith. And stay away from the eggnog." He left her and went directly to Maggie Stewart.

Judith was in a state of shock, but she moved about greeting people, her smile intact.

Maggie's smile also remained intact. She had seen Robin leave the room with Judith Austin and was aware they had stayed away some time. Judith Austin was a very beautiful woman. But the sight of the tall handsome man crossing the room and coming to her side dispelled her uneasiness immediately.

He took her arm possessively and started to ease her away from Ethel and Christie Lane. Suddenly his attention switched to the door. Everyone in the room looked at the frail girl who entered. Then a murmur went through the sophisticated group. No matter how quietly she entered, Diana Williams *entered* a room. She stood there hesitant and alone, almost childlike. Gregory Austin rushed to greet her and protectively put his arm around her. In a split second everyone was surging around her. Diana accepted all the introductions with modesty.

"Boy, Ike Ryan sure doesn't know what he's doing this time," Ethel said, as she watched the commotion. "Diana's shot. She has to go up in smoke."

Diana finally broke through the crowd and came to Robin. Gregory Austin was still holding her arm possessively. "Robin," he chided, "why didn't you tell us you had invited Miss Williams to our party? We didn't know she was in town or we would have extended the invitation personally."

"You invited me on Christmas Day at Voisin," Diana said accusingly. "When you didn't call for me, I figured I had misunderstood and you expected me to meet you here."

"Allow me to make up for my rudeness by getting you a drink," Robin said. He and Gregory both led her toward the bar, leaving Maggie with Ethel and Christie.

Ethel was talking about her new suite at the Essex House: "We just moved in yesterday," she told Maggie.

"Big deal," Christie said. "Living room, two bedrooms, and it's three times as expensive as the Astor."

"Well, I can't exactly see myself pushing a baby carriage down Broadway," Ethel snorted. "At least the Essex House is across from the Park. It will be good for the baby."

"Oh, I didn't know. Congratulations," Maggie said, forcing herself to show an interest she didn't feel.

Christie beamed expansively. "The rabbit died last week. When the doc told me the news—well, I was so happy I was ready to do anything."

"Except move from the Astor," Ethel snapped. "But he finally gave in."

"Yeah, and she's got me sleeping in the other bedroom. Only until the baby comes, then we fix it up as a nursery. But I guess she's right, an expectant mother needs all her sleep. Hey, you two broads chat a minute. I see Dan the Man, and I want to talk to him." He crossed the room and grabbed Danton Miller's arm.

Maggie felt uneasy with Ethel. She didn't know her and she wasn't especially good at girl talk. "When do you expect the baby?" she asked.

"The end of August, or the beginning of September. I'm three weeks late, but the rabbit test was positive."

There was a moment of uncomfortable silence. Then Maggie said, "I think it was very wise of you to pick a hotel near the Park. It will be wonderful for the baby."

"You don't think I intend to stay there?" Ethel asked. "Christie doesn't know it yet, but next season he's doing the show from California."

"Oh, I see." Maggie didn't, but she had to say something.

"I'll swing it. With Christie the magic word is 'baby.' I'll tell him the Park is no good for the kid—muggings and all that. And once we get out there I'm determined it'll be a whole new life—a big house, and all the right people. I'm going to make him hire Cully and Hayes—we've got to get in with the right people so our kid will know the right kids. I tell you, Hollywood is just waiting for Ethel Evans Lane."

"You might be disappointed," Maggie said. She scanned the room quickly and wondered where Robin was.

"He's in the den with Diana," Ethel said.

"I beg your pardon?"

"Your boyfriend—Diana's latched on to him."

Maggie was too stunned to answer. For a moment there was an uncomfortable silence. Then Dan and Christie joined them.

"We been talking about a new time slot for year after next," Christie said. "Would you believe it—the sponsors are lined up, doll, waiting for me for two seasons after this?"

"May I get you a refill of this sticky stuff?" Dan asked, as he smiled at Maggie.

There was a loud burst of laughter from the den. Obviously Diana was holding court. Dan smiled and lowered his voice conspiratorially. "I noticed you came here with Robin Stone. Does that mean you have to leave with him?"

"It's the normal procedure, isn't it?" she asked.

"Too bad. I was about to ask you to dinner. How long will you be in town?"

"About two more weeks."

"May I call you?"

"Well—" She thought quickly. She couldn't just say no, and it would never do to let him know where she was staying. "Let me call you," she said. "I plan on visiting my family in Philadelphia tomorrow. I don't know how long I'll be away."

"You know where to reach me?"

"IBC." She smiled. "And now I think I'd better join Robin." She left Dan and went into the library. Diana was holding everyone's attention with a funny story about her twin sons.

"God, they're getting so gigantic," she was saying, "I can't lie about their ages. And naturally the Beatles are their idols. *They* also have long hair. Oh, my dear, they are absolutely Carnaby Street. The other day I was about to introduce them as my babies and I stared at these two seventeen-year-old, six-foot hunks of children and I suddenly said, 'Meet the twin cantors.'"

Everyone laughed more uproariously than necessary. Robin didn't laugh. He watched her carefully and when she handed him her empty glass, he beckoned the waiter for a refill.

Maggie made her way to his side and slipped her arm through his. "It's seven o'clock," she whispered, "and I'm starving."

"There's a table full of hors d'oeuvres," he said, keeping his eyes riveted on Diana.

"I'd like to leave—"

"I'm working, baby." He patted his pocket. "I have a letter of agreement all ready. I've been carrying it around with me for two weeks. All she has to do is sign. And if you're a good girl you can be the witness."

"How long will it take?"

"I hope it happens tonight at dinner."

"She's coming to dinner with us?" she asked.

"She's coming to dinner with me. And if you like, you can come too."

She turned and left the room. She didn't look back but she sensed he never looked after her. She saw Dan Miller shaking hands with Mrs. Austin. His coat was on his arm. She crossed the room and joined him.

"Does that dinner invitation still hold?"

"It certainly does. Do you like Pavillon?"

"It's one of my favorite restaurants."

Pavillon was beginning to empty. As Maggie sat and toyed with a brandy, she wondered what Robin had thought when he discovered she had left. It was almost eleven o'clock. He was probably home, watching the news. Her anger evaporated and suddenly she felt guilty running out on him. What difference would it have made if Diana had gone to dinner with them? Robin needed Diana's signature for the Happening! She had been childish, and—worst of all—openly possessive! She had never acted that way with any man, not with Adam or

Andy, because she never cared enough. Perhaps that was the secret of her success. Was that really true? Did you have to pretend to be disinterested in a man to hold him? She had sat through this dreary dinner with Dan just to play a game with Robin. But it was ridiculous—she *had* Robin, she loved him. Why was she sitting at Pavillon listening to this idiot's life story?

"I'm glad there is really nothing between you and Robin," he said suddenly.

She looked at him curiously. "Why do you say that?"

"Because I don't like him."

"He's a very good friend of mine." Her tone held a warning.

He smiled. "I still don't like him—and it's not personal."

Well, she didn't like anything about Danton Miller. Especially his smug smile. "Perhaps you're afraid of him," she said coldly.

"Afraid?"

"If your dislike isn't personal, then I assume it has something to do with business. I know you're both at IBC and I know a little bit about network policy. Robin has certainly expanded beyond just the news area, so there must be some rivalry between you."

He threw back his head and laughed. When he looked at her his brown eyes were almost slits. "I'm not afraid of the Great Stone Man, and you know why? Because he has too much pride—and that will be his destruction."

"I should think pride would be an *asset*."

"There's no place for it in this business. I'll tell you something, Maggie. When it comes to infighting, I have no pride. That's why I'll survive. There comes a time when you have to crawl a little, no matter how high and mighty you are. But Robin Stone will never crawl. That's why he won't survive. And that's the only word that counts in this business. Survival."

She picked up her pocketbook, hoping he would take it as a cue to end the evening. He noticed it and signaled for the check. "I'm boring you, talking about business. Shall we go someplace for a nightcap?"

"I'm very tired, Dan, and I have to be up early tomorrow."

When he hailed a cab, she told him she was staying at the Plaza. He dropped her and waited until she walked inside. Then she crossed the lobby, slipped out the Fifty-eighth Street side and took a cab to Robin's.

There was no light under the door when she put the key in the lock. Perhaps he had gone to sleep. She tiptoed through the darkened living room to the bedroom. The room was dark but she saw the dim outline of the bed, rumpled and unmade from their afternoon of lovemaking. It was empty. She walked back into the living room and was just about to turn on the light when she saw the sliver of light under the door of his den. She smiled—he was in there working on his book. She walked to the door and had her hand on the knob when she heard the voices. It was Diana and she sounded drunk.

"This carpet isn't very soft . . ."

Robin laughed. "Well, I told you to go make the bed."

"I don't fuck in another woman's sheets!"

Then there was silence.

She opened the door quietly. She couldn't believe it. Both of them were completely nude. Robin was stretched out in the club chair in the corner of the room, his eyes shut, his arms behind his head. Diana was on her knees making love to him. Neither of them was aware that she was standing there. She backed out of the room and closed the door quietly. Then she went back to the bedroom and switched on the lights. She dragged her suitcase from the closet, then with an abrupt change of mind left it on the floor. Why bother for a few pairs of slacks and one dress? She'd never want to wear anything she had worn with him again. She collected her makeup and her wallet and started from the room. She turned back and stared at the bed. The bed she had shared with Robin just a few hours ago. The bed she had expected to share with him tonight and every night. The bed she thought was part of her future—the bed that Diana wouldn't get into unless there were fresh sheets. How many girls had slept in it? How many more would sleep in it? She rushed to the bed and tore at the sheets, but she couldn't rip them into the shreds her fury demanded. No one was ever going to sleep on these sheets again, or on that bed! She remembered there was a can of lighter fluid in the medicine chest and raced into the bathroom to get it. She poured it over the sheets and the headboard, and then struck a match, held it to the book of matches until it all flared, and tossed it on the bed. With a hiss, a hot orange flame licked across the sheets.

She ran from the apartment. She walked through the lobby and stopped at the door. In a quiet voice she said to the doorman, "I just rang Mr. Stone's doorbell and there was no answer, but I thought I smelled smoke coming from inside." As the doorman dashed to the elevator, Maggie casually crossed the street and stood watching under the canopy of another apartment house. A slow smile crossed her face as she saw the blaze of light from Robin's bedroom window. In a few minutes there was the sound of sirens. Soon the blaze of fire went dark and gusts of heavy smoke poured out of the window. She saw Robin come out onto the street with the other tenants. He had thrown his trench coat over some pants. Diana was wrapped in his overcoat but she was barefoot, hopping up and down on one foot on the cold pavement. Maggie tossed back her head and laughed. "I hope she gets pneumonia," she said aloud. Then she walked down the street.

She walked five blocks before the reaction set in. She began to shiver, and damp sweat broke out on her forehead. Good God, what had she done! She could have killed him. She could have killed everyone in the building. She felt faint as she realized the horror of her actions. Suddenly she understood how people could kill in a moment of rage and plead temporary insanity. She hadn't even thought of the danger of the fire spreading. . . . Thank God it was all right! She saw a cruising cab, hailed it and mumbled, "Kennedy Airport." Then she leaned back against the seat. She'd have to wait hours to catch a plane to Los Angeles, but it didn't matter. The cab cut through a dark tree-lined street as it headed toward the East River Drive—it was the street where the Austins lived. She glanced at the solid brownstone. There was a light on the second floor. How she envied a woman

like Judith Austin, secure in her beautiful brownstone
fortress. . . .

At the moment, Judith Austin was standing before the
mirror silently reappraising herself. She smiled at the
mirror and studied her smile. It certainly looked forced.
Well, that was the smile she had held until nine thirty,
until the last guest had finally departed. Her head ached
and she had longed to go to her room, but she had forced
herself to have a quiet snack with Gregory in the privacy
of his bedroom. She had nibbled at the cold turkey and
listened to him gripe. The parties were becoming too
goddam show-business-oriented. Next year he would
personally check the list—if there *was* an eggnog party
next year.

Ordinarily she would have argued, or soothed him, but
tonight she was too immersed in her own thoughts. When
she finally left him for the privacy of her own bedroom,
she had flung herself across the bed fully clothed and
tried to sort the events of the evening in her mind.

But now, as she stood in her nightgown, she had to
face the unhappy realization that Robin Stone had *not*
taken the bait. Suddenly her defenses crumbled and tears
rolled down her face. She had held them back all night.
She had not allowed herself to think of his rejection. She
couldn't afford to—not before all those people, not with
Gregory. But now she could give in to her emotions.
Suddenly she blew her nose. She would not cry! Tears
were a luxury she could not afford. Oh, a few nice dia-
mondlike drops at a sad play, or at the news of the death
of a friend; tears that could gently slide down the corners
of her eyes without damaging the mascara on the bottom
lashes. But no out-and-out tears, no sobbing: that meant
puffy eyelids the next day and bags under the eyes. And
she had a luncheon date at the Colony and a formal
dinner party at night.

But Robin had rejected her. No, not actually rejected
her—just ignored her veiled offer. Veiled! She had never
come on so strong with anyone in her life. In the past it
had never taken more than a look, a subtle smile, to bring
on instant reaction. Oh God . . . she wanted him so! She

needed someone to hold her and tell her she was lovely. She needed love. She wanted Robin! She wanted sex with someone who would make her feel young and desirable. It had been months since Gregory had tried. Oh God, to be young again, and have a man like Robin *want* you, to sit in dark bars and hold hands, to walk along the sand in the Hamptons and look at the moon. . . . Judith's love began in her heart and mind—the orgasm was only incidental. For her, as long as she was emotionally involved, the experience was gratifying. If she could have Robin's arms around her, feel his naked body close to her own, touch his face—nothing else would matter.

Gregory had never excited her as a man. Even when he was young, vigorous and hearty, he lacked the spark that ignited romance. Right from the start sex had never been important to him. He knew nothing about any variations in lovemaking. He said none of the right things at the proper moments—he had never gone down on her in his entire life. Perhaps it was her fault. Perhaps she had made him feel she was above it. But she had never been able to feel one tinge of the excitement for Gregory that she had felt for her "outside" lovers. He wouldn't believe the abandon she displayed in bed with them—the abandon that came from the thrill of romance. Yet there was so much she admired about Gregory. She loved him with the same devotion she had for her father and her mother. She would be lost without him. They had a marvelous life together. She was never bored with Gregory —only there was no romance and never had been. Perhaps a man who was a dynamo was incapable of expressing the sentimental little things that meant so much to a woman. But Robin Stone was just as forceful as Gregory, even more so. Yet you felt it was all pent up inside him. And tonight he had left with that washed-up actress, Diana Williams. How could a man who was so unattainable to her be available to starlets and broken-down has-beens? It wasn't fair! To have Robin would be the supreme conquest. He wouldn't be just an extracurricular lover. He had the same vitality that she admired in Gregory, but Robin was beautiful, exciting—oh God, to be loved by a man like that!

But he had rejected her. Perhaps he thought it was too

dangerous? Of course—that must be it! If they had an affair and it ended badly he might feel his career would be hurt. She had to make him understand that if they had a month together—a year together—no matter how they parted, it would in no way affect his job at IBC.

She walked to the mirror and gazed at her face. Good Lord, there was over an inch of slack loose skin. It had all happened so gradually. She pulled the skin tight. She looked marvelous! Well, that settled it: tomorrow she'd start searching for the right doctor. And she'd have to get some pills. She hadn't had the curse in five months and the night sweats were murder. You couldn't sleep with a man like Robin and wake up in the middle of the night bathed in perspiration.

She slipped into a robe. Odd that Gregory hadn't come in to say good night and hurl one final threat that this was positively the last eggnog party. She would go in and kiss his forehead and wish him a Happy New Year if he was awake. Now that she had made her decision about her face and the plan to get Robin, she felt exhilarated. She would have to tell Gregory about the face-lift and explain that it was just for her own vanity. There'd be no problem about her disappearing from the scene—she'd pretend to be visiting Connie in Rome.

Her smile vanished the moment she entered his bedroom.

He was lying across the bed, fully clothed. Alarm and conscience constricted her throat.

"Greg," she whispered softly.

"That eggnog has formed a rock in my gut," he groaned.

She breathed with relief. "You say that every year, but you drink more than anyone else. There's no rule that says you have to drink it. You could always have Scotch. Now come on, get undressed."

"I can't move, Judith. Whenever I try, the pain stabs at me."

"Shall I get you an Alkie?"

"I've had two."

"Gregory, you just can't stay like that, lying across the bed. Come on, now."

He made an attempt to sit, but doubled over. His face

was white and he looked at her blankly. "Judith, this is something different."

She was at his side immediately. "Where does it hurt?"

"In my gut."

"Then it's just indigestion, Greg. Try getting undressed, then you can relax." He tried to move and cried out in agony. She rushed to the phone and called the doctor. She noticed that Gregory did not stop her. He sat on the bed, doubled over, rocking back and forth.

Dr. Spineck arrived in twenty minutes. Judith was downstairs, waiting to let him in. "David, I'm glad you could come."

"I'm glad I checked with my service. From what you tell me it doesn't sound like heart."

"I think it's plain old-fashioned indigestion. I hate to call you out, but he's never had it like this."

She waited outside the room while the doctor examined him. When he called her in, Gregory was sitting in a chair, fully dressed, quite calm.

"I gave him a shot of Demerol to ease the pain," Dr. Spineck said. "I think it's the gall bladder."

"That's not serious." It was more of a statement than a question.

"We'll have to take some tests," he answered. "But you're right. It's not serious. Just unpleasant."

They drove to the hospital in the doctor's car. Gregory was installed in a corner room. Nurses were summoned. Blood tests were taken. Judith was shunted to the lounge where she sat and chain-smoked. After half an hour, Dr. Spineck appeared. "It isn't going to be as simple as we thought. A stone is lodged in the duct and he needs an operation immediately. I've summoned Dr. Lesgarn. He'll be here any second."

At one o'clock Gregory was wheeled out of the room. The floor nurse brought Judith some coffee. She sat in Gregory's room and waited. She must have dozed off, because Dr. Spineck touched her cheek gently. She sat up and stared in startled surprise at her surroundings. In a flash she reoriented herself and glanced at her watch—it was four in the morning. Her eyes shot to the bed where

Gregory should be. In alarm she looked at Dr. Spineck. He smiled. "Gregory's all right. He's in the postoperative room. He'll be there for hours. I've arranged for nurses around the clock."

"He'll be all right?" she asked.

He nodded. "He must have had gallstones for quite some time. It was a rougher operation than we counted on. He can't jump out of bed and be back at the office in two weeks—he's got to take the rest of the winter off and recuperate."

"He'll never do it," she said.

"He *has to*, Judith. He's not that young any more. None of us are. This operation has been a shock to his system. I doubt whether he'll feel up to any work for a few months."

"How soon will he come down?"

"Not before ten or eleven in the morning. I'll drive you home."

It was almost dawn when she got into bed. Poor Gregory—he'd hate having to take things easy. She'd have to stay in Palm Beach all winter and . . . She suddenly hated herself. How dared she think of Robin? Tears came to her eyes. "Oh, Gregory, I do love you," she whispered into the pillow. "I love you very much. Please get well." And she vowed that from now on she would never even think of Robin Stone, but even as she made the promise, she knew she would not keep it. She was filled with self-loathing because, as she lay alone in the dark room, she found herself wondering who Robin Stone was in bed with. . . .

Robin was in a narrow bed in a small room at the Harvard Club, alone.

He smiled for the first time that night. At least Maggie had seen fit to warn the doorman after she set the fire. He knew it was Maggie when he saw her suitcase on the floor and the charred matches from the Pavillon on the bed. He was beginning to find the situation amusing. He laughed aloud at the thought of her walking in and catching Diana copping his joint! And the worst thing had been that nothing was happening with him. In a way, thank God for the fire—he never would have been able to get it up for that crazy dame. She didn't even know how to go down on a guy—her teeth had been like razors. Yes, the fire had come just in time. Diana had been sobered by it too, and was delighted to be dropped at her hotel. But why had he brought her home in the first place? She had signed the contract at Jilly's. And if he felt he had to pay her off, he could have gone to her hotel. Archie would say that he *wanted* to be caught, wanted to get Maggie off his back. Well, it was all for the best, and all it had cost him was a bedroom. It had also cost him Maggie Stewart. A slight frown formed between his eyes, then he forced a smile. "No, Conrad, *you* lost Maggie. Not I. You're dead, you little bastard, *dead.*"

On an impulse he lifted the telephone and asked for Western Union. Where did she live? Well, he'd send it to Century Pictures. She'd get it.

The telegram was delivered to Maggie at the Melton Towers after it had kicked around the mailroom at the studio for three days. She read it, and then bought a small frame and hung it on her bathroom wall. It said:

> I TAKE IT ALL BACK. YOU WILL BE A STAR. YOU'RE A NUT! ROBIN.

Judith sat at Gregory's bedside every day. For the first time she realized he dyed his hair. It had never occurred to her that the red hair streaked with gray was not completely natural. But after a week in the hospital she noticed it was more white than red and on the back of his neck it was completely white. His unshaven face had a white stubble, and suddenly he looked like a tired old man. But she knew he was feeling better when he began taking an interest in the world around him. By the end of the second week he was checking the Nielsens. He also sent for his barber and told Judith to "go shopping or something." When she returned at five, his hair had its usual red tone, the hospital gown had been replaced with his own silk pajamas, he was reading *Time* magazine, and he looked every inch the chairman of IBC. But he had lost a great deal of weight and for the first time he looked his age. She shuddered and wondered how she would look if she had gone through a similar siege. André had been touching up her hair for fifteen years. Good Lord, she might be completely gray. And without makeup—!

Gregory put down the magazine, picked up the telephone and asked for IBC.

"Please, darling, both Dr. Lesgarn and Dr. Spineck say *no work*. In fact when you get out of here, they insist you take a long rest."

"I intend to," he said. "We're going to Palm Beach for the entire winter. It'll be the first vacation I've taken in years." He reached out and took her hand. "Judith, I'm so damn grateful that it was just gall bladder. I'd been having these awful pains for some time, but usually I could shake them. I don't mind telling you, I was afraid to get a checkup. I was positive it was cancer. If I'd had the strength, I'd have shouted for joy when they said it was only gall bladder. And this winter I'll enjoy playing golf and being with you. That's why I've got to get on the phone and set things in order."

His first call was to Cliff Dorne, head of the legal department. "Cliff, I want you here within the next half hour. Now switch me to Robin Stone."

At five thirty Robin Stone and Cliff Dorne arrived. Judith was sitting in the easy chair. "Would you like me to go out to the lounge while you talk?" she asked.

"No, stay, Judith," Gregory said. "This is an important decision. I want you to hear it. Robin, how would you like to be president of IBC?"

Robin didn't answer. It was Cliff Dorne who reacted.

"President of IBC?" Cliff repeated. "What is Danton Miller?"

Gregory shrugged. "Dan is president of Network Television."

"And what exactly is president of IBC?" Cliff asked.

"A new title I've just made up. It merely means a division of power while I'm away."

"But do you think Dan will sit still if Robin is placed up there with him?" Cliff asked.

"Yes, because Dan still has the same power. He's always had to report to me, only this time he'll do it through Robin. And Robin can check everything with me."

Cliff nodded. Then for the first time they both looked at Robin.

Robin stood up. "Sorry, but I pass."

"Are you insane?" Gregory sputtered.

"I'd be insane to take such a job. As I see it, I'd have two months of infighting with Dan, yet actually I'd be nothing more than a glorified watchdog and messenger boy. Then you return from Palm Beach with a nice tan and I go back to being president of News, with a brace of enemies and one of Dan's ulcers."

"Who said you go back to News?" Gregory asked.

"I assume the job is temporary. Any created title always is."

Gregory rubbed his chin thoughtfully. "Perhaps it *was* in its original inception, but the more I think of it, the more sense it makes to keep it as a permanent setup."

"But essentially I'm a newsman," Robin said.

"Balls!" Gregory shouted. "You've jazzed that Happening show into a real piece of entertainment. Without realizing it, Robin, you have unconsciously gone away from News. If I didn't know you better, I'd think you were also after power."

Robin's smile was easy, but his eyes were like steel. "Perhaps I am."

Gregory smiled. "I don't make snap judgments. I've done my homework on you." He reached for a sheaf of papers on his night table. "You doubt me? Okay: you're from Boston. You're going to come into money of your own someday. Your father was one of the biggest lawyers there. Your mother lives in Rome. She's not well—I'm sorry about that. You have a sister in San Francisco whose husband is wealthy in his own right. Now a man with this kind of background likes to do a job well. He has built-in security, so he does not hunger for power. You take me, Robin—I grew up on Tenth Avenue, one of the kids I played with went to the chair. I know it sounds like a Bogart movie, but it happened that way. Some of the kids on my block also made it big as lawyers, politicians, and doctors. Because the kids on that street *had* to have power. If they went into crime, they didn't fool around with robbery. They became killers. And if they went into business they became killers. I'm a killer. Dan's a killer. You aren't. I wouldn't trust you with running the financial end of a network for five minutes. You always went way over budget with *In Depth*. You built it into a prestige show. Now that Andy Parino is on it and Cliff, here, keeps an eye on things, the show's making money for the first time."

"It's also not as good," Robin said. "I was planning to have a meeting with Andy next Monday. We're doing too many shows based in New York. We need some European flavor."

"You'll have no such meeting," Gregory snapped. "That's what I mean about you and finances. The show has decent enough ratings. We can milk another season out of it. Fortunately we're getting a big enough price on the Happening show to make some money—even with you running it." Gregory smiled to take the bite out of his words. "But I didn't ask you here to lecture you on the economics of television. Dan knows them well enough. Cliff knows them even better. And one thing about Dan, he'll never recommend a show that won't make a profit."

"What about quality?" Robin asked.

"The public doesn't want quality. We have a few quality shows that we keep on. And they're losers. You know what the public wants. *Shit*—that's what it wants. The high ratings of the old movies prove it. I won't go that route yet. As long as I can, I'll try to create new shows for prime time. But we can still be commercial. And that's what Dan is. Now, if we combine your taste with Dan's commercialism—we've got a winning ticket."

Robin built his fingers into a pyramid. He studied them. Then he looked up. "Who moves to president of News?"

"I'll let you make that suggestion."

"Andy Parino."

"I don't think he has the ability," Gregory said.

"I'll keep an eye on him. He'll report directly to me."

Gregory nodded. "Okay, I'll go along."

"What about a contract?" Robin said.

"Dan has no contract."

"I want one."

"For how long?"

"One year." Robin did not miss the fleeting expression of relief on Gregory's face. "Gregory, this may not work out. But I want you to know something. I am not going to be just your telephone pal. I'm going to *be* president of IBC. I'm going to come up with ideas, throw them at you, fight for them if I think they're right. I need the assurance of one year. No one can tell anything in six weeks. But after a year, well, either it works or I walk away from the title and go back to News."

Gregory nodded. "That's fair enough. What do you think of sixty thousand a year plus expenses?"

"I think it's ridiculous."

"Dan started at fifty."

"What is Dan making now?"

"Seventy-five, plus expenses and stock options."

Robin nodded. "That sounds better."

Gregory was silent for a moment. Then he smiled. "I like your guts. I also like the idea that you want to carry the ball. Okay, Cliff will draw up the contract." Then he held out his hand to Robin. "Good luck to the president of IBC."

Robin smiled. "And may the chairman of the board have an excellent vacation." Then he looked at Judith with a hint of intimacy in his smile. "Take good care of him, Mrs. Austin."

The news ripped through Madison Avenue like a tornado.

Dan Miller was in a state of shock but he pretended that Robin's new title had been his idea. He faced the press with his usual smile and made a statement. "He's a good man, and I need someone to pitch in while Gregory is away."

But he spent hours staring at the skyline from his window, wondering what everyone in the business thought. He took tranquilizers and avoided "21" and restaurants where he might run into agency men. He holed in at night, and when he read that Robin was taping the

Diana Williams Happening, he prayed that Diana would do one of her famous walkouts—then Robin would be stuck with egg on his tape.

But as January passed, Dan's fears began to diminish. The cancelations had been decided several months back. The new shows had been selected by Gregory in November: a few seemed to be making it, a few were bigger bombs than their predecessors. And now it was time to start viewing pilots for the fall season.

By February he had completely regained his confidence. Then he heard about Robin's new offices. A suite on the penthouse floor! Dan went storming into Cliff Dorne's office.

Cliff tried to dismiss it. "Where can we put him? You tell *me*. Andy Parino has inherited Robin's office. There just is no space. Gregory had a thousand feet of space closed off up there. He always intended to make it into a gym and sauna bath. Because of the shortage of space, he's turned it into offices for Robin."

"How does it make *me* look—Robin sharing the penthouse floor with Gregory!"

Cliff sighed. "Okay, tell me where to put him and I'll be glad to oblige."

"They should have put *me* there," Dan snapped. "And given Robin *my* office."

Cliff smiled. "Not very good thinking for a man who's telling everyone Robin has been kicked upstairs. Put him in your office, Dan, and he's replacing *you*. Then you're kicked upstairs for real."

Dan had no recourse but to remain grimly silent. The newspapers were going all out on Robin's new assignment. In the beginning Robin had refused to comment. But he finally capitulated and gave a mass interview the day he took possession of his new suite of offices.

He stood behind the large desk as the questions were fired at him. His answers were polite but evasive. The press sensed his reluctance to talk, and feeling they were covering an important story, they zeroed in on him. As an ex-newspaperman, Robin felt an empathy for them. Their job was to get a story.

"Let's talk about television itself, rather than my new title," he said with a smile.

"What about television?" a young man asked.

"It's an octopus. It's no longer just a little box, it's the Love Machine."

"Why the Love Machine?" a reporter asked.

"Because it *sells* love. It *creates* love. Presidents are chosen by their appeal on that little box. It's turned politicians into movie stars and movie stars into politicians. It can get you engaged if you use a certain mouthwash. It claims you'll have women hanging on your coattails if you use a certain hair cream. It tells the kids to eat their cereal if they want to be like their baseball idol. But like all great lovers, the Love Machine is a fickle bastard. It has great magnetism—but it has no heart. In place of a heart beats a Nielsen rating. And when the Nielsen falters, the program dies. It's the pulse and heart of the twentieth century—the Love Machine."

The newspapers all carried the story. Dan read it and glowered. Especially when columnists began to try to tag Robin as the Love Machine. "Perhaps Mr. Stone is comparing the box with himself," wrote Ronnie Wolfe. "His way of giving unlimited time to a beautiful girl is well known. And like the machine he speaks of, Mr. Stone can also turn off with equal ease."

Dan threw the paper across the room. Dammit, that was only adding to Robin's image: call a man a heel with women and suddenly he gets charisma. He reached for another tranquilizer, gulped it down and wondered what the son of a bitch was doing in that plush new office. What new scheme did he have going? Rehearsals for the Diana Williams show had been postponed for two weeks. The newspapers reported that Byron Withers, the leading man, had bowed out, claiming his part had been cut down from the original concept, in deference to Diana. Byron Withers! Where did these has-beens get their nerve—thinking they could come to Broadway after three pictures and share equal billing with Diana Williams? Although he was rooting for Robin's demise, Dan still respected Diana's talent. He put down the newspaper and hoped it was a phony item and that it was Diana herself who was being difficult.

Robin also wondered if Diana was being difficult. Was she on the pills and booze? Ike Ryan swore she was fine and eager to begin rehearsals. "As soon as we find the right leading man," Ike said. "He doesn't even have to sing great—just look the part."

He was just leaving for the viewing room when his secretary peeked in. "A Mr. Nelson is waiting outside to see you."

For a moment Robin looked blank. As he stared at her, the secretary added, "It's Dip Nelson, the movie actor."

Robin's smile was warm. "Of course, show him in."

Dip strode in giving the secretary a radiant smile. She fluttered with excitement and stumbled out of the room. Robin laughed. "She's a forty-year-old virgin, she'll never be the same."

Dip shrugged. "If that's the case, I may even grab her by the ass when I leave—let the poor woman die happy." He whistled as he took in the office. "Well, old buddy pal, this is quite a layout you got yourself."

"How's it been going, Dip?"

The handsome blond man sat on a chair and threw his long legs over the side. "Between you and I, it's been going lousy until today."

"What happened to your Persian Room engagement? I kept watching for the announcement."

Dip shrugged. "The act bombed. We kept it on the road for over a year and milked what we could out of it, but I didn't dare bring it into New York. See, I did some analyzing. Pauli and me—we don't mesh."

"You mean the marriage is over?"

"Over! It's never been more solid, pal. It's just that our personalities don't go to form a good act. Look, when she does comedy or straight singing on her own, she's great. And when I do my old song and dance, I'm great. I kill them with my imitations. I swear when I do Godfrey with the uke—buddy boy, you can't tell the difference. Ted Lewis *knows* he's listening to himself when I say, 'Is everybody happy?' But the thing is, I'm one style and she's another. But listen, buddy boy, my agent told me

Ike Ryan is looking for a leading man to play opposite Diana Williams—and the Big Dipper is a natural for the job. You once said you owed me something. Well, how about booking Pauli and me on *The Christie Lane Show?* It would serve as an audition for me for Ike Ryan, and also we could use the scratch. I hear they pay five G's for guests. And it will give Pauli some coverage too. She's gonna be mad enough if I get the lead opposite Diana Williams and split the act—but if it comes from the Chris Lane show, it won't look as if I went after it."

"I'll take care of it. How soon do you want to go on?"

"Like *yesterday!*"

Robin picked up the phone and called Jerry Moss. "Jerry, who is the guest star on the next week's Chris Lane show? Lon Rogers? Well, cancel him out. I don't give a damn if Artie Rylander picked him—IBC will pay him off. I want Pauli and Dip Nelson booked in his place. And if there are any repercussions just say the word came from me. . . . Sure, say I *hate* Lon Rogers, that *I* want him canceled. . . . Hell no, I think Lon is as good as any baritone around—but I want Dip and Pauli in that spot. Fine."

He hung up and smiled at Dip. "It's done."

Dip shook his head in awe. "Buddy boy, you've sure come a long way while we've been out on the road."

The following morning Robin's secretary announced that Danton Miller was waiting in the outside office. Robin was on the telephone talking to Gregory in Palm Beach. "Have him wait," Robin answered.

Dan's anger blistered as he sat in the outer office. When he was finally admitted, he spat the words out before he was in the door. "Not only do you butt into my shows, but you play it cute, and make me wait."

"What's so important to bring you here in person?" Robin asked with a cordial smile.

Dan stood in front of him, his fists clenched. "Now you're in the booking business. How dare you go over Artie Rylander's head and put a crummy team on my top show."

"*IBC's* top show," Robin answered.

"What's your excuse?" Dan demanded.

Robin's stare was cold. "I stopped making excuses when I was five years old."

"Why are they on the show?" Dan demanded, in tight-lipped fury.

"Because I happen to *like* them. They're a new team. They haven't been on television. That in itself is refreshing. I'm tired of seeing the same old Hollywood names, the ones we pay five thousand—and then see them with Johnny Carson, Merv Griffin or Mike Douglas a few days later for scale. From here on in, no plugs for pictures are allowed on any of our shows."

"Listen, you son of a bitch—"

The secretary buzzed. Robin snapped the box on. Her voice came through.

"Your reservation to Rome is confirmed, Mr. Stone."

"Rome!" Dan looked like he was going to have a stroke. "Why in hell are you going to Rome?"

Robin stood up. "Because my mother is dying." He walked past Dan, then he stopped at the door. "And I have Gregory's permission to stay as long as I'm needed. I hope you can manage to get along without me for a few days." When he left the office Dan was still standing in the center of the room staring after him.


## TWENTY-SEVEN


SERGIO WAS WAITING at the airport when Robin arrived. "I did not cable you sooner," the boy explained. "We thought it was just another seizure. But yesterday the doctor said I should notify her family. Did I do right?"

"You did just fine, Sergio," Robin said. He was aware that the boy's eyes were shining with tears. He waited until they were in the car, then he asked, "How does she seem?"

Through the corner of his eye he saw the tears spill down Sergio's face. "She is in a coma," he said.

"Did you notify my sister?" Robin asked.

"Lisa and Richard are on their way. Their names were in Kitty's address book. I sent them the same cable I sent you."

It was ten in the morning when they reached the clinic. Robin was only allowed a brief glance at the waxen face under the oxygen tent. She died at eleven thirty that night without regaining consciousness. Lisa and Richard arrived an hour later. Lisa went into immediate hysterics and had to be given sedation. Richard stood by, stoic and helpless.

The following morning, Robin, Sergio and Richard met with Kitty's lawyer and discussed the funeral arrangements. Kitty's will would be probated in the States. The trust was to be divided evenly between Robin and Lisa, but Kitty had left the villa, the car and all of her jewelry to Sergio. Lisa stayed in bed all day. The following morning she appeared at breakfast, pale and silent, as Sergio and Robin were having their second cup of coffee.

"Kitty wanted to be cremated," Robin said. "We made all the arrangements yesterday. Richard sat in for you."

Lisa said nothing. Suddenly she turned to Sergio. "Do you mind having your coffee in the other room? I want to talk to my brother."

Robin's eyes narrowed. "This is *his* house," he said. But Sergio had already taken his coffee into the living room. "That was goddamned rude," Robin said tonelessly.

Lisa ignored him and turned to her husband. "Well, are you going to tell him?"

For a moment Richard looked embarrassed. Then he stiffened with an attempt at righteous courage. "We're contesting the will."

"Just what are you contesting?" Robin asked cautiously.

"Sergio getting the villa and the jewelry. We can't lose."

"What makes you so sure?"

Richard smiled. "Once we start legal action, the estate will be held up. Sergio will need money to live on. It's

obvious he has none. After a few months he'll be delighted to settle for a few thousand dollars. Of course, we
will also claim that Kitty was not sound of mind when
she made the will—that the boy used pressure to make her
draw it up."

"I'll fight you on it," Robin said evenly.

"You'd stick up for that little faggot?" Richard asked.

"I'll stick up for anyone who was good to Kitty."

"I'll have him investigated," Richard said. "I'll prove he
played on the emotions of a sick old woman."

"Who the hell are you to prove anything? Were you
ever here? Did you ever see them together? I did. And
for that reason my word will carry more weight than
yours."

"Oh no, it won't," Lisa said in an odd voice. "I happen
to hold some trump cards that might lessen the power of
*your* word. And the attending publicity might embarrass
you at your network. To say nothing of your personal
life."

Richard shot her a warning look. "Lisa, we can win
legally. Let's not get personalities involved."

"I might have expected this from you," Lisa snapped at
Robin. "After all, what are you really? Just a lucky
bastard—"

"Lisa!" Richard's voice held a warning.

"No, why *shouldn't* I shock him? I'd *like* to see big
brother lose his cool just once in his life! It only proves
that in the end class will tell. He's about as much my real
brother as that fairy in the other room." She turned to
Robin. "You were adopted when you were five!"

She paused, waiting for Robin's reaction. Richard
seemed to be the only one affected. He looked out toward
the patio to hide his embarrassment and displeasure.

Robin's gaze was level. "Lisa, at this moment, nothing
gives me greater satisfaction than the realization that we
are in no way related."

"Your mother was a whore!"

"Lisa!" This was Richard.

"Let her go on," Robin said evenly.

"Oh, I kept it a secret these past few years. I didn't
know until then. Kitty told me when she was ill. She said

if I was ever in trouble to go to you. That you were a strong person. That she really loved you as if you were her own. She adopted you because she had given up on having a child of her own, and she wanted one. Dad had a friend in criminal law and he told him about a case he was handling—about the poor little orphan in a coma in an orphanage hospital in Providence. Mother insisted on adopting him. Your real mother was strangled! You *had* no father. But Mother, *my* mother, worshiped you, because two years later the impossible happened—she had me! I can't stop you from getting your end of the estate —that's all legal, Dad made that stupid will. But I can sure stop you from letting that fairy wind up with anything!"

"*Try* it. I enjoy a good fight."

She jumped up and tossed her coffee in his face. "You knew it all along, about being adopted! You cold-blooded bastard—*I hate you!*" Then she ran out of the room.

Richard sat stunned. Robin calmly mopped his face and shirt. "Thank goodness the coffee was lukewarm," he said with a smile.

Richard stood up. "I'm sorry, Robin. She doesn't mean any of it. She'll get over it." He started from the room. "Oh, and Robin—don't worry, I won't let her contest the will."

Robin smiled at him. "Crew Cut, maybe I've misjudged you."


Kitty's body was cremated. Lisa silently took possession of the urn and she and Richard took a flight out the following day. Obviously Richard exerted some control, because she made no further mention of fighting Sergio on the will. When they were gone, Robin poured himself a stiff drink. Sergio watched him silently.

"I want to thank you, Robin. I was sitting in the other room the day your sister reacted so violently. Unfortunately I could not help but overhearing. Is it the truth about you being adopted?"

Robin nodded. Then he turned with a quick grin and said, "But it's also true that you are now a man of means."

The boy nodded. "She left me much jewelry. Pearls, a

twenty-carat emerald-cut diamond. Now I can go to America!"

Robin whistled through his teeth. "Sergio, you really struck it big."

"What I am trying to say is perhaps you want the ring or the necklace to give to a lady you care about?"

"Nope. You keep it all. You were there when she needed you."

Sergio stared at him. "What are you going to do, Robin?"

"Well, for one thing, I'm going to get pissy-eyed drunk. Tell you what, Sergio, let's really tie one on, find us some girls—" he stopped. "You really don't go for women? Not at all?"

The boy shook his head. "Even with Kitty. I was just her very good friend."

"Okay, you be *my* very good friend tonight. Let's go and get drunk."

"I will go with you, but I will not drink."

At two in the morning Robin was singing as they wandered down the cobbled streets. He was dimly aware that Sergio was holding him up. Several times he tripped and would have fallen if it had not been for Sergio. He had never gotten so roaring drunk. The last thing he recalled was falling across the bed before he passed out. He awoke the following morning with the first hangover he had ever known. He was under the covers, disrobed down to his shorts. Sergio came in with a pot of inky-black coffee. Robin took it and eyed him curiously.

"Sergio, how did I get my clothes off?"

"I undressed you."

"That figures. Did you enjoy yourself?"

Sergio looked properly insulted. "Robin, the trouble with people is that they think a homosexual will go for just any man. If you were with a girl and she passed out, would you take her just because she was a woman?"

Robin's grin was apologetic. "I had it coming. Sorry." Then, in an attempt to break the somber mood, he grinned and said, "Sergio, I should be insulted. I thought you dug me."

For a second there was a glimmer of hope in the dark

eyes. Then he caught Robin's smile. "You joke. But I will always wear this bracelet." He held out his arm. "I know you like women, but one day I will find a man I care about who also will care for me."

Robin sipped the black coffee. It tasted awful but it cleared his head.

"You hate what I am, don't you, Robin?"

"No, Sergio. At least you know what you are, who you are and what you want out of life."

"Does it bother you not knowing your real mother?"

"Yes—it makes me feel in limbo," Robin said slowly.

"Then find out who she *really* was."

"You heard what Lisa said. Unfortunately it's the truth. I have an old newspaper clipping in my wallet to prove it."

"Germany is not far away."

"Meaning what?"

"You know the name of your mother, the city she came from. She might have relatives, friends—you could learn about her."

"Forget it."

"You mean you would take the word of Lisa and a newspaper clipping? I am what she calls a fairy. It is true. But I am also a person. Perhaps your mother was a good person. Find out what she was like."

"Hell, I don't speak German. I've never been to Hamburg."

"I speak German and I've been to Hamburg, I know it well."

Robin smiled. "Sergio, you are a man of many talents."

"We could be in Germany in a few hours. I would go with you."

Robin threw back the covers and leaped out of bed. "Know something, Sergio? I've never been to Germany and I'd like to have a look at it. *Especially* Hamburg. I dropped some bombs over it once, but I only saw it from the air. Also I'm very partial to German girls. You make the plane reservations. We may not find out anything about my mother, but it's a cinch we'll find *something!*"

They checked into the Four Seasons hotel. The suite was Old World in its charm and furnishings. Oriental-type rugs, thick comforters on the bed. Sergio went right to the phone and began to call all the Boesches listed in the directory. Robin ordered a bottle of vodka and sat at the window, sipping his drink and watching the darkness fall on the city. People were waiting for buses. Mothers were dragging children down the street as the stores began to close. The Alster River looked serene and dark. So this was the enemy he had bombed. The city the British had bombed. It looked like any city in America. He half listened to Sergio's faultless German as he made call after call. On the eighth call, Sergio called to him excitedly. He was writing a number, an address.

"We have luck," he said as he hung up. "These Boesches said they are distant cousins of a Herta. We can see them tomorrow."

"Keep trying," Robin said. "There might be more than one Herta."

At the end of an hour they had located five Herta Boesches who had gone to America. One was still living in Milwaukee—that ruled her out. The others had not been heard from.

Sergio looked crestfallen. "I have not been a success and it seemed like such a good plan. I am most sorry, Robin."

"Sorry! Are you going just to sit there and cry in your beer? At least show me Hamburg. Is there any night life in this town?"

Sergio laughed aloud. "Robin—no town in the world has the kind of night life Hamburg has."

"You've got to be kidding! Better than Paris?"

"Paris! They are prudes. Their clubs are for tourists. Come, I will show you night life. But we will take no more than one hundred dollars with us, and get it changed into small bills at the desk. Where I am going to take you, it is most easy to be robbed."

They took a cab and Sergio directed the driver to a given point, then they got out and walked. "This is the St. Pauli district," Sergio explained.

They walked down the brightly lit street. "This is the Reeperbahn." It was more brightly lighted than Broadway. A skyscraper stood next to a bar called

Wimpy's. Across the street was a bowling alley. But what struck Robin most was the people. Masses of people, all walking in a leisurely way. It reminded him of a shopping crowd on Fifth Avenue before Christmas, without the frantic pace. These people were strolling aimlessly. Robin and Sergio walked on silently passing a conglomeration of stores—auction houses, furniture shops—the entire street was a maze of neon lights. Men with goods, hawking like American auctioneers and everywhere the smell of sausage. On impulse Robin stopped at a stand. "Two *Weisswurst*, please."

Sergio stared at it. "What is it, Robin? It looks like a white hot dog."

Robin bit into it and speared the hot sauerkraut. "*Weisswurst*. I haven't had it since—" He stopped, suddenly speechless. "I just saw her, Sergio! I saw a crummy little round table and a beautiful lady with black hair place a dish of this before a little boy. It was hot and good." Robin pushed the plate away. "This is junk compared to the way she made it."

They left the stand and walked in silence. "I saw her face," Robin kept muttering. "I'm beginning to see everything. She was beautiful—dark with flashing black eyes, like a gypsy."

"I am glad," Sergio said.

"She was still a whore. But at least I remember now. God, she was beautiful. Let's celebrate, Sergio. We're not going to spend the whole night walking down a German midway, are we? This may be your idea of night life, but it isn't mine."

Sergio took his arm and led him across the street. They turned right and walked a block. "Ah, this is it," Sergio said, "the Silbersackstrasse."

Robin stared as if they had suddenly entered another world. Girls accosted them openly. "*Amerikaner—Spiel?*" One of the bolder ones chased after them. "Three-way good time, all of us?"

Robin smiled and they walked on. Every few steps a girl emerged from an alley or a doorway. The proposition never varied. They made the girls who paraded down Seventh Avenue and Central Park South look like debutantes. These were rough little Fräuleins, educated to cater to the sailors with their striped shirts and eager appetites. They cut through another street and Sergio stopped before a dark, wooden planked gate. The white painted letters read: VERBOTEN! Sergio opened the door. Robin followed him in silent amazement.

"This is Herbertstrasse," Sergio whispered.

Robin couldn't believe it. The long cobbled street was narrow and lined on both sides with solid rows of tiny two-story houses. The windows of the downstairs rooms went from floor to ceiling. And in each lighted window sat a girl. A few windows were dark. Sergio pointed to the upper room: "That means she is working." People flowed up and down the street studying the girls. To Robin's amazement he saw women walking there with men. He spotted a well-known movie star with dark glasses and a bandanna—the German representative from her picture company was giving her a "tour." Robin felt as open-mouthed as the actress. He couldn't believe anything like this still existed. The girls behind the windows seemed oblivious of the people who walked along the street. They sat in tiny bras and G-strings, sipping glasses of wine. Their hard mascaraed eyes seemed to stare past the spectators. Occasionally one girl would turn to her companion in the next window and make a comment. The other would laugh. *Laugh?* How could there be laughter in a world like this? What did these girls feel and think? How could they laugh?

"Christmas Eve is the sad night," Sergio whispered. "They actually have little trees in the windows and they give each other gifts. Then at midnight they cry."

"How do you know all this?"

"My sister worked here," Sergio said quietly.

"Your sister!"

"I was born during the war. My father was killed in Tunisia. My mother did the best she could to support me and my three brothers. We were all under ten. My sister was fourteen. She began working the streets to bring us food from the Americans. Later she wound up here in the Herbertstrasse. She died last year at thirty-five. That is a long life for a girl in the Herbertstrasse. Come, I will show you where they go after they are thirty." He led Robin into an alleyway off the main section of the Herbertstrasse. Here the windows faced a blank wall. They were relegated to fat older women in their thirties. Robin looked at a blowsy hennaed woman with a gold tooth and muddy eyes. A beery-faced man with a red-veined nose knocked on her window. She opened it. He stood with three other men. A guttural argument ensued. Suddenly she slammed her window shut. The men shrugged and tapped the next window where a straw-haired woman sat with a kimono covering flattened breasts that hung to her waist. There was more conversation. She opened the door and the men entered. The lights went off as the group went upstairs.

"What was that all about?" Robin asked.

"It was a matter of price," Sergio explained. "They were willing to pay the proper amount of marks for the man who would have the affair, but the others wanted to be allowed to watch for a small bit of money."

Robin laughed. "A group plan."

Sergio nodded. "The second one agreed, but she made them promise that if they masturbated while watching she would make them pay to clean the rug."

They walked back to the main section of the Herbertstrasse. In one window, Robin saw a girl who reminded him of the prostitute he had beaten. She was standing wearing boots and held a whip.

"Advertising her talent," Sergio whispered.

They returned to the Reeperbahn and wandered into a discothèque where they were quickly shown to the door. Robin had a quick glimpse of women dancing together, holding hands at the bar. Here men were *verboten*. They stopped at a café where the barker at the door promised "wonderful nudes." Robin shrugged and Sergio followed him inside. The place was jammed with sailors and they were shown to a small table in the back. The nightclub floor was elevated and a girl had stripped down to complete nudity—no pasties or G-string. There was a scattering of applause and the girl went off. Now music began. Another girl came on—she looked about nineteen —fresh-eyed and eager in a pink chiffon dress, and her smile held the guilelessness of a girl going to her first prom. "This one probably sings," Robin decided.

She walked around the floor grinning at all the sailors and tossing greetings to them. They shouted back good-naturedly—she was obviously a favorite. Then the music began and she started to strip. Robin couldn't believe it. She was attractive and fresh—she would have looked more natural as a young junior secretary at the IBC network than strutting on that floor, chatting with the sailors. Suddenly she was completely nude. She stood there and pivoted with the same cheerful grin. The bitch enjoyed her work. Then she pulled a chair to the center of the floor and sat on it and spread her legs, grinning merrily all the while. She finally left the chair and walked around the club, leaning down to each table and allowing the men to suck at her breasts. She came to their table, looked at Robin and Sergio, then laughed and shook her head. She winked at them knowingly and went on her way.

Robin threw some money on the table and started out of the room. Sergio hurried after him. They walked down the street in silence.

"That girl," Robin said. "She couldn't have been more than twenty. Why? *How?*"

"Robin—these girls are the product of the war. They grew up struggling for food. And children like that grow up with a different set of values. To them sex is not love —sex is not even for pleasure. *It is a way to survive.*"

As they walked down the street, girls accosted them every five feet. "Look, I'm packing it in," Robin said.

"Come to one more place before we go back to the hotel."

They entered a cabaret on Grosse Freiheit Strasse. It was elegant and subdued. And attractive people were sitting quietly at tables, conversing with one another as a muted string trio played German love songs. It was a long room dimly lighted, paneled with Austrian drapes. There were groups of men, which aroused Robin's suspicions, until he saw several heterosexual couples, holding hands and listening to the music.

"The food is excellent here at the Maison Bleue," Sergio said.

"You eat. I want to get loaded."

Sergio ordered a steak which he attacked with such eagerness that Robin felt guilty—he had forgotten they had skipped dinner. Robin ordered a bottle of hundred-proof vodka to be left on the table. He sipped it straight. It felt like hot white velvet. . . .

The string ensemble stopped playing. A drummer joined the band, cymbals were crashed, a guttural announcement was made, and the show began. Robin watched without too much interest. It was obviously a high-class supper club. A French *chanteuse* named Véronique came out. She was good, a true contralto. She finished to polite applause. He poured himself another shot of vodka. He narrowed his eyes to place the next girl in focus. She was blond and vapidly pretty and she was singing something from *Gypsy*. Ethel Merman didn't have to worry. He looked up groggily as the orchestra went into a fanfare. Then the leader shouted, *"Brazillia!"* And a slim dark girl stepped into the spotlight.

Robin sat up. She was worth the fanfare. She wore a man's evening jacket over a leotard. Her black hair was tucked into a French knot under a black slouch hat worn at a rakish angle. Slowly she began an apache dance. It was amazingly good. The girl had a solid classical ballet background. She finished in a frenzy and whipped off her hat and let her black hair cascade down to her shoulders. The applause was strong, but she did not leave. She waited until it subsided, then the music began the familiar beat. She swayed suggestively and removed her coat. Slowly she fell to her knees, then like a snake shedding its skin, she writhed her way out of the leotard, revealing a smooth white body with tiny silver bikini pants and bra.

The music went faster, the lights began to flicker; he saw the silver-and-white body leaping into the air, falling into splits. The lights dimmed. She pulled off the bra and bikini pants, the lights came up to give the audience a fleeting flash of the nude slim body and the small compact breasts. Then the lights went off, and she disappeared to loud applause. The show was over and Robin was quite drunk.

"I want to meet Brazillia," he announced.

"We'll go to Liesel's down the street where they all go for breakfast. You'll see Brazillia there."

Robin looked at his watch. "Are you kidding? It's three A.M. This place is about to pack in. Nothing will be open."

"There are places in Hamburg open twenty-four hours."

Robin paid the bill, but insisted upon sending a note to Brazillia telling her to meet them at Liesel's. Sergio patiently wrote it in German and gave it to the waiter along with a handful of marks. The waiter returned and an exchange of German passed between him and Sergio. "She will be there," he told Robin. "Come—we will leave." Robin followed obediently.

Liesel's was obviously owned by the fat woman who greeted them and led them into a cellar with small tables and checked cloths. Sergio ordered beer. Robin's gaze wandered as he sipped vodka. A tall good-looking man entered and sat at a table across the room. Soon a few effeminate men joined him. The tall man stared at Sergio. Robin was drunk but he was able to detect the instant radar that went up between Sergio and the man. "You're sure this is where Brazillia comes, and not just a faggot hangout?"

"It's everything. It is also the only place on the block that serves breakfast." Sergio was staring at the good-looking boy across the way.

Robin patted him on the shoulder. "Okay. Sergy, go join the boys."

"I will stay with you. Perhaps Brazillia will not come. I do not want you to be alone."

"Listen, chum, I don't need a caretaker. And don't worry, she'll show."

"Robin, I don't like it. You know what kind of a girl Brazillia is, don't you?"

"Beat it, or the muscle man across the room will lose interest. He probably thinks I'm your date by now."

"But, Robin—"

"Do I have to toss you out?"

At that moment the door opened and she entered. She looked around the room hesitantly. Robin stood up and waved. She walked directly to his table. "Beat it, chum," he said under his breath.

Sergio shrugged and joined the table across the room. Brazillia sat down beside him. The woman who ran the place brought her a cognac.

"I speak English," she said in a low throaty voice.

"You don't have to talk, baby."

He glanced up in time to see Sergio leave with the handsome man. Sergio waved and Robin formed a victory sign with his fingers. The girl sat and silently drank her cognac. Robin ordered her another. He reached out and held her hand. She returned the pressure. A blond, effeminate young man entered the room and walked over to their table. He spoke a few words in French to Brazillia. She nodded and the man sat down. "This is Vernon. He does not speak English. He is waiting for a friend and does not like to stand at the bar alone."

Robin signaled for a drink for Vernon. To his surprise the fat woman brought him a glass of milk. "Vernon does not drink," Brazillia explained.

Just then a tall rugged man entered. Vernon gulped down the milk, and dashed to meet him. "Poor Vernon," Brazillia said. "He does not know what he wants to be."

"It's pretty obvious," Robin said.

Brazillia sighed. "During the day he tries to live like a man. At night he is a woman. It is sad." Then she turned to Robin. "Are you here for wild thrills?"

"I like any kind of thrills."

"If you expect something wild and crazy with me, go away." She sounded weary. "You are handsome. I would very much like to go to bed with you. But I would like a night of love, of beautiful sex—no sickness. You understand?"

"That's fine with me."

"It will be like that?" She was almost pleading.

"You call the shots, baby."

"Excuse me a moment." She walked to the bar and

whispered something to Vernon. He nodded with a faint smile. Then she returned. "Let us go."

As he paid the check he wondered what her deal with Vernon was all about. But then, many girls had fags as confidants and close friends. Amanda even said a model friend of hers lived with a fag. And look at him with Sergio.

A cab was parked outside but she tossed her head in dismissal. "I live near here."

She led him through dark cobbled streets until they came to a large building. They went through a wooden door into a courtyard. Suddenly there was a look of Paris about the place. The geraniums in the window boxes, a stray cat prowling around, middle-class domesticity. They walked up to the second floor. She leaned down and picked up a loaf of bread and put the key in the door. "I always have bread delivered, in case I have had too much cognac. If I eat bread, I don't wake with a hangover."

The apartment was small, but totally feminine. Sparkling clean and almost virginal with the white ruffled bedspread and the dolls on the bed. There was a picture of Brazillia on the dressing table. And on the mantel above the fireplace was a picture of one of the girls in the show—the one named Véronique.

"She's too good to open the show," Robin commented. "She could make it in New York." Then he reached out and caught her around the waist. "And you're too damn good a dancer to strip. You're really good."

Brazillia shrugged. "It gives me extra money and makes me a headline act. Ah, but what is the difference? None of us will go anywhere no matter how badly we want to. Once you live and work on the Reeperbahn, it is too late. But I was in America once. I played Las Vegas."

"You did?" Robin was surprised.

"Yes, not doing what I am doing now. I was part of a chorus. There were six of us. We did a straight dance, to support an old has-been American singer. He could barely get out the notes and we came on behind him to drown him out. That was ten years ago. I was eighteen and I had hoped to study the ballet seriously. But when the act was finished, all I had left was a return ticket home. So I came back."

"Where is home?"

"It was Milano. I stayed there for a time." She poured him a cognac. "Then I realized that trying to wait on tables and live the bourgeois life that was expected of me was as dishonest as—" Again she shrugged. "Come, are you like all the others—must the life story be part of the evening?"

"No. You don't have to tell me a damn thing, Brazillia. But you are young and attractive. Don't give up all your dreams."

She pushed him on the couch and sat on his lap. "Tonight I am having a dream come true." She ran her fingers along his profile and her tongue flicked his ear. "To have a handsome man like you want to make love to me."

"Eager to make love to you," he said. He kissed her gently, she clung to him. . . . Then she pulled him to his feet and led him to the bedroom.

The moment they were in bed she became the aggressor. Suddenly she seemed to be everywhere. Her tongue was like butterfly wings across his eyelids, her firm young breasts were against his chest, her long dark hair fell on his face. She made love to him and he lay back powerless to do more than accept her love. When it was over he lay limp with pleasure and exhaustion. In the dim light he reached out and stroked her head. "Brazillia, I'll never forget tonight. It's the only time in my life that a girl made love to me."

"I enjoyed it, Robin."

"Now it's my turn."

"You don't have to . . ."

"You crazy little idiot. I want to." He stroked her face and her body and when he entered her he moved rhythmically and held back. He wanted to please her. He moved deeper and faster. She was clinging to him, but he sensed she wasn't ready. He continued the steady rhythm for what seemed an eternity. A pulse was beating against his temple, he was using every bit of strength to hold back. And still he felt she wasn't ready. This had never happened to him before. And he had never held back this long without pleasing a woman. He gritted his teeth and kept moving. He *had* to please her! Then he felt the unbearable yet wonderful weakness flood through his groin as he reached his climax. He fell off her exhausted, with the knowledge that he had not satisfied her. She reached out and touched his cheek. Then she snuggled against him and kissed his brow, his nose, his neck, "Robin, you are a marvelous lover."

"Don't pretend, baby." He got up and went to the bathroom. It was frilly, like the rest of the apartment, and complete with bidet. He showered and returned in his shorts. She held a lighted cigarette out to him and patted the bed. He stared at her lovely body. The breasts stood upright under the sheer nightgown she had put on. She smiled. "Come, have a cigarette."

His smile was weary. "Brazillia, in my country they think I'm pretty good in the kip. But I'm not up to another session." He took the cigarette and began to dress.

She jumped out of bed and threw her arms around him. "Please, stay with me all night. I want to sleep in your arms. Tomorrow morning I will make you breakfast. And if the day is nice, we can take a walk. I will show you St. Pauli in the daylight, and then perhaps in the late afternoon we can make love again. Oh, Robin, it was so wonderful—please stay."

He began knotting his tie.

"Didn't you like me?" she asked.

"I liked you plenty, baby." Then he turned to her and reached in his pocket. "How much?"

She turned and sat on the bed. He walked over and touched her shoulder. His voice was gentle. "Come on, Brazillia, how much? You name it."

She lowered her head. "There is no charge."

He sat beside her and lifted her face. Tears were spilling down her face. "Honey, what's wrong?"

"You don't like me," she sobbed.

"I—?" He was bewildered. "Look, I'm not about to give you my fraternity pin, if that's what you mean. But I liked you plenty. I'm only sorry I didn't rate with you."

In a flash her arms were around his neck. "This was the most wonderful night of my life. Robin, you are completely straight."

"Straight?"

"When I saw you with the boy, I thought, well, you were the butch kind. But you are a man and it is wonderful."

"Sergio is a friend—a good friend. Nothing more."

She nodded. "I realize. And he took you slumming."

"Stop putting yourself down. He showed me the night life of Hamburg. Period."

"How did you feel, doing it with me?" she asked.

"It was great. I'm just sorry nothing happened at your end."

She looked at him and smiled. "Robin: it's all here with me." She touched her breast. "Holding you and loving you is my thrill."

He touched her hair softly. "You mean you never come?"

"I can't anymore."

"Why not?"

"Some things that are taken off cannot be replaced." His stare was blank. Suddenly she looked frightened. "Robin, you didn't know! Oh my God—" she jumped off the bed and ran into the other room. He followed her. She huddled against the wall and stared at him. She was genuinely frightened.

"Brazillia." He came to her. She backed away as if she expected him to strike her. "Brazillia, what is the matter?"

"Please, Robin—go." She dashed across the room and handed him his topcoat. He threw it on the couch and grabbed her. He was shaking with fear.

"Now tell me what this is all about. No one is going to hurt you."

Her dark eyes searched his face. She was trembling. "I thought you knew what kind of a place Maison Bleue was."

"No, I don't," but the first terrible suspicions were beginning to gnaw at him.

"Vernon—he is the one who opened the show, the one you admired. When he wears a wig he calls himself Véronique. He is my roommate."

He dropped her arm. "And you. What is *your* real name?"

"My name was Anthony Brannari—before I had the operation."

"You're a—"

She backed away from him. "I'm a girl now, I am a girl!" she screamed.

"But you had balls once," he said slowly.

She nodded and the tears streamed down her face. "I am a girl now. Don't hit me, don't be angry! Oh God, if you knew how I suffered to become a girl. Do you know what it is to *be* a girl and be trapped in a man's body? To *feel* like a girl, *think* like a girl, *love* like a girl? I was always a woman inside."

"But the breasts?"

"Silicone. And I took hormones. Look, feel my face—I never shave. And my arms and legs are smooth. I *am* a girl now."

He sank on the couch. A transvestite. He had banged a goddam transvestite. No wonder the poor bastard couldn't come. He looked at the cowering creature. "Come here, Brazillia. I'm not going to hit you. You're right—you are a girl."

She ran to the couch and started to snuggle against him. He unpried her arms gently. "Only now that I know what you *were*, let's have a man-to-man talk."

She moved to a respectful distance on the sofa. "All those broads in the show—they're men?" When she nodded, he said, "Did they all have the operation?"

"Except Vernon. He still holds out. He feels he won't be able to use his passport and get back to Paris if he has it. Although he wants to go—it is so sad for him. He is in love with Rick, the man he was meeting tonight. Vernon swallowed iodine three months ago over him. That is why he cannot drink. Rick is—how you say?—a switch hitter. Sometimes he goes for a real girl, sometimes he goes for a butch guy. Poor Vernon is neither."

"In Vegas, did you fool them too?"

"Oh no. Then I was a male dancer."

Robin stood up and reached into his pocket. He didn't have too many marks. But he had over a hundred dollars in American money. "Here, Brazillia—buy yourself a new dress."

"I don't want it."

He tossed the money on the couch and left the apartment. He heard her sob as he closed the door. His own throat tightened. He was not sorry for what had happened to him. He was sorry for the poor lost creature inside. He ran down the rickety steps. The first signs of dawn were beginning to streak through the sky. The night people of the Reeperbahn were going to bed. Couples walked arm in arm. Sailors with striptease girls, men with men, men with girls who suddenly looked suspiciously masculine to him. These people—all their dreams and hopes had turned to sawdust. The world was not made for losers. Brazillia was a loser.

Suddenly his own problems seemed very small and he was filled with anger. Gregory Austin was afraid of Dan. But he wasn't afraid of Robin Stone. Gregory thought he was a loser. Well, from now on, he'd call the shots. All at once he was eager to get back to New York. He was also eager to see that nut Maggie Stewart in California, -but she could wait—she could wait until he became the biggest winner of them all!

# TWENTY-EIGHT

ROBIN returned to New York in time to catch Dip and Pauli on *The Christie Lane Show.* Dip looked great, sang off key and moved woodenly. Pauli looked awful, sang great, and moved like a ballerina. He couldn't believe it. She had stopped imitating Lena, Garland and Streisand. Pauli had come into her own. She had a haunting style and unbelievable phrasing. Robin wondered when this metamorphosis had occurred. Perhaps in knocking around nightclubs with Dip she had given up the dream of making it and because she no longer had hope, she had unconsciously dropped the affected mannerisms—and Pauli herself had come through. Whatever it was, it was nothing short of a miracle. Even the ridiculous upturned nose and prominent teeth worked for her.

Dip came barging into his office at eleven o'clock the following morning. He sprawled into a chair and stared into space with bloodshot eyes. Then he leaned forward. "I'm going to kill her."

Robin was taken off guard. "What happened?"

"My agent called an hour ago. That fucking Ike Ryan. His taste is in his ass! He doesn't want me. He's settling for Lon Rogers—that broken-down baritone!"

"But you said you were going to kill *her*. Who is *her*?"

"Pauli!" Dip's eyes blazed. "Ike Ryan offered her a job as a standby for Diana Williams, and that stupid bitch is going to take it! After all I've taught her, all the class I tried to give her—she's going to be a standby!"

"Maybe it's for the best," Robin said. "At least you'll have some money coming in."

"She's getting three hundred dollars a week. I used to *tip* more than that around the Beverly Hills Hotel! Besides, where does it leave me? How do you like that cheap little cunt! Sashaying off and leaving me in the crapper." Anger gave him renewed vitality. He jumped up and began to pace. "Know something?" His eyes were black with rage. "I'm going home and pack. I won't be there when the *star* returns from signing her shitty little contract. Let her see how long she can get by without the Big Dipper. And I'll also throw her old lady right out of the house. But first I'll break every bone in Pauli's body!" He dashed out of the office.

Robin was still thinking about Dip and Pauli when his phone rang. It was Cliff Dorne. At the same moment, his secretary announced that Danton Miller was in the outer office. Before he had a chance to speak to either of them, Dan pushed his way in. "You're not keeping me cooling my heels out there. Did you see the notices on your act? The girl was okay, but Dip Nelson was the longest stage wait I've ever seen. The show never recovered after him. I hope from now on you'll keep your hands off my show!"

Robin ignored him and went back to the telephone. "Yes, Cliff, sorry for the interruption." Dan saw his expression change.

"When did it happen? Mount Sinai? I'll be right there." He hung up. Dan stood there, still glowering in rage.

Robin looked at him in surprise, as if suddenly remembering his presence. "Gregory's sick again." He started for the door.

"I thought he was in Palm Beach." Dan's anger had dissolved into shock.

"He flew back an hour ago and checked into Mount Sinai."

"Is it serious?"

"They don't know. Cliff says he's been feeling lousy for the past week. It seems he went to the hospital in Palm Beach for a checkup, but he doesn't trust them so he came here for observation."

"Want me to go along?"

Robin looked at him curiously. "Of course not."

And once again he left Dan standing in the middle of the room, staring after him.

Gregory was sitting in a chair in the hospital room, huddled in a robe and his silk pajamas. He was tan, but his face was drawn under the healthy color. Judith was also tanned but she looked tired. Cliff Dorne looked concerned. Robin forced a smile in an effort to dispel the heavy atmosphere of gloom.

"You don't look sick to me," he said cheerfully.

"It's the Big C," Gregory said morosely. "I know it."

"Greg, stop talking that way," Judith pleaded.

"No one takes this long to recover from a gall bladder operation. I know that. And I'm in constant pain."

"The same place?" Robin asked.

"Who knows? Everything hurts. I can't even take a leak without pain. It's all through me, I know it. And the hell of it is, no one will tell me. They tried to say it was prostate trouble in Palm Beach. But I know they told Judith the truth—it's cancer."

Her eyes went to Robin's beseechingly. "I've told him

over and over—it's prostate. I'm not keeping anything from him."

"Sure," Gregory snapped. "They'll put me through tests here. Everyone will show me charts that say it's negative. Everyone will give me big smiles, and then sit around and watch me die inch by inch."

"You'll bury me first, and soon, if you keep this up." It was Dr. Lesgarn's crisp voice as he entered the room.

"Look, Gregory, I've studied your tests from Palm Beach. It's prostate, all right—and we'll have to operate."

"What did I tell you?" Gregory's tone was triumphant. "You don't operate on prostate unless it's malignant!"

"Now I don't want any more of that talk," Dr. Lesgarn said firmly. "I want everyone out of here. I'm going to give you some sedation, Gregory. You've had a tiring trip and I want you in good condition for the operation to-morrow."

"You're going to cut?" Gregory suddenly sounded frightened.

"Yes. And you'll be fine."

"If it's malignant, *then* what?"

"Then we'll talk. But, Gregory, cancer is not a death sentence. There are many men who live long healthy lives after a prostate malignancy if it is caught in time."

"I've heard about those cases. They lose their balls—eventually even their pecker. They go piece by piece."

Dr. Lesgarn motioned Judith to leave. She walked across the room to Robin and Cliff. Dr. Lesgarn took out some cotton and swabbed Gregory's arm. Gregory pushed him away. "Tell me, before you knock me out. *Is* it malignant?"

"No one can swear one hundred percent on anything until we go in and see. But I will tell you this: I've operated on prostate malignancies, and you have none of the symptoms. I'd say it was a ninety-nine and nine-tenths chance that it is not."

"But there is that one chance?"

Judith swept over to his side and kissed his cheek. "Come on, now—you're the biggest gambler in the world, and never in your life have you had such odds in your favor. Why be chicken now?"

He managed a slight smile and she kissed his brow. "I'll be here tomorrow morning before you go to the operating room. Now do as the doctor says—rest and relax. I love you, Greg."

Then she quickly left the room with Robin and Cliff. The three of them walked down the corridor silently. She didn't speak until they reached the elevator. "When I looked into his eyes, I saw death." She shuddered. "He really believes he's going to die."

They reached the street. The long Lincoln was waiting. The chauffeur stood at attention. "Want me to ride home with you?" Cliff asked.

"I need a drink," she said.

"I think we all could use one," Robin agreed.

"I'll have to pass on it," Cliff said. "I have a long drive out to Rye, and I want to be here first thing in the morning too."

"I'll take care of Mrs. Austin," Robin said.

They got into the car. "There's a bar I like—unless you want the St. Regis or Oak Room or something special."

She leaned back against the seat. "No, any quiet place will do."

As she entered the Lancer Bar, Judith glanced around curiously. So this was where he went. It was dimly lit; she was grateful for that. He led her to a back booth and ordered her a Scotch. She waited until he had taken a long swallow of his martini, then she said, "What do you think will happen, Robin?"

"I think he's going to be all right."

"You're not just saying that?"

"No. People who think they're going to die rarely do. He's too frightened to die."

"I don't understand."

"During the war, after I got hit, I was in the hospital. It was a long ward with rows and rows of beds. There was a guy to the right of me who was loaded with shrapnel. He had to go through five operations. Each time he went up, he was sure it was his last day on earth. But the guy on the other side of me read the papers. He smiled a lot and all the while he was quietly hemorrhaging to death. I'm of the opinion that when death is in you, it fills you with a curious calm. After all, everything builds up its own resistance and immunity. Death probably carries its own emotional anesthesia."

"You make me feel much better," she said.

"It's not going to be easy either way," he said quietly. "The real trouble will begin after the operation."

"You mean lack of sex." She shrugged. "Robin, there's never been any wild kind of thing between us, even in the beginning. IBC has always been Greg's consuming passion. It hasn't been easy for me for years."

"I wasn't thinking of you," he said cryptically. "I was thinking of Gregory—he won't believe it's not malignant."

"And what about me?" she demanded. "Gregory doesn't know how to accept any setbacks. Illness is foreign to him. What do you think the last few months have been like for me? I've lived with a whimpering invalid. He wouldn't play golf, he kept taking his own pulse . . ."

"Isn't marriage supposed to be for better or worse?"

"Is that what you believe?" she asked.

"If I was married, that's what I'd believe."

"Maybe you *would*," she said slowly. "Only I haven't had much of a marriage."

"This is one hell of a time for you to find out."

"Don't look at me as if you hated me, Robin. I've given my share to this marriage."

"This marriage? Is that how a woman thinks of it? Not *our* marriage?"

"Now you're beginning to sound like a sentimentalist."

He ordered another round of drinks. "That's the last thing I am. But I thought women were."

"I was, once. When I married Greg I thought it would be wonderful. But he didn't want any of the things that go to *make* a marriage. He didn't particularly want children, he wanted a *wife*. To run his homes—Gregory always liked possessions—the town house, the house in Palm Beach, the house in Quogue. . . . It's been a full-time job."

"Well, running a network isn't exactly a hobby."

"I know that. I've respected his work, and I've accepted all his friends, made them my friends. But a woman needs more than a social life and playing the role of the perfect hostess. I've missed so much. When I look back it seems like a pretty empty life."

"Well, this is no time to dig up the past. Right now your main concern is to get this man well. He'll need you. So stop crying in your beer about being just a possession. From now on you'll be Florence Nightingale, Sigmund Freud and the best friend he ever had. I liked your speech at the bed—about being a gambler. Your instincts are right, Judith. You've got to know when to be tough and when to give in with a patient. An emotional crackup is harder to cure than physical illness. You've got to make sure he doesn't crack—because if he does, then you'll *really* know what trouble is. I've seen guys go that route. They're still lolling around in bathrobes, doing jigsaw puzzles at veterans' hospitals."

"But why? I mean with Gregory. Men with less strength sail through a gall-bladder operation. And even a prostate operation. He hasn't been himself since he first went to the hospital."

Robin lit a cigarette. "Sometimes illness hits a strong guy harder than the little guy. As you said, illness is foreign to Gregory. He doesn't know how to handle it. He's always been prepared for any emergency in business. It never occurred to him that his body was vulnerable. It's shot the pins from under him. And to a man like Gregory illness robs him of his dignity."

She looked at him pleadingly. "Robin—*help* me."

"I will."

She reached out and clutched at his hands. "Robin, I'll try. But I can't do it alone. I've been in an ivory tower for so long. I have no close friends. Women I lunch with—well, they tell me *their* troubles. I've never confided my problems to any of them. I felt above all that. Suddenly I have no one to turn to, and I don't want anyone to know about Gregory's operation. It sounds so castrating. Robin —can I feel free to call you, to cry on your shoulder?"

He smiled. "I have big shoulders, Judith."

She sat back and sipped her drink. Her eyes looked past him. "Greg's worried about the network too. Dan's been giving out too many interviews. Gregory gets ulcers every time he reads them. It's *his* network and he hates anyone else to take bows."

"Sometimes it's hard to avoid the press," he answered.

"I duck them, so they go after Dan. After my one mass interview, I cut out."

She smiled. "It must kill Dan. You've outwitted him without realizing it. In refusing to give interviews, you've made yourself an enigma—they write and speculate about you all the time. I rather like the title they've given you: the Love Machine."

He frowned. "They'll get tired of it. Publicity is the last thing I'm after."

"Greg knows that, and he doesn't resent your publicity. It's natural for you to get it. Dan's been in this business all his life, but even though you've been seen on TV, you're still a mystery man to Madison Avenue. You intrigue them, they want to dig, to find out what makes you tick."

"I think you're overrating their interest." He swallowed his drink. "Want another?"

"No. I have to be up at dawn tomorrow. Will you be there?"

He shook his head. "Someone has to mind the store. But please call me as soon as you know the results."

"I will. Do you have a private line at IBC?"

He took out his notebook and scribbled it down.

"Put down your home number, too," she added.

"IBC can always get to me. I have a direct line at home."

"Robin—remember what you said about your shoulders? If I find myself alone in the small hours, if it all closes in on me, I may need to talk to someone . . ."

He wrote down his unlisted home number. "Anytime." He handed her the slip of paper.

She sat in bed and wrote both his numbers in her phone book. She listed them under L. No name, just the numbers. "L" meant Love. That was how she always listed the man she cared about. She stretched out in bed. The night cream was heavy on her face and she wore a net to keep the oil from ruining her hair. She felt elated. Gregory did not have cancer. And once the operation was over, perhaps he'd snap back to his old self. And meanwhile during his recuperation she'd see Robin every day.

Gregory was on the table six hours. During this period, Judith called Robin twice for reassurance. He sounded concerned and told her he had two meetings, but would come if she needed him. It was finally agreed that he would drop by at the end of the day. He kept assuring her that everything would be all right.

Dr. Lesgarn appeared at three in the afternoon. Gregory was in the postoperative room. The news was excellent. There was no malignancy.

Gregory was wheeled down at five. He was conscious, but the tube in his nose and the needle in his arm made him seem like a vegetable. An hour later Dr. Lesgarn came in and told him the results. Gregory turned away from him with a sneer.

Judith ran to the bed and took his hand. "We're telling you the truth, Greg. I swear."

He pushed her away. "Lies! It all sounds so pat! You're a lousy actress, Judith!" She ran out of the room and leaned against the wall of the hospital corridor, trembling. Dr. Lesgarn came out and shook his head. "I gave him a shot, but it's going to be rough to rid him of this cancer obsession."

They both looked up as Robin came striding down the hall. His confident smile and healthy good looks only served to make Gregory seem like a shell of a man.

"I talked to the doctor an hour ago," he said, nodding at Dr. Lesgarn. "He gave me the good news."

"Gregory doesn't believe us," she said.

Robin looked properly sympathetic. "Cliff released a story to the newspapers. We said it was the same ailment —gall bladder. I think that will cover things."

"You've had a long day, Mrs. Austin," Dr. Lesgarn said. "I think you should go home."

Her smile was gaunt. "Right now, I just want to sit down and have a drink and some food. I haven't eaten all day."

Robin took her to the Lancer Bar. This time she dismissed the chauffeur. At least Robin would take her home without feeling self-conscious. She looked around the room as they sat in the same booth. Did he always come to this place?

Obviously he had read her expression because he said, "I would have taken you elsewhere, but unfortunately I had made a previous appointment to meet someone here. But the steaks are good and the drinks are even better."

She sipped her drink cautiously. On an empty stomach she would feel it, and she wanted complete control, tonight of all nights.

"Will I be intruding on your appointment?"

"Not at all." He suddenly stood up. Judith stared as a tall young girl headed toward the booth.

"Robin, I am late. Sorry."

"It's all right." He motioned the girl to slide in beside him. Then he said, "Mrs. Austin, this is Ingrid. She works for TWA, and we've flown together many times."

The girl turned to Robin with a warmly intimate smile. "We had to circle Kennedy for half an hour tonight, air traffic was so heavy. That's why I'm late."

Robin signaled for a drink for Ingrid. Judith noticed the waiter automatically brought her a vodka-and-tonic. That meant she had been here before with Robin. She had a slight accent—Swedish, or one of the other Scandinavian languages. She was tall and almost too thin, with long heavy straight blond hair and bangs hanging below her eyebrows. Her eyes were heavily made up but she wore no lipstick. And when her slim hand slipped possessively into Robin's, Judith wanted to reach out and stab her. Oh God, the vibrancy of youth! Ingrid in her white silk blouse and plain skirt suddenly made her feel squat and bulky in the Chanel suit. The girl could not be more than twenty-two—she was old enough to be her mother! The girl was also too young for Robin, yet she was staring at him with open adoration. Oh God, it *was* a man's world. Age didn't count with a man. Ten years from now, Robin would still have a twenty-two-year-old stewardess staring at him like this. She opened her purse and took out a gold cigarette case. Robin immediately reached over with a light—at least he still remembered she was at the table. Well, she wasn't going to give up without a fight. Not to this snip of a girl—a girl who would serve her on a plane: a *waitress!*

Judith watched Robin carefully. How could he allow

an airline stewardess to share even a part of his life? How many simple girls like this had he given his body to, while she had to sit there longing for him—planning, scheming?

Robin ordered another round of drinks. Judith wished she could eat something—she felt the first Scotch already. Robin held up his glass and toasted Gregory's health. Then he had to explain to Ingrid who Gregory Austin was.

"I am sorry." Ingrid was sincere, as she turned to Judith. "I wish him a very fast recovery. Was it serious?"

"Just a checkup, baby," Robin said. "He flew in from Florida because he likes New York doctors."

"Do you fly with us?" Ingrid asked.

"We have our own plane," Judith answered.

"Oh, how very nice." Ingrid did not seem overly impressed.

"Judith, you must get Gregory to take an interest in the network, even while he's at the hospital having his checkup." Robin's gaze was serious as he emphasized the word checkup. "I want you to force him into taking an interest. Do you understand?"

She nodded. Ingrid stared at both of them. "Well, I don't," she said. "Poor Mr. Adlen, he—"

"Austin," Robin said.

"All right, Mr. Austin. Well, my father had to go through a checkup once, and he said it was awful. Swallowing chalk, taking X-rays. Let him relax and forget business, I say."

Robin smiled. "Baby, do you tell the pilot what to do when the weather gets rough?"

"Of course not. Tower control and the navigator do that."

"Well, I'm tower control and Judith is navigator."

"I *still* think the poor man should be left to have his checkup in peace," she said.

Judith had to admire her. She wasn't cowed by Robin's dismissal. But then, she had been to bed with Robin and knew her power. And why? Just because she was young. Oh God, when she was young she had taken her youth for granted too.

"I'm hungry," Ingrid said suddenly.

Robin beckoned the waiter. "Get the lady a steak. And bring me a double vodka." Then he turned to Judith. "What would you like? I'd advise the steak and the tossed salad."

"What are you having?"

He pointed to his glass.

"I'll have another Scotch," she said quietly.

"No steak?"

"No steak."

A slow smile crept to his eyes. "Well, well. Judith, I like your style. It takes more than a few knockdowns to make you lose a fight—you're back there slugging at the sound of the bell. I guess that's why you're a winner."

"Am I?" she asked challengingly.

"You sure as hell are!" He raised his glass in salute. Ingrid looked on in bewilderment. Suddenly she stood up. "I think perhaps you should cancel my steak. Suddenly it seems I am not needed here."

Robin stared at his glass. "Suit yourself, baby."

She grabbed her coat and went to the door. Judith tried to look concerned. "Robin, perhaps I should go? You and this girl—"

He reached across the table and took her hand. "Don't play games, Judith. It's not your style. This is the way you wanted it, isn't it?"

From the corner of her eye, she saw Ingrid hesitate at the door, hoping Robin would come after her. Judith waited until she left. Then she said, "I don't want to hurt anyone."

"Ingrid won't bleed—at least not for long," he said. He canceled the steak and asked for a check. They finished their drinks in silence, then walked out of the restaurant. "I live down the street," he said.

She slipped her arm through his as they walked. This wasn't the way she had planned it, not so cut-and-dried. There wasn't any romance this way. She had to make him understand that he meant something to her. "Robin—I've cared about you for a long time."

He didn't answer, but he took her arm from his and

held her hand. "You're a winner, Judith. Don't try to qualify things."

When they entered his apartment, she suddenly felt insecure, like a girl beginning her first affair. And suddenly she felt the perspiration between her breasts, on her brow—those God-damned flashes! Little reminders that she wasn't a carefree young airline stewardess!

Robin made her a light Scotch and poured a large shot of vodka for himself. He drank it standing in the middle of the living room. She sat on the oversized couch and longed for him to join her. There was a fireplace and some fresh wood. If only he would light it, and they could sit in the darkness in the glow of the fire and play some of the records she saw stacked near the hi-fi. She wanted him to hold her in his arms. . . .

He suddenly walked over to her, took the drink from her hand and led her into the bedroom. She felt panic. Would she have to undress in front of him? Ingrid probably let him undress her . . . reveling in her nakedness and firm young body. She was wearing a panty girdle. Nothing was less sexy—despite her slimness, it pushed up her loose flesh into unflattering ripples.

He pointed to the bathroom as he loosened his tie. "No dressing room, but take that."

She stumbled into the bathroom and undressed slowly. She saw a maroon silk robe hanging on the door. She put it on and tied the sash. When she opened the door, Robin was standing looking out the window. He was stripped to his shorts. The room was in darkness, but the light of the bathroom reflected on his broad shoulders. There wasn't an ounce of extra flesh on him. She hadn't realized how well he was built. She came up behind him. He turned when he saw her and took her hand. Almost gently he led her to the bed. He looked at her and smiled. "Well, they say an experienced woman is the greatest. Prove it, dear lady—get down there and make love to me."

She was stunned, but wanted him so much that she complied. After a few moments he tossed her on her back and ground into her. It was over in less than a minute. Then he lay back and reached for a cigarette.

"Sorry I didn't put on more of a show," he said with an

apologetic smile. "But I'm never very good when I've been drinking."

"I loved it, Robin."

"You did?" He looked at her with amazement. "Why?"

"Because I was with you. That's what makes the difference."

He yawned. "If I wake up during the night, I'll try and please you more." Then he kissed her lightly and turned away from her. After a few minutes his even breathing told her he was actually asleep. She stared at him. So this was the Love Machine. Now what? He expected her to go to sleep. Ingrid would. His other girls probably did. Well, why not? Gregory was in the hospital. She had no one to report to. But suppose she got the sweats in the middle of the night, or snored? Gregory had made her sleep in the same room with him in Palm Beach, and he said she snored. He teased her about it but seemed secretly pleased—another reminder of old age.

She lay there and stared at the ceiling. Age changed everything. One couldn't spend a night locked in a man's arms because of night sweats and snoring. And if she fell asleep at a bad angle her breasts would hang. Suddenly she looked down at the maroon robe she still wore. He hadn't even bothered to take it off. He hadn't even seen her body or touched her—just entered her and pleased himself.

She slipped out of bed and went to the bathroom and dressed quietly. When she came back into the bedroom, Robin was sitting up. He seemed to have sobered completely.

"Judith, did I conk out that fast? What time is it?"

"Midnight." Back in the Chanel suit she felt poised and assured.

"Why are you all dressed?"

"I feel I should be home, in case the hospital calls."

He jumped out of bed and threw on his shorts. "Of course. I'll get dressed and take you home. It won't take a second."

"No, Robin." She went to him and put her arms around him. It was only midnight; if he was up and dressed he might still call Ingrid. Besides, he'd hate her if he had to dress and go out. "Robin, I can catch a cab. Please, go back to bed. You have a hard day ahead."

He put his arm around her waist and walked her to the door.

"Will I see you tomorrow?" she asked.

"No, I'm going to Philadelphia for a few days. I want to tape Diana Williams doing her show."

"When will you be back?"

"Two or three days—all depends."

She put her arms around him. "Robin, you've never kissed me."

He kissed the top of her head obediently.

"I mean *really* kiss me."

He smiled. "Not in a drafty doorway." He stared at her curiously, then he said, "Come here." He took her in his arms and kissed her deeply. "There," he said, as he released her. "I can't let you go home unfulfilled, not with the risk you took."

After he closed the door, she walked to the elevator wondering why she felt so let down. She had been with Robin, and she would be with him again. Only next time she wouldn't let him drink so much.

But in the two weeks that followed, the rapid deterioration of Gregory's morale precluded any thought of next time. He was recovering physically, but his emotional state frightened her. Robin dropped by but Gregory refused to talk about plans for IBC. He sat huddled in his bathrobe, staring vacantly out of the window.

When he was discharged from the hospital, he took to his bed at home and lay staring at the ceiling. He refused to believe the laboratory reports. He claimed he felt pains in his neck, in his hips. "It's all through me, I know it," he moaned.

And one morning he awoke and found himself completely paralyzed from the waist down. He couldn't move his legs or sit up. Dr. Lesgarn was summoned immediately. He stuck a pin in Gregory's leg, and when there was no reaction, he sent for an ambulance. Gregory was put through extensive tests. It was not a stroke, as Judith had feared: every test proved negative. A neurologist was called in.

Dr. Chase, a leading psychiatrist, talked to Gregory. Another internist was summoned. Their opinion was unanimous. There was no physical cause for Gregory's paralysis.

They met with Judith and explained their findings. She was terrified. She sat staring at them, mutely pleading for an explanation.

"I suggest hospitalization," the psychiatrist said.

"You mean he stays here?" Judith asked.

The psychiatrist shook his head. "No, I'm speaking of a psychiatric hospital. The New York branch of Payne Whitney or the Hartford Institute—"

Judith covered her face. "No, no, not Greg—he couldn't sit around with a bunch of idiots!"

The psychiatrist stiffened. "Mrs. Austin, most of the patients are men of high intelligence and sensitivity. An insensitive person rarely suffers a breakdown."

"I don't care. Gregory wouldn't want to live if word got out that he was there. It would ruin his life. And the IBC stockholders would panic—no, we can't risk that."

Dr. Lesgarn looked thoughtful. He turned to Dr. Chase. "What about that place in Switzerland? Gregory could go there under an assumed name. They also have bungalows where the wives can live with their husbands while the husband undergoes treatment. Gregory would receive excellent psychiatric care, and no one would know. Judith could release word to the newspapers that they were going on an extended trip to Europe."

He looked at her and managed a smile. "And you could even run over to Paris and London and send cards to your friends to keep up the pretense."

"This is ridiculous," Dr. Chase snorted. "There is nothing disgraceful about a man needing psychiatric care. There are wonderful places here in the States. And I see no need for this ridiculous secrecy."

Dr. Lesgarn shook his head. "I understand Mrs. Austin's point. The publicity would not be good for the network. IBC is known as a one-man operation; if that man doesn't function, the stockholders might panic. Switzerland is the best bet." He turned to Judith. "But it might mean six months to a year or even longer."

"I'll chance it," she said firmly. She told Dr. Lesgarn to make immediate arrangements. Then she went home and made two calls. One to Cliff Dorne, the other to Robin Stone. She asked both men to come to see her immediately.

They arrived at six o'clock. Judith didn't offer them a drink. She received them in Gregory's den and told them the entire story. Then she said, "If one word of this gets out, I shall deny it, and as his wife, I will dismiss you both. Since he is unable to make any decisions, I have his power of attorney."

"No one is arguing that," Cliff said quietly. "I think your decision is right. The stock would drop ten points in one day if word got out. And in a very minor way, I am also a stockholder."

"Then we're in full accord." When both men nodded, she went on. "I want Robin Stone to be given full command. Cliff, I want Dan informed of this tomorrow. He is to be told that Gregory will be vacationing for an indefinite time, and that he is to report to Robin. Robin's decisions will be final."

She refused to meet the expression of disbelief in Cliff's eyes. She stood up as a signal that the meeting had ended.

"Robin, if you can stay, I'd like to talk to you," she said.

Cliff hesitated at the door. "I'll wait outside, then. There are certain things I want to discuss with you, Mrs. Austin."

"Can't they wait until tomorrow? I'm very tired."

"I'm afraid they can't. You're leaving tomorrow at midnight, and there are some urgent matters that need your attention now."

Robin walked to the door. "I'll talk to you tomorrow, Mrs. Austin. How about lunch?"

"Yes. Will you come here? I'll be terribly busy packing."

"One o'clock all right?" When she nodded, he left the room.

The moment the door closed, she turned on Cliff. She didn't try to hide her antagonism. "What's so urgent?"

"Does Gregory know about this move?"

"Gregory scarcely knows his own name! Can't you understand? He's lying there paralyzed. He's a vegetable!"

"Mrs. Austin, do you realize what you are doing?"

"I'm doing what Gregory would do."

"I don't agree. He put Robin in to control Danton's power. Now you are not only giving all the power to one man, but you are making him autonomous."

"If I divided the power, the network would crumble. Danton is jealous of Robin—he would fight any ideas Robin might have, then nothing would be decided. There has to be one head."

"Then why not Danton?"

"Because Gregory doesn't trust him."

"What makes you think he can trust Robin?"

"I had a D & B on him. Robin is a millionaire in his own right. That means he can't be gotten to."

Cliff shook his head. "Power is an acquired taste. Once you get it, you find you like it. Also, I happen to think Dan is better qualified for the job."

"Dan's a lush."

"But not on the job. He's brought some good shows to IBC. He also knows how to run a network. And how do you think Dan will take the idea of Robin being put over him?"

She shrugged. "That's his problem."

"His position will be intolerable," Cliff said. "He'll have to quit to save face."

"Will it be easier for him to face the loss of a job?" she asked.

"When someone makes an emotional decision, they rarely take time to logicize. Anger often breeds false courage."

"Well, that's his problem," she said with finality.

Cliff Dorne made the announcement at a full-scale meeting the following morning at nine. At nine thirty Danton Miller handed in his resignation. Cliff tried to talk him out of it: "Stick it out, Dan. This will blow over. Gregory will return. I thought you were the one man who was born with a built-in survival kit."

Dan managed a faint imitation of his normal smile.

"Sometimes to survive, one must retreat. Don't worry about me, Cliff. Meanwhile, who are you planning to put in my place?"

Cliff shrugged. "George Anderson is the logical choice, but Robin has already sent for Sammy Tebet."

"*Fight* him on it!" Dan stated. "Sammy is a good man, but he's cut from the same cloth as Robin. Harvard, a society background—he'll go along with all of Robin's thinking."

Cliff smiled. "I have to survive too. And my idea of survival is being on the scene, keeping an eye on the store. At the moment I can't fight Robin. I can only watch him."

Robin was aware of Cliff Dorne's hostility. But he wasn't out to win any popularity contests. He worked well with Sammy Tebet, and after a few weeks most of the personnel at IBC had forgotten there had ever been a man named Danton Miller. Vice-presidents put their black suits and black ties in storage and began to emulate Robin's Oxford gray.

Robin worked hard. He watched television every night, and made only rare appearances at the Lancer Bar. Gradually he lost all contact with the world. Nothing existed but IBC and the competitive shows. He read every program idea and had a dozen new pilots lined up to view on the Coast.

He was just leaving for the airport when Dip called. He had forgotten about Dip in the frenetic activity of the past few weeks.

"How's my buddy, the big executive?" Dip's cheerful voice blasted through the wire. "I was going to call and congratulate you, but I've been so busy helping Pauli."

Robin smiled. "Seems the last time we spoke you were on your way to kill her."

"You know me, pal—I burn fast, then cool off. Besides, she can't get along without me. I cue her, work with her. It's a cinch that the way Diana Williams is hitting the sauce, Pauli will get a chance to play the part after it opens on Broadway. How's about coming to Philly with me tonight and catching the show?"

"I'm on my way to the Coast, Dip. I have to look at some pilots for next February's dropouts."

"Okay, and while you're out there, drop the word around that I'm up for something big."

"Are you?"

"Nah, but say it anyhow. They believe anything out there."

The flight to the Coast was tedious. He found himself thinking about Judith Austin. Their last lunch together had been all business, until the very end. Then she had looked into his eyes and said, "*Ciao*—for now." His first inclination had been to ignore the intimate urgency in her eyes, but she had seemed so helpless and vulnerable in that large house. For some crazy reason she had made him think of Kitty, and he had pressed her hand, forced an easy smile and said, "Yes, *ciao* for now."

Well, Gregory would be away for a long time, and Judith would probably find plenty of European companions. He pushed her from his mind and tried to watch the movie. And when it ended, he studied the presentations for the pilots he was going to view. He was eager for the goddam plane to land, eager to stretch his legs, but most of all, he was eager to see Maggie Stewart.

He called her when he checked into the Beverly Hills Hotel. She was surprised to hear his voice and agreed to meet him at six o'clock at the Polo Lounge.

When she walked into the bar he realized he had forgotten how beautiful she was. She smiled as she slid into the booth. "I thought you'd never talk to me again, after that fire."

He reached out and squeezed her hand. "Are you kidding? I thought it was very funny."

"How is Diana's show doing?" she asked.

"I wouldn't know. I haven't seen the lady except on business—it seems someone turned our budding romance into ashes. How is your new picture, by the way?"

She grimaced. "I saw a rough cut of it last week." She drained her Scotch and ordered another.

He looked at her curiously. "Is it really that bad?"

"Worse. If I didn't have a contract for three more pictures, I'd be out of the business. It won't even get a first-run release—they'll open it at the showcase theaters."

"Anyone can do one bad picture."

She nodded. "I have a chance to bail out with the next. Adam Bergman is directing it."

"He's excellent."

"He sure is. He even makes me look like an actress."

"What's the hitch?"

"He won't give me the picture unless I marry him."

He was silent.

"I'm going to refuse. Oh, don't look guilty. I refused him before last Christmas." Then her eyes blazed as she turned to him. "Yes, maybe you *should* feel guilty. You son of a bitch! You've ruined it for me with any man."

His grin was easy. "Come on, now, I'm not that wonderful."

"You're *damn* right you're not. It's me—just like you said, I'm a nut. Anyway I've been going to a shrink and I've just learned that I like myself."

"A shrink? But what's liking yourself got to do with marrying Adam?"

"I refuse to slip into a Hollywood-type marriage, at least the kind Adam wants. When I lived with him on the beach, I found myself doing things I never believed I'd do. Funny, isn't it? When I'm on the couch, I say, 'Where did everyone go? Where is the Maggie who lived in Philadelphia and loved and hoped? This girl doing the crazy things, she isn't me—' "

"What sent you to the couch?"

"The fire. When I realized that people could have been killed, it terrified me."

"Well, I've got a brand-new bed," he said. "With an asbestos bedspread." He took her to Dominick's for dinner, then they went back to the Melton Towers. He spent three days viewing tapes, and three nights making love to Maggie. The day he was to leave, they met at the Polo Lounge for a drink. She handed him a little box. "Open it," she said. "It's a present."

He stared at the little gold ring in the velvet box. "What is it? It looks like a tiny gold tennis racket."

She threw back her head and laughed. "It's an ankh."

"A what?"

"It's an Egyptian tau symbol—Cleopatra carried one. It means enduring life and generation. And that's you! *You* endure—no girl can forget you, and I think you'll go on and on. It's a sex symbol to me, eternal sex." She slid it onto his little finger. "Slim and bright and beautiful, isn't it? Just like you, Mr. Stone. And I want you to wear it. In a way I'm branding you. Of course you'll toss it away as soon as you leave me—but I'm going to pretend you're wearing it, and every girl will look at it and ask what it means. Maybe you'll have guts enough to tell them."

"I never wear jewelry," he said slowly. "Half the time I don't even wear a watch. But I'll wear it, I really will."

"You know something?" she said slowly. "I've heard of love-hate relationships, but I never knew what they meant till I knew you."

"You don't hate me. And you don't love me."

"I do love you," she said quietly. "And I hate you for making me love you."

"How long have you got until you start the next picture?"

"Ten days."

"Come back to New York with me."

For a flash her eyes brightened. "You mean that? You *really* want me to come?"

"Sure. I have my own private jet, courtesy of IBC. There's even a bed on the plane—we can hump our way across the country."

She was silent.

"Come on, Maggie. We'll catch all the shows, even go out to the Hamptons if the weather is mild enough. Can you get away?"

"Robin, I'd dump my whole career if I thought you *needed* me. I'm not even talking about marriage. I'm talking about needing. God, I'd follow you anywhere."

He looked at her oddly. "Who said anything about needing? I asked you to come to New York. I thought a change of scene might do you good."

"Oh, a little pleasure junket?"

"That's what life is about, baby."

She stood up with such force that the drink spilled on

the table. "I think I've just about had it with you. Oh I
don't say I won't take your call when you come back. I'll
probably even fall into bed with you. Because I'm sick.
But my shrink will straighten me out, and one day you'll
need *me*—only I won't be there!"

His eyes went cold. "I think you've got it all wrong,
baby. *I* don't need anyone. But maybe you need Adam
Bergman. It's a cinch you need him to help you make a
decent picture."

She leaned over and looked into his eyes. "To use a
phrase from my newly developed show-business vocabulary, Mr. Stone, I *dig* you—oh Jesus, how I dig you—but
you're the prize shit of them all!"

Then she walked away. He finished his drink slowly
and went to the airport. He was about to toss the ring in
a refuse basket, but it was tight and wouldn't come off.
He smiled. Maybe she really had branded him after all.

When he returned to New York he learned that Diana
Williams had withdrawn from the show, Pauli had gone
on in Philadelphia and received such an ovation that Ike
Ryan was chancing coming into Broadway with her.

Dip commuted to Philadelphia and besieged Robin
with daily bulletins. In an effort to salvage the Diana
Williams Happening, Robin took a crew to Philadelphia
and taped Pauli. When he viewed the tape he was
amazed to find it had tremendous impact. The first half
was Diana at rehearsal, Diana talking about her come-
back, then the newspaper headlines about her "illness."
The second half showed Pauli going on, the interview
with Pauli as she took over the star dressing room. It
sounded like a soap opera, but he knew it would draw
ratings.

The show opened in New York and Pauli's reviews
were fantastic. Yet oddly enough she received no film
offers. Dip was outraged, and refused to accept her
agent's explanation that Pauli was a stage personality,
and would become a Broadway superstar. He was
crushed when he learned that Hollywood had signed a
movie name to play her role in the picture.

Robin ran the Happening in May. It came across exactly as he had predicted, and outrated everything in its time period.

It was a good summer for him. The replacements were going well. He dated some of the girls in Pauli's show. He even tried to be nice to Pauli, but her back always went up when he was around. He ignored her antagonistic attitude and sat in Sardi's with whatever girl Dip brought along. He was getting to like Sardi's but as the legend of his power grew, he stopped going there and holed up more than ever at the Lancer Bar. In order to avoid contact with agents, agency men or stars, he also stayed away from "21" and the Colony. He had quickly learned the value of a decisive "No," accompanied by a firm smile, when he rejected a show. He had made a pledge that he would never allow himself to get angry or lose his cool. He never said, "I'll think it over." It was always a clear-cut "Yes" or "No." Soon word went around that he was a cold-blooded son of a bitch whose nod could make or break a man. The rare times he did go to "21" he was amazed at the aura of fear his presence caused.

However he found that a curious phenomenon accompanied his new fame. For the first time in his life girls were hard to come by. Starlets were out—he couldn't afford to be "held up" for a job. He stuck to airline stewardesses, but he didn't keep them long. They'd arrive in their best dresses, expecting to go to El Morocco or Voisin, but soon learned that his social life was confined to the Lancer Bar, a movie, or his apartment.

If it hadn't been for Dip he would have had no sex life at all—Dip kept a steady stream of young girls on tap. However Robin's work took up most of his time, and as long as he wound up with a girl two or three times a week, he wasn't concerned. And he wore the ankh ring. When a girl questioned him about it, he'd say, "It means I'm in love with *all* women: it's the symbol of eternal life, of eternal sex."

He received cards from Judith twice a week. Cliff Dorne meticulously saw to it that items appeared in various columns mentioning successive laps of the Austins' world tour.

The day before Labor Day, Dip Nelson tore into his

office and said he was positive that Pauli was having an affair with her leading man, Lon Rogers. At the same moment, Cliff Dorne called and announced that Ethel and Christie Lane had welcomed the birth of a nine-pound baby boy.

He told Dip it was all just "Broadway talk," and he called Tiffany's and sent Christie's baby a silver orange-juice cup. That night he walked down Broadway alone and went to a dreadful movie starring Maggie Stewart.

# TWENTY-NINE

ROBIN sat in his apartment waiting for *The Christie Lane Show* to start its new season. For the past few days the newspapers had hinted that the public was in for a big surprise on the opening. Robin's guess was that Christie was probably going to introduce his newborn baby to his public.

Without speaking, he handed his empty glass to Dip Nelson for a refill. "Make it a light Scotch, Dip." His eyes narrowed as Dip obediently went to the bar. He knew there was growing speculation about their friendship. Robin had smiled and offered no explanation when Jerry Moss told him the word around was that Dip procured for him. Actually he let Dip hang around because he felt sorry for him. He sensed that despite Dip's exhilaration about Pauli's success, he couldn't really enjoy his new role as "husband of the star." Yet Dip never complained.

Robin had booked Dip on two guest shots on an IBC variety show. Each appearance had drawn murderous reviews. One columnist even began carping about Dip's pull with a certain Mr. Big at IBC. Robin didn't give a damn about columns or rumors. If Dip had any talent, Robin would have seen to it that he worked on every IBC show. But Dip was God-awful on television: a handsome face was not enough. There were guys doing shaving commercials who were better-looking.

"Why Scotch tonight, buddy boy?" Dip asked, as he handed him the drink.

"Opening of a new season. I like to be sober when I view a show. We'll go to the Lancer Bar later and really tie one on."

"I wish you'd go to Danny's Hideaway with me, it would do me a lot of good."

"Why?" Robin asked as he tried to get the green out of the color set.

"Well, J. P. Morgan once said to a guy, 'If I walk through the stock exchange with my arm around you, that's the best collateral you can have.'"

Robin smiled. "Okay, we'll go there after the show."

Dip's eagerness was childlike as he dashed to the phone. Robin smiled as he heard him make detailed arrangements to get the proper table. Then he turned up the sound on the television set as *The Christie Lane Show* came on the air.

Robin couldn't believe what he was seeing. At first he thought it would turn into a gag—that any second Christie's white tie and tails would turn into a breakaway outfit and the slapstick comedy would begin. But when they stopped for the first commercial he realized the show was in earnest. They were actually trying to do a frothy drawing-room musical. It was so bad it was almost high camp; but unfortunately the girl playing opposite Christie was good enough to make it semiserious.

Dip went into the kitchen and got a beer. He watched the show casually, and wondered why Robin was suddenly so intent on it. He went into the den and turned on a Western on the small set. Robin would understand: it bugged him to have to watch a television show that consistently turned him down.

When it was over he returned to the living room. Robin appeared not even to have noticed his absence. He was standing in the middle of the room staring into space.

"How was it, buddy boy?" Dip asked cheerfully.

"It was terrible."

"Well, maybe it'll be better next week." Dip was eager to leave for Danny's.

"It was unbelievable." Robin seemed dazed. "NBC has a great comedy opposite it, CBS has a good action thriller. We *had* to lose half the audience during the second half —I know we'll come up lowest in the time period."

"Well, let's go to Danny's. We can't erase it, it happened—that's the way the cookie crumbles."

"My cookie doesn't crumble," Robin said coldly. He picked up his direct line to IBC. "This is Robin Stone. Get me Artie Rylander on the Coast. You have his home number. It's in Brentwood." He lit a cigarette and waited. "I don't give a damn who the hell is on the tie line. Cut in and tell them to get off."

When he reached Artie, his teeth were clamped in cold anger. "All right, Rylander—*explain*. How the hell did you let him do it? Couldn't you see it was going to bomb? . . . Well, then, why didn't you call me? . . . I don't give a damn about Noel Victor! He may be the best lyricist in the business for Tony Newley or Robert Goulet, but not for Christie Lane. . . . What do you mean, Chris threw out your writers? I know all about Chris owning the package now—but he owns it *with* IBC. And we're more than equal partners—we also own the air time. . . . What ballads? Listen, Artie, there is no such thing as good *new* music, there's only good *familiar* music—the public likes to hear something it knows. . . . Don't give me that crap about a Broadway show. Sure, a Broadway show comes up with a new score, and on opening night critics write about it, and the public digs it, *after* it's played on albums and on jukeboxes. We don't have time for that with a once-a-week shot on TV. And Chris Lane is not Rex Harrison! He's the All-American slob. In tails he looked like a fat blond penguin. You tell him to revamp the show and go right back to the old format. Hire back the plain-Jane girl singer who played in the sketches and the cornball announcer. And what genius dreamed up the line of ballet girls? Don't you know ballet is lost on a twenty-inch screen? And I'm afraid to look at the below-the-line costs. . . . I don't give a damn about Noel Victor's contract, hire back the old writers. . . .

What do you mean, he *won't?* We can force him to . . . .
No, I haven't looked at the contract, but I *will* tonight!
And I'll be in touch with you first thing tomorrow." He
slammed down the receiver.

"Robin—" It was Dip. "We'll lose the table at Danny's
if we don't hurry."

Robin crossed the room and put on his jacket. "Dinner
is the last thing on my mind." He went to the phone
again. "Get me Cliff Dorne at home. It's in Rye." He
snapped his fingers for Dip to bring his cigarettes. "Cliff?
It's Robin Stone."

"Yes, Robin, hold it, will you? I'll take it in another
room."

Robin lit a cigarette and waited. Cliff came back on the
line. "Sorry, Robin, we're having a small family party."

"What did you think of the Chris Lane show?"

There was silence.

"You thought it was that bad, too," Robin said.

"Well, to be honest, I didn't see it. You see—"

"What do you mean, you didn't *see* it?"

"Robin, it's my mother-in-law's seventieth birthday. We
have the family here. We're at the table."

"The show stinks," Robin said curtly.

"I'll look at the tape first thing tomorrow."

"Meet me at your office, right away."

"What?"

"Right away! You have the keys to the contract files,
haven't you?"

"Robin—can't it keep until tomorrow? My wife's
mother is here."

"I couldn't care if Whistler's mother was there—get
into town as fast as you can."

"Robin, if it was *my* mother, I'd do it. But my wife will
never believe this was necessary. I'm not too crazy about
her mother as it is. For thirty years we've had an armed
truce. If I walk out now—"

"You support her?"

"No, she's a garage mechanic. Of *course* I support her!
I even bought her a mink stole for the occasion. Kind of
silly to put such an investment into a lady of seventy, but
if I know my mother-in-law she'll outlive the mink."

"Then stop shooting the breeze up my ass about senti-ment. Get down to the office!"

"Robin, I'm afraid it will have to keep until tomorrow."

"If it does, there will be a new boy in your place."

There was a slight pause. Cliff's voice was cold when he answered. "I'll be there. But, Robin, I think you'd better also read over *my* contract. I don't work *for* you or *under* you. I'm head of the legal department at IBC. I am not a boy who can be replaced."

"If you're in the office within half an hour, your moth-er-in-law might be eligible for another stole next year. If not, you'd better take it back in the morning. *I'm* running IBC now, and there is no one who can't be replaced. We have a top show that's about to go down the drain if we don't do something fast. I want to find out if we can. And not tomorrow—right now."

"All right, Robin."

"And, Cliff, if you don't feel you can work with me you can clear out your desk while you're there tonight."

"Oh, I'll work with you, Robin," Cliff answered, "until Gregory returns. Then I think maybe we'd all better have a little talk."

"As you like. Meanwhile, blow out the candles, sing happy birthday, and get your ass over to IBC." He clicked the receiver and walked to the window and stared at the lights on the river.

Dip laughed. "Like I once said in a cornball movie, 'New York, I'll get you yet!' "

Robin turned. "What do you mean?"

"It's a cliché. The big daddy of them all. But that's how you looked—the giant who is going to rule Madison Avenue, bend buildings, kill, kill—!"

"I'm just doing my job."

"What about Danny's?"

"I haven't time."

"Robin, the man's coming down from Rye. He can't make it in half an hour. You can at least make an appear-ance with me at Danny's. . . ."

"I couldn't eat. I don't want to drink. We'll make it another night."

"But I happen to know some big agents are going to be

there tonight. I even arranged to get the table next to them."

"Go to Danny's. Tell everyone I'll be there. Say I'm in your pocket, if you like—I hear that's what you say anyhow. Put in a call to me loud and clear from the table, call this number. There won't be any answer. Then you can say, 'Okay, Robin, I'll meet you.' That will cover you." He reached into his pocket and threw a fifty-dollar bill on the couch. "Use this to pay for the meal." He started for the door.

Dip picked up the money and followed him.

As Robin left in the cab, Dip called, "If you get through in time, pal, come over. I won't make the call for an hour."

It was four o'clock in the morning when Robin and Cliff finished poring over the contract. "Go home, Cliff," Robin said weakly. "We've gone through every clause, every word. We're in a bind."

Cliff put on his coat and straightened his tie. "When we gave him co-ownership of the package, we kept the right of talent approval, but we gave Christie artistic and creative control."

Robin lit his last cigarette and crumpled the empty pack. "Who was the genius who came up with that ambiguous language? Why do we have cast approval if we have no artistic control?"

"It's an old hangover from the *Red Channels* days. That's the only reason it's still in. Gives the agency or network the chance to knock out an actor who might be offensive to the sponsor and his image."

Robin looked thoughtful. "Couldn't we disapprove of his entire cast? Keep saying no, until he goes back to the old stock company idea?"

"We'd have to give a valid reason. We'd have to claim it went against the sponsor image. And from what you tell me, the show was an unmitigated bore, but done in impeccable taste. So we can't reject the talent, or we'd be infringing on Christie's control."

Robin crushed out his cigarette. "Well, there goes one of our top shows down the drain."

"Was it really that bad?" Cliff asked.

"You'll see the tape later today. And I can just bet on the overnight rating." He waved Cliff off wearily.

It was beginning to get light when he walked down Madison Avenue. He knew what had to be done. No use crying over *The Chris Lane Show*. That was a sure cancelation by the end of June. He had to go after new shows —more comedy shows and more violence. He would call a full-scale meeting in the morning, send out a rush call for every new pilot around, hire writers who would develop pilots and shows for IBC.

In January, Robin made television headlines when he announced that *The Christie Lane Show* would go off the air the end of June. He told Jerry to remain calm—he'd come up with a winner for the new time period and Jerry's sponsors would have first refusal.

Christie's cancelation caused headlines in all the trades as well as the television columns of the *Times* and *Tribune*. Two days after the announcement, Christie was offered shows by NBC and CBS for the following season.

Although Christie's ratings had fallen, he continued with the sleek format. His publicity was tremendous. Christie and Ethel attended all the right parties. In hiring Cully and Hayes and Noel Victor, Ethel had gotten into the Alfie set. Alfie confided in her, adored her—and Ethel went everywhere to act as a "beard" to cover whatever boy he was romancing. The threesome made all the openings together while Christie worked on his show.

Chris did have firm offers from NBC and CBS, but he held off signing. The shows they offered gave him little opportunity to do more than act as a glorified master of ceremonies. He came to New York in February in one last attempt to straighten things out with Robin and remain with IBC. He told the Johnson-Harris office to tell Robin he was willing to go back to the old format.

The "new" format had been Ethel's idea, so she could get in with Alfie's set. Noel Victor was one of Alfie's best friends. Well, they were *in!* Hell, Ethel was so *in* now that he never saw her. He *wanted* to go back to the old show—it was a lot easier singing songs he knew than memorizing a new score each week.

When he arrived he was stunned to learn that his agent

had not been able to arrange an appointment with Robin. "Once he says no," the agent explained, "that's it. He doesn't give you a chance to argue, beg or plead."

Chris tried to reach Robin himself. Each time he was informed that Mr. Stone was "in a meeting."

He called Danton Miller. Dan was delighted to hear from him and suggested they meet at "21". It was four o'clock and the restaurant was almost empty. They sat at a front table at the bar area and for the first hour they tore Robin Stone to shreds. Chris began to feel better.

"At least you've got offers from the other networks. Now there's a guy who is a real loser." They both watched as Dip Nelson entered and ambled over to the bar.

Dan smiled. "He's been coming here almost every day, alone."

"Why?"

Dan shrugged. "What else can a guy do when his wife is a star and he has no job?"

"How are things going with you?" Chris asked.

"Well, let's put it this way: it is now survival time. And that blond ox standing at the bar may be my lifeline."

"Dip Nelson?"

"I think he's lonely enough. And I have a property . . ."

"Dip Nelson is finished. Go after his wife."

"His wife hasn't got Robin Stone in her back pocket. For some incredible reason, Dip has."

"Yeah." Christie seemed thoughtful. "In California, everyone is talking about it. They even hint there's something funny going on between them—you know: Queersville."

"I don't care if they're secretly *married*. I just want to get this property on the air."

"You mean you'd go back as a producer?"

"Producer and packager," Dan stated. "There's nothing about this business I don't know—but I want to be at IBC. I want to be there when the great Love Machine explodes. Then I'll step back where I belong, bigger and stronger than before."

Chris nodded. "At least you've got your future planned."

Dan laughed. "Christie—you've got it made. A big home in California, all the money you'll ever need—and you run with the Alfie pack. You've got a great life."

"Ethel has the great life," Christie sighed. "She's got what she always wanted. But I don't fit. Every night I come home and we either have a date with Alfie or we're going to a party. I don't even have Eddie and Kenny now. They like New York. They got a job with that new variety show on CBS."

"Maybe you've outgrown them, Chris. You've gone up in the world."

"You call it going up in the world to sit around and laugh at Alfie's jokes and watch him make calf eyes at some actor he's in love with? We all have to do whatever Alfie says. Ethel gets mad when I call her 'doll.' I'm supposed to call everyone 'luv.' You like that? A group I'm traveling with where men call each other 'luv'?"

Suddenly Christie's homely face crinkled into a forced smile. "Listen, I shouldn't kick. Like you said, I got all the money I'll ever need. But most of all, I got my son, Christie Lane, Jr." He drew out an accordion folder filled with smiling pictures of a plump little baby. "Look, if Ethel never does another thing, I'm still ahead. She gave me my baby and that's all that matters. I *live* for that kid —it's like getting an extra dividend in life." Then he looked at his watch. "Say, I got to be getting back to the hotel. The Plaza, yet. Alfie says that's where I should stay. You should see my suite, I think Lincoln was laid out in it. But Ethel is calling me at six thirty; she holds the baby to the phone and sometimes he gurgles or coos —what a kid!"

Dan watched him leave. He ordered another martini. Then he sent a note to Dip, who was still at the bar. Dip read it and walked over.

"No use both of us drinking alone," Dan said. "Thought we might sit together."

"Why should I?" Dip asked. "You're the character who raised hell when Robin put me on the Chris Lane show."

"Only because it prevented me from preparing a decent setup for you. I assure you, had I been given a few weeks' time, your notices would have been different."

Dip sat down. "People are always out to kill a movie star. They have to start out thinking he's a no-talent bum. But when I sing—especially to a live audience—pal, there's no one who can touch me."

"Let me buy you a drink," Dan said.

"Ah . . . I'm waiting for a call from Robin. I'm only nursing a ginger ale until he calls, see—then Robin and I will really go out and tie one on."

"You and Robin are still very close?"

"Like that." Dip entwined his fingers.

"Why doesn't he do something for you if you're so close?" Dan asked. "The word is out that you're really just his messenger boy."

Dip's eyes flashed in fury. "Don't you ever use a word like that about me! Robin relies on me for everything. As a matter of fact, it was *I* who told Robin he had to cancel Chris Lane! Yeah, and you want to know something? Robin was willing to let him go on next season, but I don't forget—Chris Lane treated me and Pauli like shit when we came on his show, and I got a long memory. I sit back and wait, buddy, then I send in the shiv!"

"How much longer does your wife's show run?"

"Until June in New York. Then it goes on the road for a year. I'm going too. They're building up the part of the brother. I'll play it."

"Why would you take a small role?" Dan asked.

"To be with Pauli. She needs me."

"She needs you like she needs extra teeth," Dan said.

"You looking to be slugged right here at '21'?"

"I'm looking to put some sense in your head."

"Meaning what?"

"Meaning that you're sitting around every night with the biggest power on television. No one in the business has the autonomy of Robin Stone. And you should latch on to it while it lasts. Because eventually it has to blow up in his face. I've been watching him. The way he acts, I feel he almost has a death wish—he seems to delight in making enemies. It's almost as if he's testing—seeing how far he can go, how far he can push everyone. There's some kind of a sickness behind his arrogance and drive. So if you're smart, you'll sit back and listen to me."

"I don't need advice from a has-been." Dip's voice was ugly.

Dan shot his old Cheshire-cat grin. "Perhaps two has-beens make for more strength than one. How would you like to be co-owner of a package?"

"I don't know about packages."

"What are you doing for dinner?" Dan asked.

"Nothing—that is, I'm supposed to check with Robin."

"Can you get out of it tonight?"

Dip smiled. "I can do anything I want."

"Then let's go. I have an appointment with Peter Kane from the Johnson-Harris office at Voisin. Oh—you haven't signed to go on Pauli's road tour yet, have you?"

"No. I'm waiting to see how they rewrite the part."

Dan scribbled his name on the check. "Then come with me. Listen, but keep your mouth shut."

"No one talks to me like that," Dip said.

"I can. Because I'm about to make you a very rich man." He rose, and Dip followed him out of the restaurant.

Dip toyed with a bourbon-and-water at Voisin. Dan and Peter Kane had martinis.

Dan immediately steered the conversation to Dip's career. Oddly enough, Peter Kane was interested. Everyone agreed the critics had been vindictive because of their antipathy for Robin.

"This poor boy has inherited all of Robin's enemies and none of his friends," Dan explained.

"What friends has Robin got?" Peter Kane asked. "Not even a steady girl. I hear Ike Ryan sometimes fixes him up with a scene—he likes the three-way bit. Tell me, Dip, is he queer?"

"Queer for girls," Dip answered.

"Well, I think your acting career has gone down the drain because of Robin," Peter Kane said seriously. "Everyone in the business knows Robin Stone is your best friend, and if *he* won't use you, they have to figure you're pretty bad. So they have no interest. He's hurt you very badly in not giving you a big show."

"I never looked at it that way," Dip said slowly. "Maybe that's why I get no offers."

He sat quietly while the two men discussed various shows on different networks. When dinner was over, Peter Kane turned to Dan. "I have the viewing room booked for nine—we'd better get a move on."

Dan turned to Dip. "We have a new show. It's my package, and Peter is representing it. We've just made a pilot. It's a spy series, and we can bring it in cheap. Vic Grant is playing the lead. I want you to look at it and see if you like it."

Dip's spirits soared. Vic Grant was a contract player when he was a star. Vic hadn't made a decent picture in two years.

Dan signed the check and they went directly to the projection room at the Johnson-Harris office. Dip watched the show. It was a good shoot-'em-up. Vic wasn't bad, but Dip knew he could do better—the part was made to order for him. And it would really put him right back on top!

When the lights came up, Dan looked at him. "Like it?"

"I think it could be great," Dip said enthusiastically.

"Let's go downstairs. There's a bar across the street and it's quiet. We can discuss the mechanics of the thing," Peter suggested.

"I'm with you, pal," Dip said.

They sat at a back table. Dip ordered a bourbon and drank it straight. If Dan and Peter saw him as this fast-drinking, devil-may-care detective, he couldn't let them know he usually stuck to ginger ale or beer.

"We're planning to ask one hundred and twenty-five thousand for it," Dan explained. "We can bring it in at ninety, some weeks less. We'll add the ten-percent commission to the package, and that leaves us with a thirty-thousand-dollar profit, to be split three ways if necessary."

"You mean I'd get one third of the action, instead of salary?" Dip asked.

"Oh, I think we could also arrange a token salary—say a thousand a week, plus office expenses."

"What in hell would I need an office for?"

"You'll need it for your company. You can't take the

money as salary, it would all go in taxes. My company is the Danmill—you get a name for yours. If you like, my lawyer can handle it all."

It was going too fast for Dip. "How would I know I could trust *your* lawyer?"

"Because your company will get all the profits and send Danmill its share."

"Where would we film it? Here or in L.A.?"

"Wherever IBC thinks best. They have big studios in L.A., but I'd rather get the action of the streets in New York, the feel of the city."

"Oh—has IBC bought it?" Dip asked.

"They will, I hope."

Dip nodded enthusiastically. "Well, I know I can play the hell out of the part."

Dan and Peter looked at one another. Dan spoke. "I'm sure you could, but we have Vic Grant tied up for two years. He did the pilot for scale, with the stipulation that he'd get the part if the show was sold."

"Then why am I here?" Dip asked.

"Because you can make Robin Stone buy it."

Dip started to rise, but Dan grabbed his arm. "Sit down! Tell me, would you rather be a ham actor all your life, or a millionaire?"

Dip glowered at him. "You know all evening you've been begging for a belt."

Peter cut in. "Dip, face it. You haven't *got* it. Not on television anyway. You've had every chance. Now why don't you get smart and make some *real* money? There's more prestige in being a package owner and a producer than in being an actor."

"What makes you so sure IBC will buy it?" Dip asked suddenly.

Dan's eyes narrowed. "It seems to me you sit around Danny's telling everyone you have Robin Stone in your pocket. Well, now's the time to prove it. Make him buy it. There will be a lot of dropouts in January. As further incentive, tell him that if he buys it, he gets one third of the profits. You can pay him any way he wants it—cash, trips, a house in the country."

"Isn't there trouble with the government?"

"We have an excellent tax man. There are ways to make Robin's third look like legitimate write-offs. If he wants a Cadillac, we use it in a few scenes and say it's for the show. The country home we buy because we shoot a lot of footage in it. We build sets and give him the furniture. If he wants cash, we find a million ways to build up dummy expenses. You let us worry about that."

"You mean I just go to him and tell him how it is?"

Dan shrugged. "Obviously you know the best way to handle him."

"And how much did you say there'd be in this for us?"

"With a three-way split, ten thousand apiece."

"What happens to Pete, here?"

"I just want the agency to get the commission," Peter said. "If I break through with a sale to Robin Stone, I'll get a vice-presidency out of it. That's all I care about."

Dip stared into space. "My name has to be on the screen as producer."

Dan laughed. "Everyone would know it was a phony."

"I don't give a damn. Pauli won't know. The public won't know. I want billing—bigger than Vic Grant. That'll impress Pauli."

"All right," Dan conceded. "I'll be executive producer. You'll have a frame for yourself as producer."

Dip smiled. "Give me a letter first, all signed and witnessed, saying I get two thirds of the action. After all, suppose I go in and make Robin take it and then you guys welsh?"

"I'll have the letter drawn up first thing in the morning," Dan said.

Dip met Robin at the Lancer Bar the following afternoon. He had Dan's letter in his pocket. He waited until Robin had started his second martini before he brought up the subject of the pilot. He described it graphically, acted out the role and finished with a flourish: "And one third of the profits goes right into your pocket, buddy boy."

Robin grabbed him by the coat and pulled him close. "Now you listen to me, you slob. Danton Miller got rich making deals like that when he ran IBC. I've thrown out every agent who ever dealt with him. Don't you ever toss my name around in a slimy deal like this."

"Then it's no dice?" Dip's voice was groveling.

"No dice regarding the kickback to me!" Then he turned to Dip. "Look, if you've got a good pilot, show it to me. If it's halfway good, it'll take precedence over any other show. If Dan wants to put your name up, that's his business."

Dip's smile was broad with relief. "Then you're not mad?"

"Only when you put me in your league, chum. Look, I'm always looking for shows. There's no reason why you shouldn't go into the production end. You've got a gangsterlike intelligence that I admire. If I buy this show and they put your name up as producer, I know damn well Danton will do all the work. But if you just sit around and take bows, then I take back what I said about your intelligence. Hang around, learn everything there is to be learned, watch the cameramen, learn about below-the-line costs—that's the first place where your profits go. Watch out for musicians and overtime. But as for the three-way split—forget it. Cut up the gravy between yourself and Dan, and whatever you have to give the crummy agent."

Robin viewed the pilot with Dip. When it was over, he stood up. "It's not good—it's *great!* Tell Dan he's got a deal."

Dip took a long walk after he left Robin. He decided he despised Robin Stone. He also hated Danton Miller. He hated every mother-fucking son of a bitch in the world. How had he gotten into such a situation? A wife who was a star and treated him like he was her servant. Men like Robin and Dan, who blatantly told him he was a lousy actor. Where had all the sunshine gone? The days when he used to walk into a room and light it up? The days when women clamored around him? Now they ducked him. Pauli had told him to stay away from the girls in the show—none of them wanted to go out with Robin Stone. But he had to get Robin girls to stay on the right side of him. Anyway, Robin was a weirdo with the broads—he'd never forget that whore he had beaten up.

And the girls complained that Robin was cheap—he wouldn't take them anywhere, just the Lancer Bar or the Steak Place and then a roll in the feathers. And if they didn't perform the way *he* wanted, he sent them home without taxi fare. Dip sighed, and headed for Sardi's. He had taken to dropping in for lunch, casing the place— trying to spot new eager young actresses he could get for Robin. Of course Robin never asked for a date, but he always seemed pleased when Dip winked and said, "Have I got a new number for you, buddy boy—this one really swings!"

How had he come to this? Well, from now on it would be different. He'd be big again. Thirty thousand a week split two ways. . . . Why *two* ways? How would Dan know whether or not Robin took a cut? He wouldn't. He'd take *two thirds*, plus his salary. He'd tell them Robin wanted it in cash, and let them and their fancy tax man figure a way to cover it. And he'd put those ten G's in a safe-deposit box each week. *Tax-free!* He'd be rich. But he was damned if he was going to sit around and watch cameras and learn how to be a producer—let the shmucks like Dan Miller do that for their shitty little one third. He'd take two thirds and have a ball. And in a subtle way he'd let word get around that Robin was on the take. Then every guy who wanted to sell a package would come to him and offer him two thirds—one for himself, one for Robin. He could become a real power. Pauli would be kissing his ass—she wouldn't give him the "too tired" jazz when he wanted to ball her. Soon he'd be in the position to give *her* a job! Suddenly his spirits dropped. Pauli! Jesus, she was like a sickness to him. He couldn't get her out of his system. Sometimes he wanted to kill her, but with all the gorgeous broads he met, she was the only one who turned him on. He had even tried the orgy route with Robin, one girl and the two of them. He had sat and watched Robin getting blown and it hadn't excited him. When it was his turn he had only been able to get it up by pretending the girl was Pauli. And she had been a real looker, too! Well, wait until the name Dip Nelson blazed across the television screen in living color, wait until he had a show on the air—two

shows, maybe even three—then Pauli would realize he
was the biggest man in town.

Robin slated Dip's pilot, A Guy Called Jones, to replace the first January casualty. The contract was worked
out, Dan had agreed, and now Dip had nothing to do but
wait until September and see what bombed.

Pauli went on tour in June and Dip remained in New
York. Pauli's attitude had changed when she learned that
Dip was going to make ten thousand a week. (He did not
tell her about the other ten he intended to deposit in the
vault.) She wrote him long letters from the road and
never failed to tell him how much she missed him.

In September the new shows came on. IBC had an
immediate winner in one series Robin had chosen. Two
others were shaky, but he had a solid daytime schedule.
The new soap opera was a smash, and both game shows
were going to make it. Of the two doubtful shows, one
was a cinch to be axed in January. He'd replace it with
Dip's show—that would write off any obligation he owed
for all time. He thought about Dip. . . . In the beginning
he had really liked him. He had an openness and a zest
for living that Robin found appealing. But as the months
had passed and he watched Dip take the crap from Pauli,
his respect for Dip gradually turned to revulsion. Dip
had to know that Pauli was cheating on him. In the
beginning he had tried to snap Dip to his senses and
arouse the manhood in him by treating him as a servant.
He felt that Dip would rebel, and once the rebellion
began his strength might return. But Dip took it.

The more Robin thought of Dip's subservience to
Pauli, the less he cared to become involved with any girl.
The few times he had tried to start anything that resembled a romance, his thoughts automatically turned to
Maggie, and the girl he was with suddenly seemed dull.
No, it was easier to let Dip supply temporary entertainment. He cared so little about the girls that Dip or Ike
brought around that he found himself requiring a three-
way bit. If he watched Ike make love to the girl it
aroused him, then he was able to jump her too. He was
aware that in a subconscious way Maggie was always in

his thoughts. And when he acknowledged this to himself, he became enraged. No girl was ever going to "get" to him! Running the network was a full-time job. He hadn't even gone near his book in a year—just the night before he had carefully put the three hundred yellow pages in a portfolio and stashed it in a filing case. He wondered when Gregory would return, if ever. . . . The last card from Judith had come from Cannes in August. Gregory was feeling fine, even playing *chemin de fer* for hours on end.

The Austins slipped into town quietly at the end of September. Judith planned it that way. Once she was settled, their "official" return would be heralded with a big splash. She didn't want to dissipate the impact with just the usual picture of them getting off the boat. It had to be done with a gigantic party. She might even take over the ballroom at the Plaza, invite all the exciting people, all the press. . . . Gregory was his old self, and convinced he didn't have cancer. He had even proven himself sporadically a few times in bed with her. Judith felt she deserved an Academy Award—she had acted wildly excited, told him he was the greatest lover in the world. She hadn't shown that much excitement during their honeymoon. But she was determined to do anything to get Gregory well—and most of all to get him back to New York. They had been gone a year and a half!

But she had used the time to advantage. The first three months at Lausanne, Gregory was too ill to see anyone. Forty shock treatments, then the dreadful regressive period when he even soiled himself. And then the slow process back. . . . She had taken a small apartment near the sanitarium, and during the first three months, when she had not been allowed to see him, she had put herself in the hands of an excellent plastic surgeon.

It was a miraculous job, though at first she had been disappointed. She had actually expected to look twenty again. She looked about thirty-eight, but a beautiful, well-taken-care-of thirty-eight. The doctor had been a genius. Of course there were tiny creases in front of her ears and heavy scars behind them, but she wore her hair

down now, soft and *bouffant,* a few inches below her
ears. Vidal Sassoon himself had styled it for her, and it
was a smashing look. Gregory knew nothing of the operation. He said she looked marvelous and the new hairdo
had done wonders. She smiled. Couldn't he notice how
firm her jawline was? He hadn't even noticed her breast
lift, or the tiny scars near her pelvis where her thighs
had been tightened.

Gregory looked well too. The red was back in his hair,
he was tan and lean, but he had no desire to go back to
work. They had been home a week and he hadn't gone
near the office. Each day he had come up with a different
excuse. He had to see his tailor—he had lost ten pounds
and none of his suits fitted. He had to drive out to see his
horses. At the beginning of the second week she literally
threw him out of the house, insisting he go to the office.

The moment he was gone, she placed a call to Robin.
She had deliberately waited. He *knew* they were back—
Gregory had talked to him several times on the phone.
She knew he must wonder why she didn't call. By now he
would be eager. . . .

His private line didn't answer. She was disappointed,
but no use leaving a message. He was probably at a
meeting. She finally reached him at three o'clock. He
sounded delighted to hear from her. He had spent the
morning with Gregory and remarked on how well he
looked.

"When am I going to see you?" she asked.

"Anytime," he said easily. "As soon as Gregory feels up
to it, I'd love to take you both to dinner."

"I don't mean it that way, Robin," she said quietly. "I
want to see you alone."

He was silent.

"Are you there, Robin?"

"I'm here. . . ."

"When can I see you?"

"Tomorrow at six, at my place."

"I'll be there. I'll leave word for Gregory that I've gone
to a charity cocktail party. I'll have no time limit and
Gregory falls asleep right after dinner."

She went to a new beauty parlor in the East Sixties.

She couldn't chance her regular place where all the operators knew her, unless she wanted those scars behind her
ears to be the biggest news flash along Park Avenue. The
operators had always told her who had gotten the latest
"lift."

She sat in a cubicle at the new beauty parlor. She had
given her name as Wright. She was positive that no one
recognized her. God, why should they? It had been over
a year since her picture had appeared on the front page
of *Women's Wear*. Well, in a few weeks, she'd take over.
She lay back and wished the woman wouldn't rub so
hard. She knew the operator felt the lumpy scars. The
bitch, she was jealous because she would never be able to
afford such a luxury. She glanced at the operator. She
was a woman in her middle thirties: broad hips, fingers
permanently discolored from hair dye, white space shoes
on feet that ached from too much standing—God, even
varicose veins! Why shouldn't the poor creature hate and
envy someone who could pay three thousand dollars just
to get rid of some lines?

The woman smiled as she led Judith into another booth
to await her hair set. As Judith thumbed through a back
issue of *Harper's*, the woman whispered to the young
man outside the booth, "You'll get a big tip from this one,
Dickie—it's Mrs. Gregory Austin under a phony name
with a brand-new set of scars. Take it easy with the
clips."

Judith smoked nervously as the slim young man coiled
her hair into the large rollers. She caught him looking at
her ears. "I had mastoids last year," she said casually.

He nodded. "My roommate had them too." His voice
was sympathetic.

She relaxed under the drier. She would go to the booth
after Dickie combed her out, and put on fresh makeup.
She was wearing that wonderful underwear she had
picked up in Paris. Thank God the scars under her
breasts didn't show. The breast and thigh lift had really
been painful, but it was all worth it. Tonight she'd strip
off her clothes and stand before Robin. She was a match
for any airline hostess now!

She left the beauty parlor at five thirty. She didn't want

to walk and ruin her hair. She looked marvelous—Vidal had cut her hair so well that even Dickie had been able to follow the line. She had given him a ten-dollar tip. She hadn't felt this exhilarated in years. She wanted to shout . . . to sing, but she merely went to a drugstore and had a cup of tea to kill the time. At five of six she took a cab to Robin's.

The doorman glanced at her casually, but she felt that her large sunglasses hid her identity. Of course he wouldn't recognize her—she had been away so long.

She felt short of breath from excitement and nerves as she buzzed Robin's door. He opened it and beckoned her in and returned to the telephone. God, this was an anticlimactic greeting! He was talking to California—he sounded like Gregory with all those damn ratings. She looked around the room. She had only been here once, but during the past year she had relived every second they had shared together. Every word, every piece of furniture in his apartment, was etched in her mind. She felt slightly uncomfortable in the new underwear. The naked beige bra and the tiny lace pants scratched. But any annoyance would be worth it when she watched his face as she undressed. She planned to do it slowly, deliberately. She was wearing a suit—Valentino had outdone himself on this one: the silk blouse buttoned down the front, nothing had to go over the head, and she had those marvelous individual false eyelashes—no worry about the stripped ones coming off.

Robin hung up, came and grasped her hands in welcome. He tried to smile but there were two lines between his eyes.

"Trouble?" she asked.

"Roddy Collins."

"Who is he?" she asked.

This time he really smiled. "Not only have you been away, but it's a cinch you haven't watched the box since you got back."

"No. And neither has Gregory, thanks to you."

He sat down and offered her a cigarette. The lines returned to his eyes. "Our new star, Roddy Collins—his series has zoomed to the top ten. It's a Western. He plays the fastest gun alive for law and order. A beautiful guy, six foot six and all brawn. I've just learned he's a flaming faggot."

She shrugged. She wanted Robin to take her into his arms. He was pacing the room and had scarcely looked at her. His mind was still on the phone call. "Isn't a star's private life supposed to be his own?" she asked.

"Sure, if he'd *keep* it private, I don't care who he goes to bed with. But it seems sleeping with a boy is not his bag. He likes to dress like a woman and go out cruising to pick up a *guy*. Do you get the picture—six foot six, the newest all-American sensation, sponsored by a family-type product, walking into a bar in drag trying to pick up a guy?"

She started to laugh.

"It's not funny, Judith. It seems a guy five foot eight took a poke at him and the cops arrived. Our lawyers rushed in. We got three people to swear he did it on a bet, and that they were following him. We covered it *this* time, but we can't keep a guard on him every second."

"Robin, I've been away from all this for so long. I know I've got to start living with it again soon. But not now, not our first time together?"

He looked at her as if seeing her for the first time. "Of course—would you like a drink?"

"Yes." God, anything to break the ice.

He mixed two Scotches. "Gregory looks good," he said as he handed her the drink. "I'm very pleased that he wants me to keep running things, but you've got to make him take some interest."

"Doesn't he?"

"No. He called a meeting today and told everyone how proud he was of me. Tomorrow he's playing golf. And the following day he's going to look at some new horses."

She shrugged. "It's your network now, Robin."

"Yes, it is," he said quietly.

"Then let Gregory play with his horses and golf clubs."

"Judith, I thought he'd come back and try and take over completely. I was prepared to fight him on that— thirty percent of the programming consists of shows I've personally brought in. But he has no interest at all, and that's not healthy. I like Gregory. I want to work with him hand in hand, toss ideas around, make him argue with me when he thinks I'm wrong. It will make for better programming. Besides, the word *is* around that it's my network—and I don't want him to be upset."

She put down her drink and stared at him intimately. "Let me take care of that. It's my network too, you know."

"Judith, it's easy for you to say that now, but wait until you get into the swim of things. I don't give interviews. I'm not the most lovable guy in the world, according to the press. And unless Gregory is in there punching with me, he's going to be the forgotten man. As long as he was away, it was okay, but if he comes back and doesn't roll up his sleeves, then the papers will have a field day and it will *really* be my network. There's one columnist in particular who hates my guts. I refused to let him be a panelist on one of our game shows—he's a fat slob who is a hater. He's been writing about me every day, calling me the Love Machine!"

Her eyes narrowed. "How about living up to the title?"

He swallowed his drink. "Give me a chance to get healthy. You've been swimming on the Riviera. I haven't even had time to catch a weekend at the Hamptons."

"You look strong enough to me, Robin."

He walked over and pulled her to her feet. Her arms went around his neck. Suddenly there was the shrill interruption of the telephone. "Don't answer it," she said.

"It's the IBC line!" He removed her arms from his neck gently and walked over and took the call. "Hello. Yes. Oh, no kidding, Dip. Did Dan see it? No, I've never heard of Preston Slavitt. Oh yes, he's that off-Broadway writer who looks like he never takes a bath. Well, his talent is in his ass. . . . Really great, huh? Well, how long have you got the viewing room? . . . Okay, in twenty minutes." He hung up.

"You don't have to go somewhere?" She couldn't believe it.

"Dip Nelson latched on to a pilot that just might be great." He picked up his glass and drained his drink.

"Dip claims he can get me first crack at it tonight. The other networks are viewing it tomorrow."

She looked surprised. "Who is Dip Nelson?"

"It's a long story, baby. He's an ex-movie star turned producer. We bought a series from him and Dan Miller." He held out his hand to help her up from the couch. "Look, Judith, you better go down first. I'll follow in a few minutes."

"When will I see you?"

"I'll call you tomorrow, around eleven." Then he kissed her lightly and walked her to the door but she felt his thoughts were already at the viewing room. She went down in the elevator, took a cab, and got home in time to find Gregory mixing a martini. He looked at her with genuine pleasure. "I'm so glad you're back early. I found your message and was afraid I'd have to eat alone. God, you look beautiful."

She took the martini and sipped it absently. And suddenly it occurred to her that Robin Stone hadn't even commented on the change in her looks.

When he hadn't called by one, she was furious. He probably had a lunch date so that meant he probably wouldn't call till three. But he had said he'd call at eleven! Well, he could have gotten jammed up. She stalked around her bedroom. She was all made up, but still in her negligee. She had hoped he might invite her to lunch, a long quiet lunch where they could talk and catch up on the past. Now it would have to be cocktails. She could manage to stay with him until nine. Leave word for Gregory that something had come up regarding the Orphans' Ball.

She stretched across the bed and began playing solitaire—she told herself that if five cards came up, he would call at four, just to talk. If ten came out, he would call at three, just to talk. Fifteen, he would ask her for a drink. Twenty, he would ask her for the evening. And if the game came out he would tell her that he was really mad about her and the whole thing would be as she dreamed.

Eight cards came out. She tried again. Fifteen this time —no, that wasn't fair. This time she'd do it and take the results seriously. No cards came out. Good Lord, did that mean he wasn't going to call?

At five o'clock she was desperate. She put in a call to him on his private wire. There was no answer. That meant he wasn't at his desk. When Gregory came home at six she was still in her negligee. "Are we going somewhere?" he asked as he noticed her perfect makeup.

"I wish we *were*," she said.

He smiled faintly. "We've been away a long time. People don't know we're home yet."

"You're right. I guess I'd better start phoning around."

He sighed. "I like it like this. We can have a quiet dinner and watch TV."

"What do you think I've been doing for a year and a half?" she asked quietly.

He looked contrite. "All right, why don't you put on something nice and we'll go to the Colony."

"Alone?"

"Together," he said.

"How will that look?" she demanded.

"Like we're having dinner at the Colony."

"Also like we haven't a friend in the world."

"Maybe we haven't, Judith. Most people don't, you know."

"That's nonsense, we've always been invited everywhere."

"Invitations," he said wearily. "Invitations to openings, to parties after the theater. Returning the parties—I guess we've been out of circulation."

"Let's get back," she insisted.

He shrugged. "All right, you start things going—that's always been your end."

She thought about it that night as she lay in bed. How did one get things going again? She had no real close women friends, just women she knew well enough to lunch with, discuss clothes and charities and listen to *their* troubles. Judith had never made a confidante of anyone and she had never been *out* of circulation before. Invitations for dinner parties, openings, art shows, charity balls—they had always kept pouring in. Suddenly she realized that their entire social life had centered around

Gregory's work. When a Broadway show opened, there were opening-night seats from the producer, because the producer or director hoped to work for Gregory or get one of his stars on an IBC show. When stars came to town they called Gregory and invited them out. The phone hadn't rung since she had returned. But it was her own fault. She had done nothing but center her thoughts and plans on Robin. Well, she'd start things going tomorrow. Perhaps she'd give a small dinner party. She'd call Dolores and John Tyron. They were always "in" on everything.

Dolores was delighted to hear from her. "Oh, Judith angel, how divine that you're back. Are you going to the party for Joan Sutherland next week?"

"Well, to tell the truth, Dolores, I haven't made any dates, you're the first person I've called. I'm barely unpacked."

"You must be exhausted, all those parties in Europe. I'm dying to hear about it. Did you see Grace when you were in the south of France? I heard she gave a marvelous gala."

"We were in Capri then."

"Oh, then you were at the Korda ball? Was it divine?"

"I'll tell you all the things we did when I see you. But I'm more interested in *you* and all the friends I haven't seen in so long."

"Well, you must really have had a tremendous time to stay away this long! And isn't Gregory lucky having that marvy man running things for him? Tell me, Judith, I hear such wild things about him—are they true?"

"What do you hear?"

"*Everything*, darling—orgies, and also that he's AC-DC. He's always with that handsome ex-movie star, Pauli Nelson's husband."

"Who is Pauli Nelson?"

"Darling, you *have* been away. She was the biggest sensation on Broadway last year. But Robin Stone sounds so wicked. I'd just *adore* to meet him."

"Well, I'm planning a small dinner party and I'll invite him along. How about one night this week?"

"Darling, we're dead until a week from next Thursday.

But get Robin Stone and arrange your little dinner—say in two weeks. Call me back and give me the date and I'll put it right down in my little book. Oh, angel, my other phone is ringing, and Freddy has just come to comb my hair and—good Lord, look at the time, I'm due at La Grenouille in an hour."

Judith made several calls. Everyone was delighted she was back, but each woman was booked and chatted endlessly about the excitement of the new season, and everyone naturally assumed she and Gregory had been invited everywhere. Well, a small dinner party at the Colony wasn't going to work. The solution was a large black-tie party in her home.

She decided on October first. She called Dolores back. Dolores was flying out of the door, but of course she'd look at her appointment book. "Angel—not October first! That's the opening of the New Regal Club. You've joined of course? Well, look through your mail—it's a closed membership but I'm sure they've sent you an application. Why not make your party, let's see, how about October eighth? That's open for us—I'll pencil it in lightly and you call back and confirm. I've got to dash, angel, but of course I'll see you before then."

Judith tried Betsy Ecklund. October eighth! Wasn't Judith going to the private showing and black-tie dinner at the Berner Gallery? The Duchess of Windsor was supposed to be coming in for it. Judith should check her mail —her invitation had to be there.

She hung up and stared at the mail on her breakfast tray. Some assorted bills, an ad from Saks, a letter from her sister. It was unbelievable! She was out of everything. To have to check with Dolores and Betsy on *their* availability—! In the past, she had just picked a date and given the list to her secretary. When her invitations went out, everyone came. Now she had to make dates fit in with *their* social life. Could a year and a half change things so radically?

It was twelve thirty. She had nothing to do. She dialed Robin's number with new determination. He picked up on the third ring. She heard talking in the background— his office sounded as if several men were there. "Oh yes."

He made his voice impersonal. "I'm sorry I didn't call, things have piled up. Can I get back to you, either late this afternoon or first thing tomorrow?"

She replaced the receiver. Now what? She was all made up. She had to see him. Once he saw her, he'd respond. She had seen the look of admiration in his eyes when she came to his apartment—until that damn phone call!

She'd run into him! Make it appear accidental! Yes, that was the thing to do. *Today.* Let's see—he'd probably go to lunch at one and return around two. She'd manage just accidentally to pass the IBC Building at that hour and bump into him.

She dressed carefully—no hat; the beige coat with the sable boa. She arrived at IBC at ten minutes to two. She went to a phone booth and called his office. When his secretary asked who was calling, Judith said, "Miss Weston of the Nielsen office."

"May I have him return your call, Miss Weston? He's expected back shortly."

"No, I'll call back." Judith clicked the phone. Good, that meant he was still out for lunch. There was a book-store next to the IBC Building. She took her post there and pretended to be looking at the titles. She'd stand there until Robin returned and then as soon as she spotted him, she'd pretend to be walking by and accidentally bump into him. She waited ten minutes. How long could you stare at books? And it was windy—thank God she had her hair loaded with spray net. She wondered if the doorman noticed or recognized her. It was getting chilly, downright cold. She felt her eyes tearing. Some of the mascara began to run. There was a mirror near the doorway, and she saw that the mascara specks dotted the whites of her eyes. Half her bottom lashes had disappeared. That was the awful part of having once been a natural blond—your hair darkened with age, but your lashes never did. She got out her handkerchief. The mascara had caked in small lines under her eye. She tried to wipe it away.

"Something in your eye?"

She turned. It was Robin.

In the daylight with his tanned face close to her own, she suddenly felt that the entire operation had been a farce. But she turned and managed a weak smile. "Just mascara and wind. I had a luncheon date and thought it was such a divine day I'd walk, so I dismissed my car. It suddenly seems to have turned into winter."

"Want me to hail a cab?"

"Please." She tried not to show her dismay.

He led her to the curb and signaled a taxi. "Judith, I meant to call you, but I got so bogged down."

"I understand, but . . ."

The cab arrived and she was furious—usually you could never find one, but this damn fool had driven up as if he was practicing for the Indianapolis 500. Robin opened the door. "I'll call you, Judith."

As soon as she got to her bedroom, she flung herself on the bed, sobbing off all her brand-new false eyelashes.

At five o'clock she took one of Gregory's sleeping pills and left a note that she had a headache. And as she fell into a heavy sleep she wondered if Robin suspected she had planned their "accidental" meeting.

The "accidental" meeting had disturbed Robin. He thought about it off and on during the afternoon. He found himself snapping at his secretary, being more than curt with Andy Parino, and actually rude when he turned down Jerry's invitation for drinks at the Lancer Bar. When he got home he mixed himself a drink and tried to watch television. But Judith kept coming to his mind. She had looked so pathetic standing in front of the bookstore. Her feeble excuse had rocked him—the poor thing, to be so desperate, to stand there hoping to run into him. Holy God, how had this happened? Had Kitty felt this way about her young boys?

He picked up the newspaper. He was damned if he was going to worry about it. Amanda had wanted him, a lot of girls had waited for his call—girls who didn't have double town houses or husbands who owned television networks. . . . But they were *girls*. They weren't fifty-year-old women who had gone through a face job. . . . He had been stunned when he had seen her: the smooth tight skin, like Kitty's . . . . Dammit, plenty of fifty-year-old rich women had face jobs—why did he have to feel guilty about Judith's?

He leafed through the newspaper in an effort to clear his mind. Suddenly he came upon a grinning picture of Dip Nelson. The headline read: TV's NEWEST TRANSFUSION. The interview was in Dip's inimitable style: "TV needs new blood," he was quoted as saying; "that's why Robin Stone rushed to buy the new pilot Danton Miller and I created. The trouble with TV is too many people are in it who have no knowledge of real show business."

Robin tossed the paper on the floor. He went to the phone and dialed Dip. "No more interviews," he snapped. "You talk too much! From now on, let your show talk for you. That's an order."

"Okay, buddy boy. But I still think you're wrong not to have bought the other pilot I showed you. It's a sure winner."

"It was a piece of shit."

"You're in an adorable mood tonight."

Robin clicked the phone. He poured himself a stiff drink. By eleven o'clock he was very drunk.

Judith awoke the following morning with the dull sense that something was very wrong. Then she recalled the events of the previous day and fresh tears came to her eyes. It was nine o'clock. Gregory was going to Westbury to look at some horses. The entire day stretched before her. She tiptoed into his bedroom. He was gone. He had a *reason* to get up—his horses and golf—but she had nothing. She opened his medicine chest. That green pill had been a real knockout drop. She took another. Why not? At least she'd sleep through the day—it was better than lying around waiting for a call that wouldn't come.

The pill worked quickly. She hadn't eaten dinner last night. She thought of ringing for some tea, but her head felt heavy and she drifted off to sleep.

She heard the phone ring. It sounded like it was coming from a distance, but as she shook herself awake, the sound became clear and insistent. She groped for it.

. . . Good Lord, it was four thirty—she had slept the day away.

"Hello, Judith."

It was Robin. He was on the phone, calling her. And she was so heavy with drowsiness. . . .

"Did I disturb you?" he asked.

"No, no, I had a hectic day." Why didn't her head clear? "I just got home and was trying to get forty winks."

"Then I'll hang up."

"No, I'm really awake." She hoped she didn't sound as sluggish as she felt.

"I managed to get through most of my work and I thought you might feel in the mood for a drink."

"I'd adore a drink."

"Fine. My place in half an hour?"

"Make it an hour," she said quickly. "I'm expecting a few calls for some charity events."

She staggered out of bed and rang for the maid. A pot of black coffee might help. Oh God, why had she taken that pill! He had called her! He actually wanted to see her!

She sat before her dressing table and sipped the coffee. Three cups, and still she felt light-headed. Everything seemed to be coming to her from a distance. But at least her hand was steady and she was able to apply her makeup. Her hair was a mess but she pinned on a fall. The hairpins dug into her scalp, but she had to be positive it was secure. Of course they might not go to bed, still she was taking every precaution. But she wasn't going to push things. . . . He had called! He wanted to see her and that meant he'd call again.

She scribbled a note for Gregory explaining she had been called to a charity cocktail party and might be late.

She was still light-headed when she knocked on Robin's door. He was in his shirt and had loosened his tie. He took her hands and drew her into the room. Then he kissed her gently on the lips. Suddenly with an abandon she had never known, she threw her arms around him, and kissed him long and deep. Then he took her by the hand and led her into the bedroom. She felt as if she was moving in a dream. All sounds were muted, even her movements seemed slower—yet she was without any inhibitions. She undressed slowly and stood before him. He stretched out on the bed and pulled her down. Making love with Robin suddenly seemed the most natural thing in the world. And she accepted his embrace as if she had known it all her life.

It was nine thirty when she got home. Gregory was sitting in bed watching television. She threw her arms around him. "Oh darling, I'm so sorry I missed dinner with you."

He smiled and patted her head. "Getting back in the social swim?"

"A bit. The meeting dragged on forever, and several of us went to '21' for a drink and then before I knew it . . ."

"That's all right. Shall I ring for some dinner for you?"

She shook her head. "I had two Bloody Marys. I think I'll just go straight to bed."

She *was* hungry, but she wanted to be alone with her thoughts. And she also wanted to go right to sleep and get the evening over with, because tomorrow would bring Robin—and that was all that mattered.

In the weeks that followed, Judith's entire life centered around the telephone. Robin usually called at eleven. To avoid any possibility of running into Jerry or Dip, Robin switched from the Lancer Bar to his new hangout, Marsh's Steak Place. She thought of it as "our place." And on days when he couldn't see her, she'd walk past it—just seeing the restaurant made it all seem real. Sometimes they went to his apartment; and yesterday she had driven him to the airport because he had to make a quick trip to the Coast. She wore her new European clothes and began to plan her winter wardrobe. Gregory wanted to spend the winter at Palm Beach. Fine. She'd manage to need dental work, redecorate the house—she'd get in to town often, then she'd be able to spend entire nights with Robin. She had gotten some marvelous hormone pills from Dr. Spineck and the flashes had stopped. As for the snoring—well, she just wouldn't sleep. How could she sleep if she had the chance to spend an entire night in Robin's arms, and wake with him and have breakfast

with him! Of course she'd have to pretend to wake before
him and patch her makeup. She'd buy one of those new
alligator bags that had room for everything in it. . . .

She hadn't done a thing to reactivate her social life.
She didn't care about it . . . Robin's phone call was the
only thing that mattered. Sometimes she grew frightened
at the intensity of her feeling for him. She was really in
love. The frightening thing about this romance was her
compulsion to see him constantly. At night she lay awake
and had fantasies—Gregory would drop dead, painlessly
and quickly, Robin would console her, and after a
suitable time they could marry.

*Marry!* She sat up in bed. *Marry Robin!* Oh Lord, to
kill off poor Gregory, even in a daydream—that was
awful, horrible! But she loved Robin. Yes, she loved him
—this was really it. This was the kind of love novelists
wrote about. It did exist. Her past "romances" paled in
comparison. Everything paled in comparison to Robin.
He was her whole life. And Gregory wasn't going to drop
dead quietly—he was getting stronger every day.

Suppose she divorced Gregory? No, that wouldn't
work, because Robin would have to quit IBC. Well, why
not? He had told her he wanted to write a book—he had
even finished the first draft. It was about the Great Men
who made it back from failure to the top: General de
Gaulle, Winston Churchill . . . Robin's theory was that a
true winner is the man who comes back after he's been
on top and hit rock bottom. It's easy to make it once. But
making it twice is what separates the lucky ones from the
great ones.

Well, she had plenty of money. Even if she took
nothing from Gregory, her stocks and securities were
worth more than half a million. And the D & B report
stated that Robin had real money of his own. They could
go to Majorca, take a house. . . . She would keep everyone away from him. They'd walk the beach, sail together, and at night they'd sit before a fire and he would
read his manuscript to her. . . .

The more she thought about it, the more obsessed she
became with the idea. Suddenly it was urgent that she
talk it over with Robin. He loved her—she was positive

of that. They had been seeing each other constantly for six weeks. And the nights he wasn't with her, he was home watching television. Often she would slip into her bedroom and call him. And there wasn't a night she went to sleep without calling him to say good night—and he was always there. It was so wonderful to lie in the darkness, with Gregory safely asleep in the other room, and pour out her love to Robin. Of course he never came out and said he loved her. Robin wasn't the type. But he always said, "Sleep well, my darling."

She looked at her watch. It was noon—that meant it was eleven o'clock in Chicago. She had talked to Robin in Los Angeles last night. He was flying back today. The plane stopped at Chicago to refuel at four.

Suddenly she sprang out of bed. She'd be at the airport in Chicago when he arrived. They'd fly back together and she'd tell him. She scribbled a note for Gregory explaining that she had to go to Darien for the day. . . . Thank God Gregory was always so tired when he came home that he fell asleep right after dinner.

She arrived in Chicago at four, went to the VIP lounge and had him paged. He arrived slightly breathless, and speechless with surprise when he saw her.

She rushed to his arms. She didn't give a damn if anyone knew—from now on they were going to be together all the time. They had a drink while the plane was refueling. For the first time she was glad that Robin had the use of Gregory's company plane. He seemed slightly off balance at her surprise appearance but she felt he was delighted. She held off with her news until they were seated in the plane, heading for New York. Oddly enough, it was Robin who gave her the perfect opening.

He took her hands and said, "This is all very wonderful and exciting but you must never do it again. The pilot certainly recognized you, and we don't want to hurt Gregory."

"I care about Gregory—that's why I want it to be quick and clean-cut. Robin, I'm going to ask Gregory for a divorce."

He didn't answer, but turned his attention to the clouds that floated beneath the plane.

"You want me, don't you, Robin?"

"We have each other. Why hurt Gregory?"

"I want to marry you."

He took her hands. "Judith, I don't want to get married." Then as he saw the tears rush to her eyes, he said, "I've never wanted to get married. To you, or to anyone."

"Robin, it *would* work. You could leave IBC, you could write. I'd be with you. . . . We could have such a wonderful life, Robin. Please don't say no. Just think about it. That's all I ask—*think* about it!"

He smiled and took her hands. "All right, we'll both do a lot of thinking. No more talking." He stood up and crossed to the small bar and mixed two drinks.

"To us," she said, as she raised her glass.

"To you, Judith. I never want to hurt you. Please believe that."

She snuggled against him. "Oh, Robin, I wish this plane ride would never end."

He didn't call the following morning. At first she wasn't concerned. She sat in the bedroom and waited. At three thirty she called him. He picked up the phone on the second ring.

"I'm sorry I didn't get to you," he said, "but there were several meetings this morning that I had to attend. Things piled up while I was out of town."

She giggled. "I caught you with people in the office, right?"

"Yes."

"How long will they be there?"

"It looks like the entire afternoon is jammed up."

"What about my coming by at six o'clock tonight at your place?"

"Can't. All kinds of appointments until seven, then I have to watch one of our new shows. It starts tonight."

"I'd love to watch it with you."

"I'll be at a sponsor's home. Then there's some party or something later. May I get back to you?" He sounded slightly annoyed.

She hung up. He didn't call back. She and Gregory had dinner alone. He was tired. Soon the Miltown caught up with him. He dozed off while he was watching the new show. She watched aware that Robin was also watching —somehow it made her feel closer to him. He was probably bored, and the party would be dull. She had been to parties given by agency men. . . .

The next morning she read the reviews. IBC had another winner. The *Times* gave it an excellent review and also mentioned the shot of adrenalin Robin Stone had given the network. But it was the afternoon papers that really upset her. There certainly had been a party—but it was no little agency party. They had taken over the Rainbow Room and every top celebrity and socialite had been invited. The center fold was filled with pictures. There was a large picture of Robin seated between a musical comedy star and a model. He was grinning as he listened to something the musical comedy star was saying. But the thing that ripped at Judith's heart was the way his left hand was interlocked with the model's. That gesture spoke louder than any words—they were together!

She waited a week and he didn't call. He had to be busy—he couldn't intentionally be ignoring her. Finally in desperation she called his private line at the office. The impersonal voice of the operator answered on the second ring and told her it was no longer a working number. A slow creeping fear nagged at her—he wouldn't dare! He couldn't! She dialed his private number at home. The same impersonal voice came on. "Sorry, that number is no longer in use. No, we cannot give out the new number. It is unlisted."

Her rage made her weak. He had done this to avoid her! She burst into tears and buried her face in the pillow. That night she lay awake until dawn. She wanted to destroy him! She would make Gregory fire him!

She began her attack the following morning. "He's taken the network from you. We're outcasts—do you realize that? Robin Stone is getting all the invitations we should be getting!"

Gregory listened apathetically. Then he said, "Judith, I'm sixty-two. The stock has never been higher—it's going to go two-for-one next month. The network has never been in better shape. And I don't intend to tamper with success. To tell you the truth, I kind of like the idea of checking in, finding everything is going well and slipping off to play golf or go to the track."

"And what am I supposed to do while you go to the track—sit home all day? And you're tired at night. I'm dying to go somewhere."

"I thought you were busy with your charities. Seems you've been happy enough these past weeks."

She avoided his eyes. "How many charity luncheons can I go to?" (She hadn't been to any.) "I can't keep doing that. I've forced myself to make charity dates for cocktails, but that's all over—people are beginning to wonder whether my name means that much on a patron list! They never see us anywhere. I'm embarrassed to admit we're not invited to all the 'in' parties."

"Haven't you had your fill of that? The same people at every party, the women all wearing name gowns to prove something to the other women?"

"No—I *like* going out."

"Well, I think it's a big bore. I thought you were finally getting some sense these last few weeks. It's been relaxing staying in. Now you want me to fire Robin Stone because he's invited to parties instead of us. Judith, you're acting childish."

"I'm not sixty-two and impotent!" she shouted.

He walked out of the room. She sat very still. Then the tears slid down her nice new tight face. Oh God, she moaned to herself. She had hurt Gregory. And for what? For Robin Stone, that's what! She ran into her bedroom and flung herself across the bed. Oh God, Robin was gone! He had intentionally let himself be photographed with that girl. He had walked out on her—on all her dreams. She'd never hold him in her arms again, never feel his body against her own. . . . Her sobs came out dry and harsh. Suddenly she felt her head being stroked— Gregory was sitting beside her. "Don't cry, honey, I'm not mad. I know you didn't mean it."

She turned and clung to him. "Oh, Gregory, I do love you."

"I know you do, and just let me get my sea legs back.

I'm not ready yet to tear into the aggravation of running a network. We'll go to Palm Beach this winter. We'll have fun—I promise you."

She nodded slowly. "And, Greg, you're not impotent..."

Judith made a determined effort to reactivate her social life, but she met with complete failure. Her frustration and anger almost eased the pain she felt about Robin. But there wasn't a night that she didn't stare at her phone and recall all the wonderful nights when she had been able to call him and whisper endearments. The memory would make her dissolve in tears and hug the pillow to muffle her sobs.

She decided to go to Palm Beach before Christmas. She didn't dare give her usual eggnog party—everyone was going to Acapulco, the Bahamas, or to parties given by the new hostesses who suddenly seemed to dominate the social scene.

She thought about Robin with a mixture of hate and desire. And when she reached Palm Beach she sat listlessly on the patio, played solitaire and tortured herself envisioning him making love to some young and beautiful girl.

But there weren't any beautiful girls in Robin's life. He worked ten hours a day, and kept abreast of the competition on the other networks. Dip's show was slated for February. Each day he checked with Robin. "Want any action, buddy boy?" Sometimes he allowed Dip to trail him to the Lancer Bar. And sometimes at ten o'clock when the walls would close in on him, he'd call Dip. "Meet me in front of my building. I want to walk."

"Pal, it's twenty-eight degrees, and I'm in bed."

"Are you meeting me?"

"Okay, give me ten minutes to dress."

When Dip wasn't "on call" to Robin, he sat around Danny's with the agents fawning over him. Sure, he'd see what he could do for them—Robin Stone never bought a show without consulting him. Dip reveled in his new power. He got back at every agent who had snubbed him by telling one and all that none of their clients would

ever appear on IBC. And most of them actually believed
he had that kind of power over Robin Stone. As one
agent put it, "A man will do anything for the man he
loves."

Oddly enough, it was Dan who fought those rumors.
He laughed openly at the suggestion of homosexuality
between the two men. It wasn't love Dip Nelson was
giving Robin, he'd explain: it was cash—a nice healthy
kickback.

The rumors reached Gregory in Palm Beach. When he
saw Danton Miller's new show with a separate frame for
Dip Nelson as producer, he called Cliff Dorne.

"The show is pretty good," Gregory said. "But when
that hambone of an actor who couldn't produce his way to
the men's room winds up with billing there's got to be
something to the gossip. I don't believe the fag stuff—but
there has to be a kickback involved."

"I've gone over the contracts carefully," Cliff said wearily. "If there is any kickback, it's well concealed. I came
right out and asked Robin how come he bought a pilot
from Dip Nelson, and he said, 'Cliff, if *you* have a pilot
that's any good, I'll even buy one from you!'"

Gregory hung up. Judith was sitting with him on the
patio during the conversation. "Well, what are you going
to do?" she asked.

He shrugged. "Right now, I'm going to play eighteen
holes of golf."

Nothing seemed to be able to stop Robin Stone. *Life*
magazine did a story on him, without his cooperation.
They drew from opinions of people who worked with
him and girls he had dated. One airline stewardess
claimed he really was the Love Machine. A model said he
was the most romantic man she had ever known. An
aspiring actress said he was a big zero. Maggie Stewart
was quoted as saying, "No comment." The publicity
snowballed, but Robin ignored it. He went to movies
with Dip, occasionally met Jerry at the Lancer Bar, ate
solitary dinners at the Steak Place, but most of all he
worked.

It was Jerry who brought Gregory's growing antagonism to Robin's attention. They were standing at the Lancer Bar, and Jerry said, "How often do you consult Gregory on shows that you buy?"

"Never," Robin said. "There hasn't been any need to. Right now I'm going through the pilots for the next midseason dropouts. I'll invite him to view the ones I've selected."

"That's big of you," Jerry said.

Robin didn't answer. He gave the ice in his drink his total concentration.

"He did give you your chance," Jerry persisted. "If you want to stay where you are, I'd advise you to pretend to ask his advice now and then."

"I suppose it's known as Robin Stone's network now," Robin said slowly.

"Yes, it is."

Robin smiled. "Then let Gregory take it away from me."

"Meaning what?"

"Meaning that I don't give a damn. I didn't go after the network—but now that I've got it, I'm not handing it back to Gregory on a silver platter. Let him come after me, let him fight me to get it back."

Jerry looked at him oddly. "Know something? Someone said you have a death wish. I think it's true."

Robin laughed. "You go to your couch and I'll go to mine."

By April the fall lineup was set. Robin was leaving his office when Dip Nelson came crashing in. "Listen, Pauli's winding up her road tour. She gets into New York tomorrow. I got a great idea I haven't discussed with Dan yet. Instead of using a different girl on the show each week, let's use Pauli, make her a permanent character. How does that grab you?"

"It doesn't." Robin sat down and with a rare show of tolerance said, "Look, Dip. Let's not fool around with a successful format. Pauli can have her pick of any Broadway musical—Ike Ryan is dying to get her for his new show next season."

"But Pauli *belongs* on TV."

"Look, worry about your own career. One television

show doesn't last forever. You should be finding new properties. Dan Miller has a new idea for a pilot that sounds sensational."

Dip's eyes went dark. "You're kidding! That dirty bastard! Sneaking behind my back. We got a deal—we go halves on everything."

"Have you got it in writing?"

"No, we got a gentleman's agreement."

Robin laughed. "That certainly won't hold up with either of you."

Dip's eyes narrowed. "I'll get him for this." Then with a complete change of mood his boyish smile returned. "Hey, how's about going to Danny's with me? You haven't been anywhere. People are liable to forget we're buddies."

Robin shook his head. "I'm leaving for the Coast tonight. I want to find a movie name to do Dan's pilot. And Ike Ryan has a series I might buy if I can get the actor I want."

Dip's smile vanished. "What's Ike got on you?"

"Meaning what?"

Dip sat on the edge of Robin's desk and smiled. "Look, buddy, the Big Dipper *knows* how you operate. You don't give away ice in the winter unless you're obligated. Did you beat up another whore somewhere?"

Robin reached out and grabbed his tie. "Listen, you cheap son of a bitch—no one has anything on me, including you. If Dan Miller hadn't come up with a good show, it wouldn't have gotten on. I was glad you cut yourself into the action, I thought you might try for a new career. If Ike Ryan has a good show, I'll *buy* it! But if a friend's show slips, I'll cancel it just as fast as any outside show. And you *remember* that!"

He released his hold on Dip. Dip smiled and straightened his tie. "What are you getting so riled up for, pal? The Big Dipper loves you and would kill for you. Remember that—*kill* for you! You don't come by friends like me so easy."

Robin put in a call to Maggie as soon as he checked into the Beverly Hills Hotel.

"It's eleven o'clock," she said, "and whatever you want, I'm too tired to listen."

It's two A.M. New York time," he said. "And if I'm not too tired to talk you can listen. Besides this is business. Will you meet me for breakfast in the Loggia Room tomorrow at nine?"

"Make it eleven and I'll think about it."

"I have to view two pilots between ten and eleven."

"Sorry, I don't like being sandwiched in."

"Maggie, this is business."

She yawned. "Then tell me now."

"Okay. Let's start with this: I saw your last picture."

Her husky laugh came fast. "You're right—maybe it *was* my last picture."

"It was awful. But you looked great. I want you for a new television series."

"Why?"

"Because you just might be right for it."

"In that case, call my agent. Maybe *he'll* have breakfast with you. His name is Hy Mandel and he's in the book." Then she clicked the phone.

He spent the next ten days viewing pilots. He decided to let Maggie cool down. But he wanted to see her. . . . Several times he actually reached for the phone, but he resisted—he sensed they couldn't meet, make love and part again. And he wasn't buying matrimony.

It was one of those nights . . . a restless lonely night. Robin decided nothing could be lonelier than a lonely night in Los Angeles. At least in New York he could always go out and walk. But if you walked down any of the tree-lined streets in Beverly Hills, a prowl car immediately approached you. No one walked in Los Angeles. During the week, the entire city folded at ten. Of course, he could always get a girl—the Polo Lounge was loaded with ambitious starlets and agents who were terrified of him, yet eager to catch his eye. Suddenly he was tired . . . fed up. Why the hell didn't he just hand Gregory back the network, and walk out? But walk out where, and to what?

The sound of the phone broke into his thoughts. He looked at his watch. Seven thirty—too late for a business call. The operator announced Mr. Milano. For a moment it failed to register. Suddenly Robin brightened. "Put the call through," he said eagerly.

"Robin! I am so glad to have gotten you."

"Sergio, it's good to hear your voice. Where in hell are you?"

"I just got back to town today and am reading the back trades and I learned you were here."

"God, you even talk like an actor. I read that you were doing a picture in Rome. What's happened since?"

"I am getting my big chance now—I start on a new picture here, next week. I play the lead. I am an actor, Robin. Isn't it wonderful?"

"What are you doing now?"

"I told you, I start a picture next week."

"No, I mean now, like this minute?"

There was a pause. "Robin, I have met someone I care a great deal about . . ."

"Oh, well, good luck. I'm glad for you, Sergio, I really am."

"I am having dinner with him tonight. His name is Alfie Knight."

"I think you two make a hell of a team," Robin said good-naturedly.

"But what about a drink tomorrow?" Sergio asked.

"That's a date. Five o'clock in the Polo Lounge."

"I'll be there," Sergio said.

Robin ordered dinner from Room Service and turned on the television set. Dip's show was on—he might as well catch it.

The commercial came on. The show started with the usual action teaser just as the waiter arrived with his food. Robin was just starting on his baked potato when he saw a close-up of Pauli. He almost choked on it. God damn Dip—he had *told* him not to use her! How had Dan gone for it? He pushed away the table and watched the show. It was bad. In an effort to build Pauli into a permanent character the entire show went down the drain. He put in a call to Dan immediately.

Dan was stupefied. "Dip told me it was a direct order from you. Next week's script is already taped. I gave her a contract for the rest of the season." Robin slammed the receiver and put in a call to Dip. The wire was busy. The idiot was probably busy taking bows. He made reservations on the midnight flight out. Suddenly he remembered his date with Sergio. He didn't even know his phone number—well, he'd leave a note with the captain in the Polo Lounge.

He arrived at Kennedy Airport at eight in the morning and went directly to his office. He called an immediate meeting with Dip and Dan Miller. Robin's expression was deadly as he demanded that Pauli be written out after the following show.

"I can't do it to her," Dip argued. "She has a big interview today. She's told all the press she's a regular on the show and if she got axed it would hurt her reputation."

"It's an *order*," Robin stated.

"I own the package," Dip said stubbornly.

Robin turned to Dan. "You have equal say!"

Dan stared at him curiously. "I have one-third say, and I'm willing to side with you."

"Who has the other third?" Robin asked.

Everyone was silent.

Dan looked at him. "I thought you had it."

For a moment Dip looked frightened. Then his face went hard and his body tensed as if ready for physical action. "No, chum, I have two thirds, so I have the voting stock as you might say." Then he smiled. "So I guess that settles it. Pauli stays."

Robin stood up and faced him. "Dip, once you did me a big favor. Do me one more. Never come near me again."

Dip made a pretense at a pompous bow and left. Dan shifted his feet nervously as he waited for Robin's reaction. He was surprised when Robin turned to him coolly and said, "Well, it looks like you're stuck with Pauli. Good luck."

"You can't be angry at *me?*" Dan asked.

"I'm only angry that you thought I'd deal in on anything like this."

"How does this affect my new show?" Dan asked.

"Is Dip in on it?"

"No."
"Then you still have your deal."

The ratings slipped after Pauli went on the show. In June, Robin canceled it. Dip was out of a job. But oddly enough the television exposure helped Pauli and she was signed to do a movie. Dip followed her out to the Coast and Robin concentrated on the new fall season.

Gregory Austin had scheduled the November stockholders' meeting to be held on the Coast. Usually he made a quick three-day trip accompanied by Cliff Dorne, but this time he had decided to spend a full week there. Judith needed the excitement.

Gregory stared at Robin's picture on the cover of *Newsweek*. He realized the stockholders regarded Robin as their God, and to them Gregory was a semi-retired old man. But he had never felt better, and was now eager to resume command. He had made several subtle attempts to regain control, but so far all of his efforts had failed. Robin listened to his suggestions . . . but that was all he did—listen. Then he went on to do things in his own way. And so far, Robin's way was the right way. The ratings were at a new high. IBC was Robin Stone's network.

But Gregory hadn't given up. The summer at Quogue hadn't been too bad for him though Judith had been bored. Christ—a man spends thirty years to build up a network and a good life, then along comes one illness—a year and a half away from the scene and he comes back to find a new civilization.

His heart went out to Judith. He had seen the scars behind her ears. Jesus! Did she think he was idiot enough not to notice how her breasts suddenly stood up? He knew she must have done it while he was going through those weeks of shock treatment. She had been so great to him while he was ill. It was only natural that she had come back eager for excitement. And he had failed her. Yet he had to admit that he had enjoyed the idea of Robin's take-over when he returned. In the beginning it had been relaxing to have someone else making the decisions. He had even enjoyed the summer at Quoque and tried to ignore the heavy sighs that emanated from Judith each night as they watched television. But it was her attitude when they returned to the city that finally made him take action.

Judith began taking to her bed for days at a time. Some days she took sleeping pills every four hours. On these days Gregory brought in a nurse to watch over her and at night he slept in her room—he was terrified she'd set herself on fire as she staggered around hunting for a cigarette. When she wasn't in bed, she shuffled around the house without makeup, in an old dressing gown. She refused to go out. He even offered to take her to El Morocco. She didn't want to go alone. Okay, he'd ask Maurice Uchitel to give a party for her there—take over the upstairs room. This only caused her to go into a crying spell: "No one would come." In desperation he placed a call to Dr. Brugalov, his doctor in Switzerland, and explained that Judith was going through a delayed reaction to the strain of his illness and asked if he could recommend someone in the States to help her.

Dr. Brugalov recommended a Dr. Galens. When Gregory explained the situation, Dr. Galens wanted to see Gregory each day. Oddly enough, he didn't want to see Judith. Gregory was so desperate that he agreed. They went back to his paralysis, they discussed his sex life with Judith. He told Dr. Galens about the scars behind her ears, the small scars on her body. He felt sure she hadn't done it to attract other men—Judith wasn't like that and actually sex meant very little to her. Gregory felt she had gone through the operation to hold her position as the goddess on the front pages of *Women's Wear*.

But Dr. Galens kept returning to their sex life. One day in desperation Gregory snapped, "Look, this girl was a virgin when we got married—so I started very slowly with her. And she never showed any desire to experiment. And that's how it's always been. Lately she must have read some of those 'How To' books—you know, those marriage manuals—because in the past few years she's made some amateurish attempts to go down on me.

I never would have dared to try it with her—she's just not that kind of a woman. I don't need outside sex. God knows I went through enough variations in my bachelor days to last me a lifetime. And if straight uncomplicated sex was what Judith wanted, it was okay with me. Besides, it was our *life* she loved: it was exciting, and—" He had stopped suddenly. Jesus Christ! That was it! The fear! His fear! All interwoven with IBC and Judith—Judith loved the life he gave her. He loved her—no, it was more than that: he *worshiped* her. Despite his grumbling about the eggnog parties, he was still so damned thrilled she belonged to him—thrilled with the elegance she brought into his life. When he used to survey the dinner parties and realized she had created this beautiful world for him, he had always nurtured a hidden fear that something might destroy it. Another man? No, Judith wasn't highly sexed. Money? He'd always have that. Illness? Yes —illness could destroy everything!

And now it had happened: he had lost Judith. She was courting self-destruction now. But hadn't he done the same in returning and pretending to enjoy the luxury of having Robin run the network? Suddenly it was clear to him. He could get Judith back on her feet! It wasn't going to be easy. But his fighting spirit had returned.

First he had to regain control of IBC. He took immediate action. He went to Robin and stated that the decisions for next year's lineup should be brought to him. Robin looked at him with that lopsided smile.

"Why?" Robin asked.

Gregory was embarrassed. He couldn't meet Robin's cool, direct gaze.

"Look, Robin, I promoted you from newsman to president of this network. I'm proud of you, I want to work with you—you're my boy." He had tried to be open and affectionate.

Robin's eyes had gone hard. "I'm nobody's boy!" He spat out the word. "I've been calling every shot around here for almost two years. I can't start asking your permission for every move I make. If you want someone to do that, get yourself another *boy!*"

Well, Gregory could *get* another boy but he couldn't let another network get Robin Stone. Nevertheless, each time he looked at Judith, his determination strengthened —his poor sad Judith who had gone through all those operations only to slip into oblivion because of him. He had to regain control of IBC.

He hoped the trip to Los Angeles would help. He didn't expect to stir up any real excitement with the stockholders—he had to play a waiting game. It was crazy but he had to hope that Robin's shows flopped, that the IBC stock went down. He had to root against himself and pray for big losses. It was the only way he could get his network back.

Dr. Galens felt the trip would be therapeutic for Judith, providing she didn't just sit in the hotel. Gregory had called Cully and Hayes and asked them to publicize their arrival on the Coast and get them invited to all the big parties. It galled him to have to take such measures, but Judith's well-being was all that mattered. And Cully and Hayes had come through: several invitations had already arrived by mail. And Judith had stopped taking Seconals, gone and had her hair touched up and bought an entire new wardrobe for California. Perhaps the week of excitement would snap her out of her lethargy for good.

They were due to leave on Sunday. The Friday before, he called and asked her what time she wanted to leave.

"Must I answer this very second?" she asked. "Just tell them to have the plane ready by noon."

He told his secretary to call his pilot and have him stand by. The secretary seemed surprised. "Mr. Stone took the plane two hours ago."

"He what?"

"He's flying to Las Vegas this weekend to catch some performer. Then he's going to the Coast to attend the board of directors meetings. I assumed you knew—"

"I forgot," Gregory said quickly. He sat back. How *dared* Robin take the plane! He sent for Cliff Dorne.

Cliff sighed. "Look, Gregory, what do you mean, 'how dared he?' It's the company plane, and he runs the company. You know what that plane has been nicknamed along Madison Avenue. The Flying Couch! Robin redecorated it so part of it has been turned into a bedroom with a wall-to-wall bed! And he rarely makes his flights without some girl—any girl to keep him company in that bed. I can't keep track of him. Half the time I never know where he is."

"We've got to stop him," Gregory said.

"Unfortunately when you were ill, Judith gave him complete power. I can't tell you how many times I wanted to walk out. But I knew I'd be playing into his hands. If he'd put in his own man as legal head, we'd be dead."

"We're dead now," Gregory said quietly.

"No, he'll bury himself."

"What do you mean?" Gregory asked.

"It has to happen—especially the way he's going the last six months. He makes insane decisions, and takes unheard-of chances. He put on two shows that *had* to flop and instead they came off as 'high camp' successes!"

"He's like all the rest," Gregory said slowly. "Power-mad."

"No, I don't think it's power he wants. On the one hand, he seems to want his name to blaze like headlights —and at the same time, he throws mud at it. I'll be very frank and tell you I can't figure him out. There are even rumors that he's queer, yet he always has a girl. Then there were rumors that he was getting a kickback and I spent weeks checking that. He wasn't. There's only one funny wrinkle. There's an actor—Sergio Milano. Until recently, Robin sent him three hundred dollars a week. I know this because his tax man and my tax man are cousins and I checked it out. Sergio Milano is making it with Alfred Knight."

"Then you think Robin is AC-DC?"

"It looks that way. Sergio hasn't made it big yet, but he's been getting some good parts, and he's a sexy-looking Italian. Obviously he's making enough money so he doesn't need any from Robin. Or maybe he's stopped taking it because Alfred Knight is his new lover."

"Look, can we put someone on this thing? I don't know how it's done." Gregory looked embarrassed.

"I've done it already. I have a man who will tail Robin the second he hits the Coast. I figure we owe it to our stockholders, if we think we have a guy at the top who could get involved with a morals clause."

"Cliff, I don't want any scandal. It's one thing to get rid of Robin, but another to destroy a man's life. I won't do that."

Cliff smiled. "Gregory, all I want is a written report. We're bound to unearth plenty. Then we present it to Robin. He won't want scandal either. He's got a family—a sister who's a big socialite in San Francisco—and he's bright enough to know any open scandal would finish him in the business. That's when we tell him we're putting in someone to 'help' him. We'll divide the power. You'll create another new title. Let Robin remain as President of IBC. We'll get Dan Miller back. Then the power will be divided and *you* will make all final decisions."

Gregory nodded. "I'd like Dan Miller back. I can control him. But will he accept Robin's having equal power? That's what made him walk out before."

"No, he walked because Robin had power *over* him."

"And suppose Robin walks—right to another network?" Gregory asked.

"He won't be able to, not if we have the kind of written report I think we'll have."

"Well, we can't make any move until we get such a report," Gregory said.

"We'll get *something*. If not on this trip, then on the next one. Maybe even in New York. I've hired a good outfit, they have men in every city. Meanwhile, we just have to be patient."

Gregory nodded. Then he began to plan how to break the news to Judith that they'd be flying on a commercial airliner to the Coast. Oddly enough, she took it well. "I hate that bloody plane. Sell it."

Robin landed in Los Angeles late Sunday afternoon. A stack of messages was waiting for him at the hotel. Agents, stars and affiliate station managers had called.

Everyone had sent liquor—his suite looked like a well-stocked bar. He ruffled through the messages: one was a note from Sergio.

He poured himself a shot of vodka. The Polo Lounge would be crawling with IBC personnel, let alone the goddam stockholders. It was the one place he had to avoid. He called Sergio.

"Robin, I am sending you a check next month for all the 'allowances' you sent me. I have just signed a great contract with Century Pictures."

"Forget the money, you'll only screw up my taxes. You were a good friend to me when I needed one, and I knew that the money on the sale of Kitty's estate wouldn't last forever."

"The government took so much," Sergio said mournfully. Then his mood changed.

"Robin, tonight Alfie is throwing a big party. It starts at eight. Please come."

"I don't make those scenes."

"It's not that kind of a party. Everyone will be there." Sergio laughed. "Good Lord, Robin, I'm just making it now—I couldn't afford a drag party. And I have a morals clause in my contract. So has Alfie."

"I don't mean that, in fact it never occurred to me. I mean I don't make the Hollywood scene. Sorry, chum. You'll have to celebrate without me. By the way, are you shacking up with Alfie?"

"No, he has a small house. I live at the Melton Towers. Eventually perhaps we will buy a house together. It is my dream."

"Melton Towers. I know a girl who lives there—Maggie Stewart."

"Oh yes. We see one another in the elevator. She is very beautiful."

When Robin hung up he called the Melton Towers. Maggie answered on the first ring.

"Oh it's Superman and his Flying Couch. I read in the trades that you were due in town."

"Maggie, I want to see you."

"I just finished taping a game show. Three today, two more tomorrow. I bring five different sets of clothes and kill myself trying to be bright, perky and above all sparkling with daytime personality. I tell you there's nothing like a daytime personality to kill a girl's morale."

"I want to see you," he repeated.

"I heard you the first time."

"Then why are you rattling on about taping shows and all that crap?"

"Because I'm insane. Know why? Because I *want* to see you. That means I *have* to be crazy—like asking for punishment."

"Do you want to come here? We'll order room service. Or how about Matteo's?"

"You come here," she said slowly. "I've taken off my face, my hair is limp. I have some franks in the freezer and I make a wild can of baked beans."

"I'll be right over."

"Cool it for an hour. I want to take a shower and look halfway presentable."

He poured himself a vodka, switched on television and wondered if Gregory Austin had arrived. Perhaps he should call. Then he shrugged. The hell with it—he'd see him at the board of directors meeting on Tuesday.

Gregory sat in the large living room of bungalow eight at the Beverly Hills Hotel. Ordinarily he would have preferred the Bel Air. It was off the beaten track and he wouldn't run into all the network personnel. Like tonight —it was six o'clock, but his watch told him it was nine o'clock, New York time. He was beat, but Clint Murdock had just phoned. Clint was a retired general and a very important cog on the board of directors. *Mrs.* Murdock had seen them checking in—would they have dinner in the hotel dining room tonight? He had no choice . . . the general was too important to snub. Well, it would be a quick dinner. With luck he'd be back in the bungalow before midnight. He yawned. Maybe he'd have time for a short nap. . . . They weren't meeting the general until eight. He'd better tell Judith. Mrs. Murdock was a bore, but at least Judith could wear one of her new dresses. Maybe they'd even stop off at the Polo Lounge for a drink. And from tomorrow night on, they were booked for a party every night. Cully and Hayes had earned their thousand a week. He hoped it would make Judith happy.

She came into the living room. "I don't know what to do. The valet is closed."

"They'll open early enough tomorrow," he said.

She smiled. "Well, I'll just have to wear the gold lamé pajamas tonight. They're the only things that didn't crush."

"Tonight?"

She waved an invitation. "This was here when we arrived. Alfie Knight is throwing a big party—everyone will be there."

"Judith, starting tomorrow we have parties every night. But tonight I made a dinner date with General Murdock and his wife."

"General *Murdock?* I wouldn't want to have dinner with them if I had *Nothing* to do—let alone turn down Alfie Knight's party for them!"

He rose from his chair and tried to put his arm around her. "Judith, I *need* him. Murdock can help me with the board."

Her face went ugly with scorn. "Sure. We'll sit for hours and I'll have to make idiotic small talk with Mrs. Murdock, while you listen to the general's latest story about his fishing. Do you think Robin Stone would grovel like that? He'll be at Alfie Knight's party! *Everyone* will be there!" She broke from him and dashed into the bedroom.

He felt panic as he saw her head for the bathroom. "Judith, what are you doing?"

She held his bottle of sleeping pills. "I'm going to take two! I refuse to sit and listen to those dreary people. At least if I'm asleep I won't be miserable about missing one of the best parties in town."

He grabbed the bottle. "I can't break the date with the general. But if the party means so much to you, you go. I'll invent some story for the Murdocks."

"I can't walk in to a party like that unescorted." She reached for the bottle. "Let me take the pills, *please*, Greg. I just can't face an endless dinner with those people."

"No, I'll get someone to escort you." He suddenly turned to her. "Perhaps Robin Stone will take you."

Her face was expressionless. "I'm sure he has a date."

"He can still escort you, even with a date." He went to the phone. He hated to ask Robin for a favor—then he thought of Judith. Dammit, he wasn't going to have her taking to her bed.

When Robin came to the phone, Gregory plunged right in. "Robin, there's a party tonight at some movie star's home—Alfie Knight, I believe. Yes, well, Mrs. Austin has been invited and feels it might be amusing. She hasn't attended one of these Hollywood bashes for a long time. Unfortunately, I have a dinner engagement with some of the board of directors and I would consider it an enormous favor if you'd escort her."

Judith watched Gregory's face for some sign. The silence was ominous—she could tell that Robin was refusing. . . .

"I feel the same way," Gregory answered, "but it would be a personal favor to me. Oh, I see. Well, look, Robin, can't you still keep your dinner appointment and take Mrs. Austin to the party? I doubt whether those things get going much before nine or ten. I really would appreciate it. . . ."

"Oh for God's sake, stop begging!" Judith shouted. She rushed over and grabbed the phone. "Robin, this is Judith —forget it! It was Gregory's idea, not mine."

"Do you really want to go, Judith?" he asked.

"I thought it might be fun. And I think I need a bit of excitement. But I don't want to force you to go."

"I hate Hollywood parties. But look, Judith, will it be all right with you if we make it late—say ten o'clock?"

"Ten would be marvelous. That would give me a chance for a quick nap."

"Fine. I'll ring you from the lobby."

She hung up and tried to hide her happiness. He hadn't wanted to go, but he was doing it for her. That meant he still felt something. She had given him every chance to get out of it. And he probably had a date with a girl and was breaking away just to be with her. She walked over to Gregory and kissed him lightly. "Your poor hired help, they still jump to your bidding."

He felt relieved to see her happy again. "No, he wasn't jumping—not for me anyway. You were the one he melted for. But then, you've always had that power, Judith."

She was so happy that she wanted to be kind to everyone. "Are you sure you don't mind my skipping dinner with the Murdocks?"

"Of course not. I'll tell them the trip knocked you out. And they'll never know you went to Alfie's party. It's a cinch *t'ey're* not invited."

She kissed his head. "I'm going to cream my face and take a long warm bath. Then a little nap—wake me when you leave."

She sang as she ran the bath water. She was going to see Robin again. And she felt he wanted to see her too. Of course he did. She had scared him off with that marriage talk. Well, she'd let him understand that from now on, it would be on his terms. No more ultimatums. She'd see him every night this week—they were bound to be invited to the same parties. And when they got back to New York they'd go to the Steak Place and . . . Oh Lord, it was wonderful to be alive!

Robin rented a car and drove to Maggie's apartment. It was almost seven o'clock. This was a hell of a mess, but Judith had sounded so desperate. He had stopped it cold after that marriage talk, and had assumed she had someone else by now. But that false surge of pride in her voice when she had told him he didn't have to take her —it had been a cry for help. He hadn't the heart to refuse.

He thought about it as he drove down Sunset Boulevard. He wondered why he felt compassion for Judith. He didn't feel anything for anyone. Except Maggie—hell, he *wanted* Maggie! It was a physical drive. As simple as that. Also he admired her spunk. She hit back at him. She was a challenge, not limp and sad-eyed like Amanda. Maggie was a fighter—his kind of girl. But Judith—what the hell did he owe to *her?* Why had he cut short his evening with Maggie? It bothered him. He pushed it from his mind as he eased the car into a small parking spot near the Melton Towers.

Maggie looked tired, but hauntingly beautiful. He noticed the purplish circles under her eyes. She was too thin, but for some reason she was more desirable to him than ever.

They ate on the coffee table. And when they finished he helped her with the dishes. Then with almost a shy smile she led him into the bedroom. He was amazed at the way she somehow brought out all the tenderness in him . . . and later when he held her in his arms he felt completely fulfilled for the first time in ages. God, if they could just find some kind of workable truce. He knew he wanted her with him, but he couldn't ask her just to live with him. He lay there stroking her hair, and for the first time he wondered about marriage. It might work— that is, if she could let him be free to take off whenever he wanted. Oddly enough he couldn't think of anyone he would *want* to take off with. Jesus, very shortly he'd have to take off and escort Judith to that damn party. He stole a look at his watch. Eight forty-five—he still had time.

"Maggie . . ."

"Mmm?" She stirred, and nuzzled her face into his neck.

"Have you any plans for your career? I mean aside from the game show?"

"Alfie Knight has a picture I want to do."

"My offer to star in a new television series still holds."

"I'd rather do the picture."

"Have you done anything about it?" he asked.

She stretched across him and reached for a cigarette on the night table. "I wrote Alfie a note, and Hy's been on his neck. He said he'd use me if he didn't get a jumbo. I hear he wants Elizabeth Taylor. I don't think I have much of a chance."

"I might be able to help. But why not take the television series? It would be great exposure for you, good money, and Alfie won't be doing the picture until next year."

She looked at him slowly. "And then you'll pop out

here every few months and we'll meet, fuck and talk about my career?"

"I'll be out here a lot—"

"That means we'll fuck a lot and talk a lot." She got out of bed.

"What *do* you want, Maggie?"

She stood in the center of the room. The bathroom light spilled on her body. He could see the anger in her eyes. "I want *you!* Tonight was marvelous, but as always, I'll hate myself in the morning. I'll feel like an accommodation—your West Coast lay!"

He was out of bed in an instant and took her in his arms. "Dammit, you know that's not true. I could get any girl in this town just because I have jobs to give out."

"And you've just offered me the plum—the big job, a lead in a series. And for that I'm supposed to be ready to jump at a phone call! God, it sounds like a plot for a B picture. Tell me, who is the New York girl you've got stashed away, ready to rush to the Lancer Bar at a moment's notice? And is there one in Chicago? There would have to be—you have to stop and refuel the Flying Couch."

He broke away from her and put on his shorts. She reached for a robe and lit a cigarette. She watched him as he dressed.

Suddenly he smiled. "The Flying Couch—is that what they call my plane?"

"Didn't you read *Undercover* last month?"

"What the hell is that?"

"A scandal sheet. You were on the cover. You don't only make *Newsweek* and *Time!* You make a lot of magazines. And according to *Undercover* you don't care *what's* on that Flying Couch with you, man or woman, just as long as you can hump!"

He slapped her hard. She went limp and burst into tears. Then she fell into his arms. "Oh God, Robin, why do we try to destroy one another?" she sobbed.

"I care for you, Maggie, and I want you to take this job."

"I don't want a payoff!" The tears ran down her face.

"Can't you understand? The only thing I want in this world is *you!*"

"You *have* me! More than any woman in the world has ever had me. I still wear your goddam faggy little ankh ring."

When she didn't answer, he said, "Does a wedding ring make all the difference?"

"Yes."

"Okay."

"Okay, what?" she asked.

"Okay, we'll get married." He looked at his watch. It was nine fifteen—he had to get to Judith but he wanted to settle it with Maggie. "It will mean you're Mrs. Robin Stone. But I have to be free to come and go. Like right now, I have to leave."

She stared at him. "You *what?*"

"I have to take a lady to a party."

For a moment she stared at him in disbelief. She backed away from him as if he had struck her. "You mean you came here, knowing you had a late date, knowing you were going to jump out of bed and go to another woman?"

"It's nothing like that. The lady is Mrs. Austin."

"That makes everything legal. She's not exactly Dame May Whitty."

"Maggie, let's not get Mrs. Austin involved with us."

"Oh, she's *above* all that!" She laughed. "You want to be free, yet you have to jump when Mrs. Austin snaps her fingers. Is that how you got to be head of IBC?"

"I'm going to leave, Maggie. I don't want you to say things you really don't mean. I'll call you tomorrow."

"There is no tomorrow for us." Her eyes blazed.

"You don't mean that, Maggie."

She turned away and he knew she was sobbing. He went to her and took her in his arms. "Maggie, I *care* for you. Good God, how else can I prove it? I'm asking you to *marry* me. If you want me for what I am, fine. I want you."

"I want you to *need me,* Robin," she sobbed. "I was married to a man who didn't need me, except for one thing—an heir. Robin, don't you understand? I love you so much that it scares me. I was hurt when Hudson cheated on me even though I never loved him. But I'd never survive if you let me down. Don't you think I've tried to forget you? With Andy, Adam, all my leading men. But it didn't work. I don't want you to marry me because you feel you're doing me a favor. I want you to marry me because you *want* me, because you want to share everything with me—your thoughts, your love, your problems. Not just your body. Can't you understand, Robin? *I want you to need me.*"

"Looks like we can't close the deal," he said slowly. Then he smiled oddly. "You see, baby, I don't need anyone."

She nodded slowly in defeat. "Dan Miller once said that about you."

"Then Dan is brighter than I thought." He started for the door. "Do you want the job?"

"No."

"Do you want marriage?"

She shook her head. "Not on your terms."

He opened the door. "I'll be here for four or five days. If you change your mind on either count . . ."

She stared at him, her eyes heavy with tears. "Don't call me anymore, Robin. Please. Never!"

"You really mean that?"

She nodded. "Not unless you can call and say you *need* me."

She waited until she heard the elevator close behind him before she fell on the bed and sobbed.

Robin entered the lobby of the Beverly Hills Hotel at one minute before ten. Five minutes later Judith swept down looking like shimmering gold. She had never looked better and she had never stirred more compassion within him. He thought of Maggie with her ponytail and the purple shadows under her eyes. And he knew that no matter how hard he tried, he could never make love to Judith again.

He managed a bright smile as he walked toward her. "You're going to put all the movie stars to shame," he said.

"It's the only thing that didn't wrinkle. And I've worn it to death at all the parties in New York."

"I only have a rented Rambler. It's not elegant enough for you," he said as he led her to his car.

She snuggled against him in the front seat. "I like this better than a limousine." She watched his profile as he drove up the sloping hills. "Robin, I've missed you," she said softly.

"A beautiful woman like you shouldn't miss anyone," he said easily. "Judith, watch for the signs on your side. Alfie's house is on Swallow Drive—all these damn streets have birds' names."

"We're on Doheny now," she said.

"That's where we're supposed to be. Somewhere near here we take a sharp turn."

She concentrated on the street signs.

"I acted like a child," she said slowly.

"When?"

"Flying to meet you in Chicago."

"I thought it was a bit reckless, but charming."

"I've done a lot of thinking, Robin. I can't hurt Gregory, he needs me."

"Good girl. And I think you need him, too."

"No, I need you."

"Ah—here's Swallow Drive. And that must be the house, where all the Rollses and Bentleys are parked."

A prowl car was just pulling up as Robin parked. "You going in there, mister?" the officer asked.

Robin nodded. "I believe there's a party."

The officer laughed. "This is the third time I've been sent here. Look, tell Alfie Knight I'm a fan and he's entitled to have some fun, but the lady down the street has a baby that's teething."

"I'll do my best," Robin promised. He helped Judith out of the car.

The officer stared at her, dismissed her as a civilian and then turned his attention back to Robin. "Say, don't I know you? You look familiar. Of course! I used to watch the *In Depth* show when you were on it. Robin Stone, *right?*"

"Right."

"Almost every celebrity in town is at that party. Say, you should be back doing that show. I liked you—you're almost as good as Huntley and Brinkley."

"He has the Happening show now," Judith said with a hint of possessive pride.

"No kidding. Well, I'm on night duty lately so I don't get to see much TV." He waited until Robin started up the path. Then in a low voice he called, "Mr. Stone, could I see you a second—alone?"

Robin hesitated. Judith smiled and nodded. He left her and returned to the prowl car.

"Listen, Mr. Stone. I know that broad with you isn't your wife. She's got too much mileage for that."

Robin's gaze was cold. He waited for the officer to go on.

"Look, I'm not butting in. I just want to tip you off—in case she's someone else's wife. . . ."

"I don't think I understand," Robin said.

"I don't miss anything, see. And while I was talking to you, I noticed a tail."

"A *what?*"

"A tail. I think you got a tail. Are you in any trouble or something?"

"Not any more than usual."

"Well, while we were talking a guy was driving around this street. He made a U-turn and went down, then came back, then went down again, and now he's parked down the road a piece. I just recognized him last time around. He's a private investigator."

"Maybe he's tailing someone inside. The lady I'm with is with me at her husband's request."

The officer shrugged. "Maybe he's eyeing one of the other big homes, waiting for someone's husband to come out. But he's a tail."

"Well, he's not mine," Robin said, "but thanks all the same!" Then he hurried up the path after Judith.

When they entered the house, the surprise and delight on Sergio's face made him almost happy that he had come. He recognized several top directors, a few big stars, and the usual assortment of starlets. Someone grabbed him and planted a wet kiss on his neck. It was

Tina St. Claire. He introduced Judith to Sergio, Alfie and Tina. Then he got two drinks and steered Judith toward a couch. A large Siamese cat sauntered through the room and eyed him. It let out a low growl and leaped into his arms.

Alfie almost dropped his drink.

"God, have you got sex appeal! Slugger hates everyone."

"Slugger!" At the sound of Robin's voice the cat purred. Robin scratched its ear. "Where did you get it?"

"Ike Ryan gave it to me. It belonged to his wife. Ike travels so much that half the time the poor cat was in a kennel and I adore cats. He hates strangers but you're the exception."

"No, we're old friends, Slugger and I." He rubbed the cat's neck and noticed it still wore the little silver tag on its collar.

Tina St. Claire stood before the combo and began to gyrate suggestively, staring meaningfully at Robin.

"Better cut the drums," Robin said to Alfie. "I just headed off the prowl car."

"Oh, that divine officer. I think he just used the neighbors as an excuse to come here. Personally, I think he's gay," Alfie said.

Judith smiled at Robin. "We really don't have to stay," she whispered.

"Bored already?" he asked. "Or is this crowd too much for you?"

"Any crowd is too much when I'm with you. I'd rather have a nightcap in your suite."

"I thought you wanted to go to this party."

"I've been. Now I want to be with you."

"That would be rude to Alfie, and to Sergio. He's an old friend."

He drank slowly and steadily, talking to Sergio and Alfie while Judith was trapped in conversation with a group of actors. He was determined to make it a late night—too late to take her back to his suite for a nightcap.

It was close to midnight when the party began to thin

out. Judith extricated herself and joined him at the bar. Her smile was forced. "Well, I've let you spend all your time with the two boys. Now it's my turn. How about that nightcap?"

"What are you drinking?"

"Whatever you have."

"Alfie has a well-stocked bar. Name it."

"I don't want a nightcap here," she said angrily.

Alfie ambled over. "What's the trouble, luv?"

Robin suppressed a grin. Alfie was one of the few hold-outs on television. Mrs. Gregory Austin meant nothing to him.

She smiled. "No trouble. I was just telling Robin that it was high time we got home."

"If you're tired, mate, I can always have someone drop you off at your digs."

She ignored him and turned to Robin. This time her voice was firm. "Robin, I want to go home."

His grin was loose. "Alfie, you heard what the lady said. Who's got a car going toward the Beverly Hills Hotel?"

"Johnny there lives on North Canyon—hey, Johnny, when are you packing it in?"

The young man across the room signaled that he was on his way. "There's your ride, luv," Alfie said.

"How dare you!" She turned her back on Alfie. "Robin, take me home."

"Sure, but not this moment. I want to finish my drink."

Alfie went behind the bar and handed him the bottle of vodka. "Looks like it needs freshening."

Judith watched him refill his glass. "Robin, I want to leave—with you."

"Look, luv," Alfie said, "we all can't have just what we want. Now I'd like to marry Sergio and have babies. Unfortunately, it just can't work out."

Her eyes blazed as she stared at Robin. "You like being here with all these degenerates!"

"I like being with my friends." He left her and walked over to the couch. Alfie and Sergio followed.

Judith stood against the bar. Nothing like this had ever happened to her. Alfie's easy scorn . . . they treated her as if she was a common girl on the town. She was Mrs. Gregory Austin, but she had been pushed around and ignored. She poured herself a large Scotch. The clock hanging over the bar ticked loudly in the silence. Suddenly she was aware that almost everyone had gone. Only Robin and those two queers remained, huddled together on the couch. He was doing this to her intentionally, to make her feel cheap. She got off the bar stool and something on the floor caught her eye. It was a gold bracelet. She read the inscription and a slow smile came to her lips. She held it gingerly as if it would soil her fingers and approached the men on the couch.

"Now I see why I was told to leave. The three of you really do want to be alone, don't you?"

The men looked at her curiously. Alfie saw the bracelet and leaped to his feet. His hand automatically reached for his wrist. He lunged for her but she backed away. "You bitch—I had it on tonight. Where did you get it?"

"I found it on the floor behind the bar." She dangled it before him. "The catch must have broken. It's really a very interesting bracelet."

Sergio jumped up and headed toward her. "Give him back that bracelet."

With a quick motion she dropped it into her bra. Then she brushed her hands together. "Now it's where neither of you fairies have the nerve to go."

Robin got up slowly. "Maybe you forgot about *me*. I'm not afraid of tits."

"You're a fairy too." But she backed away from him. "The Love Machine—with you it's girls for your name, but men are your game. The bracelet proves it."

"What's Alfie's bracelet got to do with me?"

"You tell me," she said lightly. "It has Sergio's name on the front, and on the back it says *From Robin Stone, Christmas, Roma, 1962*. But Alfie was wearing it. Is that why you wanted to stay, Robin? So you could have it out with Alfie for taking your real lover away from you?"

Sergio turned to Robin pleadingly. "It's the bracelet I asked from you in Rome. Remember you said that I could have anything I wanted engraved on it? So I had your name put on the back. I wore it always. It was and is my

dearest possession. But Alfie gave me his." He held out
his arm showing a similar gold bracelet. "Alfie's mother
gave him this. It was the closest possession *he* owned. So
we exchanged bracelets."

Alfie nodded. "It was something I treasured, Robin."

Judith threw back her head and laughed. "This is the
most touching scene I've ever witnessed. Well, I guess I'll
be on my way. I think Gregory will be delighted with
this bracelet. I think all the scandal sheets will enjoy it
too. We might make it in time for the board of directors
meeting on Tuesday. After all, Robin, we've got to see
that you are—what's the word—oh yes, totally unemployable."

"Judith, I don't give a damn about the network. If you
have a gripe against me—fine. But don't get Sergio or
Alfie involved. You could hurt their careers."

She looked at him and laughed. "You're making it
sound better and better." She turned to Alfie. "I think the
scandal sheets would adore knowing about you, *luv!*" Her
eyes blazed in anger. She started for the door.

Sergio lunged for her. Alfie grabbed her and pulled her
to the center of the room. Robin started toward them to
break it up, but Sergio was closing in. He had her
trapped behind the bar. She looked around wildly, like a
cornered animal. Suddenly she saw the gleaming Oscar.
She picked it up, and as Sergio moved toward her, she
brought it down on his head. He fell to the floor immediately.

"You bitch!" Alfie screamed. "He's unconscious—you've
*killed* him! Oh God, Sergio. . . ." He was on his knees
sobbing over the unconscious man.

Judith raced toward the door but Alfie leaped up and
caught her. "Oh no you don't!" His hand lashed across
her face. Robin picked up Sergio and placed him on the
couch. He heard Judith scream. He knew Alfie was slapping her, but he was sure that nothing more than her
dignity would be hurt. His main concern was for Sergio.
He got some ice and put it to his head. "Be careful!" Alfie
shouted. "His skull might be fractured."

Robin turned, took one look at Judith and rushed
across the room. Her lip was cut, blood was streaming

from her nose. Her hairpiece was askew and looked oddly comical against her battered face. Robin tried to intercede, but Alfie dragged her from his reach by the hair. Miraculously, it remained on. She screamed at the top of her lungs. Robin grabbed Alfie's arm and forced him to release her. Judith's pajamas were torn at the neckline, revealing part of her wired bra. The bracelet slipped out and clattered to the floor. Alfie grabbed it. Then, for good measure, he gave Judith another blinding slap across the face.

Robin grabbed her and she clung to him, sobbing. "I'm sorry, Judith," he whispered. "But when you play like an alley cat, sometimes you get *treated* like one."

They all froze when they heard the chimes and the pounding at the door. "Open up! It's the police," a loud voice called.

"Oh my God," Judith began to sob. "This will kill Gregory. Look at me."

"You! What about *me!*" Alfie screamed. "And Sergio! This kind of publicity can ruin us all . . . because of you —you bitch!"

Judith clung to Robin. "Get me out of this. Oh, God, please get me out of this and I'll never do anything wrong again."

"*You'll* never do anything wrong! You've got your millions to go back to. What about me? I've got a morals clause!" Alfie spat at her.

Robin held Judith against him, and grabbed Alfie with his free hand. "Alfie, I'll get you out of this—only I've got one condition: Maggie Stewart gets the lead in your new picture."

"*What* picture? We'll all be run out of town tomorrow."

"Judith!" Robin held her off and stared at her mottled face. "Your story is that I was drunk. I went on the make for you. I ripped at your dress. Sergio stepped in to help you. I went to hit him, he ducked and you got the blow —that explains your face—then I smashed Sergio."

"And what was *I* doing?" Alfie asked.

"You rushed to her defense and I clipped you." He reached out and gave Alfie a resounding punch on the jaw. Alfie yelled. Robin smiled slightly. "Sorry, chum, but if you're defending the lady you have to take your lumps." Robin noticed that the pounding at the door had stopped. He knew the police were trying to make a forced entrance from the back.

"Now, everyone know their lines? I hope so, because here comes the law—"

He turned around just as the police came in through the bedroom terrace. In panic, Judith dashed for the front door. She flung it open and faced a blinding flash of camera bulbs. The reporters tramped into the room. She dashed back to Robin, then, seeing the press and police, she backed away. Dimly she heard Alfie explaining, "It's just all a ghastly misunderstanding. Mr. Stone stayed to talk to me about Miss Maggie Stewart—I want her for my new picture—and we had a few drinks. Robin had one too many. He really didn't know what he was doing. Good God, he couldn't be on the make for Mrs. Austin if he was sober, she's old enough to be his mother."

Judith's swollen lips grimaced at him. "Why, you dreary little—"

"Easy," Robin said. "Let's just say this wasn't my night."

Then the ambulance arrived. They all watched the doctor kneeling over Sergio.

"How is he?" Alfie asked anxiously.

"Probably just a concussion," the ambulance attendant answered. "However they can't tell till they X-ray." Then he shook his head. "You movie characters sure play rough."

The policeman whom Robin had met earlier in the evening took him by the arm and stared at him with a wounded expression as if to say, "And I trusted you." Alfie was asked to come along as a witness. Judith refused to press charges, but she was taken along despite her objections.

It was all routine at the police station, except for the newspapermen. It seemed to Robin that every reporter in town was there, plus a television cameraman from a local station. Robin did not try to avoid the cameras, but he shielded Judith throughout. When one inventive cameraman darted between them and managed to get a shot of

Judith's swollen face, Robin lunged after him and smashed his camera. The other cameras picked up this byplay, but order was instantly installed by the police. Alfie refused to press charges. "After all, I took a poke at him first. And he was drinking," Alfie said.

The doctor phoned in to say that Sergio was all right —it was only a mild concussion. Robin paid a fine for disturbing the peace and wrote a check to the newspaperman for destroying his camera and it wound up with everyone being released.

Then he drove Judith back to the hotel and parked near Crescent. "We can go in this way and avoid the lobby. I'll walk you to the bungalow."

"Robin—"

He looked at her. One eye was beginning to discolor and her lips looked raw and bloody.

"Put some cold compresses on your face," he said. "Tomorrow you're going to have a real mouse on that eye."

She touched her face gingerly. "What do I tell Gregory?"

"Exactly what you told the police."

She reached over and took his hand. "Robin, I know this will sound crazy to you, but I really loved you." Tears came to her eyes. "And now I've destroyed you."

"No, baby, *I've* done it myself—and maybe it's about time."

He walked her to the bungalow. It was dark inside.

"I won't wake Gregory," she said. "There will be plenty of time to tell him about it tomorrow."

"Sleep well, Judith."

She clung to him for a brief second. "Oh, Robin, why did all this have to happen?"

"Go into your bungalow," he whispered, "and stay there. Stay where you belong from now on." Then he walked away and went into the hotel. He turned off his phone, fell across the bed and went to sleep without even taking off his clothes.

Gregory Austin was awakened at seven in the morning by Cliff Dorne. "Jesus, Gregory," he said, "I almost fainted when I heard the news. How is she?"

"How is *who?*" Gregory tried to rouse himself into full consciousness.

"Judith."

Gregory stared at the clock on his night table. "What in hell are you talking about?"

"Gregory, the lobby is filled with reporters. You've got a 'Do not disturb' on your line, but I told the operator I'd take full responsibility for breaking it. Have you seen the morning papers?"

"For Christ's sake, man, I've just opened my eyes. What is all this talk? And what's Judith got to do with it?"

"Robin Stone beat her up."

"What!" Gregory dropped the phone and raced into Judith's bedroom. She was sleeping face down on the pillow. He tugged at her arm gently. She mumbled and gradually awoke. He stared at her in shock. "Judith— your face! You've got a black eye! What happened?"

"It's nothing." She tried to bury her face in the pillow.

He pulled her into a sitting position. "Cliff is on the phone. There are reporters in the lobby. There's supposed to be a story in the newspaper. *What happened?*"

"Get me some coffee," she said slowly. "It's not as serious as you think."

Gregory raced back to his bedroom. "Judith's all right. Get up here immediately, and bring all the newspapers." Then he sent for coffee. Judith finally got out of bed and came into the living room. "I look worse than I feel," she said with a wry smile.

"Tell me what happened."

"There isn't much to tell. Robin drank a lot. Suddenly he lunged for me. Sergio tried to protect me and then when Robin lunged for him he ducked and I caught the blow. Then Robin knocked Sergio out—and then the police arrived. That's all."

"That's *all?*" Gregory thundered. "Look at yourself! Why didn't you send for me? Or Cliff Dorne?"

Judith sipped at the coffee. "Oh, Greg, you're making too much of a fuss. The police let us all off. As a matter of fact, Robin brought me home."

"He brought you home!"

"Yes, he had sobered up." She heard the door chimes and rose hastily. "That's probably Cliff. I don't want him to see me." She disappeared into the bedroom.

Cliff had all the newspapers. Gregory winced as he stared at the front pages. The big black headlines were all variations of the same theme:

LOVE MACHINE TURNS INTO WRECKING MACHINE
OVER NETWORK CHIEF'S WIFE.
A STONE'S FIST IS GRANITE.
THE NIGHT THE LOVE MACHINE RAN AMOK.

And each story was the same. Gregory studied the pictures. Everyone looked ready to fold except Robin. He appeared oddly undisturbed. There was even a slight grin on his face.

Cliff sat looking like a pallbearer. The doorbell rang constantly as bellboys delivered telegrams for Judith from her New York friends. It was close to noon in the East—the story and pictures were all over the country by now.

Gregory paced the room. "How did the newspapers get into the act?"

"Our man tipped them off," Cliff said morosely. "He couldn't know Judith was involved. He's the one who's been tailing Robin since he arrived."

Judith emerged from the bedroom. She had put Covermark over the discoloration of her eye, and aside from her swollen lips she looked fairly presentable. She even managed a slight smile at Cliff. "Well, I've certainly seen how the other half lives. And every one of our friends has suddenly remembered we're alive. Greg, would you believe they all think I'm glamorous? You should read these wires. Peggy Ashton wants to throw a big bash in our honor. She said I'm the woman of the century—having a man fight two men to get at me." Her smile was actually one of childish delight.

"We've got to write some statement for the press," Cliff said. "Of course Robin goes. It's a shame it had to happen this way"—he tossed a glance toward Judith, who was busy opening the wires—"but at least we've got a legitimate excuse for the board of directors."

"No. He stays," Gregory said.

Both Judith and Cliff stared at him.

"We've got to clean this thing up. It has to be a big misunderstanding as far as we're concerned. We'll give out a statement that Robin never went after Judith, that she slipped and fell down the stairs. We'll think of something."

"We will not!" Judith stood up. "I'm not going to be written about as if I were some idiot and make Robin a hero. He went after me and that's that!" She stormed out of the room.

"She's right," Cliff said. "A denial will only give added life to the story. Fire Robin, and in a few days it will blow over."

"*He stays!* Put in a call to Danton Miller and offer him his old job back. Tell him he'll work with Robin. They'll both have equal power, and neither can make any decision without my approval. From here on I am in control."

"Gregory, you must be mad. You've been looking for the chance to get rid of Robin. This is it!" Cliff argued.

"I wanted my network back, and I've got it. Besides, I asked Robin to take Judith to this party because Judith *wanted* to go. At least now she'll stick with her own kind. But I'm not about to toss Robin to the wolves."

"I think you're making a big mistake," Cliff said. "No other network will touch him now—he's unemployable."

"I'm not paying you for opinions," Gregory snapped. "I pay you for legal advice. Robin Stone has contributed too much to IBC to be booted out for one crazy night. This will all cool down after a time. We'll switch the board of directors meeting to the day after tomorrow. By then I'll have boned up on the reports and *I* will present them! Have Dan fly in. He and Robin will sit behind me like two co-workers while *I* speak."

Robin awoke to the banging on the door. He looked around . . . he was still lying across the bed. He felt rocky, but he made his way to the door. Cliff Dorne stalked in and threw a batch of newspapers on the coffee table.

Robin picked them up. They were worse than he expected.

"I've just come from Gregory's bungalow," Cliff said.

Robin nodded. "I suppose he wants my resignation."

"He sure as hell does, but he feels sorry for you. He's hired Danton Miller to replace you, and you can stay on until you find something else. At least you'll save face that way."

Robin went to the desk and scratched out a few lines. "I think this is the way it's done," he said. "I have no contract. It ran out some time ago. . . . Here is my resignation. You can witness it." He handed Cliff the pen and the paper.

Cliff smiled. "May I say, I've waited a long time for this moment."

"I'll leave on the first flight I can catch. I'll go to my office in New York and clear out my desk. And, Cliff— here are all the charts for the spring shows. Everything's in there—ratings, future plans, the report I was going to give to the board of directors." He handed him the attaché case.

"I'll send the case back to you in New York," Cliff said.

"Keep it. You gave it to me as a Christmas present last year." Then Robin walked to the door and held it open.

Gregory Austin stared at Robin's resignation. He shook his head. "Did you tell him I wanted him to stay, Cliff?"

"He had it all written before I arrived," Cliff said.

Gregory shrugged. "Well, he's just signed himself out of television. Damn his pride. If he had stayed on and worked with Dan, this would have blown over. . . . Maybe I should talk to him."

"You do, and I'll walk out on you," Judith said suddenly.

Both men looked at her in surprise.

"I want him out of our lives. I mean it, Gregory."

Gregory nodded. "All right. Cliff, tell Dan everything is set. But I want Sammy Tebet to take Robin's place. Sammy's a good man—nothing like Robin, but then I doubt if there will ever be anyone like him."

"Then why have him if you have Dan?" Judith asked.

Gregory smiled. "I want two men there, two of them who will be at each other's throats."

Cliff nodded and left the suite.

Robin was packed. He started to leave, then came back and picked up the phone. The operator said, "Oh, Mr. Stone, there have been hundreds of calls for you. Every newspaper has called, and there's a man from *Time* with a photographer waiting in the lobby. If you like, there's a way out on Crescent Drive—you can duck them—"

"Thanks, honey. Will you get me the Melton Towers? It's an apartment house, but it has a switchboard."

"Yes, we know the number. And, Mr. Stone, I just want to tell you that I think you're wonderful no matter what the newspapers say. It's unusual these days to read about a man who fights two men to get a woman he wants. I think it's romantic." She giggled, then rang the Melton Towers.

Maggie came on after two rings. Her voice was heavy with sleep. He realized she had probably not heard the news. "Wake up, sleepyhead, you're supposed to be at the studio for the game shows, aren't you?"

"Not until one—*Robin!*" She was suddenly wide-awake. "You're calling. Does that mean—?"

"It means I'm leaving for New York, Maggie, on the one o'clock plane."

There was a long pause, then she said, "Is that what you're calling about?"

"Yes. And, well, I just wanted you to know I didn't—" He stopped.

Suddenly it didn't seem important to tell her he hadn't gone on the make for Judith or hit her. Somehow he knew Maggie would understand. He just wanted her to know he wasn't running off without saying goodbye. "Maggie, you see, I—"

But the phone was dead. She had hung up.

# THIRTY

December 1968

DIP Nelson rushed off to lunch at Sardi's carrying *Variety*. As he entered, he felt a new sense of power. He was Dip Nelson, Broadway producer, and Robin Stone was just a name from the dim past; it was a year since the big scandal and no one knew what had happened to Robin. He had just vanished. But the Big Dipper never struck out. He had come back. Maybe not as a performer, but as a top Broadway producer. Joe Katz had no alternative but to make him co-producer if he wanted Pauli as the star. And they had the biggest hit on Broadway. He stopped at each table and showed everyone the grosses in *Variety*. Everyone at Sardi's listened. They had all seen the story in *Variety*, they all knew Pauli was the greatest, and they also knew she was having an affair with her leading man.

Christie Lane sat on the plane and looked at *Variety*. His face broke into a broad grin. Then he tore out the clipping. "What is it?" Ethel asked.

He showed it to her:

## L.A. to N.Y.

Christie Lane
Ethel Lane
Christie Lane, Jr.

He folded it and put it in his wallet. "His first *Variety* clipping for his scrapbook. I'm putting it beside the clippings of his birth notices."

Ethel smiled as she held the child. "We're going to

have a smash opening. Alfie and Sergio will fly in and so will half of Hollywood."

He nodded and lay back and tried to catch a nap. He was excited at the idea of doing a Broadway musical. He didn't even mind that it was for Ike Ryan. So far Ike hadn't had a loser. And Ike didn't take any shit from anyone. When Dip Nelson had tried to muscle in as co-producer, he had turned him down. Well, Dip had made a deal with Joe Katz. And Pauli had a big hit. Leave it to Dip—he had learned plenty from Robin Stone. Funny, Robin had been bigger than all of them, and wham, just like that he had disappeared from the scene. Suddenly he thought of Amanda—he could think of her now with no emotion; she was just a dim memory now. Ethel had given him the only thing he really wanted: his son. He smiled contentedly.

Ethel snuggled the baby and kissed his head. Funny, in the beginning she had only gotten knocked up to get her way with Christie. Now the baby was the most important thing in her life, the only thing she really cared about. All the frustrated love she had given the men who had passed through her life, she now lavished on the child. But she'd never make a mother's boy of him—she'd know when to let go. He was her kid and he was going to have the greatest life in the world. And now Christie's Broadway opening would be exciting. She had a good life —she was den mother for Alfie and Sergio, *the* hostess of Hollywood. Her Hamtramck dream had practically come true. Of course there was no handsome leading man— there was just Christie. She had plenty of time on her hands to play around, but she didn't get any offers. She was respected. She was *Mrs.* Christie Lane. Oh well, you couldn't have everything.

Danton Miller read the review of his new special in *Variety*. It was murderous. Dammit, the only shows that held up were the old ones. The shows chosen by Robin Stone. He had been a rocket all right, but like all rockets he had exploded into thin air. He drummed this into Sammy Tebet's head every time Sammy got high-handed.

Sammy was bright and he'd have to keep an eye on him —he couldn't afford another Robin Stone in his life. But Gregory would see to that. Gregory was back, riding roughshod, and Gregory was going to cancel the new variety show Dan had put on in September. Dan could feel it in his bones. It would happen at tomorrow's weekly meeting. He lit a cigarette. His ulcer stabbed him. He looked up toward the ceiling and silently promised that he would never smoke again if he got through tomorrow's meeting with his job still intact. He wondered if Gregory had read *Variety.* . . .

Gregory *had* seen *Variety.* But he was looking at *Women's Wear.* Judith's picture was on the front page. He stared at it fondly. He shuddered every time he recalled her picture on the front pages of the Los Angeles newspapers. Oddly enough, it had made her a celebrity again when she returned. She had worn an eye patch for a week. And the fact that Robin Stone had gone off the deep end over her gave her new glamour among her friends. It just proved you could never figure women. Judith was right back in the swim. God, every night this week there was a party or an opening. He suddenly remembered that he had a five o'clock fitting for his new dress suit. And of course Judith insisted on his ordering a new velvet smoking jacket for their eggnog party. It was going to be bigger than ever this year. He stared at her picture and smiled. She had never looked better, and she had never seemed happier. . . .

They all read *Variety,* but none of them read the "Literati" section, and none of them noticed the small paragraph that said, "Robin Stone, former IBC Network President, has just completed a book which Essandess will publish in the late spring."

Maggie Stewart boarded the BOAC plane for London. She was also carrying *Variety.* The big headline on the front page was a lead story about her walkout from the new Alfie Knight picture. But when the plane was airborne she wasn't reading *Variety*—she kept reading and rereading a cable:

DORCHESTER HOTEL    LONDON ENGLAND
MISS MAGGIE STEWART    MELTON TOWERS
BEVERLY HILLS, CALIF.

I NEED YOU.

ROBIN

# ABOUT THE AUTHOR

JACQUELINE SUSANN was one of the most successful writers in the history of American publishing. Her first novel, *Valley of the Dolls,* published in 1966, holds the bestselling fiction record in the *Guinness Book of World Records. The Love Machine* was published in 1969 and became an immediate #1 bestseller and held that position for five months. When her third novel, *Once Is Not Enough,* was published in 1973, it also moved to the top of the bestseller list and thus established Jacqueline Susann as the first novelist in history to have three consecutive #1 bestsellers.

A novella, *Dolores,* was published posthumously in 1976, and also became a #1 American bestseller. However, her first book to be published, *Every Night, Josephine!* was to remain her own personal favorite. Little has been written about her writing career prior to 1963, the year *Every Night, Josephine!* was published. Until the discovery of *Yargo, Josephine* was thought to be her first full-length work. In fact, Jacqueline Susann coauthored a play, *Lovely Me,* which was performed on Broadway in 1946, and she wrote several magazine articles and short stories in the 1940s and 1950s. Today, the Susann books are to be found in more than thirty languages worldwide and are estimated to have sold over 50 million copies in all editions. And now, added to this body of work, is *Yargo.*

Jacqueline Susann was born in Philadelphia. Her father, the late Robert Susann, was a noted portrait artist and her mother, Rose Susann, is a retired public school teacher. Jacqueline Susann was an actress before becoming a writer (of her career in the theater, she liked to say that the plays she appeared in broke all records too— the track records for opening and closing.)

In private life she was the wife of television and motion picture producer Irving Mansfield for almost thirty years. Jacqueline Susann died on September 21, 1974, after a courageous and privately fought struggle with cancer. With the exception of her husband and a few close friends, her twelve-year fight to overcome the disease was not known until after her death.

# Bantam Book Catalog

Here's your up-to-the-minute listing of over 1,400 titles by your favorite authors.

This illustrated, large format catalog gives a description of each title. For your convenience, it is divided into categories in fiction and non-fiction—gothics, science fiction, westerns, mysteries, cookbooks, mysticism and occult, biographies, history, family living, health, psychology, art.

So don't delay—take advantage of this special opportunity to increase your reading pleasure.

Just send us your name and address and 50¢ (to help defray postage and handling costs).